MW01383842

GOAT FOR AZAZEL

0468-LEE

GOAT FOR AZAZEL

A World War II Story

George Oscar Lee

Library of Congress Number:		99-90832
ISBN#:	Hardcover	0-7388-0544-0
	Softcover	0-7388-0545-9

This book was printed in the United States of America.

To order additional copies of this book, contact:

Xlibris Corporation
123 Chestnut St. Suite 402
Philadelphia, PA 19106
USA

1-888-7-XLIBRIS
1-215-923-4686
www.Xlibris.com
Orders@Xlibris.com

CONTENTS

LEVITICUS XVI – 10

BUT THE GOAT FOR AZAZEL, ON WHICH THE LOT FELL TO BE THE SCAPEGOAT, SHALL BE PRESENTED ALIVE BEFORE THE LORD, TO MAKE AN ATONEMENT WITH HIM, AND TO LET HIM GO FOR A SCAPEGOAT INTO THE WILDERNESS.

IN LIEU OF A PROLOGUE

****

Writers usually begin their books with quotes or prologues. The most interesting quote ever, was done by Voltaire and the most work connected with writing a book was done by Countess Leo Tolstoy, who rewrote "War and Peace" only 14 times.

I, however owe a word of gratitude to several friends of mine who shared with me, their life experiences, be it scenes from Auschwitz, Cracow, Bucharest or bordello's adventures. The army routines I drew from my own life in the Polish Army during W.W.II.

While language or uniform may differ ,the basics are always the same. The average "dog-face" soldier hates his non-coms and officers and wants to come back home from war in one piece.

I must thank Mrs.Mimi Sherman, a math teacher from N.Woodmere,N.Y. for editing my book. Her encouragement came with each written chapter. I would like to thank Ms.Cindi Richardson for typing my original manuscript while struggling with those long and "impossible" Polish names.

Above all, I would like to thank my wife Leah for putting up with me during those long evenings and/or nights spent writing the "GOAT FOR AZAZEL".

I must confess, I've enjoyed writing this novel. I gave it all I had in me,including humor,poetry,love and authentic description of the most difficult period of the history of mankind. I sincerely do hope,that the reader will enjoy the book, as much as I did writing it.

Aventura,Florida, June 1999
George Oscar Lee

PERSONAL NOTE:

****

Several people asked me why I've chosen the "GOAT FOR AZAZEL" for the title of my book? The truth of the matter is, that a year and a half into my writing I couldn't find an appropriate title.

One day, during the Yom Kippur service, I found in my prayer book a reference to the scape goat in Leviticus XVI-chapter 10. It seems that the Lord put all the sins of Israel on that goat and sent it to Azazel in the wilderness, but willed it to live. I've seen certain analogies in the case of Holocaust survivors. Indeed, I have found a perfect title for my novel.The name of the U.S.Air Force pilot belonged to a very decent and unassuming man, for whom I've had great respect and admiration. Unfortunately this man as well as his son died much too early in life. The name of "Goldie Locks" on a B-17 plane was a C.B.radio "handle" of Giselle (Golda) Lachs, the mother of my two children.

Any mistakes or historical inaccuracies are exclusively mine.

The author.

CHAPTER 1

Henryk Kaplinski was examining the 8 cm. X 12 cm. gray envelope in his hands. Although he guessed the contents of the envelope without reading it, his face still registered disbelief.

Yes, without a doubt it was a "poviestka", a notice from the Ministry of Defense of the Ukrainian Soviet Socialist Republic, better known as: Voyenkomat", an envelope similar to many that were already received by his friends.

Somehow, the green 2-kopeck stamp on the envelope depicting a Red Army tankist, brought a feeling a foreboding. With a sinking feeling, Henryk slowly opened the letter. He, that is Henryk Moyseyevich Kaplinski, residing at 22 Panska Street in the town of Boryslaw, region of Drohobycz, was requested to come on January 12, 1940 (Wednesday at 9:00 A.M.) punctually, to the offices of "Voyenkomat" for a physical examination prior to the induction into the Peasant and Workers Red Army. Punishment for avoiding the Army service would be meted out under the Article #58, Paragraph A.

"What a way to spend one's twentieth birthday," Henryk bitterly said to himself. "Maybe they will let me go because I am the sole provider for my widowed mother and three younger siblings."

The next few days were simply horrible at home. His mother, two sisters and a baby brother were crying like he was already dead. "Don't worry so much; I'll get out of this mess, somehow," said Henryk. "You will see."

And, see they did, but only Henryk standing in a long line on January 12, 1940 with many other young men from the town and surrounding villages; Poles, Jews, Ukrainians and some Armenians.

The long line went around the "Voyenkomat" building which was located not far from Henryk's favorite movie theater "Grazyna."

It took several hours before Henry's turn came. He was told to undress and walk to the next room, although the examination room was heated, and yet Henryk shivered. A tall heavyset woman doctor dressed in a white coat over her Army uniform came up to Henryk. She looked into his eyes, listened to his heart, asked him in Russian to open his mouth, put him on the scale, which registered an even 72 kg., measured his height, 1m. 85 cm., and uttered one single word, "Godien" – suitable, able bodied.

Henryk didn't speak Russian, but he understood the meaning since the Ukrainian language, which he spoke fluently, was similar to Russian.

"Tovarish comrade," Henryk started to speak, but the doctor quickly cut him off. "I am not your 'tovarish'; I am the Senior Lieutanant Piotrova." Next! Henryk was pushed to another room where six barbers were engaging in cutting the hair off the young concsripts' heads

There was something dehumanizing when Henryk felt the metal, hand operated hair cutter more suitable for sheep than for people. It touched his scalp and his short, wavy blond hair with a slight reddish tint, fell to the hair-covered floor. "Don't worry, young man, it will grow back," good naturedly said the middle aged barber.

Henryk followed the other men to another large room where he was issued a Red Army uniform consisting of a loose fitting blouse, pants, two undershirts, two sets of long underwear, boots, two pieces of cloth to serve as socks, a long woolen winter coat, a winter hat with ear flaps and the ever present red star to adorn the hat. To complete the wardrobe, he was given funny looking gloves where the trigger finger was separated from the rest.

After he was dressed in the freshly acquired uniform, he went into another room where he was given a metal pot, half a loaf of black bread, 50 grams of roughly cut tobacco known as "machorka" and 37 Rubles.

"What about cigarette paper?" asked Henryk, the Supply Sergeant. "Use the newspaper "Pravda" because for smoking it is better than "Izviestia," laughed the Sergeant. "Blankets, metal helmets, you will get in boot camp."

In a gigantic assembly hall, Henryk, along with hundreds of young men, were sworn in. After some long speeches by political officers, the "politruks" and Communist Party dignitaries, telling them how privileged they were being accepted into the ranks of the Red Army, they were ordered back to the first room, where they had left their civilian clothing. At that point, they were told to say their goodbyes to their families, who were impatiently waiting for their loved ones outside the building.

Everyone was promised a home furlough in ten days. For all practical and impractical reasons, they were considered fully pledged Red Army men subject to harsh discipline. They could not leave the premises anymore. The entire building was circled by N.K.V.D. troops with fixed bayonets on their rifles.

Henryk collected his civilian clothing and went to the gate where his anxious family was waiting. They did not recognize Henryk in his Red Army uniform. "Mama, it's me, your son," Henryk said jokingly. His mother had a look at Henryk and promptly fainted. Henryk had to shake his mother back to reality.

"Mother, please, I am going back to the nearby town of Sambor for basic training and I'll be back in ten days. Don't worry, I'll be just fine. You will see, " said Henryk, slipping into her hands all the money he was given.

Suddenly, a military band appeared on the street playing the popular, at the time, melody of "Yesli zavtra voyna." (If tomorrow is a war).

Henryk didn't have to wait for war to come because one was already going on full blast in far away Karelian Isthumus of Finland. The papers were full of articles, reprinted from "Pravda," "Red Star," and "Izviestia" about the treacherous Marshall Mannerheim attacking the peaceful U.S.S.R.

Henryk couldn't even imagine in his wildest dreams that he,

Henryk Kaplinski, would be needed to help comrade, O.W. Kuusinen and the Finnish working class. He was not that patriotic, and his further thoughts on that subject were interrupted by orders to board the trucks, which held twenty men each vehicle.

The long column of trucks with freshly conscripted soldiers reached the town of Sambor within the hour. The soldiers were dropped off in front of the barracks. Field kitchens were set up awaiting their arrival. Whatever Henryk would have to endure was better handled on a full stomach, he reasoned.

The cabbage soup, loaded with chunks of meat, tasted just fine to a twenty-year-old rookie. After the meal, the men were ordered to their rooms each containing thirty six bunk beds. Henryk was assigned the upper bed and much to his relief, the lower bunk was taken over by his former classmate and neighbor, Edward Daszkiewicz, an ethnic Pole whom Henryk did not notice at the induction center of "Voyenkomat."

Both Henryk and Edward went to the same public school and they often worked on their lessons at each other's house, being fed by the mother, at whose house they happened to be. After public school they went to separate gymnasiums (high schools).

Unfortunately, Henryk's father died of tuberculosis while Henryk was attending the second class of gymnasium. Henryk's mother couldn't afford the tuition of 36 Zlotys, thus, Henryk had to get a job with a master cabinet maker in the nearby suburb of Wolanka. In the meantime, Edward continued his education at the state gymnasium in the town of Drohobycz. He was always dressed in the navy blue school uniform with silver buttons with light blue stripes on the sides of his pants. On his left arm he had an embroidered shield with the school number #525.

Regardless of the change in their social lives, both boys remained good friends. With the Soviet invasion of their part of Poland on September 17, 1939, things changed again for the boys, back to the pre-gymnasium days, they were, indeed, kindred in spirit.

Adjacent to their bunk bed was another school friend, Roman

Baczyskiy, a Ukrainian boy who would occasionally taunt Henryk with words such as "Zhidek"(kike). Henryk, in turn, would find words that would correspond to Roman's insults, but basically, they all were getting along surprisingly well.

During their first night in Sambor's military barracks they decided on their "solemn word of honor" to stay together and watch out for each other, come hell or high water.

The next few weeks were spent on grueling exercises, long marches with heavy backpacks on their backs, attending boring lectures on military doctrine, and political sessions about Stalinism and Leninism. Needless to say, those lectures were compulsory. At night they were so tired that they would fall asleep the second they reached their beds.

Everybody was allowed to write to their families, but they were told not to complain about conditions because the ever-present "cenzura" would not let their letters through. The return address was a field post box #1342.

The promised furlough in ten days had to wait a full month. Finally, they were given a three day pass to visit their families. The Red Army provided transportation to their hometown of Boryslaw.

Henryk found his family managing under the circumstances rather well. His mother, as a mother of Red Army man, obtained a profitable job at the local food distribution center, and Henryk's sixteen year old sister became an assistant to the secretary of the Communist Youth Organization, the Komsomol. Henryk was very much relieved. It seemed that the family was functioning satisfactorily without him being there.

The same truck and the driver that brought Henryk home came to pick him up three days later. It was a tearful goodbye to the family, but Henryk was optimistic in his belief that he would be back home again very soon.

Rumors were flying high about their unit being sent to Finland. This time there was some truth to those rumors because men started to receive additional warm clothing. The winter of 1940 was the coldest on record. Even the oldest men in the village didn't remember a winter as bitter cold as this one.

A few days later an entire train pulled in to the nearby railroad station and the men started to board the individual wagons. It took two days to fully load the battalion's equipment and supplies. Luckily, Henryk and his friends and another five men were assigned to the same compartment. By that time Henryk was promoted to the exhalted rank of the corporal. It seemed that he was the fastest in assembling and disassembling blindfolded the issued rifle in fifty seconds. The train moved slowly, making many long stops. The final destination was not made available to the rank and file, but from the names of towns that they passed, Henryk deduced that they were moving northeast.

They passed the town of Minsk in Byelorrusia, Vilnius in Lithuania, went through the Baltic States of Latvia and Estonia, stopping often on the tracks for some unexplained reasons. Without a doubt, the train was moving towards the city of Leningrad. The closer they got to Leningrad, the more trains full of wounded soldiers were going in the opposite direction. Eventually, they reached the town of Primorsik, just northwest of Leningrad. Henryk's battalion was disembarked and ordered to join General Meretskov's Seventh Army. By the time Henryk's squad reached the assigned position between Lake Ladoga and Ilomantsi, it was March 11, 1940.

On the following day, war stopped and peace was declared. The situation improved considerably for enlisted men and non-commissioned officers, starting with food, clothing and entertainment. Especially popular were the concerts of the Red Army choruses and dancers. Henryk managed to see a film "Circus" four times. Veterans of the "Winter War" told Henryk what a tough opponent the Finnish forces were, quietly adding that many were killed and wounded on the Soviet side. Only years later did Henryk find out about the 200,000 Soviet casualties suffered in the Russo-Finnish war.

Henryk, Edward and Roman were inseparable. Roman, however, while on a night guard duty, suffered from frostbite on both of his ears. Consequently, he was sent to an army hospital in Leningrad. Surprisingly, Roman was happy to be in that hospital where pretty and not so pretty "med-sisters" were taking care of the "war Hero." Having their friend in the hospital gave Henryk and Edward an excuse to visit.

Without any difficulty they obtained a two day pass to Leningrad. It was, unquestionably, the most beautiful city that they had ever seen – starting with the Peter and Paul Fortress, the Hermitage Museum, St. Isaac Square, the Summer Palace and all the pretty girls whey met on the Fontanka and Moika bridges. From those bridges the young men could see big chunks of ice floating underneath. A nearby valley sprouted crocuses and jonquils announcing the arrival of spring.

Upon their return to the barracks Henryk volunteered for the much needed carpentry work. As if by magic, new shelves, desks, beds and fixed windows appeared. Everyone was praising Henryk's work. This, of course, didn't escape the notice of their platoon leader, Lieutenant Ponamarenko, for whom Henryk made a very impressive desk. Ponamarenko, in turn, must have mentioned to his superior officer, Captain Yuri Bartenev, about Henryk's "golden hands." One day Henryk was called to see Captain Bartenev.

"I hear some very nice things about you, Corporal Kaplinski. How would you like to make some furniture for me?" said the Captain. "Yes, comrade Captain, it would be my pleasure, but I have to clear it with comrade Lieutenant Ponamarenko." "Consider it done. What do you need in addition to lumber?" asked the Captain.

Henryk mentioned a few items and asked for helper, "Riadowoy", Pfc. Daszkiewicz. "No problem, in a couple of days you'll have everything and my driver will pick up both of you at eight o-clock and bring you to my house in Petrodvorets, a suburb of Leningrad. One more thing, you will have to keep your mouth shut, not a word to anyone. You'll be considered assigned to a special detail. Is that understood, Poniatno? " said the Captain.

"Da, tovarish kapitan, it is fully understood," answered Henryk. "You do a good job and there will be sergeant's stripes for you and corporal's for your helper. Dismissed," barked the Captain.

The next few weeks changed into a dream job. At the appointed hour, the Captain's truck picked up Henryk and Edward and brought them to the house where the Captain's wife, Valentina Alexandrova Barteneva, greeted them with a friendly smile. "You boys better start the day on a full stomach. Have breakfast with me." Not needing further encouragement, they ate a sumptuous meal and drank hot tea straight from Tula's samovar.

Valentina Alexandrova told Henryk what she would like to have done. Henryk measured the room and quickly sketched a double bed, two side tables, and a rather interesting chest of drawers with extra shelves. His plan was approved without protest.

It was, indeed, a cushy assignment. They started to work with real zest. Their work was frequently interrupted by Valentina Alexandrova who kept bringing food and drinks. Within sixteen working days, they had the furnishings made; the only remaining thing was to lacquer the woodwork.

The Captain seemed to have the right connections because the war-time shortages did not apply to him. Whatever Henryk needed was obtained in a day or two.

The very morning that they boys were supposed to finish the furniture, Edward was running a high temperature and was kept at sick bay for observation. Rather than wait for Edward, Henryk decided to proceed with the task on hand. Arriving at the Captain's house, Henryk apologized for Edward's absence explaining the reason. Valentina Alexandrova was most understanding.

"Never mind, so it will take you an extra couple of days." Henryk could never get used to the Russian pronouncement of his name that sounded more like Gienrik.

"By the way, my husband was promoted to major and he went to the Frunze Military Academy for a one month refresher course for senior officers, so I'll be home all alone." At noon time she called Henryk into the kitchen which also served as a dining room.

"Davay po obiedat," (let's eat) said Valentina Alexandrova. It was an elaborate meal with the ever-present bottle of vodka. "Vashe zdorovie," (your health) and they clicked glasses together. Henry, who very seldom had a drink, was flying high just after two drinks. Valentina, on the other hand, seemed to be stone sober. At one point, she reached for a pickle, leaning over Henryk, exposing her white, full breasts. The intoxicating smell of her body, mixed with strong "Moscow Night" perfume, overwhelmed Henryk. He simply took Valentina into his arms and began to kiss her. Valentina's moist lips and probing tongue were unexpected rewards.

"Come, let's make ourselves comfortable," said Valentina, leading Henryk to the bedroom. With trembling hands, Henryk helped Valentina to undress. His entire sexual experience at the age of twenty was two quick visits to a local whorehouse in Boryslaw, the city of his birth. This was definitely heaven! They made love over and over again. Finally, some hours later, they fell asleep. They woke up just minutes before the truck came around to take Henryk back to his barracks.

"Be back tomorrow morning to finish the job," sternly said Valentina. "Yes, I'll be back on time," said Henryk, not knowing which job this time she had on her mind.

The next day Edward was still sick, so Henryk went to Valentina's house by himself, wondering how he'd be received. Valentina opened the door with the biggest smile he ever saw. The day was started with a quick rumble in bed, followed by a big breakfast.

"Gienrik, I want you to know that I am twenty five years old and have been married for five years. Yuri can't make me pregnant and I would love to have a baby very much." "I'll see what I can do to help," said Henryk, with a grin. The next few days were spent alternating between making love and putting a second coat of lacquer on the furniture.

At last, the project was finished, much to Henryk's regret. Besides, the Captain returned and Henryk was assigned to different duties. By this time Edward completely recovered from a bout with pneumonia.

Two months later, Major Bartenev stopped by to see Henryk to deliver the promised promotion to sergeant. At the same time, he promoted Edward to corporal, along with a few other men to avoid any suspicion of favoritism. Beckoning Henryk on the side, the Major said to him, "Too bad your unit is moving back to the Ukraine; otherwise I would let you make a crib for our first baby." "Congratulations, comrade Major," said Henryk, more scared than relieved.

CHAPTER 2

Henryk's unit was moved to Zhitomir in the Ukraine. Here, Henryk spent several months learning about the use of mortars. The Soviet heavy mortars 120mm were simple, but of effective construction; smooth-bore barrel, the end of which rested upon a steel base-plate, which, in turn, spread the recoil shock to the ground and a supporting tripod which held the barrel at the desired elevation.

Henryk, as a squad leader, and Edward became quite proficient in using the mortar, but carrying it around was totally another matter. Thus, they spent almost four months in Zhitomir's barracks. Henryk, thanks to his additional skills as a carpenter, was always in demand. Somehow, he managed to obtain two furloughs during that time to visit his family in Boryslaw.

At home there was some talk about the Germans planning to attack the Soviet Union. These rumors Henryk dismissed as an utter fabrication of fascist propaganda.

In March of 1941, his unit was moved once again; this time to the town of Rovno, near the present Russo-German border. Seeing so many Soviet films, Henryk was convinced about the invincibility of the Red Army. During the month of May, more and more Soviet troops, equipment and supplies were moved towards the border. At the same time, trains full of grain, timber and fuel were crossing the border into Germany without any interruptions. Several times Henryk noticed German reconnaissance planes flying over their positions without alarms being raised.

One day in the beginning of June 1941, Henryk was sent to the divisional headquarters to pick up the mail for the battalion. To reach the headquarters Henryk had to walk about 6km. To his surprise, the headquarters were no longer there. According to a sub-lieutenant whom Henryk met, the entire staff moved that very morning to another location.

"I can't tell you, Sergeant, because I don't know myself. Even if I knew I wouldn't tell you. Besides, I can't even find my own unit. It is a real 'bardak' whorehouse."

Disillusioned, Henryk came back empty-handed, finding his C.O. very upset. The Captain couldn't contact the headquarters either. It seemed that a tank corps moving from one location to another chewed up all the telephone lines. Therefore, the Captain decided to lay fresh lines the very next day, but history had different plans for that morning of June 22, 1941.

In the wee hours of the day, holy hell broke out. Unending waves of planes were dropping bombs on their position, Artillery shells were exploding all around, creating an indescribable chaos. Some officers were yelling at men to open fire, but their orders were ignored in the prevailing total confusion.

Lt. Ponamarenko removed his Nagan pistol from his holster and screamed, "Fuck your mothers! Open fire in a westernly direction and keep firing or I'll kill you my.....". He never finished the sentence because a series of 50 mm bullets cut him in half.

Henryk and Edward managed to send a few salvos in the direction of incoming fire. Having exhausted their supply of mortars, they didn't have any choice but to heed an order given by an officer whom they hardly knew. "Davay na zad," (fall back immediately). There were many killed and many more wounded screaming for help. Complete panic took over Henryk's and Edward's move. They ran as fast as they could towards the east only to be encountered by units of another rifle regiment. "Don't go that way! The Germans are right behind us. Go back where you came from."

On Edward's suggestion, they started to move southeast in the direction of their hometown, They lost contact with their own unit. Soon they were joined by other stray Red army men. One of these new men said, "Let's raise a white flag and surrender to the Germans," a sentiment that Henryk and Edward did not share.

"Let's run away on our own," suggested Edward. "We'll move at night and sleep by day."

They didn't get any sleep during the day because the earth seemed to tremble under the weight of "Schwerpunkt," the epicenter of the German Sixth Army lead by Field Marshall Beck. All roads were occupied by German forces moving east.

Coming out of a clearing and trying to cross a road, they were almost run over by a truck full of German soldiers. Automatically, they raised their hand, but the truck didn't even bother to stop. One of the German soldiers yelled out to them, "Stalin kaput!" Everything around seemed to prove the soldier was right.

They kept moving like a pair of hunted animals, covering 10 – 15 km. of mainly wooded area. The first few days they ran on adrenaline, but now their young bodies demanded nourishment. Water was no problem due to many small brooks, berries and mushrooms that kept them alive. Exhausted, they fell asleep, only to be awakened by Russian voices. It was another unit of the Red Army trying to reach their own ranks. "Who are you?" asked a senior lieutenant from that group. Henryk, more out of habit than discipline, got to his feet and reported his name and unit.

Further conversation was interrupted by a sharp command in German. "Hande hoch!" (Hands up) You are totally surrounded; whoever makes a step will be shot at once," a heavy accented Russian left little doubt as to the real meaning of the order. Out of the woods came several dozen, dressed in field gray uniforms of regular Wehrmacht soldiers, each carrying fully automatic weapons. There was no sense in resisting. "Drop your rifles and pistols and form a column of four men abreast and follow Sergeant Weber," A further order was barked at them.

Resigned, dog-tired and hungry, the men followed given orders. In silence, they marched for an hour before their destination, which was a large field with thousands of assembled captured Red Army soldiers.

Walking, Henryk managed to destroy his army papers, which listed his Jewish nationality.

No food or water were given to the captured prisoners of war for the first two days. Some men ate grass. On the third day, a watery soup and bread were finally issued, but by that time, many men had collapsed and died. After the meal, the prisoners were told to get up on their feet. An order was given in German, Russian and Polish for all political officers and Jews to step forward. A number of men heeded the order and stepped forward. Henryk wanted to do the same, but Edward stopped him. "Don't be an idiot, they will kill you." "Whatever will happen to the other Jews will happen to me," answered Henryk.

"Why don't you wait for awhile and see but if you are in such a hurry to die, then go," bitterly said Edward. The order was repeated once more. "Political officers and Jews step forward. Whoever hides in the ranks will be shot at once." Hearing this, some more men stepped out. As soon as the men were assembled, they were told to walk to the middle of the field. A canvas covered truck with black crosses painted on the sides pulled in front of the men. The truck backed up dropping the gate. From the truck a machine gun opened fire, killing or wounding the men. It was a wholesale massacre. The firing finally stopped and the sergeant in charge of the execution detail inspected the corpses, administering a final coup-de-grace.

There was a terrible silence! A slight breeze was bending leaves in their tribute to the fallen soldiers. Very quietly, out of the corner of his mouth, Edward said to Henryk, "Didn't I tell you that you had better keep your mouth shut about being a Jew?" Henryk just nodded with his head because the scene left him speechless.

The reaction of the soldiers to the just seen massacre varied from utter shock to jubilation. "Gitler-molodets." Hitler is a fine fellow killing off kikes and politruks." Some more level headed soldiers would say, "Don't jump for joy yet, your turn will also come." Here and there shouts were heard, "Jude, Jude!" Obviously, some other men had the same idea as Henryk, but few were only too glad to report Jews to the Germans. Once discovered, they were shot on the spot.

Someone pointed at Henryk. "He looks like a Jew." Henryk stood paralyzed; only Edward had a presence of mind. "He is a Pole just like me. We went to church together. Maybe you would like to see my prick to find out whether it is circumcised? I'll shove it in your mouth so you can suck on it at the same time."

After this outburst, some men laughed, but they left them alone. They were not bothered by anyone. To be on the safe side, they slowly moved into a group of other prisoners on the next day.

On the sixth day of captivity, there were announcements. The Germans were looking for barbers, medical personnel, electricians and carpenters. Anyone pretending to those trades would be shot. When the call for carpenters came, Henryk and Edward raised their hands. This time quite a few men answered the call. Henryk and Edward were chosen with a first group of twelve men. A single armed German soldier escorted them to a nearby village from where they walked another kilometer to a partially destroyed bridge. Their task was to repair the bridge, over a small river, in the shortest time possible. Any attempt to sabotage the work would be punished by death. The twelve men team of P.O.W's was now supervised by two armed men. Heavy lumber and assorted tools were already provided. One of the guards, speaking a passable Polish, explained what had to be done.

The prisoners, while being hungry and exhausted, still under the influence of the massacre, were afraid if they wouldn't adhere to the given orders they might also be shot. Therefore, they applied their skills to the project at hand. Heavy logs were put across the damaged part of the bridge. Henryk's suggestion of putting a couple of logs as reinforcement came to the attention of the Polish speaking German soldier. "Say, what is your name? You seem to know what you are doing." "My name is Henryk Kaplinski, and I am a master carpenter," answered Henryk. "Your name from now on will be Heinrich, and I am putting you in charge of this group. By the way, my name is Siegfried Bodenheimer and I am from Silesia." That, of course, explained to the men his proficiency in Polish.

A motorcycle with an attached sidecar pulled in front of the bridge. An officer addressed the Corporal inquiring about the progress made so far. "These men are doing a splendid job, I think. I'll keep them for other jobs as well," said Corporal Bodenheimer. "In that case, you better feed them because even a horse can't work unless fed. I'll send my driver with some food for these bastards," said the officer and ordered the driver of the motorcycle to turn back.

Henryk perfectly understood the entire conversation since his mother was born in Vienna in second "Bezierk", the so-called "Matzoh Insel" or Matzoh Island. He grew up speaking German with his mother. One of his earliest songs was, "Gutten Abend und Gutte Nacht" set to the music of Schubert. Admitting the knowledge of German in these circumstances would raise suspicion. The same motorcycle returned, but instead of the officer sitting in the sidecar there was food for the men.

The food was swiftly distributed and swallowed within minutes. The men clearly could have eaten more, much more, but this had to suffice for now. Someone scrapped from his pocket enough tobacco to make one cigarette, which all of the men shared. Nourished somewhat, they went to finish repairing the bridge under a hot July sun.

For several months Henryk's team followed the conquering #813 "PIONIERKOMPANIE" (engineer company) across the vast Russian land, basically helping the Germans to exploit the occupied territories. Unlike other Germans, Feldfebel Siegfried Bodenheimer took good care of his men, in the same fashion that a good "Bauer" would take care of his cattle. He fed them on time in order to get the maximum out of their skills and travails. He eventually doubled the guards to prevent their escape.

"No one of my HIWIS or HILFSWILLIGE (volunteers) will ever run away," he boasted. And yet, one of the men did escape, but straight to heaven. It was Mikhail Pavlov, a twenty four-year-old lad from Odessa. He was badly injured by a mine and Bodenheimer with one shot to the back of his head relieved Pavlov of his misery. Bodenheimer killed him with the same expression and feeling that a farmer would dispatch a lame horse. Mikhail was universally liked. Many evenings he would sing in his beautiful baritone, everyone's favorite song about Kostia, the sailor.

The very next day Bodenheimer brought in Mikhail's replacement. It was a middle-aged Ukrainian from Lvov by the name of Danilo Boyko. "Heinrich, this is your new man. See to it that he does his work well; no excuses will be tolerated," said Bodenheimer. As ordered, Henryk showed Danilo Mikhail's bunk, and explained the routine and duties.

A knowing half smile and half grimace on the face of Danilo told Henryk that he was recognized as a Jew. The Ukrainians of Lvov lived and worked among Jews for centuries and they could, as the saying went, "to smell a Jew from a kilometer away."

Worried about the new development Henryk sought Edward's advice. "Ed, I'm in deep trouble. This new fellow, Danilo, saw through me. I'm quite sure of that. What can I do?"

"Let's see what can be done. I'll talk with the other guys to see if Danilo is asking any questions about you. We'll watch him very closely. Just don't worry," Edward assured him.

Subconsciously, Henryk started to avoid Danilo whenever it was possible. Danilo would greet Henryk with a facial expression that would communicate to Henryk, "I'm wise to your game. Hardly a week passed by and Danilo managed to antagonize everybody on the team.

To begin with, he took over Mikhail's bunk. If that was not enough, he started to boss everybody around. "What kind of 'Jewish' work are you fellows doing? The Germans will never stand for it," looking at Henryk at the same time. "Danilo has a point; let's finish this piece of work before the Germans will get to us," said Henryk.

The next morning Edward woke Henryk up with a big grin on his face. "Can you believe it? Danilo hung himself at night, or what was more likely, some fellows helped him to do so by putting a pillow over his mouth to stifle his cry. Someone else put a cord on his neck and pulled the cord over the beam's ceiling. He was dead within a few minutes. You don't have to worry about him any longer."

"What do you think we should say to Bodenheimer?" We'll just report the suicide and that is all," said Henryk. Bodenheimer didn't have the time or inclination to find you another replacement, you 'schweinhunds' will have to work a bit harder, 'Verstanden?'" And work harder they did. Nothing seemed to be able to stop Hitler's war machine. What the Red Army couldn't accomplish, the white, innocent, light snow flakes, like a trillion small butterflies, silently covered the Mother-Russia's earth. Snow combined with paralyzing cold congealed lubricants in the German vehicles and weapons; Hitler's "Grand Armee" came to a halt.

Henryk's team hit very tough times. They were used over and over again to help dig out equipment from snowdrifts. They were constantly cold and hungry in the winter of 1941-42. In addition, the Germans were in a foul mood; their "spaziergang" through Russia ended.

At Christmas time, Bodenheimer brought a bottle of Schnapps for the men in honor of his promotion to the rank of sergeant. "Wir gratulieren Ihnen, Herr Bodenheimer, we congratulate you," said Henryk. "Oh, by the way, Heinrich, I want to talk to you. You seem to me more intelligent than the rest. I have orders to disband this group. The men can join Die Osttruppen or Ost Legionen, Cossack units or even Organization Todt. If not, they will be sent to a concentration camp. Your job is to tell your men about it and bring me a list of their choices. One more thing, Heinrich, let me give you a piece of advice. If you want to live through this crazy war, you better join the OT (Organization Todt). I'll give you a written recommendation. If you have any German blood in you, we can make a Volksdeutch out of you yet, and now go back to your men before I kick your behind; Merry Christmas, Heinrich."

"And Merry Christmas to you, Herr sergeant. You have been good to us," said Henryk, walking out of Bodenheimer's bunker.

This new situation had to be discussed in greater detail with Edward, prior to notifying the rest of the team.

Henryk repeated to Edward his entire conversation with Bodenheimer. Throughout their ordeals they became very close, trusting each other and relying upon each other like brothers.

"Henryk, we have to get out of this God forsaken place; otherwise we surely will die sooner or later. I think our best bet is to join OT; maybe that way we'll be able to get home to see our families." "I agree with you, Ed. We don't have any other viable choice." Both Henryk and Edward went to see the rest of the men who were living in a basement of a bombed out house.

"Fellows, here is the situation. We went through hell together, but we survived because we watched out for each other. But now we have to go our separate ways. I can't do anything any more for you, and he explained their options as they were given to him by Bodenheimer. "You'll have to follow your heart; I'll need your decision by tomorrow morning."

The next day Henryk's difficult tasks became even more troublesome with the disappearance of his two key men, Andrei Komarov and Ilya Muromets. According to some men, Andrei and Ilya escaped into the forest in the hope of joining the Soviet partisans active in the general vicinity. Henryk always felt that Ilya Muromets was a high ranking army officer who was trying to keep a low profile in the captivity. His name was most likely fictitious because of Ilya Muromets in Russian folklore was legendary hero.

Henryk hardly started to speak with his men regarding the problem facing them all, when Bodenheimer suddenly appeared. "Slight change of plans. The Cossack military units are in the planning stage. You fellows are still assigned to nonombat auxiliary roles such as you are doing now. In the future, some of you will become drivers, ammunition carriers, and so on." Bodenheimer looked around to see the reaction of his own subhumans (Untermenschen).

"I don't see Ilya and Andrei? Where the devil are they? Asked Bodenheimer, looking at the surprised Henryk.; before Henryk had a chance to respond to Bodenheimer's question, the quick thinking Edward came to the rescue. "Herr Bodenheimer, a staff car came by and took those two. They said they needed grooms for the general's horses." "Ausgezeicht. Excellent! Good riddance, I never liked those two anyway. A few of you from the region of Don and Zaporozhie will be eventually sent to the Cossack units. Henryk, Edward and maybe some of you, too, will be sent to Smolensk or Vitebsk where OT could use your skills, The rest of you keep busy if you want to stay alive." With these words, Bodenheimer left.

Some of the men were disappointed because they hoped to escape the deprivations of the semi-prison life. As far as Henryk and Edward were concerned, they glad to leave the present, mostly dangerous work and move away from the front lines.

They also wondered about Bodenheimer's largesse. They were not in the position to know that the decision to incorporate former Soviet nationals and P.O.W.'s into auxiliary troops were made at the level of divisional commanders, who, in turn, were recipients of Quartermaster General Wagner's memorandum, "We are at the end of our personnel and material strength."

Henryk and Edward, along with a few remaining men out of the original dozen, labored under the strict supervision of Sgt. Bodenheimer for the next couple of months. In the spring of 1942 they were sent under a heavy guard to the city of Smolensk, the historical gateway to Mosow. Smolensk was captured by General Guderian's Second and General Hermann Hoth's Third Panzer Group tanks almost a year ago.

A constant and determined Soviet resistance in the area between Dnieper and Western Dvina Rivers caused the Germans many problems, especially regarding mined bridges. Working on one of these bridges over the muddy waters of Dnieper, Henryk's men came across several masked mines. Handled by inexperienced men, one of the mines exploded killing and severely wounding men in the immediate area.

Bodenheimer came at once to inspect the damage when someone pointed to him another unexploded mine. "Never mind, I'll handle this one by myself," said Bodenheimer, who prided himself as an explosive expert. This time, however, something went wrong because the mine exploded. Bodenheimer, who was partially protected by a heavy beam, lost only three fingers on his left hand. A German medic applied bandages to the wounded hand and rushed Bodenheimer to a nearby Army First Aid Station, leaving the Russian POWs unattended. It was ironic, because the mine which wounded Bodenheimer was of German design, the so-called "S" mine which Germans left in anticipation of a Russian counterattack.

With Bodenheimer's absence and the loss of a few of his men, Henryk requested and received several dozens of captured P.O.W.'s from Marshall Timoshenko's defeated army. The men were mainly carpenters, builders or railroad workers. "Heinrich" Kaplinski was put in charge of the "Hilfswillige Pioners" detachment thanks to Bodenheimer's recommendations. Henryk, in turn, appointed Edward as his deputy.

This new and totally unwelcome position required the knowledge of the German language, which he spoke fluently, but for the time being, he spoke a broken German. However, as time progressed, he started to use more frequently to the point that some of the German noncommissioned and commissioned officers would remark how fast did "Heinrich" learned German.

His detachment was always carefully guarded, be it in Smolensk, Vitebsk or the Mogilev regions. To the Russians of the detachment, Henryk was considered a "Paliak" because he always spoke Polish with Edward. Now with the Germans giving Henryk additional authority, the men were careful in dealing with him and that suited Henryk perfectly.

Not one of the men suspected Henryk of being Jewish. What Henryk was afraid of were the Poles and Ukrainians of his own home region.

Three weeks later Bodenheimer showed up wearing an elegant leather glove on his left hand, thus hiding the three missing fingers. "Wie gehts Heinrich? At the hospital they gave this," pointing to his glove, "and a War Merit Cross (KVK) 5th class and one full month of furlough. I'm going home to Silesia, but I requested to stay with my 813 Pioner Company 'till victory. We might be going to France. It would certainly be a better assignment than this 'Dreck.' Heinrich, what do you think about those lovely French girls? I know also that you were the first to rush to my help, even before the medic came in. As a German soldier, I want to repay my debt of honor. I'll take you and Edward in ten days to Minsk on my way home. In Minsk, there is a branch of Organization Todt (OT) where I'll drop you off and take the train to Katowitz. In the meantime, find yourself a replacement."

This time the replacement was easy to find because with the newly arrived group a man came forward and introduced himself to Henryk. He was Aleksei Gusiev, an architect from Moscow and a former sublieutenant of the Red Army. He was tall and well mannered, even in these tough circumstances, and had an aura of quiet efficiency of an experienced professional. In addition, he had a rudimentary knowledge of German.

Without much ado, Henryk transferred to Gusiev a few files and some tools that were in his possession. They shook hands warmly and wished each other good luck.

On the appointed hour, Bodenheimer stopped to pick up Henryk and Edward. Both carried bags with their few personal belongings. They climbed aboard the truck where a couple of armed soldiers were also riding. Naturally, Bodenheimer, as befitted his rank, sat in the truck's cabin next to the driver. They were frequently stopped by the Military Police, mainly on the crossroads. The Police were looking for deserters, saboteurs, and escaped prisoners. Since Bodenheimer had all the necessary papers, which he would hand over using his gloved hand, and after a few general questions, they were let go. It took twenty-eight hours to reach Minsk, a distance of 250 km. because the rain had softened the unpaved Russian roads in many places.

At the outskirts of Minsk they were stopped by a unit of S.S. Bodenheimer presented his papers, which the S.S. man carefully looked over. "What about those two?" said he, pointing at Edward and Henryk. "Oh, these two are Hiwis joining the O.T.," answered Bodenheimer calmly. Henryk's heart just skipped a beat. "That is fine. The office of O.T. is located on Hitler Strasse, #133. By the way, the fellow in charge of that office is Herr Bruno Mueller, an uncle of mine, Give him regards from his nephew. Dieter. 'Mach es Gut und weiter gehen.'"

They found the Hitler Strasse, what used to be Stalin's Boulevard, without difficulty. The main building of Organization Todt (O.T.) was a three story brick building which was requisitioned by the German authorities. Bodenheimer asked for Bruno Mueller by name, and after a short wait was directed to Mueller's office. Bodenheimer knocked on the glass door bearing a sign 'Baumeister Bruno Mueller.'

"Herein! Come in." Bodenheimer and his two proteges walked in. Mueller was a heavy set fifty something year old man who offered a chair to Bodenheimer. "Bitte, nehmen Sie Platz. What can I do for you?" "I've regards for you from your nephew, Dieter, and at the same time I would like to use this opportunity to introduce these two young men who wish to join your organization. They worked as Hiwis for our battalion for over a year and a half. We have been very pleased with their services and we do recommend both of them highly."

Mueller and Bodenheimer chatted for awhile like two old friends sitting and smoking, while Henryk and Edward stood in the corner of the room respectfully holding their hats in their hands. Mueller inquired details about Henryk's and Edward's work. He seemed to be fully satisfied with the answers. "Sehr Gut, let them fill out an application and we'll direct them to the O.T. barracks where they'll receive new and clean uniforms, food, a place to sleep and so on. By the way, Heinrich, Sprichts Du Deutsch?" "Ja, klein bischen, Herr Mueller," answered Henryk. With Bodenheimer's help they filled out applications which Mueller promptly signed and affixed his stamp to it. "On the way out see my secretary. She'll give you the 'Pasierschein' and directions to the barracks.

You are dismissed." Mueller also shook Bodenheimer's hand, clicked his heels and said, "Heil Hitler" in a heavy Bavarian slang. Bodenheimer responded in kind.

After leaving Mueller's office, Henryk said to Bodenheimer, "Auf Wiedersehen, Herr Bodenheimer and vielen Dank." (Goodbye and thank you very much). Bodenheimer wished both of them luck and left the building. "Edward, I hope it is the last time we see this son of a bitch, Bodenheimer." "I hope so too." But they were both wrong.

A Russian speaking secretary with an Estonian sounding name, dressed in the uniform of O.T. issued then "Ausweiss-Pasierschein" that served as identification cards and passed along with other needed papers and directed them to the O.T. barracks located on Gogol Strasse #16. The O.T. barracks were located in a former school dormitory, which now housed the workers of the Organizational Todt, named after its founder Fritz Todt, chief architect and whose organization carried out the most impressive construction program, building bunkers, bridges, autobahns and railroads for the Wehrmacht.

By the time Henryk and Edward joined the O.T., Todt was killed in a mysterious air accident. His successor, Albert Speer, maintained the O.T. as his predecessor had run it. Almost 80% of its members were nonGermans; many of them volunteers from countries occupied by Germans and sympathetic to Hitler's cause.

Upon entering the barracks Henryk and Edward showed their "Ausweisses" to the officer in charge. "Welcome to O.T. It's too late today for you to receive your uniforms. Go to the mess hall and get yourselves something to eat. We'll put you up on the third floor for the night and tomorrow we'll assign you to your permanent duties. Here are your food coupons."

Hungry and dog-tired, they went to the mess hall on the main floor, handing over the coupons to the waiter. He, in turn, brought them two bowls of cabbage soup, some meat and potatoes, and two mugs of coffee, which tasted like dishwater. Since they hadn't eaten anything better in almost two years in captivity, the food was just fine.

After the meal, they walked up to the third floor where a foreman pointed at two available beds right next to a public latrine and washrooms. Too tired to argue about the choice of beds, they went to sleep. The snoring of their neighbors and frequent flushing of the toilets did not wake them up, but the morning scream of "Aufstehen" had done it. They quickly shaved and got dressed, following the rest of the men to the mess hall, taking their seats at a large table marked "3rd floor only."

The breakfast was surprisingly substantial; eggs, sausages, boiled potatoes and large chunks of black bread, followed by hot, strong tea.

Another official of O.T., wearing a uniform with a swastika armband, came up to the table yelling, "Where are the two new men that arrived last night?" It was obvious who they were because they were out of uniform. The official spoke Polish with a distinct Warsovian dialect. Edward said quietly to Henryk, "Let me handle this." "Here, sir, here we are," politely but firmly answered Edward, and both of them stood up. Perhaps the tone of Edward's answer caused the official to use a more civilized way of continuing conversation.

"Herr Bruno Mueller used a code X-33 to your application, indicating that both of you are experienced carpenters. I can use you on a special project at once. Which one of you is named Heinrich Kaplinski?" "I'm, sir, but my name is actually Henryk," answered Henryk. "I'll call you Heinrich; it is better this way. Both of you go and get your uniforms and report back to me in forty-five minutes. My name is Jerzy Krygier." Henryk and Edward clearly understood that they had to deal with a Polonized German, who switched his loyalty once more by becoming a Volksdeutsch. Glancing at each other, they realized the new situation. Without a doubt, Henryk had to be extra careful.

They had done what they were told, picking up uniforms with the ever-present swastika armbands, even though they were neither soldiers nor members of the party. Next to Hitler Jugend, Organization Todt was the second organization to carry it's founder's name.

Once in uniform, Henryk looked in the mirror to see his reflection. A hard, weather-beaten face with deep, sad eyes looked back at him.

With a few minutes to spare, they showed up at Krygier's desk. "I see that you've learned the lesson of punctuality. I like that in my men. I need you two and maybe another half dozen men to fix a part of the railroad demolished by those stinking Russian partisans. You, Heinrich, I'm putting you in charge of that project. You'll be personally responsible to me for the results. I'll have these additional men within the half-hour in front of the building. One of the men, a fellow by the name of Sebastian, will have the needed tools. Sorry, but no trucks are available this morning, so you'll have to walk about 5-6 km. to the railroad. Don't bother coming back 'till you finish the job, understood?" "Yes, sir." The instructions were all too clear.

By the time they came down, Sebastian and the other five men were already waiting for them with extra spades and picks. They formed an eight-man squad and marched in military fashion through the town. The reaction they provoked in the population of the town varied from amazement to fear, especially when Sebastian sang the only song he knew in German:

> "Wenn die Soldaten durch die Stadt marchieren
> offnen die Madchen, Fenster und die Turen..."
> (When the soldiers march through the town, the
> maidens open their windows and doors)...

The task they faced after reaching the damaged part of the railroad was rather simple. A part of the track was blown up Henryk, or Heinrich as he was called now by the men, assembled his crew, to find out about each man's experience, dividing the job among his people, leaving the hardest and toughest-like carrying wooden railroad ties and rails to Edward and him. This fair distribution of labor won an automatic respect and admiration from his men. With everybody applying himself the job was finished in record time. After the customary smoke interval, they marched back to town singing the same song.

As the days changed into weeks and months, Krygier, who called himself Kruger now, started to assign Henryk, progressively more difficult projects and at the same time adding more and more people out of the vast pool of captured Soviet Red Army men. The extra responsibility and enlarged visibility was an unwelcome development for Henryk, who would have preferred to be less noticeable.

In the meantime, he didn't have much choice. He discharged each assignment as best as he could, always treating his men fairly, and making sure that they were properly fed on time. He, himself, was the first to work and the last to eat. At the end of each day he would report to Kruger about the accomplishments or the rare failures. Kruger, in turn, seemed to be very well informed about Henryk's activities. It was obvious to Henryk that Kruger had an informant or informants on each project; one or more reason why Henryk had to be extra careful.

However, two separate incidents changed Henryk's situation completely. Working on a bombed out building, Henryk noticed that one of his men from the original half a dozen man squad was shirking or what appeared to be shirking from his duties. It was none other than Boguslaw Kosciolek. "Hey, Kosciolek, what gives with you today?" asked Henryk. "Panie (Mr.) Heinrich, I don't feel too good. I think I'm sick," answered Kosciolek. Henryk took another look at Kosciolek. It was clear to Henryk that the man was, indeed, ill. Henryk touched Kosciolek's forehead. There was no doubt about it, Kosciolek was running a high fever.

Henryk told Kosciolek to lay down and rest, applying cold compresses to his head. "Panie (Mr.) Heinrich, I have something to tell you in secret. Be very careful with Sebastian. He informs on you to Kruger." "Thank you very much for letting me know. I'll be careful and you just take it easy a bit. Rest and drink a lot of water. I'll check on you from time to time."

When the other men complained that they had to do Kosciolek's work, Henryk simply told them to shut up. "Look, Kosciolek is really sick. It can happen to any of you, so let's just cover for him today." The men grudgingly went back to work, knowing deep down that Henryk was right once more. At the end of the day, Henryk removed one of the doors and put Kosciolek on it and said loudly, "I need three more volunteers to carry Kosciolek back to the barracks." Not three, but six men raised their hands. Kosciolek was brought back to the barracks where a medic called for an ambulance. That was the last time Henryk saw or heard from Kosciolek. All of his inquiries as to his fate ended in, "We don't know."

Slowly but surely, Henryk's reputation as a fair and caring individual had spread throughout the barracks. The harder Henryk tried to minimize his role, the more people would come up to him to ask for all kinds of favors or advice. Whenever he could, he would say a kind word of encouragement, which was very much appreciated by the rank and file.

One evening, after work, Henryk and Edward sat down to play their usual game of chess. The men around them spoke about women, schnapps, politics, hushing their voices when it came to the word "Stalingrad", and eventually switched their conversation about Henryk. "Our Henryk is smart like a Jew." It was a compliment that Henryk could have done without. Someone else said, "Maybe he is one. As a matter of fact, he even looks like a Jew."

Both Henryk and Edward heard the exchange. Henryk couldn't utter a word, but a quick thinking Edward again came to Henryk's rescue saying, "If he is a Jew, then I am a rabbi." Everyone started to laugh. The chess game ended with Edward beating Henryk badly. This time Henryk didn't mind the loss. He was grateful to Edward for his cool head and everlasting friendship. One thing became clear that he had to leave this place.

Another incident happened that would speed up his wish. Henryk's detachment work on widening a bridge over a tributary to the Dvina River. During a late and hot afternoon one of the men carried a heavy wooden board about three meters long, when someone else called his name. He turned around to see who called him inadvertently hitting Sebastian in the head. Sebastian was knee deep in the water reinforcing a beam when the board hit him. He lost his balance and fell into the deep part of the river screaming, "I can't swim; I can't swim, help." The wooden board must have scratched his face because it was covered with blood, adding to Sebastian's panic. Sebastian was going under fast. Henryk witnessed the entire scene and without a moment of hesitation jumped in after Sebastian. He grabbed Sebastian from the back and pushed him towards the bank of the river where the other men pulled Sebastian to safety.

Henryk put Sebastian on his side pressing his chest a few times. Sebastian coughed and spat the water out. Someone handed Henryk a clean bandage, which Henryk applied to Sebastian's deep cut on the forehead. Sebastian was badly shaken, but otherwise he was fine.

There wasn't much of the day left and they badly needed supplies to finish the job. Therefore, Henryk decided to call it a day, and the entire detachment marched back to the barracks. They arrived at least an hour earlier than usual. "Herr" Kruger jumped out of his office screaming, "Heinrich, what is the meaning of coming back in the middle of the day?" Henryk simply pointed to Sebastian's bandaged head and said, "We also ran out of needed supplies." Kruger didn't bother with any other explanation. He seemed to be totally preoccupied with Sebastian's status. "Bring Sebastian to my quarters immediately."

Henryk noticed an intense exchange of words between Kruger and Sebastian. He managed to hear some excerpts of their conversation. "He saved my life," pointing to Henryk. To follow Kruger's orders, Henryk asked a couple of workers to help Sebastian get to Kruger's office. He had never seen Kruger acting more humane or ever admitting an injured person to his office with an adjacent private room. Henryk had been to Kruger's office, but never to his bedroom.

Henryk had had enough excitement for one day. He was tired, hungry, and his boots and clothing were still wet. He, therefore, went up stairs to change into a fresh uniform and later went to the mess hall to get some food.

Well known in the mess hall he was served regardless of the time. He ate slowly, talking about the day's happening with the men of his detachment. "There is too much to do about Sebastian; it was an accident. The creep is lucky to be alive," was the general comment. "Oh, never mind, I'll go up and check on him anyway. Good night," said Henryk and walked towards the staircase leading to Kruger's office.

The door to Kruger's office was closed. Henryk politely knocked on the door and not hearing the usual "Herein" (come in), he let himself in. There wasn't anyone in the office proper, so Henryk walked towards the slightly ajar door leading to Kruger's bedroom. What Henryk saw was almost enough to change him into a pillar of salt, There in the middle of the room, Sebastian sat on an armchair and the big and powerful Kruger was on his knees performing fellatio on him. Henryk wanted to close the door, but inadvertently the door opened wide, with a slight squeak, loud enough to alert both of them that someone else entered the room.

An indescribable look of horror registered on their faces. "What the hell are you doing in my office?" yelled Kruger. "I just came by to see how Sebastian is, but I see that you're resuscitating him in a very interesting way, Herr Kruger," calmly answered Henryk, putting an emphasis on the word "Herr." "What do you want? Money, cigarettes, whisky? Just say the word," said Kruger, near panic. "Kruger, I'll take all of that and more. I want you to give me and Edward transfers from Minsk to Lemberg in the Ukraine as soon as possible, and your dirty little secret will be safe with me. Do we understand each other?" "Yes, you'll have it. No wonder some men suspect you of being a Jew."

"Oh, sure that I'm a Jew. Kruger. I would show you my prick, but I'm afraid that you might suck it the same way as you did Sebastian's. Don't be an idiot, too, Kruger. Get me those fucking papers and let us get the hell out of this place. I'll stop by tomorrow morning for those papers. They had better be ready! "Ist dass klaar Herr Kruger?" "You'll have them, but for God's sake keep your mouth shut." "Zum Befehl" (as ordered, Sir). "Und Gutte Nacht," said Henryk, closing the doors behind him.

Henryk ran up to the third floor straight to Edward, whom he woke up from a deep sleep. "Get up, Edward, get up. I need to talk to you urgently. It is very important." "It better be important, you jackass, waking me up in the middle of the night," yawning, said Edward, and both of them walked out of the room to the hallway where no one could overhear their conversation.

Henryk faithfully described the entire scene and repeated in detail his conversation with Kruger. "No shit," was the comment uttered by Edward. "That is finally our chance to get out of here." They went back to their respective beds, but Henryk couldn't fall asleep, thinking of the best way to handle this situation.

The next day he showed up at Kruger's office about half an hour earlier than usual. "Gutten Morgen, Herr Kruger, how is Sebastian this morning?" innocently asked Henryk. "He is just fine, thank you. And now back to business. I don't have an opening for you in Lemberg, not until six to eight weeks later. However, I have an immediate opening in the city of Lublin. I have to send a replacement for the local manager and a crew of about twenty-four men. That is the best I can do for you and Edward at the moment to get you out of my sight. One more thing, your transfers have to be countersigned by Herr Bruno Mueller."

"We'll take the Lublin assignment. Last night I wrote three separate letters to the authorities about your little affair and gave those letters to reliable people with the instructions to mail them out in three weeks unless they hear from me; just a little insurance."

"Henryk, you really must be a fucking Jew because you are too smart to be a Pole," said Herr Kruger, handing two transfers to him. Take them to Mueller and I don't ever want to see you again. May the devil take you." "Exactly my sentiments, Herr Kruger," said Henryk, while leaving the office.

Prior to seeing Mueller, Henryk went to look for Edward, who waited impatiently in the adjacent hall. "Look, Ed, I couldn't get the Lemberg post (city located 100 km. from their hometown). The best he could come up with is Lublin, which is available to us in a couple of days. For Lemberg, we would have to wait at least two months. I think it would be too dangerous for us to stay here any longer where Kruger has all kinds of contacts. Don't you agree?" "I think that you are right. We have to get away from here. Besides, Lublin is not bad at all. My mother has a sister living there. I'm sure they will help us. In the meantime, get those papers signed and we can pack in the evening. God only knows that we don't have a hell of a lot to pack."

Thus, encouraged, Henryk went straight to Mueller's office. "Ja, herrein," was in response to Henryk's knock on the door. Henryk entered the office taking his cap off. "My name is Heinrich Kaplinski, and I came to have these transfers co-signed, Herr Mueller," said Henryk, putting the transfers on Mueller's desk right in front of him. "Yes, I remember you. Wasn't that my nephew, Dieter, that recommended you to us? Also, Kruger had mentioned your name once or twice. He told me that you were an outstanding foreman, always well organized. Aha, the only thing he didn't like about you that you were too ambitious for him, almost like a Jew, ha, ha, ha."

"Herr Mueller, if I were Jewish, would I have been so patriotic? As far as being well organized, it must be part of my German heritage. My grandmother was part German and worked with German colonists in our area, and as you very well know that, "Gutt eingeseift is halb rasiert" (well-soaped beard is half shaven).

Kaplinski, I do like you. Maybe I'll send Kruger to Lublin and keep you here, instead, What do you say?" "Herr Mueller, I really appreciate your all too generous offer, but you see, my entire family was killed by the Soviets and the only sister of my mother lives in Lublin and I would like very much to see her."

"Du hast rechts." (You're right) Mueller signed with a flourish both transfers and handed them over to Henryk. "Good luck, Heinrich. Stop by in the afternoon and pick up all the papers from my secretary; the railroad tickets, food requisition and so on. I'll also write you a letter of recommendation. This may open a few doors for you in a strange town. Too bad that you don't want to stay because you and I would get along just fine. You can come back any time; just let me know." "So sorry, Herr Mueller, and many thanks," said Henryk, clicking his heels.

Outside of Mueller's office, Edward was waiting anxiously. "How did it go?" "Oh, everything went fine, even better than I expected."

Both Henryk and Edward didn't bother to go to work anymore. They were busy organizing the departure of twenty-four volunteers in addition to their own. There was a delay because the papers that Mueller spoke about were not ready until the next day. Henryk went twice to Mueller's secretary. Each time the Estonian secretary, whose name was Karen, would address Henryk in German, which she also spoke fluently, along with Russian and her native Estonian. "Herr Heinrich, you're such an interesting man. Why are you leaving us? Stay here and I'll make it very pleasant for you." The rumor had it that she was Mueller's mistress. The last thing Henryk needed was to have Mueller as a jealous lover.

"Fraulein Karen, you are very "simpatisch", and I'm very flattered, but in Lublin my wife and son are expecting me." "Oh, I didn't know that you're a married man. Here are your papers and goodbye." She turned around and started to type furiously.

Henryk picked up the papers and arranged for a roll call of the twenty-four Hivis. He checked each man against the master list and chatted briefly to find out their origins and experiences, finally announcing the departure time of 7:30 A.M. the next morning.

On the eve of departure, Sebastian came to see Henryk, bringing with him an envelope stuffed with money and a bottle of precious French cognac. "Mr. Heinrich, the envelope is from Kruger, but the cognac is from me to you. I just want to thank you again for saving my life as wretched as it is. I'm not a homosexual, but I must do whatever Kruger wants because he is blackmailing me." "Good luck Sebastian, but the next time you get a blow job at least close the door." They shook hands and parted.

CHAPTER 3

Henryk fell asleep, hoping that tomorrow might be a beginning of a better life, and perhaps a chance of being reunited with his family. All of the letters he wrote to his neighbor's Christian family kept coming back with a stamp "Unknown at this address."

The next morning Henryk's group was assembled on the "Appel-Platz" right on time. Two large trucks with their motors running were ready to drive the group to the main railroad station in town. The men put their gears on their respective trucks boarding at the same time. After a final head count, Henryk yelled, "Forwards" and the truck moved, slowly picking up speed.

At the station, the Railroad and Military Police carefully scrutinized their papers. Henryk dropped all appearances of pretending to speak a broken German, and switched to his pure, at home acquired Viennese German when dealing with the authorities.

"You must be from Vienna," one of the policemen said. "No, I'm Prussian," barked Henryk, knowing full well that nobody liked the Prussians, not even the Berliner, judging from his dialect, policeman examining Henryk's papers. The policeman gave Henryk a smile and handed over the papers. "You do have a good sense of humor. Take wagon #23; it is the best." "Thank you very much and take care," this time answered Henryk, very politely.

The number #23 wagon had six compartments into which Henryk placed his detachment and their gears. He also put Edward in charge of twelve men at the further end of the wagon. He and four other men were located in the largest compartment.

Like everyone else he put his own baggage in an overhead bin. His seat was next to the window, underneath which a small collapsible writing table was attached to. Here, he could also play his favorite card game, solitaire, during the trip. "All aboard," yelled the conductors and loud whistles were very welcome sounds. Finally, they were leaving Minsk and the horrible war.

The issued tickets called for a stop at Pinsk, Brest, where they would have to change trains for the city for their destination., Lublin, a trip that the station master at Minsk said would take from two to three days.

After inspecting his men, Henryk went back to his seat. He found a German book written by Courts-Mahler, a romance novel, that was once his mother's favorite. As it happened, his travelling companions were two Poles from the city of Stanislawow and two Ukrainians from West Ukraine, the city of Sumy. After reading about ten to fifteen pages, he fell into an uneasy sleep, caused perhaps by the book itself, or most likely, by the happenings of the day. The monotone of the railroad wheels coming in contact with the rails had a soothing effect on him.

Like through a dense fog, he heard the conversations held. The Ukrainians spoke about horses in their Kolhoz, but the Poles had a spirited argument. It was the word "Zhid" (Jew) repeated several times that actually woke Henryk up. He kept his eyes shut pretending to be asleep, but he listened intensely to every word said. "Ja Ci mowie on jest Zyd." (I'm telling you that he is a Jew) "Ale co, glupstwa mowisz." (You are talking nonsense) "To ja pojde na Gestapo." (I'll report him to the Gestapo) The situation suddenly became very dangerous for Henryk; he had to act at once.

With a big yawn he got up from his seat and walked slowly toward the offending Pole that was using the word "Zhid." "Say, what is your name?" said Henryk, pretending to be half-asleep. "Boleslaw," answered the fellow, with a smirk on his face. "Boleslaw, what?" "Boleslaw Chrobry," this time with a bigger smile like he would be telling a joke. And a joke it was. Henryk, with his good memory, knew that there was no Chrobry (brave) on the list of Hivis and Chrobry was the name of an early Polish king. A complete hatred pent up in three years took over Henryk.

With a clenched fist he hit Boleslaw squarely on the mouth,

splitting his lips and knocking out two front teeth. After the initial shock, Boleslaw wanted to put up a fight, but Henryk's fists, after years of hard labor, were like hammers. A fast left and right to his chin caused Boleslaw to fall to the ground, where Henryk kicked him in the ribs. A distinct crack of broken ribs was heard. For good measure, he also kicked him several times in the kidneys. Boleslaw started to cry and beg, "No more, no more; please excuse me."

Hearing the commotion, everyone in the wagon came running to see what happened. Henryk stood over the crying Boleslaw lying on the floor and started to shout curses in German, which he learned from Bodenheimer. "Himmel-Kreutz, Donnerwetter, verflucht, verdamnt and zugenaht noch einmal, Du Schweinhund." This will teach you to insult German honor. The other Pole went down to the crying Boleslaw and said, "Ja Ci powiedzialem ze to jest szwab." (I told you he was a Kraut) "Everybody back to your seats, and you tell this "Dumkopf" that next time I'll kill him for sure. I want these two jackasses out of my compartment." Edward came up to Henryk and quietly said, "I'll take care of him, don't worry."

Henryk really didn't have to worry any more about Boleslaw because by the next morning he disappeared altogether. It seemed that during the night he fell off a platform riding between two wagons, or maybe someone pushed him.

This incident changed Henryk's opinion among men. No longer was he seen as a gentle and fair man; he was now seen as a strict disciplinarian and no one 'smart' should cross him. The new role suited Henryk just perfectly.

The next day they arrived in Pinsk where another team of Railroad Police came by to check the group's papers. Henryk spoke to the sergeant in charge. "Sir, during the last night one of our Hivis deserted our unit; I would like you to note on our papers that I have dutifully reported this case to you. His name was Boleslaw Kubec. He was a new man whom I met only two days ago." The sergeant, using his Pelikan pen, duly wrote down on

Henryk's papers the time and the day of Henryk's report, adding his own name, rank and the military unit.

"Don't worry, Herr Kaplinski; we'll get him sooner or later." "Thank you very much; you can do with him whatever you please." "Oh, we surely will, and you have a good journey." Henryk went back to his seat where someone handed him a current German Army newspaper. It was full of propaganda.

Although Henryk had seen for himself the thousands of captured Soviet P.O.W.'s, it also seemed that the Russians had a never ending supply of men and material. Names of Soviet generals such as Timoshenko, Konev, Zhukov, Chernyakovsky or Rokossovsky became known as did the names of recaptured Russian towns. The tide of war started slowly to change direction in the Soviet's favor. The Germans were still a very formidable force to reckon with and that was also known to Henryk.

He was literally caught between the hammer and the anvil. He fell asleep with men tiptoeing around him. The train kept moving very slowly, making frequent stops to let military convoys or entire Red Cross trains full of wounded men pass by. Some hours later, they had reached the town of Brest, where according to their schedule, they had to change trains for Lublin. The Stationmaster, a short and fat Hessian, told them flatly, "I don't know when the next train to Lublin will leave. Maybe within a day or two, or God only knows when and check with me every couple of hours." "Look, sir, I must bring these Hivis to Lublin. They are being expected at the highest level of O.T." "I don't give a damn about your O.T. I have greater problems, just to find trains for those fucking Jews. Don't try to bribe me either or I'll have you arrested. Is that understood?" "Yes, sir, Henryk said disappointed, and went back to his unit where he told the men the results of his conversation with the Stationmaster. "We must keep together. No one can go away for more than fifteen minutes and only in pairs."

Thanks to the requisition coupons they had sufficient amounts of food augmented by local peasants selling their wares around the station. The wait for the next train was unexpectedly short, barely sixteen hours, but long enough to acquire unwelcome company in the form of lice. They couldn't do anything about it at the moment, and the moment of liberation from the lice would have to wait for their final destination – Lublin. Lublin was the solution to other problems as well.

Lublin was a beehive of activities. An ancient Polish town strategically located, it became an important point of arrival and departure for many military units during the German occupation. The ever-present "Kontrolle" checked Henryk's papers which were found "Alles in Ordnung." "You are all from O.T. There is one of your trucks outside the station. Let's see if we can catch it." Henryk immediately dispatched Edward to check on that truck. A few minutes Edward came back with a Polish speaking driver.

"It is all set; this man will take us to O.T. – Lublin barracks." With some difficulty they managed to squeeze the entire group into the truck. Henryk and Edward sat in the truck's cabin.

The large four story building to which the truck brought them was a former Polish high school on Chopin and Kolejowa Streets, now converted to the Headquarters of O.T. the guard at the entrance told Henryk to report to Dr. Ing. Hermann Oberlander's office located on the second floor. After waiting about half an hour, Henryk was admitted to the office.

Dr. Oberlander, in charge of O.T. – Lublin, was a middle aged, bespectacled man who politely asked Henryk about the trip, looked over the papers, reading with attention Mueller's letter of recommendation, while Henryk remained standing, never offering Henryk a chair.

"Very good, Kaplinski. We hope that you'll perform as good or better in Lublin. You may have the rest of the day and tomorrow off to catch up on things. However, I expect you and your team to be ready on the following day at 7:00 A.M. sharp. My assistant, Ing. Josef Keller will brief you on your duties and projects and also show you and your men to your quarters. Remember, if you ever need more men, just say it.

Further conversation was interrupted by a telephone call. Dr.

Oberlander picked up the receiver. "Oberlander hier, ja, ja," sofort (at once) getting up from his chair said, "Please wait here. I'll be back in a few minutes." Henryk looked around. Typical portraits of Hitler and Fritz Todt were hanging on the wall behind the desk, along with a couple of very good photographs of Zugspitze in the Alps in the wintertime. These were only decorations.

On the large mahogany desk were all kinds of papers and blueprints. There was also a newspaper "Berliner Beobachter." Henryk picked up the newspaper glancing at the headlines. It was September, 1943; the Allied forces landed on the Italian mainland at Salerno, Calabria and Taranto, took Naples, and were facing the Volturno River.

Hearing incoming steps in the corridor, Henryk quickly put down the paper just in time for Dr. Oberlander's return. "I'm sorry to hold you up. Just let me introduce you to my right hand, Ing. Keller. He is a very capable fellow, a former fighter pilot. I'm sure that you two will get along." He again picked up the phone saying, "Josef kommen Sie herrein bitte." A minute or two later Ing. Keller came in. He was a young man about a few years younger than Henryk. After a brief introduction, Keller said, "Please follow me," and they walked into an adjacent office which had Keller's name painted in gold letters. Henryk was invited in and asked to take a chair. He also noticed that Keller couldn't bend his right leg. Keller must have felt Henryk's look at the leg because he said, "Yes, it is wood. I lost my leg on the Eastern front piloting a Me-109. You see there are bold pilots and old pilots, but there are not bold and old pilots at the same time." He said that with an engaging smile. It was, indeed, difficult to dislike this man.

Ing. Keller was well prepared. He laid out Henryk's projects for the next month, patiently explaining different procedures, the equipment on hand, methods of communication, payments to the crew, food distribution, and other technical and purely logistic points. Noticing Henryk's eyes slowly closing, he said, "Forgive me, I didn't realize how tired you must be from the long journey.

Let me take you to your quarters and we can discuss these things at greater detail tomorrow."

"I'm really sorry, Herr Ing. Keller, but I must see what my men are doing and then get some sleep." "But of course," and they went jointly to the large waiting room where most of the men were sleeping on the floor already. "Up, up, everybody, we are going to our rooms." Eventually, everyone found a bed. Some people washed up and changed clothing, but some just fell into the beds fully clothes and dead tired. Surprisingly, nobody wanted to eat. It never happened before. The free day and a half was God sent. The men rested, ate and rested some more. They also got rid of the lice picked up at the railroad station.

In the meantime, Henryk went over the details of their assignments with Ing, Keller, and at 7:00 A.M. the unit was ready for the task ahead. This time they had to repair a stretch of the road some 30 km. away and to reinforce several telephone poles undermined by heavy rains. A small convoy of three trucks was put at their disposal, two trucks for personnel and one to carry supplies. This type of work didn't present any difficulties since the men were well versed in their chores.

During the day a large Mercedes-Benz pulled up to the place of their work. It was Dr. Oberlander, Ing. Keller and two other men well-dressed in civilian clothing who came to inspect the site, From their facial expressions, Henryk deduced that they were fully satisfied with the work done so far. Ing. Keller came up to Henryk. "Gutten Tag, Heinrich, wie gehts?" "The upper management decided to extend the project another 14 km. Do you think you can handle it? If yes, what else do you need?"

"Herr Ing. Keller, with these few men it will take quite a long time to accomplish a thorough job. In addition to supplies, I'll need at least another twenty five to thirty men." "That is no problem. By eight o'clock tomorrow morning you'll have an extra forty men. Satisfied?" "Yes, Herr Keller, that would be fine." "In that case, Heinrich, "Auf Wiedersehen." The fact that neither Dr.

Oberlander or the other two gentlemen didn't address Henryk was just as well, since Henryk preferred dealing with Ing. Keller.

In the meantime, a military type of kitchen served the men soup and bread. Henryk walked to the field kitchen to get himself something to eat, and at the same time he spoke to the cook. "Tomorrow, I expect an additional forty to sixty men. To be on the safe side, bring us an additional sixty portions of everything." "On whose authority are you ordering the additional food?" "On Dr. Oberlander's. You can check with him if you want," said Henryk. "It won't be necessary, sir. We have orders to comply with Dr. Oberlander's requests." "Thank you very much. I'm sure the men would be appreciative."

Henryk's men worked just another couple of hours and at quitting time they boarded the same trucks, taking along their tools. The heavy equipment would have been left under guard. Upon Henryk's return, he contacted Ing. Keller regarding supplies and tools for the additional promised men. "It is all done. They'll meet you at the work site at 7:30 or 8:00 o'clock in the morning." Ing. Keller kept his word because simultaneously with Henryk's trucks two other canvas covered trucks pulled in, To Henryk's total surprise, instead of expected Hivis, forty men jumped out, clad in pajama like, striped suits, being yelled at by four S.S. men toting their automatic weapons.

"Aus steigen, loss, loss, schnell." Seeing these emaciated faces and bodies, Henryk recognized them as Jews. His heart skipped a beat. As he found out a bit later, they were inmates of the nearby concentration camp, Majdanek He also had the undisputed proof of concentration camps' presence. This was an fact and no longer a rumor.

Someone barked aloud, "Mutzen ab!" (Hats off!) And forty men, like well-trained soldiers, took off their hats, displaying their shaven heads. One of the S.S. men came up to Henryk with a "Heil Hitler." "Heil Hitler," answered Henryk, who was wearing a freshly pressed O.T. uniform and swastika armband. "Sir, are you in charge?" "Yes, I am." Nonchalantly answered Henryk.

"We brought you forty "Dreckiscke Juden Haftlinge (shitty Jewish inmates). My orders are to fully cooperate with you, sir." "Thank you, corporal. I'm responsible for this project directly to Herr Dr. Ing. Oberlander, who as you probably know, is a very important party member, He and Herr Albert Speer have the Fuhrer's ear at all times. Anyone or anything intervening in my work will be guilty of sabotage. Therefore, I would appreciate it very much if you would let my men do their job and they will also supervise the "Haftlinge" during the day's work. In this way everything will go smoothly. Don't you agree with that, corporal?"

"Yes, but if any of these Jewish swines won't work, we'll shoot them right there." "Of course, you can do it, but that will only upset my men and I won't have any work done, so give me your cooperation and the right people will hear about you, corporal. What is your last name?" "Schmidt, Wilhelm Schmidt, sir! You will have our cooperation." "Alles is wieder in Ordnung" (everything is again in order), said the corporal, clicking his heels and he left.

Henryk called Edward to the side and quietly told him about the conversation with the S.S. man. "Edward, please assign each of our men to two inmates. Let them be as human as possible because they themselves were P.O.W.'s not so long ago. I can't mix with them because they may recognize me as a fellow Jew, and then the Krauts will with shoot me on the spot or send me with them back to Majdanek. So, take over for me and I'll see that they are fed on time." "Dear Henryk, did I ever disappoint you?" "No, never, no brother could be any closer. Your friendship I'll treasure to my dying days."

The next few weeks were very difficult for Henryk. He was deeply and emotionally involved with the Jewish inmates of Majdanek. On one hand his own Jewish identity had to be kept from them for fear of informers; on the other hand he couldn't visibly help them either because the S.S. men while they eased up a bit due to Henryk's understanding with Corporal Schmidt, but the S.S. kept a watchful eye on all proceedings. The only thing that Henryk did under the circumstances was to increase their daily food ration.

A few days after the inmates joined Henryk's O.T. group, one of the cooks asked Henryk, "Herr Kaplinski, I don't see sixty men, but only forty." "Count again, my friend, and you will see sixty," said Henryk, with a smile, "You are right, there are sixty of them. The way the war goes lately, one day we may need their generosity." Henryk just shook his head and walked away.

That evening Edward told Henryk that several inmates asked about Henryk's background. "I told them that you are a Volksdeutsch, but you are a very decent man and they shouldn't bother you." "Ed, you've done very well. Every time I look at those Jewish faces from Majdanek I think about my family in Boryslaw. All my letters written to our Christian neighbors came back with "Addressee unknown" stamp. I'm really desperate. I must go back to my hometown to find out what has happened to my family. I also know that your letters came back with the same results. Do you want to go with me to Boryslaw?" "Yes, very much, but how are we going to do it?" "I overheard Keller's telephone conversation with someone in Lemberg. Keller is supposed to send them some building material in exchange for badly needed pipes. I'll ask Keller if we could deliver that stuff to Lemberg. From there to Boryslaw is, as you very well know, slightly over 100 km. which we could cover in two to three hours. I've a gut feeling that Keller would allow us to do it."

Sometimes in life, problems come in bunches, but so do the solutions, The next day started like so many preceding days, but this time, the "golden Polish autumn" changed into a nasty, prewinter period, gray, rain ladden skies threatened to unleash its cargo. There was a chill in the air.

The usual contingent of forty Majdanek inmates included some new, even more emaciated faces, typical "musulmen" living skeletons that barely moved about. Also, Corporal Schmidt was replaced by another S.S. man of the same rank, a baby faced killer with ice cold blue eyes.

It was one of those "musulman" that started events that changed Henryk's life. This particular "musulman" was carrying a pail of drinking water to a group of workers. Unfortunately, he tripped, spilling the pail and some of the water, wetted the new S.S. man's boots, just as Keller and Henryk were passing by. The S.S. man removed the rifle from his shoulder and pointed it to the frightened man laying on the ground. All he could do to defend himself was to say, "Bitte, nichts schiessen." (please don't shoot) The S.S. man responded, "You are right, the bullet is too good for you." Saying that, he grabbed a spade from the hands of a nearby standing worker. He then put the wooden handle of the spade across the poor man's neck, stepping on the end of the spade with one foot, apparently with the idea to put the other foot on the other end of the spade in order to choke the man to death, when Keller yelled out on the top of his lungs, "Halt, Sofort, Halt."

The S.S. man slowly got off the spade, pointed his gun towards Keller and in a sarcastic tone of voice, addressed Keller, who was wearing his civilian suit, rather than his O.T. uniform, "Und wem habe Ich die Ehre?" (and whom do I have the honor of addressing?) Keller's face was white with anger. Through clenched teeth, he said, "Kriegsbeschadigte Kapitan der Luftwaffe Ing. Keller." (a war wounded Air Force Captain) It is because of idiots like you that we are going to lose this war. You and your lot are giving a bad name to the brave soldiers of Germany. If you are in Majdanek, then you should know or hear about my older brother, Hauptsturmbahnfuhre Karl Keller. I'll make sure that he sends you to the Eastern front. There you'll have a chance to prove how brave you are. Get the hell out of my sight and don't ever come back."

The S.S. man stood there like a wet puppy. He saluted respectfully and left. Other inmates picked up from the ground a lucky inmate, when Keller who calmed down a bit said, "This man is excused from work today," and turning to Henryk said with a smile on his face, "Heinrich, I don't have a brother in the

S.S., so don't worry, we'll manage it somehow. I'm sure that jerk will keep his mouth shut."

"Herr Keller, that was a noble thing you have done. I wonder if I may be permitted to stop at your office this evening for a few minutes. Would 7:30 be convenient?" "In ordnung, Heinrich, I'll see you then." "Mit der Deutsche Punktlichkeit." With German punctuality, Henryk came to Keller's office and before he had a chance to knock on the door, he heard Keller's, "Herrein, and do sit down."

They spoke about the day's happening. Keller sensing that Henryk wanted to speak about other matters, asked him directly, "Heinrich, what is on your mind? You seem lost in your thoughts lately." "Herr Keller, you are absolutely right. Edward and I need to get to Lemberg where we suspect our families currently are. We need transportation and documents allowing us to travel for about four to seven days." "When do you want to go?" "The sooner the better because we are very anxious to locate our dear ones." "Oh, I can understand that. Coincidentally, we have to send a truck with supplies to Lemberg and pick up some other stuff, but that truck is due to leave Lublin in a few days. Would you like to drive it?" "Yes, Herr Keller, that would be quite acceptable."

"One more thing, Heinrich, I also want to speak with you. I'm being promoted and sent to the Normandy region in France where we are going to build additional bunkers and barricades against a possible invasion by the Allies. You can come along with me as my assistant or stay here and take my place. I'm sure that you can manage either assignment." "Sir, congratulations on your promotion and I'm deeply honored by your offer. May I give you my answer upon my return from Lemberg?" "But of course. I'll get you all the necessary papers. What is Edward's last name? I keep forgetting it, it is so impossible." "His name is Daszkiewicz. D-a-s-z-k-i-e-w-i-c-z." "That is fine. I do hope that you will find your relatives. Keep in mind my offer." "I won't forget it. Thank you very much."

The next day Henryk woke up with a terrible tooth ache. Some kind of an abscess was forming on his gum, next to a molar. He was in great pain most of the day. Edward noticed it immediately and said to Henryk, "Let me take you to the dentist. There is one nearby on Kolejowa Street, so let's go, why suffer?" Although the dentist was located hardly three blocks from their barracks, yet to Henryk it seemed like an eternity. The sign on the door clearly said, "Dr. Bronislaw Drzewiecki-Stomatolog – one flight up." To get to the first floor, Edward had to practically carry Henryk. They knocked on the door and walked in.

A very pretty young woman with jet-black hair and incredibly blue eyes, dressed in a white laboratory coat opened the door wider. Seeing two men wearing O.T. uniforms with their ever-present swastika armbands, startled her. She recaptured her composure and said in heavily accented school German, Gutten Abend meine Herren. Was wunchen Sie?" (good evening, gentlemen. What do you wish?) Edward answered her in Polish, "My Polacy" (We are Poles) And proceeded to tell her pointing to Henryk that he needs an immediate doctor's attention.

She was not pacified with their being Polish and wearing German uniforms, that was quite obvious. "My father, Dr. Drzewiecki is just finishing working on a patient and you will be next. Please sit down. I'll tell the doctor that you are here." A few minutes later, a middle aged woman walked out of the doctor's office holding her left cheek, followed by a tall, almost grey haired man in a white coat. "I'm Dr. Drzewiecki, how can I help you, gentlemen?" Edward briefly explained to the doctor in Polish Henryk's condition because Henryk could hardly speak or stand on his feet.

"Take your seat in this chair," said the doctor to Henryk, pointing to a dentist chair. "And you, sir, please wait in the other room and I'll see what can be done for your friend." Edward left for the waiting room where Czeslawa, the doctor's daughter, gave him some old magazines and local papers to read.

In the meantime, the doctor examined Henryk's mouth and said, "Look, sir, I'll have to treat your tooth several times in order to save it. I would really hate to pull out your healthy molar. It will be painful for a minute, so hold on." The abscess was the size of a nut, so when the doctor punctured it, Henryk felt like someone touched it with a hot iron and promptly fainted. Dr. Drzewiecki anticipated Henryk's reaction and crushed an ampule in his fingers containing ammonia, which he put next to Henryk's nostrils, and as a result, Henryk came back to himself at once.

The doctor cleaned and medically treated the infected area of Henryk's gums. "I'm sure that you are feeling much better. However, you must come to see me every day for the next three days. I must check to see if the infection reoccurs. Please rinse your mouth with Hydrogen Peroxide mixed with warm water at least three times daily. Avoid salt or spicy foods." Henryk felt much better; he removed the white napkin from his chest and got off from the chair,

"Thank you very much, Doctor, and what do I owe you?" "My daughter usually takes care of the payments, but I can't seem to find her," and he mentioned his fee, which Henryk promptly paid. The doctor glanced briefly into the waiting room to see his daughter, Czeslawa, engaged in deep conversation with Edward. He turned around to Henryk and said, "You are my last patient of the day, Mr. Kaplinski. Judging from your Polish language you must come from the Lemberg region. Am I right?"

Henryk now had a good chance to look at the doctor. He was no longer in pain and he could think clearly. He had an eerie feeling that somewhere or somehow he had met the doctor before. All of a sudden it hit him, Of course, he knew him. The doctor was his mother's cousin, Bronek Holzman, the black sheep of the family who married a gentile Polish woman in church. Henryk now remembered, even though he was a child of nine or ten years old.

The whole family sat "shiva". Bronek's father poured ashes on his head, tore his clothing and declared Bronek's death. There were some rumors that Bronek went to a medical or dental school in a large Polish city and nobody ever heard from him again. Bronek's father died without forgiving his son for marrying out of his faith.

It was really so simple. Drzewiecki was the Polish equivalent of German Holzman.

"To answer your question, doctor, I'm from your own home town of Boryslaw. You are, after all, Bronek Holzman, my mother Esther's cousin. I'm Henio Kaplinski, the son of Szymon Koppel, who had to change his name to a Polish one in order to hold a job in the Post Office, a token Jew, even though he fought under General Haller in the Polish Legiony."

The doctor turned white, holding a chair for support. "Yes, Henio, I now recognize you, too. How is your mother? I know that my parents died of broken hearts. I caused them much pain, but I had to live my life as I saw it. You see, I never believed in God anyway. It didn't matter to me if I didn't believe in Him as a Jew or Catholic, and then I met this woman whom I loved and still do. That she happened to be Catholic was a coincidence. Her father was a professor at the university and he helped me get into a dental school, the very same school that rejected Bronek Holzman from Boryslaw, accepted Bronislaw Drzewiecki. This is my story. Tell me, please, what are you doing in German uniform? If they catch you, they will surely kill you."

"Bronek, there is not much to tell. I was taken into the Red Army in 1940, and a year later I was captured by the Germans. I kept quiet about being a Jew. They needed carpenters so I volunteered in order not to die of hunger. Later, they put me into O.T., and that is where I am now. If it weren't for Edward who saved my life several times I would probably be in Majdanek or another such place. Edward and I are school friends. We even played together in the sandbox. He is my brother whom I love dearly. Next week, we are going to Lemberg and to Boryslaw to see what has happened to our families. I'll tell you when we get back, we hope."

"Henio, for God's sake, don't tell my daughter who I am or your friend for that matter either. We'll tell them later after the war, but not now. Do you promise?" "Yes I do," said Henryk, and they shook hands and embraced each other warmly.

As they were about to part, the office door opened. Both

Czeslawa and Edward came in smiling, "Cesiu, Mr. Kaplinski is a very engaging young man, I enjoyed talking to him." "Papa, so is Mr. Daszkiewicz. I have taken the liberty of inviting him tomorrow evening to see Bertold Brecht's "Three Penny Opera." It is actually a parody, and it's playing in the Juliusza Osterwy Theatre. I'm sure that Mr. Edward will enjoy Kurt Weil's music, and now that you told me that Henryk is such an interesting man, I'm, with your permission, extending the invitation to him also. Both of you have to get rid of those awful German uniforms. I don't want my friends to see me with Germans."

Before Henryk had a chance to respond, Edward firmly said, "We both will be happy to escort you to the theatre. Where and when can we pick you up?" "Tomorrow at 5:00 P.M. in front of our building. We live on the third floor, and remember, we must be back before the stupid curfew time." "We are looking forward to tomorrow's evening," said Edward, politely kissing Czeslawa's hand. They exchanged long glances and only a blind man couldn't see that these two young people were hopelessly in love.

Edward spent the entire next day talking about Czeslawa. "She is so beautiful, so sweet, her eyes are deep as an ocean. Did you see her hair, her smile? Henryk, I'm telling you now, she is the woman that I'm going to marry, you'll see." "Edward did you lose your mind altogether? I have NEVER seen you behaving like a schoolboy. Is that the first time you are interested in a girl? Get hold of yourself. In two days we are going to our home town, or did you forget about it already?" "Yes, Henryk, I do love her. She is going to be my wife and no, I didn't forget about our trip either, but still I can't wait for tomorrow."

The next day must have been the longest day ever for Edward because he kept checking his wrist watch every few minutes. They quit working a bit earlier and rushed to the barracks to get ready for the theatre. Never before had Edward spent so much time in front of a mirror, He even borrowed a tie from a friend because he thought that his own or Henryk's wasn't elegant enough.

Czeslawa was already waiting for them in front of her house.

She was dressed warmly in a winter coat and was wearing a cute hat with a long feather. "Serwus" and how are you two? Let's take a trolley to the theatre because it's late." The wagon reserved for Poles was crowded, but Czeslawa wouldn't ride in a wagon for the Germans which was relatively empty, a wagon that Edward and Henryk could ride having the O.T. "Ausweisse." I would rather die than let anybody see me riding in a German wagon." So, all of them rode in a crowded wagon for a few minutes. They got off the trolley, but they still had to walk a good city block to the theatre. Many other young people walked in the same direction. In the middle of the sidewalk, there was a large poster pillar, full of placards, posters, announcements, both in Polish and German. One large white poster with black lettering caught Henryk's attention. It was written in German "AN ALLE DEUTSCHE" (to all Germans), something about curfews, deportations and executions.

He couldn't read it because of two large letters P.W. painted right over it. "What are these letters, Czeslawa? Are they someone's initials?" asked Henryk. "Oh no, it stands for "Polska Walczaca" (Poland fights on), or didn't you know?" "No, I didn't know either," said Edward. "I wish I could also help Poland." "Maybe you will," said Czeslawa, taking both men's arms.

The theatre was full of people. The play itself was not very popular with the German authorities, therefore, the Poles made a parody by changing the title to "Opera za dwa groszy" or "Two pennies opera" and according to Czeslawa, the play was a hit.

"During the intermission I'll introduce you to the director of this theatre, Mr. Waldemar Nowozeniec, a former captain of the Polish Army, who lost his left arm in the September '39 campaign at Kutno, where he was an adjutant to General Tadeusz Kutrzeba. He is an old friend of our family. We are very proud of him and his decorations Polonia Restituta and Virtuti Military." "Yes, we would very much like to meet him."

The play was excellent, parody or no parody, because the message was unmistakable. The prolonged bravos were the proof of acceptance by the audience. During the intermission, Czeslawa found Waldemar surrounded by admirers. She walked up to him, extending both of her hands, which he took with his only hand. "Congratulations, Waldemar! You outdid yourself this time also. I would like you to meet these two gentlemen. May I present Mr. Henryk Kaplinski and Mr. Edward Daszkiewicz, who by the way is the man I'm going to marry, but he doesn't know it yet." "Cesiu, how long do you know this handsome man?" asked Waldemar. "Two days only." Waldemar broke up with an unstoppable laugh. "And where does this prince on a white horse come from?" "He comes from the Lvov region, the same area as my own father." "Czeslawa, you are still a child." "No, Waldemar, I'm a fully grown twenty year old woman." "Very well then, don't forget to invite me to your wedding."

The bell rang for the conclusion of the play, and Waldemar shook hands with Henryk and Edward, with a facial expression dismissing the whole scene as a child's prank. The second half of the play was even more enjoyable. They left the theatre realizing that the freedom of expression can be appreciated only in its absence.

The surrealistic touch was demonstrated to them just a block on Teatralna Street, when two German soldiers and a Polish policeman stopped them. "Papiery" (papers) "Ausweisse!" It wasn't the Germans barking those words, but the Polish policeman dressed in a blue black uniform. The word "Papiery"" spoken with such an air of superiority reminded Henryk when someone would call him "Zydek" (kike). He reacted with fury, addressing the Polish policeman in German, "Warum schreist Du?" (Why are you yelling, is someone here deaf) Deliberately slowly, Henryk and Edward reached for their "Ausweisse" and handed them over to the policeman. The minute he had noticed their photos in O.T. uniforms with swastika armbands quite visible, he immediately returned the "Ausweisse" to the owners.

"What is the matter with you, do these "Ausweisse" burn holes in your hands" continued Henryk in German mainly for the benefit of the two standing German soldiers, who by this time were amused by the clear discomfort of the Polish policeman. "Przepraszam, przepraszam, excuse me, excuse me, but what about her?" "This lady is with us," said Edward, putting an emphasis on the word "lady."

The younger of the two soldiers started to laugh openly. "Kameraden, do you think that she can take care of you two?" "Don't worry, she has a sister," said Henryk good-naturedly. "Good night," said the soldiers in unison and turned around.

It was late by the time they reached Czeslawa's house. Edward told her already that they would be leaving Lublin in the morning for about a week. Henryk kissed Czeslawa's cheeks and said, "Please remember me to your father." "I certainly shall, Mr. Henryk," said Czeslawa turning to Edward. He embraced and kissed her squarely on the lips. "Czeslawa, don't let anybody else kiss those splendid lips in my absence. I'll be back on the wings of an eagle for you." "I'll miss you very much Edzio, my darling," said Czeslawa, looking adoringly at Edward. As they parted, Henryk said to Edward, "It is no longer "Pan" (Mr.) Edward, but Edzio. This is a very serious affair, my friend." "Yes, I have never been more serious about a girl before this time, I assure you. I'm head over heels in love with her." "Somehow, I believe you. Let's go to sleep, we have to get up early to pick up the truck. Hopefully, everything will be ready."

Each one spent the night with different thoughts. Edward was dreaming about Czeslawa. She was everything he ever hoped to find in a woman; beauty, brains and elegance. He was sure that his parents would approve of her. All he had to do was to find them. Since his letters addressed to them were coming back, he had a feeling that they were hiding with his aunt in the resort town of Truskawiec, just 8 km. from his hometown. These were the arrangements made before the induction into the Red Army in fear of an arrest by the dreaded Soviet N.K.V.D. Police. At the time he was told not to write, but simply to show up late at night. He was sure that his parents would wait for him, even if it took an eternity.

Henryk on the other hand, was tossing and turning, He had an ominous feeling of tragedy, hoping against hope that somewhere or somehow he'll find his mother, two sisters and a brother. He knew that his mother was a very resourceful woman, who with her light brown hair could pass for a Pole. His sister, Maryla, always displayed the same toughness as her mother, and in 1943 she was already nineteen years old. She probably could take care of herself. And maybe help with the other two siblings. In a couple of days he would have his answers, but in the meantime, he had better get some rest.

The next morning found Henryk and Edward all packed and ready to go. Henryk was familiar with Napoleon's often quoted dictum that armies march on their stomachs, which reminded him that logistics must be at the forefront of planning the trip. "Edward, while you are checking out the truck, make sure that the supply clerk gives you at least two good spare tires, extra fuel and whatever extra food you can get from him. If you have to bribe him in order to get these things, just do it. In the meantime, I'll go down to the office to pick up the papers from Keller. By the way, Edward, did you also pack our civilian winter coats?"

"Yes, I did. I was also thinking about extra tires and fuel. We both know the "famous" Russian and Polish roads. We will just have to move slowly and carefully, hoping that we won't get stuck in the mud or have flat tires. God will bless us. I'll wait for you in the garage."

Henryk went straight to Keller's office. As usual, Keller was on the telephone and motioned to Henryk to take a seat. After a couple of "Ja and Jawohl", he said, "Good morning, Heinrich. Today is your big day. Are you all set? Here are your papers; the bill of lading, invoices, packing slip, special passes, requisitions for food, fuel and the building materials you're to bring back. I also called Lemberg's O.T. office. They will be expecting you. You will have their cooperation. I have one more thing for you," and with these words he took out a Luger handgun from his desk and extra ammunition.

Seeing the surprised look on Henryk's face, Keller said, "Look, you never know on these crazy roads whom you will meet, from partisans to plain thieves. Take it, it's just a form of insurance." "Thank you very much, Herr Keller. It's a good idea. I also didn't forget our precious conversation. You'll have my answer upon my return. Auf Wiedersehen," said Henryk, pocketing the gun and the bullets.

CHAPTER 4

Henryk went to the garage where he found Edward sitting in a cabin of a captured, by the Germans, medium size, French Citroen truck. "Jump right in. Everything is in order. I have two extra spare tires and sufficient fuel. Good luck to us and let us go." Edward put the engine in gear and the truck started to roll, picking up speed slowly. It started to rain and the visibility became poor, but they just kept driving. They were stopped briefly at the outskirts of the town by the Field Military Police. The Police, seeing the two men dressed in uniforms, just waved them on.

A couple of hours later the rain changed into wet snow further obscuring the visibility. Driving became even more hazardous. The snow reminded Henryk of Moscow, Smolensk, Stalingrad, Kursk, and Orel, Kharkov. He strongly felt that Kursk was the decisive turning point of the German-Soviet war, the point after which the Red Army permanently kept the initiative, but the battle as of the beginning of December, 1943 was far from over.

These were the thoughts, which occupied Henryk's mind, sitting in the cabin of the truck, slowly inching through the Polish countryside towards his hometown of Boryslaw. Edward was totally engrossed driving the truck on snowy and slippery roads. Henryk often consulted the road map, marking progress made right on it. Every kilometer brought them closer to their destination. Several times they encountered difficulties in climbing steep hills or getting stuck in the combination of mud and snow. They would step out of the cabin, chop some tree branches, and put them under the wheels, which would enable them to move again.

One thing became clear to them that they couldn't reach Lemberg in a day. In addition, they were also very tired and needed to refuel the truck. They were stopped frequently by different Military Police or local Gandarmerie units, who would check their papers and cargo, usually on crossroads or near bridges. It was getting dark rapidly and the snowfall intensified. The need was to pull up somewhere for the night.

At the last checkpoint of the day, Henryk asked the Sergeant of the patrol where they could spend the night. "Just drive straight on this road for another 5-6 km. to a small town, or if you prefer, a large village. Ask for Tank and Truck Repair Station #118. Captain Hans Liebknecht will surely put you up, but just don't tell him that we recommended you to see him." "Thank you very much, Sergeant; it is very Christian of you," said Henryk, drawing a big smile from Edward.

A few kilometers further, they were stopped by a single soldier trying to get a ride. "Where to, Gefreiter?" asked Edward. "To the next town," answered the soldier, totally wet from the snow. "Hop in, maybe you can help us too. We are trying to locate the #118 Repair Station. Do you know where we could find the unit?" "Do I know? But of course, I am the company's cook. I'll take you there directly. I was visiting a Polish girl and on the way back the snowstorm caught me. Thank God, you fellows gave me a lift. I appreciate it very much."

A few more minutes passed and they reached the town and the #118 Station. The Gefreiter introduced himself only as Max. "Everybody knows me as Max, the cook." He reported back to his Sergeant, who, in turn, reported to his Captain Hans Liebknecht, who just happened to pass by. "Sir, these two O.T. drivers request permission to spend the night with us." "Permission granted. Give them something to eat. Let them fix the flat on the left rear also. By tomorrow morning they had better be out of my sight, Remember, no fuel for them, understood?" "Yes, sir, and thank you, sir."

Max knew all the right people because hot food was brought to them. "While you eat, I'll have my friends change and fix your tire. It will be done by the time you finish eating. I'll also see to your beds. Leave everything to me." Max arranged for them to sleep in a room where two unlucky noncommissioned officers drew an all night patrol. ."You must be out by six o'clock in the morning; otherwise I'll get myself in hot water," said Max. " No problem, Max, we'll be out by that time." "Stop in for breakfast in the morning. I'll be on duty, so you won't leave our place hungry. Don't worry about the truck either. It will be fully guarded." Max was a jolly fellow you couldn't dislike.

As promised, they were out of the room by 5:30. The kitchen, where Max presided, was just down the corridor. Max obviously expected them because a breakfast was prepared and additional "Butterbrodt" sandwiches were also packed. He joked that he couldn't get any fuel for them. "Every drop of fuel now requires at least two signatures, and for stealing they put you up against the wall. I'm too young to die."

The powdered egg omelet washed down with Ersatz coffee tasted just fine. They shook hands with Max. "Auf Wiedersehen, Max. mach es Gut, we are very grateful to you for all of your courtesies. You can always travel with us."

It took a couple of tries, but the truck's engine sprang to life and after warming her up for a few minutes, they drove through town in the direction of Lemberg. It was still dark. Partially masked headlights didn't emit too much light. Edward, fully rested, drove as fast as the conditions would permit. God must have been lifting the gigantic curtain on the horizon and a bright, sunny day was peeking carefully through. The 8 cm. thick blanket of snow, which fell during the night, was no obstacle to a loaded truck. They were moving smoothly, subject to routine paper and cargo controls. They reached the outskirts of Lemberg by midday.

Lemberg or Lvov, as it is known to the local population, was an old and historical Polish town, which escaped serious destruction, The Germans turned the town into a capital city of Distrikt Galizien. Brutal repression and mass killing of the city's 150,000 Jews in nearby Janowsky Street concentration camp was already accomplished, as Henryk found out, by the time he reached the

O.T. Headquarters on Piasecka Street. It was a large building, previously a Jewish owned business, which housed the present O.T. Warehouses. The truck was unloaded by Ukrainian workers mainly. Henryk, who was now Heinrich, again spoke only German with Edward, acting as his interpreter.

With the bill of lading signed by the receiving clerk, who checked the merchandise against the packing slip, they went to the chief of Lemberg's Section of O.T., Herr Dirk Grogge, to inquire about the shipment to be picked up and delivered back to Lublin.

"Sorry, fellows, we still don't have the complete order in stock. It will take another two or three days, and that is the best I can do for you. Your office called twice already and I promised them our full cooperation, but, unfortunately, we didn't get our deliveries on time. If there is anything I can do for you in the meantime, just ask for it."

"Herr Grogge, our boss, Herr Keller, suggested that we go down to Boryslaw, where the oil fields are. They are supposed to have a surplus of pipes, which we could use in Lublin. All we need are passes for that region." "Yes, you can have them right now, but be back on time because I have to ship the merchandise to Lublin." He then signed and stamped two passes "Passierschein" valid for travel in the Drohobycz-Boryslaw region.

"Here they are, you can either stay here or drive to Boryslaw, hardly 100 km. from here." "Thank you very much, Herr Grogge. We'll leave for Boryslaw as soon as we refuel the truck. We hope to be there by the evening so that we can have a full day to check on those pipes." "Suit yourselves, Auf Wiedersehen." "Auf Wiedersehen, Herr Grogge, and thank you very much again."

With the first leg of their trip accomplished, they were free to drive to Boryslaw. "Henryk, if we leave now, we still would have at least two hours of daylight driving and about one hour of night driving by the time we reach our destination. I suggest that we stop first to see what has happened to my parents. If they are not there and I doubt very much to find them there, because they never answered my letters. That would mean that they have gone to hide in Truskawiec, which is only 8 km. more and we would be free to go to your house and check on what has happened to them. Pending what we may find, we'll drive straight to Truskawiec and stay there overnight. I also think that it is better for you to go to your house at night, so that nobody can recognize you. Do you agree?"

"Yes, Edward, it makes perfect sense, so let's go." Having an empty truck, they moved much faster in order to cover the remaining 110 km. The roads being in poor condition and facing the possibility of additional snow accumulation, they projected the trip to take about three hours, barring, of course, the unforeseen. In general, the truck was making good progress on the roads with limited vehicular traffic. The great majority of trucks and cars were of the military type. The rest being horse driven wagons, carriages and sleds.

On the both sides of the road they would see cattle foraging on the snow covered fields, small villages, some homes had grass hatched roofs. The smoke coming out of the chimneys would go straight up like so many large fingers pointing to the blue skies.

It was dark by the time they reached the town of Drohobycz. They were stopped by the Unit of local "Schutz Polizei", just by the Tysmienica River. Their papers were "In Ordnung", especially the "Passierschein" issued by Herr Grogge, brought a dose of respect. "Where are you "Meine Herren" going to stay for the night?" one of the policemen asked politely. "Don't worry, we'll find a couple of girls willing to put two handsome devils like us up for the night," This remark drew universal laughter and they were told to proceed.

Drohobycz was a large and strategic city by Austrian, Polish and now German standards. It contained two oil refineries "Polmin" and Galicja", three railroad stations to handle the shipments of petroleum products, regimental headquarters to whatever army happened to rule, and the streets were asphalt paved and well lit. The truck moved with ease on Stryjska Street until they came to the heart of the town, where a beautiful, municipal building "Ratusz", erected by the Austrians prior to World War One, stood in the large square. From there they took Boryslawska Street, leading directly to their hometown, just another 9 km.

Henryk's heart beat so hard that he thought Edward, who was sitting next to him, would hear it. Finally, he would have the answers as to what happened to his family. As agreed, they stopped first near Edward's house on Mosciska Street. Edward jumped out of the cabin and asked Henryk to remain in the truck.

"Stay there, I don't want to create any commotion. Just wait there 'till I call you," and with these words he disappeared behind the wooded door of a three story building. Henryk waited in the truck with what seemed to be an eternity, if twenty minutes could be counted as an eternity. Finally, Edward came out all flustered. "My parents no longer live here. I went to all of our former neighbors. Nobody knows what had happened to them. Luckily, one old retired, former railroad man, who has worked with my father, told me that, should Edward come to this house, to tell him that they went into hiding and that he would know where to look for them. And that is Truskawiec. Now, let us go and look for the family."

Boryslaw was the town where both of them grew up. They knew every stone and every house. Everything looked so familiar, and yet, foreign at the same time. They passed Zielona Street, and a few minutes later, they came upon Panska Street, #22. "Henryk, let me park the truck a block away, under the trees, in a dark place. You better put on the civilian overcoat. Your uniform may draw an unwelcome attention to you or someone can recognize you and that might be trouble. I'll stay with the truck. In case of any problems or trouble on the street, I'll honk the horn twice. Agreed?"

Henryk shook his head and put on the coat, turning up the collar. Suddenly, he was dreadfully cold. He walked toward the house where he was born and raised. It was just a modest two family house in which his family occupied the upstairs. The sidewalk was full of broken household items sticking out of the dirty snow. The door handle was broken and the door was slightly ajar. A small amount of snow crept into the corridor forming a straight white line.

Unable to restrain himself any longer, he ran upstairs two steps at a time, Without bothering to knock, he opened the door leading to their "salon." He was shocked to see a bunch of strangers. A Ukrainian woman dressed in an embroidered blouse and a long pleated skirt, a couple of kids in dirty nightshirts and an old, toothless, heavily mustachioed man gave him a surprised and frightened look.

"Where are the Kaplinski family?" Henryk asked in Polish, raising his voice in anger, "My ne znaiemo." "We don't know," the woman answered in Ukrainian. We have lived here almost six months. We are from the village of Tustanowice, and they told us that we can have this empty apartment."

He felt faint and had to sit down for a minute. The Ukrainian woman swiftly brought him a glass of water, which he accepted. "Did you live here before?" Henryk shook his head and said, "Yes." Nothing mattered anymore.

"Bihme." "As God is my witness, my family didn't have anything to do with whatever happened in this house, If there is anything in this apartment that you would like to take with you, just take it." "No this house without the people in it doesn't mean anything to me anymore," said Henryk, slowly moving towards the door. "Wait, please wait, just another minute, I do have something for you. I found it in one of the drawers in another room."

She ran into the other room and a couple of seconds later came back with a large wedding photograph of his parents in an old fashioned silver frame. He turned the picture around and surely as he remembered, there was a familiar stamp: "Zaklad Fotograficzny Titiana w Drohobyczu" (Photograph Titan in Drohobycz). "This I will take," said Henryk, walking out. The woman ran after him with, "May God help you." Edward was already on pins and needles. "What happened there?" Henryk briefly told him what had transpired and handed him the wedding picture of his parents.

"Really a beautiful couple. You do resemble your father very much. You have the same shy smile." Henryk started to cry unstoppable tears were running on his face. "Edzio, Edzio, there is no one there. They all must have been killed. Oh, God, why, why?" Edward held Henryk tightly in his arms and let him cry for awhile. "You don't know that for a fact. Don't you have any Christian friends whom may know something about their fate? Let's look them up. Don't lose hope, my friend."

"Good idea, I just remembered that diagonally across the street there lived a good friend of my mother, Pani (Mrs.) Litwinowa. I'll try to see if she is still there, and you stay with the truck." With very few people on the street, preferring to stay indoors, and without any difficulty, he found the home of Pani Litwinowa. He knocked on the door several times. Nobody answered his knock. In desperation, he knocked on the window, He heard someone coming to the door. The woman said in Polish, "A kto tam stuka w nocy?" (Who is knocking at night?) "Pani Litwinowa, this is I, Henio Kaplinski." "Jesus, Maria, little Henio?" "Someone said that you were killed. You are alive, thank God, come in, come in," and she opened the door letting him in. She was smaller than he had remembered and all gray, but she had the same kind face.

"Pani Litwinowa! Do you know what has happened to my family?" "Yes, I know, you poor boy. You better sit down. It's going to be very painful. On the fourth or fifth day of the war in June of 1941 a truck came for your sister and the Russians took her with them to Russia. She was a member of Komsomol and the Russians said to your mother that if Maryla won't go with them the Germans will surely kill her. Your mother gave her the permission to leave. I'm sure she is safe somewhere in Russia. She was always very smart. Don't worry about her."

"What about my mother and the other two little ones?" "I'm just coming to it. I'm old and I must choose my words very carefully. Would you like some vodka?" "No, Pani Litwinowa, just continue."

After the Germans entered the town, the Ukrainians, with the blessings of the Germans, organized a bloody "pogrom" on the Jewish population of the town. A lot of people were killed or severely wounded. Your family was untouched because I hid them. Later on, your mother and the kids went back to their apartment. A few weeks later, the Ukrainian Police and the Schutz Polizei" came to your mother to look for your sister. She told them that Maryla ran away with the Russians and she didn't know her whereabouts. The Militia men didn't believe her and accused her of hiding Maryla. In order to force her to talk, they took the little ones away. Your mother never heard from them again." Litwinowa stopped for awhile to collect her thoughts and continued with her sad story.

"After awhile, they gave up and let her work with the rest of the remaining Jews. She turned white almost overnight, even though she was much younger than I. Henio, you must know, it was very dangerous to help or hide Jews. Those dogs would kill you for that. I helped as much as I could, but I never had much of anything, especially after my own son, Wacek, didn't return from the war in September of 1939. I didn't care if I lived or died. I didn't have anybody to live for anyway. Your mother was special. I loved her like she was my daughter. Her, being Jewish, never bothered me because we are all children of the same God. One day, I don't remember exactly, maybe five or six months ago, one of the Ukrainian Militia men, your actual neighbor, just shot her. At least, she didn't suffer much. It was Bohdan Terleckyj, the same age as you. I think he even went to school with you, if I'm not mistaken. You probably remember him. He was always a nasty, disrespectful boy who always hated the Poles and Jews just like his drunkard father. Now, Henio, tell me, what are you doing here? Do you want something to eat or drink? "Czem chata bogata" (My house is your house).

"Dear Pani Litwinowa, thank you very much for telling me

the sad truth. I'm fine, but I must go now because I don't want to cause you any trouble. I thank you for helping my mother. She was always very fond of you."

He took the old lady's hands and kissed them. ."Maybe after the war I'll come back to see you." He embraced her once more. "May God look after you", she said, making a sign of the cross after him.

Henryk left the house in a daze. His worst premonitions and fears had been confirmed. He felt all alone in a hostile world. His only hope was that his sister would survive somehow. He buttoned his coat to shield him from the bone chilling wind when from a side street emerged a figure in military uniform carrying a rifle. It was too late to turn around. They were hardly a meter apart. In an instant, they recognized each other.

"Bohdan, is that you?" It was more of a statement than a question. "Yes, Henryk, you Jew bastard! What are you doing here? I'll take you to the Schutz Polizei"

Henryk had to think fast. His life was on the line. He had a pistol under his coat, which he couldn't reach with Bohdan's rifle pointing straight at him. His only hope was to distract him long enough to be able to draw his gun or bring him closer to Edward.

"Bohdan, you and I went to school together. I was just going to see my mother whom I didn't see in a few years. My fiancée is waiting for me at the end of the block. She has a $20.00 gold piece which I'll give to you if you let me go." Bohdan's face broke into a crooked smile. Henryk could see right through him. He wanted the coin, and at the same time to bring in two new Jews to the Polizei.

"Sure Henryk, for old times sake, just walk in front of me." Henryk was walking deliberately slow in order to unbutton his coat and pull out the gun without making any abrupt moves. Seeing a large puddle, he sort of sidestepped letting Bohdan slightly ahead of him. This gave him enough time to reach for the gun and stick the barrel into Bohdan's back. "Bohdan, you stinking son of a bitch. Raise your fucking hands or I'll kill you right now. Drop your rifle now!"

Bohdan turned slightly towards Henryk and saw a Luger in his hand and a German uniform through the open coat. This time Bohdan was really scared. He was not accustomed to seeing Jews with guns and wearing German uniforms at the same time, "Henryk, you let me go and I'll arrange to have your mother released. Is that a deal?" "Bohdan, you shit. Keep your mouth shut, She is already free. You killed her, remember?" This time Bohdan kept quiet.

Edward, seeing two silhouettes approaching the truck, started the engine just in case, but recognizing Henryk he stepped out of the cabin truck. "Henryk, what is going on? Who is this man?" "Edward, don't you recognize him, its Bohdan Terleckyj. He killed my mother and probably the rest of my family," "Oh, that is him alright. He was always tormenting me in school with "Smert liacham (Death to Poles). Let's kill that creep right now." "No, Eddie, he belongs to me." "Bohdan, get into the truck!" Bohdan started to scream for help, but a rifle butt to the jaw stopped that immediately. Hardly a peep came out, just blood from a bruised jaw and split lip, which he tried to stop with his bare hand.

"I told you to keep your mouth shut, understand?" Bohdan just shook his head. He understood the new situation only too well. Only a miracle could save him now, but miracles didn't happen too often in this God forsaken land.

Edward was driving in the direction of Truskawiec where he hoped to find his family, but first he had to get rid of Bohdan. Driving at night, Edward must have taken the wrong fork on the road because they found themselves riding along Bronitsa forest. "Henry, this looks like an ideal place of rest for our friend, Bohdan."

Bohdan knew that his end was coming. He started to protest, "Not here, please not here." "Tutka ubyvaly Zhidiv." (Here Jews were killed) "Henryk, didn't I tell you that this is the ideal place," sarcastically added Edward. "Edward, you stay with the truck. I don't want you to come with me. I have to revenge the death of my family." "Bohdan, you just keep walking into the woods. Remember, I'm right behind you."

Just outside the parked truck, in the gutter, Henryk noticed an old, wet "talith", a prayer shawl, whose silver decorations were ripped off, but the black stripes and fringes were still visible. "Bohdan, come back here for a minute. Take this "talith" and put it on your head and keep walking." Bohdan started to object, when Henryk kicked him hard in the testicles. Bohdan picked up the "talith" and put it on as ordered. They walked thirty or forty steps into the forest when Henryk decided to finish Bohdan off.

"On your knees!" Bohdan started to cry and beg for his life in Ukrainian. Henryk saw in front of him a descendant of such Jew haters as Chmielnicki (also Bohdan), Petlura, Bandera, and without the slightest hesitation, pulled the trigger, aiming right between the eyes, He kept firing until he heard a click of an empty gun. He watched the dead body twisting in a crazy postmortem spasm. Through the holes in "talith", blood was coming out, making the Ukrainian soil the most fertile in the world. The eerie silence of the woods was only briefly disturbed, but the echo repeated the sound once more.

Henryk stuck his gun behind his belt and ran back to the truck. "Let's go from this place." Unknown to him, it was the place of mass executions of Jews from the area and their final rest in mass graves. Edward, without a word, turned the truck around and sped in the direction of Truskawiec. "Henryk, tell me what Mrs. Litwinowa said to you?" "I can't right now, but in due time I'll tell you."

The remaining 8 km. to Truskawiec was reached within a few minutes. Just a couple of years ago Truskawiec was a beautiful resort town, full of elegant villas and hotels, where a military band would play in the park, classical and popular tunes for the benefit of vacationers from all over Poland and Europe. Now, it had an appearance of a ghost town.

"It is very close now, another 300-400 meters. I'm going to drive very slowly, without the headlights, because I don't want to bring attention to us. So, stick your head out of the window and help me find the place." All they heard were dogs barking. Nobody was welcome on a night like this. Edward found the house and parked the truck behind the stable, away from prying eyes. A dog inside of the house started to bark, but a human voice shut it out. The door of the house opened and an elderly man, carrying a rifle in one hand and a kerosene lamp in the other, asked in Ukrainian, "Who is that?" Edward recognized the voice as belonging to his father.

"To ja, Edward!" (It's me, Edward) He answered without raising his voice and ran into his father's waiting arms. "Oh, sweet Jesus of Nazareth, its Edzio." The two men held each other, crying and laughing at the same time. "Come in, come, come in," and noticing Henryk, he asked, "Who is that?" "This is my friend, Henio Kaplinski, you should remember him." "Oh, ten Zydek." (Oh, that Jew) I remember him, but what are you doing with him and why are you both in German uniforms?" "Let's go in and I'll tell you all about it. Where is mother?" "She is bedridden already eight months. I'll tell her that you are here." "Zosiu, Zosiu! Our son, our Edzio is here! We are coming. Bless the Lord. Edzio is finally here."

They both went into another room where an old, frail woman lay in bed propped up with several dawn pillows. "Mamusiu, to ja, Edzio." (Mother, it's me, Edward) He kissed her hands and face over and over again. Henryk observed the touching scene, wishing that this would have been his mother, Alas, he decided to leave them alone with their happiness. His own heart was aching. Certainly, he was happy for Edward finding both his parents, but he, Henryk, was all alone, an orphan.

He went back to the truck where he found a bottle of homemade vodka hidden under the seat and came back to the house. He uncorked the bottle and took a big swig. A warmth started to spread in his stomach. Then, he took another swig and another, until the bottle was empty. "There is no more vodka," he said aloud and promptly passed out on the floor. It was there, where some time later, Edward and his father found him. They dragged him into another room, undressed him and put him to bed.

Edward briefly told his father about Henryk and the fate of his family. "I, particularly do not care for Jews, but killing them is totally another matter. We would never allow it in Poland." "Oh, papa," said Edward, seeing no point to argue with his stubborn father. He had so much more to tell him. Henryk slept in a drunken stupor. Dreams and nightmares were entering his head like a crazy kaleidoscope. He was again a little boy, standing with his father, during the Yom-Kippur services. He and his father were draped in long, cream colored woolen "talith" capturing God with them and isolating all the evil in the world. Henryk felt so safe standing next to his big father. He felt his strong body and gentle, warm hand, which his father put on top of his head.

This angelic picture changed into an ugly face of Bohdan Terleckyj. Henryk kept firing and firing his gun, but Bohdan was just laughing. What is wrong with this gun? Bohdan, die already, die already...

"Henryk, Henryk, get up. You had a bad dream. Get up! It's noontime already!" Rubbing his eyes, Henryk said, "Where am I?" "Henryk, you're in Truskawiec in my parents' house. Please get up." Slowly, Henryk came to himself, remembering every disturbing detail of the previous day. "Edward, I don't want to get up. I don't want to live." "Don't be an idiot, get up. We have to go away from here. I can't endanger my parents!"

Edward's father came into the room carrying a tray on which were sliced raw potatoes, a small glass of vodka and a bowl of water. He took the slices of potato and tied them to Henryk's forehead. "And now, drink vodka, your hangover will disappear." The cold potato brought some relief and his surprise, after drinking the vodka, he felt much better. He got up, shaved and washed up and reached for his freshly pressed uniform, which the old man managed to clean and press, while everyone else slept.

"Papa, when did you learn to iron?" asked Edward. "You learn fast when you must do something," answered the old man, with a smile. After eating a piece of dark, peasant bread and kielbasa and drinking boiled water, colored by some herbs, Henryk said goodbye to the elder Daszkiewiczes. Edward said his goodbye in private. The senior Daszkiewicz shook hands with Henryk once more, "My Edzio told me about you, and as I said before, some Jews are very nice, indeed." "So are Poles, Mr. Daszkiewicz, but very few of them." "My boy, you are right, we do have many bad people among us." He walked them to the barn, behind which was the parked truck. They pulled the truck out without creating much noise.

"What are we going to do now, Henryk? Should we go back to Lemberg or at least make an appearance at the local office of the oil company to find out about the availability of those pipes? What do you suggest?" "We may as well stop by to see if they have any pipes we can use. I very much doubt if they would look for Bohdan in Bronitsa Forest. We are just two O.T. men on an assignment, right?"

They located the main office of the Oil Industry Department on Kosciuszko Street in the building that belonged to Mr. Goldman. They showed their "Passierscheins" to the reception clerk and asked in German for the manager. The receptionist told them that Herr Bertold Beiz was busy, however, Ing. Koretz would see them. Koretz, Koretz; quickly thought Henryk. Koretz was a well known Jew, very capable, who knew the Kaplinski family, It was too late to back out, but Henryk was hoping that a few years later as well as the German uniform he was wearing, would make him unrecognizable. His further speculations were pointless, since Ing. Koretz just walked into the room.

Henryk introduced Edward and himself as members of O.T. looking for galvanized steel pipes 40 cm. x 10 m. at least 500 pieces. The conversation was conducted in German, which Ing. Koretz spoke flawlessly. "I think we have some, but I don't know if we can spare them. You see I am a Jew. The decision to sell or barter lies in the hands of Herr Bertold Beiz, who might be here in a few minutes." As he spoke those words, the door from another room opened and a tall, handsome man in his thirties walked in.

"I'm Beitz, what seems to be the problem?" Ing, Koretz introduced both men and explained the reason for their visit. "Alles klaar (all is clear). We may be able to spare some pipes 200-300 of the diameter you are looking for plus some of a slightly smaller dimension. However, in exchange, I need cables, chains and wires. I'll have my staff give a list of needed items. Please check with your office to see if they would accept our proposal, and check if they have those items in stock. The phone is in the other room. Sorry, I have to go now. Leave the word with Ing. Koretz. "Auf Wiedersehen."

Ing. Koretz called in one of the secretaries and asked Henryk to give her the telephone number of his office in Lublin. "I'll call you as soon as I will be able to reach your office. It'll take just a few minutes, I hope." "In the meantime, can I use your restroom?" asked Henryk, who felt the affect of the hangover. "Oh, sure," said Ing. Koretz, pointing to the door leading to the restroom. Henryk emerged from the restroom just as the secretary was paging him, "Lublin on line #3" "Darf Ich, Herr Keller sprechen?" (May I speak with Mr. Keller)? "Keller here." Henryk, after a polite exchange of greetings, repeated his conversation with Ing. Beitz. "Get out the list of items they can spare and what they want from us, but under no circumstances spend more than half a day. We badly need the merchandise from Lemberg. Also, something important came up and I need you here."

With Henryk gone to the phone, Ing. Koretz politely asked Edward, "How s your father? Is he well? I worked with him years ago for the railroad. Should you see him, please give him my regards."All that Edward was able to say was, "Thank you, sir, I will." Henryk, returning from making the telephone call, saved Edward from further conversation with Ing. Koretz.

"Herr Koretz, our chief, Ing. Keller suggested that you phone us your inventory, which you can spare long with the list of items you require of us. At that point, we shall study your request and see how we can best arrange for the exchange. Since there is no merit to our waiting, we'll be on our way. You have been most kind and cooperative, Herr Koretz." "Whatever you wish, gentlemen," said Ing. Koretz. "Let me also use the facilities. I'll be right back. Please wait for me a minute, Henryk."

As soon as Edward left the room, Ing. Koretz said, lowering his voice to a whisper, "Antloif fun do" (Yiddish – run away from here), adding louder in German, "Es war ein Gross Genuss, Herr Kaplinski" (It was a great pleasure, Mr. Kaplinski). Koretz bowed and left the room as Edward returned through another door. "Let us go back as soon as we can." With their truck fully refueled, courtesy of Mr. Beitz, they sped in the direction of Lemberg. A slight, wet snow started to fall again, somewhat slowing down the truck.

For a long time no one spoke. Each was deep in his own thoughts. "Cigarette?" asked Edward, offering a cigarette case. "Thank you. I think I'll take one." Unlike most men, Henryk only occasionally would smoke a cigarette. He developed distaste for tobacco while serving the Red Army, where he would be issued "machorka" tobacco that would give him a headache of gigantic proportions.

Henryk lit both cigarettes. Inhaling deeply, Edward said, "Henryk, Ing. Koretz knew who I was. He also knew my father. What do you make of this?" "I'll tell you a better story yet. When you stepped out for awhile, he told me very quietly in Yiddish to run away. He knew my mother very well. I think she was even related to him somehow. I'm sure that he meant well that sooner of later someone would recognize me as a Jew. By the way, I'm not worried about Bohdan. No one is going to look for him under the prayer shawl of a Jew shot in the woods."

Halfway to Lemberg they were stopped by the same local Police. "You are the same O.T.'s who passed this way the other day, carry on." They reached Lemberg in the early afternoon, They requested that the local O.T. load their truck because they were rushed by their Headquarters to bring the badly needed supplies as soon as possible. Herr Grogge approved the request with a smile. "So soon back? I guess you didn't like the girls in Boryslaw?" "They are very nice, but duty calls, and we had to rush back." Grogge issued orders to load their truck with the utmost dispatch. The loading was supervised alternatively by Edward and Henryk. In less than an hour their truck was fully loaded and they were on their way back to Lublin.

Henryk wondered why Keller wanted him back so soon? Was Keller being sent to another position ahead of time, and he wanted Henryk to come along? Henryk decided to move out with Keller in any case because Lublin was becoming a bit too "hot" for him. Working along with the inmates of Majdanek was too much of an emotional burden.

Edward, on the other hand, had only one reason why he was rushing back Czeslawa. "Listen, Henryk, I've decided to marry Czeslawa upon my return, and I want you to be my best man. I never had and probably never will have a better friend than you." "Ed, did your mother drop you on your head when you were a child? You hardly know the girl, but if you want to get married so badly, then all I can do now is to wish you both much happiness. I'll be honored to be your best man. Your first child better be named after me." Edward. With his left hand on the wheel, embraced Henryk with his right arm and said, "Thank you, I love you like a brother."

It was past midnight when they reached The Tank and Truck Repair Station #118. This time, instead of asking for Captain Liebknecht, they asked for Max, the cook. The sentry smiled when he heard Max's name mentioned. "Max is sleeping." "Wake him anyway. Tell him his two cousins are back and don't worry." The sentry called the duty sergeant, who, in turn, woke up Max. A few minutes later, Max showed up, dressed in an army coat, the long white underwear visible above his boots.

"Hello, Max, sorry to wake you, but we don't know anybody else as nice as you." "Don't worry, you can sleep in my bed and I'll go to the kitchen. I have to be there soon anyway. Get yourselves a couple of hours of shut-eye and stop in the mess hall for breakfast on me." "Thanks. Max, you are the greatest." "Yah, yah, that's what everybody tells me. Come along and I'll show you to your "Gast-zimmer." You sleep here, and I'll see you at breakfast."

They took off their boots and jackets and fell asleep on a single bed immediately. They snored almost as loud as the other men in an adjacent room. The ruckus of the morning revile woke them up. Quickly they washed, shaved and went to the main mess hall, where the men of Station #118 were already assembled. They were mostly mechanics from the Wehrmacht, who didn't pay any attention to the two O.T. men. Henryk and Edward sat at the same table as last time, with the noncommissioned officers of the #118 unit company. The discussion at the table was about the merits of their own tanks, the Mark III with a 37 mm. gun, and the Mark IV with a short 75mm. piece having an armor thickness of 30 mm., put against the superior Soviet tank T-34 with an armor of 45 mm. They were also excited about the captured Soviet tank 43-ton KV-1B.

As interesting as that conversation was, Henryk and Edward had other objectives on their mind good old Max saved them a trip to the kitchen. He stopped by their table and wished them God speed. "Good, hot meal picks up a man's spirits. Don't you think so?" asked Edward as they both got into the truck's cabin. "Let's go, let's go, we don't have time to waste." The trip was uneventful with the exception of a stop made due to the load in the back of the truck, shifting on a sharp curve. Working in unison, they corrected the situation in a relatively short time and continued on their journey.

It was already dark when they reached the city of Lublin. Although they were gone just a few days, it seemed that an eternity passed. In a way that was true, especially to Henryk. Dutifully, they drove the truck to the warehouse, where they left the unloading of the truck to the night crew. Tired, but satisfied that their mission was accomplished, they went to the barracks where they were greeted by the rest of their unit. "We missed you fellows." "Not as much as we missed you."

A hot shower did wonders for their tired muscles. Edward was whistling a popular tune about meeting a girl at nine o'clock in the evening, He was truly happy finding his parents and having the next day off. He was going to spend the day with Czeslawa, whom at the end of the day he would ask for her hand in marriage.

Henryk, on the other hand, couldn't fall asleep. The happenings of the last few days were pressing on his mind like a ton of bricks. The loss of his family was paramount in his thoughts. The killing of Bohdan didn't affect him at all, even though he was the only man that he ever killed. Surprisingly, he felt good about it. It was his "Nekumah." (his revenge) He felt as much remorse as he would if he had killed a bedbug. Would he kill other such "bedbugs"? Without hesitation, of that he was quite sure.

As far as his early morning appointment with Ing. Keller was concerned, he was ready to throw his lot in with him. Of all things, a Russian proverb came to his mind, "The morning is smarter than the evening." At that point, he fell into a deep sleep.

It was Edward that woke him and not the noise usually associated with a large group of men getting up. "Get up. Get up! We both have important things ahead of us." Henryk attended to his toilette, being extra mindful of being properly dressed in a freshly pressed uniform and shoes shined to mirror-like perfection. Somehow, he felt that today's meeting with Keller would be a very important one. In his respect, he was not disappointed.

Henryk met Ing. Keller just as he was opening the door to his office. He greeted Henryk with a big smile and said, "'Herzlich, willkommen.' (Hearty welcome, Heinrich) How was your trip? We missed you around here. Please sit down. I have several things to go over with you. Just let me get my papers out. I want to thank you for an excellent job done. You know, that we needed those pipes and you went all the way to Boryslaw to look for them. Hopefully, they will be able to spare some. This you have done on your own, and this to me shows initiative that only men in O.T. have.

There are several problems connected with our pervious, present and future projects, but they all can wait. However, what can't wait is this letter. It seems that you applied for commission in the Pioneer Battalions of the Wehrmacht, and your superior, Herr Krueger, gave you his highest recommendation by being a Party member. You'll have to report to the Induction Center within forty eight hours. With Christmas and the New Year holidays around the corner, we could get you a postponement of two to four weeks at the most. Why didn't you tell me that you want to join the Wehrmacht? I always knew that you had a German heart beating in your body. One can't eradicate German roots in a single generation."

"Dear Herr Keller, this application is as a big surprise to me as it is to you. Herr Kruger, whom I caught in a homosexual act with one of the younger boys, simply wanted to get even with me. Personally, I would much rather join you at your new post. After all, O.T.'s missions are very important to the defense of our Fatherland."

"Very well then, let me get in touch with the Induction Center and see what can be done about your case. We'll continue tomorrow. Take the rest of the day off." "Thank you very much, Herr Keller. I do appreciate your efforts on my behalf."

Henryk left Keller's office dazed and worried about the latest development regarding the induction into the Wehrmacht. At the first medical check up, the doctors would discover his circumcision and Majdanek's striped suit would be his end. What was he supposed to do to get himself out of this jam? To run away, but where? According to rumors, the forests were even more dangerous to a Jew than the Germans themselves. He had to speak with Edward. Maybe, he had some ideas on the subject, but that young fool was in love and was spending the day with Czeslawa, only God knew where. Maybe he could find him at Dr. Drzewiecki's office or home. He would try Dr. Drzewiecki's first; at the same time he would have a dental check up.

It took only minutes from the barracks to reach the dental office. Henry expected Czeslawa at the office, but another young woman dressed in a white coat was the receptionist of the day.

"Good morning, where is Czeslawa today?" asked Henryk in German. "She took a day off and I'm filling in for her. My name is Helga. How can I help you, sir?" asked Helga in fluent German. "I'm a patient of Dr. Drzewiecki. I'm due for a gum check up." "I'll tell the doctor that you are here. Please take a seat." The waiting room was full of people. He counted five adults and two kids. He was resigned to a long wait.

To his surprise, about fifteen minutes later, the door from the doctor's cabinet opened and Dr. Drzewiecki motioned to Henryk and said in German, "Bitte, kommen Sie herrein." Henryk was embarrassed to be going ahead of everybody else, but the patients waiting said encouragingly, "Bitte, Bitte". Rather than object, he went inside. Dr. Drzewiecki spoke in German as long as Helga was in the same room. "Miss Helga, will you please go to the Apothecary and fetch Mrs. Skowronska's prescription. I need it." "Surely doctor, I'll be right back."

With Helga gone, the conversation shifted to Polish. "I just came back from Boryslaw. The Ukrainian Militia killed my mother, sister and brother. Maryla, my sister, managed to escape to Russia. I hope she will be safe there. Can you imagine? I have to report to the German Induction Center in two days. They started to conscript O.T. men. Do you have any advice or ideas as to what can be done to avoid it?"

"Henio, I'm very sorry to hear about your mother and the kids. We know what is happening with the Jews. Unfortunately, I can't talk to you too long because Helga is due back any minute now and I don't trust her at all. Come to our apartment this afternoon at five o'clock. Our apartment number is 3B. We'll talk then. One more thing, what do you know about Edward Daszkiewicz? He seems to be in love with our daughter. She told me that unless we give her our blessings, she'll run away with Edward. Knowing our Cesia, she'll do it. History repeats itself."

"We know each other since we were little kids. He is the finest and the most decent human being. He saved my life on several occasions. I do love him like a brother."

A knock at the door and Helga walked in with a package from the Apothecary. "Sie sind fertig, aber Sie mussen zurueck kommen in eine Woche," (you are finished, but you must come back in a week) said the doctor, more for Helga's benefit than Henryk's. Henryk checked his pocked watch. He still had almost three hours 'till five o'clock and his meeting with Dr. Drzewiecki. He had a feeling that he would meet Edward there.

The idea of going back to the barracks mess hall for lunch was revolting. He didn't feel like seeing or talking to his O.T. comrades. On the spur of the moment, he decided to head towards the center of the town to a small café-restaurant just off Mickiewicza Street. He was totally oblivious to the cold weather and the people passing by.

He reached the welcome warmth of the café named appropriately, "Under the White Eagle." This was the place that he visited from time to time on his days off, looking for brief and not binding sexual encounters. This afternoon, it was only a question of spending a couple of hours, 'till his meeting with Dr. Drzewiecki. For this time of day, surprisingly, the café was full. Probably a number of people went inside the café to keep away from the cold. The waiter whom Henryk knew as Wincenty showed Henryk to a small table for two located in a far corner of the room.

"Don't bother with the menu. Most of the listed dished you don't have anyway. Just bring me a Schnapps, something to eat and coffee or tea." "Very well, sir. I'll bring you the Schnapps first." Henryk took a cigarette out of the box and was just about to light it when he was asked in German for a light. Keeping the match lit, he turned in the direction of the voice. Henryk almost fainted when he saw the S.S. man lighting his cigarette. He recognized him at once He was a Jew like himself from his hometown of Boryslaw. It was Edek Nadler, whose nickname was "Panczyk."

He was to a large degree a local hero, at least to the Jews of the town. A taxi driver by profession, extremely good looking, tall and blond, who unlike his co-religionists, was constantly involved in fights with Polish and Ukrainian anti-Semites. It was during one of those fights that Nadler was accused of stabbing a man with a knife and was sentenced to a few weeks in jail. The judge, a Pole, himself, not a Jew lover, when he learned that Nadler fought against three rowdy Poles, beating the living daylights out of two men and allegedly stabbing the third with a knife, said, according to the town's rumor, "If three Poles couldn't beat one lousy Jew, then they should go to jail." But since Nadler used a knife he had to send him to jail to cool off a bit.

Nadler came back from jail to a welcome home party. Everybody wanted to buy him a beer. Since that time, nobody tried to mess with Nadler – "Panczyk". Now, the same Nadler was in the uniform of a S.S. man. "Henryk, what the devil are you doing in a O.T. uniform?" asked Nadler. "I was just about to ask you the same question. Why don't you pull up a chair and sit down." Wincenty, the waiter, brought Schnapps to Henryk, then Nadler ordered in German, "You better bring us a bottle." "Yawohl, mein Herr, sofort," said the waiter, shrewdly appraising the new situation.

"Well, Henryk, how did you get yourself into the O.T.?" Henryk briefly told him his story from being conscripted into the Red Army and to finding himself in the O.T. He stopped short of telling him about his upcoming induction into the Wehrmacht.

"Now, what about you?" "In late June of 1941, I managed to run away to Cracov, where I found a job as an auto mechanic. As you recall, I used to own a taxi and was always handy with cars. I told the owner of the garage that I was a Pole from Lemberg fleeing the Soviets. I gave him my name as Tadeusz Kierod, and he, somehow, through his connection, obtained a "Kenn-karte" for me under that name. I was his best mechanic and customers liked me.

One day, a young and beautiful German woman pulled into the garage with her Sport-Opel. I fixed that car in minutes. She asked me how much she owed me for fixing her car, and I told her, "Just one kiss." Well, that is how our romance started. She fell in love with me and would show up at the garage almost every day.

One day, my boss called me into his office and said, "Tadeusz, do you know that Fraulein Luise von Spandorf is a niece of a German general?" I was shocked to hear it because I thought that she was just another secretary. One thing lead to another and we became lovers. That was the time when she discovered that I was a Jew. As a good catholic, she decided to save my life. She also told me about her uncle, the general in the Wehrmacht. He was impotent, and it was very important for him to be seen at all social functions in the company of a beautiful woman. Childless, he would do anything for her."

His further story was interrupted by Wincenty who brought a bottle of Schnapps and some nondescriptive food. Nadler took several larger bills out of his pocket and gave them to the waiter. "Take this "dreck" back and bring us something more substantial, but make it snappy." The waiter had another look at the money and his face broke into an approving smile. "Yes, sir, I'll be right back." With the waiter disappearing into the kitchen, Nadler continued with his story.

"Fixing cars in the time of shortages can be very profitable. I was making real good money. Luise lived in the elegant part of Cracov on Karmelicka and Straszeckiego and she rented a small bachelor's apartment for me on Szewska and Plant. We would meet many times in Jordana Park."

"I'm sorry, but I don't know Cracov." "Sorry, I keep on forgetting. Cracov is really a nice city, but I was caught twice by the Gestapo on the street. Only by mentioning her uncle, General Eugen von Schobert, was I able to escape their net. It was then that Luise suggested that I become her uncle's driver. I accepted that offer because it gave me papers that nobody could touch me.

A few months later, the General was appointed the Chief of Staff of the 22nd Freiwilligen-Kavallerie Division der S.S. Maria Theresia, a unit composed largely of foreign personnel and Volksdeutsche. As a Pole, I fitted right in and now I'm his personal valet and driver. I'm here with the General, whom I do have to pick up in an hour. I don't know what the future will bring, but I always can get a car for my Luise and go."

The waiter brought a piping hot, deliciously smelling Sauerbratten and fried potatoes and a couple of beer steins just in time because there wasn't much Schnapps left. Mostly consumed by Nadler. They finished eating the tasty meal, smoked a few cigarettes and when Henryk checked his watch it was the highest time for him to leave. He surely didn't want to be late for his meeting with Dr. Drzewiecki.

"Look, Henryk, I do know your family, and I know you as a decent boy, but we are living in horrible times, If you ever need my help, look me up at Karmelicka #42, apartment 24. I even have a telephone, number Cracov 4224. Submit those numbers to memory. Just reverse 42 into 24; the combination of those numbers is my telephone number. Good luck to you and take care of yourself. Let's meet in Boryslaw after the war." They held each other's hand, and without a further word, Henryk left the restaurant.

Henryk walked fast, like a man with a purpose in life. His spirits were lifted by Nadler's sheer personality and optimism, not mentioning the consumed alcohol. He now was seriously considering Nadler's offer of help. In the meantime, he would see what Ing. Keller was able to do on his behalf at the Induction Center

Without any difficulty, he located apartment #3B, and before he had a chance to knock at the door, Dr. Drzewiecki opened the door for him. "Witamy" Greetings! Please do come in. First of all, I would like to introduce you to my wife, Elzbieta." Henryk politely kissed Elzbieta's outstretched hand.

"It is a pleasure to meet you finally. I heard so much about you from my husband. You do already know our daughter, Czeslawa, and of course, her fiancée, Edward." "The pleasure is all mine, and I am very pleased that Edward became engaged to such a lovely young lady. Congratulations all around." Dr. Drzewiecki smiled broadly and said, "Henryk, these two young fools want to get married in a couple if weeks, you being the best man naturally." "I hope I can make it." Said Henryk, having the Induction Center on his mind. "Everybody please step into the other room, we'll have a drink in honor of our daughter's engagement. It will be just our immediate family and one more old friend, whom I do believe you have already met in the theatre, and he should be here any minute now."

The knock at the door was answered by Czeslawa herself. To Henryk's surprise, it was Mr. Waldemar Nowozeniec. Dr. Drzewiecki, noticing the surprised look on Henryk's face said, "I served with Waldemar in the September 1939 campaign. It was I, the company's dentist, who removed Waldemar's shattered arm. It wouldn't have been for me, he would have bled to death. He knows very well who I am (the emphasis was on the word 'knows'), and we became best friends since."

"Nice seeing you again, Mr. Kaplinski. It looks like your friend, Edward, is stealing our only treasure." "Mr. Nowozeniec, I have a feeling that those two are made for each other." "We all have the same feeling, but why rush with the wedding in these crazy times?" "You do have a point, but they are so lost in each other that nothing in the world matters, only their love." "Well, in that case let's have a drink."

Dr. Drzewiecki poured a straight vodka for everyone from a pre-war bottle marked "Monopol Spirytusowy." "To the young couple! We welcome Edward to our family with our open arms and hearts. We do trust our Czeslawa and her choice of a mate. We wish the young people all the luck in the world." "Na zdrowie!" (To your health)

Elzbieta Drzewiecka invited everyone to the table. "We are sorry for the modest reception, but I was told about it at the last minute. We'll make a large reception after the war." From a large porcelain tureen, Mrs. Drzewiecka served the gathered guests a delicious smelling and tasting "bigos." The tureen seemed to have an inexhaustible supply because everyone who asked for more received seconds and some. Hot tea and sweet cookies "caluski" completed the meal.

With the ladies gone into the kitchen, Dr. Drzewiecki opened up a serious conversation. "Our friend, Henryk, has a major problem on his hands, I'll speak frankly in the presence of his best friend, Edward, and my friend, Waldemar. The very reason why I am so protective of Henryk is because he is the son of my own cousin from Boryslaw. This may come as a surprise to Edward, but not to Waldemar. He and I have no secrets."

Edward just opened his mouth, but didn't utter a word listening to Dr. Drzewiecki continuing his speech. "Henryk has to report to Wehrmacht's Induction Center in a couple of days. There is a remote chance that his chief will be able to get him off or at least to postpone it awhile so that Waldemar, through his underground connections, can arrange for a "Kennkarte" under a fictitious name an a possible job with reliable people."

Dr. Drzewiecki lit a cigarette and continued further. "Considering Henryk's military background with the Red Army, he would have been an ideal candidate for the Polish underground army. Unfortunately, for the same reason, he can't join Wehrmacht, being a Jew, which also might be a problem with the Polish partisan group, even though he would be fighting the same enemy. Therefore, we advise a 'wait and see' policy for the next couple of days. Hopefully, Henryk's chief will get him a postponement, thus giving Waldemar's people a chance to prepare a thorough cover that would not fall apart at the first Gestapo investigation. Any questions or ideas?"

CHAPTER 5

There was a silence. Dr. Drzewiecki's speech mad a lot of sense to everyone concerned, especially Henryk. "Since there are no other ideas on the subject, I'll take Henryk to the other room to take his photograph for the "Kennkarte." I need another jacket for him and a tie. Also, Henryk, part your hair in the middle. The rest of you can have another drink. After all, this is a party."

Edward gave Henryk his jacket and tie because no other jacket would fit him properly, After parting his hair in the middle, Henryk looked in the mirror. A strange and yet familiar face looked back at him. His slightly amused expression would now be permanently registered on the photograph. The mere fact that other people also worried about him, added a dose of optimism into his future, a future that looked less threatening, even if for awhile.

After having another glass of tea and a cigarette, Edward said, "I, out of all people, really hate to break up the party, but we must be getting back. I would also like to avail myself of Waldemar's help, and perhaps move out with Czeslawa to some small town. I have had enough of O.T. its time to help Poland."

"It may be in Poland's interest to have a Polish patriot within the ranks of O.T. to know about their building plans and repair jobs. In this way we will know where the different partisan groups were active. In any case, let me think about it," said Waldemar.

Henryk kissed Elzbieta and embraced Dr. Drzewiecki, and thanked them for a memorable evening. He also shook Waldemar's hand. "I do thank you for your willingness to help me." "We are all fighting the same enemy," answered Waldemar. "I do have something to say to all of you," said Czeslawa. "I want everyone to turn to the wall because I don't want you to see how I am going to kiss my Edward." Everybody obliged her with a smile. In all probability, it was most likely history's longest kiss.

It was quite late when Edward and Henryk reached their barracks. Henryk found a note waiting for him, It was short and to the point. "See me at 4 P.M. tomorrow, Keller." No other explanation. Henryk was totally exhausted by the events of the day. In a way, he was glad that he didn't mention his accidental meeting with Nadler. It was an option that he decided to keep to himself.

Henryk spent the entire next day on odd jobs near the home base, delivering supplies or supervising small road repair jobs. At 4 P.M., he reported, as ordered to Keller's office. Keller was tied up in a conference with O.T. management. Raising both hands, Keller gave Henryk to understand that he would be busy for another ten minutes. Henryk just shook his head indicating that he understood the message.

The ten minute wait stretched into an hour, when Keller finally called Henryk in. "Gutten Abend" Good evening, Herr. Ing. Keller, you wanted to see me, sir?" "Yes, Heinrich, I did and I do. Please sit down. I do have some interesting and good news for you. We were able to get you a postponement of four weeks. At the same time, we were cautioned by the authorities that in a case of an emergency they may recall this arrangement. This will give us time to figure out our next move. Are you pleased?"

"Yes, very much, Herr Keller. That will give me a chance to put my private life in order and give me a possibility of attending the wedding of my best friend, Edward Daszkiewicz." "Starting tomorrow, you are back on your regular schedule, I'm counting on you as always, Heinrich, Gutte Nacht." "Good night sir," said Henryk, very much relieved with Keller's news.

Meeting Edward in the mess hall, Henryk told him about his conversation with Ing. Keller. "Since you are going to see Czeslawa this evening, please tell Dr. Drzewiecki about my postponement. He, in turn, should let Waldemar know about it."

"Hey, Henryk, this is good news. I was worried that you won't be around for my marriage. I'll give Dr. Drzewiecki your message.

You had better go in and rest because you look like a mess." "As soon as I grab something to eat, I'll go up to my dormitory. Give my regards to Czeslawa."

This time Henryk ate more out of habit than anything else. He washed up and went to his dormitory. From someone's radio in the room, Chopin's Andante Spianato and the Grand Polonaise Brilliante Op. 22 mixed beautifully with the peaceful snoring of the sleeping men, created a blissful atmosphere lulling Henryk into a deep sleep. The next morning, at breakfast, Edward told Henryk that his message was delivered. "I was told to remind you that it would take a good few days to get you quality papers."

"That is fine with me. We'll just have to be patient. I understand that today we drew different assignments in the area." "Well then, we'll see you in the evening. Good luck"

With the coming of the Christmas holidays, the tempo of work came to a halt. Most of the men were loitering around the barracks, separated by distance from their families, Some of them decided to go to church and after the services get drunk and sleep it off.

Ing. Keller unexpectedly took a two week vacation in order to visit his wife's family in Bad Wiesee in Bavaria, leaving Henryk as his replacement. Henryk managed to wring a concession from Keller regarding Edward. "Herr Keller, Edward is getting married on January 2, 1944, and we should grant him a two week furlough starting tomorrow. He is a very good man." "Heinrich, kurz and bindlich," (short and sweet) he can have the furlough as a wedding gift from me." "Thank you, Herr Keller. May I wish you happy holidays and a pleasant journey."

In a way, Henryk was glad that Keller was leaving for a few weeks. He needed the extra freedom to move unhindered, to see to his new identity papers, to spend the holidays with Edward and his future in-laws, and above all, to attend the wedding.

Just before Christmas evening, a fresh snow blanketed the city covering the dirt and the drabness of everyday life. More and more horse driven sleds made their appearance. On Christmas evening,

Henryk entered Drzewieckis' apartment bringing gifts for the family and a silver cigarette case with the initials E.D. engraved for Edward. He also had a bottle of vodka in his coat pocket, which he forgot to take out when he hung up his coat.

To his surprise, in addition to the people invited last time to the engagement party, Helga, the doctor's assistant, was also present. Dr. Drzewiecki must have read Henryk's mind because he lifted six fingers behind Helga. It was an old sign known to every school kid in Drohobycz, so-called "zeks", meaning danger. Henryk just smiled in the acknowledgement. Very gallantly, Henryk kissed Helga's hand, "How nice to see you again, Miss Helga." "Did you know, Henryk, that Helga didn't want to spend Christmas Eve with her family so that she could be with you," said Czeslawa, flirtatiously. "In that case, I'm deeply honored, indeed. I couldn't think of another person more interesting than Miss Helga," half seriously, added Henryk

The compliment hit the mark because Helga visibly turned red. What Henryk really wanted to say was that his mother didn't raise stupid kids. When needed, Henryk could turn on his natural charm that few women could resist.

At the table, he was seated right next to Helga. This time, Mrs. Drzewiecki outdid herself. According to Polish tradition, several kinds of fish were served. Where she obtained the fish was a mystery. Most likely, some of Dr. Drzewiecki's patients from nearby villages paid their bills with various food articles.

The beautifully decorated Christmas tree held several lit colored candles. The warmth coming from those candles seemed to embrace everyone in the room with a promise of tomorrow. The assembled dinner guests were in a very jolly mood. While vodka was flowing freely, Henryk noticed that Helga kept on filling his glass, and at the same time would rub her leg against his under the table. He well understood the conveyed message, but decided to be very careful with the drinks. The "Vino Veritas" approach could work both ways. Every time she would refill his glass he would do the same with Helga's glass, making sure that she drank her vodka as well. Every chance he had he would stretch his arm holding the glass of vodka and promptly would empty it into a cactus plant located near the window.

He wondered if a cactus could get drunk. Eventually, he got Helga where he wanted her to be, i.e. quite high, but he had to admit to himself that she held her liquor superbly. As far as he was concerned, a quotation from the only Shakespearean play, "The Tempest" he remembered was:

> "You taught me language, and my profit on't
> Is, I know how to curse."

Thanks to the Red Army, he knew well how to curse and drink.

Waldemar Nowozeniec started to sing the Polish version of "Silent Night" and everybody joined in. Henryk knew all the Christmas songs because as a young boy he would go with other friends to carol in front of Polish and Ukrainian homes. Czeslawa, holding Edward's hands, asked Helga to sing something appropriate with Christmas spirit. Helga obliged by singing, "O, Tennenbaum, O, Tennenbaum" in German. Her voice was rich, almost a perfect coloratura soprano. Just the fact that she sang in German put everyone in a serious mood. To break the uneasy silence, Henryk politely applauded, soon followed by the rest.

Mrs. Drzewiecki used the moment to serve tea and cakes. After such a rich diner, the tea was welcomed by all. With the meal finished to everyone's satisfaction, Dr. Drzewiecki got up and made a short speech welcoming Edward to the family, announcing the wedding date of January 2, 1944 at 2:00 P.M. at a small R.C. church "Our Lady of Mercy" on Kollontaia and Solna Streets, about a ten minute walk from their house.

"By the way, Father Bykowski is looking forward to meeting us all at tonight's midnight Holy Mass. So, let us go. A little walk will do us good." Henryk out on his winter coat, scarf and hat. Reaching into his coat pockets for gloves he found in one pocket a bottle of vodka which he forgot to take out, and in the other pocket he found Helga's cold hand. "I hope you don't mind it, Henryk, I forgot my gloves." "Not at all. You can wear mine. They are just a bit too large, but they will keep your lovely hands warm." "No, I prefer to hold hands." The entire Drzewiecki party walked down the steps, greeting neighbors and strangers with "Merry Christmas."

A very light snow still falling, each flake illuminated by street lamps, appeared for a brief moment, like a white crystal. Leading the group were the Drzewieckis' and Waldemar followed by Czeslawa and Edward. Henryk and Helga were closing the ranks. Helga didn't mince words with Henryk. "After the mass I want you to take me home because, and she started to sing, "I'm afraid to sleep by myself," a title of a very popular song. "That sounds very interesting," agreed Henryk, squeezing Helga's hand in his coat pocket.

The midnight mass was celebrated in a solemn ceremony, Henryk briefed by Edward on all church procedures, just went through the motion of a devout Catholic. He was sure that his own prayer to the God of Israel would be heard within or outside the confines of the church, With the services concluded, they all met with Father Bykowski briefly and in front of Dr. and Mrs. Drzewiecki, Henryk offered to take Helga home.

Henryk kissed Mrs., Drzewiecki on both cheeks and thanked her for the lovely dinner, Dr. Drzewiecki embraced Henryk whispering into his ear, "Be very, very careful with her. She works for the Gestapo." "Don't worry, I'll be extra careful."

It was a very long walk to Helga's home. They encountered a couple of German patrols who gave them a smile usually reserved for loves. "Here we are," said Helga, pointing to a small house. "The apartment belongs to my friend currently vacationing in Zakopane, and she gave me the keys to it." "That is just fine; nobody is going to bother us then."

Helga opened the door with a key that was hidden under the doormat. It was a small, one bedroom apartment, tastefully furnished. A few female nude figurines added a slightly erotic flavor to the room. Henryk, noticing that Helga was becoming stone sober, suggested that they have "just one more" drink.

"Henryk, I don't know where my friend, Maria, keeps her vodka." "Don't worry, Helga, I just happen to have a bottle to keep us going." "Alright, remember just one drink, you promise?" Henryk poured two stiff drinks while Helga put on a record player. The Latin beat of "La Cumparsita" filled the room. "Helga, how about a dance?" asked Henryk. "With pleasure, just let me change from my sweater into a blouse. I'll be back in a minute." While Helga disappeared into the bathroom, Henryk quickly emptied his drink into the kitchen sink, replacing the contents with tap water.

Helga came out of the bathroom wearing a low cut blouse, clearly showing the outline of her magnificent breasts. Henryk, putting down a book of poems by Adam Mickiewics, said, "Helga, you do look and smell fantastic. Come here, let's finish our drinks and dance. So, bottoms up!" He drank his glass in one large gulp, Helga made it in two gulps. Henryk got up and took Helga in his arms, holding her very close to his body. Being a fair dancer, he confidently led her about the room.

The consumed alcohol started to influence Helga's steps. She started to step on his feet. Ignoring that, he lifted her face and kissed her eager lips. She responded with her probing tongue. The record ended, but Henryk managed to move the needle, starting the tango all over again. "Henryk, take me to bed already, I can't wait any longer." "I can hardly wait myself, but shouldn't we have a tiny drink in honor of Edward and Czeslawa's engagement?" "Of course, but a tiny, tiny one, agreed?" "Let's have that drink and go to bed, darling."

He gave her another, not so tiny drink, which she drank at once. He swept her off her feet and carried her to the bedroom.

Looking straight into her eyes, he slowly removed her blouse and the brassiere, admiring her chiseled like breasts and proceeded to undress her completely.

She stood naked in front of him, a sight for hungry eyes.

"Do you like what you see?" she asked him smiling.

"Not even Venus de Milo is prettier than you."

"Henryk, I want to see you naked too."

Here came the part that Henryk was afraid of: having Helga the Gestapo informer see his circumcised penis would betray him as a Jew. On the other hand so much pent up sexual tension had to be released, no matter what the consequences.

Henryk removed his tie and shirt, displaying his hairy chest, the sight of which drew a comment from Helga:

"Jesus, Maria!"

"Turn around, let me see your lovely neck."

He cupped her breast with one hand and released his trousers with the other while kissing her neck. He bent her body, entering her with his erect and throbbing member. She was like a bitch in heat, fully allowing Henryk's every move within her. She reached three climaxes before he had his ultimate release.

"Henryk, I never had a man like you. I think that I'll love you forever."

"The evening is still young and you are not going to waste night like this on sleeping. Let's make love again." Helga shut off the light, explaining that she preferred the darkness in a romantic situation such as this. So did Henryk but for different reasons.

Methodically he massaged her breasts and covered every square centimeter of her body with kisses; aroused sufficiently they reached climax simultaneously.

She rested her head on his chest and started to cry.

"Henryk, I am a real whore. The Gestapo made me do it, They are holding my father in Auschwitz and they will keep him alive as long as I bring them information on anti-German activities. My father was on of the A.K. leaders, so everybody is trusting me.

"They told me to spy on Dr. Drzewiecki and Waldemar. When I met you, I thought you were Jewish. I'm sure that Dr. Drzewiecki suspects me. God, what shall I do? Henryk, please help me. On my bended knees I beg you to help me."

Henryk put on the light and looked at Helga's face. It was a face of a young and totally scared child.

"Listen, first things first. Are you getting any letters from your father?"

"Yes, I received three letters from him?"

"Were there any dates on those letters?"

"Yes, but it looked to me that someone else added those dates. The handwriting and the ink were different."

"I must be frank with you. That is a very bad sign, The Gestapo most likely forced him to write a few letters, which they are releasing whenever it suits them I only hope he is still alive. As far as Dr. Drzewiecki and Waldemar are concerned, I doubt it very much if they are involved in anything or in any struggle against the Germans. Especially Waldemar, with his one arm. They are like the rest of us Poles, we do not like the Krauts. Most likely you know it from my dental charts that I had a big problem with my gums. You have no idea what the O.T. or Army dentists are like."

"Edward brought me to Dr. Drzewiecki because I couldn't even walk by myself. Dr. Drzewiecki cured my gums and in the meantime Edward fell in love with Czeslawa. Me being Jewish that is very funny. My grandfather on my father's side was as Armenian and that may explain my slightly Mediterranean looks. My grandmother on my mother's side was a German colonist from the First World War and because of her they took me to O.T. and now they want me in Wehrmacht. Do you think they would let a Jew serve in Wehrmacht? Next week it will be January of 1944 and look where is the Red Army now. They already recaptured Vitebsk, Mogilev, Smolensk, Zhitomir, Kiev and Vinnitsa. Another 100 km. and the *Moskals*[1] will reach the old Russo-Polish Border of 1939. In another year they will take Warsaw and if the Americans will open the Second Front they will take Berlin too.

"Remember Helga, they are using you. Pretend that nothing has changed. Just string them along for awhile. Time is on your side but for heaven's sake don't involve the Drzewieckis or Waldemar in anything that can bring harm to them and if you love me as you are saying, don't even mention my name to them. Remember, when the war will finally be over, you'll pay dearly for any cooperation with Germans. Pity will be because you won't be able to help your father, I think he is beyond any help."

Helga started to cry again. Henryk took her into his arms and began to rock her back and forth like a small child. Soon she fell asleep. Henryk was just able to stay up for another few minutes and he too drifted into an uneasy sleep.

He was also the first to wake up. The morning sun was peeping through the kitchen curtains. It took him a while to realize his whereabouts.

Helga was asleep, lying on her stomach with both of her hands and head covered by a large pillow. Only her long blond hair was sticking out.

He observed her wondering if the Gestapo's hold over her would still exist in view of their last night's lovemaking. Come what may, he better be very careful.

He went to the bathroom where he found someone's straight razor and proceeded to shave himself. On a whim he left out the mustache area, promising to himself to raise one, never realizing that this would save his life in the near future.

He washed up and got dressed while Helga was still sleeping. Rather than waking her up he wrote her a note which he left near her side of the bed. A note which she found sometime later:

> Dearest Helga:
> I have never met a woman like you. You must be an angel because last night I was in heaven with you. Now it is time to be back to earth. I must report to my unit, will try to obtain a New Year pass and definitely will see you at the wedding. Counting seconds till I again kiss your ruby lips.
> Love, Henryk

A bone chilling wind hit him unexpectedly as he left Helga's warm apartment. He walked quickly in the direction of the barracks, thinking as to his next move in view of Helga's admission of being a Gestapo informer. Surely, Dr. Drzewiecki had to be notified but that would have to wait a few days since the Drzewieckis were visiting relatives or friends.

Upon return to the barracks, he found several urgent messages from the upper management. He had to dispatch a few teams of workers to fix the damage caused during Christmas by the partisans of *Armia Ludowa*[2] sympathetic to the Soviets.

Direct orders reinforced with a promise of two days furlough for every day spent working during the Holidays brought results. Grudgingly, workers went to their designated places.

His staff was reduced by one man, Pawel Mienta, who hanged himself during the previous night.

The Military Police had jurisdiction over the O.T. It was they who forced open the poor man's hand, extracting a letter written by Mienta's mother.

She wrote among other things that Pawel's wife was having an affair "with every man in Sandomierz who wears pants."

The Police Investigator made a remark: "He isn't the first man to do so and he won't be the last either to commit suicide." The investigator took statements from Mienta's friends and promised to notify Mienta's mother.

Henryk had to write a report for Keller regarding Mienta. Exhausted and disgusted he went to sleep.

Next day brought other problems. He was too busy to think about Helga, but she found a way to get in touch with him by showing up at the gate of the barracks.

"Heinrich, there is a woman asking for you at the main gate. What a pair of tits on her."

He came down to the gate and kissed Helga in full view of the guard.

"Henio", she started to call him Henio rather than Henryk.

"I missed you and had to see you."

"I missed you too but I can't get away for a few days. I have a big mess on my hands. One of my men hanged himself. Desperate people are doing desperate things. Let's keep our heads cool for a while but on Sylvester Night we'll go someplace crowded with good music and plenty of vodka and very dimmed lights."

"I know such a place and I'll take you there."

"Hopefully your friend is still in Zakopane."

"She is, she is, Henio." Helga's face turned beet-red and she cast her eyes downwards.

"Barring anything unforeseen, I'll pick you up around 10 P.M. Will you be ready?"

"Yes my darling. I'll be ready and willing."

He kissed her goodbye and went to his duties.

This affair has been developing much too fast, thought Henryk. Who was seducing whom? That was the question.

First things first. He had to notify Dr. Drzewiecki about the latest happenings. A sudden toothache gave him a good excuse to leave the barracks for a while but several pressing matters prevented him from leaving the post before noon of the next day.

One of the supply trucks was going in the direction of the city just a few blocks from Dr. Drzewiecki's office. He asked for a lift and the driver readily obliged.

"Heinrich, I'll drop you off at the door," said the driver.

"Thanks, but that is not necessary. I'll walk the block."

"Suit yourself then," and dropped off Henryk just a block from his destination.

A few doors from Dr. Drzewiecki's office, two men in long winter coats stopped him.

"Ihre Papieren, bitte – your papers please." The accent was on the word "please." He instinctively knew that he was dealing with the Gestapo.

He reached for his "Ausweis" usually kept in the inside pocket of his jacket. The papers weren't there. A cold sweat took over.

"Don't bother looking for your papers. We have your "kennkarte."

"This can not be. Let me see it." The conversation took place in German. With exaggerated politeness they handed over to him a "kennkarte."

He recognized his picture taken during Edward's engagement party. He understood at once. They got hold of "his"' papers, but how?

"Who is this Zdzislaw Slowikowski? These are not my papers, I just remembered where I put my papers this morning rushing from my office. Here they are," and he took out his O.T. Ausweis from his jacket's side pocket.

"My name is Heinrich Kaplinski and you can verify it very easily by calling my office. I see there is a slight resemblance, but that individual must be at least 5 years younger, he parts his hair in the middle of his head and doesn't have a mustache.

Please look at my head without my hat. Am I your man? Of course not. One more thing, here are my Wehrmacht induction papers."

By this time he was totally relaxed, even smiling. The two Gestapo men again compared his face with the "kennkarte."

"Looks like he is right. Wier mussen immer vorsichtig sei. We must always be careful."

"Ja, meine Herren, it is your duty. Happy Holidays."

"Happy New Year. Heil Sieg!"

Henryk kept going around the block and not seeing anyone suspicious he entered Dr. Drzewiecki's office.

His knock was answered by Czeslawa, who gave him a quick kiss on his cheek and said:

"My father wants to see you right away in his study."

Henryk entered the doctor's office where he found Dr. Drzewiecki in a somber mood. They shook hands briefly.

"We have a major problem on our hands. A messenger was supposed to deliver your 'kennkarte', which he kept as agreed in a book to identify himself to us. Czeslawa was also carrying a book as a sign of recognition. They were told to exchange the books. Unfortunately a random street inspection of papers caught up with this young and inexperienced boy, who panicked and dropped his book on the pavement, which the police picked up. Fortunately, he managed to get lost in the crowd of people. All this was seen by Czeslawa who was on the other side of the street, trying to cross the street to meet that messenger. Thank God she escaped their net. The papers are gone now and we'll have to make others."

"I know about it because I was stopped on the street by the Gestapo. Thank God I parted my hair differently for the picture and started to grow a mustache and when I showed them my O.T. papers and my Wehrmacht induction notice they let me go.

One more thing, Helga is an informer. She told me that herself. The Gestapo are holding her father. She is blackmailed that way."

"We know about her. It's better to know who is informing about us rather than someone else whom we may not suspect at all. We are extra careful with her and so should you be."

"Dr. Drzewiecki, things got a bit out of hand with Helga," and Henryk told him about his affair with Helga.

"This is suicidal, how can you do this?"

"I managed to do it without her seeing me naked."

"Listen, things are getting really hot around here. Stop coming to this office. I might be arrested any day now and so can Waldemar. Edward and Czeslawa have very good papers and they will disappear in a small town with relatives. My wife will go with them, while I'll go to a T.B. clinic somewhere in the Tatra Mountains under a different name. Don't worry, I don't have T.B. but that is a very good cover. A young dentist, a Polish patriot will fill in for me for the duration of German occupation. If we all survive we shall meet in this office.

Dear Henryk, many years ago when I still lived in Boryslaw I was and still am a 'Cohen' a priest. Therefore, I'm giving you my priestly blessing in Hebrew, which I remember better than my Latin."

He put both of his hands on Henryk's head and recited the "Shma" – "Hear o Israel, Our God is one."

They embraced and held each other very closely. Tears were flowing unashamedly from their faces.

"Thank you very much, uncle, for everything." It was the first time that Henryk called him uncle.

"I would like to say good-bye to Edward too."

"No problem, he is in the other room waiting for me to finish with you. And now I must attend to my patients."

He knocked on the other three times and Edward walked in. It was a different looking Edward. His hair was blond instead of being dark. He wore a peasant's rough and dirty clothing, like so many other folks in the region.

"My other brother Henryk! Time has come for us to part. I don't know for how long, maybe even for eternity. God blessed with me with your friendship and Czeslawa's love. I also consider myself privileged to marry into your family Yes, Drzewiecki told me everything. As a child I loved to come to your house. It was always so warm and full of love and I wished that my own parents would be more like yours instead of being cold and bigoted. May God grant us that we should meet after the war either here or in Boryslaw. Good-bye dearest brother."

Henryk shook Edward's hands and kissed him on both cheeks.

He wanted to say so much more. Brothers couldn't have been any closer. Edward saved his life on several occasions. From now on, he would have to take care of himself. The safety net for his wire walking act in this crazy world was removed.

"I have one final favor to ask of you. Please repeat with me words of an ancient Hebrew prayer. Shma Israel, Adonoy Elohenu, Adonay Echod." Thank you very much Edward. Will I see you at the wedding?" Henryk asked hopefully.

"Sorry I forgot to tell you that we are postponing the wedding for another few months. We'll be getting married under assumed names in a town where we are going to live. Don't worry our first boy will be named after you."

There was nothing more to say and Henryk left the room. On

the way out, he briefly said good-bye to Czeslawa, wishing her luck. She ran after him in the waiting room and loudly announced:

"Mr. Kaplinski, please see the doctor in 3 weeks at the same time." It was said with someone sitting in the waiting room in mind. He was sure that one was or another, we won't be able to keep that appointment. Fate probably had other plans in store for him.

With so many men away for the holidays and increased demand on O.T. services, caused by the weather and ever present partisans, Henryk had to improvise as best as he could in the absence of Herr Keller and his authority.

Several men from his unit came to see him with pre-induction notices for January 3, 1944. That was the same day as his own notice.

"Yes, I know about it, Maybe I'll join you too."

"Are they taking Jews into Wehrmacht too?" Myroslaw Skoryk asked. It was the same Myroslaw Skoryk who sometime ago baited Henryk with anti-Semitic remarks. He would have to be dealt with once more. Henryk addressed Skoryk:

"Ty chuju niemyty – you unwashed prick – one of these days I'll knock out the rest of your teeth."

"I'm truly sorry. I won't do this anymore." Said Skoryk, scared.

"You fellows are full of jokes, I have to write a report about that poor guy Pawel Mienta. The poor old woman, he was her only son. Couldn't you see that something was wrong with him? Don't you understand that we have to watch for each other?"

"You are absolutely right, Herr Heinrich."

Henryk was left to his thoughts and his still unwritten report. He wrote down facts about Pawel Mienta as it was given to him by the men of his unit. He also included the name of the Police Investigator for the case.

Having finally finished the report, he brought the finished report, along with the other papers, to Keller's office, leaving them on Keller's desk when the phone rang. He dutifully picked up the phone. It was Herr Keller calling from Germany.

"Heinrich, I'm glad that I caught you in the office. I want to tell you that I can't come right now. I have to bury my parents who were killed in an air raid by the *VERFLUCHTE*[3] Englander. How prophetic, it was my father that kept saying "who lives by the sword dies by the sword." How right he was. In the meantime, do the best you can."

"Sorry to hear about your parents, they seemed to be such nice and religious people."

Germany being bombed into oblivion might shorten the war, he hoped. Tomorrow will be another day, a day when he will meet Helga again. How shall he act now, being a lover of a Gestapo informer?

CHAPTER 6

September 1, 1927 was not an average day. It was a day that the 7-year-old Edward Daszkiewicz went to school, a first grader. He was so proud that his father brought him to school on the first day.

Some of the boys were crying and holding onto their mother's skirts, but not Edward. He felt like crying too, but was afraid that his father would not approve of such behavior. Edward was always afraid of his father, not that he ever hit him. He only had to look at Edward and Edward would freeze in his tracks.

Edward wanted very much to please his father, but hard as he tried, he never succeeded in getting his father's approval and praise was something he didn't think his father was able to bestow.

It was always: "Don't do this and don't do that. Don't play with the Jews, they are all dirty, they killed our sweet Jesus and so on."

And now, he, Edward, had to go to school with so many Jewish and Ukrainian kids. He was sure that at least half of the class was Jewish and that was in Public School named after a great Polish poet, Adam Mickiewicz, even the street was named Mickiewicza. Everybody called that school "White" because there was another school called "Red". Maybe because it was all red bricks. Maybe it was easier to remember colors rather than the names. Years ago his father told him it was an Austrian school and he told him the names of those two schools but Edward couldn't remember those names in German. It was such an ugly language.

"Edward," said his father, "pay attention to the teachers, always respect them and you had better behave. Otherwise there will be hell to pay."

Why he always used the word "hell" to scare me, thought Edward and then something happened that never happened to him before or almost never. His father embraced him and kissed him on the forehead. He loved his father in those rare moments.

"Good luck, Edzio." Mr. Daszkiewicz turned around and left Edward with the rest of the screaming kids.

The first grade classroom was located on the main floor just to the left. Edward sat on the third bench near a large window. Next to him sat another boy just as scared as Edward was. To break the ice, Edward introduced himself.

"My name is Edward Daszkiewicz. What is your name?"

"My name is Julek or Juliusz Weissman, Serwus."

Hearing the name, Edward asked Julek: "Are you a Jew?"

"Yes, I am and you?"

"I'm Roman Catholic," said Edward with pride. "Is it true that you killed Jesus?"

"Who me? I don't even know Him, then how could I have killed him?"

Further discussion was interrupted by the teacher:

"Quiet class, please take your seats, I need a few brave boys to sit in the first row. Don't worry, I won't eat you up in spite of my reputation. All you boys from the last row do come and sit here in the first row. I want to see you better. I'll wait. My name is Mr. Kobryn. You probably heard of me. Remember no talking during the class. If you have to go to the bathroom, raise your hand. Anybody who disobeys me will be put in the corner or will have his hands spanked with this wooden ruler. Class, is that clear? I can't hear you!"

"Yes teacher, we understand."

"That is much better, class."

Edward was so excited that he hardly heard what the teacher was saying. Somehow the first two lessons passed by, quickly followed by the great "pause" of twenty minutes.

Julek took a large pretzel out of his pocket.

"Edward do you want a piece?"

"Yes, Julek, thank you very much." The boys ate and talked and talked some more. They even forgot to go to the bathroom. Julek is very nice thought Edward to himself.

"Are all Jews like you?" "No, I don't think so. Some are larger and some are smaller. Why do you ask? Do you want to fight?"

"No, I don't want to fight. They will kick us out of school and my father will surely murder me."

"So let's stay friends, *SHTAMA*[4] ? They shook hands on it just as the school bell rang. The rest of the school day went without any major problems. One boy by the name of Katz was spanked, another boy landed in the corner. Both Edward and Julek raised their hands to go to the bathroom and the teacher told them: "Next time, only one boy at a time."

At the end of the school day, Edward said good-bye to Julek and ran home happy as a lark. He survived the day without crying. He was happy. The school was fun and he made a new friend. Being an only child he didn't make friends readily.

"Mama, I am home. Mama I'm hungry." His mother gave him a big hug and a kiss.

"How was your day dear? I'll warm up your favorite mushroom soup. Did you meet any nice children?"

"Yes, mama. His name is Julek. He shared his pretzel with me. I asked him if he was Jewish and he said he was. I also asked him if he killed Jesus. He told me that he didn't know him and that he didn't kill him either."

Mrs. Daszkiewicz started to laugh.

"Mama, he is not dirty. He was wearing very nice clothing, is blond and even a little bit taller than I and what's more he speaks Polish as well as we do. I'm going to bring him home tomorrow."

"That would be nice, dear, but he will have to leave before your father gets home. You understand?"

"Mama, can I bring him home then?"

"Of course, he can even eat with us."

"I'll ask him."

Edward was looking forward to the next day of school. By the time his father came home, he was fast asleep.

The second day of school brought relief to many boys in the first grade, including Edward. There was nothing to be afraid of with the exception of "Pan Professor" Kobryn. Julek was sitting right next to Edward and his first words were: "I brought two pretzels for us." "And I brought two apples, listen, after school come with me and visit me. My mama will give us something to eat."

"I'll come but I can't stay too long. My parents are at work and only my older sister, Rose, is at home but she won't squeal on me."

"Daszkiewicz, Daszkiewicz, pay attention. You can talk later," reprimanded the teacher.

"Let's take a short cut through the church's property." Julek hesitated a bit but encouraged by Edward's "nobody will bite you", ran along him and within minutes they arrived at Edward's house.

"Mama we are home. This is Julek, mama."

"How are you Julek? I'm glad that the two of you are going to be friends. How about some delicious pierogi with sour cream?"

"Mrs. Daszkiewicz, thank you very much. I can't stay too long because my sister will look for me."

"Where is your sister going to school?"

"She is attending the Queen Jadwiga School for girls. She is 4 years older and very smart."

"Oh, I'm sure of that. Please sit down and eat something." The boys ate heartily, laughing amongst themselves when unexpectedly, Mr. Daszkiewicz made his appearance. He greeted his wife and turned to Edward:

"Edzio, how was your day in school?"

"Very good, I like school and, papa, this is my friend, Julek."

"Julek what?"

"Julek Weissman", answered Edward.

"Weissman, Weissman? Which Weissman? What does your father do?"

"My father sells lumber on Stryjska Street."

"Yes, I know him. He is Jewish but a decent person." There was a distinct chill in the air. Julek looked around uneasily and said:

"Sorry, Edward, but I must run home. Thank you Mrs. Daszkiewicz for pierogi, See you in school tomorrow, maybe you would like to visit me?"

"Mama, may I?"

"Sure son, but be home by 7 o'clock at the latest."

"Thank you mama, you are the best mom in the whole world."

The next day the boys went to Julek's house. It was Thursday and Mrs. Weissman was home early in preparation for Friday and Saturday, the Jewish Sabbath.

Edward was never inside a Jewish home. What surprised him was that the house was similar to his, maybe a bit nicer. The wooden floor was so highly polished that each parquet was clearly visible. Edward was actually afraid to walk on it.

"Don't worry, Ed, this floor is meant for people to walk on. Come and have a bite to eat and then you boys can play."

Julek's mother was very nice, Ed thought. Much taller than his own, her grey hair was tied in a bun in back of her head and above all she had a kind face with an ever present smile.

Mrs. Weissman prepared for them hot potato soup and fresh kaiser rolls with butter. Mrs. Weissman kept adding soup to their plates.

After the meal, Julek showed Ed his chess set and his prize possession – a stamp album with 24 stamps of different countries and his most precious triangle stamp from the Belgium Congo.

"Did you know that it is in Africa?" "No, I didn't know."

"It is very hot there." Both boys tried to imagine life in those far away countries.

"Julek, I don't know how to play chess. Can you teach me?" For the next couple of hours they were much absorbed by the game of chess, without realizing that it was late and dark outside.

"I'm afraid to go home so late. My father will kill me."

"Don't worry, I'll go with you and talk to your parents," said

Mrs. Weissman. And so the three of them went to the Daszkiewiczes house.

Mrs. Weissman politely knocked on the door, which was opened by Mrs. Daszkiewicz.

"Good evening, I'm Julek's mother, I'm terribly sorry that Edward came home so late but they were engrossed in the game of chess and we all didn't realize how the time flew. It was my fault, because Edward told me that he had to be home by 7 o'clock. I must say that the boys are getting along very well."

"So the boys played chess? I didn't know that my Edward knew how to play it." interrupted Mr. Daszkiewicz. "I always wanted to teach him but never got around to it."

"He knows now. Julek taught him and Edward quickly grasped the concept. Your son is very bright."

"That is very nice. I'm glad the boys met. Would you like a cup of tea?"

"No thank you. We must be getting back. Tomorrow is another school day and I have to get up early to help my husband in the business."

Since that time, the boys were inseparable. It didn't matter in whose house they played. They were always fed and always loved. Mr. Daszkiewicz changed his attitude slightly towards the Jews:

"The Weissmans aren't like the rest of them. They are different." He even went out and bought Edward a chess set and a set of large wooden bowling pins to be played on the outside using a wooden ball attached on a string to a tree branch. This was a lot of fun but only on nice days. On rainy days they would play jacks made out of highly polished ordinary stones and they devised a game of soccer using large buttons taken from old winter coats.

Edward, being very inventive, made army tanks out of wooden spools of thread. Using a knife, he cut out "teeth" on the rim of the spools, inserted a rubber band and a wooden match to wind the toy tank, so that it would slowly move on the kitchen table.

The inevitable winter came and with it snow. Edward's father would insist that Edward go out and wash himself with snow.

Both Edward and his mother would scream with fright but Mr. Daszkiewicz insisted and Edward had to comply.

"This will make a man out of you. You'll never be scared of the cold."

Julek couldn't do it because he developed a whole series of never-ending colds, which kept him out of school for long periods of time. Edward would stop at Julek's house and brief him as to what transpired in school in his absence.

Every chance Edward got he would go sledding, ice skating or skiing.

Late spring was followed by early summer and with it the summer recess. Julek remained in Drohobycz but Edward and his mother were invited to spend the great part of the summer with Mr. Daszkiewicz's sister, who was married to a Ukrainian, Ivan Bozyk. He was an owner of a large farm and several orchards, in a resort town of Truskawiec some 9 km from Drohobycz.

Edward insisted and got permission to invite Julek for a week-end to Bozyk's farm.

Everybody was surprised when Mrs. Weissman brought Julek to Mr. Bozyk's house. By sheer coincidence Mr. Bozyk knew Mrs. Weissman, having bought lumber in their warehouse for his farm.

While the grownups were talking and sipping tea, the boys and Mr. Bozyk's three daughters showed Julek the stable, farm and orchard. Bozyk's middle daughter, Oksana seemed to be totally fascinated with Julek. The kids spoke a mixture of Polish and Ukrainian. There was no language barrier among the very young. Julek was enchanted with the farm never having seen one before. He came back to the house and said to his mother:

"Mama, I love it here. Can I stay, please?"

"Sure son, I'll leave you here for two days. Behave yourself and don't cause any trouble."

"No, mama. I won't, I promise."

The next couple of days were the greatest in Julek's life. He was grateful to Edward for the invitation, He went horseback riding without the saddle just like the rest of the kids, falling off the horse only once, to everybody's delight. He helped to bring in the fresh hay, worked alongside the peasants in the field and listened to their songs at the end of the day.

He knew many of those songs taught to him by his Ukrainian nanny, Kasia:

> "Yichav kozak na viynonku, prashtchav svoyou divchinonku."
> "Kozak going to war was saying good-bye to his girl."

Oksana holding onto her two blond pigtails was watching him sing.

In a couple of days, Julek's mother came back, bringing with there Zalewski's famous chocolates, a local treat of unmatched taste, for everyone. Working outside on the field under the strong August sun had put color on their faces. They both looked tan and fit. Julek looked even more self-reliant.

"Mama, can I stay another few days?"

"I don't think so, son. We shouldn't take advantage of Mr. Bozyk's hospitality."

"Te Pani Weissman, puskay chloptski ihrayout." "Mrs. Weissman, let the boy stay. My daughter, Oksana, likes your son. She doesn't stop talking about him."

"Well, if he isn't too much trouble, let him stay until Thursday." The summer in the foothills of the Carpathian Mountains was coming to an end but the work in the field was far from over. Everyone, even the smallest child had to help, especially in the orchards where boys were boys were most helpful reaching apples and pears from the furthest branches."

It was quite late when the boys went to sleep exhausted from working and climbing trees in the orchard. Shortly after midnight, the entire Bozyk's household was awakened by the vicious barking of their dog Brandy, Everyone ran out of to see the causes of the barking and Mr. Bozyk was the first to act, dressed in long underwear and holding a hunting rifle in his hands.

In the middle of the yard, next to an old maple tree, Brandy the black and white mongrel held in its bleeding mouth a porcupine with protruding needles. Brandy would swing the porcupine and let it hit the tree. The dog proceeded this way several times until the porcupine lost consciousness and the dog slowly turned the porcupine on its belly. Having accomplished that, the dog sank its teeth and claws into it.

Mr. Bozyk yelled at the dog to stop, even shot his rifle in the air but the dog refused to listen to the command, it was her kill. After Brandy finished with the porcupine she ran to the doghouse where she licked her wounds. Next day, Brandy was the hero of the day.

Finally, the day came when the boys had to return home. Mr. Daszkiewicz, who was in Truskawiec on business from his company, came with a horse driven carriage to pick up his wife and the boys.

"Serwus Julek! I spoke with your parents and told them that we would pick you up and drop you off on the way. You all look great. I see that the Bozyk's were nice to you, even though they don't care for *LACHY*[5]

The boys didn't pay attention to Mr. Daszkiewiczes remark. What was going on between Mr., Daszkiewicz and Mr. Bozyk was grownup business. All they wanted to do now is to say thank you and good-bye to Bozyk's and their daughters.

Oksana approached the boys holding two packages wrapped in a newspaper.

"These are presents for you", she said blushing. The boys opened the packages, which contained two identical hand-embroidered linen, peasant shirts. The embroidery on the collars and sleeves had clear Ukrainian designs and motifs.

"Thank you very much for everything. Go with God and come back to us."

An hour later the boys were back in Drohobycz and ready for city life.

There were just a couple of days left in their summer vacations but those were filled with preparation for school.

Their parents brought them some new clothing, leather backpacks, which they used in wintertime to slide down the hills. The backpack was from the best store in town, Einsiedler's and the school supplies from Werdinger who had the nicest selection and was located in the main square of the town.

As always, school started on September first. The boys, now second graders, didn't cry anymore and came to school on their own.

A big surprise awaited them. The easygoing Mr. Kobryn was replaced by Mr. Dumin, a mean, harsh disciplinarian who used to come to class with his large, black Doberman dog. Everyone in the class was sure that the dog was indeed the devil reincarnated. "Pan Professor" Dumin would hit the kids indiscriminately over their heads or hands with his long wooded stick. Coming across a Jewish boy he would occasionally pull him by the hair in the vicinity of the victim's ear. The kid would scream in pain and the class would laugh, even though each kid knew that sooner or later he would be in the same position.

The class was petrified of their teacher, however they paid very close attention to him. Their home assignments had to be done on time and certainly without any erasures. No one, absolutely no one, wanted to have Mr. Dumin's scorn on their head, unless your name happened to be Marcel Klinghoffer, who used to get more than anybody else. He complained once to his parents about it. And what his parents told him served as a reminder to the entire class: "If you didn't deserve it, you wouldn't be punished. The teacher is always right. That's why he is a teacher."

The Edward and Julek duo admitted another boy, Eli Reissman, a very good soccer player, and they became a trio.

In March of the next year, Mr. Daszkiewicz told Edward that he was promoted at work, therefore they will have to move to Boryslaw about 9 km from Drohobycz.

"You will be going to another school there." Edward started to cry. He didn't want to go to another school and he didn't want to leave his best friend, Julek.

"Don't worry, my son. You'll see Julek. We'll have him over as soon as we get situated. Besides, you will make new friends, maybe even better."

Edward decided to tell Julek about their move to Boryslaw at the end of the school year. Little did he know at the time that in Boryslaw he would meet a new friend who would have a profound impression on his life in the years to come.

CHAPTER 7

The next day, for a change, was totally quiet and problem free. He slept the entire afternoon, never realizing how tired physically and emotionally he was.

Waking up he washed and shaved once more. With satisfaction, he trimmed his mustache, got dressed into his new dark suit which he purchased for Edward's wedding, that wasn't taking place.

He would probably be early at Helga's place and perhaps he would have a chance to take her to bed before leaving for the New Year's party.

A leisurely half hour walk brought him to Helga's hideaway. A small pink envelope was stuck in the door frame. He took it out because it was addressed to him. He opened the envelope expecting some form of delay. Instead the note read:

> Dear Henio!
> I have to see my employers regarding the health of my father. I'll get back to you as soon as possible.
> With all my love,
> Helga

He re-read the note several times. Unfortunately or maybe even fortunately he couldn't fine a better explanation. He tried to open the door. Nobody answered his knock. Deep down he was glad that she was away. One problem less, he thought, putting the note into his pocket.

It was New Year's Eve. People rushed to each other's homes with smiles on their faces. He was all alone with no one to speak to or with.

A few blocks from Helga's house, there was a small bar. With time on his hands he walked in and ordered a couple of double vodkas, which he drank in quick succession. The bartender tried to make small talk but finding Henryk unresponsive, he left him to attend to more gregarious patrons.

Slightly tipsy he continued walking towards his barracks. The idea of spending the New Year's Evening with his O.T. buddies became revolting.

From the shadow of a tree a female with too much rouge and lipstick on her face approached him.

"Good evening, handsome. All alone on New Year's? Would you like some company?"

"Yes, it sounds like a good idea. I need to talk to someone and why not you?"

She took his arm and they walked to a nearby building that had a separate entrance leading to her apartment.

The apartment itself had a pleasant ambiance, a large comfortable bed, a lamp with shade that had erotic figures painted on it. Next to the bed stood a washbasin with a couple of white, clean towels.

"Why don't you make yourself comfortable. I'll put some soft of music on for you or perhaps you prefer another drink?"

"Both if you don't mind. What is your name?"

"My name is Lucyna. My regular customers know me by that name. You can give me your name if you wish or any other name that suits you. I can see that you are greatly troubled, do you care to tell me, friend?"

"You know, Lucyna, your profession is the noblest and at the same time the most honest. You do provide pleasure and relief to lonely men like me. Some so called "good" people, they are the whores of the world. They talk nice, go to church on Sundays but they will rob you or kill you. Lucyna pour me another vodka."

"Sure friend, I'll just call you friend. Do you want to spend a short time with me or the entire night? I must ask you for money up front."

"No problem, Lucyna. I do like you, you are honest and direct. I'll pay you for the night but I may leave sooner. Fair enough?"

He took out of his billfold several larger bills.

"Would that be sufficient?"

"Yes, my friend that is enough, you are very generous."

He could tell she was no shrinking violet when it came to handling money.

"Let me look at you again. I know people and certainly know men, all kinds of men after all that is my business. I think that you and I are from the same stock, of that I'm sure. It takes a Jew to know a Jew."

Henryk was speechless. He must have been really drunk to get himself in such a situation.

"Lucyna, I didn't come here to be insulted. I came here to get laid."

"No, friend, you didn't come here to get laid. You came here to talk and talk we shall. The reason why I am so sure of you even before you've dropped your trousers, is that I'm rabbi's daughter from Piotrkow..."

"Wait just a minute. As a child I had many Jewish friends and classmates. One of them taught me how to say the mornings prayers. If you are a rabbi's daughter as you say, then surely you must know the words of that prayer."

"Oh, you mean 'Modi ani Lefunechu..."[6] There was no longer any doubt in Henryk's mind as to her being anything else but Jewish.

"But how can this be?" he asked, confused.

"You see friend I'm a prostitute, that is my profession, but I'm not a whore. There is a world of difference. Before the war, I studied linguistics at the Jagielonian University in Cracow, where I met and fell in love with a fellow student, a Gentile boy. He was the son of Count Potocki. He was so gorgeous and totally irresistible. I became pregnant and Jerzy promised to marry me. I was so naïve in those days that I believed him. For a while he set me up in an apartment in town while he went to Paris to continue his studies. He prepaid my expenses for about a year until my daughter was born and then he disappeared. All my letters came back unopened. I couldn't go back to my parents. I brought them too much shande[7] as it was. I needed money to live on and to support my daughter. I took in a few lovers who paid me for my favors. They, in turn, brought their friends and willingly or unwillingly I was in the business of the oldest profession in the world. One of my steady customers was and still is a priest who obtained for me baptismal papers of a deceased person my age and with changes that war brought I came to Lublin where I opened the only business I know. I still see that priest. He hears my confessions and I do his. We are good for each other."

Lucyna stopped talking and the room was strangely silent. Henryk sat with his mouth slightly open. Lucyna's words had not only the sound of truth but it was the truth, he just didn't know how to react to it. He wasn't the only person who was in deep trouble, that's why misery likes company. He couldn't tell his story because the words didn't come out of his mouth.

It was Lucyna again who was more realistic:

"Friend, let me put out the light by the window, so that my walk-in customers will know that I'm busy. Tonight I don't want to see anybody else."

She went to the other room and shut off the light facing the window.

"What would you like to do? Tell me your story but I see that you are not up to it at the moment, so let me make us something to eat. Would you like that?"

Henryk just shook his head in affirmative.

"How about some scrambled eggs with delicious kielbasa?" He again shook his head, as Lucyna gave him a warm smile."

"It will take me just a few minutes."

She put on an orange apron and from a small pantry she brought six eggs, butter and a big ring of kielbasa, which all soon landed on a frying pan.

Within minutes a small kitchen table was set for two people, plates, napkins, silver cutlery, kaiser rolls and delicious smelling scrambled eggs.

Henryk didn't have to be asked to sit down. For some strange reason he was hungry. They both ate the meal with real gusto.

"Would you like to have some coffee?"

"Lucyna, how can I say no to good coffee?" They both laughed. By the time she served him coffee, laced with French cognac, Henryk was totally relaxed.

"Lucyna, my name is….."

"Please don't tell me. I don't want to know your real name. I'll call you "friend" from now on. You can tell me about yourself, only if you wish to do so."

"I agree. I'll just tell you a little bit. The Russians took me into their army in 1940. A year later I was captured by the Germans. I was able to join the O.T. as a non-Jew and now I have to report in two days for a pre-induction examination to Wehrmacht. The minute I drop my pants it is going to be the end of me. I'm afraid. As you see, I'm facing an insurmountable problem."

Lucyna started to laugh so that tears appeared in her eyes. Henryk, full of indignation asked her:

"What is so funny?"

"Sorry, friend, I do owe you an explanation. You see, one of the medical orderlies in charge of the so called 'Schwanz-parade' who squeezes pricks of the recruits for discharge associated with gonorrhea or syphilis is a good client of mine. He is 'Der Kleine Hansl'. Actually his full name is Hans Alfred Mahler. The coffee and cognac you drank is his. And do you know what I do for him? I piss on him. That's right. I piss on his face and head. He is completely impotent and that is the way he gets his kicks. Me, rabbi's daughter, is pissing on that Nazi worm. If only his sleazy Nazi friends knew. He is coming to see me tomorrow. Do you have any idea how much water I have to drink so that I can give him his "golden shower"? Don't worry about the examination either. I already sent him some men with similar problems. All you have to do is tell him that Lucyna sends her best regards. I'll set it up for you. You can trust me. You can't miss him. He is short, fat and is bald like a billiard's ball. Look, we talked so much without realizing that we have barely 5 minutes to midnight. Our meeting calls for champagne. I kept that bottle for a special occasion and for me, this is it."

She opened a bottle and the cork flew all the way to the ceiling. They drank to Victory over Germany, for the liberation from the Nazi yoke and finally for their respective health. Lublin's churches were ringing in a new 1944.

"Lucyna, where is your daughter?"

"You mean Irena. She is 7 years old, smart and beautiful and lives nearby with the sister of that priest I told you about. I do get to see her every couple of weeks. She was told that I am a runner for the Polish Underground Army and that required secrecy. You see she is very patriotic."

"Lucyna, I don't know how to thank you. I do hope to God that your wishes should materialize."

"Well, friend, did I earn my money for the evening? You see in my business I can't afford 'dormoche'[8] ." Now it was Henryk's turn to laugh uncontrollably.

"Friend, I am very tired and so are you. Let's go to bed."

They got undressed. He remained in his underwear and Lucyna put on a sexy negligee. No sex was intended, they slept next to each other like good friends.

Some hours later, some drunk kept knocking at Lucyna's door, waking them up.

"Lucyna, Lucyna, open the door, this is Grzegorz."

Lucyna didn't bother to answer. Henryk took the initiative to get rid of the drunken man. He simply shouted in German:

"Mach das Du verschwindest" – disappear – and disappear he did.

It was the noon sun that woke them up. Both felt wonderfully refreshed. They stayed in bed for another hour at least, reminiscing about pre-war years.

"Lucyna, again, I don't know what to say or how to thank you."

"Never mind. Let me make you some fresh coffee and we still have some rolls and cheese left."

"That would be just fine. Can I wash up and maybe take a shave in the meantime?"

She showed him to a small bathroom and handed him a fresh towel and razor.

By the time Henryk came out of the bathroom a breakfast awaited him. They ate in silence, realizing that in a few minutes, each of them would go their separate ways. He to an unknown and unsafe future and Lucyna being a captive of circumstances would have to continue in her not chosen profession until the end of the war. Lucyna looked into Henryk's eyes and said:

"We have to say good-bye to each other. Before you go I want to tell you a story. When I started in this business just before the outbreak of the war in September, 1939, I operated under the name of 'Krystyna.' One evening three young Lyceum students came to see me. They introduced themselves as Goldstein, Glick and Rappaport and they asked me to choose any of them to be my first client. My answer was 'Sol sein mit Glick (let it be with luck). And now that you are leaving I'm saying the very same words. Let it be with luck. For heaven's sake, go before I start crying and ruin my makeup."

Henryk got up and without a word kissed both her hands and left the room.

Leaving Lucyna's apartment, he felt strangely elated by the experience they both shared. Here and there he would smile to passerby's, some of whom, probably braver, would smile back in spite of his O.T. uniform. Streets weren't crowded this New Year's day. The sidewalks were swept clean of last night's slight snow fall. Wherever ice was formed, some kind soul spread ashes to prevent people from falling. The air was cool and crisp but the sun tried unsuccessfully to peek through cloud-laden skies.

Henryk reached the barracks and reported to the duty officer. It was a formality that he adhered to because it was a way of checking what transpired in the last two days. There were few cases that required his immediate attention. One of them was an urgent note from Helga, which he chose to ignore for awhile. He was afraid that she might show up in the most inopportune moment. Therefore he decided to join a squad of men sent to repair a small bridge that was close to the barracks. He intended to be as busy as he could, because in a few days he was due for Wehrmacht's pre-induction examination.

Quickly he changed into his overalls, emptying pockets from his uniform. Among the assortment of items he usually carried in his pockets he found a small envelope marked with only one word 'Friend'. He ripped the envelope open and in it he found money and a brief note:

> Since you didn't avail yourself of my charms,
> I'm returning your money because only a satisfied
> customer comes back. Good luck friend. Lucyna

"What a woman," he said aloud to no one in particular. He joined the squad of men leaving for their assignment. A canvas covered truck brought them to the spot where the bridge needed some repairs. Like in the past they had an armed escort. Someone had a bottle of Schnapps which he passed around, somebody else contributed cigarettes which everyone lit, deeply inhaling the satisfying smoke. The holiday spirit probably had something to do with people's largesse.

Having finished their smoke, men slowly applied themselves to the task at hand, finishing the job just before dusk. The same truck took them back but it was dark when they reached the barracks. The guard on duty approached Henryk.

"Heinrich, you have a visitor. She wouldn't go away until you came back." As he suspected it was Helga. He would have to deal with her carefully. A scorned woman would complicate his life even further.

"Serwus Helga. How are you? Good to see you again."

She removed her scarf which hid most of her face in the poorly lit street. His heart skipped a beat. Her face bore marks of a brutal beating. Her left eye was completely closed and swollen, upper lip cut and front tooth was missing.

"What is God's name has happened to you?" asked Henryk petrified.

"The Gestapo tortured me. They wanted information on Dr. Drzewiecki and Waldemar, but I didn't tell them anything, I swear to Virgin Mary. They told me that my father died of a heart attack, those bastards, you were so right."

"You are so brave. A real heroine. Poland is proud of you. Don't worry about the tooth. Dr. Drzewiecki will put in a false one. You won't know the difference. The swelling will disappear in a couple of days. Just apply ice or snow. In no time at all you'll be pretty as ever."

"Henryk, I want you to come with me and spend the night."

"Darling, I would love to do it but I can't. I just returned from work and tomorrow I have to appear before the induction commission. If I don't show up there, they might put me against the wall. I'm sure you don't want that for me."

"Oh, no. I love you too much as it is already."

"Then please Helga, go home and take care of yourself. I'll be in touch with you as soon as I know the results of the examination. Usually they give you a few days before they ship you off. Let me see what can be done but in the meantime you go home and be of good thoughts. Remember saying: 'The devil is not as black as the people paint him.'" Henryk kissed her forehead and softly said to Helga:

"Everything will be fine, don't worry, God won't let us perish."

Helga kissed both his cheeks and said:

"You are right my noble knight." Much at peace now, she made a sign of the cross and left him standing for a while until he could not see her anymore.

Henryk returned to his room and after washing up he joined the group of men working with him on today's project, in the mess hall. He ate fast, swallowing the food. With the examination on his mind, he was considering various options still open to him. One of them was to obtain papers directing him to Cracow where his fellow countryman Nadler, promised him a place where he could hide from the German authorities.

He went to the office where he calmly took O.T. stationary in full view of other office workers and typed himself a letter of transfer from Lublin to Cracow. He forged Keller's signature and for good measure affixed his stamp to it.

Office workers were used to Henryk's presence, for all practical reasons he was Keller's deputy. For appearance sake he also straightened out and dusted off Keller's desk drawing a remark from a typist: "Sauberkeit ist eine Gewohnheit" – cleanliness is a habit – to which Henryk just smiled and left them with a "Gute Nacht und angehneme Ruhe" – good night and pleasant rest. He fully realized the danger, should he be caught with those forged documents. Tomorrow is going to be his encounter with fate.

CHAPTER 8

The cavernous, former warehouse on Mariacka Street #7 was now the Wehrmacht's induction center. Henryk, accompanied by 35 of his own O.T. men reported to the duty officer. Like everybody else, Henryk was given a number and had to wait his turn to be examined. Told that he had to wait at least 30-45 minutes, he decided to look around for himself.

It wasn't so simple, his group was kept under a guard and all the movements were controlled. Henryk excused himself to go to the restroom. His stomach was acting up after last night's rushed meal or perhaps it was his nerves.

In front of one of the stalls, someone hung a white laboratory coat. Henryk took that coat, checking if anyone noticed and put the coat on himself. In one of the coat's pockets he found a stethoscope which he promptly displayed on his neck and a fountain pen which went to the upper left pocket. He walked out to the hall. No one paid the slightest attention to him. The place was a beehive of activity.

What Henryk noticed was that prospective soldiers were admitted 10 men at a time. At the first desk each new man was registered and given a sheet of paper upon which each subsequent medical orderly or physician would enter his or her remarks. Altogether there were six stations. Only one station was covered with a white curtain which, upon closer inspection, Henryk discovered the bald head of Hans Alfred Mahler. This was the last medical stop. There was one more desk where recruits were handing over their forms and seemed to be briefly interviewed by the man sitting behind the desk. Henryk was sure that it was only a formality.

A sense of de ja vou overtook him. He was in the same position just four years ago. The only difference was that the music of "International" was replaced by "Horst Wessel" song and the German doctors seemed to him to be a bit more thorough, but the results were the same. Once they got hold of you, they had you by the short hairs, that much was obvious. He had seen enough.

He took off the coat on the way to the bathroom, just as some highly irritated doctor was yelling:

"Who the devil took my laboratory coat!" Henryk walked in with the coat folded on his arm.

"Here sir, someone left it in the other room." The doctor wearing captain's insignia smiled and politely thanked him. Henryk joined his men. A few minutes later his number 187 was called.

At the first desk, he was asked for the date of his birth, home address, marital status, education, religion, which he submitted as Catholic and his nationality, Polish, and his mother and grandmother being Austrian. He was also asked to produce his O.T. card which the clerk compared to the information just given.

At the second station he was put on a scale and measured. He had gained 3 kg. since his last induction but he shrank by a centimeter.

In quick succession his blood pressure was noted at 120 over 80, pulse at 88, respiration at 16. The eye doctor established his vision at 20/20. The following doctor was the man whose white coat Henryk wore for a while.

"Ah, this is the young man who found my coat. Let me check you out myself." His listened to his heart again, checked his spine and his feet and said:

"You don't have flat feet. You are a fine specimen of a perfect Aryan." And signed the form that Henryk carried from desk to desk.

The major hurdle was the remaining "Schwanz-Parade" but Henryk was hoping that Lucyna spoke to "Der kleine Hansl."

He moved the curtain slightly and entered the cubicle. The man standing next to Hans said:

"You, just wait a moment."

Hans was talking to the other, middle-aged man wearing a white coat and rubber gloves.

"Peter, I have to take care of something personal. Be back in a few minutes. Please cover for me in the meantime."

"Sure thing Hans. I'll take care until you come back, just go ahead." Hans left before Henryk had a chance to say something to Hans.

"Next!" The next person was Henryk.

His heart started to beat violently. He had a sudden stomach cramp and he couldn't hold his bowels anymore.

"Herr doctor! I have a bad stomach. I must run to the toilet and clean up."

Whether it was the title of doctor that Henryk bestowed on the medical orderly or the unmistakable stench, because Peter reacted with:

"Scheisse! Shit! Go and come right back, I'll hold onto your papers, you idiot."

"Thank you, thank you, Herr Doctor. I'll be right back." Henryk didn't mind being called idiot as long as he could be back to see Hans instead of Peter.

"Die verfluchte Auslander! Those damned foreigners. Next!"

Henryk ran on the double directly to the bathroom where he bumped into one of his men, from his own squad, Ryszard Strzelecki, who suffered from a weak bladder and was the subject of many jokes.

"Hey Ryszard, I finally managed to soil my underwear, would you have another pair for me?" "As a matter of fact I always carry one with me just in case. You always were on the level with me. This is my chance to reciprocate." From a side pocket of his uniform he took out a pair of underwear shorts.

"Thank you Ryszard, I owe you a big one."

He washed up as best as he could and went back to Hans' cubicle, praying that Hans would be back. Also his papers were left there. He waited outside to see who was coming out. When he had seen Hans' bald head yelling "Next" he pushed the other man standing in the line with:

"Excuse me, I was here before, they have my papers. I had to go to the bathroom."

"Let him go or he may shit in his pants again", someone remarked. Henryk of course didn't pay any attention to the heckler. He walked in. Hans looked at him for a while and said:

"Are you the fellow who had to run to the bathroom?"

"Yes sir, it was me. Sorry but I had an upset stomach."

"Drop your pants, hurry up!"

"Herr Mahler, I'm a friend of Lucyna, she sends you her very best regards." Hans gave him a big smile of recognition.

"Why didn't you tell me before. How is the old girl?"

"She is just fine, she is very fond of you, Herr Mahler."

"Is she? That's great. Here are your papers signed. Good luck! Next!"

Much relieved Henryk left Hans' domain.

At the next desk sat a man in a white coat but whose rank Henryk couldn't tell. Whatever his rank the man spoke with certain authority in his voice.

He asked Henryk numerous questions regarding Henryk's experience with the O.T. and his previous military background. Henryk was stressing his O.T. past, minimizing his Red Army years. The man listened attentively, making some notes in Henryk's file and then he fired a direct question at Henryk:

"Are there any reasons in your mind why you should not join the Wehrmacht's ranks?"

Remembering his meeting with Ryszard Strzelecki in the bathroom Henryk tried:

"Sir, I have a very weak bladder, I continue to wet my bed a night."

"Where we are going to send you, not only will you piss at night but you will also shit. Let me see your O.T. Ausweis."

Henryk handed over to him his O.T. identity card, which the man barely looked at, and instead of returning the card he gave him a replacement, a temporary Wehrmacht's I.D. card valid only for the transport to his next assignment, subject to Wehrmacht's discipline and military law.

Henryk fully realized that his option of traveling under the auspices of the O.T. evaporated. Unless he somehow obtained other papers.

A loud, shrieking voice brought him back to the new reality again.

"Malcontent! Get the hell out of my sight before I put you in the brig. Next!!"

Henryk didn't need another invitation, he left immediately only to be stopped a few meters away by a captain who must have noticed or heard the exchange of words between Henryk and the man whoever he was.

"What seems to be the trouble, son?" The captain was a tall man with gray hair, an army chaplain with Protestant markings on his military tunic.

"No problem, Herr Kapitan, just a slight difference of opinion. I wish that the war would end soon."

It was not a talk that officers of the Wehrmacht would encourage regardless of their religious denomination.

"Yes my son, we all feel that way from time to time. But we must ask God for help to defeat our enemies."

"Maybe God will listen to your prayers."

"You see my son, I'm in sales and not in the management." Smiling said the captain. Henryk was left to his own thoughts. There was nothing else to do but to move on to the next room, where over 100 men were already assembled. Most of the men smoked cigarettes and talked with each other.

"Attention, men! In a few minutes you are going to be sworn in. After the swearing in ceremony you will be given your rations, uniforms and individual orders as to your next post. Is that understood?" The last word had a threatening tone to it.

"Is that understood? I don't hear anything!"

"Yes, sergeant", men answered.

"That is much better! You will learn fast I see." A few officers walked in and the sergeant reacted at once:

"Attention everyone, no smoking." And turning to the officers he reported:

"Sir, the men are ready." A lieutenant took over the proceedings. "Repeat after me." He read the oath of allegiance to Hitler which each man repeated. Only God knew what was in the men's hearts.

Another sergeant with a booming voice, ordered the men to another large hall where a group of non-commissioned officers, mostly middle-aged men took over.

"Loss, schnell." Get a move and hurry up. The men were issued dry food rations and blue/gray Wehrmacht uniforms.

At the uniform counter the pot-bellied corporal didn't bother to ask Henryk for his size. He just looked at him and handed him a patched up tunic that was freshly washed and ironed. However, the trousers were new just a bit too long. At the next window he received additional items like a blanket, underwear, knapsack and high boots. Boots were used too, but soles and hubnails seemed to be recently put on them. Henryk wondered what had happened to their previous owner. He tried on the boots and they fit. In a way he was glad that he was given an old pair of boots. It would save him the trouble of breaking them in. He still remembered vividly the pain caused by wearing a new pair.

In some cases it was a matter of life or death, especially on long marches.

"Here is your belt, General." Someone handed him an old belt laughing. It was indeed an old belt that someone had used also to sharpen a straight razor. The belt had a buckle with words "Gott mit uns" – God is with us. Henryk took that as a very good omen. He felt that God was with him. He, the son of a Jewish couple from Galicia in the German Army. What an irony!

Men from Henryk's squad approached:

"Listen, Heinrich, we've got to get back to our barracks to collect our things. You better speak to someone in charge."

Henryk didn't mind being the spokesman for the group, he just wanted to get back himself. He also wanted to pass a word to Edward and Drzewieckis, even though he was told not to do it. The O.T. group walked up to the sergeant and requested to see the officer in charge. The sergeant seeing so many men, obliged and brought them to the captain in charge of the Induction Center.

"Sir, we are a group of 36 O.T. men. We respectfully request permission to get back to our barracks to collect our belongings and straighten out our personal affairs. Personally I have to turn over to the office important papers dealing with O.T. projects in the last three weeks. We are asking for 48 hours leave.

The captain listened carefully, watching the men.

"What is your name?"

"Heinrich Kaplinski, Sir."

"I like it when somebody shows initiative and cares about his men. I am hereby promoting you to the rank of 'Feldfebel' (corporal). However you can have only 24 hours. Kaplinski, I'm holding you personally responsible for the group to report tomorrow morning at 8AM sharp. Sergeant, assign one armed guard to supervise this group. Dismissed."

The O.T. group accompanied by a soldier with automatic Schmeisser went back to their barracks. Once they reached the barracks they went on their own, leaving a very frustrated guard.

Henryk knew full well that without his O.T. identity card he couldn't get very far. He would be stopped at any railroad station or even at a street crossing. At the moment there was no other choice for him. He would have to go along with his induction until a more opportune possibility.

"Heinrich, the same broad came to see you again. She is waiting downstairs for you, you lucky stiff." One of the guards came to tell him.

"Thanks. I'll be right there." He didn't see any harm in seeing her or in saying good-bye.

Helga looked much better. The swelling on her eye disappeared and the cut on her lip was just slightly visible. If not for the missing tooth there was no permanent damage done to her face.

Henryk embraced and kissed her gently. "How did it go?" Helga asked.

"Not so good. I'm in the Wehrmacht as of tomorrow morning."

"What about you?"

"I went to see Dr. Drzewiecki about the missing tooth but he was not there. Some young doctor is in charge now. He told me that Dr. Drzewiecki contracted T.B. and had to be rushed to a sanitarium in Tatra Mountains. Czeslawa and Edward eloped to get married and I have no idea as to their present whereabouts. In addition you are leaving too. What am I going to do?"

Drzewieckis and Edward disappeared as planned so there was no sense in going there and looking for trouble. Joining the Wehrmacht may not be such a bad idea after all. First chance and he'll surrender to the Allies. In the meantime he'd better pacify Helga.

"Pull yourself together, you still have some relatives. I'm sure they will help you. I'll write to you and as son as I get my furlough I'll come to see you. Darling I have to go but you be brave, the war cannot last forever. Try to survive, that is what we all have to do. Promise?"

"Yes, I promise."

Henryk felt sorry for Helga but in his life there was no room for her. She probably felt it because there was an awkward moment. Their lips met briefly and they went their separate ways.

The next morning's reveille sounded even sharper in Henryk's ear. This was the day that he was due to report, along with other man at the Induction Center. There was no doubt in his mind that his days in Lublin were numbered. The sooner he would leave Lublin the better and wasn't the Wehrmacht's uniform his best cover?

Henryk packed up his belongings making sure that he had his civilian suit, shirts and tie with him in any case. That was the suit purchased for Edward's wedding. Henryk wanted to get some use out of that suit. Whether he'll get that chance was an open question which remained to be seen.

The cook in the mess hall prepared an extra large breakfast for the men leaving the O.T. for the Wehrmacht.

"Is this our last meal?" someone joked.

After the breakfast the inducted men left the barracks in loose formation only to be stopped a few blocks away by a "Lapanka", a round-up of able-bodies men for work in Reich. For a split second Henryk thought that an arrest might be a form of escape from serving in the German army, but he put aside that idea after the policemen, having seen the temporary Wehrmacht Kennkarte, which was signed by the captain of the Induction Center Bernd Schmalhausen. For whatever reason he lost interest in Wehrmacht's recruits.

There is one procedure known to the soldiers world over, regardless of the armies in which they serve – "hurry up and wait."

It took almost the entire day to be finally processed. The O.T. group was split. The majority of the men were transferred to the Eastern Front, which was hardly 175 km away. Henryk and five other men including Strzelecki were assigned for temporary duty in the vicinity of Munich in Bavaria. They would have to travel to Cracow and Vienna to get there.

One of the army clerks said to Henryk:

"I see that Herr Kapitan Schmalhausen promoted you to corporal. Well Corporal, Munich might not be your final assignment. More likely it will be France or Italy. I wish I could draw such a duty."

The inductees were given all kinds of papers, forms, coupons, money and dry food rations.

Cracow was a God sent opportunity to locate his fellow countrymen, Nadler and perhaps take advantage of his offer. Because of the late hour they had to sleep at the Center and on the following morning they would begin their journey in all directions.

Henryk decided to call Nadler and let him know that he was

coming to Cracow. The only telephone at the Center was hopelessly tied up by men eager to reach their loved ones. His chances of using the phone at the Main Post Office were much better, but to get there, he needed a special pass. He located the sergeant in charge of the gatehouse.

"Sergeant, may I speak with you in private?"

"Yes Corporal, what is on your mind?"

Henryk took out a package of Polish, pre-war cigarettes, the elegant "Egipskie" and handed it over to the sergeant.

"Sergeant, I need to see my girl this evening. I want to give her a bang or two. She lives not far from here. One hour will do the trick. I'll be back, I'm leaving all my things here."

"Keine Sorge, Feldfebel – No worry, Corporal, but if you don't show up it will be my ass on the grill and not yours."

"As you have said Sergeant 'Keine Sorge'. I'll be back. She wants to get married and I don't. Besides she has an ugly mother and who would want that old bitch for a mother-in-law?"

"Alright already. Let me give you a pass for two hours. Give her another bang on me, you son of a bitch. You better be back and thanks for the cigarettes."

He quickly walked out of the Center in the direction of the Post Office. Here and there people on the street would stare at his O.T. uniform always trying to avoid any contact with him, whether it was physical or verbal. He didn't blame them. Most of the Poles didn't want to have anything to do with the Germans, at least the decent ones, thought Henryk with bitterness.

Some minutes later he reached the Post Office. Individual windows were closed due to the late hour but the three phone booths were open. Two out of three were occupied. Henryk couldn't see their faces because they sat with their backs to the door. The third booth with a large sign over the "Fur Deutschen" – for Germans— was vacant.

Henryk walked in and lifted the handle requesting in German Cracow #4224, the number that Edek Nadler gave him.

The telephone operator kept telling him over and over again

that she couldn't get through to Cracow:

"There are some problems on the line, Sir."

"I'll wait a few minutes." He sat in the booth afraid to leave it. Nobody wanted to use the phone anyway. Half an hour later he tried the number again with the same result.

"Operator, I must get through, is that clear?"

"I do understand, Sir, but I don't control the lines."

There was no point in antagonizing her. He waited another 45 minutes and tried again.

This time the operator reached the 4224 number in Cracow. Alas, there wasn't anyone on the other side of the line to pick up the receiver.

"Your party is not at home, Sir. Sorry, try later."

There was nothing else to do but go back to the Center. Nadler could have been out for the evening or altogether not in town. He'll have to try to see him when in Cracow. Dispirited, he came back to the Center barely on time.

"Corporal, how did it go?" asked the sergeant.

"Scheisse (shit), she had a red flag day, can you imagine?"

"It happens 12 times a year only, better luck next time."

Henryk joined the O.T. men, most of whom were asleep already, only Strzelecki waited for him with some extra food he managed to obtain.

"Eat Henryk eat."

"I really can't, I had a very lousy day, Strzelecki. You're a good friend and I appreciate everything you are doing for me."

"Well, there is always tomorrow", half jokingly remarked Strzelecki.

"You are so right, let's hit the sack. We need all the rest we can get."

The much needed rest they didn't get, awakened after a few hours of sleep to the sound of "Aufstehen, Aufstehen, Raus! You lazy bums this is not a hotel, this is the Wehrmacht."

It took Henryk a few minutes to realize that the semi-military discipline of O.T. was replaced by the Wehrmacht's own and old

Prussian tradition of obedience. Gone forever were the easy camaraderie of working men. He would have to adjust to the new situation and fast. There was no alternative at the moment.

He divided his belongings into two piles. The Wehrmacht's issued items went to the rucksack and the O.T. uniform along with his suit were carefully folded and put into a small valise that Strzelecki thoughtfully provided. He was now prepared for different options, come what may.

The fat sergeant from the Quartermaster's Unit was screaming orders even before the men had a chance to swallow their Ersatz – coffee and bread with margarine.

Henryk's name was called with a first group of 20 men. They were issued some additional papers and were told where to board the truck taking them to the town's Railroad Station.

Henryk checked his papers. It was the Wehrmacht's authorization to the Station Master for tickets to Milano, Italy via Cracow, Bratislava, Vienna and Brenner pass.

Only five other men had similar documents, they were Strzelecki and four former O.T. men with whom Henryk worked on several projects. Three times they were counted before boarding the truck. The same fat sergeant and an armed guard kept them company until they reached the railroad station where the railroad police and the military police took over. The papers were again checked and rechecked.

After a two hour wait, a train marked Radom-Kielce-Cracow pulled into the station. Henryk's group entered a wagon marked "German Military Personnel Only."

What looked like a comfortable compartment for six men, became less comfortable with the addition of two more soldiers. To kill time, the men smoked, played poker or read. A couple of hours later the train pulled into Radom station, their first stop. Given half an hour, Henryk decided to look around the station. One thing was obvious to Henryk's experienced eye. The station was well guarded by uniformed and civilian personnel. Paper of travelers were carefully scrutinized.

Acting nonchalant, Henryk bought a newspaper and walked into the men's room stinking of urine and disinfectant. On the wall housing urinals, someone scribbled with big, black letters:

"DEUTSCHLAND SIEGT AN ALLEN FRONTEN" – German is victorious on all fronts. The same 'someone' crossed the letter "S" in "SIEGT" and changed it to the letter "L" making it "LIEGT" – is lying.

Henryk smiled with satisfaction, the resistance to German occupiers was visible even here.

Loud whistles and 'All Aboard' reminded Henryk to get back to the train. The next stop was Kielce, but Henryk didn't bother to leave his compartment.

Almost every hour on the hour the conductor and Military Police would come and ask for "papieren". With a bored facial expression, Henryk would hand over the group's papers. The other two soldiers had to do the same.

"Alles in Ordnung" or "Alles Klapt", everything is in order was the usual answer.

It was late in the evening by the time they reached Cracow.

Checking the departure schedule for Bratislava with the Station Master of Cracow, Henryk's group was told that the next train for Bratislava was due some 26 hours later. There was nothing else to do but wait.

The Wehrmacht's duty officer directed them to a small room and advised them to catch up with sleep on any available bench.

"In the morning I'll be able to help with accommodations for the day till your departure. That is the best I can do for you at the moment."

On the spur of the moment, Henryk decided to speak with the officer.

"Pardon me, Herr Lieutenant. May I ask you for a favor?"

"Yes, Feldfebel, what is it? I'm very tired and sleepy, so make it snappy."

"Sir, my older brother is a personal driver to General Eugen von Schobert. He is located on Pomorska Street right here in town.

I didn't see my brother in several years and tomorrow night we are leaving for Bratislava. Could the Lieutenant issue me a pass for a few hours?"

Whether it was the General's name or the sentimental side of German soul, which could be at times very cruel, the Lieutenant reacted with:

"Kein Problem, Feldfebel. By all means go and see your brother. Here is your pass, just fill in your name. I have no time."

Henryk clicked his heels and saluted smartly. The Lieutenant without acknowledging the salute turned around and left Henryk holding the pass.

Now Henryk had the means of leaving the Station without any hindrance. The next stop was to try the telephone and contact Tadeusz Kierod AKA Edek Nadler from Boryslaw.

He dialed the number Cracow #4224 which was etched in his memory. On the fifth or sixth ring, a sleepy female voice answered the phone.

"Wer ist dass? – who is this?"

"I'm very sorry to call so late, Fraulein. I'm Tadeusz's cousin. I just arrived in Cracow. Is Tadeusz at home?"

Henryk hoped that the female was the niece of the general, Luise von Spandorf, but knowing Edek's reputation with ladies he couldn't be sure.

"Yah, ein moment bitte." "This is Heinrich Kaplinski, how are you cousin?" Henryk stressed the word cousin which Edek was quick to pick up because he responded in kind:

"Heinrich, my favorite cousin, how are where are you?"

"I'm at the main railroad station in town."

"Can you spend a few days with us?"

"I'll be delighted."

"In that case, can you meet me tomorrow morning at 9:30 in front of 'Esplanada' coffee house on Szewska Street right across from 'Bagatela Theatre'. Any 'droshky' (horse driven carriage) driver knows that place."

Tadeusz put an emphasis on the word 'droshky' giving Henryk

an indication as to preferable method of transportation.

"Very well Tadeusz, I'll see you in the morning and again I apologize to the lady for calling so late."

"Don't worry, Luise doesn't mind."

So it was Luise von Spandorf.

Breathing a sigh of relief, Henryk took out of his pocket a fountain pen, his favorite 'Pelikan' and using Gothic script he filled his name on the pass. Having done that he went back to his bench where Strzelecki and other former O.T. men were sitting.

"Henryk, I saw you talking to an officer, what was that all about?"

"It is very simple, you see my girlfriend has a married sister here in Cracow whom I wanted to meet for some time now so I asked for a pass for you too, but the son of a bitch gave me only one. He said don't press your luck, so I took just one pass."

"How long is the pass for?"

"Just for a day but someone told me if you go to the hospital they can extend it for another day or two."

"So what are you going to do?"

"I don't know yet. I'll see how Helga's sister will receive me, seeing me in German uniform. Maybe I'll put on my O.T. uniform. I really would like to see Cracow. I'm told that it is the most beautiful city in Poland and maybe in the world. If it doesn't work out I'll join you in Italy. Have you got a butt?"

"Good luck Henryk, let's get some sleep now."

Henryk stretched out the best he could on the wooden bench and to his surprise fell asleep despite all the station's commotion and noise.

The morning found Henryk refreshed and eager to meet with Edek Nadler/Tadeusz Kierod. To that end, he gathered his belongings consisting of an army rucksack and the small valise. He shook hands with Strzelecki and the other men from his group. He walked towards the exit where he was stopped by guards.

"Where to soldier?" The questions was asked by a stern looking Military Police Sergeant. "Your papers!"

Henryk handed over his Wehrmacht traveling documents and the pass issued to him only yesterday. The sergeant looked over the pass and said sarcastically:

"This pass is not valid." Henryk's mouth opened but the words didn't come out.

"The pass doesn't have the length of time added to it. For how long was it issued?"

"Four days only."

"That we can fix ourselves." With those words, the sergeant added the words, 'four days only' to the pass.

"Now everything is in order and you may take off."

"Thank you very much, sergeant." "Enjoy yourself, make the most out of those precious days." "I'll do that, I promise."

Outside the railroad station stood a line of horse driven carriages. Some caring drivers put blankets over the backs of the horses.

A man wearing a black derby hat and heavy woolen scarf asked Henryk in broken German:

"Wohin, Herr Offizier?" Where to Mr. Officer?

The driver clearly saw Henryk's rank of a corporal and yet he addressed him as an officer in shrewd anticipation of a bigger tip.

"Caffee-House 'Esplanade' on Szewska Strasse"

"Gutt" and the driver put Henryk's luggage in the back of the carriage. Henryk took a seat in the carriage while the driver gave him a blanket for his legs. Henryk wondered if that blanket was the same that was given to the horse. Henryk lifted the collar of his coat to shield him from the wind.

"Have you been to Cracow before?"

"No, only in my dreams."

"If you wish I'll point out a few places as we drive. You see Cracow is a city that we are all very proud of. We are driving along Straszewski Strasse, soon we'll see the famous St. Florian's Gate."

Henryk was observing the city with keen interest, watching the people on the sidewalk, he couldn't find a Jewish face. A trolley car was making a turn with difficulties on Planty Park and

Szpitalna Street. The sparks from an overhead cable were flying all around.

The driver, assuming his role as tourist guide, pointed with his whip to the beautiful theater named after a Polish poet Juliusz Slowacki.

"Even Paris doesn't have a nicer theater because the interior of the Theatre is enhanced by an illustrious curtain made by Siemiradzki. Right near the Theatre is a nightclub 'Cyganeria' with the most beautiful girls in the world. 'Dort mussman haben viel Geld' there you must have a lot of money. Would you believe that in 1942 some Jews threw grenades at German officers. Imagine the nerve of those Jews. Good thing that Herr Hitler liquidated Jews for Poland."

"We are coming close to Karmelicka Strasse. Please look to your left and you'll see a XV, century Castle Barbakan and after that in a few more minutes the Herr Offizier will be on Szewska Strasse and the 'Esplanade' coffee house. I do hope that the Herr Offizier enjoyed the tour."

The anti-Semitic remark uttered by the driver about Hitler and the Jews long ceased making an impression on Henryk. He heard it too many times already. However Cracow as a city was something to admire. Just after half hour in town, one forgot any other city. He barely remembered Vienna, he had visited as a small child, even Leningrad which he had seen almost four years ago couldn't compare to Cracow, soaked in the history of Poland, history that he remembered vividly from his school days. His further thoughts were interrupted.

"Mein Herr, here is 'Esplanade', your destination. The driver put Henryk's belonging on the wet sidewalk.

Henryk paid the driver adding a few Zlotys as a "Trinkgeld."

The driver took off his derby saying: "Danke, danke."

Henryk glanced at his pocket watch. He still had another 10 minutes to wait, providing of course, that Edek would be on time.

He didn't need to worry about Edek being on time. A long, black Deimler limousine pulled to the curb, where Henryk was standing. The door opened and a man dressed in the black uniform of S.S. jumped out. It was Edek himself.

"Come, get it, let me help you with your luggage."

Henryk put his stuff on the back seat and sat in front, next to Edek. Once in the car they started to speak Polish, the language they both used in Boryslaw.

"How are you, Henio? What is happening with you? Last time I saw you in Lublin you were with O.T. and now I see you in Wehrmacht's uniform?"

Henryk patiently told him how he was conscripted into the Wehrmacht and his reasons for leaving the city of Lublin.

"It is a smart thing you have done under the circumstances."

"Sooner or later the Gestapo would have caught you. They have thousands of informers. Do not trust anyone. Your idea of getting to Italy and surrendering to the Americans or the British might still be a good option. Here in Cracow, things are getting progressively worse. The Jewish Ghetto was liquidated entirely just a few months ago. Most of the Ghetto inhabitants were killed in nearby Plaszow concentration camp. Very few Jews escaped to the Aryan side, but unless they have close friends who are Poles and some money, they won't last long. There are few Jews that Gestapo knows about and they are using those Jews to fish out other Jews, otherwise they themselves will be killed."

"You seem to be very well informed." Said Henryk.

"General von Schobert for whom I work as a driver, has a friend another General in the S.S. Gen. Kruger and that whore's son was bragging one evening,, while having drinks with Schobert, that he keeps a Jew Dr. Rosenhaugh, Poland's foremost ophthalmologist in permanent "house arrest" to treat his eyes. He believes that Jews are better doctors."

They sat in silence for a few minutes and the Nadler continued:

"Look to your right, that is Sukiennice (Cloth Hall), not so many years ago, many Jews had their stores there and now nobody is left. If you wish to see the Ghetto area we can drive through

Limanowska, Jozefinska Streets or through Plac Zgody. Maybe tomorrow, if we have time, I'll show you the Jagiellon University, Matejko's Square, Pilsudski and Kosciuszko Mounds. To Wawel the Royal Place we won't be able to go. Now I'll take you to my own room which I rent from a widow of a Polish high ranking officer who disappeared in the east during September, 1939. Her name is Anna Szczucka. She is glad that I'm the tenant otherwise she would lose the apartment altogether to other German civilians. She'll make you something to eat. You relax, wash up and tonight General von Schobert is giving a little party and I can use your help as a waiter. I'll get you a white jacket. Make sure that your fingernails are absolutely clean. The General has an obsession about clean fingernails."

"How do you manage to survive among the S.S.?" asked Henryk.

"The same way that Daniel in the lion's den survived. It isn't easy. I assure you. A Chinese philosopher Confucius once said that the darkest place is always under the lamp. Tell me who would suspect a Jew as a driver to a S.S. General? The only person besides you is Luise von Spandorf. She is Catholic and in love with me, made her mission in life to save me and convert me to Catholicism. I told her that after the war I'll think about it. Maybe the time will come when she may want to embrace Judaism for what Christians have done to Jews. Of course, there is also the possibility that she may fall out of love and report me to the Gestapo. Imagine what a scandal that would create! General's niece and a Jew? What a 'Rassen Schande'[9] ", he added with a smile.

"You see Henio I'm not afraid of dying. After all you live only once, but still I have no intention of dying. I want to live and survive this lousy war. I want to live long enough to tell the world what I've seen. I'm just worried that nobody is ever going to believe me. I do carry poison and if I have to, I'll take it. I'm not a coward, but I don't want to die a thousand deaths either.

Here we are in front of my house. Come, I'll give you a hand with your luggage. The apartment is on the third floor. When you speak with my landlady Mrs. Anna Szczucka use German only. She is also totally fluent in French and English. I suspect that she taught languages at the Jagiellonian University. Since the time when the Germans killed over 168 faculty members she had kept a very low profile and who can blame her."

The elevator in the lobby had a sign in German and Polish: "Elevator out of order."

"It has been like this for a while. They can't get a missing part to fix it. Let's walk. It's only three flights."

Edek Nadler, better known as Tadeusz Kierod, opened the door with his key just as Mrs. Szczucka was trying to do the same. Henryk was introduced in German as Heinrich Kaplinski, a friend who'll be staying in the apartment for a few days.

"Frau Szczucka, could you make something to eat for my hungry friend? I have to run and pick up the General and you Heinrich be ready by 5 o'clock. I'll be waiting downstairs for you."

"Fine, that will give me plenty of time to rest. I'll be on time."

"Herr Kaplinski, just give me a few minutes and I'll have something for you to eat. Would a cheese omelet suffice?" We also have real "Bohnen caffee" with compliments of Herr Kierod."

"Thank you very much. I'll just put my things away in the meantime."

Henryk brought his luggage to Tadek's room. It was a nicely furnished room with a comfortable looking bed near the window. A large oil painting of Black Madonna of Chestochowa hung over the bed. At the opposite side of the room stood a desk and an old hand carved chair. To the right of the desk there was a door leading to the bathroom, as Henryk soon discovered.

Henryk took out his O.T. uniform and his civilian suit and hung them in the wooden closet with outside carvings matching the desk and the chair. His toilet articles he put in the bathroom on the shelf right over the sink.

"Herr Kaplinski, the food is ready," announced Mrs. Szczucka.

"Thank you. I'll be right there."

Lunch prepared by Mrs. Szczucka was served on an elegantly

set table. The food pleased the eye as well as the palate.

"Good appetite, Herr Kaplinski. Do you mind if I join you for coffee?"

"Not at all, please sit down."

Henryk had a closer look at Mrs. Szczucka. She was at least ten years older than Henryk and that would make her 34-35 years old and yet she looked considerably older. Most of her black hair had changed into gray. Her once beautiful face bore the imprint of years of war. The shapeless black dress masked a nice figure and only her large eyes betrayed both her real age and her native intelligence. There was an awkward moment of silence, that Mrs. Szczucka broke:

"Herr Kaplinski, do you speak Polish?" Henryk, mindful of Edek's words answered in German:

"Very little I'm afraid, surely not enough to carry on an intelligent conversation but I have noticed that you speak a very good German. Where did you learn your German?"

"I took it at school and later when my husband Jerzy was the Polish Vice-consul in Berlin I had lots of practice."

"Where is your husband now?"

"I'm afraid he was captured by the Soviets in 1939. I did get regards from him through a Polish soldier who worked as a railroad man. Jerzy sent his greeting from Smolensk. Hopefully he wasn't executed with the rest of the officers at Katyn."

"For your sake let's hope for his safe return."

"Thank you very much, Herr Kaplinski. By the way, how long do you know Herr Kierod?"

"Sorry Mrs. Szczucka, I really don't know him at all. He is a friend of a friend. He is just letting me use his apartment for a few days because I can't afford the hotels on corporal's pay and army barracks or Red Cross crowded facilities I can very well do without. Please pardon me I want to wash up and use this 'Mittagspause' to rest for a while because Herr Kierod is going to pick me up. Should I fall asleep please wake me at 4:30."

"Yes, I'll do that gladly for you."

"Thank you very much, Mrs. Szczucka."

Henryk went to the bathroom, shaved again and washed up, taking special care about his fingernails, as suggested by Edek. Having almost two hours before picked up, Henryk lied down on the bed. Looking for something to read for a while he noticed two books on the night table. The top book was Hitler's 'Mein Kampf' and the other book of poetry by Heinrich Heine. Not exactly Nazi recommended reading.

Henryk opened Heine's book and started to read the marvelous poems. A couple of minutes later the physical tiredness took over and he fell asleep.

"Herr Kaplinski, Herr Kaplinski, bitte stehen Sie auf."

"Mr. Kaplinski, please get up." It took a good while for him to wake up. He looked around the unfamiliar room and slowly remembered how he got here.

"Thank you Mrs. Szczucka, I'm up." He washed his face with cold water and now fully awake, got dressed. A few minutes before 5PM he went downstairs to wait for Edek's arrival. He stood in front of the house watching the meager traffic when a gray Opel Kadet pulled to the curb. The door of the car opened and a tall, well dressed, attractive brunette approached Henryk.

"Are you Heinrich Kaplinski?" It was more of a statement rather than a question.

"I'm Luise von Spandorf. Tadeusz was busy with my uncle and asked me to pick you up. You'll see him later."

"Good evening, Fraulein von Spandorf. It is a pleasure to meet you." She just gave him a polite smile.

"Please get into the car."

Henryk didn't have any experience with women drivers but Luise was an exceptionally gifted driver.

She drove with ease, shifting gears whenever the need arose.

"We are almost there. Can you see the Wawel the Royal Palace?"

Even though he couldn't see too well in the distance, he said

"Yes". She pulled to the front entrance of a modern looking four-story building.

A doorman and a uniformed guard acknowledged her with "Good evening, Fraulein von Spandorf." The guard looked suspiciously at Heinrich.

"He is with me. The general is expecting us."

"Otto," she said to the doorman, "Please put my car in the garage."

Luise and Henryk entered the lobby of the building, and took the small elevator to the top floor.

"Heinrich, please use the servant's entrance to the kitchen. You'll find Tadeusz there. Our butler got sick and we need someone to help us this evening. The General is giving a small cocktail party for some of his friends. It was Tadeusz's idea to bring you here."

Henryk did as he was told. He entered the kitchen where he found Tadeusz busy supervising two cooks, a man and a women.

"Now that you are here please take off your coat and put this white jacket on instead. The butler caught pneumonia and you'll have to serve drinks. Let me see your hands."

Henryk extended both his hands for Tadeusz to see.

"They are fine." He looked around and not seeing anyone nearby he lowered his voice and continued speaking in a hushed voice:

"Tonight some of the worst S.S. people involved with the Jews of Cracow will be here. In some cases they helped people to escape but for very big money but most were sent to concentration camps. Hope no one will suspect you here. Remember you're my cousin's school friend. Things are not good around here at all. Tomorrow, unfortunately I must drive the General to his new divisional headquarters and I don't know how long I'll be there. Luise wants to go skiing with her girlfriend in Zakopane and visit Krynica. I asked her to take you along. She is not too crazy about it, but as long as you are with her you'll be safe. You can go back to my apartment for a day or two. Mrs. Szczucka is a very suspecting person but she'll keep her mouth shut as long as I'm around. Your idea of going to Italy is good. I understand that many German soldiers are giving themselves up to the Allies. Should you go to the Russians however and tell them about being Jewish in the German Army, they will shoot you as a spy. You are better off with the Americans or the British. Raising his voice for the benefit of the cooks who walked in, he continued:

"Heinrich, look where we are storing extra bottles of Schnapps, Cognac and wines. I'm keeping several bottles of champagne on the windowsill to keep them cold. Get busy, the guests will be arriving shortly."

"Ist alles bereit?" Is everything ready? These words were spoken by a gray haired, tall man dressed in full general's regalia.

"Who is this man?" The General asked Tadeusz pointing to Henryk.

"Herr General, he is the man who is going to help out this evening because the butler got sick."

"You come over here. What is your name?"

"My name is Heinrich, Herr General." Said Henryk standing at attention.

"Show me your hands, Heinrich." Henryk walked up another step and showed the General his hands, both sides.

"Ausgezeichnet – excellent as you were."

Henryk took a kitchen towel and started to wipe various sizes of glasses.

Tadeusz introduced Henryk to the cooks.

"Heinrich is going to help this evening, please show him around a bit."

"Heinrich, I need you by the bar come with me."

"Sofort, Fraulein von Spandorf." – At once Miss van Spandorf.-

She took him into a large salon and pointed to the bar and a table laden with several decorated silver trays containing assorted artistically arranged and deliciously looking canapés.

"Heinrich, offer our guests drinks of their choice and every few minutes walk around with food trays. Make sure that you have enough napkins and matches to light cigarettes with you." Said Luise von Spandorf.

"Yawohl, Madame."

First to arrive was the General's Aide de Camp, Captain Fritz Knackendoeffel.

"Oh, Fritz, how good to see you." Luise extended her hand, which Fritz promptly kissed.

"You are looking marvelous this evening, Luise."

"Thank you very much. The General is looking forward to seeing you."

"And I'm looking for him. I have a bunch of letters and documents for his signature."

"Here you are, Sir, how is the General this evening?"

"Never mind Fritz all that flattery, did you bring me papers from Headquarters?"

"Here they are, sir do you need any help with those papers?"

"Just give them to me. If I need your help I'll ask for it."

The General was in a lousy mood, that much was obvious to everybody including Henryk.

A polite knock at the door and three people walked in. Fritz announced their presence:

"General der S.S. Kruger, Countess Tatiana Dlugorukaia and Lieutenant Klaus Volkmann."

The group was followed by other people and Fritz kept introducing them:

"Obersturmfuhrer and Mrs. Theodor Heinemayer, Lieutenant and Mrs. Oswald Bousko and S.S. Sturmscharfuhrer of the Sicherheitspolizei Wilhelm Kunde assigned to the Jewish affairs."

The last remark drew a universal laugh. Henryk not only didn't laugh but his stomach turned sour with fear. To his mind a prayer came of Daniel in the lion's den.

An exceptionally beautiful young woman arrived with Kunde. Her long blond hair covered half of her face. Herr Kunde introduced her as Klara Cybulska of Silesia.

Henryk started to circulate with glasses of champagne between the guests. Here and there he was able to listen to parts of their conversation starting with "prosit", "your health".

The guests kept drinking and asking for more keeping Henryk quite busy.

From time to time, Tadeusz made his appearance by bringing additional trays filled with food.

Fritz put on the Telefunken radio and a sentimental song "J'Atten drais" filled the room. Led by General Kruger and Countess Tatiana everybody started to dance. Tatiana sang in French the words of the song, soon followed by Klara in German:

"Kom Zuruck, Ich warte auf Dich denn Du bist fur Mich, Einmahl Gluck komm Zuruck..."

That music was succeeded by the popular Rakoczy March which brought the dancers and almost everybody else to an upbeat mood, only to be interrupted by Berlin's radio announcement of "Ansage Ansage":

"The Germany Army Group North in operation code 'Blue', fought one of the war's hardest battles against superior enemy forces of Meretskov and Govorov, inflicting tremendous casualties on the attacking Soviet Armies. Under the unrelenting attacks of Asiatic hordes, the valiant soldiers of the Reich took a phased retreat to pre-arranged positions. The enemy paying a very high price was able to remove the blockade of Leningrad."

"Donnerwetter", screamed General Kruger and turned off the radio.

"Forgive me Fraulein von Spandorf. I didn't have the right to do that and spoil the evening for everybody. I was just too upset with the news. It looks like the only war we are winning is the war against the Jews. Badly needed transport is being used to resettle the damned Jews and in the meantime the Bolsheviks are already on the Polish border of 1939. I hope and pray that our Fuhrer Adolf Hitler will finally unleash his secret weapons."

He put the radio back on, but nobody was dancing anymore. The magic bubble of the evening was busted.

"Hey you," pointing to Henryk "bring us another round of

drinks and make it a double." General Kruger once more took over.

Henryk kept refilling glasses even faster.

"Say what is your name?" asked General Kruger.

"Heinrich Kaplinski, Herr General."

"Where are you from?"

"Galizien, Herr General."

"Is it true that people from Galizien have a well developed sense of humor? In that case do tell us a 'witz' (joke). Henryk had to think fast and one joke came to his mind.

"Herr General, this is about the English. Oscar Wilde was invited to the Earl of Essex for dinner. The next day, Oscar was asked about the dinner and answered: "Everything was cold with the exception of Champagne."

Everybody started to laugh. General Kruger had tears in his eyes.

"That is splendid, Heinrich. What are you doing here?"

"I have a few days of furlough, Herr General. I've been assigned to the Italian Front for which I'm leaving in two days."

"Pity, I could use a quick-witted fellow like you. I'll have my adjutant write you a note of recommendation to my colleague in Rome. Good luck!"

"Much obliged Herr General. Would the General care for another drink?"

"I think I've had enough, let me just say good-bye to our charming host and hostess."

He shook hands with General von Schobert and kissed the hand of Fraulein von Spandorf. His escort, Countess Tatiana Dolgorukaia politely thanked everyone for all the courtesies extended to her during the evening, in her heavily French accented German. A slight yawn betrayed her utter boredom with the present company, almost saying that she, the White Russian émigré Countess from Paris knows how to have a good time.

Henryk, in the meantime was helping Mrs. Heinemayer to her coat, his back was turned on S.S. Sturmscharfuhrer Wilhelm

Kunde and Klara Cybulska, thus he heard the exchange between Kunde and Klara.

"Wilhelm, I think that fellow Heinrich is a Jew. I'm telling you because we Poles have a nose for those things." She spoke lowering her voice and so did Kunde.

"Halt die Schnautze, keep your trap shut. Do you think that a General of the S.S. would keep a Jew on his staff? I hate Jews for political expediency but you Poles hate them for no reason at all, even though you do passionately worship another Jew on the cross."

"The matter is closed. Verstanden? Understand?"

She kept quiet like a beaten dog.

Slowly the salon emptied of the guest, while General von Schobert made a brief appearance in the kitchen.

"Thank you Heinrich for saving the evening. The cooks will clean up and the rest of you can go home. Tadeusz you'll pick me up at 6:00AM sharp. Good night everybody."

"Gutte Nacht, Herr General und angenehme Ruhe."[10]

"Heinrich, I'll drive you home because I've got to get a few items for tomorrow's trip and thank you again for your help this evening."

"Good night Fraulein von Spandorf." Said Henryk removing his white jacket and putting his clothes back on.

With General von Schobert retired for the night and Fraulein von Spandorf taking her car to go home, Henryk said good-bye to the cooks and left with Tadeusz. Tadeusz drove home swiftly even though a slight snow was falling in Cracow.

"Look Henryk, things are heating up for me. The General is being sent to Balkans or another God-forsaken place and I have to go with him. How long I will be there is another question. In any case, I can't be here to help you. I can give you some money. That always comes in handy in any situation. After I take a few of my things I'm going back to Luise to spend the night there. Since I have to leave early in the morning I have asked Luise to take care of you for two more days, until your departure for Italy. Tomorrow, around 9:00 in the morning, she'll pick you up and take you to

Zakopane, her favorite skiing spot. It is about two hours by car. By the way, please wear civilian garb and take your papers just in case. If you don't have what to wear, you can take anything you need from my closet, especially sweaters. She also might go to Krynica to visit her friends. It is up to you if you want to go there or stay in Zakopane. Here we are back home."

Tadeusz opened the door to his apartment, trying not to make any noise to wake up Mrs. Szczucka. He moved around the room with cat-like grace. He packed a small valise with a few articles of clothing, toilet accessories, some papers and a Luger pistol.

"Listen, Henryk, I don't know if I'll see you upon my return, or if at all for that matter. Remember whoever survives this war, will have to tell our relatives what happened to us." He embraced Henryk and held him close, adding in Hebrew "Chazak v' yamatz.[11] This envelope is for you, use it well."

"Thank you very much, I'll never forget your help and generosity."

In silence they shook hands. Words were not needed. Tadeusz took his valise and left the house. Henryk packed up civilian clothes for two days borrowing Tadeusz's white woolen sweater and a black winter coat with "Karakul" fur collar. He set the alarm clock for 7:30 in the morning, which should give him plenty of time for the 9:00 meeting with Luise. He was too tired to put on the pajamas, he fell asleep in his underwear as soon as he hit the pillow. He slept so soundly that he didn't hear the buzzing sound of the alarm clock. It was Mrs. Szczucka who woke him up.

"Herr Kaplinski, good morning. I guess you wanted to get up at this hour, no?"

It took Henryk a few moments to clear the cobwebs from his mind.

"Thank you very much. I almost overslept an important meeting. Do you think that you could get me a cup of hot coffee and nothing else?"

"No problem, Herr Kaplinski, just give me a few minutes." Henryk quickly shaved and washed up. He put on Tadeusz's white turtleneck sweater over dark slacks and followed the delicious aroma of freshly brewed coffee.

"Herr Kaplinski, you look very handsome in this outfit. The civilian cloths is much more becoming of you."

"You certainly have a point there, Madame Szczucka."

The coffee tasted great but the bread he left untouched.

"Madame Szczucka, thank you very much for everything. I'll be back in a day or two to collect my things."

He went to his room to put on the coat and take his piece of luggage. He went down to the street where Fraulein von Spandorf was already waiting for him. The car was the same as the night before the only thing that was new was a pair of skis attached to the back of the trunk.

"Good morning, Fraulein."

"Good morning Heinrich, how did you sleep. You worked very hard. I was watching you."

"Very well indeed, Fraulein."

"Are you all set? Hop in. We have a couple of hours drive to Zakopane. Have you ever been there?"

"Regretfully, never."

"It is really a beautiful place, as you'll soon see for yourself. Do you ski?"

"Just a little bit. I'm sure you are a much better skier than me."

"I used to spend my winter holidays in Garmisch-Partenkirchen. I love to ski. Heinrich, let's get serious. Tadeusz told me very little about you and I don't want to hear anything else. He asked me to take care of you for a couple of days and that is exactly what I'm doing. I have booked two separate rooms at the 'Kasprowy Wierch" in Zakopane. I do know the manager of the hotel very well and some of the more permanent guests. Please keep a low profile whenever it is possible. If you want to ski, you can rent them for the duration of your stay. You can also read in an enclosed glass porch and get a suntan at the same time. I have dark glasses for you. You'll look and act like a typical tourist. I can always tell the curious that you are a friend of a friend or that you are recuperating from some disease or broken love affair. Your choice. I also must phone my friend in Krynica. There is a strong possibility of me driving there today or tomorrow. I'll be staying there at Hotel 'Patria' with Mrs. Kramer. You probably heard of that hotel. It is owned by your Polish singer Jan Kiepura whose wife Martha Eggerth is very fond of some of our high ranking officers. You can call me there but only in an emergency. In that case all you have to do is to tell me that you have regards from my brother Bernard. In that case I'll come back immediately."

"I understand fully and I'll try not to cause you any trouble, Fraulein von Spandorf."

"Very well then, we do understand each other."

"Perfectly, Fraulein."

Henryk marveled at the ease which she drove the car, climbing slowly but steadily on serpentine narrow roads. The snow covered Tatra Mountains were fully visible in their eternal majesty. From time to time, they would overtake civilian and military transports.

They were stopped a few times on the road by the Military or Border Police. Each time when Luise showed her papers they were told to proceed without any further question. Only on the last inspection a sergeant checking Luise's papers made a nasty remark:

"Not everybody can go skiing these days, you must know somebody."

"It's true, but not everybody has an uncle who's a General in the S.S."

Hearing this the sergeant handed back her papers as if they were hot coals.

That drew a laugh from Luise and put her in a good mood. She had a pretty smile, displaying a row of white teeth.

"Heinrich, if you want to get a little sleep, go right ahead. We still have almost an hour before we get to the hotel. I'll wake you in time."

"Good idea, hope you don't mind, Fraulein."

"Not at all that's why I suggested it."

Henryk wasn't sleepy but he found the conversation with Luise taxing. He was afraid to say something that would put him or Tadeusz in jeopardy.

Once he closed his eyes without realizing it he fell asleep. The car came to a sudden jolt. Henryk opened his eyes. They were in front of a hotel built in the Swiss-Alpine chateau style and bearing a large sign "Kasprowy Wierch."

"Here we are. Don't touch anything. The hotel bellhop will pick up our things and bring them to the lobby. Let's register in the meantime."

The hotel manager came to greet Luise, personally. He kissed her hand, barely giving Henryk a second look. Later he introduced himself as Timoteusz Karpowicz.

"We have everything ready, Fraulein. Your regular room is waiting for you. Unfortunately the adjacent room is fully occupied. Therefore we'll put your friend into a room one flight above you. Hope you don't mind."

"Not at all, Timoteusz. Thank you for being so nice." All formalities were streamlined for Luise.

"Heinrich, I'm going skiing as long as the daylight lasts. I'll see you at suppertime. The bellhop will bring your stuff to your room. The restaurant is open if you'd like to have something to eat. If you change your mind, you can go downstairs and rent a pair of skis. I suggest that you use the beginner's slopes. Auf Wiedersehen."

Since Luise was already dressed in her elegant ski outfit, she put her skis on her shoulder and walked out of the hotel's lobby. The bellhop waited patiently with Henryk's luggage.

"I'll take you to your room, Sir."

"That will be fine. Lead the way."

A small elevator, high enough to accommodate skis brought them to the fourth floor.

The bellhop opened the door letting Henryk walk in first. He put Henryk's valise near the bed and the door keys on the dresser.

"Will that be all, Sir?"

The young boy spoke a passable German with a distinct Polish accent.

"Thank you that will be all."

He handed him a decent tip. Henryk looked through the window, and saw a modest slope. That was probably the beginner's slope, he thought. Mostly young people were on it and everybody had a smile on their faces. The war might as well be on the moon. He unpacked his few belongings and put them in the top draw of the modern dresser. Toilet accessories were placed in the bathroom and the pajama's he stuck underneath the bed's pillow. On the bottom of the valise was the thick envelope given to him by Tadeusz. Now was the time to check out its contents. There was a substantial amount of money in various denominations and currencies. There were Polish Zlotys, German Reichmarks and Italian liras.

Henryk divided the money into three piles. Some of it he put into his wallet for immediate use, some he stuck with his toilet articles and the rest he put in the coat where he discovered a hole in the lining.

The trip and the fresh Zakopane air sharpened Henryk's appetite. He realized that with the exception of this morning's coffee he hadn't eaten anything.

He decided to go down to the restaurant for a bite to eat and then to rent skis and try his luck on the beginner's slope.

The hotel manager, Pan Karpowicz was standing near the entrance to the restaurant. Noticing Henryk he called over a waiter and said to him in Polish:

"Take good care of this gentlemen. He is a friend of Fraulein von Spandorf."

The waiter brought Henryk to a small table, handing him the menu.

"Please bring me a bowl of 'bigos', a cabbage-meat dish. That will keep me going until this evening. He said in German, which the waiter understood perfectly.

"Sofort, mein Herr" – at once, sir.

A few minutes later the waiter brought a piping-hot, large

bowl of 'bigos' and a few freshly baked kaiser rolls.

He ate with gusto because the 'bigos' was of superb quality. He paid the bill and tipped the waiter at the same time.

A sign in German and Polish "This way to the ski-rental shop" led him down stairs to a large, musty smelling room. All kinds of skiing and sledding equipment were displayed on shelves. Ski boots and ice skates were neatly stacked in small wooded boxes. The clerk was coming down the ladder carrying a pair of gloves for the only customer at the moment, a young woman.

There was something familiar about the clerk's posture and voice. The clerk turned around and faced Henryk. They both almost fainted from the surprise. It was Edward Daszkiewicz, his very best friend.

CHAPTER 9

In the middle of August, Julek came to see Edward. A big truck stood in front of the house loaded with household items. Four husky men carried chairs, tables, sofas and all kinds of boxes. Mrs. Daszkiewicz was running from man to man yelling "Be careful with that, don't drop it."

Men listened politely and kept working. Nobody wanted to antagonize Mrs. Daszkiewicz, after all it was the company's truck they were loading and they themselves worked for the same company. Mr. Daszkiewicz worked in the front office where he held a relatively high position.

The boys admired the strength and skills of the workers. They were lifting heavy objects as if they were feathers.

"When will I see you again?" asked Julek.

"As soon as we settle down. I'm sure that I'll miss you and the other kids from school."

"I wonder how the Boryslaw's kids are? I hear that they are being called 'malachs.'"

"You'll find out for yourself, Edward."

"So long Julek. Come to visit us. It is only 9km from Drohobycz to Boryslaw."

The boys shook hands not knowing what else to say to each other.

"Do widzenia Pani Daszkiewicz, good-bye Mrs. Daszkiewicz." Julek hop-scotched the invisible squares in the direction on his home.

Edward was sent on an errand for his mother to buy bread and kielbasy for the men loading the truck. Finally the truck was fully loaded. Mrs. Daszkiewicz and Edward sat in the truck's cabin next to the driver.

The Boryslawska Street in Drohobycz leading to Boryslaw was unpaved and the truck had to move slowly, otherwise as Mrs. Daszkiewicz would say, they would break all of the possessions. The driver of the truck managed to reach its destination at Panska Street #24 without breaking anything.

Mr. Daszkiewicz awaited them with a grin on his face. Those people who knew him would know that the grin was his way of smiling. Next to him stood a young woman of 20, dressed in a Ukrainian folkgarb.

"This is Kasia, our new maid. Your brother-in-law, Bozyk, sent her to us from Truskawiec. She looks like a good worker."

"We'll see. Come Kasia. Let's help these men unload and put away the household goods where they belong."

"Mrs. Daszkiewicz, where do you want to put this sofa?"

She would show the men where she wanted the furniture. Sometimes she changed her mind until she was satisfied with her choice.

The men quietly complied. They knew better than to argue with sharp-tongued Mrs. Daszkiewicz.

Edward would occasionally carry a small breakable item to its designated place. He also took care of his personal items, unpacking his school books, toys, collection of fountain pen parts and his newly acquired chess set. At last the workers brought into the room Edward's chest of drawers, containing his clothing. He was proud to have a room to himself. Many of his friends had to share their rooms with brothers and sisters. He was all alone, wishing that he too, had someone to share the room with. He missed Julek already and hoped to meet a boy like him in school.

He went out of the house, neighbors or onlookers or maybe both categories, were watching the men empty the truck of household items. Mr. Daszkiewicz checked the back of the truck to see if the men had "overlooked" anything. Satisfied, he handed a silver 10 Zloty coin to each man and the driver received a 20 Zloty banknote. He was extra generous and wanted the men to know it. After all, they worked for the same company. Each man took off his cap and thanked and blessed the Daszkiewiczes. The truck left, leaving a small dust cloud behind.

At the entrance to the house a woman in her thirties made her appearance. In one hand she carried a dish covered with a linen hand towel and with the other hand held the hand of a small boy approximately Edward's age.

"Excuse me. I'm Mrs. Kaplinski and this is my son Henryk. We live in the adjacent house. We greet you with bread and salt."

"Nice to meet you. This is very thoughtful of you. We're the Daszkiewiczes and have a son the same age. Let me call him. Edek, come here for a minute." Yelled Mrs. Daszkiewicz.

Edward was watching the entire scene from the small balcony. He came up to his mother, shy when meeting strangers.

"Come closer, Edek, nobody is going to eat you up."

Hearing this both boys smiled at each other. The grownups are sometimes so silly. Who is going to eat up whom? Slowly at first the boys started to ask questions of each other, totally oblivious about parents and their conversations.

"Where are you from? Where did you live before?" Asked Henryk.

"I'm from Drohobycz, that's where we lived before. I also went to school there."

"What grade are you in?"

"I'll be starting the 3rd grade in September. And you?"

"Me too, I guess we'll be going to the same school, maybe even to the same class. That would be fun, right?"

"Where is our school?"

"Just down the road on Panska Street, about a ten minute walk. Would you like for me to show you the school?"

"Mama, Henryk wants to show me the school. Can I go with him?"

"Go ahead but be right back, do you hear?"

"Yes, we'll be right back."

"Let's go!"

Their school on Panska Street was located across the street from the P.K.O. Savings Bank. Edward looked at the school, thinking that his "white" school in Drohobycz was nicer.

"Can we walk to school together?" asked Edward.

"Of course, you silly goose. I'll stop for you in front of your house and whistle three times, That's how you'll know it's me."

"Do you know something Henryk? The streets in Drohobycz are much nicer. They are asphalt covered. Here in Boryslaw everything looks so dirty and dusty. How come?"

"My father told me that because of the oil pipes underneath the streets, they can't be covered. Do you understand?"

"That must make a lot of mud when it rains."

"Ha, ha, ha. You are so right. Just wait for the first rain, you'll see our famous Boryslaw mud."

Laughingly they ran home. Edward felt that he found a new friend in Henryk, Boryslaw wasn't such a bad place after all.

As usual the school opened on September 1st, welcoming boys and girls of Boryslaw. Mr. Daszkiewicz had the foresight to register Edward in this school where boys and girls attended together, because in Drohobycz only boys went to the "white" school.

The co-educational school posed a slight problem for Edward because he didn't know how to speak to girls. Luckily, that lack of knowledge lasted only a few days. That task was made easier for him by the fact that his teacher was a lady by the name of Mrs. Bogdanowiczowa.

By comparison to Edward's former teachers, Kobryn and Dumin, Mrs. Bogdanowiczowa was an angel. She smiled a lot but still kept up the discipline in the class.

"Remember kids, I know everyone of your tricks. A kid who can trick me hasn't been born yet."

The class understood in the very beginning of the school year that she could be very tough and whoever tried something, was caught and punished. She didn't hit anybody, but made the trouble maker write on the blackboard in full view of the class 25 times

"I'm a dope" and who wanted to do that? Edward was thinking less and less about Julek, because Henryk replaced him as Edward's closest friend. Every free moment they spent together, only occasionally getting into trouble.

It wasn't anything premeditated. It just happened on the way from school. They watched a new three-story building being constructed. So far it was just a shell of the house made of bricks. No stairs were built, just wooden boards with narrow wooden strips nailed across those boards to prevent the workers from sliding down. That day, there wasn't anybody at the building site.

"Why don't we have a look inside." Suggested Edward.

"Why not? Let's go inside. We'll leave our school backpacks in this corner."

Having done that they ran up the boards till they reached the top. There was no roof, just a single board connecting one side with the other.

"Henryk are you brave enough to walk on this plank to the other side?"

"Sure Edward. Just you watch."

He walked carefully and slowly, balancing his hands like a trapeze artist in the circus. The plank was creaking with each of his steps. He was scared to look down, it was 3-stories high. With relief he reached the other side holding onto the chimney for safety.

"And now, you my hero", said Henryk.

Edward looked at the narrow plank. He was truly scared but if Henryk made it, he would too.

Instead of walking slowly like Henryk before him, he decided to run across the plank. With each stop, the board behind him started to move away from the wall, something the boys were unaware of. Edward barely reached the other side when the supporting board fell to the ground. Luckily for Edward, Henryk was able to grab his hand and pull him towards himself. With the other hand, Henryk held the chimney.

They started to cry because without help, they couldn't get down.

"My father will surely kill me."

"Mine too, let's call for help."

"HELP, HELP, PLEASE SOMEBODY HELP US!"

In no time at all a large group of people gathered in front of the building site.

A clerk from the nearby bank had the presence of mind to call the Fire Department because within minutes a fire truck pulled alongside. The wailing of the truck's sirens scared the boys even more. The firemen extended their ladder and brought the very grateful boys down to the applause of bystanders.

The Fire Chief himself, wearing a shiny brass helmet asked the boys for their names.

"Edward Daszkiewicz, sir." Crying said Edward.

"Does your father work in Polmin?"

"Yes, sir, but please don't tell my father. He will murder me for sure, I beg you."

"And you my boy, who are you?"

"Kaplinski, sir. My father works at the post office."

"All right boys. I won't tell this to your parents but don't you realize you could have been killed or remained crippled for the rest of your lives?"

"We are very sorry", and they started to cry again.

"Stop crying. Go home now, and to the rest of the people he said:

"The show is over, you can go home too."

The boys picked up their school bags and ran home on the double. No one questioned Edward but Henryk's mother asked him why he came home so late? He gave his mother an evasive answer.

The next day Mrs. Kaplinski found out about Henryk's heroics from a friend in the marketplace.

"I'm going to punish you for lying to me. You are getting a dozen lashes on your behind and you are lucky that I'm not telling your father on you. Lie down on your stomach and count slowly to 12."

She meted out the lashes methodically. She acted on an old Jewish principle: "If you hit 'Toches" behind, it will reach your head."

It hurt a lot and he cried in silence. He knew very well that he deserved that punishment. He was glad that his mother did the punishing, who knew what would have happened if his father applied his heavy hand.

Their escapade became known in school. For a while the kids would tease them about it.

"The firemen are coming." To a degree the boys were the unsung heroes but that fame, like other fame, evaporated soon enough, much to their relief. The boys were left alone.

Basically the boys learned their lesson and truly tried to behave themselves. But, try as they did, they would occasionally get into minor or not-so-minor trouble. In wintertime a snowball fight would sometimes end with a fist fight and bloody noses, but always outside the school perimeter.

Spring followed a long winter, mud was everywhere. The famous Boryslaw mud had the consistency of clay. It was easy enough to put one's feet into but to take them out was another matter entirely. Many a shoe or galosh were lost that way and continue to be lost to this very day.

The Jewish Passover and the Easter Holidays came together that year late in April and the beginning of May. Enjoying the sunshine and their new wardrobe, the boys took a walk towards the town's river, Tysmienica. It was truly the most polluted river in all of Poland. At the time a popular song about the river sounded this way:

"Tysmienica modra rzeka kto sie zbliza ten ucieka."

"Tysmienica beautiful river, who comes close, runs away."

Petroleum waste floated on the surface of the river creating a new industry for poor people. The so-called "Lebaki" using mopsticks would skim the surface of the river, removing the petroleum flotsam and squeezing it into pails. Later they would mix the petroleum with wood shavings, creating large balls to be used to ignite the firewood used universally for heating or cooking purposes.

Boys watched the "Lebaks" work for a while. Walking alongside the river they came upon an old boat with two oars intact tied with a rope to a small makeshift pier.

"Let's borrow the boat," suggested Edward and he was the first to get in.

"Henryk untie the boat and join me."

Without hesitation or afterthought, Henryk untied the boat and jumped in, breaking the bottom of the old boat. The dirty Tysmienica's water soon filled the boat. Their beautiful new suits were soaked throughout with a black petroleum. To top it all, Henryk also ripped his new pants.

They jumped out of the boat. As soon as they fastened the boat back to the pier, they moved away trailing water behind them. They certainly didn't want to be accused of damaging the boat. All of a sudden Edward started to laugh.

"Look at you, you look very funny."

"I've got news for you, you don't look any better. Look what has happened to my pants! My mother will murder me. Just this morning she told me how expensive my suit was. What are we going to do?"

"I don't know. We can't stay here, so let's go to my house, maybe my mother will help."

Walking through the fields rather than through the town they reached Edward's house. Mrs. Daszkiewicz was sweeping in front of the house when she noticed the boys coming her way.

"Jesus Maria, what do we have here. Did you boys swim in Tysmienica?"

The boys nodded their heads and that was when Mrs. Daszkiewicz started to laugh.

"Next time put on your bathing suits."

Indeed they were a sorry looking bunch.

"Mrs. Daszkiewicz, I also ripped my pants. I'm afraid to go home."

"Don't worry Henryk. I'll fix it for you, but first we have to wash your pants. Get undressed and Edward bring him some dry clothes. Let's get going."

Mrs. Daszkiewicz filled the sink with hot water and washed both pants on a metal washboard using a brush and soap, repeating this process several times until she was satisfied with the results obtained.

By the time the boys played a few games of chess, the noon sun dried the pants. Still slightly moist she fixed the torn pants so well that the damage was hardly visible especially after she had pressed them.

"Here you are my boy. Run along now."

"Thank you, thank you, Mrs. Daszkiewicz," said Henryk much relieved.

He came home and changed at once into his everyday clothing. When asked why he wasn't wearing his new outfit he answered that he didn't want to dirty it.

The following school year they were transferred to another school. It was the T.S.S. "Towarzystwo Szkoly Ludowej" – Society for Public School.

They were together until the time when both went to different Gymnasiums[12]. Both wore beautiful navy blue school uniforms with silver buttons and light blue stripes for school uniforms. Different school numbers were embroidered on their left sleeves.

Edward went to the Jagielly Gymnasium in Drohobycz where his former classmate, Julek Weissman, also attended. Henryk remained in Boryslaw attending the only private Gymnasium near Zakarpacka Brama.

The distance between the schools, new sets of friends, difficult time of puberty, slowly eroded their close friendship. They managed to see each other occasionally, fully recognizant that they were friends.

Soon a new reality crept into their individual lives. For Henryk it was a sudden nightmare. His father started to cough persistently, spitting blood. Diagnosed as having T.B. he became very weak, lost his job at the post office, the only Jew at that location. The best doctors of Drohobycz and Lwow couldn't help. The sickness was spreading rapidly. Mrs. Kaplinski, Henryk's mother, afraid that the children would be affected, sent her husband to a costly T.B. Sanitarium in Worochta high in Carpathian Mountains. That stay prolonged his life for a while, but emptied her meager savings.

By the time Henryk completed his second year of Gymnasium, his father died. At the funeral, in addition to family members and some close friends, two of Mr. Kaplinski's co-workers and Edward, the only Gentile friend of Henryk, showed up.

After the customary, "Shivah" mourning period of seven days, Mrs. Kaplinski addressed Henryk:

"Son, I'm very sorry to interrupt your studies. We have no money left for tuition. I spoke with the director of your school, Mr. Remer, regarding our situation. He lowered the fee somewhat but not enough, we still can't afford it. Son, you have to help me to raise your sisters and brother. I have arranged for you to work for a cabinetmaker on Wolanka. You'll be getting some money – not much in the beginning. Later, if things go right, you'll be earning more."

Henryk understood that his mother didn't have another option left. His father, the breadwinner of the family was dead. He was the oldest, and it was his turn to pitch in.

Edward concentrated on his school and sports. He became a proficient soccer player. At home, the picture was less than rosy. He and his father were constantly at each other's throats. The smallest thing created a big argument, especially if the subject was Jews.

"What I don't understand father, are your complaints about the Zhids (Jews) and yet at the same time your lawyer is Advocate Katz, so is your dentist, Dr. Kranz and your physician is also a Jew, Dr. Mischel. How come you are dealing with them if you despise them so much?"

"You don't understand, Edward. They are the best. I trust

them more than I trust my own Poles, but overall I still dislike them."

During the summer of 1939, the political situation of Poland vs. Germany seemed to be ready to explode. Still some people were surprised when Germany attacked Poland on September 1st. Poles were confident that their brave army would stop Hitler.

Edward and Henryk volunteered to fight the Hun. On the way to the recruiting station, Henryk met a friend coming out of the recruiting office.

"Don't bother to go in. They don't take Jews."

Henryk turned around and went straight home. Edward however had more luck, being a Gentile. He went directly to the regimental headquarters of the 6th Battalion. There were several dozen young men ahead of him. Some men were processed very quickly, others were questioned at length. After waiting in line for almost two hours, Edward had just one more man ahead of him. He was close enough to hear the conversation between the recruiting sergeant and the man:

"Dear doctor, we will win the war against "Schwabs" (Krauts) without Jewish help."

The young doctor, a recent graduate of Bologna Medical School, turned red and left the office.

Here is a new way to cut off one's nose to spite one's face, thought Edward to himself, but he wasn't about to argue with the sergeant. Maybe he knows more than I do.

Edward submitted his name, mentioning that he completed two years of P.W. Officers Candidate School. He was accepted at once.

Short of uniforms and supplies, he was issued a four-cornered hat with a long feather attached to the hat, a rifle and several clips of ammunition.

"Go home and wait for further orders." And so he did. As a Pole and a patriot he felt good about joining the Army in defense of "Deus at Patria" – God and Motherland.

Wailing sirens announced an enemy raid. People around him

ran to houses, windows of which were covered with strips of tape to prevent the glass from flying around.

Two German planes, their black crosses quite visible to the naked eye, flew over the main square of the town. Even the sky seemed to cooperate with the enemy because not a single cloud could be found on a perfectly blue sky.

Edward heard some rifle fire so he took off the rifle from his shoulder, reached for a clip of ammunition and his great surprise and frustration, the issued ammunition didn't fit the caliber of his Mauser rifle.

"Holy God, we'll lose the war," he said aloud to no one in particular.

Some ten days later the Germans marched in to town to be greeted wildly by the Ukrainian population. Four or five days later, the Red Army occupied the town and the Germans withdrew their troops.

Mr. Daszkiewicz retired from Polmin shortly before the outbreak of hostilities. That probably saved him from being arrested by N.K.V.D. the Soviet Secret Police. To cover their tracks and to be less visible they moved to Truskawiec to be closer to the family Bozyk, their sister and husband.

In 1940, Edward was inducted into the Red Army. He was toying for a while with the idea of deserting the Red Army to cross the Carpathian Mountains to Hungary but learning about the fate of his school friend Wacek Litwin who was killed by the border guards, changed his minds.

It was in Przemysl at the basic training that he was reunited with Henryk. That meeting changed their lived forever.

CHAPTER 10

They both stood like two pillars of salt, unable to utter a single word. The always quick-thinking Edward was the first to break the awkward silence:

"Mein Herr, I'll be with you in just a moment, I'm just about finished with this young lady."

It was clear to Henryk that caution was required in this case. The young woman who was trying poles for size spoke German with Edward. She paid the rental fee and left the shop while Edward addressed Henryk in German.

"How can I help you, Sir?"

"Do you have a pair of skis in my size?'

"Of course, sir, please come this way." And he led him to the corner of the store away from the open front door. Seeing no one and not being seen by anyone they embraced each other warmly.

"What in the world are you doing here in Zakopane? How is Czeslawa? How are Dr. and Mrs. Drzewiecki?" asked Henryk.

"I'll tell you all about it but first let me close the shop. I work here also as a ski instructor and you are going to be my student for the next hour. Remember, we have never met before and my name is now Edward Jaroszczyk. I kept the name of Edward to prevent any slip-ups. On the slopes we'll have all the privacy we need."

Henryk lived with Edward through so many difficult if not impossible situations, that he knew when not to ask questions. There will be time for that on the slopes.

"Let me enter your name in the log book. Is it still Heinrich Kaplinski?"

"So far I'm keeping it."

"Please try on these boots and skis. They should fit you well."

They put their skis on their shoulders and walked out of the hotel, towards the beginners slopes. The slopes themselves were covered with fresh snowpowder, looking very inviting. The sun played peek-a-boo with the clouds, flooding the area from time to time with its golden rays. The crispy mountain air was swallowed by everyone on the slopes. Those who ski know that exhilarating feeling.

"I want to get you out on the open field away from people. Should anybody come around, I'll pretend to teach you how to ski and you just follow my instruction. Let me bring you up to date about what has happened to us since we left Lublin. As you know, Dr. Drzewiecki and Waldemar provided Czeslawa and me with 'Ausweises' and we moved to a small town, Hajnowka, where we joined the A.L. Peoples Underground Army. Sometime later we were ordered to join a unit of A.L. in the famous, thick Bialowierza Forest. It was relatively safe because German troops avoided the partisan-teeming area."

"One day, unfortunately, we came across another partisan group. It was the N.S.Z. (Narodowe Sily Zbrojne), a Polish unit with fascist orientation. For a couple of weeks, we had a loose co-operation, watching each other's flanks. A small group of Jewish partisans, two men and two women, attracted by Polish voices and smoke coming out from a fire, were able to pass by the guards, standing on the outer perimeter of the camp, showed up undetected, at the center of the camp. The N.S.Z. unit commander, Ardrzej 'Kuty' Nowosad didn't like the idea at all: 'If the Jews could waltz in with such ease, what would have happened if the Krauts had gotten in here first?"

Edward's story was interrupted by a middle-aged skier who was coming almost directly at them. Edward switched to German:

"Mein Herr, to go up the mountain you must use a method we call 'herring bone'. Keep both skis in sort of acute angle and slowly climb the hill, like this, please repeat it."

Whoever watched Edward had seen how Henryk clumsily stepped on his own ski, falling to the ground.

"No, this way," reproachingly said Edward. "Please watch me. That's much better."

Whatever his reason, the man in question moved away.

"Henryk, I'm sure that I'm under surveillance, but I don't know by what agency, Krauts or N.S.Z. Be that as it may, let me continue with my story.

"Actually the rest was told to me by Czeslawa, because I was not a witness to what happened. I was posted on guard duty, some distance from the camp itself."

"According to Czeslawa, 'Kuty' invited the Jews to partake in the evening meal. He even half-jokingly said: "Sorry, we don't have Kosher food." Everybody around laughed even the Jews. 'Kuty' took out a bottle of 'Bimber' homemade vodka and passed it to all. The older of the two Jewish men, a short but powerfully built man said: 'Sir, we are grateful for food. If you could spare us some ammunition, we'll be on our way.'

'Kuty then said: let me see your rifle, maybe we have bullets of your caliber.'

"It sounded quiet innocent and the young man handed over his rifle to 'Kuty'. It was the single biggest mistake in his young life. Once 'Kuty' had the rifle in his hands, he checked to see if it was loaded, and it was. He pointed the rifle towards the older man, who had just a pistol in his holster. 'Hand over your gun, the Jews don't need guns. They are so brave that they can fight the Germans with their bare hands. Besides you have the Talmud to shield you.'

"One of 'Kuty's' men took the pistol out of the holster. They were hopelessly disarmed.

The older of the Two Jewish men started to reason with 'Kuty'.

'A joke is a joke, but we too, sir, are fighting the same enemy. Poland is our Motherland too. Please give us back our weapons and we'll be gone and out of your way.'

'I see your point, but if we share our food and our ammunition with you, then you should share your women with us. Right boys?'

"Yes, yes, they should do that' echoed the men of 'Kuty's' squad.

'Sorry, sir, we can't do that. The women are my daughters and the oldest is married to this young man.'

'Kuty' kept on drinking 'Bimber' straight from the bottle.

'This is war, we have to share everything. I'll start with the young one first. And 'Kuty' grabbed the young woman by the arm. The father pushed 'Kuty' away. 'You'll have to kill me first.'

"Kuty' pulled out his revolver and shot the father. It took four more bullets to kill him. The other younger man was clubbed to death with the butt of his rifle. After that, they grabbed the women into the bunker where they repeatedly raped them. Czeslawa couldn't stop those wild beasts. They threatened her too. It was the scream of those girls that brought Dr. Drzewiecki to the scene."

'Stop it at once. In the name of God and the Polish Republic I'm ordering you to stop!"

"Get the hell out of here. It is none of your business. Why do you want to protect these Jews? Maybe you are a Yid too?"

"Yes I am!"

"In that case you can join them too." And so he shot Dr. Drzewiecki with one bullet to his head, in full view of Czeslawa and her mother."

Mrs. Drzewiecka, a gentle soul, a nurse to the unit and doctor's able assistant, yelled out:

"Then I'm a Jew too, you bastard, you killed my husband!"

'Kuty' as drunk as he was didn't miss the first or the second not even the third shot. All his bullets found their mark on Mrs. Drzewiecki. It was then that Czeslawa ran out to find me, that's because no one tried to stop 'Kuty'. She found me on my designated post. Actually I heard her crying as she was coming towards me. Hysterically she told me about the death of her parents. I left my post unattended and ran to the bunker, leaving Czeslawa behind. The door to the bunker was slightly ajar. They were all there, with their pants down, watching each other perform. I had only one hand grenade in my possession which I threw in, killing and wounding everyone in sight. I used my 'Schmeiser' to finish off those who were still moving. Miraculously the girls were spared, protected by the bodies of the men that lay on top of them. They asked me to kill them too. Of course I didn't do it. Some men and women came to their rescue, nursing their bloodied and abused bodies Czeslawa was howling like a wounded animal. She kept fainting on and off for the rest of the day. My officer took me on the side and said to me:

"I'm afraid that the N.S.Z. will want to avenge the death of their entire squad by killing you. You and Czeslawa had better disappear from here, I can't trust any of my own men. Here is the name and address of your contact in Cracow. I trust this person with my life because it's my own daughter. She will arranged another identity card for you and possibly a job. You had better hold guard at that time and will tell them that you were killed in an ambush. I'll let a few salvos in the air and move my base somewhere else. May God keep you and Czeslawa. I'll miss both of you and people like Drzewieckis, Poland's best and bravest."

"My biggest problem was not the Germans or N.S.Z. but Czeslawa. She was in sort of a daze. She didn't eat or sleep and she stopped crying too. By the time we reached our contact on Cracow, Czeslawa was seven months pregnant and she lost our baby. It was a girl."

"The underground was very helpful, starting with our 'Ausweises' and ending with a job for me at this hotel as a ski instructor. The biggest help was for Czeslawa by getting her a five year orphaned girl of Jewish origin, whom she adores. She named the girl Danuta after her mother."

"Maybe we can meet this evening near the hotel. I'll bring Czeslawa and Danuta with me. And now Henryk tell me what has happened with you during all this time."

The same curious man who hung around before, showed up again, this time pretending to adjust the bindings on his ski boots.

"Sir, try to turn around on skis. It's very simple actually. All you have to do is to move one leg and follow it up with the second leg, placing it parallel to the first. Please watch me and do the same."

Henryk tried it and promptly landed on his behind. Whatever the suspicious man wanted to know he must have learned because he left in a great hurry. Edward stretched out his hand and helped Henryk to his feet.

"I don't like that man. You continue doing the 'Herringbone' while telling me your adventures."

Henryk told him what transpired in Lublin during Edward's absence. Edward stood still for a while and gave a low whistle.

"Holy God! It is a miracle that you are still around. I don't know what to say, how to be of help. We ourselves are on very thin ice. I have a foreboding that I might be arrested any day now. I'm worried sick about how Czeslawa and Danuta will be able to survive. Let me talk to Czeslawa. Maybe she has some ideas. I'm afraid to contact the underground. The underground is compromised, that I'm sure of. In any case we'll be taking a walk in front of the hotel this evening between 8:00 and 8:15. If either of us can't make it whatever the reason, I'll be in the shop tomorrow at 9:00, my regular hours. Otherwise my absence may raise unwelcome curiosity. You can take the skis with you to your room. You can bring them back tomorrow any time during the day. Stay well my brother, may God keep us all under his wings."

With these words, Edward left but Henryk remained another ten minutes, practicing the 'Herringbone.'"

Having done that he took off his skis and marched back to the hotel. Reaching his room he cleaned his skis of snow, leaving them outside the door which he opened with his key. To his surprise, two men were there already.

"I'm terribly sorry, I must have opened this door by mistake, I apologize."

"No need to apologize Herr Kaplinski. This is your room, please come in."

"What do I owe the pleasure of your visit, meine Herren?"

"May we introduce ourselves. My name is Eberhard

Schoengarth, I'm the Befehlshaber der Sicherheitspolizei und der S.D. im Distrikt Krakau and this is my associate Herr Bruno Streckenback."

Henryk recognized the suspicious man on the slopes, it was Bruno Streckenback. Edward was right. He was under the Gestapo surveillance. From now on, both men had better be very careful.

"How do you do, gentlemen. How can I be of service?'

"Do you want to see our credentials?'

"No, I believe that you are who you say you are."

"Then your papers, please."

Henryk showed them all his papers. He wasn't worried at least the papers were authentic, issued by proper authorities.

"They are fine and now pray tell us where did you get so much money that you had to hide it in your toilet articles."

Henryk was relieved because they over looked the money that he had left in his coat.

"The simple explanation is I've won that money in a poker game at the O.T. You probably know that I came to this hotel with Fraulein von Spandorf. Being worldly gentlemen you surely know that to entertain a lady of her class, much money is needed."

It was Schoengarth who changed the subject of the conversation.

"What is your business with the Polish ski instructor?"

"None whatsoever. I have never seen him in my life. Fraulein von Spandorf selected this hotel and she is the one that suggested that I take a few ski lessons before I join her on more advanced slopes. She is due tomorrow and you can verify my story. Her uncle is a General in the S.S. von Schobert. Both he and the General of the S.S. Kruger know me personally. Would you want to check with them too?"

"That won't be necessary, but do not leave this hotel without checking with us first."

"Does that mean that I'm in sort of house arrest?"

"Not at all, we just want to corroborate your story with Fraulein von Spandorf and to show you that we don't harbor ill will towards you, please join us downstairs for a coffee."

"I appreciate that very much but I must decline your generous offer. I'm so tired from skiing and all I want to do is take a bath and relax a bit. Perhaps Fraulein von Spandorf will come sooner and I might be otherwise engaged."

"Ha, I've seen him falling on his back." Said Bruno Streckenback.

"Very well then, perhaps some other time," and they left the room. Henryk started to breathe a bit easier. He filled the bathtub with hot water and got in. The hot water was an elixir for his tired muscles and thoughts. In his mind he went over the conversation held with the Gestapo. He would need Luise to pacify these two. Of that he was sure. He would have to call her even though he didn't plan on it.

His meeting with Edward this evening would definitely have to be postponed until tomorrow when he'd be returning the rented skis. A word of caution would be slipped there. He just realized where he had left the skis. He would have to bring them in as soon as he got dressed. He pulled the plug out and the water rushed down. That is how life could go down the drain, he thought to himself. That's how innocent lives of Drzewiecki's went, killed by another Pole. Doctor Drzewiecki-Holzman, his uncle, he'll say the immortal words of Kaddish if he ever got the chance. Dressed, he opened the door of his room leading to the corridor. His skis were standing where he had left them. A puddle of water bore witness that snow was on them before.

He brought the skis inside his room and changed into more suitable evening wear. The bath that he took relieved him of the tension caused by the unexpected visitors and at the same time made him hungry. But first things first. He had to make a call to Luise. He went down to the lobby of the hotel and asked the desk clerk to get the telephone number that Luise left with him.

It took a while to get through to Luise. The telephone operator connected him in the second booth. Henryk had a feeling that somebody else was also on the line.

"Hello, Luise. How are you? I just wanted to know how your trip on those famous Polish roads was? Frankly I was worried about ice because you have a tendency to drive too fast."

He heard her laugh. "Don't worry Heinrich, I can handle that car in any situation."

"How is your brother? I hope he is fine?"

"He is well, thank you for asking. I'll be back in Zakopane by tomorrow noontime, Liebling."

Henryk never called Luise by her first name. Always addressing her formally a Fraulein von Spandorf. Of course, she never called him 'liebling' either. She understood that Henryk was in some kind of jam and she was willing to help.

On the way to the restaurant he met the two Gestapo men in the hallway.

Henryk politely said to them: "Good night again. I spoke with Fraulein von Spandorf, she should be here by noontime tomorrow."

"That will be fine. We're looking forward to that meeting."

Henryk knew full well that the Gestapo would find out about his telephone call to Luise anyway. Having Luise's backing he felt reassured about his personal safety. On the other hand he had doubts if he could have done anything to help Edward and Czeslawa. The sooner Henryk and Luise got back to Cracow the better. The idea of submerging in a gray and blue sea of Wehrmacht seemed less frightening.

After all, the best way of hiding a tree is still in the forest. Perhaps he wouldn't have to sell his soul like Faust to Mephistopheles, maybe just rent it out for the duration of the war.

A long hallway led to the hotel's dining room. The head waiter greeted Henryk with "Guten Abend, mein Herr."

While shaking his hand, Henryk managed to slip him a neatly

folded banknote. The head waiter's face registered the universal recognition of 'bribes gratefully accepted.'

"We have for you a very nice table. Are you alone?"

"Yes, at the moment", and he ordered whatever was available, just as long as it was hot.

To his pleasant surprise the food was well prepared and tasted delicious. He ate slowly, enjoying each bite. To a casual or maybe not-so-casual observer, Henryk appeared a picture of a contented man with no worry in the world.

He went back to his room, undressed and went straight to bed. Being physically tired and emotionally drained, he fell asleep at once.

He rose in the late morning, totally refreshed. Today he was expecting Luise back by noon time. He felt confident that she could handle those two Gestapo men amicably. His worry was Edward and how to warn him of eminent danger. If everything went smoothly, Luise should be here within two hours. During those two hours he had to find a way to contact Edward. Quickly he shaved and got dressed. With skis over his shoulders he went downstairs to the restaurant for breakfast, where a number of skiers had the same idea.

He left his skis in a rack provided for that purpose, near the entrance to the restaurant itself.

A hot cup of ersatz-coffee and a piece of cheesecake "sernik" kept his soul and body together.

The ski slopes were busy this morning, some people, judging by their red and smiling faced had been there for a while already.

Henryk fastened the bindings of his skis to his boots just as some skier made a sharp stop in front of him, spraying snow all over him.

He lifted his face to see who was the culprit. It was Herr Bruno Streckenback of the Gestapo.

"Guten Tag, Herr Streckenback, wie gehts?" politely inquired Henryk.

"Den schlechten Leuten gehts er immer Gut." The bad people

have it always good" and with a sardonic smile he continued skiing.

Having the Gestapo watch you was synonymous with having snakes under your own skin. They were toying with him, that much was clear.

To occupy his time he started to 'herringbone' up the hill. Turning around and leaning hard on the bamboo ski pole he heard a distinct crack. He leaned on it even harder, breaking the pole. Now he had a perfect excuse to visit the ski shop. With one good pole and the other broken one in his hand, he managed to ski down the slope and went straight to the shop with Bruno Streckenback trailing behind him.

Edward was engaged in a deep conversation with a teenage couple. Looking at Henryk walking in with an unknown man, he said:

"I'll be right with you gentlemen."

Henryk held up six fingers a signal to Edward of eminent danger. It was the same sign of warning they used as children way back in Boryslaw.

Edward slightly nodded with his head acknowledging the signal. He went back to his customers giving the final instruction, how best to wax skis. The couple seemed to be satisfied with the answer because they purchased a can of wax and left the ski shop.

"Are you gentlemen together?" asked Edward.

"No we are not. This gentlemen was ahead of me." Said Bruno Streckenback visibly annoyed.

"How can I help you? Oh, I see that you have broken a ski pole. Hopefully you didn't get hurt."

"It was my fault. I'm just a beginner and I must have leaned on it too hard. I'll gladly pay for it."

"Don't worry. The pole probably had a crack to begin with. The ski poles are in this corner of the shop, please follow me. Let me see the other pole. I'll try to match the length."

They walked towards a wooden barrel containing several individual poles of different sizes and types.

Edward bent down to the barrel covering his face but Henryk heard him say in Polish:

"I'm clean, just remember you have never seen me before in your life."

"Yes, sir, this one is almost the same size and weight."

"Just a moment, hold it right there, I'm with the Gestapo", said Bruno Streckenback holding the Gestapo Identity card.

"You!" he said to Edward. "Have you ever seen this man before?"

"No sir. I've never seen this man in this hotel or any other place."

"What about you Herr Kaplinski?"

"Perhaps I can shed some light on the subject." These words were spoken by Luise von Spandorf who just walked in.

"Look, who do we have here? Ihre Papieren?' "Your papers!"

"You may live to regret it. I'm Fraulein Luise Wilhelmine von Spandorf. I suggest that you change your tone of voice Mein lieber Herr" (my dear man). You want to see my papers, how about this piece of paper."

All of this was said in upper class German. She took out of her pocketbook a long, narrow envelope and handed it to Herr Bruno Streckenback.

He read it and reread it. It must have been something out of ordinary because his eyes were bulging. He clicked his heels and stood at attention.

"Please forgive me, Fraulein von Spandorf. I didn't mean any disrespect, I assure you." And turning to Edward and Henryk he said:

"This investigation is officially closed."

"Thank you Herr Streckenback." Said Luise.

"I'm at your service, Fraulein von Spandorf." He turned around and left the shop.

"What was that all about?" asked Edward innocently.

"I have no idea. I came here to exchange a broken pole. It was probably a case of mistaken identity. It does happen occasionally.

Thank for your help. I'll be back later to return the skis. We are checking out this afternoon."

"Come Heinrich. Let's go I still want to ski a bit."

"On the steps leading from the shop to the main lobby, Henryk asked Luise:

"How did you know that I was in the ski shop?"

"It was the bus boy who told me that you went down the stairs with a broken pole. I was afraid that you broke something else too."

"Could we leave for Cracow right now?"

"No, Heinrich. That would not be very smart. It would raise suspicion all over again. As I said before, I'm going to ski for an hour or so and then I intend to have a nice long hot bath, relax a bit, get something to eat. After that, we'll check out jointly and drive home to Cracow. I see that you have a set of skis so put them to good use and later pack up your things. We'll be leaving in about three hours."

What Luise said made a lot of sense in the present circumstances. She certainly knew how to handle Gestapo functionaries. Henryk realized that he was at her mercy but so far she didn't steer him wrong. He might as well use the remaining few hours to ski and using the pretext of returning skis to speak with Edward as to their further course of action.

He made his way to the more advanced ski slope where he spotted Luise from afar, zigzagging down the hill with the ease of a bird, totally absorbed with the speed and challenges of the slopes. It was fun watching her ski, unquestionably she was in her element.

Edward went back to his beginner's slope, managing to fall a couple of times, much to the amusement of the young children.

After his last and not so gentle fall, he took off his skis, walking back to the ski shop. This time nobody was trailing him.

The shop was empty of people except for Edward and a woman who was in the far corner of the shop, engrossed in reading a brochure.

Hearing steps, the woman lifter her head and turned and faced Henryk.

"Oh my God, it's Czeslawa!"

He ran up to her, taking her in his arms, kissing both her cheeks.

"Henryk you talk to her. I'll be standing at the door pretending to repair the lock. Should anybody come, I'll hit the lock twice with the hammer.

"Czeslawa, Czeslawa, you are a sight for sore eyes. I'm so sorry about your parents. They were such wonderful human beings."

"Henryk, I know that you are my cousin, my father told me everything. Now I understand what your, I mean our people, went through. What was that commotion with the Gestapo men?"

"I don't rightly know, but in the meantime everything seems to be fine. The woman who bailed us out is a friend of a friend of mine, but I can't rely upon her for too long for several reasons. We are returning to Cracow later this afternoon. From there, courtesy of the Wehrmacht, I'll make my way to Italy where I intend to give myself up to the Allies. What about you two?"

"Edward and I are good skiers. During the winter the Germans are less careful guarding the border crossings. We intend to get on skis to Kosice and from there to Hungary or Rumania with the help of the Polish underground."

"Will I ever see you both again?"

"Only God knows the answer. If we survive the war look for us at this hotel. Ask for an old caretaker, Jan. He'll get you in touch with us. Or possibly in Lublin where my father had a practice or maybe in Boryslaw. Edward wants me to meet his parents."

Two hammer knocks interrupted their conversation. Czeslawa immediately continued reading her brochure and Henryk started to put back his ski boots.

The cause of the alarm was a young girl of 9 or 10 years, who wanted to buy white shoe laces. Edward didn't have any in stock so he took out a shoe lace from a man's boot, cut it in half and gave it to the little girl free of charge.

"It's time for me to go, Czeslawa. May God protect you and keep you and Edward."

"The same to you, dearest Henryk." She kissed him tenderly and wiped the tears forming in her eyes.

Edward came over, shook hands with Henryk and kept him in his silent embrace. Word weren't necessary. No brothers could have been closer.

Henryk left the ski shop in deep thought. It was almost funny how Providence affected different people at different times. In a way he was grateful to the capricious and totally unpredictable Providence for giving him a chance to see Edward. Will she do it again?

It didn't take long to pack up his belongings. Money hidden in his toilet case was still there. Waiting for Luise he stretched out on the freshly made up bed. Tired, he dozed off only to be awakened by a pre-arranged double knock on the door.

Henryk opened the door and let Luise in.

"Are you ready? We have to move at once. There is no time to waste. The kitchen prepared some sandwiches for us which we'll eat while driving back to Cracow. My luggage is already downstairs. Meet me there in five minutes." Said Luise leaving the room.

Henryk double-checked the room for any items left behind. He took his luggage out of the room which he then locked with the hotel's key, walking down to the lobby.

Luise was near the front desk and the two Gestapo men were next to her.

It was Herr Streckenback who asked her:

"Are you leaving us so soon? What is the sudden rush?"

"Unfortunately we have to get back" said Luise putting down her room keys on the counter.

"Heinrich, don't forget to leave your keys, otherwise these gentlemen will be following us. I want to do just one more thing," said Luise, walking towards the grand piano standing in the corner of the lobby.

She sat on the stool, adjusting it to her height. She took of her black onyx signet ring, putting it on the top of the piano, lit a cigarette and started to play.

The Gestapo men were totally dumbfounded and so were the rest of the people in the lobby.

She played brilliantly. Luise became an extension of the piano itself. The first sounds of the keyboard brought everyone from the hotel to the lobby.

By the time she finished playing Schumann's Fantasiestucke, op. 73 her cigarette was all gone.

She put out her cigarette in the ashtray and continued to play. Her second number was Smetana's "Aus der Heimat" (From the Homeland).

A thunder of applause followed her performance. The loudest "Bravos" and "Bis" came from "her" Gestapo men.

It was Herr Streckenback again who approached Luise and kissed her both hands.

This beast had tears in his eyes.

"Hoch Gnadige Fraulein, I never heard anyone play Schumann with such a "Zart und mit Ausdruck lebhaft, leicht Rasch und mit Feuer", with feeling, expression and fire. Please forgive me if I made you feel uncomfortable at any time and should you ever need my help all you need to do is ask."

"I don't think it will be necessary but thanks just the same." Said Luise, putting her ring back on her finger.

She threw a kiss to the appreciative audience. Several porters fought for the privilege of bringing Luise's and Henryk's luggage back to the car.

Luise seemed to be the master of the piano as well as the car, which she drove with the ease of a professional driver.

Henryk lost his speech or simply he didn't know what to say. Luise had many aspects to her personality, therefore he started cautiously:

"Fraulein von Spandorf, I don't know much about music but I do know that you played beautifully."

"Thank you Heinrich. I had to do something to cast off

Gestapo's suspicion about us. Playing the piano seemed like a good idea at the time."

"May I ask you a question if I'm not too impertinent. What was that paper that you showed to those Gestapo men that changed their attitude towards you?"

"Heinrich now you are really impertinent but I'll tell you. It was a letter signed by Heinrich Himmler himself, stating that anything I do is for the good of Deutsches Reich and what I do, I believe sincerely is for the good of my country. I don't want you to ask me any more questions. The less you know the better off we'll all be. As soon as we arrive back in Cracow, I want you to go away and stay away. You do represent danger to Tadeusz and me. Tadeusz told me that you are reporting to a Wehrmacht Unit on the Italian Front and from there you'll try to reach the Allies. The idea in my opinion is totally crazy, but with a bit of luck and so called 'chutzpah' you may succeed. The only thing I can still do for you is to drive you to the railroad station tomorrow at noontime. From that moment you are on your own. Is that clear to you?"

"Yes, Fraulein von Spandorf, perfectly clear."

They drove in complete silence almost half an hour longer. Tadeusz told Luise everything he knew about Henryk, her use of the Yiddish word 'chutzpah' made it only too clear.

"Heinrich," she said in a much softer tone, "behind you in the blue zipper bag are some sandwiches and a thermos with hot coffee, Please help yourself and get me a cup. I'm sorry if I sounded so cruel but we live in very trying times. Tadeusz and I are going away for a couple of months and maybe longer. Cracow became a very dangerous place for people like you. I'll get a letter of recommendation from General Kruger's adjutant to the General's friend in Rome. Use is only with extreme caution. Remember, the letter may backfire."

Henryk ate all the sandwiches because Luise didn't want any. She seemed to live on coffee and cigarettes, which she chain smoked. The road home appeared to be shorter or perhaps Luise drove faster, slowing down for an occasional police check or a sharp curve on the road.

It was well after 11:00 in the evening when Luise dropped him off in front of Tadeusz's house.

"I'll pick you up tomorrow around noontime, be ready."

"Thank you very much, Fraulein von Spandorf for everything."

"You are most welcome", and she took off.

Henryk walked into the house. The same sign "OUT OF ORDER" on the elevator told him that nothing had changed in Cracow but those few days in Zakopane changed his life and his outlook on many things. The unexpected meeting with Edward was a bonus.

In all likelihood, Mrs. Szczucka heard him fumbling for the key and opened the door for him.

"Good evening, Mrs. Szczucka. I'm sorry to bother you so late in the evening but I just arrived."

"No problem. I was about to make myself a cup of tea. Would you like some?"

"I'd be very grateful for a cup. Let me put my stuff away and I'll join you in a couple of minutes. Any messages from Mr. Kierod for me?'

"Just one: Take good care of yourself."

"Thank you very much."

Henryk put his belongings into Tadeusz's bedroom, hung up his coat, washed his hands and joined Mrs. Szczucka in the kitchen. A large cup of piping hot tea and bread and a cheese sandwich awaited him.

A polite conversation took place. Mrs. Szczucka asked him how he liked Zakopane.

"It is really a most beautiful place. Were it not for the war, one could have enjoyed the resort even more. I'm sure you've heard the song of "Es geht alles foruber, es geht alles forbei nach jedem Dezember kommt wieder ein Mai." Everything passes, everything passes by, after each December comes May again."

"Hopefully the war will end soon and you will be able to join your dear ones. Are your parents alive?"

"No Mrs. Szczucka, they are not. I'm all alone. Forgive me, I'm going to bed. Good-night and thanks again for the tea."

"Good night I'm going to go to sleep too."

The conversation with Mrs. Szczucka upset him because he wanted to tell her more about himself, but that wasn't advisable in his present circumstances. Tadeusz's words were still embedded in his memory: "Be careful with Mrs. Szczucka, I don't trust her."

"Herr Kaplinski, don't hesitate to ask if you need anything."

"Thank you again, Mrs. Szczucka. I'm so tired that I can only think about going to sleep. I'll pack up my belongings right after breakfast. Good night."

"Good night to you, Herr Kaplinski and sweet dreams." She looked straight at him with her blue eyes. She is looking at me like a cat about to devour a mouse, thought Henryk to himself. He went to his room, quickly undressed, donning his pajamas he went to bed.

He was asleep in minutes. The happenings of the last few days came back to him in a kaleidoscope-like dream. Edward with his shy smile, Dr. Drzewiecki, Luise von Spandorf, Gestapo men in Zakopane were soon replaced by Helga and her moist lips. He felt her smooth skin, her probing tongue and her hands playing with his hairy chest.

A painful erection woke him up. That wasn't Helga of his dream in his bed, instead it was Mrs. Szczucka. Like a cat she sneaked into the bed. He wanted to object to her presence but she blocked his mouth with her lips.

"Don't say anything please. Just hold me tight. I need a man, I really don't know what came over me. It's this crazy war. Whatever you do just don't send me away."

"Don't worry, I won't," said Henryk. He also didn't care if she was or wasn't ten years his senior. Her body doused with Koln Wasser-parfume #4711 was the same fragrance used by Luise and smelled wonderfully erotic.

He brutally entered her and yet she was more than ready for him. Keeping up the tempo he made love to her several times. Her sobbing was mixed with her requests for more. Henryk kept obliging her and finally they stopped and an awkward silence took place. She put her head on his chest and a few minutes later they were both asleep.

For Henryk all the pent up tension and problems of the last few days simply evaporated. He woke up refreshed, optimistic and quite hungry and all alone in bed. He didn't hear her leaving the bed. The happenings of last night were dreams or reality?

Since Luise was coming for him at noon he allowed himself an unheard of luxury of remaining in bed an extra hour.

A knock at the door was followed by Mrs. Szczucka carrying a tray with hot coffee, scrambled eggs and kaiser rolls.

"Good morning, Herr Kaplinski. I thought you may like breakfast in bed," she said giving him her warmest smile.

"Mrs. Szczucka, is this the prisoner's last meal?"

"Oh, no. You have nothing to fear from me. We Poles either love or hate. There is nothing in between and I don't hate you. I have sinned last night. It's 'mea culpa, mea maxima culpa'. May Holy Mother forgive me."

Henryk being very hungry ate quickly while Mrs. Szczucka was asking him to erase last night from his memory.

"Mrs. Szczucka," said Henryk wiping off his mouth, "having said all that, are you ready to sin once more, if so come to my bed."

It took her but a second to take off her dress, she was stark naked underneath.

This time he was very gentle with her. She held onto him and yet her warm, salty tears were streaking her face. Henryk kissed off those tears and at the same time he was moving his fingernails along her spine.

Inadvertently, during their lovemaking, Mrs. Szczucka said some very endearing words in Polish rather than in German and Henryk, without realizing answered her in Polish. They simply continued their conversation in Polish.

"Henryk, I spoke with my brother who is a priest about Tadeusz, seeking his advice. I already suspected that Tadeusz is one of you.

He told me to keep my mouth shut. He was sure that we Poles are destined to the same fate as Jews. I have a feeling that my husband will never come back and although I know you for such a short time, I feel very comfortable with you. You can return here any time you wish."

"Thank you very much indeed, I'll consider your offer."

Her speech about her priest/brother and the fact that she knew Tadeusz's background, brought Henryk back to reality. Tadeusz's suspicions were well founded.

"Fraulein von Spandorf is going to pick me up soon. I better be ready. I still have to pack."

"Please forgive me Henryk. I rattled like an old woman that I am." And she left the room.

With no time to waste, Henryk quickly shaved and washed up. His belongings were expertly put in the valise. Dressed in Wehrmacht's uniform, he went to say good-bye to Mrs. Szczucka. She was in the kitchen. Henryk embraced her and bent down, kissing her fully on the lips. He handed him a small packaging saying:

"Henryk, I prepared for you a couple of sandwiches and a bottle of vodka. It may come in handy. I also gave you a rosary that was in our family for years. It was blessed by the bishop of Czestochowa. I know that you don't believe in it, but this one will protect you from all evil. Had my husband taken it with him, he would have been alive today. May God who is the Father of all bless you and keep you."

At this point she started to cry. "Mrs. Szczucka," he kept on call her Mrs. Szczucka.

"I'll be just fine. I trust that your rosaries will do their job. I'll write to you if it is at all possible. Thank you for your good wishes and please thank Tadeusz for his help. I must run now. 'Do widzenia' – good-bye".

He ran downstairs and none too soon because Luise was just turning in from the adjacent street.

"Good afternoon, Fraulein von Spandorf. How are you today?"

"Hop in Heinrich. You seem to be in excellent spirits."

"There is a Polish saying 'raz kozie smierc' – a goat dies only once."

"That might be good for a goat but you want to live or don't you. Then you must move on."

"Did you hear anything from Tadeusz?"

"He is fine and sends you regards>"

"Should you speak to him soon, tell him that his suspicions regarding Mrs. Szczucka were well-founded. However I have reason to believe that she will keep her mouth shut."

"We are aware of her, but under torture everyone eventually talks. Tadeusz is not going back there so there is nothing to worry about. By the way, I brought you a letter of recommendation from the General's friend in Rome. I have a gut feeling about it. I suggest that you burn it. It may complicate matters and bring unwanted attention to yourself. Remember, keep a low profile and never volunteer for anything. I brought you a little 'Proviant', some Wurst and cigarettes and writing paper. Every 'real' German soldier writes letters."

"I'll do as you say." He tore the letter into very small pieces and threw it out the window where it mixed with light snow falling in Cracow.

"It is very funny but you do resemble our Rudolf Hess albeit with much lighter complexion. You'll be fine just don't show your dick around."

They approached the Main Railroad Station in Cracow. The traffic around it was mainly military. She was stopped by the Railroad Military Police. Luise was flirting unashamedly with the sergeant.

"Here is where we are going to say good-bye to each other." She embraced him and for the first time kissed him.

"Stay well and take good care of yourself."

Henryk took his luggage out and watched Luise's car disappearing at the end of the street.

Once more he was left to his own devices. There was no safety net.

CHAPTER 11

Henryk lifted his valise and turned around only to be confronted by the same sergeant with whom Luise flirted.

"I would give a month's pay just for a roll in the hay with that lady. Where does a dog face like you deserve such a classy woman?" said the sergeant with mock self-pity.

"Sergeant, you have to have the right equipment."

"What a cheeky bastard you are, Feldfebel, get the hell out of here."

"I will sergeant, just tell me where do I report for the trip to Italy?"

"I personally would send you to the Russian Front."

"Oh, I have been there. Now I want to see the 'romantic' Italy, Sergeant."

"I hope the 'Englander' will cut your balls off." He said smiling. "Go to window #4 and make sure I don't see you around anymore."

Henryk walked through a large hall teeming with civilians and soldiers in a wide range of uniforms. He located the window marked #4 partially hidden by a massive pillar. At least a dozen or more soldiers of assorted ranks and ages were ahead of Henryk. Some of the men came back from home furloughs and some with pale faces undoubtedly came from army hospitals. The clerk at window #4 was taking his sweet time processing soldiers to their assigned destinations.

"It's going to be a long wait," said Henryk aloud to no one in particular. There was nothing else to do but wait.

A few minutes later, two young recruits joined the line. It was obvious to Henryk that these boys were identical twins. Their

German language was heavily accented. They addressed Henryk respectfully.

"Pardon us, Feldfebel, do they issue tickets for Italy at this window?"

Judging by their baby faces, Henryk put their ages to be 17 or 18. He felt much older than the difference of six years.

"I'm due for the same area. Why don't you guys stick with me? Where are you from?"

"Our names are Anton and Bonifacy Swiderski. We're Volksdeutsch from Katowitz in Silesia."

"Who was German in your family?" asked Henryk.

"Our grandmother. Our father being German and Polish hated the Bolsheviks and he joined Wehrmacht. He died fighting them near Smolensk."

"Did you volunteer?"

"No Herr Feldfebel we were conscripted," said Anton, hastily adding, "we are ready to fight for our Fuhrer." Bonifacy's face said something opposite. They kept on chatting until Henryk's turn came to speak with the clerk behind the window #4.

"Your pay-book and orders, Feldfebel."

Henryk handed over to him the requested papers. The man was close to 50-years old with a thick neck and protruding eyes. The neck seemed to be squeezed by the tight collar of the jacket. He surely wasn't an officer but he acted and sounded like one.

"Your destination is Milano. I can forward you only as far as Vienna. From there you'll be shipped out further. Too bad you have missed your train. The next one for Vienna will be at 2200 hours or so. You still have about seven hours wait. So far I have eleven men going to the same destination. With you it will be an even dozen."

"Sir, right behind me are two young boys also going to Italy, could you please add them to our group?'

"Oh, sure, let me see their papers."

Henryk asked the Swiderski brothers for their traveling documents and gave them to the clerk.

The clerk had a good look at the boys and said to Henryk:

"Kaplinski, I'll put you in charge of the 14 men. I'll make up one list and one pass for all of you. You all will be responsible for each other. Is that understood?"

"Yes sir. 'Alles in Ordnung.'"

What was in his personality, he wondered, that caused complete strangers to look to him for guidance? He was mad at himself for taking under his tutelage these two young Polish Volksdeutsches. He needed that like proverbial hole in the head.

"Are you Feldfebel Kaplinski?" That question was asked by a Master Sergeant in a polite but firm tone of voice. Three other soldiers were right behind him.

"Yes, I am, sergeant." Henryk had a good look at him, recognizing a seasoned soldier.

"What can I do for you, sergeant?"

"We were told that you are in charge of the group going to Italy." These four men were missing until now from Henryk's list.

"Yes I am, but since you do outrank me, would you like to take over this group, sergeant?"

"Hell, no. You can have that pleasure but I do appreciate the offer, Feldfebel. I was discharged from the hospital recently. I still walk with some difficulties. Had a few days of furlough so I went to my home in Cologne. The British bombed the house, nothing was left, only rubble. Couldn't find anybody alive, although one neighbor said that my mother left the town a few days ago, but where to? The bloody English. 'Gott strafe England'[13].

"Sit down, sergeant, take a load off your feet. Have some Schnapps and Wurst. You'll feel better. Surely better days are coming."

"I'm afraid they aren't."

"Scheise (shit). Sit down and let's have a drink."

Henryk pulled a bottle of Schnapps and poured a healthy slug into Werner Gastfreund's outstretched cup. 'Prosit' – health to you all."

The bottle was passed around and by the time it came back to

Henryk it was empty. There was another bottle in Henryk's valise but he decided to keep it there for a while yet.

Master sergeant Werner Gastfreund ate in silence. Finishing eating he wiped his face with a clean handkerchief and went to his corner where he fell asleep almost immediately.

"Would Herr Feldfebel like a piece of Silesian Wurst?" asked Bonifacy Swiderski.

"'Danke schoen' – thank you very much."

"Anton is bringing you some hot tea. Here he comes."

"You boys are something special. Thanks for the Wurst, tea, if only you would have something to read. We have almost five hours to kill."

"Herr Feldfebel, my brother has a book by Karl May. Would you like to read it?"

"Indeed very much. What is the title of the book?"

"Old Shutterhand. We've read it several times over."

Bonifacy took out the book from his backpack and gave it to Henryk.

"Papieren, Kontrolle" A couple of Military Policemen stopped to check everybody's papers. Henryk handed over the group's list, explaining that the list represented traveling documents for fourteen men.

"What about that fellow in the corner?" asked the policeman pointing to Werner sleeping in the corner.

"He is with us. Don't wake him up, let him sleep."

"I don't like his looks, we'll wake him up."

It wasn't necessary to wake Werner up because the tumult caused by the Policemen woke him up. It was like waking a bear from hibernation. Werner was in a foul mood.

"You don't like my bloody looks, stay at attention when addressing superior rank!" Werner let a volley of obscenities at the Policemen and ended with: "I'll have you court-martialed for showing disrespect to the German Uniform. About face! Get the hell out of here and don't come back!"

The Policemen turned around, hiding their embarrassment.

"Werner, forget about that 'Dumkopf', let's have a smoke."

"Thanks Heinrich. I'll go back to sleep."

"Good idea, I think I'll do the same."

Henryk took off his boots and opened the book by his favorite author of his teen year's, Karl May.

The ugly war and his masquerade in the German Army soon disappeared. He was with his hero, fighting the bloodthirsty Indians, riding the fastest horse in the Wild West and hunting majestic bisons. His eyelids became heavy and he fell asleep with a smile on his face. The noise of the waiting room was replaced in his mind by the wind of the prairie.

"Feldfebel, Feldfebel, it's time to move." It was Anton Swiderski who shook his arm and not a Redskin about to scalp him.

"Yes, what is it?" Half asleep asked Henryk.

"Our train just pulled into Track 22. Let's go Feldfebel."

"Where are my boots Did you see them, Anton?"

"Here they are. Don't you recognize your own boots, Feldfebel?" The shoes were gleaming with fresh polish, they looked like brand new pair. Someone had done an excellent job of polishing.

"Who is the joker?"

"We did it, Herr Feldfebel," answered the twins, "we wanted to surprise you."

"Thank you boys. It wasn't called for." It was difficult to get mad at them. Henryk quickly checked the men against the list. Everybody was present and accounted for.

They marched two men abreast with Henryk and Werner leading the group.

Prior to boarding the railroad wagon, they were held up by a conductor claiming that a stamp from local authorities was missing from their papers. Someone had to go back to the window and obtain the overlooked stamp. Werner volunteered.

"Give me those papers. I'll speak with the asshole at the window." And speak he did because he returned in a few minutes with an additional stamp affixed to the papers.

"Es macht keine Unterschit" – it doesn't make any difference- they told me at the window. Idiots!"

"Werner, dome a favor and keep those papers."

"Alright, but only until we get to Vienna."

Sometime after midnight, the overcrowded train started to move slowly at first and eventually picking up speed. Destination Vienna.

It was also Werner who managed to get the most comfortable compartment for the men. He took a seat by the window and invited Henryk to sit across, also a window seat.

"We may as well enjoy the privilege of our ranks."

The train kept moving in total darkness. After a while the conversation died and silence took over. Here and there one could see the tired and worried faces when someone inhaled a burning cigarette.

The monotone sound of the railroad wheels put Henryk to sleep faster than a sweet lullaby. He was aware of the train making frequent stops while still being asleep. It was Henryk's wonderful ability to sleep during artillery barrages or the noises of O.T. barracks. What was that predestined fate, which was sending him to the city of his mother's birth and yet he felt like a wind-driven leaf.

It wasn't the noise of the men but rather the sun creeping through the masked window that woke him up. The Swiderski boys brought two pails of water from somewhere. It was enough for the men to shave since there was no water available in the bathrooms. Having brought the water, the twins and Werner disappeared only to return later with some watery soup and stale bread. The food was distributed and quickly consumed.

Werner offered Henryk a cigarette which they smoked deeply in their own thoughts.

"Say Heinrich, you're from Vienna, aren't you?"

"Yes sort of."

"We should be in Vienna for a few hours at least. If you are afraid to go home to find what I found, I'll gladly go with you for company."

"Thanks, Werner. I have to do it by myself. It's a painful story."

"I understand. Forget I even mentioned it."

The Austrian landscape was moving like a gigantic conveyor belt with snow covered trees, homes, bridges, small villages and Gothic style churches. The war hadn't reached this area yet. Henryk went to the bathroom located at the other end of the wagon. At least seven or eight other soldiers had the same idea, forming a line in front of the door leading to the bathroom.

Henryk stopped an elderly-looking conductor.

"Pardon me, when do you think we'll get to Vienna?"

"Well, young fellow, we have some major problems. A couple of days ago the Allies bombarded the fuel works in Vienna, ball bearings and aircraft industries in Steyn, steel industries in Linz, even Innsbruck and Wiener Neustadt didn't escape their wrath. Since Berlin and Rome formed close political ties, our Austria became a roasting pit on which the country was to be 'browned'. Ha, ha, do you get it? Browned."

"I got it all right. Aren't you afraid to talk like this?"

"What can they do to me? My only son died in Stalingrad. They sent me his medals which they can shove up their asses. I want my son back."

His voice was bitter, full of disillusionment, frustration and discontent.

"'Es tut mier sehr Leid, Vaterl' – I'm really sorry, Pops." Said Henryk walking into the vacant restroom. He still heard the old man say: Go with God and come back in one piece."

Meeting the old man gave Henryk food for thought. Did he, like so many Austrians, greet Hitler's appearance in Linz and Vienna after the Anschluss in March of 1938 or did he belong to the minority like Schuschnigg who opposed Hitler? Who knows?

Back in the compartment, he continued reading Karl May's book. Just taking out time to eat or drink he finished the book by the time the train pulled into the magnificent, albeit slightly damaged building housing the main railroad station.

Whatever the damage Allies managed to inflict upon the Vienna's Communication Center, the Austrians were able to repair it in record time.

The main hall represented a mess of gigantic proportion. Hundreds of soldiers mixed with groups of refugees who, judging by their unwashed faced and unkempt hair, must have been in this hall for some time now seeking ways to reach their destination. The military always had priority.

"Give me the group's papers and your own. I'll try to get you a pass to the city, should time allow."

"Werner, that is fantastic. Do you want me to go with you?"

"No. You don't know how to talk to them because you are one of them," he said laughingly.

Truthfully, Henryk was puzzled by Werner, who didn't act like an average army sergeant. It was evident from Werner's speech and manners, that he was an educated man, who moved with ease when dealing with Army's "red tape" and inflexible rules.

Henryk's hunch about Werner was demonstrated when Werner came back in relatively short time, bringing the group's travel papers to Milano and a pass for Henryk, good for the entire day. Werner kept the same nonchalant composure.

"We still have almost five hours until our departure for Milano, don't lose any time, go to town. Leave your belongings with Swiderskis and I'll supervise the group in the meantime."

"Werner, could I have a word with you?" Henryk asked.

"Sure, what is it?"

"I would like to ask you a personal question. Who are you?"

"If you are that curious, I'll tell you. This is not for publication. Can I have your word of honor on this?"

"Absolutely."

"Not so long ago I was a major who disobeyed a direct order. You see, we were surrounded by the Russians. The bastards had a numerical superiority of four to one. Our situation was hopeless and I was ordered not to retreat. However to save the 400 lives of my men. I did retreat, thus getting myself court-martialed with the reduction of rank to sergeant, and that was only thanks to the intervention of my ex-neighbor, Lieutenant Colonel Ernst Bloch. The funny part was that Colonel Bloch himself was of Jewish parentage, whom Hitler declared to be of German blood. So now you have it. The fucking war is as good as lost, but I'll keep fighting because I have no one to live for. Now you my friend take off."

Werner turned around, leaving Henryk astonished by those revelations.

"Herr Feldfebel, I'll take care of your things until you come back from the city. Enjoy yourself if you can."

"Thank you Anton. I'll do just that."

Henryk put on his coat, where inside the lining he had some extra money thanks to Tadeusz and his Cracow escapade. The local Gandarmaire stopped him briefly with a warning:

"Be back in time, Feldfebel. We would hate to look for you in the city."

"Don't you guys worry. I'll be back. Adieu."

A few taxis and several horse-driven carriages were lined in front of the station. He decided to take a taxi. The driver, a small man wearing thick glasses, who was surely seventy years old, but still spry, asked him:

"Where to Feldfebel? Perhaps to the nearest bordello?"

"Not this time. Please take me to Number Two Lichtenfels Gasse in Zweiten Bezierk."

"That used to be a Jewish section. What is your business there?"

"My father used to be the building superintendent, working for the Jews. Another friend eventually got that building and I want to visit him. Besides, what the hell do you care?"

"Sorry, just making conversation. That should be near the Rathouse (Municipal Building) between Leopold and Malz Gassen if I'm not mistaken."

"No, you are not mistaken, you're right on target. Let's go

already, otherwise we'll both freeze to death, Weitermachen. Here Pops have a cigarette."

"Thank you very much. I'll keep it 'Fur Spater', for later. Do you know something funny? I do miss those Jews. Life in Vienna was somehow different. At least bombs weren't falling in our heads. Ha, Ha."

Some 20 – 25 minutes later, the taxi pulled in front of a non-descript four-story building.

"Here you are Feldfebel. Would you like for me to wait for you?"

"That is a very good idea. Here is some money in the mean-time. I'll be back in ten or fifteen minutes. From here I want to go to the Sachar Hotel on Kentner Strasse and after some coffee and their famous torte we'll go back to the station. I'll take good care of you."

"Ich danke Ihnen vielmals" – Thank you very much. I'll wait here on this spot, sir."

This was the house in which his mother was born and lived until the age of seventeen. It was here where she had met her future husband. Henryk heard so much as a child about the house that he could almost describe it to the smallest detail. The apart-ment was on the second floor, first door to the right. She also used to tell him about the friendship with Ilona Weisskopf, the daugh-ter of the building's superintendent. A friendship that was deeply discouraged by the parents of both families.

All Henryk wanted to do was to see the apartment for himself. The large oven lined with ceramic tiles from Holland and the highly polished mirror-like parquet floor in the 'salon'."

He would invent some excuse to enter the apartment for a few minutes. A closer look at the door on the second floor revealed a small sign in Gothic script: "Families Weisskopf".

His heart skipped a beat and yet he knocked at the door. After a moment that seemed like an eternity, he heard:

"Ein Moment bitte – one moment please," and the door was opened by a pleasant-looking middle-aged lady about his own mother's age. Seeing slightly puzzled look on her face, Henryk said:

"Excuse me, I'm trying to locate parents of a friend of mine killed in Russia. They lived on this street at number 2, 22, or 42 but their name is Schwarzkopf, not Weisskopf, like yours."

Having solicited some sympathy, Henryk was invited in.

"Please come in. You look so tired. Can I offer you a cup of tea? I just brewed a fresh pot."

"Thank you very much, I really could use a cup. I hope that I'm not intruding?"

"Not at all, please sit down. I'll be right with you."

Henryk looked around. The apartment was the way his mother used to describe it. The oven was still there but the floor was covered by a large Persian carpet.

"Here is your tea, Herr....?"

"Heinrich Kaplinski, at your service."

The name Kaplinski didn't mean anything to Mrs. Weisskopf, because she knew his mother as Koppel.

"Herr Kaplinski, you do bear an uncanny resemblance to the fiancée of my friend from childhood. He was a handsome man, just like you are."

"He and his bride moved to Galizien in Poland and last I heard from them was before the Anschluss. They were fine people even though they were Jewish."

"Dear Mrs. Weisskopf, thank you for the tea but I must hurry because my unit is at the Station and we are being shipped to Italy."

"You poor boy, what this war had done to all of us. 'Gott behute' – God protect us and keep you safe. Should you find yourself back in Vienna, don't hesitate to visit us."

"I surely won't forget you, Mrs. Weisskopf."

That was that. He finally managed to see his mother's apartment and meet her childhood friend. The remark about his mother's family 'being nice even though they were Jewish' was probably said for the benefit of his uniform.

The taxi drive was downstairs, exactly where he left him, blowing into his hands to keep them warm.

"I'm glad that you are back, I was beginning to freeze. Are you going to the Hotel Sachar? Or did you change your mind?"

"Not at all, let's go there."

"Herr Feldfebel, you're in luck. My brother-in-law, Hupert is the hotel's doorman. He knows everybody there including the maitre d'hotel. Hate to tell you but in that Hotel, they don't bother with privates or Feldfebels unless they have the Knight's Cross. Don't worry, I'll talk to him and we'll see what can be done."

"Thanks for telling me. If I can't get in I'll just look around but it sure would be nice to taste their coffee and torte. Whatever you can do I'll appreciate."

The taxi stopped in front of the Hotel a large edifice built in Rococo style in time of glory and splendor of the Austro-Hungarian Empire.

"Please wait a minute, let me speak with Hupert, my brother-in-law."

The driver walked towards a man standing in the vestibule, dressed in an elaborate coat with brass buttons and gold embroidery. They talked for a while and then shook hands. The driver came back with a large grin on his face.

"It's all arranged. He'll take good care of you. I told him that you have single-handedly captured 150 Russians. They will have a table near the window for you. I have to run an errand for him. I should be back in an hour. Should you finish earlier and I'm not around, just take another taxi. Hupert will find you one. Hope you've enjoyed my service."

It was a delicate hint about payment. Henryk had shillings given to him by Tadeusz Kierod while still in Cracow. He was generous with the man that was so helpful.

Hupert the doorman, directed Henryk to the opulent main

dining room. The head waiter, alerted by Hupert, escorted Henryk after a greeting, to a table near the window.

"Hope this is satisfactory to you, sir."

"Very much indeed."

"Nothing is too good for our heroes. I understand that you've captured 150 Red Army men."

"It is a slight exaggeration, only 149 were there." They both had a good laugh.

"What would you like, sir. I'll tell the waiter."

"For me a cup of 'Bohnen Kaffe mit Schlagsahne' coffee with whipped cream and a piece of your famous Sachar torte. I have one more favor to ask. You see, I have fourteen friends waiting for me at the railroad station. We are all being shipped to the front. I'll gladly double the un-official price if you could get me a whole torte. It would mean a lot to me and the boys."

"I'll see what can be done."

"Thank you very much," said Henryk, shaking the head waiter's hand, while slipping a folded large bill at the same time.

"You're most welcome, Sir. Your coffee and the torte will be brought to you momentarily."

There were many high ranking officers of different branches of the military including the S.S. Some smoked cigarettes or cigars, deeply engrossed in their conversations with their friends or elegant ladies. No one paid any attention to him.

Through the window Henryk could see a charming park where maids were pushing white baby carriages on small wheels or walked their French poodles.

"Your coffee, sir." Said a soft-spoken waiter well past his 65th birthday.

"Thank you, the coffee smells delicious."

Henryk slowly drank his coffee and ate the torte. It was sheer heaven. He was as close to paradise as he would ever get, sitting on a plush red armchair. He savored every sip and every bite. Unfortunately heaven was short-lived. Just two tables away sat four devils personified by their black uniforms. The waiter brought a package containing the torte just as Henryk was finishing his coffee.

"Thank you very much. How did you manage to get it? You didn't tell them per chance that I'm Hitler's relative?"

"You guessed it right, that's what I told them."

"'Rechnung, bitte' – my check please."

"Everything is already paid for. Good luck and come back to us. We wish you 'Mazl'."

"I'm sorry but I'm not familiar with that expression."

"It's an expression that we use around here."

Henryk walked through the entire length of the dining room, saluting here and there some officers, some of which saluted back. Surely the Feldfebel was here on business and had every right to be here. Henryk thought that way too.

Hupert the doorman delivered a message from his brother-in-law: "Please don't wait for me. I won't be back in time. Hupert will get you another taxi. He also gave these newspapers which you have left in the car. He thought they belonged to you."

Henryk wanted to object that these papers weren't his, but since he didn't have any reading material, he decided to take them. Most likely whoever was riding the cab before him must have left the papers on the backseat.

"Fine, I'll take the papers. Please get me another taxi."

"I'll be glad to. It will take a minute or so." At the whistle blow, a taxi came around the building and stopped at the front entrance of the hotel.

The invariable question of 'where to?' was answered by a laconic 'main railroad station.'

Riding through town, Henryk observed the broad streets and boulevards, many parks and considerable military traffic, canvass covered lorries, moving slowly through the town and spewing dark, stinking exhaust onto the streets of Vienna.

Some twelve minutes later, the taxi reached the station. Henryk paid the driver while other people got into the cab. Carrying the precious Sachar torte, Henryk walked to the corner of the hall where his group was located on the same spot where he left them hardly four hours ago.

"How are you Heinrich? Did you get laid for us at least?"

"No, but I've got the second best thing, a Sachar torte."

"Hurrah for Feldfebel Kaplinski," said the Swiderskis.

"Heinrich, hold it till we board our train. I think we're being routed through Ljubljana in Slovenia and then to Triest-Milano. We've got to move now. In the meantime you fellows just sharpen your appetite." These words were spoken by Werner whose authority nobody could or would challenge.

"Herr Feldfebel, I'll carry your things and you just carry the torte," said Anton.

It took a few minutes of confusion to find the right track and the right train, but finally the group was directed to a wagon where the sign 'Reichs Bahn' was stenciled over some French markings.

By the time everybody settled down, Werner ordered the Swiderski twins to bring hot water coffee or tea – "Whatever they've got as long as it's hot. Otherwise, don't bother coming back."

And come back they did with a large kettle full of steaming hot liquid. It looked too weak to be coffee and too strong to be tea. After a few trials it was decided that it was indeed coffee but of unknown origin.

"I need someone with a sharp knife to cut this cake into fourteen equal pieces, any volunteers?"

"I'll do it Feldfebel, I used to be a butcher."

"Go ahead Adolf."

The cake was expertly cut and distributed among the appreciative group of men. If food finds its way to the heart of a man, cake does it faster, especially such a delicacy as Sachar torte.

The finger-licking Sachar torte put everybody in a good mood. Adolf the butcher had also another talent. He had a better than average voice. He started to imitate Zara Leander's style of singing.

"Ich mochte so gerne aber Ich weissnicht was. Mein Herz mochte dieses und mein Verstand mochte dass" (I don't know what. My heart wants this and my brains want that.)"

He followed with "Zwei rote Rosen und ein zarter kuss" (two red roses and a strong kiss...), and the very popular: "Dein ist mein ganzes Harz..." from "the Land of Smiles."

Prompted by the appreciative audience, he sang a couple more songs and then announced:

"That is all fellows, I'm going to sleep."

Most of the men agreed with Adolf. It was time to hit the sack. Werner was sitting next to Henryk, both were enjoying Adolf's singing while smoking their cigarettes.

"Heinrich, how was your trip to the city? Did you get to see the people you wanted to meet?"

"Yes I did, Werner. It was a disappointment, sometimes it's better to leave certain things as they were."

"I fully agree with you, let's go to sleep."

"You go ahead, I'll read for a while. Goodnight Werner."

Henryk removed the newspaper from his coat pocket which was given to him by the doorman at the Sachar hotel. It was an old issue of the "Neue Zuriche Zeitung', a German-Swiss paper dated Thursday September 9, 1943. The following headline caught his eye: "GERMANS CHARGE BETRAYAL BY ITALY". "Berlins newspapers branded Italy's capitulation as cowardly treachery. The German press abounds in denunciation of Premier Pietro Badaglio and King Victor Emmanuel, as well as the Italian people." "Mussolini was too great a person for a nation like that." "The King left Germany in the lurch just like in 1915."

The rest of the article was missing, however another page dated Wednesday, November 24, 1943, also caught his attention:

R.A.F. BOMBERS RETURN TO DEVASTATED BERLIN AFTER 2.300 TON ATTACK, GREATEST IN HISTORY.

Reich's Capital set afire. City's heart blasted by 775 four motor planes.

The British armada lost 26 craft. The Germans claim, that in the terror Raid, the British lost 'a considerable number' of attacking planes.

On the Russian Front, The Red Army scored important advances on most fronts but admitted withdrawing from Chernyakhov-Brusilev area.

"Are you still reading, Heinrich. Why don't you go to sleep?"

"Werner, I found this old Swiss paper, do you want to glance at it? You may find it very interesting."

"Fine, let me have a look." Once he started to read the paper, he read it with great interest.

"Heinrich, I agree, it doesn't look good, but I believe that Der Fuhrer will find a way out. The war is far from over."

"It seems so, we'll get a chance to lose our asses yet."

"That's for sure. Goodnight."

The train made numerous stops throughout the night. Some wagons were attached and some disconnected and yet all that commotion didn't prevent Henryk from sleeping soundly.

It was an early morning when a sudden jolt woke everybody in the compartment. The sun's rays were coming through an occasional cloud. The train stopped in the middle of nowhere. After a while soldiers and some civilians left the train to stretch their legs and to attend to their bodily functions since most of the toilets weren't working properly.

The distance between Vienna and Ljubljana was approximately 300 km. It was unlikely that the train covered that distance during the night.

Henryk headed towards a large tree while the rest of his group preferred bushes.

A hum of incoming planes hardly caused a worry. Three planes flying from east made their approach. Some soldiers said:

"Not to worry, they are ours." Werner was the first to recognize the planes.

"ALARM, ALARM, those are the British, take cover, take cover!!" It was too late, the R.A.F. planes with their marking quite visible now, opened fire at the entire length of the train, killing and strafing people and the wagons.

The two powerful Vickers and one Halifax VI unleashed their bombs. Most of the bombs missed their intended target but one did, hitting the last four wagons, destroying everything in its path. The Vickers continued flying but the Halifax turned around for another pass. The anti-aircraft gun located on a flat platform near the locomotive, opened fire at the plane. The tracer bullets coming out of the four barrels didn't even come close to the plane, because the Halifax's own machine gun silenced the anti-aircraft gun, spraying death along.

Screams for help came from the bushes, hiding members of Henryk's group. The voices belonged to Swiderskis. Anton was shot in the elbow and his twin Bonifacy was wounded at the knee. Adolf lying in a puddle of blood was dead, caught literally with his pants down. Luckily for the men a medical team was present and functioning.

Once Werner located the medics he took over the rescue procedures. He directed the medical personnel to the most critically wounded first. He was briefly challenged by a very young lieutenant whom Werner was able to shut up immediately. The lieutenant as green as he was, was smart enough not to interfere with an experienced soldier.

Unknown to Werner, the whole scene was observed by a tall colonel, whose right hand was in a cast. He walked straight to Werner, who with Henryk tried to comfort Swiderskis.

"Werner, what the hell are you doing masquerading as a sergeant?" These words were spoken by a good friend of Werner's from Heidelberg's days, Oberst Olaf Gustafsen. It was easy to recognize Olaf by the dueling scar of his face. Werner should have known it because he was the one who put it there.

"It's a long story Olaf. I'll tell you the first chance I get."

"See me later after you clean up this mess. You'll find me in the second passenger wagon."

"Zum Befehl, Herr Oberst" as ordered, colonel. Olaf just shook his head.

The medical officer holding Anton's almost totally severed hand, turned to Werner and said:

"There is no way in hell to save his hand. We'll have to cut it off completely to stop the flow of blood."

Unaware of the doctor's words, Anton blissfully passed out.

"Are these fellows brothers?" asked the doctor.

"Yes they are. Could you administer morphine?"

"We don't have any but in this case we might find some." Orders were given to disconnect the damaged wagons and to load the wounded into remaining wagons. The dead were quickly buried near the big tree, which gave Henryk a hiding place during the raid by the British.

A rifle with a fixed bayonet and a steel helmet were the only memorial.

Henryk was shaken by the fate that befel the twins, at the same time realizing what these two Volksdeutsche were capable of doing to him, should his Jewish origin be made known, still it was difficult to dislike these two.

Some railroad rails in front of the locomotive were severely damaged and had to be replaced, if the train was ever going to move again. The task of removing rails from the back of the train and transferring them to the front was given to Henryk's group. It was a job performed by the men of O.T. many times in the past. While they were busy doing that, another team repaired the locomotive.

The time was of essence, since there was fear that the British may come back to finish their job. No one had to encourage the men to work faster. Surprisingly, just a few hours later the train moved again, albeit with wagons much overcrowded.

The windows in Henryk's compartment were shattered by bullets and to keep the cold from entering the compartment, someone hung an old blanket. Still the cold air was coming through, making everybody uncomfortable and irritable at the same time.

Nobody felt like talking.

After a while Werner said to Henryk"

"I'm going to see Olaf and check on Swiderskis."

Henryk just shook his head in acknowledgement. He closed his eyes pretending sleep and without realizing, he dozed off only to be awaken by Werner a couple of hours later.

"Are you asleep, Heinrich?"

"Not anymore Werner, what's up?"

"I did visit the Swiderskis for a few minutes. A pitiful scene, one boy lost his arm and the other a leg. They cut it off just above the knee. The entire medical team is talking about this case. "Vive la guerre" at least for the moment both boys were sedated. It is almost funny, I have seen so many dead people and nothing touched me more than these two brothers whom I hardly know. As I said "vive la guerre". I also did see my friend Olaf. The son of a bitch is related to Karin the wife of Reichsmarschall Herman Goring. I told him the circumstances of my court-martial and he promised to pull a few strings in Berlin on my behalf, we shall see what we shall see. He gave me a bottle of Aqua-Vita so let's have a slug and go to bed. I have had enough excitement for one day, don't you think so?"

"Yes I do so let's have that drink." They poured themselves a stiff drink and passed the bottle around. By the time the bottle came back to Werner it was empty.

A few minutes later everybody was asleep. The loud snoring of some men didn't bother the rest.

CHAPTER 12

Another few minutes on the Brooklyn's L-line and Captain Paul Krafchin would reach the destination of his parents home on Bay Parkway in Brooklyn, N.Y. he was given 3 days home leave before being shipped overseas. He really deserved the brake.

Just to think about what he had to do to get that second silver bar on his shoulder. He felt very proud of himself. He the only son of immigrants from Buczacz and Stanislawow in Poland.

Having completed 2 years of engineering school at Cooper Union he was accepted by the Air Force in the early days of 1942. His first assignment was pre-flight training at Maxwell Field in Alabama. It took 6 tough months of studying engines and codes with strong emphasis on physical endurance. It seemed that the "Jew boy" from New York found admiration and respect from his instructors and classmates. He was scholastically and physically (best soft ball player) in the top 10%. By the summer of 1942 he was sent to Bennetville, S.C. flying school for Primary Training lasting 4 grueling months followed by a 3 month stunt at Bainbridge in Georgia for Basic Flight School. It was only after completing the Advanced Training School in Marianna, Florida that he got his wings and a commission as a 2nd lieutenant in the U.S. Air Force, graduating with top honors in the Class of February 1943-B. Bona fide fighter pilot.

Like any other branch of the Armed Forces, the U.S. Air Force was doing everything in 3 different ways. The right way, the wrong way and the Air Force way. After training so many fighter pilots they had decided to retrain some of those guys as multi-engine pilots and Paul became one of them. Again the Air Force in it's wisdom sent Paul to Boca-Raton in Florida to learn the uses of

Radar. It was in Lockburn, Ohio at the Central Instructors School where Paul learned to fly the 4 engine B-17 after additional 4 months of extremely hard training. He was afraid that the war would end before he would have a chance to fight the Huns.

Finally he was transferred to McDill School in Florida where he was ordered to pick up his 10 man crew and a brand new B-17, which he promptly named Goldie Locks after his childhood sweetheart Goldie. Now at last he was a full pledged member of the 8th Army 486 Bomber Group. His co-pilot was Lieutenant George Perry an easy going New Englander from Fall River, Mass. The rest of the crew represented a cross section of America. The bombardier also a Lieutenant was the oldest of the group, he was 30 years old and totally bald. No wonder he received a nickname of "Curly" that Chris Pasek of Allentown, PA. acknowledged with a smile. The navigator, aircraft engineer, sight gunner, ball turret and tail gunner were from "shining sea to shinning sea" the exception was Moe Samuels the radio operator of the Bronx, N.Y. formerly of Great Britain, whose voice was pure silk. All were young and eager boys well trained in reconnaissance, artillery observation, bombings (tactical & strategic) strafing and air fighting. What experience they lacked they made up on enthusiasm. It was a very good crew.

It was in McDill where Paul became a Captain. It seems that the Air Force accepted his recommendations of how to better pack his own parachute and improve the exit and landing techniques. He was offered an immediate position as an instructor which he politely declined, stating that as a Jew he had special reasons for dropping bombs over Germany. No one on the board opposed that.

So it was today on Friday, December 24, 1943 a day when he was coming home to spend one day with his family and to celebrate also his father's 50th Birthday. The train slowed down and pulled to the station, where Paul got off. It was late afternoon and a slight snow mixed with rain was falling on Brooklyn. From the station to his parents apartment was 14 solid blocks. This time

Paul was in a rush and to boot he had a heavy overnight bag, containing his personal effects as well as some presents for his folks.

He hailed a cab and gave the driver the address of 8910 Bay Parkway.

"Yes, Sir, Skipper, I used to live across the street from that number. I'll get you there in a jiffy."

The driver, wearing a cap and smoking a cigar looked intensely into the rear view mirror.

"Pardon me, skipper. Aren't you the little Paulie who delivered my newspapers? I would recognize you anywhere. To think what became of little Paulie. Can you imagine?"

"I recognize you too, but can't remember your name."

"It's Sam Goldstein. I used to play pinochle with Isaac, your father. How is he? We moved from there some years ago and now we live in the Mill Basin section. You are hardly little. How tall are you?"

"Slightly over 6 feet, Mr. Goldstein. I do remember you well. You used to tip me well, you were a good sport."

They both had a good laugh. The driver expertly pulled in front of the wrought iron gate leading to 8910 Bay Parkway and jumped out of the cab opening the car door for Paul and grabbing his bag.

"Please let me carry your bag in."

"Thank you Mr. Goldstein. It isn't necessary, how much do I owe you?"

"Not a penny, not a penny. It is my pleasure and privilege to drive you to your parents home. Please give them my best regards and may God bless you. We are so proud of you. Our little Paulie a captain in the Air Force. Isn't that something?"

Paul's parents lived on the main floor, right next to the steps leading to the upper floors. The house didn't have an elevator.

He knocked twice at the door, the same way he did as a teenager when he forgot his keys to the house.

"This must be our Paulie" he heard his mother's voice even

before the door was opened for him and there stood his mother and father.

They embraced and kissed each other warmly. To Paul, his parents looked much older than when he had seen them last, especially his father, who had a long history of heart ailment which kept him from any strenuous job. The only job he held for any length of time was as a minor official with the Ladies Garment Union and that was thanks to Mr. Dubinsky a Labor Leader who was related to Paul's mother.

"How are you Paulie? You must be very tired. Do you want to wash up? We are going to eat as soon as I light the Sabbath candles. Your room is the way you had left it. Your father doesn't allow me to touch anything in that room."

Paul went into his room. It was true, nothing there changed. The same pennants and posters of the Brooklyn Dodgers were displayed on the walls. His attempt at oil painting of the Brooklyn Bridge was also hanging at the same spot. His bat, glove and Jerseys were there where he had left them. Nothing was touched, even his "Superman" comics and baseball cards. His cloths hung in the closet were hopelessly outgrown as he found out after trying on his favorite sport jacket.

"Mom, I guess I'll have to wear my G.I. outfits till the end of the war. Let me wash up and I'll be with you in a minute."

Both Paul and his father put on their yarmulkes as Yetta, Paul's mother made the blessing over the 8" candles put in the silver candle holders, an heirloom from Buczacz. Isaac, Paul's father made a blessing over the wine and round Challah.

"Now we are ready to eat Yetta, what goodies have you prepared this time? After all we have a special guest this evening."

"Don't worry Isaac, you won't go hungry, I assure you. I made a carp the way Paulie likes it with white horseradish, so let's have some more Manischewitz's wine."

"Papa, if you want something stronger. I have brought you from the PX a bottle of your favorite rye whisky Canadian Club."

"Thank you Paulie, maybe a bit later, because we have invited your girlfriend Goldie and her parent for tea. They live in Englewood, New Jersey now and Max works so they will be here in a little while. Isaac was referring to Max, Goldies father who had a candy store in Jersey.

The excellent fish was followed by a delicious chicken soup with noodles and extra carrots and fresh dill, just the way Paul liked it.

"Would you like more soup, Paulie?"

"No mama, unless you don't have anything else."

"Don't worry son, there is more coming."

The next dish was flanken beef and roasted chicken, mashed potatoes, noodle pudding and "tsimes" followed by home made compot of apples and prunes. This was served in a crystal bowl. The small chip in the crystal was caused by Paul himself when some years ago he tried to dry the dishes.

Having finished with dinner, Yetta Krafchin announced:

"We'll wait for tea and coffee when the Wohls arrive. They should be here any minute."

"Mama, Papa have you noticed anything new about me?" asked Paul.

"Paul I think you became even more gray" Isaac was referring to Paul's premature gray hair, which gave Paul a distinguished look and many admiring glances from the females. It was Isaac's standing joke about gray hair. He claimed that gray hair was hereditary because in his case he got it from his son. Of course, he himself was totally white.

"No Papa, I was walking about my second silver bar and not my silver hair, I'm a captain now."

"Dear Paulie, by me you're a captain, by Papa you're a captain, I only would like to know if by captains you're a captain."

"Mama, they know that I'm Jewish, I'm not hiding it. I feel 100% American and where I'm going I'll soon find out if by captains I'm indeed a captain."

Further discussion was interrupted by the knock at the door.

"That must be the long awaited Wohls" said Paul who went to open the door.

"Gut Schabbes" Sorry we're a bit late, the traffic was horrendous. How are you all? What to we have here? A Captain in U.S. Air Force? How are you Paul?

Max Wohl was the first to shake Paul's hand, his wife Simca kissed him on both cheeks, only Goldie their daughter a bit shy at first kissed him fully on his mouth in full view of both sets of parents. The Wohls and the Krafchin's were friends of long standing even though Max and Isaac were a study of opposites. Where Isaac was stocky built and gray, Max was thin, tall and bald. While Isaac was basically shy and reserved, Max was anything but shy. Their friendship was solid. The women looked and acted more like sisters than friends, since early days in Buczacz, Poland. Both obtained much coveted in Poland Teacher's Certificates and both migrated to the U.S.A. at the same time. While living on Pitkin Ave. in Brooklyn, they met Isaac and Max, double dated and eventually got married.

That Paul and Goldie would be a couple was always assumed by both families. Even a blind person could see that Paul and Goldie were in love since their childhood.

Goldie was a tall girl at 5.7 who appeared even taller. Her smooth copper-red hair was worn in Veronica Lake fashion which almost covered half of her face. Her green eyes and full lips accented her sensual face. This evening she looked absolutely radiant. The pink angora sweater probably one size too small, emphasized her shapely breasts. She surely was a 'dish' to be admired.

For Goldie there never was anybody handsomer than her Captain Paul Krafchin.

"Come to the table, let's have some tea or coffee, please."

Everyone sat around the table laden with all kinds of home baked cakes and cookies and artistically arranged fruits.

After several cups of tea the seniors sat at the table discussing the war and wondering what has happened to their respective families left in Poland, leaving Paul and Goldie to themselves.

They sat in the living room deeply engrossed in the conversation. Paul looked at Goldie holding both of her hands tightly. After he had said something to her she shook her head in the affirmative and became red like a beet.

Paul got up and approached the Wohls, the animated conversation at the table stopped.

"I've just asked Goldie to marry me and she has accepted my offer. We do hope to have your blessings. We've decided to get married upon my return Stateside, after the end of the war. Should anything happen to me she is free to marry whom ever she pleases."

"Mazel tov, mazel tov" this calls for a drink, we couldn't be happier. We always loved Goldie like a daughter that we never had. Isaac get some whisky."

"Mom, we'll do better than that. I have a bottle of champagne in the freezer" said Paul.

Simca brought out the champagne glasses and everybody toasted the young couple.

"My Goodness I forgot to give Goldie a small gift." He ran to his room and took from his bag a small box, neatly wrapped in foil paper.

"This is for you, Goldie."

"Open it, silly girl."

Goldie opened the box which contained a beautiful 14 karat Benrus bracelet-watch.

"Thank you Paul very much, I'll always treasure it." And she gave Paul a long kiss. A knock at the door and Krafchin's uninvited neighbors came in.

"We've heard that Paulie came home, we just wanted to see him."

"Come in, come in, have a drink. Our Paul just got engaged to Goldie Wohl."

"Mazel tov and our very best wishes."

Within the next fifteen minutes, half of the inhabitants of the building came in. The party started in full swing. Gone was the bottle of the Canadian Club which Paul brought from P.X. and so went the entire stock of Isaac's liquor. It became noisy and crowded.

"Paul let's go to your room I want to talk to you."

"Sure Goldie, let's go."

"When are you going back to your unit?"

"Unfortunately by tomorrow noontime. I've to clear this place. I must report to my unit in Florida in two days. We're being shipped overseas. I expect that Raykovik Iceland will be our first stop and after that good old England."

"Paul, I just want you to know that I shall wait for you forever and I'll be a virgin till our wedding night."

A long kiss sealed the agreement.

Finally some kind soul said aloud:

It's late let's allow the young couple some privacy. Grudgingly everybody obeyed.

"Simca, Isaac and Paul, we'll do the same. We have a long trip back to Jersey. Paul when are you going back. Perhaps we can get together for lunch or dinner?"

"I'm afraid it wouldn't be possible I have to leave tomorrow 1300 hours that is one o'clock."

"So soon what a pity."

"There is a war going on and I want to do my share."

"We understand that. Go with God and come back to us safely. We all love you."

"Thank you. I'll walk you to the car."

"Go ahead Paul, Papa and I will cleanup in the meantime."

Paul put on his coat and walked the Wohls to their car parked about 2 blocks away. He was holding Goldie very close to him. He felt her heart beating like a church bell.

"Don't worry so much, darling I'll be back, you just keep those home fires burning." They kissed again.

The Wohls got into their old Chevy. The car started on the third try. "Good-bye everyone."

Paul was watching the car disappear around the block. He stood there a minute and then rushed back to the apartment.

"Can I help with the dishes, Mom?"

"Thanks son, we'll take care of the dishes. You had better go to sleep, Good Night and sleep tight."

Paul went to his room, he was dead tired. He quickly undressed, brushed his teeth and went pronto to bed. He was asleep within a minute.

It was past 9 o'clock in the morning when his mother walked into his room carrying a tray with a glass of orange juice and French toast, Paul's favorite breakfast dish. A neatly folded New York Times was next to the plate.

"Good morning sleepy head. It's time to get up, don't you think so?"

"Good morning, mom, let me stay in bed for a while. That is something I don't do very often in the Army."

He drank his juice glancing at the paper's headlines of Saturday, December 25, 1943:

> "EISENHOWER NAMED COMMANDER FOR INVASTION. 3000 PLANES SMASH FRENCH COAST. BERLIN HIT. ROOSEVELT PROMISES NATION A DURABLE PEACE."

He ate in a hurry now, got up, shaved and showered and got dressed. He heard his mother shout:

"We have ordered a taxi and we'll take you to Grand Central Station in Manhattan since today is Christmas, the trains aren't going that often and the traffic is light."

"That will be just fine, mom."

"Paulie, do you have anything to wash? Any laundry?'

"No mama, don't worry about my laundry."

Paul started to pack up this things when the phone rang.

"It's for you Paulie. It's Goldie."

The phone was in the hallway. Paul picked up the receiver and spoke with her for a few minutes. Whatever the subject of that conversation was it left a big smile on his face.

"You are really crazy about that girl, aren't you?"

"Yes mom, totally."

"If we ever want to catch that train, we must leave now." It was Isaac rushing everybody now.

"We are ready Isaac, the cab is probably outside already."

Paul's look prevented Isaac from grabbing Paul's bag.

"I'll take it, papa." They locked the door and left the apartment. Isaac noticed that Paul kissed the "mezuzah" on the door. "That's right papa, there are no atheists in the trenches."

The cab was parked in front of the house right by the fire hydrant.

The driver turned up to be Mr. Goldstein himself.

"Mr. Goldstein, how in the world did you know when to come?" asked Paul.

"Your mother's call to our dispatcher's office came while I was there, so I asked for this job."

From Bay Parkway via the Belt Parkway and the Manhattan Bridge to Grand Central Station was a record ride in 35 minutes. Paul kissed his parents Good-bye and shook hands with Mr. Goldstein.

His mother was crying "Paul be careful, please be very careful."

"I will mom, I promise. Did you ever hear of Simca's from Buczacz son to have his 'toushie' shot off over the Atlantic? Of course not. I'll be just fine. Mr. Goldstein I thank you once more and do take them home."

He went straight to the station where after a while he located his train and compartment. There was someone occupying the top tier of the bunk bed, lying with his face towards the wall.

Hearing Paul's entrance to the compartment the man turned around and said:

"Welcome Captain. I hope you don't mind me taking the top. I'm Lieutenant Bill Beilleux from Shreveport, Louisiana, where my name is pronounced Bay-u but my friends call me Bee-Bee, just like in bee-bee gun."

"Nice meeting you, I'm Paul Krafchin."

"Don't think of me being rude but I need to catch up with

sleep. I had a heavy date with a dancer from Roxy Music Hall and I'm totally exhausted, I haven't slept in 28 hours."

"Go right ahead, lieutenant. I'll just read for a while and take a bit of shuteye myself before dinner."

"That sounds like a good idea."

Paul read The New York Times, President Roosevelt sounded very optimistic in his Christmas broadcast from his Hyde Park home. The appointment of General Dwight D. Eisenhower as supreme commander of the Anglo-American invasion force was well received. General Montgomery would be chief of British Army units, General Alexander would head the Allied Forces in Italy and General Spaatz would be American Air Force commander against Germany.

"Forts", Liberators and medium bombers into thousands hit special military targets along the coast of Northern France. The Red Army advanced to Vitebsk.

There is the action and I am still here thought Paul to himself.

Killing the time Paul opened his book by Rudyard Kipling and reread some of it's poetry. One about "Soldier, Soldier" struck home.

"Soldier, Soldier come from the wars,
I'll down an' die with true love!"
The pit we dug'll 'ide 'im an' the
Twenty men beside 'im-
An' you'd best look for a new love."

The light snoring of the lieutenant in the upper bunk had a contagious effect upon Paul because he also fell asleep. It was dark already when Paul woke up when he heard his neighbor coming down from his bunk.

"I guess it's time to get some chow" suggested Lieutenant Bill "Bee-bee".

"Go ahead I'll be there in a few minutes."

Paul washed his face, he also could have used a shave but that function he left for the next morning. Pullman's black porter came in and introduced himself as Harry.

"I'll be taking care of your compartment till we get to Florida.

What time do you wish to have your bed made, Sir?"

"Around 10:30 and I could use another pillow."

"It will be taken care of, Captain Sir."

Paul inquired as to the whereabouts of the dinning car and proceeded in that direction.

The dinning wagon was crowded by mostly military personnel and a few civilians.

"Oh Captain Krafchin, please join us. We have reserved a seat for you."

It was Bee-bee sitting with two other lieutenants.

"I don't mind if I do."

Bee-Bee introduced the other two gentlemen: "Lt. Jim Wilson and Lt. Gene Brady, Both of Dayton, Ohio."

"Paul Krafchin, it's a pleasure. Gentlemen, please sit down."

"How about a drink?" On the table was an opened bottle of Wild Turkey.

"I'll have a short one, your health gents."

"Captain Sir, you're 2 drinks behind everyone at this table, Sir."

"I'll stay with this one for a while."

The waiter asked Paul, what he wanted since everybody else placed their order.

Paul studied the limited menu. "I'll have a steak, medium rare and French fries and plenty of ketchup."

"Very well, Sir. I'll put your order right in."

"Where are we by now?" asked Paul

"We passed Philadelphia, Camden, Baltimore and we should be approaching Richmond, Virginia."

"Captain, may we refill your glass?" asked Jim Wilson.

"Thanks I'm waiting for my steak."

"The Captain is from Brooooklyn" stated Bee-Bee.

Paul didn't like the prolonged "oooooo" but he kept his cool. It was Brady who asked Paul:

"Is that true that lots of Jews live in Brooklyn?"

"That is quite true but not enough. As a matter of fact I'm one of them."

"I meant no offense, Sir." An awkward silence took place, you could have heard a pin drop.

Brady started to speak about Jewish contribution to the world of science followed by the influence of Jews in Hollywood. Mercifully the conversation was interrupted by the waiter who brought dinner to the table as well as another bottle of Wild Turkey.

The food was hot and surprisingly delicious. The chef knew his art because Paul enjoyed his meal. By the time the coffee and deserts were served the subject of Jews sprang up again.

What became abundantly clear to Paul was that Bee-Bee was tipsy and trying to belittle Paul.

"Listen, Lieutenant, let me paraphrase the British Prime Minister Disraeli from the Queen Victoria era when he was heckled by a Member of Parliament about his Jewish origins said: "Sir, when my forefathers knew how to write and read yours were still living in a cave."

"Bravo, Captain, that was a hell of a good answer."

"Captain, Sir." As drunk as Bee- Bee was "Let me quote to you from Rudyard Kipling, whose book you were reading this afternoon:

"By living God that made
you,
You're a better man than I am'
Gunga Din!"

"You bet your sweet southern ass."

Paul got up and took out of his wallet a sufficient amount of money to cover his meal and tip and he put an additional twenty dollar bill down saying;

"The second bottle is on me fellows and thank for an interesting evening."

Everyone got to their feet sending Paul a sharp salute.

"As you were" said Paul walking away leaving the trio standing with their mouths wide open.

CHAPTER 13

Paul walked the length of three wagons and stopped to look into the moon lit night, watching trees, barren fields and small peaceful towns passing by.

"A penny for your thoughts, Captain..." Paul turned to locate the source of the melodic voice. It was a pretty brunette wearing a Red Cross uniform.

"You seem to be miles away from here. Thinking perhaps about the girl or girls left behind?"

"You are quite right, just one girl occupies my mind."

"How refreshing, would you have a light?"

"I'm sorry, I don't smoke."

"I'm beginning to like you even more. My name is Vivian, Vivian Holmes."

"I'm Paul Krafchin from Brooklyn, U.S.A."

"And I'm from Boulder, Colorado, we're both very far from home. Would you like to join me for a cup of coffee?"

"Sorry, Miss Holmes, I had a very tough day."

"Perhaps at breakfast tomorrow morning?"

"Perhaps, Miss Holmes."

Paul was shy with women despite all his sophistication. He never knew if women wanted to baby him attracted by his gray hair and baby-face or simply to seduce him. Paul wanted desperately to be faithful to Goldie but with the war going on who in the world would believe that Paul at age 24 was still a virgin?

He went back to his compartment, where he found his bed turned up for the night. Mint candy was laying on his pillow. Harry had done a superb job.

Paul took off his jacket and his shirt. His dogs were dangling over the khaki T-shirt, when lieutenant Beilleux walked into the compartment, still slightly loaded.

"Paul, I want to apologize for this evening."

"It's Captain Krafchin, in case you haven't noticed, apologies accepted and the case is closed. I don't want to hear a peep coming from you is that clear Lieutenant?"

"Yes Sir, Captain Sir, corrected I stand."

Bee-Bee climbed into his bunk and true to his promise he kept quiet much to Paul's relief, since he didn't feel like getting into a lengthy and totally unnecessary conversation.

He still had another day's journey to reach his destination but he'll manage it without companionship of Bee-Bee. "I'll be captain among captains" he said to himself falling asleep.

And sleep he did because he didn't hear Bee-Bee coming down from his upper bunk bed. Having attended to Army's 3S (shit, shave, shower) he went to the dinning car, meeting Harry in the hallway.

"Good morning, Captain, did you sleep well, Sir?"

"Just fine Harry, just fine."

"Begging Captain's pardon, Lieutenant Bay-u is leaving at the next station at North Carolina's City of Raleigh. Would Captain like to be by himself for the rest of the trip?"

"Indeed, I would Harry, thanks." Said Paul handing him a few dollars.

"Thank you very much Captain."

The idea of loosing Bee-Bee as a roommate was very appealing.

Wearing a big smile on his face he entered the dinning area. The hostess seated him by the window at a table for four, where two other seats were already occupied by two middle aged ladies.

"Good morning ladies."

"Good morning, Captain."

A young waitress handed Paul a menu. He glanced at it briefly and placed his order:

"May I have a glass of orange juice, couple of sunny side eggs, over lightly, crisp bacon, home fried, toast and plenty of hot coffee."

"Right away, Sir."

"Our Captain seems to know at all times what he wants."

That was spoken by Vivian Holmes whom he has met last night. She was sitting with her back to him and now that she turned around, she was even prettier in the morning than he remembered her to be.

"I've finished my breakfast but I'll be glad to join you for coffee, that is if I'm being invited."

"Of course the Captain will invite you, we are just leaving anyway, aren't we Gertrude?"

It was one of the two ladies sitting at Paul's table playing Cupid.

"By all means Miss Holmes, please sit down and let me get you a fresh cup."

The waitress who brought Paul's breakfast also brought a cup for Vivian.

"Please eat, Captain don't disturb yourself. There is no sense in eating a cold meal. I'll enjoy seeing you eat, dig in."

"Thank you Miss Holmes."

"You can call me Vivian."

"That will be fine Vivian."

His breakfast was interrupted however for the second time by the appearance of Bee-Bee.

"Good morning, Captain, I just want to say Good-bye. I'm getting off at the next top and again Captain, I..."

"Never mind Bee-Bee take care of yourself and good luck to you."

"Thank you Sir, if you are ever in Shreveport look me up, we are in the telephone book."

"I'll do that, Lieutenant." As he turned towards Vivian, Bee-Bee saluted sharply. Paul responded in kind.

"Is that one of your officers?" asked Vivian.

"No, thank God."

The pleasant conversation was to be interrupted for the third time. This time by the appearance of 3 other women dressed in Red Cross uniforms. The oldest and the most senior of the group addressed Paul.

"Pardon us, Captain but Miss Holmes is needed at the meeting which will take place in 5 minutes." And she kept murmuring to the other Red Cross ladies: "At least she found an interesting looking young man."

"Sorry Captain, I must run. If I won't see you at lunch time perhaps I'll bump into you at dinner time."

"I'm looking forward to it." Paul said gallantly.

He finished his third cup of coffee and left the dinning car. Passing by a compartment filled with non-commissioned officers he heard a song that brought a chuckle:

"Hey, Baba-reeba, mama in the kitchen
Papa in jail
Sister on the corner
Has pussy for sale."
Hey, Baba-reeba..."

Let them enjoy themselves, nobody knows what tomorrow may bring.

Harry brought to Paul's compartment the latest issue of "Stars and Stripes". He always enjoyed the paper, especially the cartoons. The spirit of G.I. Joe was unbeatable, so were the optimistic headlines:

RUSSIANS BREACH LINE ROUT 22 DIVISIONS
BIGGEST U.S. AIR ARMADA SMASHES REICH

RAF reports more U-boats sunk by planes in 1943 than in 3 prior years combined.

There was nothing mentioned about the fate of the Jews under the German occupation. Paul's parents were probably mislead by propaganda and false rumors.

The train made frequent stops on the way to Tampa, Florida,

his destination. Between reading and stopping off at the dinning wagon, the time flew rather fast.

At lunch time he tried for the first time in his life to eat cat fish, which turned to be a pleasant experience. He managed to say "Hello" to Vivian sitting in the company of Red Cross workers. She in turn said something that sounded like "I'll see you later."

Paul knew pretty well that once he reached his base the Air Force would demand his pound of flesh.

With another 4-5 hours of free time a catnap might be advisable. He stretched out on his bed and closed his eyes listening to the car wheels making contact with the rails.

A gentle knock at the door, interrupted his sleep.

"It's open, come in." Paul thought that it was Harry but to his surprise it was Vivian.

"May I come in?"

"Please do Vivian, how did you find me?"

"Last night I saw the compartment you went into."

Paul reached for his shirt to put it on.

"Don't bother Paul, I'll take mine off too."

Paul became speechless as Vivian pulled the shades down and locked the door from inside.

"What are you doing Vivian?" stuttering said Paul.

She didn't bother to answer. Once she took off her shirt, her pink brassiere was next, exposing her firm breasts and large dark nipples.

She walked slowly to Paul who was on the bed until her breasts encompassed his face. The irresistible smell of her body caused an instant combustion. Paul pulled her roughly towards himself, kissing her with passion he didn't know he possessed. He quickly removed her skirt and matching pink panties. In a split of a second he was naked, oblivious to the voices of people walking in the train's corridors. He entered her and all his pent up energy was released a few movements later in a series of explosions over and over again.

"For a quickie it was very good, Paul. You have promises of

being a very good lover but ask your girl friend to teach you how to slow down a bit."

She dressed herself as fast as she got undressed.

"Paul, stop looking at me like you have seen a prehistoric animal. It wasn't that bad, was it?"

"Not at all, but it was so...so... unexpected."

"That's how life is, my friend. Stay well and always expect the unexpected."

She kissed him slightly on the lips, lifted the shades and opened the door walking out with an amused expression of her face.

"So long Paul and always support the American Red Cross."

Paul was shaken a bit as he reached for his shirt. His virginity and his principles were gone within a few minutes. Wasn't that a laugh.

Harry stopped by to see if Paul wanted anything. "We'll be reaching Tampa within an hour or so." "Thank you Harry, I don't have much to pack I can do it in a few minutes."

The compartment became too oppressive for no reason at all. He walked out to the hallway to watch the country side. A stocky Master Sergeant was standing next to him smoking a cigarette.

"Good afternoon Captain."

"Good afternoon, sergeant, what is that you are smoking?"

"Camels Sir. Would the Captain care for one?"

"I don't mind if I do."

Sergeant offered Paul a fresh pack of Camels and Paul took one cigarette. The Sergeant obligingly lit it for him. After a first puff on the cigarette, Paul started to cough.

"Begging Captain's pardon, is that the Captain's first cigarette?"

"Not really, I've tried some years ago to smoke but not lately. After this butt I won't smoke anymore, I don't think that Camels agree with me anyway."

They chatted amicably for a while. "I have to get my gear ready, thanks for the cigarette. Sergeant."

"You're welcome Sir."

Paul's few belongings were expertly packed in a couple of minutes. The train slowed down and came to a complete stop. Over the public systems an announcement came: TAMPA-TAMPA. his destination.

Paul left the train in a hurry, somehow he tried to avoid meeting Vivian and he was anxious to get back to his base still some distance away on Dale Mabry Highway. About half a dozen Army 2.5 ton trucks and a few jeeps were at the station. Paul started to look for a chance to hitch a ride when he heard a familiar voice:

"Captain Kravets, this way." The voice belonged to his C.O. the "old man" himself Lt. Colonel Gary J. Cotshott, who was motioning for Paul to approach the staff car.

"Krafchin Paul, Sir."

"Kravets, Krafchin what difference does it make, hop in."

Lt. Col. Cotshott better known to his men by his nickname "Gary the Hotshot" was a 34 year old dedicated airman, well respected and feared because of his sharp tongue and short temper. The staff learned to avoid him whenever it was possible. The popular saying was: "keep away from the icebergs."

"Driver, step on it, we don't have the whole day to waste, let's go."

"Yes Sir, Colonel."

"Well Krafchin, did you have a nice Holiday? I remember something about your father as the reason for your furlough, how is he?"

"The Colonel is too kind, my father is well, thank you Sir."

"Good because from now on you won't have the time to take a piss." He closed his eyes indicting that no further conversation is indicated or desired. Paul kept his mouth shut till they reached the base, romantically located between Hillsborough and Tampa Bays.

The sentry recognized the C.O.'s car and lifted the ramp. The car proceeded to the unit's Headquarters.

"Thank you for the lift, Colonel."

"Get your ass out of here and be ready for tomorrow's briefing."

Paul saluted the Colonel who just waved his hand. Another privilege of rank, Paul thought.

On the double he went to the Officers Quarters, where he shared a room with 3 other captains. Everyone seems to be highly agitated.

"Hello, what gives in here, fellows? I've just seen the "old man" it looks like someone stuck a dynamite stick up his rear end."

"Paul, don't you know? We are moving out in 48 hours."

"What about the New Year Holiday?"

"Forget about it, all leaves are cancelled, we are working around the clock now. The Colonel wants everybody at 7A.M. sharp in the Operations Room for a final briefing."

With no time to waste. Paul located his co-pilot George Perry.

"Good evening, skipper. You've probably heard the news, we're moving out in 48 hours. I have taken the liberty of preparing our baby for the flight. I've checked and rechecked every single item personally.

"Fuel?'

"All 3000 gallons of it."

"Bombs?"

"12.000 lbs. all incendiaries. I was told."

"Ammo?"

"For each of the seven 50 mm guns 300 rounds."

"You have done a good job, George."

"Thank you Sir, anything else Skipper?"

"No, George, I'll see you in the morning."

His throat became dry and off to the canteen he went for a cup of coffee.

He slept poorly thinking about Vivian and the high state of alert. He got up earlier than usual. At the crowded dining room he just grabbed a cup of coffee and blueberry muffin. When he reached the Operations Room at 6.45 he found everybody assembled there already.

Exactly at 7 o'clock Lt. Col. Cotshott walked to the podium. Everybody stood up.

"Good morning Gentlemen, please sit down. Smoke 'em if you got 'em. The time has come for us to earn our pay. First of all, the big news. We're moving out in 24 hours and not in 48. I repeat in 24 hours, Is that clear? We are flying to Iceland, which as you know is a sovereign state handled by Dennmark. In 1940 the British landed there to pre-empt the Krauts, promising not to interfere with the country's internal affairs. Canadian troops followed the Brits, however in July of 1941 the area came under U.S. protection. Our troops relieved the British-Canadian garrisons. You must understand that whoever controls Iceland commands the North Atlantic sea lanes and the naval exits into the Atlantic from Europe and that is where and why we come in.

My deputy, Major Lars Nyburg will brief individual wings and answer all pertinent questions. One more thing, I can't stand SNAFU or excuses, Major carry on."

Everybody got to their feet. "Sit down, please."

Major Nyburg along with his operational officer Captain Duane L. Burnham started to brief individual crews, as far as logistics, flight plans, order of take offs, detailed heights and other concerns connected with an operation of this magnitude.

Paul's plane was assigned as number seven for take off. He promptly gathered his crew in front of his plane "Goldie Locks."

"From now on, we are going strictly by the book. I won't tolerate the smallest violation of the military discipline. Remember that the tiniest mistake may cost the lives of the entire crew. I'll never ask for the impossible, if you have a problem come to me or Lt. Perry BEFORE it becomes a major problem affecting us all. We are one for all and all for one, agreed?"

"Agreed Skipper." Fully energized everyone attended to his duties. Paul again checked and rechecked every bothersome detail, leaving nothing to chance.

Next morning at 5.30 with sun rays barely coming from the east, the first group of planes started to take off. The sluggish, heavy planes once they reached the speed of 150 miles per hour became airborne climbing 500 feet a minute. Some three minutes later they turned 90 degrees and flew straight in a northerly direction.

The sixth plane couldn't get stated holding up Paul's plane. He heard on the earphones "Gary the Hotshot" yelling "Get that fucking crate out of the way."

Once the runway was cleared Paul's crew didn't have any problems. There was a sigh of relief among the men but still the crew was very apprehensive. Their experience was limited to the basic training and required logged hours. Some men were still afraid of flying, although no one would admit it aloud. It was just like a fear of darkness, either you were afraid or not.

Once they reached the proper altitude and the place in the formation, everybody's mood improved. The radioman found a station out of which sweet words of a popular song lifted their spirits even more:

"Why do robins sing in December
long before their time is due."

That song was followed by: "Give me 5 minutes more, only 5 minutes more, let me stay, let me stay in your arms."

Paul didn't stop anyone from listening in, he felt great and so did everybody else on the plane. Flying a powerful bird and being a part of a large formation of 39 planes gave him a feeling of security only obtained in numbers.

Above him was the purest, never ending, blue sky and underneath clouds that reminded him of dirty white sheep skin. Like everybody he chewed gum and was addicted to sweets but he could never get used to the relief tubes. Smoking was another taboo, that he was adamant about. Whoever smoked had to chew tobacco instead. He liked to watch at high altitudes the moisture trail smoke, leaving straight white lines on the horizon.

The flying weather was perfect until they reached Canada, where they encountered a strong wind which kept them company until they approached Reykjavik, Iceland. Here in the preparation for landing they had to loose altitude and they came across a blinding snow storm. With the visibility close to zero, the instruments took over.

Flying in sunny Florida was very easy by comparison, but Iceland was something else entirely. "Goldie Locks" touched the snowy runway a bit too hard, but overall the plane and the crew performed superbly.

Other planes were not so lucky. Two planes behind Paul's collided in mid air, another plane crashed, killing the pilot and wounding the remaining crew.

The crew disembarked leaving one of the gunners to guard the plane. The men were driven to the barracks for hot meals and ever more appreciated hot showers. Paul made sure that every two hours someone else would be guarding the plane.

The next few days were sheer hell. The sudden change from Florida to Iceland was very hard on the men. The bone chilling wind seemed to penetrate layers and layers of clothing. They worked very hard to keep the plane free of snow and ice. It was a loosing battle. On the fourth day the snow stopped falling. Having been already refueled they cleaned up the planes and the runways they were getting ready for the second leg of their trip to their final destination the USA Air Base at Sudburry-Sussex in England.

The flight itself was routine if you want to forget a couple of German Me-109 fighters, who plunged into the mid of formation only to be scared off by the concentrated fire of the deadly 50mm guns.

The snow of Iceland was replaced by rain and fog. The rain was nasty as it was couldn't compare to Florida's hurricanes, but the fog lived up to it's reputation. The RAF Liaison Officer Richard Hunt-Evans would joke that in Essex the fog is so thick that one can pour black ink over it, cut it to pieces and sell it as coal.

Weeks later the men got used to the new surroundings and to the custom of high tea. The Yanks were generally welcomed by the British population, especially by the ladies. Some British men complained that the problem with Americans was that they were overfed, oversexed and over here.

However, the men of the 486th Bomber Group had another thing to worry about because after a very lengthy briefing they got their first mission to bomb the synthetic oil plant at Mersburg in Germany. The strength of the 486th was soon increased to 42 planes. Paul and his crew were ready for this assignment and were looking forward to it's implementation.

CHAPTER 14

The train making explained and unexplained frequent stops somehow reached Ljubljana Station in Slovenia.

The heavily wounded soldiers, among whom were also the Swiderski Brothers were taken off and put aboard Army Ambulances. The Military Police discouraged everybody trying to contact those wounded and about to be evacuated.

By the time Henryk's group reached Triest, the group itself was split in half. A high ranking officer countermanded the original orders by assigning seven of Henryk's men to a temporary duty in Triest.

Werner, Henryk and Ryszard Strzelecki, the same fellow that helped Henryk at the Induction Center, along with four more men were allowed to continue on their Milano destination.

The group's papers were often checked and questioned. Werner who became the defacto group leader was most resourceful and most experienced in dealing with higher-ups.

Italy in itself was a totally new experience for Henryk, he even asked Werner about the population looking so much like Jews of Poland.

"For all I know, some of them might be Jews but the population considers them to be Italians. Only the "Fascisti" occasionally send them to our S.S. units for "relocation". As a student not so many years ago, I've spent several summer vacations in Italy. I love their music, songs and women, I even speak some Italian. Heinrich, I forgot to tell you, I'm ordered to report at once to the Headquarters' Personnel Department. You, however, are included in tomorrow's transport to Pignatoro in Liri Valley, some 110 kilometers from Rome. You are assigned there to a Special Engineering Battalion attached to the 15th Panzer Grenadier Division. You still have a couple of free hours, so take a walk to the nearby Museum on Via dei Rustici. Anybody will tell you how to get there. By the way we may be separated if that is the case let me tell you that it was a pleasure to have known you. I'll have to say what Michael Angelo said back in 1564: "The span of life has run it's course..."

"Thank you Werner, it was a pleasure to have met you, but in life who knows, maybe we shall meet again. "Beinbruch" break a leg, Good Luck!"

"Well, I might see you tonight. In the meantime, take care of yourself."

They shook hands and Werner left for the Personnel Department.

Henryk decided to adhere to Werner's suggestion to visit the local Museum. He left the Assembly Hall that was located in the former barracks of the crack Italian Alpine unit. The guard at the door didn't even bother to verify the pass.

He stopped a few people for directions to the Museum on Via dei Rustici, the standard answer he got was: "no capisco" or "nichts verstehen". Henryk understood the reluctance of the population of getting involved with "Tedeschi" (Germans) whom they avoided like a plague.

Finally a middle aged priest, carrying under his arm "Il Messaggero" "newspaper" took a pity on Henryk.

"Sprechen Sie Deutsch?" asked Henryk

"Ich kann mich in dieser Sprache verteidigen. Aber Italianisch ware mir lieber. "I can hold my own but I would prefer Italian."

"Das leider kann ich nicht." "I'm sorry but I can't speak it."

The priest gave him direction to the Museum located within a 5 minutes walk. He was praising the Museum as "Das Weltberuhmte" (world-famous) and "unglaublichen" (unbelievable) or "unbeschreibbaren" (undiscribable) place that is "zu besuchen" (be visited) and "zu geniesen" and enjoyed.

After thanking the priest Henryk walked to that Museum only

to discover that the Museum was closed for repairs. Deeply disappointed after the priest's build-up. Henryk went back to the Assembly Hall, where Strzelecki who was caring for Henryk's belongings asked him:

"Back so soon?" "Yah, the place was closed."

With nothing better to do, he went to the canteen to get something to eat. In another room two soldiers were playing chess, he watched the game for a while and when asked to join he agreed and played five games out of which he lost three. He fared much better at the ping-pong table. His fourth match was interrupted by exited Strzelecki:

"Heinrich, Heinrich! You'll never believe who came in?"

"Don't tell me it was Rommel."

"No, silly. It is our very own Werner Gastfreund but as a Kapitan Gastfreund, can you imagine him as a Captain. He asked about you, he wants you to see him right away."

"Well, I better go to see the Captain."

Henryk located Werner speaking to a group of officers. Henryk stood by the door, waiting for Werner to finish his conversation. With the conversation finally finished he turned to face Henryk.

"Ich meldete gehorsam, Herr Kapitan" "Feldfebel Kaplinski, reporting as ordered."

"At ease, Corporal."

Both looked around to check if anybody else was in the room, they were alone.

"I went to the Personnel Department. They restored my rank to a captain only. I think that it was the best deal that my friend Olaf was able to get for me. I still like being an officer better than a sergeant. I'm taking over a Company whose C.O. was killed in action. It is also in the 15th Panzer Grenadier Division, the best god damn unit of the Germany Army in Italy. I already requested you as my adjutant. You just stick with me. Heinrich. One more thing, among men you'll address me as Captain, in private continue calling me Werner."

"Thank you Herr Kapitan, I understand fully and I'm grateful for your attention. Soldiers of armies world over salute the uniform. I'm saluting the man."

"Nicely done, Heinrich. We're leaving with a supply column at 6.00 A.M. Strzelecki has been posted to another unit. It will be just you and me."

"Very well, Herr Kapitan."

"Dismissed!"

Henryk saluted Werner and made a full about face. He found Strzelecki in the same place where he left him before.

"How is that possible to become a captain from a sergeant?"

"I don't rightly know Ryszard, perhaps he is on a special assignment for the Military Counter Intelligence? Who knows."

"Everything is possible. Where did they assign you?"

"The 15th Panzer Grenadier Division wants my ass this time, what about you?"

"I don't know yet, have to hang around this place for another day or two. I don't mind as long as they don't send me to the front."

"You're quite right. Take it. "langsam aber sicher" (take it easy), maybe I'll bump into you somehow or somewhere."

"Stay well, Heinrich."

Another couple of days and he'll be in Pignatoro in Liri Valley facing the Allied forces. Would that be the British or the Americans. He was hoping for the Americans.

CHAPTER 15

The long, military relief column left Milano at the appointed hour. For security and practical reasons the column itself was divided into two parts. The part going to Monte Cassino left an hour earlier, followed by the second group destined for Pignatoro, Captain Werner Gastfreund and Henryk were among them.

The canvass covered camouflaged trucks carried troops, supplies, ordnance, precious fuel and the ever present field kitchen.

Werner with four other officers were driven in a staff car, proceeded by two motorcycle riders and followed by the entire column. There were additional two other motorcyclists constantly circling the convoy like a pair of watch dogs.

Due to the foul weather the trucks were moving slowly. While the poor visibility was a hindrance, at the same time it was a blessing in disguise because the enemy curtailed its air activity. At night they kept moving with partially covered headlights, emitting just enough light to see the next 20 meters. Bad roads and partisan's activity contributed to further slowdown. Frequent flat tires were promptly repaired while trucks that suffered major breakdowns were temporarily abandoned and their cargo shifted to other trucks.

In the wooded area the convoy was attacked by guerillas, killing two motorcyclists and wounding one of the truck drivers. Soldiers jumped out of the trucks and opened a concentrated fire repulsing the poorly organized attack. Later on two half-trucks joined the column scaring off any future hostile action on the part of partisans.

Henryk was assigned to the kitchen detail for the duration of the trip which lasted two days by the time they have reached their destination, Pignatoro.

The Company which Werner was supposed to take over had a task of protecting a segment of the most formidable Gustav Line, a system of sophisticated interlocking defense, located across the rugged part of Italy along the Garigliano and Rapido rivers.

Upon his arrival, Captain Gastfeund ordered a meeting of all officers and platoon leaders. He wanted a detailed report regarding unit's strategic situation, troop morale and logistics. The provided information helped him to assess the combat readiness of the Company. The report was delivered by a tall Lieutenant Kurt Haber, who was the acting C.O. until Werner arrived.

It seemed according to Lt. Haber, that the growing Allied superiority in men, air power, armor and material was negated by the skillfully conducted German defense of the region, thus able to halt the American 5th Army near the Garigliano and Rapido rivers at the base of Monte Cassino. The facts on the ground supported his view.

Werner had told Henryk later that:

"I couldn't design a better defense system. Also we're very lucky facing green inexperienced and poorly led troops of the U.S. 36th Infantry Division, if we are to believe reports of our intelligence gathering unit. I'm also afraid Henryk that sooner or later I'll have problems with Lt. Haber, who had his eyes on the command of this Company. I also found out that other officers nicknamed him "Professor" which he was at the University of Stuttgart where he taught Spanish and Italian. I also managed a brief glance at his file. Lt. Haber fought in Spain along Franco. He is a Nazi through and through, one of those "Alte Kampfar" (old campaigner). I don't trust him

There is something very odd about him. See what you can find out from other men."

"I'll do my best."

It was easier said than done, because men shied away from Henryk often seeing him in proximity to the C.O., a situation that was actually welcomed by Henryk. Getting "goods" on Lt. Haber will have to wait. In the meantime Henryk was glad to be with the kitchen detail and occasionally with the maintenance group.

Allied troops were unable to move forward because of a merciless pounding by the German artillery, through the seemingly endless daylight hours. By comparison the German losses were negligible therefore there was no need for the scarse reserves to be committed.

The German units were well fortified and held the high ground, confident that they could repel any Allied attack, with the exception of an air attack.

A couple of weeks later. Werner along with the other company commanders were summoned to the 15th Panzer Grenadier Headquarters, leaving Lt. Haber as the company's most senior officer in charge.

That day Henryk and the chief cook were preparing lunch for the troops when two Italians, holding vintage rifles emerged from the woods, soon to be surrounded by the men, who took the rifles away from them.

Lt. Haber came out of his bunker to investigate the commotion. In fluent Italian he asked the reason of their presence among German troops and their names.

They claimed to be hunters on the way to their village Sant Apollinare and their names were: Carlo Battaglia and Maximiliano Cervantes Camhi.

"These fellows are partisans and we had better shoot them" said Lt. Haber to the other officers who came to see the excitement.

"Herr Lieutenant, maybe there is a chance to obtain valuable information from them, including the identity and whereabouts of other guerrillas."

"No, there is no point in taking prisoners, because there is nothing to be gained from the information they might share. Let me speak with that Spaniard, he is Spanish that much I've detected from his Italian."

"Maximiliano Cervantes, do you have anything to say so that

we can spare your life? And you Sancho Panza?"

The men kept quiet. Lt. Haber waited a minute or two and then switched to Spanish:

"En un lugar de La Mancha, de cuyo nombre no quiero acordarme, no ha mucho tiempo que vivia un hidalgo…" or

"In a certain village of La Mancha, which I shall not name, there lived not long ago a gentlemen…"

"Let's kill those idiots. You! Come here!" Lt. Haber yelled pointing to Henryk who was just passing by with a tray of sandwiches.

"Take those two imbeciles into the woods and shoot them."

"Begging Lieutenant's pardon, I don't carry a weapon."

"Oh, you don't then take my pistol and go." He took out his Luger and handed it to Henryk.

Pointing with the pistol to the prisoners Henryk said: "Hande hoch und weiter gehen" "Hands up and keep going."

The prisoners lifted their hands and resigned walked in the direction of the forest with Henryk following them a few meters behind. Once they had gotten deeper into the woods Henryk was sure he was hallucinating because he clearly heard a Hebrew prayer: "Shma Israel, Adonoy Elohayno, Adonoy echad.." coming out of the Spaniard's mouth.

Henryk repeated the same prayer pointing to himself and said aloud" "Fuggio, fuggio, run away." But the men didn't budge. Carlo Battaglia pointed to Henryk's pistol. They probably think that I am going to kill them once they turn around.

"No, no, don't worry, run." And he stuck his pistol behind his belt, but the men still didn't make a move. Henryk seeing that turned to the side and started to urinate. It was then when Maximiliano Cervantes started to laugh "Grazia mile, grazie mile" Thank you, thank you and they disappeared in the woods. Henryk waited a few minutes and took out the pistol and shot it four times into the air.

Slowly he came back to the unit and reported to Lt. Haber.

"Feldfebel Kaplinski reporting. Prisoners shot as ordered, here is your pistol, Sir, I've cleaned it."

"Tell me, Kaplinski, is that the first time you've killed an enemy?"

"Yes, Sir, it was Sir."

"Well, well you've finally become a soldier."

"Thank you, Sir."

"Dismissed!"

Toward the evening the same day, Werner came back from the meeting.

"Anything new around here I should know?"

"Not really, Lt. Haber gave an order to execute two partisans."

"Anything else worth mentioning?"

"No, Sir."

"Heinrich be a good fellow and bring me some hot coffee, I'm dead tired."

"At once, Sir."

Henryk was glad that Werner didn't ask him for details. After all what was so special about two prisoners that was worth talking about? He went and brought Werner his coffee. Everything was quiet. A quiet before a storm that broke out on January 20, 1944.

Soon "Amis" after a lengthy artillery barrage began the Rapido river crossing, but before they even reached the river, the men of the 1st Battalion came under heavy mortar, artillery and small-arms fire attack.

The Rapido, true to its name was a small but swiftly flowing river about 12 to 24 meters wide and 3 to 5 meters deep and well protected by the numerically superior 15th Panzer Grenadier Division.

Werner was watching the action through a pair of powerful binoculars, safe in a bunker with Henryk next to him.

"Heinrich, those idiots are sending their men in a frontal attack to a certain death. They have rubber and wooden assault boats and pontoon bridges but it will be simply a turkey shoot. Poor bastards, they are being led to slaughter. Sorry to say we also have such officers."

Werner was proven right, because soon all boats and bridges were destroyed, communications were out and the units were cut off. At that point Werner gave an order to counterattack and to concentrate their efforts to wipe out stranded men, killing or wounding nearly all officers. NCO's enlisted men and capturing some.

"Let me tell you Heinrich, the American attack failed so dismally because they selected a poor crossing site, their flanks were exposed, our positions were well prepared, their bridging equipment was inadequate for the job. The element of surprise to which our troops pay lots of attention, in their case, that element of surprise was squandered by many patrols, most of them spotted or captured by our men prior to the attack. However this victory might be one of our last one. The stinking, gum chewing Yankees remind me of hyenas, because they are coming for the kill when their opponent is already tired and wounded, like us after 3 years of fighting the Bolsheviks and their General Winter. We have left behind us, on Russian steppes the very cream of our youth and I ask you for what?"

Henryk kept very quiet. There was nothing that he could or wanted to add to it. That kind of talk could land both of them in jail.

"May I have Captain's permission to return to my bunker?'

"Of course, I'm sorry Heinrich if I sounded a bit too pessimistic, I tend to worry about the men in my command."

"I fully understand, Sir."

A few weeks passed by there were skirmishes and Werner's Company held it's own, inflicting heavy casualties on the attacking Allied Forces.

March 15th, 1944 changed everything for everybody. A massive American air strike and artillery bombardment on the nearby Monte Cassino and Werner's position reduced the targets to rubble.

Many were killed and wounded. Among the dead were Werner and Lt. Haber.

Henryk lived through the worst pounding. The majority of American attacking planes turned north. There was one plane left and it looked like the pilot in an afterthought decided to make one more pass to drop the remaining bomb load. It wasn't a direct hit on Henryk's bunker but the exploding nearby ordinance was able to penetrate the damaged wall separating Henryk's bunker from the one that took the direct hit.

Something incredibly hot like a burning sun hit Henryk's left leg between the hip and the knee. Every cell of his body was filled with pain and then he saw his leg swimming in warm, red liquid. The life was slowly ebbing out of severed veins. With the last vestiges of self preservation he wanted to shout for help but his lips formed one only word: "mama" and he passed out.

CHAPTER 16

To his surprise Captain Paul Krafchin found out that neither he or his crew were quite ready for a bombing mission. The next few weeks were spent learning new tactics to suit present conditions.

The emphasis was put on aircraft speed, armament, maneuverability, rate climb, turning ability, improving pilot's ability for quick reaction and the use of sun and clouds as a weapon.

"Remember" the instructor has said "The guy you don't see will kill you."

The silhouettes of enemy planes were as familiar to Paul's crew as the pictures of their own mother. From Heinkel 111, H-6 Dornier 17 Z-2, Junkers 88-4, to Messerschmidts 163 and Focke-Wulf or Fieseler 156 Storch, awaken from sleep in the middle of the night, the crew would recognize the planes.

Paul also learned the German designation of each type: Kampf, Stuka, Schlacht, Jagd, Nacht Zerstorer, Aufklarungs, Fernaufklarungs, Heeres and the names Gen. Erhard Milch, Gen. Albert Kesselring and Gen. Lohr.

The proper maintenance of the plane was of paramount importance. No wonder that Lt. George Perry would kid Paul saying that no baby in the world was better taken care of than their "Goldie Locks."

In their spare time, the crew visited the pubs in nearby towns, making friends with the local population and occasionally fall in love with their pretty and often not so pretty daughters. Lt. Perry summed that all up:

"What do the English girls have over the American girls?"

"What?"

"They are over here." That remark was always good for a laugh.

The same evening Paul met Vivian Holmes at the Red Cross Canteen. They chatted amicably for a few minutes.

"Paul I would like you to meet my fiancée, Flight Lt. Richard Hunt-Evans of the RAF."

"How do you do, Sir. I had the pleasure of meeting you in your capacity as the Liaison Officer."

"Captain Krafchin, right? I was just going to get a couple of pints of bitter, could I get you some?"

"Thank you, I'll go and get it."

"No, stay here and talk to Vivian, I'll be right back."

"Vivian, I didn't realize that you're engaged."

"Don't let this bother you, Paul. Anytime you'll change your love making skills from rabbit to turtle, call me, will you?"

"I'll do that, Vivian."

Flight Lt. Hunt-Evans came back with several bottles of not so cold Guinness' stout from St. James's gate in Dublin.

"Cheers, how do you like out stout?"

"It's different. I'm more used to drinking Miller's beer, what we call in the States the champagne of all beers."

"Vivian tells me that you are from Brooklyn. Is that near Coney Island?"

"That's right, almost on top of it."

"One day I would like to visit Brooklyn."

"I'm sure that one day you'll see it."

They kept talking about the war and switched to the weather when Paul said:

"My goodness, it's late for me, duty calls. I wish you both much happiness but I must run."

On Tuesday, March 7th, 1944 Paul attended a briefing, Among those present were pilots of the Mustang fighters, freely discussing their experiences after returning from their first attack on Berlin. According to them it was a huge one, 800 U.S. Bombers, Fortresses and Liberators dropped over 2.000 tons of bombs on Berlin that day.

Paul spoke with Lieuts. Carl Bickel, Charles Koening, Felix

Rogers and James Keane to find more details. That mission had a price tag of 68 planes lost in battle.

"George" said Paul to Lt. Perry. "These guys are just like you and me. If they can do it so can we."

"Skipper, I knew that all along, our turn at bat is coming up, I feel that in my bones. I'm ready and I'm sure that you are too."

"Absolutely."

The next couple of days were nerve wracking, because they were called in twice and twice their mission was aborted the last minute and no explanation was given.

On Wednesday, March 15th, 1944 Captain Krafchin was awakened at 4.15 a.m. was served a breakfast of steak and eggs, but could not manage to eat more than a few bites, because he anticipated his first combat mission within a couple of hours.

The pre-launch briefing at the 486 Bomber Group's ready room, covered the targets of today's attack.

"Our campaign in Italy has clearly been disappointing and negative in results, from the short range view point. However in an effort to expand the Anzio beachhead and simultaneously to penetrate the Liri Valley and Monte Cassino areas, it is necessary to view certain positive accomplishments in terms of the broad strategic picture. In other words you're going to bomb the hell out of those targets."

Paul listened carefully to the briefing officer and came away with the impression, that March 15th was going to be a big day in his life. Lurking in the back of his mind was an awareness, that the day could easily be his last on earth. He pushed that thought away, realizing that dwelling on that possibility would not help him to do his job, for which he was being paid.

The crew was assembled and counted for. It was still dark but the planes were visible in the dim starlight, looking like giant sleeping eagles or voltures.

The idea of going head-to-head and toe-to-toe with German pilots didn't seem so strange anymore. His self confidence was strong, bordering on arrogance. He surely felt that he was on the first team, he had the best crew in the man's Air Force and the best plane in the world. After all he had spent the last couple of years perfecting and polishing his skills. He was ready for this day. He was also ready to prove to his mother that among captains he will be a CAPTAIN. His daily ritual of walking around the plane was increased to seven times.

"Captain, did you loose something" asked a worried gunner.

"No, not at all, but it is the custom of my people to walk around the bride 7 times on the wedding day. I can do no less with this beauty."

The crew went inside the plane taking their positions. Paul laced his shoulder harness and adjusted it properly.

His plane was an amazing conglomeration of hydraulic pumps, gauges, indicator switches, wiring, instruments, fuel lines, radios, machine guns, tires, flammable liquids, bombs, bolts and nuts and above all the crew. Everybody and every little gadget had better be working fine.

When Paul got the signal to start his engines, he leaned forward to double check the area on both sides of the plane. His field vision was somewhat obscured. He had to trust the land crew for what he could not see. He gave the plane handlers a thumbs up signal and called out "CLEAR."

The roar of engines was deafening in the early hours of the morning. The engines that were firing on half of its cylinders, were not running smoothly. Until the monster warmed up a little, the plane shook badly, even reading anything on the instrument panel created a problem.

Finally, the engines came up to their proper RPM and manifold pressure. With his head back firmly against the headrest, he had a flying machine underneath him now. Th engines were running like a fine Swiss watch.

"Goldie Locks" took her place in the formation.

The day was slowly rising and Paul could clearly see Capt. Carlton Black's plane on his wing. He lifted his left hand from the throttle just long enough to give him a thumbs up signal. Puffy clouds were floating below formation at 10.000 feet in a not so perfectly clear sky. At 25.000 feet the visibility improved to an incredible view of the world. Through the scattered clouds he could see the English Channel and the coast of France.

The heavily armed B-17 Fortresses and the B-24 Liberators flew the classic 54 aircraft combat wing formation.

Three 18 aircraft groups were brought together, in a compact unit, which was 2.000 meters wide and 800 meters deep with 550 meters between the first and last aircraft. This increased mutual fire support gave maximum defense, using 75% less air space. Such a formation presented truly formidable concentration of fire power as well as a reduced target for the head-on fighter attacks that the Luftwaffe had recently developed.

Word came in that German fighters were spotted. Numerous enemy planes were headed to attack the American formation. Moe Samuels, the radioman switched to the combat frequency briefly to see if he could pick up anything on the action. There was much traffic, that nobody could make sense of. A mumbo-jumbo of excited voices were calling contact and reporting kills. He switched back to the fleet frequency, just in time to hear:

"Bandits, Bandits, at 2 o'clock high."

As if from nowhere a perfect fighter formation "Schwarme" "Four Fingers" of two pairs of ME-163 appeared, greeted at once by several P-51 Mustangs with their highly visible red tail markings. The Mustangs announced on the radio to bomber formation:

"Your escort is the 332nd and you'll be protected."

This was no idle boast because so far the 332nd never lost a bomber to enemy air action.

"Hooray for the Tuskegee Airmen" yelled out "Curly" Chris Pasek.

The combined fire of the formation in addition to Mustangs fire chased away the German planes. After a while the 332nd escort aircraft shook their wings and turned back to their bases for refuel. By that time the 54 plane formation was high enough for oxygen to be used and proceeded on the way to its targets.

Paul eagerly drank hot, black coffee from a thermos bottle, instead of sugar he ate his favorite Hershey chocolate bar.

Crossing the French-Italian border they encountered anti-aircraft flak. Looking down it seemed like somebody was throwing cigarette puffs at them. Out of reach the formation kept flying in a south-east direction.

If Italy looked like a boot, their destination of Monte Cassino and Liri Valley was an ankle.

The tranquility was soon disturbed by an attack of German fighter planes coming out of clouds and having the sun behind them.

The few seconds of an element of surprise were sufficient to spread death and destruction. The sky was a turmoil of battle and things became rather sticky.

Paul could see two of the formation planes twisting in dances of death. One of them was his wingman Capt. Carlton Black's plane that was hit at a shallow angle, skipped and cart wheeled endlessly, leaving a brilliant plume of explosions and fire on the ground.

"Goldie Locks" opened a series of five-seconds bursts. The glowing tracers went towards the attacking Messerschmidts, their paths met. The 50 mm shells hit their target before the "Bandit" had a chance to return the fire. The Messerschmidts blew up and the falling pieces hit Paul's plane.

"Oh, shit" screamed Paul checking gauges and he looked his plane over for damages. He could see some dents and several holes in the wings, yet everything seemed to be in fine working order.

The crew of "Goldie Locks" was elated to have knocked down the enemy plane, the very same one which destroyed Capt. Black's aircraft.

Looking back Paul noticed two brilliant white parachutes.

"I hope these fellows will make it." It was his not so silent prayer.

The elimination of Black's plane left Paul even more determined to reach his target.

From this morning's briefing he knew that the bombing of the 6th century Benedictine abbey at Monte Cassino won't be an easy task. A veritable fortress, manned by crack troops, backed by an impressive and deadly array of firepower will be a hard nut to crash. He had better feelings about his own assignment. Not surprisingly the formation was to be split, with 36 planes attacking Monte Cassino and the smaller group of 16 planes now including Paul's were destined for Rapido river in Liri Valley.

It was "Gary the Hotshot's" voice that brought "Goldie Locks" crew to immediate attention:

"30 more minutes to the targets. Get your asses ready!"

The men were ready indeed, their nerves stretched like violin strings. The tracer bullets came up from the ground to the planes in a unwelcome greeting. Plane after plane started to unload their deadly cargo on the head of the defenders of Liri Valley. With Capt. Black's plane gone, "Goldie Locks" was the last plane to bomb the target.

"Captain, captain" screamed the bombardier "I can't release the load, something is jammed."

"Release the fucking bombs, we can't take them back with us!"

"Curly" was working frantically jiggling various instruments but to no avail. A cold sweat of fear came over Paul, because they had missed their target.

"God damn it, let's make another pass, hurry up!"

While other planes proceeded north for their rendezvous with the Cassino group, Paul tried one more pass to drop off his bombs. This time "Curly" succeeded and the assortment of fragmentation, incendiaries and general purpose bombs hit their targets, due more to plain luck than the properly selected trajectory, range or deflection.

Unburdened by it's cargo "Goldie Locks" ran like a bitch in heat after it's group.

"Kravets what the fuck you think you are doing?" the "sweet" voice of "Gary the Hotshot" was heard.

"It's Krafchin, Sir, had to unload my cargo. Didn't want to bring it home, Sir."

"Well done, Krafchin, but watch you ass do you hear."

"Thank you, Sir."

"Goldie Locks" caught up with the rest of the group. At the rendezvous point, the Monte Cassino group arrived albeit with four planes missing. The combined now formation continued flying north-west to their home base in England. Nothing was sweeter than the sight of P-51 Mustangs of the 332nd escorting them on the last leg of their journey. They couldn't stop one plane from crashing into the English Channel due to mechanical difficulties. The crew parachuted and was picked up by a U.S. submarine answering the plane's "Mayday" call.

Once they landed safely on the "terra firma" Paul was the last person to leave "Goldie Locks" into the caring hands of the ground crew.

"Welcome back, Skipper."

"It's really good to be back." Turning into the westerly direction he said aloud:

"Yes, mama, even by captains I Am a captain."

CHAPTER 17

The totally unexpected appearance of Henryk in the ski shop upset both Edward and Czeslawa. For Edward, Henryk represented a brother that he never had and Czeslawa has seen Henryk as a link to her father and his mysterious family.

"Czeslawa, I think that we have seen the last of Henryk in our lives."

"Don't bet on it. I fervently hope that he'll survive the war and we shall see him again."

"Amen."

Through a coded message, Edward notified his underground contact in Krakow about his brush with the Gestapo agents visiting the hotel where Edward was working.

He was advised to lay low and stick to his routine and report any changes. In compliance with the instructions, Edward continued running the ski shop and giving ski lessons to the guests of the hotel.

While Edward worked, Czeslawa and Danuta started to help their landlords Cyprian and Malgorzata Bujnicki in making local, hand made gift items for the tourists trade.

The Bujnickis were a childless couple, native Gorals of the Podhale region, who supplemented their income, like so many other peasant/artisans carving wood objects and painting the high Tatra Mountains.

Czeslawa displayed a rare talent for painting, starting with water colors and progressing into oil painting. Urged by Bujnickis she brought samples of her work to the "Haus der Zakopaner Kunst" on Hauptstrasse. (The house of Zakopane Art on Main Street).

The proprietor Herr Horst Fischer bought the paintings at once and asked for more. The demand for her work grew and Herr Fischer started to pay her more and more for her work. The more she painted the better she got. Slowly the word spread about Czeslawa's artistic ability and her paintings started to make a good income. Danuta started to copy her mother's style and she became successful in her own rights, even though she was still a child. No matter where they went they always wore the colorful native dress, thus blending well with the local population.

With the money coming in they could have moved out of Bujnicki's house. Czeslawa was against it and so were the Bujnickis themselves but for all together different reasons. They fell in love with Czeslawa and Danuta. They started to tell everyone willing to listen, that Czeslawa was their daughter and Danuta their grandchild. That warm feeling was reciprocated soon because both Danuta and Czeslawa began to address them as grandpa and grandma and Czeslawa would call them father and mother.

After another peaceful month Edward was called to the office of Herr Hoffmann the hotel's manager.

"Edward, I was watching you for a while now, you're doing an outstanding job. I may have something else for you to do. Look at this newspaper. Who do you see on that picture?"

Edward looked at the "Einzige deutsche Zeitung des General gouvernements-Krakauer Zeitung" (the only German newspaper of the government in Cracow) there was a picture of a smiling couple celebrating their 25th Wedding Anniversary.

"Do you recognize this man?" asked Herr Hoffmann.

Edward looked intently not knowing what to say.

"I think that man stayed in our hotel recently with his pretty wife."

"You're right but is that the same woman?"

"No, I don't think so. The other one was nice and slim, this one looks a bit on the heavy side."

"Your right again. When they stayed with us they looked and acted like any other married couple. As a matter of fact they are married but not to each other. This fellow left some incriminating or let's say embarrassing papers and pictures. He called me up and he wants me to deliver these papers to him in Cracow personally. I don't have the time or the inclination. Our regular driver is sick therefore I want you to go to Cracow, return these stupid things to him and to pick up some supplies and one dozen of assorted sizes of skis from our regular sources at the same time. His name is Augustus Kleinert of the MER-Reiseburo on Adolf-Hitler-Platz number 41. His telephone number just in case is 23243. That is on the old Plac Mariacki. Can you manage all that, Edward?"

"Keine Sorge, no problem Herr Hoffman when do you want me to go there?"

"Tomorrow morning, bright and early."

"It will be done, Herr Hoffmann."

That evening Edward came home and after a light super as their custom was, he told Czeslawa about his trip tomorrow to Cracow.

"Listen, Czeslawa, maybe I can get traveling permits for us. Sometimes a little squeeze can go a long way, long enough to reach Hungary or Roumania or some other places."

"What other places? I'm going nowhere, I'm staying right here with Danuta. This is my home now, here in Zakopane, here in Poland. We are not moving. If you want to go, let me not stop you. I had enough of being brave, look what has happened to my parents. They are dead, do you understand DEAD. I also lost my own child and now, thank God, I have Danuta. She is my whole life, I'll dedicate my living days to her welfare. We are doing just fine and we live a peaceful life. I even got her a tutor to give her private lessons. I'll educate her and make a decent person our of her, I don't want to become a Gypsy. We'll stay with Bujnickis, they are very good to us almost like our own parents. I told you if you want to go I won't be in your way and may the God's mother of Czestochowa keep you in her care. I'll wait for you for as long as it may take."

Edward never heard an outburst like that coming from

Czeslawa. She was no long the meek Czeslawa, she was now a lioness guarding her cub.

"Czeslawa, I understand you very well, I'll see what will happen in Cracow and then I'll tell you about my decision."

"Fair enough."

Next morning, Edward came to the hotel to pick up the small panel truck, the papers for Herr Augustus Kleinert and the requisitions for supplies. On the chair next to the desk was yesterday's copy of the "Krakauer Zeitung". Not so innocently he "borrowed" it for the trip.

From the Hotel, Edward took the nearby Route #21-B leading to Cracow. Not surprisingly he was stopped a couple of times. Cracow claimed 345.000 inhabitants but the 25.000 Germans ruled the town.

Every Cracovian knew where the Plac Mariacki was, therefore Edward found the number 41 of Adolf-Hitler-Platz with ease. It was close to the famous "Mariankurche" a church built in 1537 yet.

The "Reiseburo" had interesting neighbors, NSDAP the main office of the Nazi Party at number #25 and a German Apotheke "Zur Sonne" at number 42 and corner Johannisgasse.

He parked his truck almost in front of the "Reiseburo" just as the spot was vacated by another truck pulling out.

Edward went inside the office carrying the large manila envelope.

"What is it?" asked the receptionist.

"I have a delivery for Herr Kleinert."

"You can leave the package with me."

"I'm sorry, my orders were to hand deliver it to Herr Kleinert personally."

"Herr Kleinert is very busy right now."

"In that case I'll come back when he won't be so busy."

"Wait a minute. I'll check with Herr Kleinert." She went inside the other room. A few minutes later she came out.

"Alright, Herr Kleinert will see you now."

Edward walked into the other room, took off his cap and closed the door behind him.

"Do you have my papers?" asked Herr Kleinert.

"Yes Sir, but first I must check the picture in the paper to see if it corresponds with your face. We wouldn't like these papers to fall into the wrong hands, would we? It is you but who is this charming lady, she doesn't look a bit like the woman you were with in our hotel. Isn't that interesting?"

"Alright, I know when I am being had, what do you really want?"

"Herr Kleinert, nothing really much. My wife and I would like to visit Hungary and Roumania and we need traveling papers, tickets and permits. We don't need money."

"You are a Polish swine."

"I agree with you Herr Kleinert but do we have a deal?"

"What name should I put down on those papers?"

"Don't bother Herr Kleinert. I'll do that myself to save time."

Herr Kleinert removed two sets of traveling documents from a large office safe.

"Herr Kleinert while you are at it, kindly add another set. It's for our dog. We wouldn't like to leave him behind you understand."

Without a word he added another set.

"Is there everything I need for traveling. If not your picture will be on every billboard in Cracow. That I promise you. If I don't have a life neither will you."

Kleinert added a few more sheets to it.

"Thank you very much Herr Kleinert you are a real gentleman." The emphasis was on the word gentleman.

"Take those papers and go to hell. If anybody will ever ask me about those papers, I'll tell them that they were stolen. "Du Sweinenhund."

"Danke schoen Herr Kleinert." And he left the office carefully checking his rearview mirror for anybody following him. There was nobody there.

His next stop were the suppliers where he picked up the merchandise and a dozen of assorted sizes of skis for his shop.

The trip home was even faster since nobody stopped him on the road this time. He drove to the hotel where he unloaded the supplies and reported back to Herr Hoffmann returning the keys from the panel truck.

"Did you get at least a decent tip from Herr Kleinert?" laughingly asked Hoffmann.

"Indeed Herr Hoffmann, may I go now?"

"Go ahead, you must be tired by now."

Upon his return he contacted his handler code "Monika." He told "Monika" about the obtained papers and reminded him about having the old O.T. papers and uniform.

"We'll check those papers and if need be we'll update them and we'll let you know about your next step because we understand that you want to join the Anders Army. You should hear from us in about a week. Do not try to contact us in the meantime, we'll contact you, understand?"

The week was stretched to 17 long days.

One day "Monika" called him that "Kciuk" will bring him a "present."

Edward waited and waited. Finally one evening someone knocked at their door late and an old man came in and introduced himself briefly.

"I'm Kciuk and I have a present for you." He handed Edward papers wrapped in a clean white handkerchief. Without another word he left their house.

Edward opened the package. It contained perfectly executed travel documents with all the necessary stamps. The papers were for one person only. The other two sets were probably needed somewhere else. For good measure "Monika" included a "Monatskarte mit Lichtbild, unbergranzte Fartezahl" A monthly permit with his picture allowing for unlimited travel on trolleys and a receipt of 25 zlotys purchased at the Fahrkartenverkaufsburo on Lorentz Strasse #13.

He didn't see an immediate use of it but he took it anyway. The papers issued to Edward Daszkiewicz of the O.T. brazenly permitted for travel to Kosice in Slovakia by any means of transportation to visit his sick mother. Any help in this regard shall be appreciated by O.T.

"It is so outrageous and that is why it may work" he told Czeslawa.

A few days later he was told the name and the method of contacting the Polish underground people in Kosice. He was all set to go.

At work he told Herr Hoffmann that he volunteered into the German Army to fight the Bolsheviks. Mr. Hoffmann was so pleased that he paid him an extra months wages.

"Remember, Edward, when you come back your job will be here waiting for you."

"Thank you Herr Hoffmann, maybe by that time I'll come back as a new owner."

"Ha, ha. And I'll be the new ski instructor." Herr Hoffmann was laughing so hard that Edward though his sides may split.

Saying good-bye to Czeslawa was the hardest and the most difficult one he has done in his entire life. There was nobody in the world whom he loved more and yet he had to leave.

"I understand you Edward and understand why you are doing it. I prayed last night and I know that you will return to me and Danuta."

She kissed him so hard that his lips were bleeding. Danuta was told that daddy is going on a trip and will be back sometime later.

"Will you buy me a new toy?"

"Sweetheart, I promise." He kissed her and she went back to sleep. Her brown hair was spread on the white pillow case. Edward wiped the tears from his eyes.

He still had to see the Bujnickis who knew about his plans from Czeslawa.

"Don't worry Edzio, we'll take good care of Czeslawa and

Danuta. We want you to know that we have made a will and left it with Father Pankracy Galczynski. Should we die the house will belong to Czeslawa. We have some nephews and nieces but we don't know where they are and besides we never cared for them. There is nobody whom we love more than Czeslawa and Danuta. We also know that your going to fight for Poland, so this is our debt and we are paying it off."

Edward held both Bujnickis in his arms. The tears were flowing on their worried faces.

"Edward before you go sit on the bed for a minute, it will bring you luck."

That was the custom of the people. He also knew that a team of horses were in front of the house. The orders given to the driver was to take Pan Daszkiewicz to the nearest railroad station. Edward wad dressed in a warm civilian coat underneath that coat was a freshly pressed O.T. uniform. He had only one valise with well selected items for the journey. In his head he had memorized the name, the code and the method of contact his "angel". Edward was on the first leg of a long trip. As Confucius said: the longest trip starts with the first step. Today Edward made that step.

CHAPTER 18

The horse driven carriage brought Edward to the railroad station at Chabowka. He dismissed the driver about 100 meters from the station itself.

"Should I wait here for a while. Pan Daszkiewicz?"

"It is not necessary, Jan. You can go right back."

Edward took his suitcase and walked towards the station. At the window marked "KASA" there was a "Bekanntmachung-Obwieszczenie" an announcement in German and Polish that the train to Kosice was canceled till further notice. When asked, the stationmaster himself didn't know when the connection would be resumed.

Edward ran out of the station in an off chance that the driver might still be in the area, however, there was no trace of the driver or the wagon.

While contemplating his next move. Edward noticed a small convoy of three trucks pulling in front of the station. Out of the cabin of the first truck a man dressed in the uniform of O.T. emerged stopping a passerby, a local peasant dressed in "Goral" style in sleeveless, embroidered fur jacket "sierdak", wearing a black felt hat and carrying a heavy, hand carved wooded cane the "ciupaga."

Whatever question the O.T. man asked the "goral" just shrugged his shoulders.

Without hesitation Edward walked up to the O.T. man and asked in German if he could be of help.

"I asked that idiot for the road to Presov or Kosice, but that fellow either didn't understand me or didn't want to give the right directions. By the way, how come you speak such a good German?"

"Kamerad, I'm also with the O.T."

"Then why are you wearing a civilian coat?"

"Look underneath that coat. I have a girl in this region and her family doesn't want anybody wearing a German uniform of any kind to come around. Do you understand my situation if so can you give me a ride to Kosice. I'll show you how to get there the best way."

"It is not up to me. I have to check with my Chief, Juozas Petrauskas."

"If you want me, I'll talk to him myself."

"No, you just wait here a minute."

He didn't have to wait a minute because the Chief came to see what was going on.

They started to speak German but later switched to rapid Lithuanian, which Edward couldn't follow, but working at O.T. with so many Lithuanians he picked up a few words, especially the word "spiegas" was similar to Polish word "szpieg".

"No, I am not a spy. Here are my papers, I was supposed to take the train but the train was canceled. If you don't believe me send a man inside and verify my story. I'll wait here."

The Chief Petrauskas sent a man to check on Edward's story. The man came back and reported back to the Chief.

"Alright, you can come with us, sit in the front truck and point out the road."

"Thank you Chief Petrauskas."

The foremost Polish poet Adam Mickiewicz spoke of Lithuania as his motherland. Maybe it was true at that time. Now Edward hated the Lithuanians as the worst German Vassals.

The truck loaded with supplies including cement were moving slowly.

The driver introduced himself as Jonas Zemaitis and offered Edward a cigarette, they talked about the war and women, without realizing they had reached Kosice.

"The Chief forbade me from telling you that we are continuing to Debreczen."

"In that case, just drop me off in the center of the town. Auf wiedersehen."

Edward got off because Debreczen was in the opposite direction of his journey. Kosice was only the first stop, he still had to make his way to Budapeszt, where he was ordered to contact the Polish underground organization.

On the next crossroad he found a little kiosk. He asked the man in the kiosk for a way to reach Budapeszt. The man speaking in Slovak, a language similar to Polish, told him that a few blocks further was a bus stop for buses going to Budapeszt.

"You had better hurry up if you want to catch a bus today."

Edward didn't need further encouragement he walked as fast as he could on broken down sidewalks along the unpaved road. Small houses on both sides of the street had windows so low that he could see the people sitting at their tables.

He kept shifting the valise from hand to hand. Although he packed into that valise a minimum of items, but whatever he packed in it, he would surely need and that would include an innocent looking tin of black shoe polish. On the bottom of which he hid four gold British sovereign. On the inside of the box, with a nail he also scratched slightly the street name and the number of the house in reverse, the Istvan street number 63 was supposed to be read as 36.

After a couple more blocks he came upon a much wider asphalt paved road. At the bus stop there were several people lingering about. A large wooden bench was occupied mainly by old men and women, Some of the younger women congregated separately, holding their packages in large scarves or baskets. There were no men barring few young boys.

While Edward approached the bus stop from the opposite side came two members of the Hungarian Border Police the "Csendor" wearing colorful hats adorned with feathers somewhat resembling roosters rather than policemen.

The older and probably senior of the two policemen asked in an "official" tone:

"Igazolvany" which Edward understood as "papers". He complied and showed his O.T. papers. The policeman looked at Edwards "Kennkarte" and kept asking questions, which Edward didn't understand.

"Ich verstehe Sie nichts." I don't understand you.

The policeman started to speak German, albeit a very poor one but Edward understood him this time. "Why the civilian coat?"

"Mine was stolen the other day in a restaurant. I didn't have a chance to find another one."

The policeman seemed to be satisfied with the answer.

"Noch eine halbe Stunde zum Autobus Abfahr." Another half an hour till departure.

They saluted and walked away.

The entire scene was watched by the people at the bus stop. There was nothing else to do but to wait. Eventually, an old crowded blue painted bus pulled to the bus stop.

The old men and women that were sitting on the bench, ran towards the bus with a speed defying their ages.

Edward helped an old peasant woman to put her packages on the top of the bus along with the other passengers who were doing the same. With a piece of cord that the woman gave him, he fastened the packages to the bus railings. By the time he boarded the bus and paid the fare, there wasn't a place where to sit for the long trip to Budapeszt.

The same old woman whom Edward helped had a seat secured by a friend of hers She motioned for him to sit next to her. Still there wasn't enough room. Edward improvised by sitting partially on a valise and the little room that the woman provided.

She kept asking him questions in Hungarian while pointing to him with her finger:

"Lengyel". To which he responded with: "Ich verstehe Sie nicht."

Finally, someone else said: "Du bist ein Pole?" He shook his head and the conversation died out.

They drove in silence on mostly paved roads, hitting a pothole from time to time. Each pothole added to Edward's discomfort.

The old woman took a salami sandwich out of her bag and without a word gave it to Edward. The wonderful smell of Hungarian salami made Edward aware of how hungry he really was. He had some food in his valise, but the bus was too crowded to open the valise. He ate that sandwich with gusto and drank red wine from a bottle that the woman gave him. The bottle had a label with a picture of a bull. He welcomed that drink with a smile.

Smiles are contagious and the woman gave him her best toothless smile. Most of the passengers either ate or slept but the bus kept on moving, passing several villages and small towns. In some of those towns the bus stopped for refuel and let the people use the toilet facilities.

A few kilometers outside the last service area, the bus slowed down to let a large herd of cattle cross the street. In doing so the bus stalled right in the middle of railroad tracks.

The driver and the fare collector jumped out of the bus and lifted the hood, working feverishly to get the engine started. The bus wouldn't start and was too heavy to be pushed. From afar a whistle of a locomotive was announcing its arrival. Some of the passengers started to panic and abandoned the bus. Edward jumped out of the bus and went to the desperate driver. He quickly assessed the situation.

"Give me a screwdriver" he said pointing with his finger while turning it at the same time. He was understood immediately. In less that a minute he had the engine perking like a kitten. It was a trick he has learned in O.T. and in Russia. The bus got off the tracks just in time, when a long train roared by. The bus collected the passengers, who left the bus in fear of loosing their lives. Someone started to applaud, soon joined by the rest of the passengers, including the grateful driver and the fare collector who made room for Edward to sit up front. Once comfortably seated for a change, the bus driver handed Edward a bottle of Slivovitz. Another woman handed him a large sausage and piece of black bread. They drank and ate, conversing only in German. They asked where in Budapeszt he was going to. Edward gave them the name of the hotel where he was going to stay for a few days. There was a smile on their faces when he mentioned the name of the hotel:

"Szent Kiralyi Pensio."

"It is more of a rooming house than a hotel" and after a heated conversation in Hungarian between the driver and the fare collector, the driver said:

"Your "pensionat" is just a few blocks away from our regular run, we'll drop you off right there. At least we can do that for rescuing our bus."

That was really god news because it was very late in the evening and Edward didn't know Budapeszt at all. He had never been there.

He was dropped off with everybody on the bus waving to him. One old man handed Edward a piece of farmer cheese wrapped in a clean handkerchief, but Edward declined the offer. Just by seeing a small part he deduced that Budapeszt must be a beautiful city, but right now all he could think of was a nice, clean bed. All his bones ached from sitting on the valise.

The "Szent Kiralyi Pensio" was an old dilapidated 2 story high building. In the lobby of the "hotel" the office manager was just locking up his tiny office when Edward walked in.

"I would like a room" politely said Edward.

"So would I, we have no rooms whatsoever." Replied the old office manager.

"I'm a friend of Father Bela Vary." Said Edward while at the same time handing him a 5 Reichsmarks.

"That's different, why didn't you say that in the first place." He gave him the keys to the room #210 on the second floor.

"Come down tomorrow morning and sign in. I have to keep some of your papers. It is too late for it tonight. I'll see you in the morning. Good Night."

"Thank you very much Herr...." "Felix is my name". "Then Good night, Herr Felix."

Edward found the room and the bathroom down the hall. The room itself was occupied basically by a bed, there was no room for anything else. The only window faced the side street, it was nice and quiet. That was all that Edward needed, because he was sound asleep in minutes. There was a smile on his tired face. He was in Budapeszt.

Edward slept like only tired people sleep, but he was awakened by a loud conversation of hotel guests walking up and down the hallway.

It took a few minutes for him to realize that he wasn't home any longer. Czeslawa's voice and touch were missing and so was Danuta's bubbly laughter.

For the first time since he has left his home in Zakopane, a doubt crept in. Was he doing the right thing, leaving his family behind? The die was cast.

He went to the bathroom at the end of the corridor only to discover that the bathroom was occupied. After a while he came back to his room. On the second try he found the bathroom vacant. Finished with that chore and dressed in a black turtle neck sweater and gray trousers he went down to register.

Herr Felix greeted him with "Jo reggelt."

"Good morning to you too, Herr Felix."

"I need you to leave me any kind of identity card that you could do without for a while. It is only a formality."

"Will this do it?" Edward left an old O.T. Kennkarte.

"This will be just fine. Father Bela Vary should be here shortly. He is interested in people from Poland. In the meantime "Kerek egy csesze kavet." The last word wounded like coffee.

"If you are speaking about coffee, the answer is gladly."

"Go to the room on your right hand side. It serves as a cafeteria. Ask for Magda, she'll serve you breakfast. Just show he your room keys."

"The cafeteria" was just another room with four small tables, all of them occupied, and a counter behind which stood a middle aged, plump woman.

Edward came up to her and asked: "Are you Magda?" showing her the keys. She shook her head and pointed to the items on the counter: coffee, rolls, marmalade and hard boiled eggs.

A chipped crystal salt shaker completed the choice.

Edward learned to eat whenever food was available and today was no exception. Since there was no room at the tables he ate at the counter standing up.

A few feet away at one of the tables, four men were having breakfast. Edward thought that they conversed in Polish. To be sure he moved a bit closer to them and then the conversation stopped altogether. The face of one of the men at that table was very familiar but Edward couldn't place it at the moment.

By the time he had finished his coffee it came back to him. It was a fellow combatant, who participated with Edward's partisan group in destroying a small railroad bridge near the town of Sobieszyn, some 24 kilometers north-east of Pulawy, about a year ago. He was an explosive expert but he lost half of his pinky finger in his left hand, the only casualty of that mission.

Amazing how much blood came out of that finger, Edward was the person, who stopped the blood flow.

It was Bolek Skurka. Edward remember his name too. Perhaps it wasn't he just another fellow that resembled him. Bolek had a busy mustache ala Marshal Pilsudski and didn't wear glasses. Their eyes met for a split second and the man turned his head without a sign of recognition. After all, Edward changed too.

After finishing breakfast he went back to Felix at the reception desk.

"Father Vary should be here any minute now, have a cigarette."

"Thank you Herr Felix." He lit the offered cigarette, inhaling it's aroma deeply.

Half way through the cigarette. Father Bela Vary made his appearance. A pleasant looking, middle aged completely bald man of ruddy complexion dressed in a black suit with white collar walked straight to Felix.

They spoke Hungarian, which Edward couldn't follow, after a while Felix switched to German:

"This is a lost sheep from your herd, Father."

"Lets you and I take a walk in the fresh air." Said Father Vary in a combination of Chech and Polish.

"Very well, Father, after you."

"My name is Bela Vary, I was instructed to provide you with any help I'm capable of giving. My designated name is "Angel."

Edward started to laugh. While in Cracow he was told that he would meet his "Angel". How apropos.

"Forgive me Father, but I don't see your wings."

"They are well hidden in the day time."

"Are you helping us because of your church affiliation?"

"Partly only, don't forget also that our Istvan Batory became your King Jan Batory."

"I didn't mean any offense, Father."

"I know that son, so let's get to the business at hand. You will have to meet with "Eva."

"Who is she?"

Now it was Father Vary's turn to laugh.

"It is not a "she". Eva stands for Evacuation Team. They will send a person to meet with you on any of two bridges. On even numbered days it will be on Elizabeth Bridge called in Hungarian Erszebet between 11-12 o'clock or on odd numbered days on another bridge called chain bridge Lanchid, hours 10-11 in the morning. Always keep the third button on your coat unbuttoned. The contacting person will have the same and will address you in the following manner: "Pardon me Sir you have lost a button" to which you'll reply" "I didn't loose it, I just forgot to button it." Follow that person about 20 feet behind him and wait till the person talks to you. Is that clear?"

"Yes, Father crystal clear."

"Any other questions, son?"

"Just two, Father. How long do I have to show up on those

bridges? The other question is if you know any of the men sitting in the cafeteria?"

"The answer to your first question is about four days. If nobody contacts you during that time, just tell Felix that you were stood up and he'll get in touch with the proper people. As far as the other question is concerned, remember and remember it well. I don't know anybody, you don't know anybody and the less curious you are the better off we all will be. Otherwise, you and many good people will find themselves on Andrasy Utca."

"What's that?"

"It's just a jail. I need you now to follow me to the church to take your picture, but I need you in a white shirt and a tie in order for you to look respectful on your new papers. Go upstairs and change. If you don't have a shirt and a tie. Felix will provide you with it."

"No need to bother Felix. I have them both. It will take me but a minute, Father."

He ran up quickly to his room and changed. Working with underground teams he learned not to ask too many questions. It was exactly the same.

When Father Vary saw Edward emerge from the door he started to walk. Edward followed him in a distance. From time to time Father Vary would exchange few words or a smile with parishioners in the area. Once inside the church, Father Vary knelt down and crossed himself. Edward followed the suit.

Father Vary pointed to a confessional booth. Edward entered it. Suddenly one of the walls opened up to display a small room serving as a photo studio.

"I'm going to take your picture, be yourself and look natural, that is fine. You are all done. I just looked at the watch, you still have time to reach the Elizabeth bridge in time for your rendezvous. Here are some Pengos and change in Filers and a sketch how to reach that bridge. If you need to ask for the bridge just say: "Hol van az Erzsebet hid? Do you think you can memorize that?"

"I'll try, father, let me just repeat it a few times."

"You are doing fine, son. Good luck."

There was no problem in finding the bridge. He could read a map since his scout days. Budapeszt reminded Edward of Cracow. Both old, historic towns that remembered the medieval times. He reached the beautiful bridge, walking slowly across like so many other people on their "Mittag-pause". In his white shirt and tie he blended with the crowd. The third button of his coat was intentionally left unbuttoned. He carefully observed the people around him but nobody wore a coat in similar fashion.

An hour and fifteen minutes passed by but to no avail. He smoked during that time six precious cigarettes, got some encouraging smiles from young women but no contact. There was nothing left but to return. On the way back to the rooming house he walked briskly like a person with things to do.

Felix had one look at Edward's disappointed face and said to him:

"Magda just made a delicious goulash, go and get yourself a bowl. One always thinks better on a full stomach."

Some people were already in the cafeteria. Magda without being asked, handed Edward a bowl with goulash.

The goulash was the very best that Edward ever ate. Afraid to have his shirt spotted he went upstairs to change back into his turtle neck sweater. Someone knocked at his door. Edward opened it for the house maid who said but one word: "Felix" and pointed down with her hand. The message was understood. Felix wanted to see him. He found Felix in a deep conversation with an elderly lady. He was telling her something in a soothing tone of voice, because the woman seemed to be in a highly agitated state. After a while she calmed down and gave Felix a friendly smile. He responded by kissing her hand. After a brief good-bye she left the room.

To answer a puzzling look on Edward's face, Felix said:

"You don't want to know about her. This is not why I asked for you. I just received word from base 'Romek". They want you to go there at once. The address is Vaci Utca #167. It is about three blocks from the former Polish Consulate. Take the trolley car #6 around the corner from us till you reach Dob Utca, walk east one bock. The number 167 should be on your left side. Knock slowly on the door four times and ask for Bilewicz. Do you have enough change in Fillers for the ride?"

"Yes, Felix, I have."

"Very well then, take off."

As told, Edward walked to the nearby corner where the trolleys made their infrequent stops. The third trolley bore the sign #6. The car was crowded but Edward managed to get a seat. Somehow being seated was to be less visible.

He was grateful to the conductor for announcing each stop. The trolley was moving along the most elegant part of the city.

One of the riders pointed to a large edifice bearing Moses' tablets, Edward caught the word "Zhido Tabak-Dohany Templum. The street swerved to the left and the sight of the Jewish Temple disappeared.

Some minutes later the conductor yelled out" "Dob Utca" and Edward pushing some people out of the way stepped down from the trolley car.

The number 167 was exactly where Felix described. Four slow knocks at the door and the door was opened by a young woman in a black skirt and white blouse.

"I was told to ask for Mr. Bilewicz."

"Your name?"

"Edward Daszkiewicz."

"Please follow me" she led him through a long corridor. On the walls hung several large oil paintings depicting Polish kings. She knocked on the door marked number 2. He wondered if the number 2 belonged to the second department dealing with intelligence matter.

"Come in" they heard an authorative, man's voice. She introduced both men to each other.

"Captain Bilewicz please meet Edward Daszkiewicz."

Captain Bilewicz was a man in his early forties with a receding hair line and well trimmed mustache. The man was every bit of a soldier but wearing a civilian suit.

Behind the desk, on the wall was a large white-red Polish flag and two pictures of Marshals Pilsudski and Smigly-Rydz.

"Panno Agnieszko, please leave us alone."

"Of course, Captain. Should I bring in some tea?"

"That would be nice."

"Daszkiewicz, do sit down. It is our understanding that you wish to join our fighting men."

"Yes captain."

"It is my job to send the best and the most qualified men. Smuggling men over borders is a costly and dangerous proposition. Is that clear, Daszkiewicz?"

"Yes Sir."

"Where do you hail from?"

"I was born in Drohobycz in 1920, Sir."

"Wait a minute,

does the name of Kazimierz-Josef Daszkiewicz ring a bell?"

"It's the name of my uncle, my father's younger brother. We didn't hear about him since the September Campaign of 39. We were told that he was killed."

"No, Edward he is very much alive and doing a fantastic job for us. He was also my roommate in Officer's School."

"Where is he now?"

"I can't tell you but he is fine and safe. Have you heard about Stanislaw Maczek from Drohobycz?"

"I heard my mother mention that name, she is related to that family, a second cousin or so, I can't tell you more."

"That is fine, you told me what I wanted to hear so far."

A polite knock at the door and Miss Agnieszka walked in carrying a tray with tea, sugar and cookies.

"Please ask Chaplain Ziemba to join us. Let him bring a bible and you bring a steno pad."

Miss Agnieszka went out of the room and in a few minutes came back with an elderly gentleman, stiff as a rod, dressed in a black suit. Underneath his arm was visible a bible and a large wooden cross.

"Kapelan Ziemba. I would like you to swear in this young fellow."

"Please put your left hand on the bible and lift your right hand, repeat after me: "I, say your name, do solemnly swear that the deposition I am about to give shall be the truth, the whole truth and nothing but the truth, so help me God."

After the swearing in, the Chaplain left the room and Captain Bilewicz took over.

"Tell me everything about yourself from your childhood till the present. Don't skip anything no matter how ugly or unpleasant. So go right ahead. Miss Agnieszka, are you ready too?"

Edward started to speak about his years in Public School, Scouts, Gymnazium, his friendship with Henryk Kaplinski the war of 1939, his induction into the Red Army his capture by the Germans in 1941, their escape from captivity together with Henryk, their O.T. period, his love for Czeslawa (he broke down for a short time) their partisans activity, the death of Czeslawa's parents, his escape to Zakopane the unexpected meeting with Henryk and finally his decision to join the Polish Army.

Miss Agnieszka wrote down every word, she was visibly moved.

"Yes Edward, we can definitely use you."

"Captain, the tea is completely cold."

"Never mind, we'll drink it cold. I'll add some "Malinowka" to it. It will be fine."

From his desk he took out an original Baczewski's raspberry liquor from Lwow and poured a generous amount into each glass.

"You shouldn't be drinking, Miss Agnieszka, you are still a child."

"Begging Captain's pardon, may I remind the Captain that I am a sergeant of the Polish Army."

"Yes I know, I was just kidding."

"Edward finish your tea and get back to your hotel. We'll get back to you within a few days. By that time we shall have the proper papers and assignment for you. One more advise. Stay low, don't go out unless you must. Is that understood?"

"Yes Sir and thank you Sir." They shook hands.

"Sergeant Agnieszka, show Mr. Daszkiewicz to the door."

Edward walked back to the trolley stop at Dob Utca just in time to see a large Police contingent surround the trolley and checking each passenger's papers.

He kept going, after all it wasn't the number 6 that he was concerned with. By the time he came back, everything was peaceful again. A number 6 trolley pulled in with a screech. The trolley was even more crowded than before. Most likely a lot of working people were returning home by this hour.

Edward reached his oasis the "Szent Kiralyi Pensio" without a mishap, totally emotionally exhausted. It was an unusual day in his unusual life. Just to hear about his uncle being alive and to find out that he was an officer was exciting.

Edward never thought about his uncle being officer material. Once Edward's mother showed him a school report belonging to her brother Kazimierz-Josef there were 5 Fs and 2 Ds. Uncle Kazimierz had to repeat that school year. Edward's mother wanted to scare him from doing the same as Kazimierz.

"Don't worry mama' he remembered saying at that time "I'll do much better in school, even better than my friend Kaplinski."

And now his uncle according to Captain Bilewicz was a good officer. God really works in mysterious ways. Felix was gone for the day and nobody knew his whereabouts, but Magda was still at her post. All she had to offer at this time of the evening was some ersatz coffee and bread with jam, for which Edward was grateful.

Having had a bite he went back to his room, got undressed and with his thoughts about Czeslawa he fell asleep.

The next morning didn't differ from the previous one. After a breakfast at Magda's he went out for a possible early meeting, this time at the chain brige-Lanchid.

The beautiful bridge over the Danube, connected Buda with Peszt. While observing people passing by he still managed to notice the splendid panorama of Peszt with its Parliament Building from the Buda side of the bridge.

Another pearl was Margit Sziget Isle quite visible from the same place on the bridge. Strauss must have been color blind because the murky waters of the Danube hardly resembled any shade of blue.

An hour and half passed by and nobody contacted Edward, who disappointed came back to the rooming house.

Felix whom Edward was about to greet, put his finger over his mouth, pointed with his finger to Madga's cafeteria and then to the ceiling.

The message was clear, not to talk to Felix now, see Magda and to go back to his room.

This time he didn't have to show Magda his room keys. She gave him two heaping plates, one with stuffed cabbage and the other with boiled potatoes. He moved to the table with one chair vacant. He sat down to eat, paying no attention to the other people at his table. The two men and a woman spoke Hungarian. Edward concentrated on his meal, the food was simply delicious, Magda was an outstanding cook. In gratitude he blew her a kiss to which he responded with a rare smile.

He found his room freshly made up especially the bed that looked inviting. He took off his jacket and sweater and laid down the bed wondering if Felix would come up or he simply meant for Edward to remain in his room.

Closing his eyes to recapture the day's happenings he fell asleep until the middle of the night when he woke up and realized that he was still dressed. A nearby church bells struck three times. It was three o'clock in the morning. He got undressed and went back to sleep.

Two more frustrating days, spend on walking the bridges passed by. On the fourth day as he was about to give up, a young girl, maybe 10 or 11 years old came up to Edward and addressed him in Polish:

"Sir, it looks like you've lost a button on your coat."

"No, I just left it unbuttoned, the same as you."

"My mother wants to speak with you, please follow me."

The young girl, dressed in a navy coat with a gray fur collar was walking ahead of him. Her two braids were shaking with each step. She reminded Edward of his own Danuta. He felt a pang on his heart.

At the end of the bridge, the girl stopped a woman pushing a baby carriage. They both turned around and faced Edward. The woman, smiling broadly said to Edward:

"Sorry, I'm late, I couldn't help it. Please talk to me and in a while look inside the carriage. Next to my baby there is a newspaper "Szabadsag" inside which are your documents. Take out the newspaper carefully and walk with me another few minutes, then take off your hat as to say Good-bye.

"I understand" and he kept a pleasant enough conversation, smiling frequently. She must have liked him, because his smiles were reciprocated.

"By the way, my name is Aniela."

Was that a coincidence because her name was a variation of the word "Angel".

In a while, Aniela pushed her carriage to the side, Edward stuck his head inside the carriage, next to the sleeping baby there was a newspaper which he took out. Through the midst of the paper he felt a hard envelope, containing his documents.

They kept walking and talking like old friends. To a casual observer at least.

"You can leave now. Go with God."

"Thank you very much Aniela, I didn't see the baby but I'm sure she or he will be as pretty as you."

"It is a girl."

On impulse he kissed the young girl, walking beside her mother, on her head and went back to his hotel.

Not until safe in his room did he have a chance to examine his papers.

He was still Edward Daszkiewicz, but now he was an employee of Schenker G.mb.H, a large export-import company also dabbling in transport. Also included was a letter of introduction singed by the company's branch president Herr Friedbert Kuezel and countersigned in green ink no less, by the vice-president Herr Peter Johannes. The branch itself was located in Cracow on Dluga Street #16. Herr Edward Daszkiewicz "spediteur" acting on behalf of the company was charges with the responsibility of arranging transportation of goods from Port of Constanza to Turkey and Syria. Schenker Co. being a Treuhandler fur Reichssicherheit Hauptamt (S.S.) requested any and all help to be given to Herr Daszkiewicz. A bunch of calling cards with the name of Edward Daszkiewicz were also included. It was a nice touch, Edward thought. The stationary was undoubtedly original, signatures and stamps probably not.

The name of Schenker Company was vaguely familiar. As a ski instructor at "Kasprowy" he rented a pair of skis to a clerk of that company by the name of Bozydar or Edzio Kubec. He also remembered that the A.K. the Polish underground Army killed a high ranking officer of that Company by the name of Gogulka or Kokulka. In reprisal, the Gestapo killed 25 Poles.

The rest of the evening he spent on memorizing the names of "his" Company executives and the telephone numbers.

Someone was walking in the hallway and stopped in front of Edward's room #210. The knob of his door started to turn. Edward went to check who the intruder might be. To his surprise it was Felix.

"Listen carefully, I don't have much time. You are leaving tomorrow morning at 6 o'clock sharp. You'll be picked up in front of "Szent Kiralyi Pensio" and driven to Keleti Palya Udvar, the East Railroad Station on Rakoczy Utca. Here are your train tickets to Constanza via Bucarest and 25 British pounds. This is all the money we can spare. Should you meet any other people in the morning, keep you conversation to a minimum or even better, don't talk at all. My gift to you is this bottle of Tokay wine-Voros Bor. Your

O.T. Kennkarte will stay here, we may use it in the future. God bless you."

Felix shook Edward's hand and left the room. Patience was never one of Edward's virtues, he still will have to wait for the morning. In the meantime, he carefully repacked his valise. The contents of his shoe polish can, wasn't disturbed. He had better get some rest, he thought, tomorrow is going to be a big day. A day that will bring him closer to Bucarest and closer to his destination: The Free Polish Army of Gen. Anders.

CHAPTER 19

Some people have inborn alarm clocks and nobody has to wake them up to tell them what time it is. Edward belonged to that type of people. During his brief stint with the partisans group, he was ready for his watch, no matter what time of the day or night.

This time he woke up at 5 o'clock in the morning giving himself a full hour to get ready. As befitted a Schenker's employee, he was dressed in his only civilian suit. He went down the stairs, carrying his valise. The door to Magda's cafeteria was open. Magda was busy preparing breakfast for the "hotels" guests. Noticing Edward she invited him in and put a bowl of hot porridge and a cup of tea and saccharine. He quickly consumed the food in front of him and said good-bye to Magda.

It was still dark and chilly outside. A couple dressed in winter clothing, their coat collars upturned, stood nearby. At 6 o'clock sharp a slow moving vehicle stopped by the curb. The couple got in the back of the vehicle with their two pieces of luggage. Edward hesitated at first but the driver mentioned his first name, dispelled his doubts and he jumped in, right next to the driver. His valise had to be put in the back, next to the couple.

An eerie silence prevailed during the first 20 minutes of the ride. Edward heard a whisper in French, but he wasn't sure. The driver whose face seemed to be chiseled in stone concentrated on driving. After a while he took two cigarettes out, offering one to Edward, who promptly lit both. Still no words were spoken.

The closer they came to the railroad station, the more traffic they encountered, traveling on Rakoczy Udca. The Eastern Station- Keleti Palya Udvar was somewhat illuminated and visible from a distance.

The driver stopped near the station, allowing the couple from the back to get off. They proceeded to the station on foot.

"You stay!" and the driver moved to the main entrance. He stopped the car again, got off and opened the car door for Edward and took his valise and put it down on the sidewalk.

With a friendly wave of the hand he got back into his car and drove off without saying a word.

Edward picked up his suitcase and went inside a very large and ornate hall.

A red cap porter approached Edward and asked if he could be of help, to which Edward agreed.

He still had some Pengos, for some reason he felt that Police don't stop passengers whose luggage is being carried by porters.

"Where to, Sir?"

"Bucharest."

"Do you have your ticket already?"

"Yes, I do."

"In that case, I'll take you directly to your train, please follow me, Sir."

They were stopped only once and that was before boarding the train itself.

Edward's "angel" furnished him with a ticket for the first class wagon. The rationale most likely was that any member of Schenker's traveling on Company business would automatically travel first class. Also the Police don't look for criminals and escapees within the confines of the first class.

The porter brought Edward to the first class wagon, where the conductor seeing how generous Edward tipped the porter, took over.

The conductor, carrying Edward's valise brought him to the assigned compartment. He politely knocked on the door and upon hearing the word "come in" he walked in and put the valise in an upper, overhead bin.

There were two people inside, a ranking officer of the Rumanian Army and an unlisted man who was busy assisting his officer in taking off a pair of gleaming riding boots.

The officer smiled and said something to Edward in Rumanian or Hungarian, Since Edward didn't understand either, he answered in German:

"Guten Morgen, Ich sprech nur Deutsch." I speak German only.

The officer replied in German introducing himself as Major Petru Enescu of the Rumanian Army.

"Edward Daszkiewicz" but he pronounced his name sounding more German-Dashkievitz.

"Are you related to the famous composer Enescu?"

"Yes I am said the Major beaming." So you've heard about Enescu?"

"Of course, good music doesn't have boundaries, but you Major seem to be far from home"

"Army business, just a short trip to Budapeszt and back. What is bringing you to Budapeszt and taking you to Bucharest, Herr Dashkievitz?"

"I'm with the Schenker company but not at liberty to discuss the nature of my assignment. Hope you don't mind.."

Major Enescu was so pleased to hear that Edward knew about his composer-relative that he didn't mind whether Edward told him about his activities or not.

"I understand your situation completely. Would you like some coffee? I'll send Corporal Mirceu to bring it. I hope that you'll do me the honor and lunch with me later on."

"I'll be delighted, Major."

Further conversation was interrupted by a loud: "ALL ABOARD" and series of whistles. The train started to move slowly picking up speed. A few minutes later, Corporal Mirceu came in carrying a tray with coffee and fresh kaiser rolls.

"Herr Dashkievitz, make yourself comfortable and give your shoes to Mirceu and by the time you finish your coffee, your shoes will shine like mirrors. No one in the Rumanian Army can do a better job, trust me, I know."

His shoes could really stand a shine, so he took off his shoes and gave them to the Corporal.

"When in Rome, do as the Rumanians do."

"Herr Dashkievitz, that is very funny."

Their conversation covered topics such as food, wine, women and finally war. They both agreed that the war will be won by Hitler despite the temporary setbacks.

In the meantime Corporal Mirceu brought back Edward's shoes. The shoes shone like mirrors, even the shoe laces were replaced. Major Enescu was right, his man servant was the best.

"Please forgive me Herr Dashkievitz, I have some paper work to do, that requires my attention."

"You go right ahead, Sir. Don't disturb yourself on my account."

"In that case, I'll take off my tunic. Might as well be comfortable."

To Edward's surprise, the Major wore a corset. Up to this moment Edward thought that corset wearing by Rumanian officers was just a rumor, but it wasn't as he could plainly see.

The Major was talking to the Corporal at length in Rumanian and then addressed Edward back in German.

'I've asked Mirceu to prepare lunch for two of us, right here in our compartment. I still have lots of work to put up with, I hope you don't mind if we eat here. It would simplify my life."

'No at all, my dear Major. It will be much nicer to eat here instead of a crowded and noisy restaurant wagon."

Edward was genuinely pleased, because he noticed that the Major and his compartment were seldom disturbed by conductors or other officials.

While Mirceu went out to prepare lunch and the Major was busy with his work, Edward to show his indifference took out a German newspaper purchased in Budapeszt.

The Major finished his work about the same time, that Edward completed reading the newspaper, Once the Major's papers were removed from the drop-leaf table. Mirceu covered it with a white table cloth, plates and the napkins and silverware were elegantly set up.

Edward removed from his valise a bottle of Voros-Bor wine, given to him by Felix.

"My contribution, Major."

"It is quite timely, Herr Dashkievitz. I've asked Mirceu to prepare a few Rumanian dishes, that you may enjoy. We're going to have "Mititeu" sausages, "Carnati" chopped meat and "Branza" cheese with "Mamaliga" a corn meal. Your wine will compliment Mirceu's menu."

"Just to listen to that delicious food makes my mouth water, Major."

Corporal Mirceu really outdid himself. The food was simply put, excellent. They raised their glasses to toast when the door to their compartment was opened and four uniformed men walked in.

Two of them were the Rumanian Border Police the "Graniceri" and the other two belonged to "Vama", the Customs.

They all saluted the Major, a brisk conversation in Rumanian followed which Edward didn't understand a word. One of the "Granicer" pointed to Edward, to which Major replied in German:

"He is with me."

Further conversation in Rumanian ensued.

"Herr Dashkievitz, they want to know how long and where are you going to stay in Bucharest. What should I tell them?"

"I don't know myself. Can you recommend a decent hotel in Bucharest?"

"Certainly, the Hotel Athenaeum and you'll be my guest."

Major repeated Edward's answer in Rumanian, which seemed to satisfy the "Graniceri".

Major's offer of a glass of wine was politely declined and as he told Edward later, they all apologized for disturbing their lunch.

The meal and the host turned to be a very enjoyable experience for Edward. The cigarettes at the end of the meal never tasted better.

"Forgive me Herr Dashkievitz, but I just recalled that I have some unfinished paper work."

"By all means, Major. Don't mind me. I'll just read or even better, I'll take a nap."

Edward was able to read for a few minutes. The combination of heavy food, wine and the motion of the train, put him to sleep. He didn't know when Mirceu put a blanket over him.

He slept soundly and only his urgent need to go to the bathroom woke him up.

"Did you have a nice nap?"

"I did, Major, I did. It seemed to me that I sleep on trains the best."

"Isn't that a truth, I need to stretch my legs a bit, would you care to join me for a little walk?"

"Gladly, Major, just give me a minute, I'll be right back."

They walked the length of the train several times, back and forth.

"How about a cup of tea, Major?"

"That's not a bad idea, we still have a few good hours till we get to Bucharest. Why don't you stay a few days and see the sight?"

"Nothing would please me more, however, I must get to Constanza. My orders call for getting there as soon as possible."

"I can appreciate that, duty above all. It's a pity that you don't have the time to see our city and the beautiful lake Lacul Cismigiu. Maybe on your way back. Perhaps I can be of help, once we get to the Bucharest's Gara De Nord Station, I'll buy your ticket for Constanza."

"Major, you are the most understanding and the most charming man I have ever come across. I don't know how to thank you or repay your kindness."

"Never mind, consider it done. Now let's go back to the compartment. Do you play cards or chess?'

"Just chess Major."

"What about our tea? We can always send Mirceu to fetch some."

"Let's go then. There is no sense in wasting time."

"I'm ready if you are, Sir."

They walked back to their compartment elated with the prospect of the chess game. Edward glanced through the window of one compartment, he was sure that he recognized the face of Bolek Skurka, one of the four men he met in the rooming house in Budapeszt. If the face looked a bit changed, the hand that held the newspaper had a half of a pinkie finger missing. That was Bolek.

As soon as they reached their compartment, Major Enescu sent his man servant for tea and out of his attaché case he removed a small travel size chess set.

Edward drew white pieces, giving him somewhat of an advantage at least in the beginning of the game. Sicilian defense or no Sicilian defense didn't help him against a superior player.

Although he managed to win two games, the bulk of games played were won by the Major, who was as pleasant in winning as in loosing.

Edward threw his king down and said:

"Major, I surrender to the superior forces."

"In that case I accept your surrender and suggest that we adjourn to the dinning car, my treat. Mirceu's tea is cold anyway."

The Major was very worldly, he reminded Edward of some of the higher class guests at the "Kasprowy" hotel in Zakopane.

At the dinning car they ordered a light supper of bread and cheeses, hot coffee and hot milk completed their meal. They went back to their compartment where Mirceu suggested that they get some sleep. The train was due to arrive at Gara De Nord station at 2.17 in the morning.

And sleep they did, awaken by Mirceu just as the train pulled into the main station of Bucharest.

"Major, this is where I get off. I don't know how to thank you for all your courtesies. Maybe in the future I'll have a chance to reciprocate."

"Wait a while, let me see if I can get you a ticket to Constanza. Just follow me. Give your luggage to Mirceu. He can carry two valises for balance."

One side of the large hall was lined with windows. Major walked to the window marked "Military Personnel only."

He emerged a few minutes later, triumphantly holding up a ticket for Constanza.

"All I could get is a 2nd class ticket in a rather crowded compartment. Nothing else was available. You still have a full 45 minutes to catch your train."

"Major let me compensate you for the ticket."

"I wouldn't hear of it, especially after winning so many chess games."

"Major, you are an impossible man. How will I get in touch with you?"

"Here is my card. You have a train connection and I have to get to my Headquarters."

"Auf wiedersehen" and good luck."

Edward took his valise from Mirceu while slipping him some Hungarian money, since he didn't have any Rumanian Leus.

A railroad employee directed him to track where the train for Constanza was puffing. He still had in his hand the Major's calling card. To his total amazement he noticed that in the front of Major's name there was a title of Count.

He found the second class wagon and the conductor after checking Edward's ticket and documents, pointed to the compartment, down the hallway on the left side.

Edward went inside the compartment assigned to him only to find another six people occupying it. The French couple who drove with him in the car to the station in Budapeszt as well as the four men he noticed while in the rooming house. Bolek Skurka was among them.

CHAPTER 20

The contrast between the 2nd class and the 1st was appalling. Not only the compartment itself but also the traveling companions were different. Major Enescu was a friendly, congenial and very helpful man. These four men sitting in this compartment greeted him with open hostility and suspicion. If glances could kill, Edward would have been dead already.

The train moved but the silence still prevailed. The first thing Edward had to do was to change the icy atmosphere. He addressed Bolek Skurka in Polish:

"Bolek, do you remember me?"

"You do look familiar, but I can't place you at the moment."

"Have another look. Do you recall who attended to your hand, when you were wounded?"

"Yes, of course, you are Edward. I forgot your name, I think you are from Drohobycz or Boryslaw if I'm not mistaken."

"I am from there and my name is Daszkiewicz."

"This big guy is also from your area, his name is Szczepan Woloszyn."

"We had a kid by the name of Woloszyn in our Boy Scout Troop."

Szczepan Woloszyn got up to his full 2 meters and he started to laugh.

"I know you too, Jesus, Maria, what a coincidence. My parents always spoke about your family that you are good Catholics and patriots."

Szczepan then introduced the remaining men: Mietek Michalski of Lvov and Onufry Barszcz of Stary Sambor.

"This calls for a drink" said Szczepan and took out of his rucksack a bottle of vodka, ring of kielbasy and bread. Someone else contributed a can of sardines. Before they had a chance to open the bottle, a conductor and a railroad policeman came in to check tickets and papers.

The four men identified themselves as marine engineers hired to fix a disabled vessel at the Port of Constanza. The French couple were teachers of French and Latin hired by the Major of Constanza. The biggest trouble Edward had to explain in German his reasons for traveling to Constanza. In all likelihood they didn't understand German too well and wanted detailed information.

"Can anybody in Romania verify it?"

"Of course, How about my friend Count Major Enescu" and he showed them Enescu's calling card.

"Thank you, that will be all." They saluted and left the compartment.

"Now I really could use that drink. Go ahead Szczepan and pour me one."

Szczepan had two small metal cups. He filled them to the top, giving the first to Edward and the second to Mietek.

"Fellows, we'll have to take turns." The bottle and the cups were passed from person to person.

"What about the French couple?" asked Edward.

"They don't drink. Did you ever see Yids drink?"

"How do you know that they are Jewish?"

"I know, even my nose knows. They represent danger to us. Let's throw them out of the train at night."

It was Edward's authoritarian, icy voice that brought back a sense of sobriety:

"Ty pacholku w dupe jebany" "You ass-fucked stable boy" you'll do nothing of the kind. This is not Poland. We are on foreign territory and we have a mission to uphold the honor of our Motherland. Should anything happen to these people during this trip, you'll answer with your own life. Is that clear Szczepan?"

Although Szczepan was taller and heavier than Edward, somehow he felt that in hand to hand fighting he would loose.

"Alright fellows, let's get some sleep. That is our Polish problem, we fight among ourselves instead of our enemies." Said Mietek.

The French couple sat in their corner, oblivious to the storm that raged about them, they held hands and spoke lovingly to each other.

Looking at them, Edward for the first time, since Zakopane, regretted his decision in leaving Czeslawa. He was too upset to sleep. Next to him was Mietek Michalski sitting, a medium built man who was the only one in the group who was an actual marine engineer, who had worked in Port of Gdynia on Baltic Sea, as Edward found out after a few minutes of conversation.

"Is there a disabled vessel in Constanza?" asked Edward.

"There are few of them, I'm sure, there always are in each port. Our orders are to join our troops by any means."

"So are mine, but I'm at a loss as to what to do once we get to Constanza."

"We have to contact a Polish-Rumanian family, that should be able to help us to locate a ship or boat going to Turkey, Greece or maybe Italy. Do you want to join our group?"

"Yes, that might be a good idea to join forces, do you have to check with the rest of the guys?"

"Not really since I'm in charge of this group. By the way, I'm glad that you put Szczepan down. Sometimes I'm so mad at him that I want to kill him myself."

"Let's save our strength for the Krauts."

"Well then, let's get some shut-eye. The distance from Bucharest to Constanza is about 240 kilometers, it will take us 7-8 hours to get there if we are lucky."

The train made several stops and they arrived in Constanza in the early hour of the next day.

Everyone reached for his belongings, only Szczepan went up to the French couple and helped to take down the two pieces of luggage from the upper bin.

The French lady gave Szczepan a most charming smile and a loud "Merci".

This scene was watched closely by Edward and Mietek Michalski.

"Hopefully, he'll forget about throwing people out of the train." Said Edward

"Not until he gets drunk again." Answered Mietek.

They carried their luggage out of the train into the station. An early, bright and sunny day welcomed them to Constanza. The smell of the Black Sea hit their nostrils.

Now Mietek Michalski assumed the leadership of the group.

"We have to get to our local Polish friends, the Kmieciks. See if anyone can find a taxi or a horse driven carriage. We can't stay here forever!"

Everybody started to look around but it was Onufry Barszcz who found a taxi willing to take five passengers and their valises. The driver like so many Rumanians spoke French. Mietek gave the address to Onufry who in turn repeated it in French to the driver: 87a Bratianu Street near Calea Victoriei.

Edward admired Onufry's fluency of French and said so to Mietek.

"Onufry's father worked for many years in a French coal mine, when the family came back to Poland. Onufry had to learn Polish all over again. He is also a Doctor of Veterinarian Medicine, which he keeps secret from everybody and that means you too."

"Why is that?"

"Nobody wants to be treated by a horse doctor."

The taxi driver after a few attempts finally located 87a Bratianu Street. It was a large, white painted house, some 100 meters from the street, almost totally hidden by an orchard. The gate leading to the house wasn't locked. A dogs barking brought a large man out of the house wearing a hat, covering a sun burned face.

Mietek Michalski addressed the man:

"Panie Kmiecik, let the Lord's name be praised."

"Forever and ever."

"We brought you regards from "Eva."

"Come right in, gentlemen, our house is your house. Alina!

Alina! We have guests, five handsome men."

From the house emerged a short, heavily built woman, who was just wiping her hands with her apron. She introduced herself to each man separately, saying "Alina Kmiecik" and shaking each man's hands.

"You all must be hungry and tired. Please come with me to the kitchen. I have some "mamaliga" and milk. If anybody wants to wash up, do that in the barn behind the house."

"We are very grateful for your hospitality, we intend to stay here as little as possible. After we have eaten, we would like to go to the Port to inquire about the possibility of catching a boat for Bosporus or Istanbul. Do you know of any ships going in that direction?" asked Mietek.

"No, I don't but we can find out at the Port. We have three bicycles only, two men's and one ladies. There is no sense in bringing too many people at this time and create unnecessary attention. Whom do you want to take along in addition to myself?" That last question was addressed to Mietek.

"We'll take Onufry with us."

"Let's eat and go, Alina will show the men where they can rest."

Alina Kmiecik had to cook some additional "mamaliga" because she wasn't prepared for the unexpected arrival of five men with healthy appetites.

The host Konrad Kmiecik brought up three bicycles. Mietek took a man's bicycle and Onufry got stuck with the ladies bicycle, which squeaked with each turn of the wheels.

Edward, Bolek and Szczepan remained behind. Alina Kmiecik showed them to a large room where several mattresses were piled, one on top of the other. The only real piece of furniture in the room was an old-fashioned chest of drawers, above which on the wall hung a large wooden crucifix, and Christ looking sadly down.

Bolek and Szczepan took out a deck of cards, inviting Edward to a game. Edward had an excuse: "I have too much dirty laundry to take care of."

Alina offered to wash it for him but he politely declined, he preferred to do it himself. By the time he came back from washing his laundry he found both Szczepan and Bolek deep asleep. He decided to do the same. He took off his shoes that still bore Corporal Merceu's shine, and went to sleep.

They all woke up a few hours later to discover that their friends didn't return from the Port.

Alina, yelled through the door: "Do you boys want something to eat."

A joint "YES" was the answer.

Alina managed in the meantime to prepare a meal consisting of hot potato soup and pierogis with sour cream. She watched with satisfaction how her food was devoured by the young men and especially by "big" Woloszyn.

"I see that you boys are worried about your friends. I trust in God. Everything will be fine. My Konrad is a very resourceful fellow, you just wait."

And wait they did till the end of the day. First the dog barked and later they heard a familiar squeak of Onufry's bicycle.

They came in very tired but smiling at the same time.

"We came, we saw and we conquered" boasted Mietek. "It was Onufry's doings. We found a ship of Panamanian registry "The Silver Albatross", that requires some repairs. The ship is due to leave Constanza in 5 days if we can fix it on time. The Captain wanted to hire us on the spot, but our papers had to be verified by the office of the Director of Port of Constanza, so we went to that office. The Director was out and his Assistant was occupied with his wife's French poodle, who was choking on something. I told the secretary that Onufry was a veterinarian and she admitted us at once. Onufry worked on that poor dog for a few minutes, forcing the dog to vomit. Once the small rubber ball came out, the dog was fine, licking Onufry's hands. Later he also charmed the wife of the grateful official, who in turn to show his gratitude stamped all our papers and even added Daszkiewicz's name to the list. He misspelled his name only three times. With legalized papers we went back to the "Silver Albatross". The Captain was very glad to see us. We do report for duty, tomorrow at 7 A.M. Mr. Kmiecik was kind enough to arrange for our morning's transportation. We are leaving the house by 6.30 the latest. Any questions?"

There were none.

"In that case let's eat something. The rest of you can keep us company or go and pack."

"I forgot to take my laundry off the line." Said Edward.

"Don't bother Edward, you'll fine your stuff ironed and folded. I put it on the top of the chest of drawers in your room."

"Thank you very much Mrs. Kmiecik, it was very kind of you."

"We try to help our people where and when we can."

With an early reveille in mind, everybody went to sleep.

This time it was Bolek who woke everybody up on time. Men quickly got dressed and packed the few remaining toilet articles. Alina and Konrad were also up. She prepared a breakfast of boiled eggs, bread and hot milk. After the breakfast she kissed everyone and wished them God's speed.

A horse driven carriage stood in front of the house.

"The man knows where to take you. I already paid him. Long live Poland!"

"Long live Poland." They replied boarding the wagon.

The two horse team briskly moved from the house on Brataniu Street through empty streets of Constanza. Half an hour later they stopped at Pier #16 alongside the "Silver Albatross".

Mietek Michalski familiar with nautical customs and routines shouted:

"Request permission to board the ship, Sir."

"Permission granted. Welcome aboard."

They walked single line up the gangplank each man saluting the Captain, Dimitri Demitrius.

"My Petty Officer Jorge Rodriquez will show you to your quarters. You'll find overalls there. I expect you in the engine room within 45 minutes. That is all, dismissed!"

The cabins were very cramped and had to be shared with another person. Edward bunked with Mietek and Bolek with Onufry. Szczepan because of his size was given a single cabin.

"I can't stay here, I'm claustrophobic. I'll have to sleep on the deck." Said Szczepan.

"Suit yourself. In the meantime put your things away, get into your overalls and come with us. We have no time to waste. This is it."

Dressed in overalls they went to the engine room. The Captain and his crew were waiting for them. The Captain introduced the men. After a brief explanation as to what has to be done, he pointed to the tools and said:

"We have 4 days maximum to finish the job or there will be hell to pay."

"Captain, it will be done on time." Said Mietek.

There was a lot of work involving cylinders, shaft, o-rings and pins. Mietek the only engineer insisted on finishing the job in two days.

"If we have to, we'll work around the clock. We must prove to the Captain that we are a seaworthy crew."

Mietek was an experienced man and at the same time a good teacher, who didn't blow his stack when something was done incorrectly. He would again explain what has to be done and how, always systematically helping others.

The Captain often stopped by but he kept quiet, preferring to see the end result. Mietek asked the Captain if food and drinks could be brought down so as not to waste precious time. The Captain complied with Mietek every wish.

Mietek's crew worked long, uninterrupted hours. The sweat of their bodies mixed with oil, grease and effort brought the desired results two days later. The engine worked with clockwise precision. The work had been completed in record time. Mietek knew that now he could get anything they needed from the Captain. Everybody was happy and hopeful. The happiest was Mietek himself who at the spur of the moment recited to Szczepan a poem about a locomotive standing in a station and ready to move:

> Stoi na stacji lokomotywa
> Ciezka, ogromna I pot z niej splywa
> Tlusta oliwa
> Stoi I sapie, dyszy I dmucha,
> Zar z rozgrzanego jej brzucha bucha..

"I know that poem, it is by Julian Tuwim."
"Did you know that Tuwim is Jewish?"
"I thought that he was Polish."
"Yes, Jewish and Polish at the same time."

CHAPTER 21

"Schau mahl, Gustav"

"Look here Gustav, this one is still kicking."

"He looks badly wounded, maybe we can find other men in better condition."

"Rudolf. I don't see anybody else. The "verfluchte" Americans unfortunately have done a very good job of it. Let's see what we can do for this poor fellow."

"First thing first, let's stop his bleeding and bring him to the collection point for the hospital."

The medics cut open Henryk's trousers, exposing the large wounded area.

"It doesn't look good at all, I can't tell if the femoral artery was damaged or any other branching system of muscular tubes?"

"Let's clean him up the best we can, the rest will be up to the doctors anyway."

Gustav applied iodine gauze pads and fastened it using a tourniquet approach.

"This will have to hold until he gets to the Army Hospital. Let's pack him up and put him on the stretcher, one, two three..." and Henryk landed on the canvass stretcher.

Henryk heard the conversation like in a fog. He couldn't tell if they spoke about him or not because he just passed out again.

In a way he was lucky, because he didn't feel how many times he was less than gently put down on the ground on the way to the collection point, located in a deep valley of the Apennine Mountains, a place almost invisible from the air.

There were many wounded men, some expired on the way.

Doctors and nurses rushed from soldier to soldier, administering whatever their meager resources would allow.

"Move that soldier to the Hospital as soon as you can, the bandages should hold till that time" said a doctor pointing to Henryk. "There is an ambulance coming, put him there."

The trip to the hospital was the worst experience of Henryk's life. Each pothole or even a crooked cobblestone was a pain, magnified many times over. The nurse sitting next to the driver, was oblivious to many calls of "Hilfe" "Help", she was too busy smoking a cigarette to pay attention to the wounded men. Henryk was too weak to say or ask for anything.

The Hospital near Pescina was located 20 kilometers from the front and housed in a former girls grade school. The classrooms and the corridors were filled with hospital beds. Due to the shortage of beds, two soldiers were put in the same bed.

Henryk woke up in a large room with 15 other beds in it. The bed next to him became vacant, because for the occupant of that bed the war just ended. The linen was quickly changed and another patient was unceremoniously put in it. The nurse addressed both Henryk and his new neighbor:

"I'll be right back, don't you go away now, do you hear."

Very funny, where could he possibly go? He couldn't even move let alone walk. The entire body felt heavy and the pain was excruciating. As a patient, Henryk was never in a hospital in his life. The smell of carbolic acid, formaldehyde and other disinfecting agents was a smell of death.

He was sure that death didn't have a face only a smell. The smell that he had in his nostrils. A nurse and an Army Doctor approached his bed.

"How do you feel soldier? What is your name and your unit?"

Henryk replied in a weak voice.

"I'm Astrid von Vietinghoff, senior nurse for this ward and this is Captain Doctor Scharf. Let's have a look. What do we have here?"

She gently removed the field bandages. The wound started to bleed again.

"This is one holy mess. Nurse have him cleaned up. We have to prevent an infection at all costs. Otherwise he can say good-bye to his leg. Apply the usual sulpha. If he is up to eating, he can have some blended food. I'll be back later on to check on him."

She cleaned the area between his hip and his knee, as best as she could, applying fresh bandages to stop the bleeding. For a nurse a man's body was no secret. Even in shrunken from fear state, she recognized a circumcised penis. Or that was her imagination. It must have been, because, when she tried to hang Henryk's army tunic a set of rosary beads, a gift from Mrs. Szczucka, fell out of it's pockets.

"Is that better, Heinrich? I like that name, it is also my father's name. Can I bring you something to eat?"

"Nurse, I'm very thirsty, could I have some water, please?"

"The doctors don't like when patients drink too much liquids. I'll bring you some, after that you'll have to wait for your regular meals with the rest of the men of this ward."

"I understand that Fraulein von Vietinghoff. I'm in terrible pain, do you have something for it?"

"Unfortunately, all we have at the moment are Aspirins. Let me bring you some water."

Minutes later she brought him a bowl of lukewarm, nondescript soup and a glass of water to go with a couple of Aspirins.

"Eat something and try to get some sleep."

"Thank you Fraulein von Vietinghoff."

"Just call me Astrid, everybody does."

A medical orderly came running in and shouting:

"Attention, attention! Generaloberst Heinrich von Vietinghoff is making as unexpected inspection of the premises."

The doors were opened and several high ranking Army officers escorted by doctors walked in. Heading the group was General Vietinghoff, dressed in a gray leather coat. An Iron Cross was dangling from his neck, a man in his mid fifties wore a mustache similar to Hitler's. An expression of permanent tiredness and many un-slept nights were registered on his face.

He started the inspection of the ward by questioning the doctors as to the status and treatment given to each soldier, comparing it with the chart at the end of the bed.

After speaking with some of the men, the General would remove a medal from the box held by his Adjutant and pin it on the wounded soldier.

Stopping at Henryk's bed the General asked:

"Where is this man's chart? Who is his nurse?"

"I'm Papa, he was just brought in from the field. Didn't have the time to prepare one."

"That is different, Liebling. Good to see you. Carry on, nurse."

"What is your name and where are you from?"

"Feldfebel Kaplinski Heinrich aus Galizien, Herr Generaloberst." He told him also about his unit and the casualties.

"Yes I know about the terrible beating you've got from the air. That is all the Americans are capable of. On the ground one of our men is as good as 10 of theirs anytime. I also know that some of our best soldiers are from Galicia. Adjutant a medal for this man."

It was a War Merit Cross (KVK). Henryk was do dismayed that he couldn't say a word.

"Take care of yourself soldier, good people are scarce."

"Yes, Sir" he finally managed to say as the General left the hospital ward.

Some nurses, among them Astrid, and patients that could walk, came over to Henryk to offer their congratulations. All that Henryk could think about was how to use this medal as a ticket to get away from the hospital.

Astrid von Vietinghoff faced a real dilemma. What to do about Corporal Kaplinski. Last night while Henryk was sleeping, she lifted the covers, pretending to check on his bandages, there was no mistake, his penis free of fear, relaxed to his normal size, the ring of circumcision was clearly visible, that he was a Jew. Her duty was to report him to her superior, Captain Scharf.

She the only daughter of the Generaloberst Heinrich von Vietinghoff of old Prussian, Military family, knew what duty was or meant. Growing up in their vast estate, near the city of Konigsberg, just where the river Pregel emptied in Frisches Haff, the concept of Fatherland was repeated over and over again. That she was born a girl and not as a boy, was a great disappointment to her father, who was hoping for a son to carry on the family name and it's traditions. She excelled on horse back, shooting, played the violin and spoke Latin, French and English fluently, but she still was a woman.

Both of her parents knew and worked with Jews, until Hitler's rise to power. The manager of their estate, their doctors were Jewish, known for their honesty and patriotism. The General, who at the time of the First World War was a major, had Jewish officers. He recommended few for bravery on the field of battles. She couldn't understand what was the fuss about the Jews. Maybe the Jews of the East, certainly not the German Jews. On the other hand "Der Fuhrer" knew better.

Astrid completed Nursing School in May of 1941 and shortly after joined the ranks of Wehrmacht. She could have had any assignment, but she preferred not to use her father's influence. She wanted to do what was expected of a daughter of the German nation in time of war.

Many times she wept over the flower of German youth being cut down on so many fronts. A never ending stream of wounded would come through the hospitals doors, where she worked. After meeting her former lover from the days of Bund Deutsches Maedels (B.D.M.) in a field hospital near Smolensk, she stopped counting the wounded. Poor Rudi, as a teenage he suffered from premature ejaculation and now a grown man he lost the ability of walking since he became a double amputee.

Her second lover a captain named Theodore von Hippel hung himself, using his suspenders, in Dorfen Hospital near Munich.

As a result she kept away from men, at best she would mend them for other women to enjoy.

Captain Scharf must be told about her discovery. She knocked on the door of his small office.

"What brings you in, Astrid? What is that troubled expression for? Whom did we loose this time?"

"Captain I've found out that Feldfebel Kaplinski is circumcised, what are we going to do about it?'

Captain Scharf broke out laughing. "Astrid, how many circumcised penises have you seen?"

"None, Captain."

"What makes you so sure that he is a Jew? Maybe he was operated on some venereal disease or maybe he is a Moslem from the East. He sounded to me like those Volksdeutsches class #2 from Russia? Do you want to announce to the world that the man your father, Generaloberst Heinrich von Vietinghoff, the Commander of the 10th Army a commander over 215.000 troops gave a medal to a Jew? Do you want to ruin his career? Or as a catholic you want to "assere piu papisti del Papa" be more papal than the Pope? Astrid I suggest that you forget all about it. You did find him wearing a German uniform, right? The man was wounded defending our Fatherland, then he certainly deserves to be treated, like any soldier, with respect and dignity. Remember also, that we are not the Gestapo, we are medical officers, isn't that enough? Astrid, I'm very, very tired. I consider this case closed, do we understand each other?"

"Perfectly, Herr Doctor."

She has left his office even more confused than before. If he was Jewish, why would he keep rosaries? Did those rosaries save his life or was he wounded because of them? The first thing she would have to do is to nurse him back to health, to make sure that he doesn't loose his leg. She also had to admit to herself that Heinrich was a handsome man and she was strangely attracted to him. Perhaps later, she will be able to convert him to Catholicism, that surely would meet with the approval of her family priest in Prussia.

"Gesagt und getan." Said and done. This is going to be my own, rather than Martin Luther's "Da stehe Ich" "Here I stand" project.

CHAPTER 22

With the engines of the "Silver Albatross" running smoothly and the formalities at the Port taken care of, Captain Dimitrius, the master of the ship, gave an order to his first officer, to lift the anchors and head for Bosporus.

Nobody was happier than the "Polish crew" as they were now being called. Mietek Michalski, who had proven his engineering skills, was given the job of running the engine room. Edward, Bolek, Onufry and Szczepan became his helpers. Mietek reported directly to Captain Dimitrius, who took an instant liking to the quiet and respectful Pole. In the privacy of the Captain's cabin, Mietek would make suggestions as to the improvement of the ship's performance. Those recommendations were made only if nobody else was around. Captain Dimitrius, being a Greek was smart enough to take advantage of Mietek's ideas.

"The Silver Albatross" contravened the 200 nautical miles from Constanza to Bosporus in good time. It was here in the Bosporus area that the "Silver Albatross" had to refuel and purchase enough of other supplies to last them till their port of call in Arabat, Algeria.

Captain Dimitrius was hoping that the "Polish crew" would stay with the ship for the duration of the voyage, but he couldn't be sure that they would do that. The "Polish crew' wanted to persuade Captain Dimitrius to navigate the ship through the Straits of Messina, which would take the "Silver Albatross" some 300 miles off it's chartered course. Failing that, they would ditch the "Silver Albatross" and look for another vessel. Bosporus offered all kinds of possibilities.

The Captain asked Mietek to locate in the Port, hardware and tools needed in the engine room. Mietek gladly took that assignment, because it gave the freedom to explore other eventualities for the group. Mietek asked for and was granted the permission to have Edward to come along.

At each port there seemed to be a surprising number of enterprising commercial agents, who for a fee will find you anything from soup to nuts and more. The omnipotent word of "Bakshish" opened many doors. A number of Turkish merchants spoke German but the currency they wanted to get paid was British Sterlings, American dollars, Swiss Franks or gold. This in itself spoke volumes as who the victor might be.

Mietek located the needed hardware and Edward got the best price by haggling that met with the admiration of the sellers and a smile on the ship's purser.

Walking back to the ship, they crossed a small park where a monument of Kamal Ataturk sitting on a horse, was erected. Half of the face of the fierce warrior was covered with birds' deposits. Next to the monument three women dressed unlike the locals were making remarks in Polish.

"Mietek, look, these are Polish women, let's find out what they are doing in this place?" The women were very glad to meet their fellow countrymen, however they refused to say, what they were doing in the area, where they came from or where they were going.

"You'll have to speak with Pan Kazimierz. He is the only person that can answer those questions for you."

"Where can we find him?"

"Come with us, we'll show you, but you have to get rid of that man" one of the women said pointing to ship's purser.

Mietek told the purser: "You go ahead, we'll be back shortly, as soon as we take care of a delicate matter."

"I understand boys, you give them one for me."

Two short blocks from the park, on a narrow street, stood a small hotel with a sign in Turkish and English "Grand Hotel", that seem to be teeming with Poles. Edward couldn't believe his own eyes, where did these people come from or where were they going? He was getting the same answer from everyone: "You have to see Pan Kazimierz."

Everybody on the other hand, wanted to know what Mietek and Edward were doing in Istanbul and where they were from?

"We are from Lvov region, town of Drohobycz."

"Our Pan Kazimierz is from the same area."

"We would like to meet him now."

"And so you shall. Let me have a better look at you. "Rany Boskie" Holy God, it's my nephew Edward!"

Edward almost fainted from shock. That was his uncle Kazimierz-Jozef Daszkiewicz, his father's younger brother.

They held each other embraced for several minutes. Witnesses to that unexpected meeting had tears in their eyes.

"We all thought that you were killed in September Campaign. Only recently someone mentioned in Budapeszt that you're still alive and well. How did all that happen?"

"I was captured by the German but was able to escape from their P.O.W. Stalag and today Edward, I'm proud to say, that I am a Major in the Anders Army."

"That is great, uncle."

To Edward, his uncle looked older than his forty or so years, maybe the gray hair and gray mustache had something to do with that.

"My friend here and three more friends on the ship would like to join the Army."

Edward introduced Mietek and told him about the other fellows.

"I'll be able to help them all, but first let's get something to eat and then I would like to speak to my nephew alone."

One of the women took a hint and invited the men to a hotel room that served as a canteen for the Polish guests of the hotel. The food was simple, a pile of pita bread, chalvah and olives washed down with strong Turkish coffee.

Mietek finished his meal and said:

"I have to get back to the ship. Edward you stay here with

your uncle. We all will se you tomorrow morning. Have to procure additional supplies, so don't worry about the Captain, leave him to me."

"Good-bye Mietek, Edward and I we have a lot of catching up to do. See you in the morning."

Uncle Kazimierz led Edward to a small room on the third floor. The entire furniture of the room consisted of a narrow metal bed and a rocking chair.

"Sit down Edward and tell me what has happened to our family since September of 39?"

Edward collected his thoughts for a while and the words came out like a torrent, he couldn't stop, occasionally holding tear:

"Your parents or my grandparents died of natural causes in December of that year, just three weeks apart. I was conscripted into the Red Army in 1940 and a year later was captured by the Germans, was able to get into the O.T. with a friend of mine Henryk Kaplinski. Wearing an O.T. uniform I managed to visit my parents in Truskawiec My father is holding up nicely, but I can't say the same thing about my mother. In Lublin I joined the Underground Army, met a girl by the name of Czeslawa, whose father came from our area. We moved to Zakopane where I had the Gestapo briefly interested in me but thanks to Kaplinski's friend escaped their clutches. To make sure I left Zakopane went over the "green" border and here I am. My heart aches for Czeslawa and our five year old girl, Danuta. That is our adopted child of Jewish origin."

Uncle Kazimierz listened to Edward's emotion laden voice:

"Poor boy, you went through hell."

"What about you uncle? Who are all these people?"

"I can't tell you too much, but basically I was given an assignment by the Political Department of the Polish Army to gather our people, especially the young ones, capable of bearing arms, from areas of the Middle East, stragglers from Iraq, Syria, Palestine, Iran, men and women who left Russia and change those people into fighting men. I have here with me over 100 mostly men, some are murderers, thieves, rapists and con men. The bulk came from a jail in Kirkuk, Iraq where our army base was situated. To get them out wasn't easy or cheap. We have also about 10% of Jews who didn't want to remain in Israel, because the bulk of Jews that came out with General Anders from Russia, changed their Polish Uniform for their own of the Jewish Brigade. We also have a few Ukrainians as well as Byalorussians, who claim Polish citizenship."

"That sounds almost like a French Foreign Legion, uncle."

"You are right, in many ways they are. Poland was always a multinational country but we Poles have to stay on the top of the situation, don't you agree?"

Edward didn't answer and uncle Kazimierz continued:

"Between your experiences in the Red Army and the underground plus your education, you may qualify as a Lieutenant-candidate, a "Porucznik". I'm sure I could get that approval for you and by the powers vested in me I can put you in charge of this group or I should say a platoon."

"Let me think about it for a while, but how do you expect me to feed, train, equip and transport these people to the front lines?"

"The biggest problem is to get these people to Italy, everything else will be taken care of over there. I have some money for food and shelter in the meantime."

"Tomorrow we'll speak with Captain Dimitrius of the "Silver Albatross". Perhaps some deal can be made."

Edward's eyes closed, totally emotionally exhausted he fell asleep on the rocking chair. He never felt his uncle take his shoes off or put a blanket over him.

The crying singsong of the Muzzein, calling the faithful to morning prayers, from nearby minaret woke Edward up. He was by himself in a strange hotel room. The door opened and his uncle came in carrying a copper feenjan with hot Turkish coffee. In Poland any coffee was a luxury and to have coffee so thick that a spoon got stuck was an unheard of extravaganza. In addition to the heavenly smelling coffee there were also two pieces of local cakes, reeking with honey.

"Good morning, Edward. How did you sleep? I was thinking, maybe we can use the "Silver Albatross" to move our people to Italy."

"I don't know uncle, it is after all a small cargo vessel with no accommodations for people."

"We could set up tents for a couple of nights, that shouldn't be a problem."

"In that case let's see Captain Dimitrius. He is a Greek and a businessman. Money talks."

"I have 300 British pounds left. For that money I have to feed my people and cover any medical emergency. Let's see him anyway."

A short cab ride brought them to the pier where the "Silver Albatross" was anchored. Mietek Michalski spotted the cab from the deck of the ship and was surprised to see Edward and his uncle so early in the morning.

"What is going on?"

"We would like to speak with Captain Dimitrius about transporting our people to Italy. If we grease his palms do you think he may do it?"

"I really don't know. One hundred people is a lot for such a small ship, but there is no harm in talking to him. Let me see if he'll receive us."

Edward excused himself, saying he wanted to change his shirt and remove something from the valise. Mietek Michalski, who always had the Captain's ear, came down to tell Kazimierz that the Captain will see them in his cabin in 10 minutes. They waited for Edward's return and the three of them went to the Captain's cabin. Mietek knocked at the cabin's door.

"Come in, please."

In English, Mietek introduced Major Kazimierz Daszkiewicz of the Polish Army.

"How do you do sir. Your name seems to be similar to Edward's Are you related?"

"As a matter of fact, we are. Edward is my nephew."

"What can I do for you, gentlemen?"

"We would like to discuss a certain delicate matter with you."

"In that case let me order coffee or tea for you in the meantime."

The entire conversation took place in English. A language that Edward didn't know. His uncle Kazimierz translated the words and the local customs. The coffee broke "the ice" so to speak.

"Captain, I have about 100 people that I would like to bring to Italy. Can you help?"

"Major, I'm flying a neutral flag. What you are asking me to do is highly illegal, I can get myself into a lot of troubles. Do you realize that? Besides, how in the world could I squeeze in so many people?"

"Captain, we have tents and our own food, we won't be in your way. It's only for a few days anyway. We'll make it worth your while." With these words, Kazimierz put down on the table 200 pounds sterling.

"Don't make me laugh, for 200 pounds you want me to take such chances?"

Edward reached into his pockets and took out four gold sovereigns, that had traces of black shoe polish on it and put it next to the money.

"That is a little bit better but not quite."

"Captain, the Axis Powers are loosing the war. Sooner or later the Allied Forces will win this war. Every peddler in the "souk" market knows it. We will give you papers that you have helped in the war effort. With papers like that you'll be welcome in every port. I'll try to get you a medal too, what do you say Captain?"

"It sounds very interesting but I need some more money. I have to take care of some people too."

Kazimierz took another 50 pounds and added it to the other.

"Captain, you drive a hard bargain. Shall we shake hands on

it?"

"Not yet, I need Michalski to come with me to Rabat. We'll be coming back this way two weeks later."

"This would be strictly up to Mr. Michalski. He is not under my jurisdiction."

"I'll go Major, if that is all that is needed to close the deal."

"Captain, Mr. Michalski kindly agrees to the terms. Shall we shake on it now?"

The Captain shook Major's outstretched hand. From his cabinet he brought out a bottle of Gold label. Seven stars Metaxa, Liquor from Piraeus his native city in Greece.

"Your health, gentlemen."

The liquor went smoothly down their throats.

"When can I bring my people, Captain?'

"We'll be busy loading supplies and extra water, the whole day tomorrow. However I want everybody on this ship on the following morning by 5.30 A.M. sharp. Everyone will have to stay inside, till we clear the Port."

"As you've ordered, Captain."

They left the Captain's quarters, satisfied with the arrangements made. Major Kazimierz-Jozef Daszkiewicz had to rush back to the "Grand Hotel" to get his people ready for the voyage.

"Edward, just one question, please. Where did you get those gold coins and why were they black?"

"It is a long story uncle. The color I couldn't help, because I've kept it in a tin of shoe polish."

"Are you coming along?'

"No, uncle. I'll stay here. To make room for as many people as we can possibly fit in the engine room, for the duration of the trip."

"So long, I loved you as a child and I love you as a grown man. What Poland needs is more people like you."

"Thank you uncle. In a few days we'll be in Italy and from there like in the words of our national anthem "from Italian soil to Poland" and I to my Czeslawa and Danuta."

CHAPTER 23

An old German Kubelwagen made several trips from the "Grand Hotel" to the "Silver Albatross" each time dislodging a group of Poles, who quickly disappeared in the bowels of the ship.

Literally by 5.30 A.M. everybody on Kazimierz's list was safely tucked away. A few minutes later, anchors were lifted and the ship was on it's way to the Straits of Messina.

Kazimierz-Jozef Daszkiewicz may have been a poor student in Public School but he became an excellent organizer.

Most of the men in his group were "housed" in the engine room, the rest were spread wherever space was available, including hallways and corridors. The only exception was made for the five women, mostly nurses, who were given a cabin, previously occupied by the ship's crew.

There were no complaints, since everybody knew that these were temporary accommodations. By noon time, Captain Dimitrius gave permission for the Polish group to move freely on the deck, with a stipulation to go below in case of sighting airplanes. Any other emergency would be announced by three whistles.

The fresh sea air was a blessing for the men from the engine room. The combination of heat, smell of oil and ship's motion, caused sea sickness for many.

The sky was overcast with no planes in sight, Kazimierz called a meeting of his group, in order to introduce Edward as a future commanding officer. A couple of hours prior to the meeting, Kazimierz went over the discretionary file of the group with Edward.

The file contained the names of con-men, thieves, larcenists and a couple of murderers, not to mention a couple of soldiers convicted of insubordination.

A file bearing a name of Ursyn Niemcewicz accused of killing an Iraqi in Kirkook, caught Edward's attention.

"Uncle, this case interests me. I would like to speak with that man."

"I'll call him in for you."

"Within minutes a tall, young man, who reminded Edward of Henryk Kaplinski made his appearance.

"Major, have you sent for me?"

"Yes, I did, but it is Lieutenant Edward who wants to talk with you."

Edward glanced into the file once more.

"Are you Ursyn Niemcewicz, born on May 3rd 1921 in Pinsk, son of Marek and Rozalia?'

"Yes and no Lieutenant."

"How could that be?" Edward asked puzzled.

"Yes, I'm Niemcewicz but not Ursyn but Asher. My parents were Moses and Rose."

"Are you Jewish then?"

"Yes Sir, I am."

"It says in your file that you have killed an Iraqi. Could you tell me how did that happened?"

"I'll be glad to, Lieutenant. I was posted on midnight guard duty, when I noticed two Arabs trying to steal our supplies. I yelled out to them to stop but they didn't obey. I proceeded as per my instructions to shoot first in the air and shouted for them to halt but they kept running, I took aim and shot one of them. The other managed to escape. The dead man was one of our suppliers and related to a bigwig in town. If he was our supplier what was he doing in the middle of the night, near our storage bins? The investigating officer didn't like my Jewish background and he recommended to the military judge advocate a minimum sentence of one year. I didn't have anybody to defend me and if it weren't for the major, I probably would still be in that lousy jail."

"Is that the "Emes", the truth?" asked Edward.

"Yes, that is the "Emes", the whole truth" said Niemcewicz a bit perplexed, realizing that Edward knew the Jewish word for truth.

"If the major agrees, we'll destroy your file as well as the files of the rest of the group and we shall start with "tabula rasa" a clean slate for everybody in the group. We'll be fighting for the independence of Poland. Our blood will wash all of our intransigence. A precedence has been established by the French Foreign Legion. We could do no less."

"As of this moment, the files are officially destroyed. Niemcewicz you are dismissed. Edward, it is almost 3 o'clock. Time for our meeting."

They walked to the middle of the ship, where the group was already assembled. Kazimierz addressed his people:

"Fellow countrymen, we are on our way to Italy to join our brothers and our allies in a noble fight against our greatest enemy of all times, Hitler's Germany. Once we reached our destination, I in all likelihood will be assigned to another function or post. Therefore I would like to hand the command of this unit to Lieutenant Edward Daszkiewicz. Most of you know by this time, that he is my nephew, but this has nothing to do with my selection, I assure you. He is simply the highest ranking soldier among you. It is also upon his initiative, that all of your files dealing with your past have been destroyed. Your starting your new life as Polish soldiers, free of any stains or blemishes."

At this point his speech was interrupted by a joyous "Hurrah".

"Well, I'm glad that you approve. I hope that the Army will also approve my choice of squad leaders. Will the following individuals step forward:

Szczepan Woloszyn, Boleslaw Skurka, Przemyslaw Nowacki and Asher Niemcewicz. Stay at attention! I bestow upon you the rank of "plutonowy" sergeant. Each one of you will be in charge of 25 men. About face! Dismissed."

Three ear piercing whistles had been sounded sending everybody below the deck in panic.

The First Officer shouted to Captain Dimitrius."

"Kerios Kapetanos, Kerios Kapetanos! Echete to karawa!"

"Captain, Captain a war ship is approaching!"

It was a frigate of the British Royal Navy. It's Union jack fluttering in the wind.

"Ahoy there Captain, we are coming aboard the ship to inspect the cargo." A voice over the bull horn was heard.

"We are flying a neutral flag, we are not a combatant vessel, Sir."

"Our sources informed us that you're transporting a hostile group of passengers. We are coming aboard with or without your permission."

Captain Dimitrius called in Major Kazimierz.

"What are we going to do now, Major?"

"Don't worry, Let me handle this."

All the guns of the Frigate were aimed at the "Silver Albatross."

A small boat filled with a dozen heavily armed sailors and one officer approached the "Silver Albatross and quickly boarded the ship.

"Who is the Captain of this vessel?' demanded the British officer.

"I'm Captain Dimitrius at your service. Whom do I have the honor of addressing?"

"Sir, I'm Lt.-Commander Norman McLachlan of the Royal Navy. May I see your ship's travel, cargo and passengers documents."

"Of course Sir. But first may I introduce you to Major Daszkiewicz of the Polish Armed Forces. He wishes to have a word with you."

Major Daszkiewicz pulled some papers out of his wallet and spoke at length with the British officer. Nobody else was present during their conversation.

"Let me verify it with my superiors at Headquarters." And he immediately dispatched two sailors back to the Frigate.

"In the meantime Captain, let's have a look at your ship."

"By all means, please follow me."

Captain Dimitrius showed Lt.-Commander McLachlen his papers and took him on the inspection. Four of the sailors went along, their guns ready.

The crew as well as the Poles were scared by the armed sailors. Reassured by smiling Major Kazimierz that these sailors were British and friendly, they continued with the inspection tour.

"Commander, we have aboard this ship some o Ceylon's best tea, may we offer you a cup?' asked Captain Dimitrius.

"If a kingdom could be given for a horse, why not for a cup of hot tea? Sometimes I think that the tea is the most important ingredient that will see us through this war."

"I fully agree with you Commander, we Greeks need Oyzo, the Slavs need their Vodka but you the English need tea, so be it."

"Major" said Commander McLachlen "If I were a betting man I would say that you have spent some time in Scotland, isn't that so?"

"Right Sir, I trained for a special mission, not very far from that Loch monster. Your country reminds me very much of my own region in Poland, however yours is greener. I was there a short time, yet long enough to fall in love. If I ever live through this war, my first stop will be at number 15 on Newark Street in Glasgow, that is where my Maud lives."

"We wish you luck, Major."

Someone knocked at the door of Captain Dimitrius' cabin where the three gentlemen were having their tea.

"Come in." both Dimitrius and McLachlan said.

It was one of the British sailors with a message for Commander McLachlen. He quickly read the message and smiled broadly.

"Very good news, Major. I have been ordered by the Admiralty, to take your people off this ship and transfer them to the nearest Italian port, to see to their safety, comfort and transportation to the Polish operational section of the front without further ado. Please tell your people to get ready. We shall move out at once."

"Captain Dimitrius, I'm glad that you tilted your neutrality our way. I also would like to thank you for all your help. Can we take Michalski with us now?" asked Kazimierz.

"No, he has to stay with me, I need him. A deal is a deal."

Never did Kazimierz see his people move so fast, they were ready in record time. He still had to see Michalski.

"I'm sorry Michalski, I tried to spring you loose but Dimitrius insisted that you make one more trip with him. Here is my field post number, write to me. I'll make sure that you get a medal and an advance in ranks. Take care."

"Thank you Major, I'll see you in a month, maybe the war will end by that time."

Even more than the Poles, the crew of the "Silver Albatross" and it's Captain, were glad to get rid of the semi-welcomed, trouble inviting passengers. Now that the British took them off their hands the crew became really friendly.

Several rescue boats were bringing Poles from the "Silver Albatross" to the frigate.

A long whistle and stiff salutes from both decks and the ships went their separate ways.

Once upon the deck of the "Admiral Nelson" frigate, Bolek Skurka removed from his satchel a white-red flag of Poland and started to sing the Polish national anthem "Jeszcze Polska nie zginela" "Poland shall not perish" soon joined by the rest of the Poles. Lt.-Commander McLachlen didn't waste any time. He ordered his medical staff to check out the health of the group.

The Polish nurses helped out a great deal. They still managed to look prettier for their British hosts than for their own men. Where clothing was needed, the stock room found replacements.

The mess hall was open around the clock now. The powdered eggs and the Canadian bacon were a great hit with the Poles, however they didn't find the fish n' chips much to their liking.

"Admiral Nelson" skirted the coast line, mindful of it's human cargo and present assignment reached their destination two days later.

Motor boats ferried the Poles from the "Admiral Nelson" to the makeshift port facilities, where a large convoy of trucks awaited them.

A large contingent of British, tight lipped Military Police supervised the transfer. The convoy moved for a couple of hours when it suddenly came to a halt in the middle of nowhere.

Major Kazimierz jumped out of the leading truck to find the reason for the delay. He was told by an officer in a staff car, that a unit of the British Army stopped on the road for tea.

"You chaps will have to wait or get your own tea."

Half an hour later the column started to move again till they reached the Polish Basic Training Base at Reggio-Catanzaro.

Kazimierz's group were isolated from the rest of the camp's population. Health and processing procedures were given as the reasons for the quarantine.

The medical report from the "Admiral Nelson" was barely looked at. The doctors of the base thoroughly checked every man and woman, declaring most of them fit for combat with the exception of two men who had T.B. and one of the nurses was 4 months pregnant.

The G-2 Section took a much closer look at each individual, using Major Kazimierz's detailed report as a guidance.

Major Kazimierz Daszkiewicz was promoted to lieutenant-colonel and promptly given another assignment. He hardly had the time to say good-bye to Edward.

His recommendation as to keeping the entire group intact and putting Edward in charge was adhered to. The group was split and the men were posted to units that suffered most of the casualties. Edward's rank was only recognized by "pod-porucznik" sub-lieutenant. He and Niemcewicz with his squad were sent to the 10th Battalion of heavy artillery located near Monte Cassino.

CHAPTER 24

Henryk Kaplinski was running a high temperature. His thoughts were like a crazy maelstrom of dreams and reality. One second he was back in Leningrad and a second later he was having coffee in Vienna, hearing the song:

"Das ist die Liebe der Matrosen von dem kleinsten und Gemeinsten Mann bis rauf zum Kapitan. Jawohl Kerr Kapitan..."

Was he himself singing that song or his neighbor Erich-Maria Kusnitzky, whom everybody called "Klavier Zahne" due to his incredibly beautiful, white teeth resembling piano keys.

Henryk was sure that Erich-Maria would gladly exchange those teeth for the leg and part of his hip lost when he stepped on a mine.

Was that Erich- Maria who invited Henryk to spend their next furlough at his parents home in Berlin on Dorotheanstrasse #61? Or did he say for them to visit his uncle in Wilno, where his uncle took over a Jewish business "Wilejka"?

His thoughts came back to his own wounds. He had to see it for himself. He unbound the bandage from his leg and peeled back the pad, that was caked with dried blood and pus. It was a shock indeed.

Astrid von Vietinghoff was just passing by and did see the look of horror in his eyes and face.

"I've seen worse" said Astrid looking at the wound and trying to sound unruffled. Henryk was badly hurt, the wound was deep, inflamed and oozing pus. She knew that the loss of blood caused the heart to pound as it tried to supply oxygen and glucose to the brain. Henryk's face was white due to the blood vessels contracting as they tried to help the heart to do its job. She also knew what she could find but took his pulse nevertheless.

The pulse was irregular and the body temperature was now low. All these were bad signs.

"Heinrich, try to relax, I'm going to bring Dr. Scharf here to have him look at your wound."

She found Dr. Scharf removing pieces of shrapnel from a soldier's backside.

Dr. Scharf looked very tired but seeing Astrid, he gave her a pleasant smile.

"What now, Astrid?"

"Doctor, could you have a look at Kaplinski? I think he took a turn for the worse."

"I'll be right over, as soon as I finish with this man."

"Can I be of help, Doctor?" Without waiting for an answer she quickly dressed the superficial wound.

"You are all set soldier, I'm afraid that you are going to live." Said Dr. Schard jokingly.

"Well, lets attend to your pet project."

They walked the entire length of the makeshift hospital to the ward housing Henryk.

Dr. Scharf examined Henryk's wound once more.

"Astrid, we'll have to clean the wound much more thoroughly and let's try sulpha again. He seems like a strong individual and should pull through the ordeal. Sorry Astrid, I have to run, I have a couple of rally bad cases today."

"I understand that Doctor and thank you very much for your time."

The next few days were critical. Astrid spent an unusual amount of time with Henryk, causing some men on the ward to remark, that Astrid didn't want to loose a soldier whom her father, the General gave a medal.

Slowly Henryk started to improve. The crisis at the moment was averted, but he was far from being out of the woods.

The loss of blood left him weak and unable to stand on his

feet. A long process of rehabilitation was still ahead of him.

"Welcome back to the living, Heinrich" said Erich-Maria Kusnitzky, whose bed was parallel to Henryk's.

"I'm not sure if I want to be back." Truthfully answered Henryk.

"I know what you mean only too well."

The extend of Erich-Maria's injuries were known to Henryk. There were days that Erich-Maria didn't speak with anybody, including nurses and doctors. For some strange reason, today he was very talkative.

He spoke about his childhood in Berlin, his favorite Tiergarten, Olympic Games of 1936, University days and the marriage to his High School sweetheart who became a well known opera singer.

"Heinrich, do you know the Toreador song from the opera Carmen?"

"Sorry, I just know the music, I don't remember the words."

"The part sang by Escamillo goes like this:

Votre toast, je peux vous le rendre,

Senors, car avec les soldats,

Oui, les toreros peuvent s'entendre."

"I'll translate it for you:

I can return your toast, gentlemen,

For soldiers –

Yes- and bullfighters understand each other."

You see Heinrich, soldiers have nothing in common with bullfighters. What soldiers have is with the bulls, they are both led to the slaughter. Let me show you a picture of my wife Anne-Sophie."

Indeed she was an exceptionally beautiful woman.

"Well now, Heinrich, now that you have seen her, tell me how can a cripple like me come back to her?" "Das ist lacherlich" It is laughable."

With these words he took out of the draw of his night table a package that held a freshly ironed pair of pajamas. Hidden inside the pajamas was a small automatic Sauer Model 38.

It was an elegant gun used by high ranking army officers or party members. Using both hands he removed the slide of the gun, injecting a round into the chamber. He pressed on the exposed cocking lever and the gun was ready for instant use.

Horrified Henryk looked at Erich-Maria, the words of "Don't do it" froze on his lips.

"Well, take care of yourself, old boy, here is where I'm getting off."

Nonchalantly he put the gun against his right temple and pulled the trigger.

A shot like a dozen of busted balloons reiterated throughout the ward. The bullet went through his brains and hit the picture of Adolf Hitler hanging on the wall.

The blood started to flow from his head down to his right arm and the hand that held the gun in post mortem spasm. The drops of blood traveled along the barrel of the gun and from there onto the highly polished wooden floor.

A bedlam of officials and curiosity seekers came up to the body. It was too late, Erich-Maria was not to be reached again.

The Commanding Medical Officer came to investigate the incident.

On the top of Erich-Maria night table lay an envelope with three words on it: To the Authorities. The C.O. major Aufgang read the note several times and than turned to Henryk.

"Did you see what happened?"

"Sir, he talked to me for a minute or two and then he took out his gun and shot himself before I had a chance to say or do anything."

"What did you two talk about?"

"He asked me how I was feeling?"

"Is that all?"

"Yes Sir, that was all, Sir."

Major Aufgang asked other patients whose beds were not far from Erich-Maria's. Everybody who witnessed what has happened confirmed Henryk's words.

"Have the body removed at once." Hissed the Major.

"Just a minute, Sir, let me say prayer." Said the Army's Catholic Chaplain.

"Ego te absolvo ab omnibus censuris, et peccatis, in nomine Patris, et Filii et Spiritus Sancti, Amen."

Two orderlies placed the body of Erich-Maria Kusnetzky on the stretcher and removed it. The ward was quiet like a morgue itself only the priest's words from Ecclesiastes #4 disturbed the stillness of the ward:

"Again, I considered all the acts of oppression here under the sun. I saw the tears of the oppressed and I saw that there was none to comfort them Strength was on the side of their oppressors, and there was none to comfort them.

I counted the dead happy because they were dead, happier than the living who were still in life. And more fortunate than either, the one yet unborn, who had not witnessed the evil deeds done here under the sun."

Some men openly started to cry and the nurses had a difficult time quieting them down.

The next day there was another brief investigation of the incident by different branch of the Wehrmacht, only to be interrupted by a sudden order of evacuation of the hospital unit.

Lightly wounded men were moved to a larger hospital at Pescara near the Pescara River and the more critical cases, including Henryk's were brought by ambulances to a train, marked with gigantic Red Crosses.

The railroad wagon, supervised by Astrid, into which Henryk was placed was terribly overcrowded.

The peculiar stench of disinfectants mixed with disagreeable odors that warm bodies provide when put together in a closed room and the cries of the wounded for help, represented a modern version of Dante's inferno.

One of the nurses at the end of her patience, yelled at the men:

"You are still soldiers, behave yourselves as such."

"Shut your fucking mouth, you whore, we have been soldiers

and now we're just cripples." shouted an ashen faced double amputee.

Strangely enough, after that exchange it, became quiet again and the medical orderlies started to distribute food and drinks.

Major Scharf came to the wagon.

"Gott im Himmel" does it stink here!"

"Major, nobody died of stink yet." Someone said it to everybody's delight.

"Jungen, wier fahren zuruck nach Heimat" Boys we're going back to the Fatherland."

As if in response to Major's statement, one of the wounded gave a muffled cry but then went quiet again. For the majority of the wounded including one shell shocked young man, who kept repeating:

"Wein nach Bier das rat Ich Dier. Bier nach Wein lass alein." (Wine after beer I advise, beer after wine leave alone.) war has finally ended.

Henryk was shaken up badly by the suicide of Erich-Maria and everything that followed. On one hand he was glad that he was leaving the front lines. On the other hand he missed the chance of giving up to the Allies. It wasn't that simple as he found out. He was wounded and his situation was very precarious.

As long as Astrid was in charge he had a chance to survive but what if someone else would change his bandages and discover his Jewish origins?

Astrid passed by and seeing his worried expression said to him:

"Don't worry Heinrich, everything will be fine. After all I'm your guardian angel or don't you believe in angels and miracles?"

"Astrid, I do believe with all my heart."

He closed his eyes and fell asleep with a smile on his face.

CHAPTER 25

Shortly after completing his first bombing mission, Captain Paul Krafchin had an unexpected visitor. It was an Army Chaplain who introduced himself as Rabbi Jerome R. Rifkind of Mill Basin in Brooklyn.

Seeing him Paul immediately thought about his father. Rabbi must have read his mind because he put Paul's fears to rest:

"No, this is not about your parents, they are just fine. I've met them about a month ago in Fort Hamilton in Brooklyn. They have given a small gift for you and here it is. I had a tough job to locate you because I wanted to give it to you personally both the gifts and the regards."

Rabbi Rifkind took out of his pocket a small box and gave it to Paul.

Paul promptly opened the box. It contained a gold signet ring with a black onyx stone and gold initials "P.K." There was a short letter included, telling Paul that the ring was made out of the parents wedding bands and the words of love.

"Thank you very much Rabbi for all your trouble. May I offer you a cup of coffee or tea?"

"Sorry son, I must run, I still have many errands to take care of. Maybe the next time." From his memory, the Rabbi recited a blessing "Tvila Derech" for people about to take a perilous journey. Finishing the prayer he stuck a stick of Wrigley's chewing gum into his mouth and left the room.

Paul put the new ring on the pinkie finger of his right hand. The ring became his good luck charm. He believed that as long as he had his ring with him nothing bad would ever happen to him.

Vivian Holmes was the first person to admire the ring. Lately he was seeing Vivian rather often. Officially engaged to Flight Lt. Richard Hunt-Evans, Vivian managed to see Paul in all kinds of places day or night. Ironically professed undying love for Richard and so did Paul about his Goldie, but their love trysts were so explosive in their animal magnetism, that neither of them could or wanted to explain. For Vivian it was even more physical that she had ever experienced with Richard.

Seeing Vivian after each bombing mission became a necessity for Paul. It seemed to Paul that Vivian was bringing him back to the sane world, especially after his fifth mission over Germany. A mission that he will never forget as long as he remained alive.

That day started with a vociferous argument taking place in the Quonset hut, that served as dormitory for his crew. Two men had an argument that soon spread to the rest of the men. Paul having very little time before his final briefing, was highly irritated, he just told everybody to shut up and to stop their silly arguments, which to the crew wasn't silly at all. Foul weather also added to his discomfort.

At first the droplets of rain hit the windshield of his plane like so many pearls, slowly changing into ribbons of tears, A sense of foreboding took over, reinforced by the realization that he left his ring on the sink in the bathroom, shared with six other officers.

He still had a few minutes before the take off. He jumped out of his cockpit and approached a member of the ground crew. Yelling over the deafening roar of the engines into the ear of the crewman, Paul told him to find the ring and keep it till his return. The man shook his head understanding Paul's request.

There was nothing else to do but to climb back into the plane. The control tower was already screaming for Paul's plane to take off.

Getting into the formation in lousy weather was a mean task. Nobody every heard Paul curse so much. "Idiots and imbeciles" were the more polite words, causing Moe Samuels, the British born radioman to remark: "The Captain has a bee in his bonnet."

This time the mission's target was the industrial town of

Chemnitz. The closer they got to the target the more flak and hostile fighters they encountered.

Just as "Goldie Locks" was unloading it's deadly cargo, the plane was hit by shrapnel of exploding shells, killing at once two of his gunners. The tail of his plane looked like a sieve, steering the plane became progressively more difficult, especially after his co-pilot Lt. George Perry was wounded in the shoulder. The wound itself wasn't serious, once the bleeding had been stopped by "Curly" however he was in no position to fly the plane at the moment.

Paul reported the condition of his plane to his wing commander Col. Cotshott. Told to get into the middle of the formation, Paul managed to execute the given order. Shortly after his plane started to fall behind.

Two B-24's were escorting Paul's plane, giving him and his crew a measure of security. The closer they got to the English Channel, the slower and lower did "Goldie Locks" fly.

Paul desperately tried to raise the altitude of the plane to no avail.

Without realizing he was singing "I'll be with you in apple blossom time," a song he sung usually in distress.

Concentrating on the instrument panel he was perspiring profusely. "Goldie Locks" like an injured bird, simply refused it's master.

The White Cliffs of Dover were rapidly approaching. The escorting planes were hundreds of meters above Paul.

"We'll never make it and it is all because I forgot my ring."

The top layer of the cliffs was illuminated by sun's rays, peeking through the grey clouds.

"This is the end! Bitch, go up!" he screamed on top of his lungs, to no one around.

Miraculously, the plane lifted a bit, barely clearing the cliffs, much to close for comfort. The control tower advised by Moe Samuels, the radioman, prepared a reception consisting of several fire trucks and ambulances.

By the skin of his teeth, Herculean efforts and sheer luck, Paul brought his plane down safely struggling with the landing gear at the last moment.

Ambulances removed the killed in the air battle. George Perry's wound was declared superficial, according to the attending medics.

"He'll be back in action within a month and he'll have a "Purple Heart" to show for it."

Paul was told that as soon as he sees to the comfort of his crew, to write a detailed report about the air battle, status of his remaining crew and the condition of the plane.

"These God dam reports!" muttered Paul.

"Captain, Captain, I have something for you!" It was the Flight Sergeant Jimmy the Beanstalk, Sullivan, whom Paul asked to locate the ring.

"Here it is, I found it exactly where you told me."

"Thanks, Jimmy, I owe you one, a big one."

"It's OK Captain, I understand that you had a rough trip this time. You look like you could use a drink."

"Boy, could I."

"Here Captain, take a slug of this" and Jimmy handed Paul a pocket flask of Scotch Whisky.

Paul drank it like water "Thanks again, Jimmy. I've got to get to bed."

Dead tired he went to his quarters and promptly fell on his bed, not bothering to undress or answer any questions from roommates.

There was no resting because Paul was summoned to see his C.O. Col. Gary the Hotshot for debriefing.

The colonel was a very demanding officer but he knew when a man reached the end of his rope, clearly Paul was a that point.

"Captain Krafchin, you have done a superb job. Get yourself some shut eye and then bring me in triplicate a detailed report. You'll also have to write to the parents of the killed men. Make sure that your plane is being repaired and only then take a 4 day R&R. That is all Captain."

Paul went back to his dorm, undressed and went straight to sleep. He spent a restless night, tossing and turning.

He woke up with a sour taste in his mouth. Someone gave him a cup of hot, black coffee and a lit cigarette. It took a supreme effort on his part just to shave and take a shower. Feeling a bit better he got dressed into a clean, fresh uniform. The first thing on his agenda was to visit Lt. George Perry, whom he found smiling, surrounded by nurses, who nicknamed George, "Tyrone Power".

Being of Portuguese descent George resembled Tyrone Power in his looks.

"Hello Skipper, how are you? These ladies intend to keep me here forever, what do you say to that?"

"George, you better get your ass out of here A.S.A.P. I have lots of work for you, I need you badly. The plane suffered several flak hits, the rudder and some panels will have to be replaced. After all the repairs, we'll have to test the plane for air worthiness."

"Yes, Sir, Captain, I'll see to it."

"Good man, George. Sorry about the ladies but there is a war and we all have to make sacrifices."

In quick succession he went to the hanger to examine the plane, afterwards he met with his crew and talked with each member at length, listening to their concerns and praising their morale.

Then came the toughest part of being a Captain- writing letters to the parents of the boys killed in action.

He poured his own heart into those pages. The report in triplicate to his superiors was an easy task by comparison. Having taken care of all things for which he was responsible, he finally got his precious four day leave.

Vivian Holmes whose fiancée was shipped off to North Africa, was able to secure an apartment of White Street in Brighton, belonging to her friend Alice Spencer a member of W.A.A.F. (Women Auxiliary Air Force).

Knowing how to avoid SNAFU (Situation Now All Fucked Up), Paul managed to get a jeep from the Motor Pool and from the

P.X. all kinds of supplies, including whisky, cigarettes, chocolates and several cans of Spam to last them at least four days.

The jeep was fully refueled and the Supply Sergeant gave Paul an extra 5 gallons of precious gasoline. Smiling they drove off in the direction of Brighton.

"The sun may never set on the British Empire, however the sun never visits, the British Isles either." Remarked Paul to which Vivian sung: "What do we care, let it rain, let it rain" to the tun of "Let is snow, let it snow."

Alice Spencer's apartment on the second floor of a 3 story house was comfortably and cheerfully furnished. Vivian knew the apartment well and like a lady of the house she took over.

"Paul, I'll whip up something for us to eat, in the meantime you prepare drinks for us, later on we'll take a bath and hit the sack."

"I would prefer a different program but I'll agree with your plan of action this time." Said Paul with a boyish grin. Paul went up to Vivian and gave her a long kiss.

"You keep that up Captain and I won't be able to do anything."

They drank and ate forgetting the ugly war. The World didn't exist. It was just Paul and Vivian. A man and a women and the union of their bodies.

"Paul let me wash up, the bathroom is hardly big enough for one person."

"Go right ahead" gallantly offered Paul, but a few moments later he took off his pajamas and went after Vivian.

"Oh, my Goodness" said Vivian seeing naked Paul. His erected penis left little doubts as to his intention.

"So soon again?" His answer was a kiss on her wet lips. Having one cake of soap for the two of them, they explored every crevice of each others body. Vivian being the more practical suggested that they adjourn to bed once they remove the foam from their skins.

Without bothering to shut off the water they ran still wet to bed. Impatiently they reached their climaxes in rapid succession.

Totally exhausted but happy Vivian put her head on Paul's chest and fell asleep soon to be followed by Paul and his slight snore.

They slept for almost 16 hours straight waking up totally famished.

"Paul, do stay in bed and I shall prepare a breakfast for us."

"Vivian, I think it's closer to lunch than to breakfast. Why don't you stay in bed and I'll cook up something."

"OK Captain, you are the boss."

Paul put on his pants and went to the kitchen, Using powdered eggs and "Carnation" condensed milk, bought at the P.X., he made some sort of an omelet. He brought the omelet and hot coffee to bed, where Vivian imitating a Hollywood star, was sitting up propped by several pillows.

"Here you are your Majesty."

The breakfast was consumed with relish.

"I didn't know, that among your many talents you also have a culinary one."

"To tell you the truth I didn't know either."

As soon as he brushed his teeth, Paul was back in bed with Vivian. The rest of the day and the next day they spent alternating between making love, sleeping and eating. Only on the third day did Vivian suggest that they go out to see the city of Brighton.

Paul shaved off his three day old beard and once dressed they left their little paradise.

Without difficulties they located an Officers Club where the movie "Gone with the Wind" was shown, later on they danced cheek to cheek and listened to some very good jazz and captivating Benny Goodman recordings.

"Nothing seems to go faster than a furlough. We have just a few more precious hours left, so let's make the most out of them."

"I whole heartily agree."

They returned to their "Shangri-La" somehow aware that after these few days, they would go their separate ways.

Paul dropped Vivian off at her office. He kissed her in full view of pedestrians and said:

"Vivian, we shall always be friends."

"Of that I'm convinced, good luck and I thank you Paul. It was nice while it lasted."

He returned the jeep to the Motor Pool and the unused 5 gallon can of gasoline.

"Captain, said the Supply Sergeant "You can have a jeep anytime you want, just see me."

"Thanks sarge,. You can never tell when I might need it."

Reaching his own unit he was completely relaxed and ready for his next assignment. There was some good news for a change. Lt. George Perry was back from the hospital ahead of time and the Air Force sent him replacement for the two killed gunners. The new men were Stanley Wieczorek of Chicago and Raymond Taylor of Tenafly, New Jersey.

Judging from their files and the brief interview, they both seemed to be fit and made a good addition to his crew.

"Wieczorek, do you think that an English typewriter will be able to type your name?"

"Yes Sir. I have lot of trouble with my name, but if it was good for my old man, it will be good for me too."

"Well said Stan dismissed."

Everyday Paul checked on the progress made by the plane's repair crew, to the point of making himself a nuisance.

"If you're that much in a hurry to get your ass shot off, we'll get your crate ready in 7-10 days, Captain." Said one of the aeronautical engineers in charge of repairs, whose rank Paul couldn't determine because of the well worn overalls.

The following day, Paul was ordered to appear at 14.00 hours in full dress uniform in the office of Col. Gary Cotshott. Similar orders were given to a few more officers of Col. Gary's squadron.

In the waiting room, of Col. Gary's office, Paul met some of these men.

"What is this all about?" asked Paul.

"They will either give us hell or pin a medal" a red-haired Major Ames answered.

"You're so right, Ames, it's party time." Smiling said Col. Cotshott who overheard the last remark made by Major Ames.

Several high ranking officers, a few secretaries and reporter from "Stars and Stripes" entered the room.

"ATTENTION!!" Everybody stood erect like a billiard stick. "Men" continued the Colonel "The Air Force is very proud of you and in recognition of your bravery above the call of duty and your battle achievements, you are being decorated today. Will the following individuals come forward..." He started to call names and pinned medals on their chests. Each decorated officer was given a certificate and a firm handshake.

Paul was the fifth person called up. While Col. Gary pinned the medal, Paul was thinking about his mother. Too bad that she wasn't here to witness the ceremony. "Yes mama, even by Captains I AM a captain, I'll mail her the certificate to see."

Having finished with the decoration ceremony, Col. Gary took out a bottle of Chivas Brothers Royal Salute 21 year old Scotch Whisky and poured each person in the room a generous drink.

"TO VICTORY!"

"To Victory" everybody replied.

"The Russians are throwing their glasses away after each drink, so that nobody else will ever drink from them again. Why the hell don't we do the same." He threw his glass against the fire place, followed by everybody else.

"Well fellows, the party is over. I've a tone of work to do and I bet that you also have things to do. Dismissed!"

Paul and the rest of the decorated men were in festive moods, but the celebration of the occasion will have to be temporarily postponed till further notice.

He went to his room where several times he reread the certificate. There was no mistake.

THE UNITED STATES OF AMERICA
TO ALL WHO SHALL SEE THESE
PRESENTS GREETINGS;
THIS IS TO CERTIFY THAT
THE PRESIDENT OF THE UNITED STATES
OF AMERICA
Authorized by Executive Order #987490 Wed. March 11th,
1944
HAS AWARDED
THE BRONZE STAR MEDAL
To
CAPTAIN PAUL KRAFCHIN, U.S.A.F.
For
MERITORIOUS ACHIEVEMENT
IN AIR OPERATIONS AGAINST HOSTILE FORCES
During the period of February 1944 in Germany and Italy
GIVEN UNDER MY HAND IN THE CITY
OF WASHINGTON
This 2nd day of March 1944

Glenn J. Collins
Brigadier General

Signature

Commanding Officer

CHAPTER 26

Sub-lieutenant Edward Daszkiewicz completed an accelerated course in handling the 5.5-inch artillery field gun, where each shell weighed 45.5 kg and had a maximum range of 14.815 meters and muzzle velocity of 510.

The gun somewhat reminded Edward of the Soviet 152 mm artillery pieces. The British weapons were more complicated and they lacked the simplicity of design and the ease of maintenance prevalent to Soviet weaponry.

He was very impressed with the caliber of the British instructors. They were easygoing, confident, mild-natured, friendly and yet reserved with occasional flashes of humor. He genuinely liked these men. Their lives were light years apart from his Polish background. They spoke using their strange military jargon, but there was no doubt as to their professionalism. Still, he never saw a sign of bad temper from any of them.

On the other hand, he had problems with his own fellow Polish officers. What is really found hard to stomach, was their religious fervor, although he himself was Catholic. They all used the same rhetoric, riddles with asinine metaphors and moronic approaches when it came to the question of Jewish soldiers in the unit.

Once finished the training period Edward had a foretaste of the great battles of Monte Cassino by savoring fighting on the banks of the Garigiani and Sangro rivers.

Maybe the great Allied generals of the Italian Campaign wanted to distract German Forces from France and the Eastern Front, however, they didn't envisage fighting up every centimeter of the Italian peninsula in general and Monte Cassino in particular.

The rugged Italian landscape confined any armored advance to the narrow, winding roads, making the terrain unsuited to mobile warfare and ideal for defensive purposes. Despite Allied command of the air, as Edward could observe, Jerries always escaped to fight another day.

Just by watching occasional "Movietone News" described by an American commentator Lowell Thomas, Edward deduces that Allied didn't do so well in Italy. In the States, civilians were getting per week a class A-ration of 3 gallons of gasoline that was 12 liters. What a luxury. In Zakopane one could live a whole week by selling that on the black market.

Edward's thoughts came back from Czeslawa and Danuta in Zakopane to the cold Italian reality.

Mark Clark's Fifth U.S. Army had a go at Monte Cassino. American Forces suffered appalling losses into thousands just over 11 km. He thought that Americans valued life more than Russians. Was he wrong?

Edward had a feeling that sooner or later his 10th Battalion of the 3rd Division, Anders 2nd Polish Corps will be put to a severe test of skills and wills.

As of March 22nd, 1944 the battle of Cassino settled down to a stalemate-with Germans infiltrating back around the town and still firmly holding the approaches to the Liri Valley gateway to Rome.

Edward used the lull in action to further improve the fighting edge of men under his command. He pushed them to the limit and then some more.

Somehow his obsession with constantly training men, came to the attention of his C.O. Col. Zabkowski, because a few days later he was ordered to report to Divisional Headquarters.

Orders are orders and Edward reported to the office of Col. Zabkowski. The good Colonel was busy and Edward had to cool his heels in the waiting room for over an hour.

"Yah, this is the Army for you, always hurrying up and waiting." Thought Edward to himself.

Finally a pretty female sergeant came out of the office and said:

"The Colonel will see you now, please follow me, Lieutenant."

They went through several offices to reach the door marked Colonel Krzysztof Zabkowski. She knocked at the door and a loud "Wejsc" come in, announced the presence of the colonel.

Edward walked in, saluted and reported. The colonel saluted back.

"At ease, lieutenant." The colonel was a tall man with gray hair and a bushy gray mustache, looking more like a university professor, which he had been, than a professional soldier that he became.

"I'm sorry you waited to long, I expected two more officers whom I wanted to be present at the meeting. They just arrived. Gentlemen please do come in."

From another room two officers came in. The first one was Lt. Col. Rudolf Nitecki, whom Col. Zabkowski introduced and the second was... and here Edward had a second shock of his life, was Mietek Michalski from the "Silver Albatross" wearing a Captain's uniform.

Edward was confused and speechless.

"Lieutenant, let me put some light on this mystery." Started the Col. Zabkowski. "We've received a number of complaints from your men, that you were driving them too hard and yet in each complaint was mentioned that you were a fair man and that you wouldn't ask anybody to do things that you yourself couldn't or wouldn't do. That made us think. At the same time we've received a letter recommending you for a Citation, connected with helping our people to join our Forces. However, that letter was signed by Maj. Kazimierz-Jozef Daszkiewicz, your uncle. Of course, you can only imagine what other members of the board said about Polish nepotism. Capt. Michalski, who was also directly involved with "Silver Albatross" affair, supported your uncle's statement on your behalf and as a result you're being promoted from sub-lieutenant to lieutenant. Congratulations, Lieutenant Daszkiewicz. And now, if you will excuse us, Col. Nitecki and I have to rush off to another meeting. Captain Michalski wishes to talk to you in private. Good luck, Lieutenant."

Edward saluted both men as they left the room, he still didn't know what to say or do. Words slowly came out of his mouth:

"Mietek or should I call you Captain Michalski, what is this all about? How come you're a Captain?"

"You can call me Mietek, however, I am a naval Captain. I have briefly served on our submarines "Wilk" and "Orzel" in Gdynia. Later I was transferred to the Naval Intelligence and now I am with Second Corps' counter Espionage and Intelligence Group, Section #2.

I really shouldn't tell you all of this, but I have seen you in action and I know you are a good Pole and genuine Patriot. We would like to have you on our team as soon as it will be feasible, providing of course that you agree. It is a voluntary move, I can't order you in this case.

One more thing, I've something for you. Here are the gold coins that you gave Captain Dimitrius of the "Silver Albatross."

"I don't understand this all together." Said Edward. "If one Jew is as smart as 10 Poles and one Armenian is as smart as 10 Jews and one Greek is as smart as 10 Armenians, than how come this Greek returned the gold coins?"

"That is a good one, Edward, but you see I managed to have him decorated by the Polish Government for his efforts and risks in helping Poles to reach Italy. He was so moved that he returned those coins with instructions that they be returned to you personally by me."

Mietek gave those coins back to Edward. Every trace of black shoe polish was gone.

"I don't need them, perhaps you can send them to my wife Czeslawa in Zakopane? I'll give you the address."

"Yes, Edward, it can be done. If not coins, we can arrange for her to have American dollars or Swiss franks an equal amount."

"That would be great if you could also deliver a letter or a verbal message."

"Consider it done. I'll contact you after our next assignment. You see the Brits of the 8th Army sent to Monte Cassino the newly organized New Zealand Corps commanded by Lt. Gen. Bernard Freyberg. Their massive artillery bombardment supplement by aerial bombing destroyed the sixth century Benedictine monastery overlooking the town of Cassino.

Due to their extraordinary blunder, the ruined monastery is now an ideal defensive site for the Jerries. The unquestionable courage, sacrifice and the sheer endurance of his troops was unfortunately not compensated for by a significant advances on the ground. So "bless 'em all, bless 'em all." And who do you think has now the honor of capturing Monte Cassino? You guessed it, us Poles! We are sure to loose lots of good men and wherever a Pole will die an Italian soil a red poppy will grow. Should we both survive this forthcoming battle, I will send for you. Will you join me?"

"Yes Mietek, I'll. Let the Holy Mother of Czestochowa keep us in Her care."

In the first week of May 1944 the Polish Second Corps swung into action. All the units moved closer to the target area. "Diadem" operation started.

To a large degree, the almost useless aerial bombing was followed by an early morning massive artillery barrage. Fusillade after fusillade of various guns were hitting the monastery.

Lt. Edward Daszkiewicz was running like a mad man from one gun emplacement to another, waving a pistol in his hand and yelling; "Keep on firing, keep on firing."

Only now did his men recognize the advantage of prolonged training. They kept firing till the barrels of the guns became red hot. The order of "seize fire" came just in time. The infantry, pioneers engineers and every available man, including cooks and supply personnel, were sent into the battle.

Despite the heavy onslaught some Germans escaped and fought back having the advantage of height. The layout of Edwards's unit's perimeter contributed to a situation common to many similar battles. The troops nearest the fighting were unaware of what was happening. When the firing started, men in positions to the left or right of Edward wondered what others were firing at, because they didn't see any targets in the smoke and confusion. Also any markers indicating cleared paths were destroyed or lost. Infantrymen refused to cooperate with the engineers, men wandered away or were separated from their units, stepping on land mines.

When it quieted down a bit, Edward ordered his men to find any German stragglers and try to bring them back as prisoners. Most of the men ignored that order preferring to shoot them down in the belief that a good German is a dead one.

Edward had to make the body count and relay the number of killed Germans to the regimental command.

Always skeptical, the battalion commander asked Edward how he had reached that figure. He replied:

"Simple Sir, I just piled the arms and legs and divided by four."

Edward came back convinced of the old Von Clausevitz doctrine that whatever the infantry doesn't cover it isn't captured. His unit suffered losses of over 40% in casualties both dead and wounded. Edward, not counting a slight wound on his neck, escaped any major harm. So did Sgt. Niemcewicz, who was the artillery observer in a most dangerous position.

Only after June 4th of 1944 when Rome finally fell to the Allied Forces, did Captain Michalski arrange for Edward's transfer to his unit in Section #2.

CHAPTER 27

The German hospital train marked with large red crosses was moving slowly in the northerly direction, zigzagging between Italian cities of Florence, Bologna and Milano often making prolonged stops. The Germans were hoping that the allied planes would respect those red crosses, because they themselves were hardly adhering to the Geneva Convention.

The conditions within the train changed from bad to worse. The chronical shortages of medical supplies were only a part of it. Food and water were also scarce. Overworked nurses, doctors and other medical staff started to snap at the wounded:

"Now, what do you want? You aren't the only one, just look around!" were typical answers to calls for help.

The irritated wounded started to argue among themselves. Whenever they had a chance they would curse the doctors and nurses, blaming them for their discomforts.

"What are you going to do with us? Send us back to the Russian Front?"

At each railroad station more wounded were pushed into the wagons, making an impossible situation.

In Milano, Major Dr. Scharf refused to let anymore wounded on the train. A Panzer Colonel wearing a black uniform, who just brought almost 25 more wounded, removed his pistol and pointed it at Maj. Scharf:

"Either you take my wounded or I'll blow your head, so help me God."

"You may as well pull the trigger, Colonel. Come in and see for yourself. I have no beds, no stretchers, no medicine, no water and no help. Many of beds have two men in one bed."

"This is your headache, Major. I have a war to fight, just step aside if you value your life."

"Bring in the wounded" he said to his men. "Leave them here on the floor. Don't worry, the Major will take good care of them. Aren't you Major?" Still holding his pistol pointed at Maj. Scharf. The threat was unmistakable. In one respect the Colonel was right it was now Major Scharf's headache. A big one too.

With those conditions on the train it was no surprise to anybody that a number of heavily wounded men expired making room for the newcomers.

Thanks to Astrid, Henryk was located in the far corner, away from the door. What little food he was given he didn't eat. He lost his appetite, he felt weak. A few attempts at walking ended almost with a disaster. A drunken sailor was steadier on his feet than Henryk.

Henryk's condition and behavior didn't escape Astrid's notice. Having the very best intentions towards Henryk, she could do very little to change the situation. Never in her life did she have a heavier load of wounded and sick on her hands. Only God knew when the linens were changed the last time. If somebody died, his body was removed and into the same bed was placed another wounded from the floor. Small or skinny men were put two in a bed.

Henryk knew perfectly well what was going on around him. He also realized that his chances of surviving this hell were next to none. That single realization brought him to the present state of depression.

Too often had Astrid seen those signs in her patients. Once they gave up morally, they were as good as dead. She decided to have a heart to heart talk with Henryk, to shake him out of the state that he was in, at the first chance. That chance came a couple of hours later.

"Heinrich, I don't like the way you act and behave, you're giving up already."

"Astrid, there is no sense to all of this, I can't escape, I might as well be dead."

"Not on my watch. I didn't bring you all the way up here, just to have you die in my hands. No, Sir! This is not going to happen. Now let me tell you a story that my own father used to tell me when I graduated from Nursing School:

In a small village near Konigsberg there lived an old Jew. He had children when he was young. The kids eventually grew up and migrated to America or Canada, forgetting about their parents. Then his wife of many years died leaving him all alone in the world. He made a meager living by collecting dried out tree branches and selling them to the villagers for kindling the fire. The people were sorry for the old man, and always gave him a few "pfennings" whether they needed the wood or not.

He carried those branches in a large cloth bag, his only posession. One day the bag tore apart and all the branches fell out. "God" he cried out of pain "I had enough of this life, send me Death and take me to you."

"As you wish, my son." God replied.

The old man looked around and there stood Death, dressed in a white bedspread and holding a scythe in its hand.

"What can I do for you?" asked Death

"What do you mean? Help me carry the wood."

Henryk was laughing now.

"I'm getting your point, I'll try my level best."

"You'll have to do better than that. In a few days we'll reach "Heimat" and we'll be put into a regular hospital. The conditions will also improve, but I can't do anything for you if you don't help yourself. Is that clear to you now Heinrich?"

"Yes, Astrid, I understand." Further conversation was interrupted by calls of "Nurse, Nurse" coming from several beds.

"I must go, Heinrich, just remember what you have promised me."

"I shall this time, Astrid." He looked at her kind but determined face. It was a face that he would have liked to have around him in the future too.

It took several more days full of confusion by the time the

train reached it's final destination "Sanatorium Dorfen" located near the town of Wolfratshausen, some 30 km from Munich in the picturesque Bavaria.

By that time enough wounded died to make room for all the ones left on the floor by the Panzer Colonel in Milano.

If the train's medical staff worked hard till this time, their workload was actually doubled. They had to move everybody from the train, bathe and put them into finally clean beds. Local volunteers and BDM girls helped with the wounded. Their help was very much welcomed by the staff and the patients themselves.

Henryk was put with nine other men, next to a large window, through which he could see the spiral road leading to nearby Wolfratshausen.

Astrid stopped by for a minute to see where Henryk was put. "You'll stay temporarily here until I can find you something else."

The "temporary" arrangement became a permanent one. Henryk liked his corner, the next bed was occupied by a heavily wounded man, whose entire head was bandaged, leaving just openings for the nose and mouth.

To combat the loneliness Astrid gave Henryk a set of charcoal pencils, water colors, brushes and precious pad.

Years ago in prewar Poland when Henryk was a student in local Drohobycz Gimnasium he had a teacher of arts and crafts a certain Mr. Bruno Schultz, who insisted that Henryk had a talent for drawing, a talent that should have been developed. Henryk was aware that his family was related to Maurycy Gottlieb a painter of some renown.

More out of sheer boredom than anything else, Henryk started to draw his immediate surroundings and then the outdoors. The more he drew or painted using watercolors, the better he got. It was wonderful therapy for him. He became more relaxed and his appetite came back and with it also a sense of well being.

From time to time his condition was reviewed by the Military Medical Board. One look at his wound or rather a hole that the wound had left, the doctors would stamp his papers "six months postponement.

Other veterans weren't so lucky, quite a number of them, still barely recuperated from their wounds were sent back to the front line. The war had a "healthy" appetite for cannon fodder.

"Six months is a long time, maybe this crazy war will finally end Henryk told Astrid while going back to his drawings.

For a change he started to draw a caricature of Astrid as Eve, all dressed in white, handing over a stethoscope, instead of an apple to Adam. This drawing became a huge success. Many doctors and nurses started to ask Henryk to draw their caricatures and portraits.

Portraits were definitely outside Henryk's capabilities, caricatures were another matter. Henryk was very careful not to offend anybody and wherever he could he would oblige people with drawings.

He liked to walk by himself on the outside of the "Sanatorium Dorfen", slowly dragging his right leg as he walked.

The winter ended but the spring didn't arrive yet. It was chilly especially in the late afternoon, when the sun disappeared behind the Alps. Tired he sat down on a wooden bench to rest.

Unwittingly, he fell asleep, while looking at the bare panorama of the Bavarian landscape with a mountainous region in the far focus and the needle tree forest much closer and the river Isar flowing right through it.

Someone gently put a blanket over him, waking him to the reality. It was Astrid leaning over him.

He gave her a smile of sheer pleasure, her face was so close to his that he raised his head a bit and kissed her fully on the lips.

At first she froze not expecting such a move from Henryk but it took her only a heartbeat to respond to him fully and warmly.

Henryk felt her whole gamma of emotions expressed in her kiss. It was a moment of clear realization for him that he loved her and everything about her. He held her hands next to his face as a single tear appeared in his eyes spilling on her hands.

"Astrid, I know this is all crazy, but I do love you."

"Heinrich, I never in my life felt like this for anybody else. I'm now sure that my own feelings as being reciprocated. Nevertheless, we have to be practical and at the same time very careful.

The first thing is for you to get better. Now we both have something to work for. Will you help me to do that?"

"Yes, dearest, just give me one more kiss and I'll be your obedient servant for ever."

If the first kiss was good, the second was even better. There was no doubt in their mind as to the force of their feelings, brought together by an ironic twist of events, they belonged to each other. She, the General Vietinghoff's daughter and he a Polish Jew out of Galicia.

CHAPTER 28

"Captain, Sir, are these the papers you were looking for? They have been just decoded."

"Let's see, Walery," said Capt. Mieczyslaw "Mietek" Michalski, Chief of the Department Two-Intelligence and Counter Espionage sections of the Polish 2nd Corps.

"Indeed, they are, thank you Walery. That will be all." Sgt. Plutonowy Walery Slawek saluted smartly leaving the room.

Out of the pile of papers, Mietek first reached for the communication from the "Directorate of Underground Struggle" which ran the Welfare, Relief and Education Service of the underground Polish State. To get that information Mietek had to tap his personal contacts with the upper echelon of the A.K. (Home Army).

As he read and reread the message, his mouth opened wide in disbelief. Hem the tough, battle hardened soldier started to cry. At first just sobs, changing into a torrent of unstoppable cries of pain.

Sgt. Slawek and a few other officers from adjacent rooms in the comfortable house in Villa Borghese in Rome, barged into the Capt. Michalski's office.

"Captain, what has happened?" begged, concerned Slawek.

"Out! Out! I don't want to see anybody, just out!" Ordered, everyone left the office.

Mietek read the letter once more this time aloud:

"Dear Capt. Michalski:

We regret to inform you that the subjects of your request, Czeslawa and Danuta Daszkiewicz of Zakopane couldn't be located. Our most reliable sources informed us that Danuta Daszkiewicz, a child had been denounced to the German Authorities as being Jewish, by a Pole "Szmalcownik". Czeslawa Daszkiewicz, mother, who wasn't at home at the time of the child's arrest, went straight to the Gestapo, claiming to be of Jewish faith. Her only request was to be reunited with her daughter. The elder Bujnicki went to the Gestapo, claiming Czeslawa as his own daughter. The Germans checked Bujnickis record, finding that he was childless. He was severely beaten and as a result he lost his power of speech. Mother and daughter with a group of other Poles captured in "Lapanka" (round up) were shipped to Oswiecim. We will follow up this case and try to extend any and all help. The "Szmalcownik" in question was thoroughly interrogated. He proudly admitted his bastardly act claiming that he was helping Poland to get rid of Jews. The court sentenced him to death. The body was disposed of in a Christian manner. Advise as to further steps.

Signed: Porucznik Eligiusz Niewiadomski.

Mietek started to bang the tabletop with his bare fists shooting "Why? Why?" He, Mietek liked Edward since they first met. To him Edward represented the best that Poland had to offer. A highly intelligent, patriotic man, ready to sacrifice everything for his Motherland. How is he, Mietek going to break the sad news to him? He didn't know how to proceed. He lifted his head noticing Walery standing by the door and not moving.

"Walery, bring me a bottle of vodka and don't let anybody come to my office, until I tell you otherwise, understood?"

"Yes Sir, I'll be right back, Sir." Walery has never seen his captain in such a state and acting so strange. It must have been some bad personal news. Walery couldn't possibly imagine Captain Michalski reacting in such a manner on someone else's behalf.

Walery was back in a minute with a full bottle of vodka and a glass that still bore somebody's toothpaste on it.

Mietek poured himself a full glass of vodka, tilted his head back and swallowed the contents of the glass in two gulps. Having done that, he put the glass in his desk and poured another drink. Noticing Walery he said:

"Are you still here? Didn't I tell you to get lost? Out!!" Walery left the room and stood guard in front of the office. "Let the man mourn in private."

Mietek started on the second drink. His thoughts went back to teenage years in Warsaw. His father Andrzej Michalski was a member of the Polish Sejm, a very respected man, totally dedicated to Marshall Pilsudski with whom he has served in the Legiony.

.... And then came May 12th 1935 and "Marshallek" died. Poles and Jews by the millions came out weeping on the streets of cities and villages.

With time, other policies took place in Poland, starting with Smigly-Rydz a stiff and unimaginative officer, who inherited Pilsudski's mantle as "the Commandant".

The economic situation became progressively harsh, especially for Jews, a 10% minority. In universities, Jews due to "numerous clauses" were forced to sit on odd numbered ghetto benches. Rather than to sit there and being humiliated, most of the Jewish students preferred to stand as did Mietek's friend Martyn Goldsztajn. Another mutual friend a Catholic girl also stood up in sympathy. Seeing that, a bunch of Fascists students, members of the Falanga and others wearing a miniature sword of Chrobry on their lapels, addressed Martyn:

"Why are you standing up rather than sitting down?"

"I'm standing up because I'm a Jew." Was his answer.

"And you?" addressing the young woman standing next to Martyn.

"I'm standing up because I'm a Pole." She was at once beaten up as a "Jewish whore."

Mietek jumped to her defense. He was worked over by several students wearing brass knuckles. Shortly after, he transferred out from the Uniwersytet Warszawski on Krakowskie Przedmiescie to Politechnika Warszawska.

Upon his graduation in Engineering he was offered a commission, joining the very modest Polish Naval Forces in Gdynia in 1937.

From many heated discussions with his father, Mietek knew of the traditional Polish Alliance with France. To Poles, France always presented the second Motherland, Pilsudski, however was highly skeptical of France's reliability as a guarantor of the Polish Western Frontier. Pilsudski to his credit was also doubtful of West's will to construct a collective security arrangement in Europe. He decided that Poland would find safety through an expansion of it's own military might and as a "Great Power" balancing between Germany and Russia.

This was the policy that the Polish Government pursued after Pilsudski's death.

Polish strength, as Mietek soon found out, was an illusion, because as a backward, agricultural country with a narrow industrial base, it couldn't support a modern military force and then there was no time, to make it a reality. Nevertheless, the armed forces were large in numbers and their morale was high but they failed to modernize. The need for motorized cavalry, modern anti-aircraft guns, bomber and fighter squadrons, armored units, heavy naval cruisers was never in sufficient quantities. By 1939 the Germans had an advantage of 10:1 in tanks alone. In the air they were hopelessly outclassed.

On the first of September of that year, with no declaration of war, German troops in full force crossed the Polish frontier. On the 3rd of September, Britain and France declared war on Germany.

Poles thought that the war was already won. Two weeks later, the Red Army entered Poland from the east.

Poland ceased to exist but would not cease to fight simply because it's armies had been defeated and it's territory was occupied by enemies. There was no surrender, the fighting went on. Poles fought Germans from the first day and they would continue till the last, on land, at sea and in the air. (From Poland itself, Russia, North Africa and Italy where Mietek's unit was stationed at the moment.)

Captain Michalski's resistance to alcohol was legendary. He could and did on many occasions out-drink many of his friends.

Now after consuming most of the bottle, he was still sober but deeply hurt emotionally.

What was the Polish character that on one hand was able to achieve extraordinary heroism and on the other, condone and promote the suffering of his fellow Jews? What possibly could that "Szmalcownik" gain by denouncing to the Gestapo a Jewish child adopted by a Polish family? Yes, Mietek had to agree with a statement of Cyprian Norwid an 18th century poet, that "the patriot in each Pole was a giant while the human was but a dwarf." How very true!

Someone entered the room and before Mietek had a chance to say "get out" he noticed Edward Daszkiewicz standing in front of him with a worried expression on his face.

"What's wrong, Captain?"

"Just everything, Edward. I'm afraid that I have some very bad news for you. I wish to God that I didn't have to give it to you." Saying that, he handed over the letter from the Directorate.

Edward read the letter, his face becoming chalk white.

"Jesus, Maria, no Jesus, Maria, No, No!" A primordial scream was heard in the room as Edward ran out of the building.

The entire staff of the Department gathered in Mietek's office. He read them the letter that Edward had left. They all stood horrified. Each of the assembled was thinking about their own families left under German occupation.

"Shouldn't we be with him right now?" someone said.

"Let's leave him alone for a while so that he may grieve in private."

An hour later, Capt. Michalski sent Walery to find Edward Daszkiewicz. Walery came back reporting that he couldn't find the Lieutenant any place.

"Take six men and find him. Don't come back without him and that's an order."

Walery with six other soldiers were looking for Edward in all the usual and unusual places from the sleeping quarters, dining rooms, bathroom even at the nearby cemetery. Lt. Edward was no place to be found. He just disappeared into the thin air. There was no other choice but to report the mission's failure.

Capt. Michalski requested and received immediate help from the Polish Military Police. Six jeeps with four fully armed men were at each jeep, combing the entire area, checking all possible hangouts, restaurants, bars, churches without results. 48 hours later, Capt. Michalski still didn't declare Edward as being AWOL (absent without official leave). He intensified the search for him. On the 3rd day, Michalski received a call from the British Military Police.

"Well, Sah. Lieutenant Woodward speaking, Sah. We're holding one of your boys here, Sah. Wish you come here and take him off our hands, Sah."

"What is his name, Lieutenant?"

"I am not sure if I can pronounce it right, Sah. Sort of Dasckvitz."

"Close enough. We'll be right over, do give us your location, lieutenant."

"Suggest, Sah, that you bring along a medic with you. He thinks that we are all Jerries, Sah."

"Confounded Walery, my jeep at once. And find Dr. Zenon Kociolek wherever he is, he is to come with us. Hurry up man."

Walery burned rubber to get to the British unit.

Lt. Woodward summoned by the desk sergeant came in momentarily.

"Well, Sah, it didn't take you long to get here, Sah."

"Could we see the prisoner?"

"All in good time, Sah, we have some formalities to take care of. You really have a bad boy on your hands."

"Let us be the judges, lieutenant."

"I meant no offence, Sah."

Reconstructing the scene of Edward's capture, it seems that he gave the British a beating.

"We found out that Lt. Edward walked into a house a few days ago, that was occupied by a minor German Consulate official's family. The official himself was long gone, leaving his parents and children behind. It seems that the truck that was supposed to evacuate them never showed up. In the garage adjacent to the house, Edward found an almost new black Mercedes-Benz limousine resting on four wooden blocks, albeit without the wheels. Edward inquired as to the whereabouts of those wheels. He was told that the wheels have been requisitioned by the German Army. To Edward's thinking why would the Germans take only the wheels when they had the entire car. He told them to find those four wheels and bring them to him. When they didn't respond, he started to shoot. At first at the crystal chandelier hanging in the main dining room and then Maisel's porcelain figurines with no results. Next he threatened to kill the old lady and the children, leaving the old man for the last. It was the grandmother who broke down and told Edward where to find those tires, burried in the garden. He made the old man dig them out. They were nicely wrapped. Next the old man had to put those wheels back on the car. Having done that the old man produced a can of gasoline. The car started immediately. The old man cursed Edward to hell.

"You damned German, you're lucky that I didn't use this gasoline to burn you all."

He then, as we found out later, sold the car to some Italian black marketers for a dozen or so gold sovereigns and a few bottles of stolen whisky. He then asked them to find him a priest, which wasn't hard to do in Rome and to drive him to the nearest whorehouse, which was just being opened "under new management" catering to a new and eager clientele. He indeed gave a few gold coins to a priest asking the priest to pray for him.

For the rest of the coins, he reserved the exclusive service of four prostitutes for the remainder of the day and night. There, he organized a sort of musical chairs game. The madam of the fine establishment was playing the piano and the four ladies were parading stark naked around Edward, who would hit them, not so gently, with his army belt on their delightful derrieres.

Your man drank two bottles of whisky if you can believe and then he emptied the bottle of champagne into a bowl where he put his dick. Having his dick wet with champagne, he requested one of the ladies to perform a sexual act, popularly known among the troops as a blowjob, which in itself, being done in a bordello didn't shock anybody. The problem arouse when he started to shoot at all the mirrors in the house. It was then when one of the scantily dressed ladies ran to the street and stopped the first Military Police patrol and that was us.

By the way, Sah, it took three burly M.P.'s to subdue your boy. One of my men, a Canadian by birth, understood some Polish and kept telling Lt. Edward that we were British and not Germans but he kept on fighting us until he passed out. I really should file a complaint against this ruffian, Sah."

"Please don't Lt. Daszkiewicz was decorated for bravery at Monte Cassino. He just got some bad news from home, his wife and daughter were dragged to a concentration camp. It could have happened to me or you, lieutenant."

"Not to me, Sah, I'm not married, but I do understand the situation, just sign those papers for me, Sah."

Capt. Michalski signed those papers without a word.

"Sergeant, bring out that bothersome Pole."

A few minutes later, Edward was brought to the room. In his dirty and disheveled uniform, unshaven beard of a few days and several black and blue marks on his face. He presented a sorry sight.

"Serwus Mietek, what brought you here?"

"Nothing Edward, we were just in the neighborhood worrying about you. What are friends for? Come, let's get you home."

Without a word of protest, Edward left the room. The jeep was surrounded by Mietek, Walery and Dr. Kociolek.

Upon reaching their own housing, Dr. Kociolek gave Edward a sedative and put him to bed. Mietek was more careful, assigning a 24 hour guard near Edward's bed.

Eight times the guard was changed but Edward slept on. Worried, Mietek asked the doctor as to the reasons for it.

"Just let him sleep, it might be the best medicine for him at the moment. When he wakes up, make sure that he takes a bath and puts on a fresh uniform and above all, even before breakfast, give him some hope. After all, not everybody is being killed in the camps. It might be a lie but he'll grasp it. Like a drowning man a straight razor."

"Yes, Doctor, I see what you mean, but please stop by in a couple of hours."

Mietek followed the doctor's instructions to the letter. He also prepared a copy of a dispatch to the Headquarters of A.K. in Poland requesting every possible help, at all costs to Czeslawa and Danuta Daszkiewicz, formerly of Zakopane.

"Thank you Mietek very much, you are a true friend. The truth must be said. I was planning to kill myself right after breakfast. Somehow I hated the idea of dying on an empty stomach, but now I must live for them and keep on fighting until we stop Krauts from annihilating our people both Catholic and Jewish.

CHAPTER 29

The morning of Saturday, April 22nd, 1944 was long, tedious, anxious and altogether too quiet for Captain Paul Krafchin. He had an appointment with Col. Gary "the Hotshot" regarding ideas which could possibly improve the success of bombing missions.

Morning briefings were not the place or time to discuss anything so important without interruptions.

Engaging in combat thousands of feet above the earth, pilots had long been recognized as daring, larger-than-life individuals, and Paul especially after his last mission, when he received a citation, that called him "superb airman, determined fighter against overwhelming odds" was becoming comfortable in that role.

Reaching Col. Gary's office he was ushered in at once.

"Good Morning, Colonel."

"Good Morning, Captain, coffee?" "Thank you, Sir."

"How do you take your coffee, Krafchin?"

"Black, Sir, no sugar."

"Here you are. And now what is on your mind? You have 10 minutes, Krafchin."

"Sir, I was just thinking...."

"That is dangerous, Krafchin. The Air Force doesn't pay you to think, but go right ahead, let me not interrupt you."

"Sir, we're flying in sufficient strength and numbers against major targets. We probably could score more, it would be possible to send some fighters over the nearby targets, prior to the bombers arriving there."

Seeing a puzzled look on the colonel's face, Paul continued:

"In all likelihood, the enemy would dissipate some of their interceptor aircraft. The outcome would be, that the enemy fighters would be short on fuel, about the time our bombers arrived, and be forced to land without making contact, thus the bombers could do a more thorough job without being pestered by nagging enemy fighters."

"Hmm, I'll admit that the fighter sweep sounds like a good idea. I'll take it up with the proper people, that I promise you. At the same time, have you noticed that as the time goes, the crapshoot is changing more into a turkey shoot. We are growing stronger everyday. We are getting ready for the invasion, Krafchin. Our victory is only a matter of time."

Colonel glanced at his wristwatch. "Your 10 minutes are up, Krafchin. Thanks for stopping by."

Paul saluted and left Colonel's office. Paul was sure that the Colonel, the no-nonsense officer would submit his ideas. Whether he, Paul, would get the credit for it, remains to be seen. The blame for it might be another matter altogether.

As long as the Air Force was paying "for not thinking" Paul might as well collect his pay. Today was the "Pay Parade". He was planning to stop at the P.X. shop to pick up a farewell gift for Vivian. She was leaving on an assignment. He recalled her words: "Paul, I'll be gone for a while. I've asked my girlfriend Lydia to take care of you until my return. So don't fall in love with her, she has a bad Irish temper, but otherwise she is lovely, so have a good time."

"No, thanks, Vivian, I'll wait for you."

"Don't be an idiot Paul. By the time I return we might forget about each other. There is a war do you remember?"

That a war was going on, he was perfectly aware of because on April 24th he was due to take his 13th bombing mission. Somehow that number sounded ominous, not that Paul was superstitious but that number made him somewhat uneasy.

In the meantime he had to pick up his pay at the Paymaster's cubicle. He submitted his serial number, which was checked against a master sheet. The clerk handed him the pay and saluted. It was then, when Paul acknowledged the salute that Paul noticed that the black onyx stone from his ring was missing. With the stone gone, the ring looked like an empty socket of an eye.

Since that time when he temporarily misplaced his ring, he looked upon that ring as a good luck charm, created by his parents from their wedding bands. Nothing was more precious or meaningful to him than that ring.

"I must find that stone," he said to himself. "I must."

He started to trace his steps and every place he had been so far, from his sleeping quarters, dining area, Col. Gary's office but the stone couldn't be found. It was probably easier to find the proverbial needle in a haystack than a black stone in that large, traversed by many vehicles, base.

There was one more place that he forgot to look, the hanger housing his plane "Goldie Locks."

On the way to the hanger he was stopped briefly by Lt. George Perry.

"Skipper, I'm all squared away."

"In that case, George help me look for the stone from my ring."

Lt. George Perry gave him a look usually reserved for feeble-minded individuals.

"Captain, the hanger is at least 25.000 sq. feet, how are you going to find it there? If any plane or vehicle moved about, that stone is powder by this time."

"I still have to look for t, can you help me George?"

"Sure thing. Let's have a look, maybe we'll be lucky."

And lucky George was because he spotted the gold initials of P.K. on the black stone, resting next to the gigantic wheel of the plane.

"Here you are, Captain. Don't ever say that I didn't do anything for you."

"Thanks George, thank you very much. I need to put that stone into the ring. Let's find some glue."

Paul asked a mechanic working on a plane for glue to fasten the stone to the ring.

"Let me do that for you Captain. I will take me but a minute. It will hold forever, I guarantee it, Sir." said the mechanic.

"Captain, you look very happy, like a kid on Christmas."

"Yes, George, very happy, come let me buy you a couple of beers, my treat."

"Sorry Skipper, I'll take a rain check, I have a date, so long then."

"Me too. I forgot to call Vivian in all that excitement."

They both went their separate ways. Paul managed to reach Vivian and before he had a chance to say that he was unavoidably detained, Vivian said to him:

"Paul Darling! I'm running behind my schedule, I'll meet you in our usual place about an hour or so late. Please forgive me. I'll have a big surprise for you. Tally-ho." With these words, she hung up.

Now, that he had his ring repaired and an extra hour to get there, things started to improve. He arrived at Woodbury Common's just minutes ahead of Vivian and her friend, wearing a British Army uniform.

"Oh, here you are, darling. I want you to meet a school friend of mine Cynthia Epstein."

So that was the big surprise. No Lydia with a bad Irish temper, but a quiet mouse of a Jewish girl, probably from London's Whitechapel district.

"Cynthia, this is Captain Paul Krafchin of U.S.A.F. I told you so much about."

"How do you do, Captain." Paul was charmed by her voice so full of dignity.

"It's a pleasure Miss Epstein."

"Please call me Cynthia."

"Now that you two have met, let's have some drinks."

Paul ordered drinks for everybody. He and Vivian had a few but Cynthia nursed her single drink the entire evening. Paul discovered that Cynthia was a witty and brilliant conversationalist and a historian by profession.

The evening was very pleasant especially for Paul who was the center of attention by two attractive females. He wished that he could have spent more time with Cynthia alone.

Vivian must have read his mind because she said:

"I do see that the two of you are getting along splendidly. Hate to brake up this lovely party but Cynthia and I must leave. Paul she is a good girl so don't try to seduce her because she is still a virgin."

Paul turned his head towards Cynthia. Her face was crimson in embarrassment.

"Sorry, Cynthia, I guess I shouldn't have said it. I do apologize for that remark."

"Sorry ladies, but I didn't hear anything."

"Our Captain is very gallant. We do appreciate that. Here are my telephone numbers, both daytime and evening. Should you be free this coming Friday evening, perhaps you would like to taste a home made dinner? My parents and I would be delighted to host an American serviceman for Sabbath."

"Cynthia I would be honored. I don't know my schedule as yet. Hopefully I shall return from a visit to Germany. I shall telephone you by Thursday the latest, if it is acceptable with you?"

"Yes Captain, it will be acceptable with us. God's speed and the very best of luck."

Paul shook hands with Cynthia and Vivian, who gave him a kiss on the cheek also.

"Take care of yourself, Paul. Good people are scarce these days. This is good-bye." The two women left the room. They didn't want to be accompanied to the car.

Paul having some time on his hands ordered another beer for himself and struck up a conversation with a bunch of RAF fliers sitting at the next table.

It seems that these boys came back from a large four-pronged assault on three Reich cities of Duesseldorf, Brunswick and Mannheim and a locomotive depot at Laon in France, asserting that a death blow was being given to Luftwaffe.

"I'm sure, that there will be also a bit left for us to do. There always is. Good show, gentlemen and good night." He paid for his drinks and left for the base.

Paul was right. There was plenty of war left for him too, as he was about to find out.

The greatest sustained air offensive the world has ever know, seemingly unending streams of Allied planes, shuttling back and forth between Britain and the Continent, blasting the military installations and traffic centers of western Europe, that are the backbone of Hitler's defenses against impending invasion.

Sunday, April 23rd was Paul's day of preparations and briefings.

Col. Gary "the Hotshot" would start his monologue with his customary: "Here is the scoop" and proceeded to tell them all that they needed to know to carry out the assignment, and ending with:

> "Gentlemen, do remember always, that the sky is even more unforgiving than the sea. Your smallest mistake will cost you dearly, so keep your eyes peeled. By the way, some of you, looking straight at Paul, came up to me with very good suggestions, rest assured, that they are being implemented as of now. So good luck and good hunting. DISMISSED!"

Paul went to his plane and found the entire crew assembled and ready to roll. One couldn't help being exited, but not as much as on the first bombing mission. They were old hands, everybody knew his task and what's more what to expect from each member of the crew.

It seemed like an eternity. "Goldie Locks" was ready for the take off. From the controlling tower came a torrent of instructions, often contradictory.

"Keep the radio on Channel Baker."

"You are taxing too slow. Check the canopy."

"Steady, steady, keep it straight!"

"Easy on the stick, just a bit."

"You own the sky now Mac."

Paul had about enough of this. It wasn't his first flight and he hated being called Mac. This was his 13th mission and he had to get back at that jerk at the tower.

"This is NOT Mac, buddy. This is Captain Krafchin!"

"Good Luck, Captain Krafchin."

Paul looked at his ring once more. His luck was with him, 13th or whatever mission. He had to get back and see Cynthia. No fucking Germans are going to prevent him from returning.

CHAPTER 30

That Henryk Kaplinski was deeply in love with Astrid and vice versa was obvious to everyone. Somehow the hospital's atmosphere was very tolerant of lovers. Patients were falling in love with their nurses all the time and Henryk wasn't the exception.

Having so much time on his hands, Henryk wondered if his love was based on the fact that his very life depended entirely upon Astrid. After a long self-examination he concluded that he was in love with her because she was the type of human being that appealed to him in every respect, intellectually, spiritually and physically. It was also a question of mutual attraction.

Every free moment she spent with Henryk. They talked about a variety of subjects, starting with religion, literature and ending with politics and the war.

Reading between the lines, Henryk could deduce from the newspapers, that the irresistible tide of Soviet arms moving steadily westward and unless the Allies reach Bavaria first, Dorfen might be occupied by the Russians.

Astrid would tell Henryk about occasional conversations with her father, Generaloberst Heinrich von Vietinghoff. As dedicated an officer as he was, he didn't have any illusions about winning the war. Five years of war had decimated the ranks of the Wehrmacht. Many of its best soldiers lay buried in military cemeteries stretching from the burning sands of North Africa to the frozen tundra around Murmansk. Divisions had been reduced to size of reinforced regiments and replacements were slow in coming. There was no way to compensate for the tremendous superiority in men and material that the Allied forces possessed. It was simply a question of time till Germany's capitulation.

For Henryk it was a question of survival and to reach that point. In the meantime, he would have to take one day at the time.

From the local volunteers at the hospital, Henryk found out about a very good restaurant in nearby town of Wolfratshausen. He therefore decided to take Astrid out on a date.

"Astrid, do you think, that we could get a Sunday afternoon off, just to have a meal at "Haderbrau" on Untermarktstrasse?"

"That is a lovely idea. I'm sure that I could arrange it for this coming Sunday, but don't tell anyone keep it to yourself. We'll have to leave the hospital separately and meet at the restaurant."

"Whatever you think is most prudent."

Astrid was able to obtain passes for herself and Henryk from Dr. Scharf. There was no need to hide anything. They both left the Sanatorium in a supply truck from the town of Wolfratshausen itself. The distance from Dorfen to town was hardly 3km, a distance that Henryk couldn't possibly cover, still limping on one leg and supporting his body with a cane.

The driver was a man in his late sixties, wearing a Tyrolean hat. His Bavarian German was difficult to understand even for Astrid. When asked to drop them off at "Haderbrau" on Untermarktstrasse he answered "Gel" for yes and "nein" for no. He further explained that "Haderbrau" was located on Obermarktstrasse and not Untermarktstrasse. He further recommended to ask Herr Jaeger, the proprietor, for duck and Weiss beer that sparkles like real champagne. "It is a costly restaurant and they may not have it on the menu anymore, unless you are a Party member."

They thanked the driver for the lift and his recommendations." The "Haderbrau" was a typical Bavarian eating place, full of heavy, dark highly polished wooden tables and chairs. The shelves were taken by a collection of old and beautiful beer steins above which there were several stuffed animals from the region.

A waiter came up to them and said: "I'm very sorry but the kitchen is already closed and we have nothing to serve."

Astrid looked around, noticing several occupied tables and people consuming their food.

"What about those people, how come they are being served?"

"Oh, they came before you, I'm sorry to say."

"Could we speak with Herr Jaeger. It is a special evening for us."

"I'm sorry Fraulein, Herr Jaeger is unavailable, you'll have to leave."

"Waiter "Ein moment bitte" perhaps you WILL find a nice table for the daughter of Generaloberst Vietinghoff."

They both looked in the direction of the voice. It was said by a tall, distinguished looking man, whose left sleeve was neatly tucked into the pocket of his jacket. He not only had one arm but also one eye, the second was covered by a black patch.

"Jawohl Herr Major."

Astrid looked at the man totally puzzled. "I see that you don't recognize me Fraulein von Vietinghoff. I can hardly blame you. Let me than reintroduce myself. I'm Major Georg-Hans Dennhard, your father's former Aide-de-Camp. We met a couple of years ago when I had both hands and both eyes."

"I'm so sorry Major. The war and all, please forgive me. May I present my fiancée, Oberfeldwebel Heinrich Kaplinski (master sergeant).

"How do you do Sergeant. You do have a lovely fiancée. Speaking of lovely ladies, here is my own, Frau Gretchen Dennhard."

"How do you do, Frau Dennhard" Henryk clicked his heels and kissed her outstretched hand.

Herr Jaeger alerted by the water came around.

"Herrshaften" can I be of service?"

"Herr Jaeger, this lady is the daughter of my former commanding officer Generaloberst von Vietinghoff. Do you think that you could find a nice table for this young couple and Herr Jaeger let them have anything they want and please put it all on my account. Is that a problem Herr Jaeger?"

"Not at all Herr Major. It will be my greatest pleasure. I'll attend to them myself just give me a minute or so."

"Much obliged, Herr Jaeger."

"Herr Major, we appreciate your gesture but I have the money to pay for the evening."

"Sergeant, listen to me. You're still a sergeant and I'm a major in this man's army. This is an order," said the major laughingly. "You, young people go and have a good time, enjoy yourselves and don't worry. This Jaeger bastard will take good care of you that I'm promising you. After all I am the Burgermeister of this town and he owes me a few favors. If there is anything at all you need, just come to see me at City Hall. I wish that we could stay with you but my Gretchen made other plans for the evening." So Mach es gutt."

Henryk saluted as the Dennhards left the restaurant.

Herr Jaeger was as good as his word. He brought them to the best table in the place and said:

"Please leave the menu to me."

Both were so flabbergasted with meeting Dennhards that they agreed to Herr Jaeger's suggestion. A decision they didn't have to regret because dishes after dishes, course after course, drinks after drinks were brought to them. There was a crisp duck, delicious venison, roasted potatoes, red cabbage, "spetzels", mushrooms and other local specialties.

They were enjoying themselves to the fullest.

"Astrid, I have two questions to ask you. The first one is why did you introduce me as Oberfeldwebel, while you do perfectly know that I'm only a corporal? The second and the most important questions is, when did I become your fiancée?"

"All right, Heinrich, I do owe you an explanation. You're a corporal but you'll soon be promoted to Oberfeldwebel. After all do you expect me to marry just a corporal? That also explains your second question. What is the matter with you? Don't you want to marry me, after you have broken my heart? Or are you in love with some other "Krankenschwester?" Heinrich, don't you think it is the right time for you to make love to me? It's time for you to make a dishonest woman out of me. After all I want to check out the man I'm about to marry. I was told to do that between two bed sheets."

She was laughing so hard that she had tears in her eyes. Now it was Henryk's turn to laugh.

"Let me address myself to the issues raised. As far as being a sergeant I really would prefer to be a civilian and the second issue, the most important one, how about right after this dessert, if that suits you."

"Absolutely, Herr Oberfeldwebel, I'm all yours."

"I'll ask Herr Jaeger for a room, after all this is also an inn. I'll tell him that I need to rest for a couple of hours."

As unusual as the day turned out, Herr Jaeger surprised them even more.

"If the lady is tired after the meal, I have available a small room upstairs. It is clean and freshly made up. Why don't you both relax for a few hours and then I'll get you transportation to wherever you wish to go."

"Herr Jaeger, we'll be going to the Sanatorium Dorfen."

"Than you are a wounded veteran. In that case it was a double honor to have you here as our guests. Please come by anytime you are free."

"Thank you very much Herr Jaeger, in addition to being a perfect host you're also a great German patriot."

Herr Jaeger was beaming from ear to ear, that he was called a great patriot by the general's daughter was the highest attribute ever given to him.

Inasmuch as the Major Dennhard picked up the tab for the evening, Henryk could afford being extravagant by leaving discretely a large tip, which wasn't overlooked by Herr Jaeger either.

"Please follow me, it's just one flight up. I'll have the maid prepare the bed for you."

"Thank you again, Herr Jaeger, You're too kind." They went up the creaking wooden stairway.

"Katia, Katia, make the bed "fur die Herrschaften, loss."

From a small room or large closet, came out a young Russian

woman. She wore a "babushka" covering her yellow hair. Her four front teeth were missing and he eyes had a look that Henryk had seen on concentration camp inmates, when worked for O.T. near Lublin. It was a look of a hunted animal.

Katia quickly opened the room with her key and removed the cover from the bed and went to fill the small basin with water.

"I do hope that everything is satisfactory." Angenehme Ruhe "Have a pleasant rest." Said Herr Jaeger leaving the room.

Minute's later Katia returned with an extra pitcher full of water. Henryk noticed her hands, they were yellow just like her hair.

He asked her in German pointing to her hands: "Was ist dass?"

She replied in heavily accented German: "Ich arbeit Ammunition Fabrik in Buchberg, chemikalien, Sie verstehen?"

"Ja, Ich verstehe sehr Gutt, Katia. Danke."

No further explanation was necessary. He just shook his head as Katia left the room.

"Heinrich, I'm going to wash up in that alcove, so don't look," she said coyly." After that I'm going to bed. You can wash up too and join me."

Astrid removed her blouse and began to wash up.

"Don't worry, I'm not looking." He was very tired, his stomach was full and he couldn't get the picture of the yellow-haired Katia out of his mind. Should he be caught, surely he wouldn't get the "luxury" of working in an ammunition factory, he would be shot outright.

His thoughts went back to Astrid. She looked very inviting dressed only in her brassiere and her undergarment. There was only one problem, she was totally asleep.

Funny, he may as well get some sleep also. The lovemaking will have to wait for a more opportune moment. He got dressed and laid down next to her on the large and comfortable four poster bed. At least they snored harmoniously in unison.

CHAPTER 31

The peculiarity of the Italian Campaign was that while it involved large armies, very tough fighting, it felt like a sideshow in comparison with the Eastern front.

The above wasn't of concern to Edward Daszkiewicz. He was lucky to come out alive from fighting at Monte Cassino. There he had a fight for every meter, the terrain around the town and monastery was honeycombed with tunnels and other earthworks that defied the efforts of allied artillery and Air Force to dislodge the defenders.

Edward knew of the American, Canadian and French attempts, but it was the fate of Poles to fight triumphantly for Cassino, where two Polish divisions, dismounted cavalry for most part, were to finally expel the Germans from the commanding heights. Capturing those heights, defended by German paratroopers cost the Poles, according to Captain Michalski, 4.000 casualties.

And now they have reached Rome, the first European capital to fall to Allies. It wasn't a simple triumphal procession into the heart of Rome. It meant going along Highway #6-the Via Caselina in careful infantry columns along the sides of the road. Most men had their bayonets fixed and they wore deadly earnest expressions.

A huge column of smoke billowed up from the southwest corner of the city, indicating a demolition greeted Edward's unit. Although Rome was declared an open city, still Edward's unit had to fight German rear guards at the edge of the ancient Forum. He was instrumental in destroying an enemy scout car in front of the Bank of Italy, within the shadow of Trajan's Columns. He didn't know at the time that Captain Michalski recommended him for another medal. This time it was "Polonia Restituta."

It was also here in Rome that Edward found out that Czeslawa and Danuta were in Auschwitz and Captain Michalski's efforts to liberate them thus giving Edward another lease on life.

With a million or more refugees in Rome, Captain Michalski's unit was quite busy hunting German deserters and saboteurs. Edward was asked frequently by the sappers to help to dismantle hidden mines and the great variety of German booby-traps. Edward had to admire the skillful German engineers and their tactics.

"If they are smart, we have to be smarter." He would say to the young sappers.

The very next day after the liberation of Rome, the Allied landed in France. The Polish Army newspaper of June 7th, 1944 quoted Eisenhower's broadcast to the people of Europe:

> PEOPLE OF WESTERN EUROPE
> A landing was made this morning on the coast of France by troops of the Allied Expeditionary Forces. This landing is part of a concerted United Nations plan for the liberation of Europe, made in conjunction with our great Russian Allies. I have this message for all of you. Although the initial assault may have not been in your own country, the hour of your liberation is approaching. All patriots, men and women young and old, have a part to play in the achievement of final victory!

These were very encouraging words. Hopefully the war would end soon and Edward and so many others would return to Poland, there he firmly believed he would find his beloved Czeslawa and Danuta.

On the spur of the moment both Michalski and Edward decided to go to the Vatican to pray for Victory.

They were lucky because Pope Pius XII appeared on the balcony of St. Peter. The St. Peter's Square and the new broad Via

Della Conciliazione were densely packed with thousands of Romans.

The Pope thanked both belligerents-the Allies and Germany-for having left Rome intact. He went on to say, he hoped that Italians would be worthy of grace shown them and put aside hatred and all personal vendettas.

After a prayer of thankfulness to the Blessed Virgin and Saints Peter and Paul, guardians of Rome, the Pontiff gave his blessing "urbe et orbis" as the immense crowd knelt before him.

Greatly uplifted both men walked slowly back to the place, where they have left their jeep.

"Edward, do you have a cigarette on you?" asked Mietek Michalski.

"Yes, Sir, here you are." Said Edward offering a pack.

A tall, straight as a rod, well dressed man approached and asked in Polish:

"May I also have a cigarette?" "By all means here you are."

"How did you like Pontiff's speech?" continued the stranger in Polish with an accent typical of Silesia's region of Poland.

Edward gently switched into a mixture of German and Polish used by the inhabitants of Silesia.

The man continued in the same vain for a while and when Edward started to speak German only, the man spoke it without realizing that the conversation was entirely in German.

To Edward, the man didn't appear to be malnourished. To the contrary, his face was the face of a man exposed to sun and wind. His bearing was unquestionable of a military man. But it was captain Michalski who noticed that the man's shoes didn't have any shoelaces, for the simple reason, because they were boots most likely officer's boots.

Michalski quickly took out his gun and addressed the man in German:

"You are under arrest. Pull up your pants and let's have a look at your boots."

The man did as he was told. Michalski was right, those were

officer's boots, that is German officers boots.

"What happened, didn't they have any civilian shoes in your size? You're coming with us. Should you try to escape, you'll be shot at once, as a spy."

The man shrugged his shoulders and asked for another cigarette. Edward obliged him with another cigarette.

Edward was driving the jeep with the prisoner sitting next to him. Captain Michalski sat directly behind the prisoner, his gun was touching the prisoner's back.

Once they reached their Headquarters, Michalski expertly frisked the prisoner. There was no hidden weapon on him.

"Take off your jacket and shirt, let's have a look under your arm!" ordered Captain Michalski.

"Captain, there is no sense in removing my shirt, you'll find a S.S. tattoo anyway. I am S.S. Standartenfuhrer Fritz Blau of Generalkommando 5th S.S. Gebirgskorps at your service. Do you want my serial number, Captain?"

Captain Michalski gave a long whistle of surprise. It was not everyday that a full colonel of the S.S. was being captured.

"We'll get to that. In the meantime would you like a cup of tea or coffee?"

"Coffee, please. I can't stand tea. It reminds me of the British too much."

"Well Colonel, perhaps we can be civilized to each other. The war as you see is almost won. It is only a question of time. Why keep on killing innocent people on both sides?"

"I agree with you Captain and that is why I thought I would save myself by offering you my full cooperation. I would like to discuss certain issues of great importance to your staff and the General Staff of the U.S. 5th Army. I respectfully suggest that you notify your superiors of my presence."

"Colonel, you are in no position to demand anything, is that clear?"

"Yes, Captain, very clear and that is why I "suggest" only that you contact your superiors, because the information I carry might be simply above your head."

"Maybe I will or maybe I won't. I think it might be lots of fun getting that information from you. Do you see this man? He said pointing to Edward. "This man's wife and daughter were recently sent to Auschwitz. Nothing would please him more than to cut of your balls and have you eat them."

"Captain, Captain, I thought that we are going to have a civilized conversation. Whatever you do or don't do, please try not to scare me. You don't think for a moment, that I became a colonel in the S.S. by being slouch or a softy, do you? Believe it or not I can save his family and that is a fact. If your people in the Underground in Poland can deliver a message to one of my friends at Auschwitz, we can get them out, providing of course that they are still alive. Do we have a deal Captain?"

"I believe so. How about another cup of coffee and a cigarette? If you will excuse me, I'm going to get in touch with my C.O."

Captain Michalski left the room leaving Edward and two M.P.'s in charge of the prisoner.

"Colonel Blau, where did you learn your Polish?"

"There is no mystery behind it. I was born in Katowice to German parents. Once upon a time I spoke Polish really fluently, but I see that you speak German rather well and to show you my good will, Lieutenant, write this down:

"To S.S. Hauptsturmfuhrer Helmuth Berger: "Lass Frau Daszkiewicz und tochter frei"-signed Winnetou."

"But Colonel, Winnetou as I remember was a character out of Karl May's book?"

"Correct, when we were children we used to play cowboys and Indians. I was Winnetou and he was Old Shutterhand. This way he'll know that the message came from me. Honestly, I do hope that the message gets to him in time. I may as well do something good if only to please my priest brother."

"Do you have a priest brother in Rome?"

"Yes, Lieutenant, right here in Rome."

"What is his name, Colonel?"

"Sorry Lieutenant, I can't tell you. He had nothing to do with my life ever. Besides, the church will protect him anyway or didn't you know."

At this moment Captain Michalski returned.

"It looks like we are going to lose you Colonel. They are sending a staff car for you. You'll be out of my hands. Too bad, I wanted to keep you long enough to find out if your message to Auschwitz would bring results."

"Captain, I assure you that if those people are still alive and my friend gets the message, he'll move mountains to comply with my request. You see he owes me his life several times over. Besides, you'll be doing me a favor as well. This way he'll know that I'm still alive and kicking."

"You see Colonel, unlike you, I'm a soldier, not by profession but out of necessity, brought by your kind. I do not kill innocent civilians and as a soldier I'll turn you over as ordered to my superiors. But Colonel make no mistake, nothing would please me more than to shorten you by a head."

"Yes, and I imagine many others. However, I intend to stay alive and trust me, I'll live to a ripe old age."

"Bastards like you usually do." Ganz Genau Herr Blau. "Exactly so."

"My Goodness, Captain. You can even rhyme in German."

Further exchange of words ended with the entrance of the room of several armed soldiers and staff officers.

"Captain Michalski, we came to claim the prisoner. Here are your written orders."

"He is all yours. I do hope you'll know what to do with him."

"Don't worry, Captain, justice shall prevail." Said one of the staff officers, putting the handcuffs on the S.S. Colonel Blau. The Colonel lifted his head and gave Captain Michalski a smile and said:

"Captain, thank you for your hospitality."

"Oh, go to hell!" "The place is too crowded already, they don't have room for me."

"Get going?" said one of the soldiers,, giving Col. Blau a punch in the kidney.

"Edward!" said Captain Michalski "I'm going to send the message to the A.K. unit in the vicinity of Auschwitz. Hope to God, for your sake, that that bastard was saying the truth.

You get some sleep. That's an order. Tomorrow we are going to chase the "Tedeschi's" in Bracchiano and if we are lucky in the Port of Civitavecchia, about forty miles northwest from here. Good night Edward."

"Good night Mietek, Captain, Sir and thanks again for thinking about my family."

"Glowa do gory" Keep your head up. Tomorrow is another day."

CHAPTER 32

After her outburst, Czeslawa Daszkiewicz was sorry that she and Danuta didn't join Edward on his trip to Hungary and Romania. It was too late to change her mind, he had left already.

Her neighbor, Mrs. Elzbieta Baranska noticed the team of horses that took Edward away.

"Where is our Pan Edward going this time?" she politely asked.

"He went to the Chabarowka railroad station to catch a train. His boss sent him to get something for the hotel."

"Czeslawa that is strange, because as far as I know there are no trains running today."

"Are you sure Pani Baranska?" "I'm quite sure, my nephew came back this morning from the station. There are no trains?"

Czeslawa was totally confused. Why didn't he then come home, perhaps he is still at the station, waiting for the train. She had better go there and find out for herself, running upstairs to get dressed and take some money with her.

Hurriedly she instructed Mrs. Bujnicki to take care of Danuta, till she returns from Chabarowka.

"Go ahead and don't worry. I'll take good care of her. It isn't the first time, besides she is a big girl by now."

Czeslawa ran out of the house towards the intersection of Tatrzanska and Gorska streets, where the "droshkys' were located.

Without asking the price to Chabarowka, she pressured the driver to get there as quickly as his horse could make it.

"I need to catch my husband at the station, please hurry up."

"Lady, the trains aren't running. If he is there, he'll be there when we arrive, so don't worry."

"Please hurry anyway."

The driver whipped the horse on both sides, the horse got the message because he went into the gallop.

They arrived at the practically empty station. There was no trace of Edward, Czeslawa started to make inquiries, but people learned not to get involved. Nobody knew anything. However the man at the small kiosk, who knew Edward slightly was more helpful. He volunteered some information:

"Yes, Lady, I saw him hitching a ride with an O.T. truck." "Thank you very much." And Czeslawa took the same "droshky" back to Zakopane.

Relieved somewhat, she asked the driver if he knew a fellow driver by the name of Jan.

"Lady, almost everyone around here is named Jan, what does his horse look like?"

She described the horse the best way she could.

"That is enough, I know who he is. Do you want me to stop at his house? It's on the way home anyway."

"That is a good idea, thank you."

The driver located Jan's small house. Czeslawa was in luck because Jan was home having his meal.

"Let the Lord's name be praised." Said Czeslawa entering the house.

"For ever and ever, Jesus, Maria, it's Pani Daszkiewicz."

"That's me I only want to find out what has happened to my husband. You took him to Chabarowka, right?"

"Yes Pani Daszkiewicz, I brought him to the station, but he asked to be dropped of some 100 meters from the station itself, not wanting to bring attention to himself. I was glad, because I was in the same situation. I don't mind to help the Underground but I have a family to feed. You do understand? I dropped him off as told and went straight home. Assuming that he took the train. I didn't see him anymore."

"Thank you Pan Jan." and they left the house.

Deep in her thoughts she kept silent all the way home. She

paid the driver, who surprisingly asked for little money. She even asked why so little and he answered:

"If this is all for the Underground than I want to be of help." She simply thanked him.

There was nothing else to do unless she contacted "Kciuk" and requested from the Underground that she and Danuta be able to join Edward.

Cyprian Bujnicki whom Czeslawa called "tata" knew "Kciuk" personally, therefore he offered to speak with him on Czeslawa's behalf.

A few days later Bujnicki came home from seeing "Kciuk".

"The man didn't promise anything but to relay the message. We'll have to wait a couple of weeks for their answer."

Czeslawa didn't put much faith in "Kciuk" and his organization. Nothing most likely will come out of it. Besides, Edward by that time would be kilometers and kilometers away from home.

With Edward being absent, their apartment became a lonely place. Danuta would ask Czeslawa almost everyday "when is papa coming home?"

"Darling be patient, I miss him too. There is a war going on as you very well know and he has an important task to fulfill. One day you'll be very proud of him."

"Mama, I was always very proud of him but I would have preferred that he stayed home."

"I know that too, Danuta, just keep being busy and the time will fly faster."

They both applied themselves to painting and to church activities.

Czeslawa like the rest of the Poles was a firm Catholic and now she spent more and more time in church. At the confessional booth, the priest wanted to know Edward's whereabouts.

Warned that some priests worked for the Germans, Czeslawa took a cautious line:

"Father, I think that my husband left me for another woman."

"I always knew that that husband of yours was no good. No wonder he never came to church."

Czeslawa ignored the last remark and continued with confessing her "sins".

The long and slow days changed into quick weeks and even faster months. Only once during that time did Czeslawa have indirect news about Edward. Someone from the "White couriers" had seen Edward in Budapest on his way to Romania. No details were given her.

Married women whose husbands are away have a special attraction and unwelcome in most of the cases, attention, by other married men.

This was the case with a certain Mr. Kajetan Burczyk, who was in charge of the distribution of ration cards. The man had an eye on Czeslawa for some time now.

"Pani Daszkiewicz, if you want cards for your husband and daughter, you have to bring both of them here, unless you decide to be more friendly to me."

"Thank you Pan Burczyk, I'll bring my daughter but my husband is currently traveling on behalf of his firm."

"That is fine, just bring your daughter then."

The next day, Czeslawa brought Danuta to Burczyk's office. "This is my daughter, Pan Burczyk."

"Do you know something, Pani Daszkiewicz, she doesn't look like you at all. She looks like a Jewess. Is your husband Jewish?"

"Of course not what an idea? You Pan Burczyk are an idiot."

"Maybe I am and maybe I'm not. It remains to be seen. We'll have a closer look. You're not from Zakopane, are you?"

"What has that to do with cards?"

"Everything my dear Pani Daszkiewicz, everything as you'll soon see." There was a threat in his voice. "Next!" The interview was over.

"Why was that man so angry, mama? Who is Jewish? What was he talking about?"

"Don't worry precious. That man is an idiot and I told him so. Forget all about him."

That evening after Danuta went to sleep, Czeslawa went downstairs to speak with Bujnickis. She told them about the conversation she had with Burczyk.

"That is indeed unfortunate, because Burczyk is one of those "szmalcowniks" people who denounce other people to the Gestapo. He is without any scruples. Keep away from him as much as you can. He can do lots of harm. I would offer him a bribe but I'm afraid that he'll keep asking for more and more. Czeslawa, we never asked you to tell us if Danuta is of Jewish origins. She is your daughter and that is good enough for us. Jewish or not Jewish it doesn't matter to us at all. We love her as much as we love you, perhaps even a bit more. We see that you take her to church all the time. She'll be a good Catholic just like us."

Czeslawa embraced and kissed both of them. She started to tell them all about her past. Her marriage to Edward, the loss of her parents and the tragic loss of her own child and adopting Danuta. They all started to cry while she told her story. Finally Bujnicki through tears said:

"I believe that God has sent you to us for our old age. You'll be our daughter forever. Let the Holy Mother of Czestochowa keep us in Her care. Amen."

Czeslawa received several notes from Kajetan Burczyk, requesting that they meet. She ignored all those messages. Each time the note became more threatening. Finally Czeslawa agreed to meet with him but only across the street from his office.

"Pan Burczyk, what is the purpose of your letter? My husband has connections with the A.K. and he'll kill you."

"Not so fast my dear. I don't think he is alive any longer. Otherwise he would have been here by this time. Like it or not Germany is going to win this war. I applied to become a Volksdeutch, so you had better treat me with respect."

"Pan Burczyk, you're a handsome man. You can have any woman

you want but you're not my type I'm sorry to say, so please leave me alone."

"I'll stop as soon as you will spend a little time in bed with me. Do you understand me?"

"Only too well but not as long as you live. I would rather die than submit to you!"

"If that is what you want that you'll get. Your final yes or no?"

"No, Pan Burczyk and a thousand times, no. Is that clear to you?"

"It is clear to me that you and your daughter are as good as dead. One day you'll beg me on your knees to change my mind but it will be too late."

A whole month passed by peacefully and Czeslawa didn't hear anymore from Burczyk. She was sure that the matter was forgotten, although Cyprian Bujnicki mentioned that he came across some strangers loitering near the house. He even stopped one man inquiring as to what was that man doing in the area. The man explained that he was lost and needed directions to the center of the town. That incident was soon forgotten.

Czeslawa exhausted her art supplies which she replaced usually by going to Cracow to her sources, a trip lasting an average one or two days. On such occasion she would carry some butter and kielbasy to barter for needed items. She would always return with gifts for the entire family.

She left Zakopane without a single worry. It was a routine trip, like so many other trips she had undertaken. Having accomplished the purpose of her trip, this time she obtained even nicer gifts for Danuta and Bujnickis. Therefore in a happy mood she rushed home.

The door to the house was opened by Mrs. Bujnicki. She looked very distraught.

"What has happened, mama?" scared asked Danuta.

"Tragedy, the Police took away Danuta, claiming that she was Jewish. Cyprian went after her to the Police, where he was beaten so badly, that he can't speak at all."

"When did that happen?" "This morning, a couple of hours ago. We're waiting for you."

"Where is Danuta now?" "As far as I know still at the Police Station."

"I'm going there right now. Where is "tata"?"

"In the bedroom, but don't waste any time with him just go and bring Danuta home>"

Czeslawa ran to her room to retrieve Danuta's Baptismal certificate and went to the Police Station. Her heart was beating like a church bell. Will she get there in time?

CHAPTER 33

"Goldie Locks" crew was always sad to leave the friendly base in Eastern Britain, whether it was their first or 13th bombing mission. This time too "Goldie Locks" had plenty of company, because it was going to be a massive raid to targets directly related to the future battle in the Calais area of the Northern France. The presumed place where landing would be made.

The precise targets were bridges, tunnels, railroad junctions and locomotive depots. Captain Krafchin's four-engine "Goldie Locks" carried enough heavy bombs for giving the enemy target a crippling blow. Should the bombs miss their intended target, the power of detonation would do the rest.

With her new Norden bombsight and devices such as "H2S"-radar scanner, "Oboe" and "Window", "Goldie Locks" was more accurate than ever. She was not as well armed as the B-17 and less agile, she still had enough defensive guns to keep enemy fighters at a reasonable distance.

Personally, Captain Krafchin was grateful for the presence of the improved P-51 Mustang fighters, a highly successful combination of British engines and American technology. Now the Mustangs had detachable fuel tanks that enabled them to fly deep into Germany, where after jettisoning their extra tanks became very advanced fighters.

Their counterparts, the Me-110 a great, twin engine aircraft, performed actually admirably in the fighter-bomber, reconnaissance and night-fighters role. However, they could not win a dogfight with the lighter, single engine P-51 or Hurricane or even the Spitfire. The Me-109 also a great fighter lacked the range to escort bombers past London and had only few minutes of battle time over the target.

After bombing the Calais area, the armada of American planes turned towards Furth, Stuttgart and Regensburg in Germany. Some of those older towns, where the centers were congested and largely of wooden construction suffered badly when incendiary bombs were dropped. The areas would burn so fiercely, that the combustion produced winds, which raised temperatures even higher, not simply burning but cremating Germans by the thousands.

American losses were small that day. Almost 1.000 bombers were sent against a dozen targets over France and Germany and only 21 planes were lost.

Luckily, "Goldie Locks" was not among them. With the exception of some minor damages caused by enemy flak guns mounted on rail cars, the plane and crew returned safely to the base.

After changing into his regular uniform, Captain Paul Krafchin attended the debriefing session and filled the usual routine reports.

Following the local custom, the pilots of successful missions would gather in the nearby pub to exchange their various experiences. On such occasions, the drinks would flow freely. The young warriors had to prove to themselves that they are still alive. It was still early in the evening but a party was going on full blast. The tobacco smoke was thicker than the English fog. An airman was playing the out of tune piano and next to him, a blond lieutenant in a smart crew cut was singing a popular song to the melody of Colonel Bogey:

> "Hitler-has only got one ball
> Goering's two are far too small
> Himler- is rather simpler
> But Goeballs-has no balls at all."

The last refrain would be sung by all the pub: "No balls at all, no balls at all, he had no balls at all." It was the airwomen who sung the loudest to everybody's delight.

After a couple of hours of unwinding in the easy company of men in uniforms, Paul's thoughts would turn to females in general and Vivian in particular, realizing that she was gone and he had a date with Cynthia Epstein the very next day, which was Friday night for the Sabbath meal with her family.

He was debating with himself if he should keep that date. Paul missed Vivian already, he missed her proximity. They knew and understood each other's need perfectly. There was no demand on the individual partners. Vivian never wanted or asked for prolonged foreplay. A few minutes after they were alone, they would find themselves in bed making love. There was no false pretense of any kind. For Paul who was an actual beginner in this game, she was an ideal woman, deeply satisfying his every wish or whim. For Vivian, the relationship was more complex, because she required a variety of men, including her fiancée. It was a flaw in her character that Paul had to put up with, but that never prevented him from enjoying her as a woman.

Vivian did mention to Paul that Cynthia was still a virgin and with the reputation, deserved or not deserved, brought from home, that Jewish girls don't "put out," Paul was doubtful how far he would be able to get with Cynthia. With no other options left for that Friday night, he called Cynthia's house.

Cynthia wasn't home, informed her father, however, everyone in Epstein's family was looking forward to meeting a fellow Jew from the New World. Mr. Epstein sounded exactly like Anthony Eden that is very pleasant. Paul was in a tight spot. "I'll be glad to come. May I have directions to your place?" Mr. Epstein obliged him by giving him detailed information.

"You couldn't possibly get lost."

"I hope so, it's easier for me to navigate in the air, than on the streets of British cities."

They both had a good laugh.

The next day, Paul attended to his plane, making sure that every small detail was taken care of and that the plane was flight ready. Whatever problems were with the crew he left it to his right hand man, Lt. George Perry. With some difficulties he obtained a 24 hour pass to leave the base.

He packed few personal items and a few small gifts, purchased at the P.X. store and picked up a Jeep from the motor pool.

He was recognized by the same sergeant, who was most helpful, the last time he needed the Jeep to go to Brighton. The sergeant greeted him like a long lost friend:

"Captain I have a brand new, in mint condition vehicle for you, with just few miles on it."

"Sorry, sergeant, I'm not buying it today, maybe after the war, sarge, but as long as it will take me where I want to go, I'll take it. Thanks."

"Don't worry Captain, it will get you there."

Having gotten lost only twice despite the "excellent" directions and being very careful to drive on the left side of the road, Paul finally located Epstein's house.

From the upstairs window, a young face was watching Paul's arrival. It was Cynthia's 16 year old brother who came down to fetch Paul.

"I'm Lloyd Epstein" he introduced himself "and you must be Captain Krafchin."

"It's me, alright or should I say it is I?"

"Anyway you wish, Sir. Please follow me, can I take your bag?"

"Go right ahead, Lloyd."

The door to their apartment was ajar. There stood a middle aged man with a large forehead, about 5'4" and a most pleasant smile:

I'm James Epstein, Cynthia's father, please do come in."

Paul walked in to be greeted by Mrs. Epstein. "I'm Eva Epstein. By this time you have met our entire family. "She was slightly plump, an elegantly dressed woman in her early forties, shaking hands with Paul.

468-LEE

"Cynthia just called. She is unadvertantly detained at her office. The Army as you very well know. She suggested that we don't wait and start without her. She'll come as soon as possible. She sounded very sorry."

"James, how about a drink for our guest."

"I was about to ask him. Is Scotch whisky alright?"

"That will be fine, are you going to join me?"

"Of course, but we drink it without ice."

"Personally I do prefer it with ice but I can drink it without."

Everywhere Paul looked were books and more books. Mr. Epstein who followed Paul's surprised look, said:

"Sometimes I myself think that we do live in a library. You see, both Cynthia and I are historians, we teach medieval history at the local university. My wife Eva teaches organic chemistry and that to some degree explains the presence of so many books. Lloyd's books are in his room."

"I'm impressed, Mr. Epstein. I, however, with the exception of technical books, must have read in the last few years hardly a novel."

"I suppose the war had something to do with it?"

"It surely has."

"Let's forget the war for a moment. Eva prepared a nice, typical Jewish dinner in your honor, please come to the table."

"What about Cynthia?"

"What about her? She'll eat whenever she comes home, I hope not too late. She has that hush-hush job which she never talks to us about. We know that much that part of her duties is to record and analyze everything that is connected with the war. As a historian I can tell you how quickly memory vanishes if it isn't recorded. At the end it is the victor who will write the history."

"That means us, we hope."

"Gentlemen, please come to the table, the food is getting cold." This time Eva was wearing an apron. The men came to the table. The lit Sabbath candles kept the room in a warm embrace.

The food, similar to the one served by his parents in Brooklyn, was served. The only difference was obvious, the portions were much smaller.

"Is that true that the steaks served in America could feed an entire family in Britain?"

"True enough but that was in prewar America."

"Since 1940 we in England learned to eat less, but we are far from starving."

"I'm sure of that." The telephone rang interrupting the conversation. "That must be Cynthia."

Mrs. Epstein picked up the receiver and spoke briefly with the caller.

"Captain Krafchin, it's Cynthia, she wishes to speak with you."

"Paul, I'm terribly sorry, but I can't make it home in time. One of the German flying bombs hit a nearby building and we have to evacuate our files and archives in case of a fire. Since I'm in charge of this unit, I must make sure that everything is taken care of. I will see you, I hope, some other day. I'll make it up, I promise." And she hung up without him having a chance to say a word.

"Captain, we are very disappointed that Cynthia couldn't join us, she asked that you stay with us over night and relax a bit. It would be such an honor for all of us. You can have her bedroom."

The idea of spending the night at the Epsteins actually appealed to Paul. He was tired and didn't feel like driving back at night through the dark and winding streets.

"I'll take you up on your kind offer. Truthfully I'm beat and could use some rest."

"That's great. Let's have some tea and cookies and then you can retire anytime you wish."

By the time Paul finished with tea, he was literally falling asleep.

"Please excuse me I think I'm ready for bed. Thank you very much for a most delicious dinner and your hospitality."

"Let me show you to the room, Paul. May I call you Paul?"

"By all means, that is my name."

"In that case please call me Eva."

Eva opened the door of Cynthia's bedroom. Light blue colors

dominated the pleasant room. Excellent oil paintings depicting London, Hyde Park and Picadilly Circus graced the walls. Next to the bed, on the night table, there was a large photograph of Cynthia with a handsome man in the British Royal Navy uniform.

Paul picked up the picture to have a closer look. The photographer captured a rare moment of a couple in love.

"Yes, Paul, that is Cynthia and her fiancée, Jason. They were never officially engaged. The war changed their plans."

"Where is he now?"

"His ship was torpedoed, some survivors were picked up by the German submarine crew. That was according to a BBC broadcast. We don't know if he is dead or alive. Cynthia and Jason know each other since they were both children in kindergarten. His parents are our best friends and colleagues at the university."

"Sorry to hear this."

"It is a bloody pity, Paul, but life has to go on and Cynthia is entitled to some measure of happiness, don't you agree?"

"Oh, absolutely. The man might be in some Stalag. Being Jewish may complicate matters somewhat."

"There is no problem in that respect, Jason is not Jewish."

"I see."

"Well Paul, I shall bid you goodnight. Breakfast, anytime you feel like having one."

"Thanks Eva, wish James pleasant dreams."

"If I know my husband he is asleep already, Goodnight."

Paul undressed and slipped under the covers. Next to the picture of Cynthia and Jason there was a thick book about Napoleon. Paul read barely few pages when the book fell out of his hands and he was deep asleep with the lights still burning bright.

CHAPTER 34

Herr Jaeger kept his word, because a horse driven carriage brought Astrid and Henryk back to the Sanitarium Dorfen.

"Please give our thanks to Herr Jaeger" Astrid said to the driver just as they were getting off.

"Fraulein, I don't know who you are but in all the years that I have known Herr Jaeger he never sent a carriage for or took anybody home."

"There is always the first time." Said Astrid smiling.

The guard at the Sanatorium entrance recognized Astrid: "They are looking for you everywhere, please report to Maj. Scharf at once.""

Dressed as she was she went straight to see Maj. Scharf.

"Astrid, where the hell have you been? We received another transport of 76 wounded soldiers. I have no idea where to put them. We are bursting at the seams as it is. We'll have to send some of the convalescents back to their units. Every room and hallway will have to absorb additional people. There is nothing else we can do. I'm near a nervous breakdown myself. Why are you still in your coat, change and let's go see what can be done."

Astrid was an excellent problem solver. She achieved more with a smile than with a direct order "Befehl."

Besides wounded soldiers didn't take too kindly to orders. They lost their fear of authority in the bloodied, snow covered fields of Moscovy.

In a response to an order, some of the tough veterans, aged beyond their years would comment:

"Do you know what to do with that order? Stick it up your arse." Or a more refined:

"Take a flying fuck at a rolling doughnut." Reducing many nurses to tears.

Astrid usually pacified some of the most difficult cases. Small wonder that Maj. Scharf needed her around the clock. She has been known for going without sleep or with very little sleep for days if need be.

Henryk, upon his return, was not at all missed. He was just another dogface. He kept to himself, reading whatever book he could get hold of or painting when his mood pushed him to it, playing a game of chess when asked.

During the next two weeks he had seen Astrid from afar only. He was aware of the additional wounded that were put into the already crowded Sanatorium. Astrid had her work cut out for her. In order to accommodate the newly arrived some of the previous, not fully recovered patients, were sent home with orders to report to their units a few weeks later.

Every available German soldier was desperately needed. Allied Forces landed in Normandy, to the surprise of many and the Red Army was already on the territory of prewar Poland. The radio and the newspaper reports were very optimistic that the Allies would be shortly pushed back to sea and the Asiatic Hordes would be punished by the new weapons that Adolf Hitler promised the nation.

Henryk was still too weak to walk any distance and any furlough to the area taken over by the Soviets was out of the question. He would listen to the discussion among the men. Nobody asked for his opinion and he wasn't about to volunteer.

Lately he started to playa solitaire card game in the large room that served as a lecture hall, library and card game room at the same time. He sat behind a small table, playing the newly acquired game, but try as he did, the cards didn't cooperate, game after game ended unsatisfactorily.

Someone touched his neck. He recognized that touch immediately. The fingers belong to Astrid.

"Liebchen, how are you? Remember, unlucky in cards, lucky

in love. I have a big surprise for you. You'll never guess what is it?"

"Alright, I give up, what is it?"

"Major and Mrs. Dennhard invited us to their house in Icking for dinner."

"That is very nice, however I don't feel comfortable in their company for obvious reasons. Also being a non –com I'm out of place among the high brass."

"I knew that and that's why I arranged for you to wear a dark civilian suit. It's hanging in your locker already together with a new shirt and tie."

"You seem to think of everything, Liebchen."

"Being a general's daughter, it comes naturally to me. Don't forget Saturday at 6P.M. we'll be picked up by Maj. Dennhard's driver at the entrance to the Sanatorium."

"At your service, Madam." He got up and gave her a mock salute. He played out another game of solitaire. This time he won. Henryk picked up his deck of cards and went to his locker to check on his latest acquisitions.

There it was, an elegant charcoal gray, striped suit next to which hung a white, freshly starched shirt, black and red dotted tie complemented the suit. Who ever selected that suit had an excellent taste in clothing. He tried on the jacket and the pants, both were like made to order. It must have been Astrid. That woman had so many desired qualities that sometimes scared him. She seemed to anticipate his every wish or thought. And yet he still didn't take her to bed. It was something that both of them desired. Intuitively they felt that each will be able to satisfy the other.

It was more of a question of when rather than where. "Haderbrau" Inn would have been an ideal place to conclude the union of their bodies, unfortunately or fortunately she fell asleep and he was too tired to initiate anything else.

Perhaps tomorrow after the dinner at Dennhards there might be a new opportunity.

Saturday morning at breakfast time Henryk met Astrid.

"Liebchen, here is your 24 hour pass and a lab coat."

"What is that lab coat for?" puzzled asked Henryk.

"Put that coat over your suite when you walk out of the Sanatorium, you can take if off before you enter the car, that the Dennhards are sending for us at 6P.M. It also might be a good idea to shave once more before you leave." She gave him a disarming smile.

"Is there anything else that you didn't think of?"

"Yes there is." She sung a line from a popular folk song:

"Meine Liebe und Deine Liebe sind beide gleich." "My love and your love are both the same."

"Astrid...." He started to say something.

"I know, I love you too. By the way, Maj. Scharf is also invited, I have to run, see you later."

Henryk was watching her leave, she walked proudly, gracefully with undeniable purpose in each of her steps. That was Astrid a woman of his choice.

The rest of the day seemed to drag forever. He played few games of chess, losing each time even to a much inferior player, causing the man to comment:

"Heinrich, your head is someplace else."

"Yah, it is one of those days my friend."

Something is going to happen. Of that he was sure. Astrid getting him a civilian suit and generally acting a bit strange or what was even more worrisome like a woman smitten by love.

Henryk took his suit, shirt and tie out of the locker and went to the general washroom. He hung up his suit on a hook and covered it with the lab coat. He swiftly shaved and washed up.

In one of the cubicles he put on the suit however tying the tie was a major effort, which he somehow overcame. Once dressed, he put on the lab coat and walked out of the restroom area.

No one paid the slightest attention to him. One more medical orderly walked the corridors. He walked toward the Sanatorium's exit almost colliding at the end of the hallway with Maj. Scharf.

"I beg your pardon, Sir."

"Watch where you are going soldier. Isn't that Kaplinski? What the hell are you doing in a lab coat? Hold it, this gives me an idea. Sooner or later we have to discharge you and send you back to your unit, which you are not in a position of doing as yet. In the meantime we could use some help right here in Dorfen, I'll arrange for your permanent transfer to our Medical Unit. I'm sure that will meet your and Astrid's approval."

"Major is very kind and understanding."

"I was a doctor before I became a Major, don't you forget that, Kaplinski. Looks like we are going to spend this evening together. Tell me, what did a beautiful woman like Astrid see in you?"

"I surely don't know, Sir."

"But I do and that counts the most." Said Astrid who overheard the latest exchange.

Next to a shiny, black Oppel stood an elderly man. Seeing Maj. Scharf, he took off his cap.

"Are you Major Scharf and the party?"

"Yes, we are, my good man."

"Please get in, it is a short 10-15 minutes ride, Sir."

They all sat in the back of the car with Astrid sitting between the men.

Maj. Scharf kept asking Astrid about specific cases under her care. Henryk just sat there listening to the conversation. In no time at all they reached the small town of Icking.

Judging by the size of individual homes, poor people didn't live in that area. Probably among them lived also party bigwigs and a variety of notables. In respectful distance from those houses, Henryk spotted several stables.

The chauffeur pulled into a circular driveway in front of a large and modern villa, almost totally surrounded by fern trees and quite a few thick oaks.

The door to the house was opened by a maid, who politely curtsied seeing Maj. Scharf in his dress uniform. She took Astrid's coat and hung it in the guest closet.

Only now for the first time did Henryk see Astrid in all her splendid glory. She wore a long black dress, cut out in the back, displaying her beautiful, alabaster like skin. A single string of pearls emphasized her quiet elegance.

Through a double glass door, both Gretchen and Georg-Hans Dennhard came to greet them. His only eye was focused on Astrid.

"Fraulein von Vietinghoff looks absolutely ravishing, doesn't she, Gretchen?"

"I agree with you Georg. Herr Kaplinski you had better watch out because in the salon there are a few wolves in sheep clothing."

"Thank you Mrs. Dennhard for the warning. Half of the hospital staff and all the patients are already in love with Fraulein von Vietinghoff."

"They say that competition is good for business, but I'm not sure in this case."

It was Maj. Dennhard who introduced Maj. Scharf, Astrid and Henryk to the other four couples already assembled in the oak paneled salon that served as a sitting room. Two of the men wore their party lapel pins on their jackets. Astrid stole the scene, because all the men started to flirt with her much to the annoyance of their wives.

Maj. Dennhard noticing the attention that Astrid caused, said jokingly:

"Gentlemen, gentlemen, Fraulein von Vietinghoff is already spoken for. This young fellow is engaged to her, isn't that so Fraulein?"

"It is absolutely true, although my Heinrich doesn't know it yet. When I met him for the first time, I like Elsa pleaded with Lohengrin to tell me his name. He wouldn't say it because he was brought to the hospital heavily wounded. Now I just want to be Juliet to my Romeo or Brunnhilde to my Siegfried, is that too much to ask for?"

All eyes turned on Henryk. The situation in the room changed drastically, everybody wanted to be a matchmaker.

Henryk was a perfect picture of an embarrassed groom. Astrid who caused all of this came over to Henryk and put her hand on his shoulder. It was Henryk's turn to speak:

"Ladies and Gentlemen, I thought that I would propose to Fraulein Astrid in private. If she would turn down my proposal I would be the only one to know about it. Now that I have all of you cheering for me, I'm going to ask her to marry me. Fraulein Astrid, will you marry me?" he said facing Astrid."

"You have to get down on your knee."

"And now?"

"Yes, a hundred times yes." She kissed him to the sound of applause coming from everybody in the room including the maid.

"Georg, this calls for our best champagne."

"Absolutely Gretchen. As a Burgermeister of Wolfratshausen I'll be honored to see you both in our "Standesamt" at City Hall.

"In that case I'll give the bride away." Said Maj. Scharf. "Let's have some more Schnapps."

The party started in an upbeat mood. The maid and the chauffeur, who acted as the bartender, barely were able to keep up with requests for drinks.

The guests were far from being sober when Gretchen Dennhard announced dinner, much to Henryk's relief; the food was now the center of attention.

Venison in various forms, from hunter's soup to ragout and chops, was served on large Rosenthal trays with delicious smelling home fried potatoes. Many toasts were made to the health and happiness of the young couple and every toast was also matched by toasts for Germany's victory over her enemies.

Next to Henryk sat Herr Ludwig Stumpf, whose brother was a general in the Luftwaffe. He displayed an interest in Henryk's background. Lucky for Henryk that Maj. Scharf answered the questions addressed to Henryk.

"Herr Kaplinski is on our medical staff despite the fact that he was wounded in action. General-Oberst von Vietinghoff himself decorated Heinrich for bravery. We are very proud of him."

Herr Stumpf was very much impressed and for reasons known

only to him, he started to address Henryk as Herr Doctor. No one tried to correct him, especially Henryk who was watching Herr Stumpf getting drunk. It was Herr Stumpf who in his drunken stupor didn't notice when he knocked down a crystal goblet.

Both Maj. Scharf and Henryk bent down under the table trying to retrieve it. Their hands met over the goblet. The thick Persian carpet prevented the glass from breaking Maj. Schard said quietly to Henryk:

"Too bad that you didn't step on the glass, that would have made everything Kosher."

Henryk sobered at once. He suddenly understood that Maj. Scharf knew about his real identity. Henryk like the biblical Daniel was in the lion's den.

"Don't worry Heinrich, remember what I've told you. I was a doctor before I became a Major. It was my step father, a Jew who put me through Medical School and I'm paying him back through you."

CHAPTER 35

The German Fourteenth Army has been "Dispersed to the four winds" Allied Headquarters declared on June 13th, 1944, but as far as Capt. Michalski and Lt. Daszkiewicz could see, the Krauts still were putting up a stiff resistance as their depleted units fell back towards the Florence area.

Capt. Michalski's company instead of going to Civitavecchia had been ordered to move towards vital points near the important highway hub of Grosseto some 14 road miles northwest of the Capital and Terni just 62 miles north of it.

Bursting through another line of defenses, hastily thrown up by the retreating Germans, Terni an important industrial and communication center was captured, including vast quantities of Nazi food supplies.

Fighting along the British 8th Army, Capt. Michalski's unit helped to clean lateral highway #74, running inland from the coast past the northern shore of Lake Bolsena.

Friday, July 21st, 1944 was a day that Michalski and Daszkiewicz will never forget as long as they both shall live, for two unrelated reasons.

Adolf Hitler had a narrow escape from death by assassination at his secret headquarters. A few hours later in a radio broadcast to the German people, that both of them heard Hitler blamed an "officers" clique for the attempt to kill him. He also announced that a purge of the conspirators was under way.

"What unbelievable luck, the son of a bitch has, can you imagine?" frustrated said Edward, sitting with Michalski in the Officer's Mess and discussing the latest news and what that might mean to end the war. Their further discussions were interrupted by a motorcycle messenger from the Divisional Headquarters, who came up to Capt. Michalski, clicked his heels and saluted:

"Capt. Michalski? I have an urgent communication for you. Kindly sign the receipt."

It was a very short message which he read aloud"

"Be advised that S.S. Col. Fritz Blau escaped. Your presence at Headquarters is at once requested."

Signed: Maj. Wieslaw Krzemien

Capt. Michalski started to curse, using a language that even Edward's not so tender ears never heard before.

"We should have shot the bastard while we had a chance and now he is loose. Those lazy bums let him escape. You better come along to Headquarters."

The reception at Headquarters was icy and brief as they reported to Maj. Krzemien.

"You two are ordered back to Rome to launch an investigation of circumstances leading to Blau's escape. If within 3 weeks you can't locate Blau, you are to return to this unit. That is all. Dismissed."

They packed up their gears including submachine guns, extra ammunition and fuel for their Jeep. They drove back to Rome. Every where they saw signs of the retreated German Army, that left in many places trails of smoke, abandoned vehicles and many loose-covered shallow graves.

Driving carefully, allowing for many pot holes and craters, caused by the weather as well as by heavy tanks that traveled this road, Michalski after being lost in his thoughts, started to speak:

"I'll court-martial whoever was directly responsible for Blau's escape and the supervisory personnel for dereliction of their duties."

"Mietek, didn't Blau mention that he had a priest brother in Rome? We should try to locate him through the Vatican or with the help of the Polish clergy. The priest may know about his brother's whereabouts, although I doubt it very much if Blau would want to involve his priest brother. It's too obvious."

"On the other hand he may do it because it so obvious. I'll have to start the investigation from the beginning and see where it will lead us."

Edward sharply braked the car to avoid hitting a woman, dressed in black walking with a child along the road.

"You almost ran her over, Edward."

"I didn't see them, was too busy talking to you."

What looked from the back to be an old woman, was actually a person in her late twenties with her young, maybe 8 years old girl, who reminded Edward of his own Danuta, his Danuta was at least six years older.

"Santa Maria, Santa Francisca, Santa Sevira, Santa Magdalen. . . ."

"Basta, basta!" Michalski who could speak some Italian asked her what was she doing in the middle of the road? The woman kept pointing south "Roma, Roma."

"I guess she wants to go to Rome, but we are not allowed to transport civilians, are we?"

"Who the hell cares, tell her to get in the back and cover herself and the child with the blanket."

"Grazia, grazia mile." Agitated she spoke fast using local dialect, which Michalski couldn't follow.

"Por favore, non parlare il dialecto."

The woman just kept talking. To shut her up Michalski gave her two bars of chocolate, which she promptly shared with her daughter. She was very thankful and pointing to herself and her daughter she introduced herself as Marcella Zurlini and the girl as Clara.

From now on Marcella concentrated her attention upon Capt. Michalski. He spoke some Italian, had an extra star on his uniform and had a driver and drivers didn't amount to much according to street smart Marcella.

"Mietek, ask her where is her husband?" Whatever her answer was, Edward understood two words "morte" and Stalingrad.

The jeep they were driving approached the northern outskirts of the neglected part of Rome of row after row of gray 4 story buildings. Marcella pointed to a house in the middle of Garibaldi Street. The number #125 was barely visible.

"Edward, stop here, that is where they live."

Capt. Michalski talked to her for a few minutes but whatever he told her she reacted by kissing him squarely on the lips and than she walked to Edward who was sitting behind the wheel and shook hands with him.

Michalski's parting words to Marcella was: "Retorne subito" I shall soon return, Ciao."

"Edward, what are you looking like that for? You are a married man and I'm still single, besides I do like her. She is direct without false modesty."

"Good luck but be careful." "I promise, I'll do so."

Driving another half an hour they reached the building, that served as a temporary stockade, from which Col. Blau escaped.

Capt. Michalski identified himself at the guard house and requested to see the officer in charge. Soon they were escorted by another guard to see Capt. Zygmunt Kapusciak.

"Capt. Michalski, we have been expecting you. Unfortunately, a serious neglect of duties has occurred for which we are very sorry."

"Captain Kapusciak, I'm not a bit interested in your apologies. I want to interrogate everyone involved or connected with Col. Blau. Can I use your office for that purpose?"

"Surely, Sir." "Let me have the guard roster for the day, I presume that you have one?"

"Yes Sir, here are the papers pertinent to the case including my own, detailed report."

Capt. Michalski looked at the roster first.

"Let me start with two men who have seen Blau last."

"That would be Corporal Roszyk and P.F.C. Majewski, I'll get them for you at once."

A couple of minutes later, two very scared and very young soldiers came into the room.

"Corporal Roszyk and P.F.C. Majewski reporting as ordered, Sir."

"At ease. Now tell me exactly what and how did it happen? Don't overlook even the smallest and the most insignificant detail, otherwise the both of you will rot in jail and that I promise you. Corporal you start first."

"Captain, Sir we swear to God that we'll tell you the truth."

"Go ahead, Corporal."

"We took over guarding Col. Blau from P.F.C. Rozpedek and P.F.C. Kotowicz at 9A.M.that morning. They informed us that Col. Blau had an upset stomach and required several trips to the restroom. Each time he went to the toilet one of the men went along. We were told to expect the same. Col. Blau asked to be taken to the toilet exactly at 9:12 because he was due to see Capt. Kapusciak at 9:30. Col. Blau was always polite and friendly. He spoke Polish with us, explaining that he was a Pole wearing a German uniform only to fight Bolsheviks and Jews. As a matter of fact, the day before when being lead to an interrogation, Blau pointed out to us that his handcuffs were not locked properly and he even said "Don't worry boys, I'm not about to run away." We all had a good laugh."

"You are not laughing now, or are you?" "No, Sir. No, Sir, we are not."

"Continue!"

"We waited with the prisoner till 11:30 for Capt. Kapusciak. We were told that Capt. Kapusciak was too busy and to bring Blau back at 14.00 hours the same day. Leaving Capt. Kapusciak's waiting room, Col. Blau asked if he cold use the nearest toilet because he had an urgent need after waiting two hours. So we did let him use it."

"Did any of you geniuses inspect the toilet before you let Blau ue it?"

"No Sir, we didn't think he would run away."

"Continue."

"We removed his handcuffs and let him use the facilities. He asked if any one of us wanted to join him. We both refused, seeing him running to the bathroom so often. To us it smelled, sorry for the pun, dysentery."

"What happened next?"

"We waited on the outside having a cigarette. Some 15-20 minutes later I ordered P.F.C. Majewski to check on the prisoner. A minute later Majewski came out screaming "He ran away." I went inside to double check. The prisoner's overalls were on the floor and the relative large window was half opened. I looked out of the second floor bathroom, just 2 meters lower was the roof of a small edifice attached to the main building. I sounded a general alarm, but Col. Blau was no longer on the premises, we checked it over and over again. The guard at the gate confirmed the exit of our Army Chaplain, father Lenartowicz was a civilian wearing horn rimmed glasses, incidentally the same pair of glasses that one of our clerks left on the window in the bathroom."

"Did anybody interview Father Lenartowicz?"

"Sergeant Woloszyn and I did' answered Capt. Kapusciak.

"What did he say?"

"He said that a civilian wearing glasses came up to him asking for the correct time. I gave it to him and a conversation in Polish developed. He didn't know that the man was an escaped prisoner. They went through the gate and since everybody on the base knew Father Lenartowicz, they were not stopped. They spoke amicably for a couple of minutes. The man asked Father which way he was going and Father told him "Sorry," he said, "I'm going the opposite way." He shook his hand and unhurriedly went the other way."

To verify this version of the event, Capt. Michalski requested the presence of Sgt. Woloszyn. A tall man wearing a sergeant's insignia reported to Capt. Kapusciak.

"These officers wish to speak with you." Both Michalski and Daszkiewicz recognized Woloszyn from the "Silver Albatross".

"Serwus Mietek, Serwus Edward. How are you?"

"It is Capt. Michalski and Lt. Daszkiewicz to you!" Intervened Capt. Kapusciak. "Stand at attention."

"At ease Sergeant." And turning to Capt. Kapusciak, Capt.

Michalski said: "We know each other from another campaign."

"Sorry, Sir"

"Sergeant, we are here to investigate the escape of S.S. Col. Blau. How did this all happen?"

"Sorry Captain, we goofed very badly. The guards were totally green. Blau fooled all of us. He seemed to be so cooperative. Another Pole who wanted to fight communists and Jews."

"Woloszyn, you are an idiot. How many Poles do you know that are colonels in the S.S.? I thought that you knew better. As big as you are there isn't a gram of brains in your head! Dismissed!"

"Captain Michalski, I...."

"Dismissed!!!"

The next person to undergo Capt. Michalski's wrath was Capt. Kapusciak, who basically repeated what the other men said already.

"I have never seen a more sloppy run outfit." He started to allude to Capt. Kapusciak "Cabbage" brains. (Kapusta in the Polish word for cabbage.

"Capt. Michalski, you can't talk to me in that tone of voice."

"I can and I will." Here Michalski identified himself as the 2nd Department operative-intelligence and counterespionage.

Capt. Kapusciak's face turned white. "I'm afraid Capt. Michalski that a number of mistakes were made."

"Who is in charge of this unit? Aren't you Capt. Kapusciak? Anything else you wish to say?"

"No, Sir. I'm very sorry."

"It is only fair to tell you that I'll recommend court-martial proceedings. In your case, reduction of rank to Lieutenant and transfer to the front lines. Sgt. Woloszyn and Corporal Roszyk to the rank of P.F.C.'s, the rest of the guard's two weeks of incarceration. Any questions, Kapusciak?" Captain Michalski didn't bother to call him captain anymore.

"No Sir."

"Is that your updated file on Col. Blaue?" "Yes, Sir."

Capt. Michalski read it carefully. "There is no new information of any kind?"

"I'm sorry, Sir."

"You really should be. In your report you wrote that Col. Blau was very cooperative. Do you still maintain that in view of his escape, Lieutenant!"

Captain and now Lt. Kapusciak totally downbeat just kept quiet.

"Lt. Daszkiewicz, we are finished here. Let's go to the Vatican. We have one more lead to pursue and after that it's like looking for a needle in a hay stack."

It took them two full days of going from one office of the Vatican to another, trying to locate a priest by the name of Blau a native of Katowice, Poland. A lucky brake came from another, Polish priest a classmate of Friedrich Blau, who now had a small parish in the nearby town of Velletri.

With the help of a detailed map they located the town of Velletri and Father Blau's church. They parked the jeep some distance from the church. Walking in from the sun lit street to the church, it took a couple of minutes to adjust their eyes to the semi-dark interior.

With the exception of several, black dressed old ladies, praying on their knees, there wasn't anyone else that they could see.

The squeaking door of a confessional booth attracted their attention. It was a priest, a shorter, heavier and older version of Fritz Blau.

Capt. Michalski with Lt. Daszkiewicz right behind him approached and addressed the priest in German:

"Friedrich, wo ist dein Bruder Cain? Antworte Mench!" Michalski, changed the biblical "Where is your brother Abel?" to suit the present conditions and he got unexpected results.

From the other door of the confessional booth came out S.S. Col. Fritz Blau.

"Here, I am."

Seeing him they both drew their pistols. Col. Blau's reaction was just a smirk of a smile. This time he spoke upper class German "Hoch Deutsch."

"Meine Herren" are you going to shoot me in church? After all, you are not the S.S., with your noble Polish chivalry you are not going to violate the sanctity of the Holy Church or are you?"

Michalski and Daszkiewicz kept coming closer to Blau in pincer like approach, their pistols still pointing to Col. Blau.

"Not a step closer!" The tone of voice was so threatening that they hesitated for a moment, but that moment allowed him to put a pill, which he held in his hand into his mouth.

"Heil Hitler!" was his last words. He was dead. The smirk on his face remained undisturbed. His death was confirmed by a summoned British constabulary unit and signed by Lt. Woodward, whom they met already under different circumstances.

Father Blau claimed the body of his brother, with British and Polish acquiescence he took the remains for burial.

Capt. Michalski got unexpected orders to remain temporarily in Rome and Lt. Daszkiewicz was ordered back to his old unit.

"Mietek, what are you going to do?"

"I got myself a few days of furlough before my next assignment. I'll locate Marcella Zurlini at Garibaldi #125 and fuck her till I won't be able to get a hard on. That will take some time I hope. Should I hear anything about your Czeslawa or Danuta I'll let you know immediately, you can count on that."

"I know that, I know that Mietek, go with God and bring me good news."

CHAPTER 36

Czeslawa Daszkiewicz ran as fast as she could towards the Police Station located on Piekna (Beautiful) and Szeroka (Wide) streets. While none of the streets were beautiful or wide, nevertheless it was where Danuta was held.

The small waiting room was full of local and transient judging by their attire, people forming a line to speak with the only available policeman on duty. A more than slightly obese policeman sat on a raised podium, behind a large metal desk, looking quite content. Unquestionably he was the master of the situation, answering questions asked by perplexed people or directing others to various departments or offices.

Finally, Czeslawa's turn came to speak with him. He uttered only a single word: "Yah?"

Czeslawa spoke with him in German.

"My daughter was arrested this morning for no apparent reason."

"There is always a reason, "Meine liebe Frau," what did she do? Was she a thief or a prostitute?"

Czeslawa wished that she could slap his face, but that wouldn't help her case.

"Sir, she is a child of 13 years."

"We have known thieves and prostitutes at that age."

"Someone accused her of being Jewish."

"That is much worse, she would have been better off if the other accusations were true."

"Sir, who can I speak to regarding this case? I have all her documents to prove otherwise."

"Go to see Herr Inspektor Bade in room #114, that is the fourth door on your right."

"Thank you very much, Sir."

Room #114 was clearly marked with a large sign in blue Gothic letters: Inspector Bade.

Czeslawa knocked at the door and moment later she heard a guttural: "H-e-r-r-e-i-n" come in.

She walked into a surprisingly large office. Inspector bade sat on the chair facing the window, rather than the door through which Czeslawa walked in.

Czeslawa waited a minute or so until Inspector Bade turned around.

"Fraulein…?" Started the Inspector.

"Frau Daszkiewicz" she corrected him.

"What brought you here, Frau Daszkiewicz?"

"Herr Inspector, my daughter was arrested this morning. Someone denounced her as being Jewish. Nothing could be further from the truth. I have her baptismal Certificate signed by our parish priest."

"Ein moment bitte." He pulled a thick file, marked with a large letter "J" on the outside.

"What is her name?"

"Danuta Daszkiewicz, Herr Inspector."

"Yes, I have it. Let me just glance through it."

She kept standing while Inspector Bade was reviewing Danuta's file.

"Here it is. She was identified by an impeachable source as being Jewish and you are claiming that she is an Aryan?"

"Herr Inspector, here are her papers. Please see for yourself."

Inspector Bade looked through a large magnifying glass at the stamp next to the priest's signature and then he lifted the certificate against the light checking for watermarks.

"Frau Daszkiewicz this piece of paper is what you Poles call "lipa" a bogus." With these words he tore the certificate into small pieces and threw them into a wastebasket standing next to his desk. With the torn certificate went Czeslawa's hope of freeing Danuta.

"Frau Daszkiewicz, tell me, how much money did the Jews give you to hide their child? By all rights I should arrest you too for harboring a Jew, but in your case I'll make an exception. Bring me the money and you can go free."

"Herr Inspector, she is my daughter, I swear to God."

"Stop pretending, I'm giving you a chance to save your own life, can't you see that, foolish woman?"

"Herr Inspector, Danuta is my daughter, she is my whole life, please let her go."

"You say that she is your daughter, than perhaps your husband is Jewish? Sign this paper stating that he is or was Jewish and I'll let you go but the girl has to stay. Wait just a moment, it says here that you threatened a certain individual with retribution from A.K?"

Now everything became crystal clear to Czeslawa. It was Kajetan Burczyk who denounced her to the Gestapo.

"Herr Inspector, that man was Burczyk. He was after me to sleep with him and to scare him off I told him that my husband was with the A.K."

"Talking about husbands, where is your husband?"

"Herr Inspector, I'm ashamed to say that my husband has left me for another much younger woman whom he has met in Cracow. All men in Zakopane think that girls from Cracow are the best."

Inspector Bade started to laugh. "I think so too."

"Herr Bade, I beg you Sir, please let my girl go."

"No Frau Daszkiewicz, you can go as I told you before, but she must stay."

"Herr Inspector, you are making a big mistake."

"To the contrary Frau Daszkiewicz, I would be making even a bigger mistake if I would let her go free."

"Herr Inspector keep me too as long as I can be with my daughter."

"You must be then her Jewish mother. I feel like biblical

Solomon. You will be together, that I promise you. You won't be separated. What do you think, we Germans don't have hearts?"

He picked up the phone and said something fast into the receiver. There was a knock at the door and an armed guard walked in.

"Leave all your belongings right here, rings, watches, jewelry, papers, We are going to double check, if you have hidden anything on you, you'll be severely punished and you won't see your daughter."

Czeslawa did as she was told. Inspector bade didn't bother to frisk her. His experience taught him that she had left everything on the table just grasping her only hope of seeing her daughter.

"Wache" Guard, take that piece of garbage and put her in cell #3. She wants to be with her daughter.

"Loss" the guard led Czeslawa to the end of a long corridor, forming a giant letter "L".

At the end of that corridor to the left, a Roman numeral III attached to an iron gate was the place where the guard left Czeslawa to the care of a woman warden. The uniformed woman built like a professional wrestler pushed Czeslawa into a small room.

"You, Jewish swine get undressed and spread your legs. Do you have any diamonds on you?"

"No, madam."

"We'll see, spread them wider you bitch!"

The matron pushed her fingers into Czeslawa's vagina, probing the insides. Feeling violated Czeslawa started to cry.

"Keep your Jewish trap shut, do you hear!"

Failing to find any diamonds the matron pushed her out of this small room into a large, overcrowded cell.

Czeslawa started to look around trying to locate Danuta. Against the opposite wall there was a long wooden bench occupied by rough looking women, some who still had too much rouge on their faces. Everybody else sat on the cement floor. Lying down was prohibited as the sign said.

One of the women braided a young girl's hair. Czeslawa recognized Danuta at once.

She walked straight to them and trying to hold back the excitement said:

"I'll take over from here on."

Danuta hearing her mother's voice, yelled out:

"Mama, mama!" they embraced and kissed each other. "Mama, mama, I knew that you'd come for me, can we go home now to grandpa and grandma?"

"Not yet darling, we'll have to wait for a while. With God's help we'll get there somehow."

The scene was so touching that many women witnessing it started to cry themselves. Soon there was room made for them to sit on the bench.

Czeslawa held Danuta in her arms. She didn't care where they might send them as long as they were together. Rocking Danuta like a small child, Czeslawa started to sing a popular lullaby.

The cell became quiet, some women got on their knees and started to pray others just kept crossing themselves. Czeslawa always sung that song when Danuta couldn't sleep and this time too Danuta fell asleep.

The women who tried to braid Danuta's hair came over and introduced herself as Amalia.

"What are you in for?" Amalia asked.

"The German accused us of being Jewish."

"You are not Jewish, I can tell."

"Of course not, but how can we get out of here?"

"I don't know, it isn't going to be easy that is for sure. The Germans are forming a transport and we are going to be on it. Nobody knows where. Maybe they will ship us to work on their farms or factories? Maybe it is going to be easier to escape from there?"

They both looked at sleeping Danuta. A pleasant smile surrounded her dimple. She didn't have a single worry, her mother was with her.

Czeslawa totally exhausted both physically and mentally soon fell asleep also. Sitting on the bench, not realizing that Amalia, a stranger was making sure that nobody would disturb their sleep.

Every few minutes another female was thrown into the already overcrowded cell. It was a miracle in itself that Czeslawa slept the entire night on that bench.

To the scream of: "Aufstehen! Aufstehen!" –get up, get up, Czeslawa woke up. It took her awhile to realize that she was in jail still holding onto Danuta.

Ten women at a clip were brought to the bathrooms, allowing for a very short time to attend to their biological function. Rushed, kicked and beaten some of the prisoner women wetted their undergarments.

Shortly after the prisoners were issued a lukewarm, dark liquid masquerading as coffee. They barely had the time to swallow the "coffee" when they were rushed to board canvas covered army trucks.

To the accompaniment of "Loss" and "schnell" the cell #3 was emptied into 4 trucks with everybody standing up. Each truck was surrounded by armed soldiers riding in staff cars and motorcycles with sidecars.

Czeslawa counted 11 trucks full of female prisoners. What seemed to be like a half an hour into the trip. Amalia started to sing the Polish national anthem with everybody else joining in.

The officer in charge stopped the column and came over to the truck from which the song came out first.

"Somebody on this truck has a very nice voice. I would like to meet that person."

Amalia stepped out.

"Let me congratulate you, it was indeed beautiful, unfortunately illegal." He took out his Luger and shot her dead.

"Any more nightingales on this truck?" Silence is also an answer.

"FORWARD!!!"

It was very clear to everyone on that truck that this killing was only the beginning of their ordeal.

What seemed to be an eternity, was actually a couple of hours when they reached their destination, but whatever their destination was it was surrounded by barbed wire and mean looking watch towers.

"Heraus! Heraus! Everybody, who could, jumped out of the truck. Other, less lucky or older women fell to the ground badly hurt.

Czeslawa asked a man, dressed in a striped suit like so many other standing on a platform, "Where are we?" in Polish.

"Lady, you just arrived in Oswiecim-Brzezinka, better known as Konzentrationslager Auschwitz-Birkenau. Welcome to the death factory."

CHAPTER 37

In took Paul a few minutes to realize that he woke up in Cynthia's bed. There was something very erotic about it, to think that the same bed was occupied by a desirable female only 24 hours ago. He had to admit to himself, that Cynthia was an object worth pursuing. She had all the attributes plus an outstanding intellect.

The war had a way of warping many issues, everything had to be done at once, because lives were surprisingly short and in many cases also violent.

As far as being intimate with Cynthia, he doubted very much if the very proper Epsteins would ever allow Cynthia a patent cohabitation until the vows were exchanged.

Clouding the issues were also the fact that Cynthia had a sort of fiancée, who might be in German hands and he himself had a girl back in the States.

On the other hand, Brooklyn and everything connected with it seem to be far away and long ago. He was now in England, in the Air Force and by 11.30 A.M. he had to report back to his unit.

Paul reached for a cigarette, which he had never done on an empty stomach. With a lit Camel cigarette he walked towards the window, silently watching the peaceful street until the softened edges of daybreak greeted him.

Paul opened the door to a gentle knock. It was Eve. "Good morning, Paul, I hope that I didn't wake you up, but you had mentioned last night that you have to leave early. We are ready with breakfast anytime you are."

"Thank you very much Mrs. Epstein, I mean Eve, I'll be right down, don't bother with breakfast. A cup of coffee or tea will do the trick."

"Once you try our kippers you might change your mind."

"Very well then, just give me a few minutes please."

Paul swiftly shaved and washed up. Dressed he came down to breakfast, which was delicious.

"Paul, we heard from Cynthia. She is still tied up in her office. She'll try to come home this afternoon if at all possible."

"Unfortunately, I must rush back. There is a slight possibility that on Sunday in the late afternoon I might be free. I'll be in the same place where I met Cynthia the last time. I'll call her anyway. Sorry but I must shove off. Thanks very much for your hospitality. I really enjoyed meeting you folks."

"Paul it was a sheer pleasure meeting you, don't be a stranger. Come over whenever you feel like it."

"Thank you again."

Cynthia's brother carried Paul's bag into the jeep. This time Paul reached his base without getting lost. He reported to his unit just in time. The duty officer joked: "Captain, another 5 minutes and I would have declared you AWOL."

Paul remembered reading in an Army newspaper, Gen. George S. Patton's maxim:

"Wars may be fought with weapons, but they are won by men."

Well, if that is the case, I'll start with weapons, he thought and ordered Lt. George Perry to see him. Both checked and re-checked every component of their great flying machine. The plane and the weapon systems were in excellent shape, however with flying, the longer you did it, the greater your chances of some-thing-bad happening.

Paul took pride in the personal knowledge of his crew, but men were getting sick, hurt or even killed in the battle and had to be replaced from time to time.

Paul couldn't control the replacement system that sent fright-ened and untrained in many cases, young men to the front, where too many died foolishly and needlessly.

Interestingly the new airmen were actually eager for combat, only to learn by bitter experience just how psychologically ill prepared they were for the stark reality of air combat, an enemy intent on killing them and the awful realization that they were just expendable cogs in a gigantic war machine. The war possessed also a power to dramatically change in so many ways, those whom it did not kill.

Most airmen had a hearty disdain for military discipline and regimentation, which Paul remembered only too well from his own days as a cadet.

Now, being the MVP of the plane, he made sure that his crew didn't suffer from boredom or discomfort. Each member of his crew knew that he could always discuss any problem, both personal or military with Paul.

At the same time, Paul demanded and received the utmost of what each man could give, thus forming a solemn bond of comradeship that was repeatedly tested in combat.

The combination of love and respect for their captain, a sense of patriotism and duty, a grim determination to survive without letting down comrades in arms, were ingredients that gave Paul his confidence in his bombing missions. That confidence was contagious, the men simply trusted their captain and his magic ring.

With half of his crew attending Sunday services, Paul was quite busy. He had a gut feeling that Monday or Tuesday the latest, something important is going to happen. Perhaps another mission.

He was called to the phone. Expecting a call from Cynthia, he was duly surprised by the deep voice of Col. Gary "the Hotshot."

"Captain Krafchin, would you mind stopping over for a few minutes? I need to talk with you."

"Yes, Sir. I'll be right over."

Paul wondered what the hell, Col. Gary wanted this time. He sounded very polite almost apologetic which wasn't his style at all.

He reached the colonel's office and knocked on his door to a friendly "Come in, Paul."

"Nothing serious, I just wanted to chat with you and since it's Sunday I'll speak with you. "Excathedra." I do value your opinion on tactics, equipment and people. This time it is people that I'm interested in. That is your honest opinion about your own Lt. George Perry?"

"Colonel, he is a damned fine officer."

"Remember Paul, I understand and appreciate loyalties but I'm talking about what is good for the Service. Can he fully take over your duties?"

"Unquestionably yes. I have no reservations regarding his abilities at all, Sir."

"Well, that's great then. Aren't you wondering what we are going to do with you?"

"Hopefully, you won't demote me." The colonel cracked a smile and said:

"No, Paul, to the contrary, we intend to kick you upstairs. With the invasion at Normandy behind us, we'll have to move some of our bases to France, Low Countries and eventually Germany. Frankly I could use some help in planning, logistics e.t.c. Think about it. I can give you a direct order but I would prefer if you would accept that idea voluntarily. The long and the short of it is that I need your decision by Monday 1300 hours. And now that I've spoiled your day let's go someplace for a beer."

Paul knew that one way or the other the "old man" had him by the short hairs.

"Colonel, you can have my decision right now. I'll be honored to serve you at any function you choose for me."

"Captain, I knew that you'll see it my way. Let's go now and have a drink."

If the colonel needed a drink, Paul needed it even more.

They arrived at the Officers Club just as two junior officers, too young even to shave, were involved in a fist fight. One look from the Colonel and they both froze in their tracks.

"Sometimes the beer suds makes them braver then they actually are. Come, let's order our drinks, we'll start with double shots. I don't like anything piecemeal. We're in England, so here is mud in your eyes."

"Your health Colonel."

"Yours too, Captain. Down the hatch."

Paul didn't know what his assignment was going to be, but whatever the colonel will dish out, he'll have to handle it, probably a responsible, 24 hours a day, 7 days a week job. Just the idea of it made him sober up.

"Why so glum, chum?" Paul recognized the voice belonging to Cynthia.

"Colonel, may I present a friend of mine Cynthia Epstein of the British W.A.C."

"How do you do Miss, may I answer your question addressed to our Captain Krafchin? All work and no play makes John a dull boy."

"Colonel, you are 100% right and believe it or not, only last night, the Captain here, slept in my bed while I was on duty."

"Well, he'll have to remedy that real soon. Pardon me, there is someone trying to catch my attention."

"What is it?" he asked the airman who held up a sealed envelope to the colonel.

Colonel Gary ripped the envelope open and read the letter.

"Captain, I'm afraid that our party is over. Let's get the bill and get to Headquarters on the double."

"Yes Sir, I'm ready." Turning to Cynthia he said: "Sorry, we have to rush off but I'll be in touch."

"Gentlemen, it seems to me that powerful forces are conspiring to keep the Captain apart from me."

"Miss, I'm afraid that it is your turn to be 100% right this time."

Colonel Gary "the Hotshot" was driving this time. The jeep's tires hardly touched the road surface.

"Captain, consider yourself transferred to my command as of tomorrow morning 9 A.M. I'll cut the necessary orders, which will be hand delivered to you. In the meantime, notify Lt. George Perry about taking over your own duties. I'm sure that you would want to say good-bye to your crew since they are due to take off a few hours later."

"Thank you Sir. It's very considerate of you, Sir."

"Let's not overdo it, Captain. Good luck Paul and now get the fuck out of my jeep."

"Yes Sir!" Paul smiled, it was the old man himself again.

Upon his return to his own unit, Paul ordered his crew to assemble for an important announcement. At the same time he spoke with Lt. Perry in private.

"George, let me give it to you straight. I'm being transferred as of tomorrow morning to Headquarters. I really don't know what they have in store for me. It was Col. Gary's idea. I recommended you as my replacement and I'm sure that you'll do a bang up job."

"Thank you Captain, the crew and I will miss you terribly. We always felt safe with you, but orders are orders. It has been a privilege to serve under your command."

"Thank you, Lieutenant, your words mean a lot to me."

They both walked into the room where the crew was already assembled. Someone yelled "ATTENTION" and everybody stood up.

"Captain, will you permit me to address the men?"

"Permission granted."

"Men, we have been through a lot together. We all felt like a family. One for all and all for one, but there is also a larger family – the U.S.A.F. Starting tomorrow, our Captain is assigned to bigger and we hope better or more important things. May I therefore in the name of the men assembled here wish you good luck and God speed."

"Thank you Lieutenant. I assure you all that in this man's Air Force, nobody has a better or more dedicated crew than I have. I'll be leaving you in the capable hands of Lt. Perry. He'll be your new skipper from now on. If he permits me I'll be looking on you guys from time to time. I thank you from the bottom of my heart for a job well done and now I would like to shake hands with each one of you."

The first one in line was Lt. "Curly" Pasek.

"Captain, it won't be the same without you and your magic ring."

"One more thing, men! I'm lending my ring to Lt. Perry for your next mission, under one condition that the planes name remains "Goldie Locks." What do you say men?"

Everybody started to applaud. Paul mingled with the men for a while and then spoke with Lt. Perry again.

"I'll pick up my ring after your return from the mission, George."

"I appreciate this gesture, Sir."

"Lieutenant, you are on your own, it is either shit or get off the pot."

"Captain, I'll manage it alright. After all I had a good teacher."

"Touché! I'm leaving now."

"Attention, men, The Captain is leaving." Everybody stood up and saluted.

Paul saluted back. "At ease men." And he left the room.

Tired and exhausted he reached his bed. It has been a long day of many surprises and tomorrow who knows? Let tomorrow take care of itself. Still he couldn't fall asleep. His thoughts shifted from Vivian to Cynthia, to Col. Gary and his new assignment. He wondered about the lack of letters from his parents. Goldie wrote to him regularly. Her letters were always warm and cheerful.

Paul started to write shorter and shorter letters since he met Vivian, always blaming the war and the lack of time, to the point when he stopped writing all together.

The physical tiredness took over and finally he fell asleep.

He woke up eager to meet the challenge of the day.

Promptly at 9 A.M. he knocked on the Colonel's office.

"Come in." and Paul walked in.

"Come in, Major" said the colonel without lifting his head from the papers in front of him.

Paul looked behind him but there wasn't anybody there.

"I said come in Major Krafchin."

"It's Captain Krafchin, Sir."

"I said major and I meant major. Learn not to contradict me, Major Krafchin. You are promoted to the rank of Major. Congratulations. By the way you are not the only one to be promoted around here."

Paul only now noticed a new insignia on Gary's uniform, it was now Brigadier General Gary Cotshott.

"Congratulations to you Sir." Paul could hardly speak.

"Major, you should know by now, that if you keep throwing shit at the ceiling, some of it is bound to stick to it."

It wasn't exactly a state secret that under that folksy manner of Gen. Cotshott there was also a brilliant mind, aristocratic-southern background to a graduate of Air Command and General Staff School and Air War College.

Here are your major's insignia and you can take your own silver bars and give them to your replacement Capt. Perry. I'm off to another meeting. I should be back by 1100 hours the latest. You had better have your ass here by that time, Major."

"Yes Sir, General Sir." He saluted and made a full about face.

Paul's next step was to reach "Goldie Locks" before she took off.

"It's the Captain coming our way." Screamed radioman Moe Samuels. "You guys better make it Major Krafchin. Hey boys, our Captain is now major, hip, hip, hooray."

"Good morning men. I just came by to see you off and wish you luck and to turn my silver bars to your new Captain Perry."

The men were deliriously proud and happy, the only spoiler was the controlling tower informing "Goldie Locks" that she was next for take off. Paul watched his "Goldie Locks" taxi on the runway, soon to be followed by hundreds of similar planes.

He rushed back to Headquarters. This time he was stopped in front of Gen. Cotshott's office by an Airwoman Sgt. Olivia Hughes.

"Major Krafchin? The General is still tied up in the Staff meeting. He asked that you wait for him. A cup of coffee in the meantime?"

"That would be very nice. Black no sugar please."

"I'll be right back with coffee, please take a seat." She pointed to several chairs lined up against the wall of the waiting room.

It's just like the Army, hurry up and wait. He finished 2 cups of coffee and smoked at least 4 cigarettes by the time Gen. Cotshott returned.

"Major, I have yet another meeting to attend in just a few minutes. I planned the day differently but a number of things came up unexpectantly, those things with top priority. However, I was made aware of contents of this letter, which I have for you. I'm afraid it's bad news."

With these words the General handed Paul a letter. He recognized his mother's handwriting, the familiar address of 7402 Bay Parkway, Brooklyn, N.Y. And the customary red 7 cents airmail stamp.

"Go ahead and open it. It has been opened already. I'll be in the other room for a while if you need me Paul."

He opened the letter. His worst fears were confirmed:

Brooklyn, N.Y. June 30th, 1944

Dearest Paulie:

It is my sad duty as a mother and wife to let you know that your father died peacefully in his own bed on May 6th, corresponding to the Hebrew calendar in the month of Iyar the tenth. Blessed he was. He didn't suffer at all. His heart just gave up. His wish was to notify you about his death six weeks after he was buried and a grave stone was erected in Pinelawn Cemetery on Long Island, N.Y.

He didn't want you to worry about him, saying that you were making our whole family proud by fighting the Nazis. That was his wish, which he made me swear on the bible to uphold.

I have the moral support of our entire family and especially Goldie, who comes to see me everyday. Had I had a daughter she couldn't have been closer to me.

My dear Paulie, do what you have to do and come back to us in one piece. You are all I have in this world.

Your ever loving Mom.

Paul cried as he read and re-read the letter. His tears were wetting the onion skin of the letter. Since his boyhood he was made aware of his father's heart condition. He knew that sooner or later, the heart of that wonderful man, who was his father, will give up, hoping that would occur later rather than sooner.

"Paul, are you alright?" It was the general himself. "My sincere condolences, Regretfully I need you badly in the next few weeks. After that I'll arrange for an emergency leave for you. I know that you have to say "Kaddish". If you wish you can take the rest of the day off."

Seeing the puzzled look on Paul's face, the General continued:

"I see that you are surprised that I know the meaning of the word "Kaddish". After all, my first wife was a Lowenstein of Rock Hill, N.C. or didn't you know. It was the talk of the South. Me a scion of confederate, ante-bellum family, marrying a German-Jewish woman, whose parents owned the largest textile plant in the South. Incidentally she died in an automobile crash. Paul, I'll have a Jewish Chaplain to speak with you."

"It isn't necessary Sir. The chaplain will tell me what a wonderful man my father was, even though he had never met him. However, if there is a way that I can place an overseas priority call to my mother, that would be the greatest kindness."

"Consider it done. I'll place that call myself. Give me the number, Paul."

"It's Lowell 7-5569."

The General went to his office and a couple of minutes later he returned saying:

I've placed the call, top priority, for you. I've instructed Sgt. Hughes to let you know when the connection will be made. I also left you some papers with her for you to have a look at, but only if you are up to it."

Thank you very much, Sir. I'll be just fine. As long as I have to wait for the call I might as well do something useful. I'm sure that my dad would want it that way."

"In that respect, your father and I are very much alike."

The general rushed to his next meeting and Paul started to sift slowly through the pile of papers on the desk, which Sgt. Hughes brought for him. She also expressed her condolences.

Some of the papers dealt with logistics. Paul spotted immediately items that were unnecessarily duplicated and other items were shortchanged. If that was true of his own plane, multiplied by the thousand of other items were short changed. If that was true of his own plane, multiplied by the thousands of other aircraft could result in tremendous savings for the Air Force and much better distribution of needed items. He wrote down his recommendations and reached for the next file.

However, his thoughts went back to his father, wondering about the coincidence of receiving the bad news on the same day that he lent his ring to Lieutenant or rather Captain Perry. Was he becoming superstitious? He doubted that very much.

"Major Krafchin! I have Brooklyn, New York on the line for you, Sir."

He picked up the receiver and heard Sgt. Hughes voice:

"Mrs. Krafchin? I have Major Krafchin on the line, Madam."

"But my son is a captain."

"He was a captain Mrs. Krafchin, he is now a major."

"Paulie is that you?"

"Yes, ma, it's me. I'm so sorry…." It was his unstoppable sobbing that blocked their conversation for the next couple of minutes. Finally he collected himself:

"Ma, I'll be home in a few weeks. The General is letting me come home."

"I'll wait for you son…"

CHAPTER 38

Czeslawa and Danuta pushed by hundreds of other people, mostly Jews from all the Nazi occupied countries, who were directed towards a specially built platform where S.S. physicians selected people fit to work, from elderly, invalids, pregnant women and children-usually unfit for any type of work.

The S.S. doctor noticed Danuta and pulled her to a spot where the S.S. men hung a bar at the height of 120 cm. and all those children who passed under the bar went straight to crematoria.

Czeslawa watched the scene in total horror, as Danuta whose height was 121.5 cm. was saved and the doctor lost interest in her. Czeslawa quickly grabbed Danuta's hand and followed people who were sent to the left. People directed to the right followed the road to showers and dis-infection rooms. No one ever saw them come out.

Surely Dante's hell was a comedy by comparison to Auschwitz-Birkenau.

Still holding Danuta's hand, Czeslawa along with many other prisoners stood in the line to list their particulars and to be given numbers, because the camp number was the only identification sign of the inmate. It replaced his or her name.

She was watching the "Schreiber" clerk who wrote down each person's data. The face was very familiar. Try as she did, she couldn't place him, the shaved head, the inmate's striped suite, threw her off.

Her turn came to see the clerk. He lifted his head from the thick folder and looked at Czeslawa:

"Miss Drzewiecka? Is that you? What in God's name are you doing here?"

Suddenly Czeslawa recognized the man. It was Count Stefan Czartoryski, a former patient of her father, back in Lublin. The name of Czartoryski was synonymous with aristocracy and the history of Poland.

"My dear count, I was just about to ask you the same question."

"Please Miss Drzewiecka, I'm known here only as Stefan Burda. It is a very long story, but what about you?"

"I was accused of being Jewish together with my daughter."

"That is really bad. Jews are the first to leave this hell through the chimney."

"What are you saying Sir? That means that they are burning people alive? Do civilized people do that?"

No wonder the air smelled of burned hair and nails.

"I must hurry. Under what name did you come here?"

"Under my husband's name Daszkiewicz Czeslawa and Danuta."

"Let me change that back to Drzewiecka and list you both as Catholics. With little influence that I have here I'll try to help you. You'll be going to the barrack, where the block "elteste" and "Aufseherin" are Katarzyna and Jadzia. Just tell them that you are Burda's cousins. They will know what to do. You can trust them. I can't talk any longer. Someone may get suspicious."

It was just in time because S.S. man came to check what was holding up the line.

"Sir, this woman had the longest Polish name that I have seen."

"Tell her, we can cut her name and her body in half." The S.S. man said smiling and went on his way quite pleased with himself.

Czeslawa couldn't tell if the number tattooed on her left arm or cutting her hair was the worst experience. The needle hurt a bit as the ink penetrated layers of her skin, but a blouse with long sleeves could hide that ugly mark. Loosing her shoulder long hair and Danuta's beautiful braids were especially painful.

"Ma don't we look like monkeys in the zoo?"

"Yes we do." Poor Danuta, she didn't realize the danger they were both in. Depression and fear took over Czeslawa. Thoughts like that were doing her and Danuta no good. If they were going to survive this hell, she had to remain focused, believing that she would outlast the forces marshaled against them.

Like the rest of the prisoners they were marked with triangles. Unlike the Jews who wore stars made out of a yellow triangle crossed with a second triangle, the color of which depended on the reason for the prisoner's arrest. Black triangles were worn by Gypsies, criminals had green ones, most of the prisoners had red ones, sent to the camp as enemies of Hitler's Reich for political "crimes". Czeslawa and Danuta had violet ones-Bible students.

Along with prisoners striped clothing, they were issued green, metal bowls. At the distribution point, the inmate in charge told Czeslawa to guard those bowls with her life. She soon found out why.

Upon entering the assigned barrack that housed the former Polish Army or it's stable just a few years ago, the inmates were greeted by a broad shouldered woman holding a whip in her hand.

"My name is Jadzia and this is my penis." She said pointing to the whip.

"You'll soon find out what it can do for your whores! Katarzyna, did you ever see a worst bunch of garbage, than these street walkers?"

"Never, Jadziu, they are the pits!"

"We'll have to teach them some manners!"

"That is for sure. You fucken whores find your bunks on the double."

There was a frantic scramble for bunks, encouraged by lightning strokes of Jadzia's whip.

Czeslawa simply froze holding Danuta's hand.

Jadzia noticing their violet triangles came up to the two very scared females.

"Are you some kind of princesses, that you need a special invitation?"

"No Pani Jadziu. We are cousins of Stefan Burda."

"You two, just wait a minute." Jadzia went to Katarzyna and spoke quietly to her. Katarzyna walked towards bunk beds located next to a separate room that housed Jadzia and Katarzyna.

"You and you" pointing to women on the upper and lower bunk "Find yourselves other bunks at the end of this row. On the double, do you hear!"

Disposed women knew better than to argue with Katarzyna. Jadzia approached Czeslawa saying:

"You two take their bunks, put the youngster on the top."

Czeslawa felt guilty about this, but there was no other solution and they moved to bunks still warm with others body heat.

Once they got to their new bunks, Jadzia told them loud enough for everybody around to listen:

"Starting tomorrow morning after the "appell" you will clean our room. If I find just a speck of dust, I'll personally beat the living daylights out of you, is that understood?"

"Yes madam." Czeslawa heard that threat clearly and so did the rest of the barrack.

"Attention all new inmates. There is no food for you tonight, you all will have to wait for tomorrow."

Everyday life in the camp was much the same. Almost simultaneously with the morning gong, which marked the time to get up, the block "elteste"-warden would rush into the room shouting and beating for no reason at all, supervising the clean up.

Regardless of the weather, the inmates of Birkenau were forced out into the camp streets. The female prisoners took advantage of every pool of water, left by rain or snow, to wash themselves. Any water available in the washrooms were allotted first to the German criminal element. Later the same water was used by Polish, Jewish and Gypsy women.

For breakfast there was a liter of bitter liquid called "coffee." Having that green, metal bowl was a lifesaver. Inmates having those bowls stolen were in deep trouble.

After the "coffee" the inmates were assembled for a "Appell"-roll call in the main square. Depending upon the mood of the guards, the inmates stood there from merciful 20 minutes to long hours. Once finished with the roll call, the inmates marched out in columns of five for 12 hours of labor performed in "Laufschritt" often running without time to catch a breath, under the supervision of S.S. men, their dogs and "kapos" holding truncheons.

After a few days of introduction to the life in Birkenau, Czeslawa realized that to survive the terrible unhygienic sanitation and living conditions, hunger, inadequate clothing is going to be next to impossible.

The first glimmer of hope was when Jadzia called Czeslawa into her room. Jadzia changed her rough language to a mild and surprisingly elegant manner of speaking:

"Mr. Burda instructed us to take good care of you and we wish to comply with his request. You will always find some extra food left for you in this room. Remember not a word to anybody including your daughter and especially your daughter. Among the other inmates I'll curse you up and down, I may hit you once or twice, just to make sure nobody suspects anything. We have plenty of informers among our people. We still don't know if we can get you a more suitable job at IG-Farbenindustrie, Hermann Goering Werke, Siemens-Schuckertwerke or Krupp.

"You'll have to be patient. One more thing, do not tell anybody that Danuta is your daughter. You'll be much better off saying that she is your sister from the same father but different mothers. Is that clear to you?"

"Yes Pani Jadziu. Thank you very much for everything."

"And now start cleaning." Jadzia opened the door and started to scream:

"You ass-fucked whore, you better clean the place once again, if you know what is good for you!"

"Yes, Madam." Czeslawa started to clean the room as if her life would depend on it. In a way it did.

Czeslawa watched at the end of the day, the returning work groups that carried, dragged or wheeled in barrels, murdered prisoners and those that had been injured by clubs or shovels.

Inmates burdened today by the bodies of their fellow sufferers knew that tomorrow may be the last day for them. They knew that their friends would bring them back to the camp for roll call, during which, everyone, both living or dead had to be accounted for. The evening roll-call lasted up an hour and sometimes even longer, rain or shine. The wooden shoes worn by inmates were an additional torture as they made it difficult to move around in the muddy ground.

After the roll call the inmates received the long awaited "supper" which consisted of about 300 gr. of bread, 30 gr. of margarine and a drink brewed on herbs. Some inmates divided their portion of bread into 2 or 3 pieces with the idea of having a piece of bread in the morning, often keeping the precious slice under their heads at night, only to find out by morning that someone stole that bread.

It was rumored that the Germans were adding chemicals to their food to make sure that the women wouldn't menstruate. In fact most of the women lost their periods including Czeslawa.

Thanks to the arrangement made by Jadzia, Czeslawa started to adjust to camp's routine but still lived in an atmosphere of constant threats day and night. The children were subjected to the same camp regulations as adults. Curiously Danuta made the adjustment much faster because of a friendship with another girl, barely a year older, who was in Birkenau longer and knew all the ropes. The girl, Janka Bialogora had a smiling face that everybody simply loved. Her sparkling personality combined with better than average voice was her meal ticket in the camp. It was Janka who taught Danuta all the do's and don't of Birkenau, how to avoid punishment and keep away from harm's way. They kept away from block #11 and the Death Wall where the executions took place and block #25 which housed the "musulmen", the ill and convalescent females that showed no signs of regaining strength.

Danuta and Janka became best of friends, an inseparable pair of Siamese twins.

Rumors were flying in the camp, that Russians were already

in the Eastern part of Poland. Maybe Germany suffered defeats on all fronts but at camp, the S.S. deliberated how to kill more people by effectively directing the trains bringing in thousands of people to the special platform in Birkenau and keeping the crematories working day and night.

Czeslawa felt that there was camp resistance whether it was unorganized or spontaneous she wasn't sure. Probably organized judging by the relationship between Burda and Jadzia.

Katarzyna were most likely involved too. Nobody discussed that issue with Czeslawa a relative newcomer. Sure that Burda knew Czeslawa back in Lublin but lots of time passed since those carefree days in prewar Poland.

In the meantime the sophisticated system of extermination crushed every visible sign of resistance. The constant struggle for life and for retaining human dignity was resistance in itself.

Each day alive was a victory.

Somehow Czeslawa managed with Danuta to survive a couple of months thanks in great measure to Jadzia, who made sure that the work that Czeslawa was assigned to, gave her a chance of coming back at the end of that day.

Everyday there was an extra piece of bread for Czeslawa in private Jadzia's quarters, thus enabling Czeslawa to give her own ration to Danuta.

Unexpectantly one day after the morning "Appell", both Jadzia and Katarzyna viewed ranks of the barracks inmates, when Katarzyna stepped back lifting her whip to punish one of the women, unfortunately for her the end of the whip touched the cap of S.S. Hauptsturmfuhrer Helmuth Berger, who happened to walk alongside the assembled group of prisoners.

"This is an insult! You!" pointing to Jadzia" take away the whip from her and give her 12 blows. Do it right otherwise I'll have another "kapo" give you 25, is that clear?"

"Do it Jadzio, do it fast." Begged Katarzyna.

Flogging was performed on a special horse, much to the amusement of some of the women who were punished by Jadzia and Katarzyna.

Jadzia was hitting her best friend with the same well practiced effort while Katarzyna the recipient of those blows had to count loudly: eins, zwei, drei.....while the S.S. Hauptsturmfuhrer Berger was watching the whole scene with a smile that never left his face.

Once flogging was finished two inmates helped Jadzia to get off the wooden horse.

Hauptsturmfuhrer Berger went up to Jadzia and Katarzyna and said:

"I hope you've learned your lesson."

"Jawohl, Herr Hauptsturmfuhrer."

"I came to your block to pick up a woman that could speak German, clean and cook and take care of my little girl? Do you have someone here that could fill my request?"

"Yes Sir." They both answered pointing to Czeslawa. "She can also paint very nicely."

"You, step forward! Do you speak German?"

"Jawohl mein Herr." Czeslawa indeed spoke a more than a passable German.

"Show me your hands and open your mouth." Czeslawa did as she was ordered.

"That will be fine. From now on your name will be Lisl, all our maids are called Lisl. It makes it easier to remember that way."

Czeslawa was scared out of her mind. She gave Jadzia a look, which Jadzia understood, because she said quickly in Polish" "We'll take care of Danuta, go."

Sturmbahnfuhrer Berger noticed the violet triangle on Czeslawa's dress, now he was doubly pleased with his choice of the new Lisl.

CHAPTER 39

Maj. Scharf's words were still ringing in Henryk's ear. How did he find out about my being Jewish? Henryk was asking himself. The only other person who knew his secret was Astrid. Did she tell him? He'll have to find out from her but the party at Dennhards was hardly the forum for discussions on this delicate subject.

"So when will you two tie the knot?" Gretchen wanted to know.

"I still have to talk with Heinrich about it but Sunday September 17th of 1944 sounds like a good day for it."

"My goodness but that is in two short weeks. Will you Astrid be ready by that time?"

"I'm sure that I could arrange it in time. I obtained permission to marry from my C.O. and have my father's blessings. I also hope that you and Major will give me away. Major Scharf volunteered to be Heinrich's best man. Basically we're almost set."

Henryk listened to the conversation with his mouth wide open. Actually he wanted to get married to Astrid sometime in the future. The way the war was going on, it was only a matter of time till Germany's total capitulation. Paris was already freed by Allied Expeditionary Forces of Lt. Gen. Omar N. Bradley's four spearheads. Reading in the National Socialist party organ, the Nationalsozialistische Parteikorrespondenz DNB, Henryk found out about the incredible, though it may seem, the treachery of Romania declaring war against Germany.

He was also aware that his home region of Drohobycz-Boryslaw was captured by the Red Army on August 7th. His further thoughts about reaching his home was interrupted by Gretchen:

"I'm going to leave you love birds for a while, I have to speak with Georg-Hans. I'm sure that he will be delighted to see you two married."

"Thank you very much, Gretchen."

"Astrid why is there a sudden rush to get married? Couldn't we wait for the end of the war?"

"Heinrich, a couple of nights ago I had a terrible nightmare. I dreamt that the war ended and you left me for another woman in Galicia and I died without ever marrying you."

"Astrid, that was only a dream. If you wish we can get married. By the way, Maj. Scharf gave me to understand that he knew who I am. Did you tell him?"

"I did Heinrich. He was and is instrumental in saving your life."

"I'm much obliged to him."

"Come, let's join the rest of the guests."

A heated conversation was taking place in the living room about the perfidy of Germany's allies. Herr Ludwig Stumpf was speaking in rage:

"Machiavelli was right when he said that it is better to be feared than loved. We Germans are the undisputed Herrenvolk. The only opposition we have is from Bolsheviks and Jews. We trust that our Fuhrer will take care of them real soon."

The host, Maj. Dennhard was quietly listening to the conversation without participating in it. He was not about to have an argument with "Partei Genossen" of the town. He knew the reality only too well, paying for early victories with one of his arms. The reality was not pleasant at all. The whole German position in Eastern and Southern Europe was now on the point of disintegration. The retreat from Russia was a terrible affair. The esprit de corps of German Armies were but a memory. The Dumkopf in Berlin repeated Napoleon's mistakes. It might be easy to go to Russia but coming out alive was another matter. The Russian dictator seemed to have a never ending supply of men and material. To him the war was just a "diplomacy carried on by other means." As the matter stood at the moment, it was obvious to Dennhard that Ivan would achieve his goals. And what about the second front? What about the Americans? Major Dennhard was sure that it also was clear to the most stupid soldier of the Reich, that the war was as good as lost. There was absolutely nothing more to gain- no military honors, no decorations, no promotion, no special leave, just a "cold arse" to use the apt expression of the Landser. It had become a pitiless battle for sheer survival. Especially now that the Soviets were fighting well beyond the historic borders of Russia. Soon the will be screaming in Berlin: "Stalin Ante Portas" – Stalin at the gates.

"Meine Herren and Damen" it is late, we have to get back to the Sanatorium. Duty calls. It has been really a delightful evening for which Heinrich and I thank our gracious host and hostess. Auf Wiedersehen."

Saying good-bye to all took another half hour. It has been a long evening and everybody was looking to get a good night sleep.

The same driver took them back to Dorfen. Sitting in the car Maj. Scharf remarked:

"I understand that Astrid wants me to be Heinrich's best man at the wedding. Nothing could please me more. Tomorrow I shall officially arrange Heinrich's transfer to my staff. I don't know if I could get him a higher rank but I'll try that. And now I must go to bed otherwise I'll collapse right here in this car."

There was no need for that because the driver pulled in front of Sanatorium Dorfen's gates. Henryk put on his laboratory coat and everyone went to his and hers quarters.

The very next morning, Henryk reported to Maj. Scharf's office.

"Well Kaplinski, you'll be working with male-nurse Erwin Boeselager till further notice. Dismissed." That was it. He located Boeselager and introduced himself to him.

"So you're the fellow that Maj. Scharf transferred. Welcome aboard. I was given to understand that you're actually one of the wounded who volunteered to help. I'll go very easy on you and have you just empty bedpans. This shouldn't be too tough for you."

"Whatever you say, sergeant. Someone has to do it, might as well be me. Where do I start?

"I do like your attitude. You and I will get along just fine. The rumor has it that our head-nurse is in love with you. You had better watch out because there is a nasty Hungarian by the name of Miclos who is after her in the worst way."

"I'm sure that he is not the only one, besides Fraulein Astrid von Vietinghoff can take care of herself."

Boeselager was clearly needling Henryk but was doing that good naturally, there was no menace in his voice. Henryk was sure that he would get along with him.

Henryk started his job of emptying bedpans of the heavily wounded soldiers. After a while, all bedpans smelled equally bad. Some of them in addition to urine and feces also had blood. He would report each such case.

There was no sense of complaining. He knew that sooner or later he would be transferred to another duty. He was just a part of Sanatorium Dorfen's tradition where everybody started by emptying bedpans.

Only once in the last three days did he come across Astrid. She just smiled seeing him carrying bedpans: "Don't worry Heinrich, I've done it many times." And undoubtedly she did.

A few days later Boeselager switched Henryk to an area where all medical utensils were washed boiled and dried. The chrome or nickel plated items didn't give Henryk much trouble but steel, be it "solligen" or not "solligen" utensils seemed to rust in front of his eyes.

Delivering some of these utensils to a nurse's station he was stopped by a giant of a fellow on two crutches:

"So you are the fellow that Astrid is in love with." He spoke German with a distinct Hungarian accent. A strong smell of alcohol was coming out of his mouth.

"You must be Miclos, then...?"

"So, you know about me already?"

"All I know is that you are drunk. Just get out of my way!"

"You look to me like a Jewish swine, remember, I'm going to fuck her whether you like it or not. After all she is but a "Offizier matratz" (officer's mattress). Let her try a non-com's prick for a change."

"That is enough Miclos, get back to your room. One more outburst like this and I'll have you court-martialed, wounded or not, is that clear?" It was Boeselager's authoritative voice that put the encounter to an end.

Miclos slowly moved around dragging one leg in a cast, being supported by two wooden crutches.

"Heinrich, forget him, the man is crazy, we are going to transfer him to Munich anyway. Let them deal with him. Here he is only trouble. Don't get involved, do you hear me?"

"Very well Erwin." Henryk was more amused than worried. He had much confidence in Astrid's ability to handle unruly patients.

A couple of days passed by and Henryk put that scene out of his mind until the time when Astrid came to the small laboratory where Henryk was removing sterilized surgical scalpels, retractors, clamps and ever in demand sautéing needles from the autoclaving unit.

"I need a few utensils for my unit."

"Go ahead and take what you need, I guess you'll have to sign for it."

"Of course, that is the standard procedure around here."

With no one within an earshot Henryk asked Astrid:

"What is the story with that Hungarian Miclos?"

"Never mind him, he is a harmless idiot, I can handle him. Don't worry. Some men see me as their mother, sister, wife, daughter or mistress. They have seen terrible things and have done even more horrible things to other people. Some of course are dying of their wounds, some will be crippled for the rest of their lives. Others worry about their families in the East and what Ivan will do to their dear ones. You would be surprised to know how many heroes cry at night for their mamas. Heinrich let you and I have the comfort in each other and let's forget about the ugly world. Remember my darling it is four more days to our wedding. Any butterflies in your tummy?" She kissed him slightly on the cheek.

"Well than, good luck to us."

"Luck is when preparation meets opportunity and I'm staying prepared." With a friendly smile she collected her utensils and left the laboratory.

The rest of the day went peacefully enough. After the evening meal, Henryk retired to his room where he was soon asleep. In the past he slept in trenches with shells flying overhead, therefore he didn't have any problems with noise coming from his snoring neighbors.

It was way past midnight, when his sleep was interrupted by Boeselager:

"Heinrich, get up! Maj. Scharf wants to see you at once. Something very bad has happened."

"What time is it…?" sleepily asked Henryk.

"It's after two o'clock, please hurry it's urgent."

"What has happened? Are the Russians in Dorfen already?"

"Much worse, please hurry up!"

Alarmed by Boeselager's voice, Henryk quickly got dressed and rushed along Boeselager to the other side of the building, housing the most heavily wounded soldiers.

They both entered a hall already crowded with medical personnel. In the corner of the room stood distraught Maj. Scharf holding a small caliber pistol in his right hand. Next to him on the floor lay the large body of Miclos clutching a crutch, blood was still slowly oozing out of several bullet holes in his chest.

"Major…." Said Henryk. Maj. Scharf lifted his arm and pointed in the direction of the other end of the room. Henryk looked at the eagle-spread figure of a woman laying on the bed, her dress in disarray, face covered with blood mixed with crushed bones from her skull, a bloody crutch touching her head. Henryk moved towards her if paralyzed. There was no mistake. It was Astrid.

"Oh God, no, it can't be." Henryk knelt by the bed trying to find a pulse. There wasn't one. Astrid, the love of his life was gone. An emptiness took over and he passed out.

What seemed like an eternity was just a couple of minutes till he was revived by the strong smell of salts.

Henryk opened his eyes seeing several concerned faces, among them Maj. Scharf's.

"Major, what has happened here?" meekly asked Henryk.

"We have pieced the story quite accurately. Astrid who was on duty came to check on a dying patient, sometime after 1 o'clock. Returning back to her station she was accosted by Miclos, who put one hand on her mouth to prevent her from screaming and with the other hand he tried to rip off her clothing. He was a very powerful man, standing on his good leg.

Astrid, as some of the men laying in nearby beds told me, kicked Miclos in the cast covering his shattered ankle, causing him a lot of pain. Enraged he hit her face with his fist breaking her few teeth and than proceeded with hitting her over the head with his crutch. Several men, sick as they were, tried to stop him, but to no avail. Someone else got me out of bed. I tried to separate them but he threatened me with his crutch and it was then when I shot him and kept firing till I emptied the chamber.

Unfortunately there was nothing else I could have done for Astrid. Out of all the people she didn't deserve to die in such an ugly manner. I really don't know what to tell you and I was looking forward so much to your wedding. Now instead of a marriage we will have a funeral. God, Almighty what a mess. Nothing makes sense anymore."

The medics were removing the dead bodies from the hall as Henryk watched helplessly. It couldn't be a reality, maybe just a very bad dream from which he'll wake up soon but the gnawing feeling in his stomach told him something else entirely. Was it possible that Astrid had a prophetic dream just barely ten days ago?

Boeselager held Henryk by the hand and led him to a small room previously occupied by an absent doctor.

"Take this and drink a bit of water, it will help you to sleep better. We'll talk in the morning."

Like a small child Henryk swallowed whatever Boeselager gave him and in a few short minutes he fell into a deep, troubled sleep.

CHAPTER 40

To join his unit, Lt. Edward Daszkiewicz was driving north on the same road that brought him and Capt. Michalski to Rome. This time the traffic was considerably heavier. Long columns of British and American forces, their trucks full of soldiers, a variety of field guns, kitchens supply trucks and Sherman tanks with 155 mm guns mounted on their chassis jammed the few available roads.

Edward was stopped a few times by the over eager Military Police of different divisions but his British style of uniform and lately popular white-red flag with a white eagle emblazoned, acted like passes and he was simply waved on.

With no one to talk to, he took out K-rations of biscuits and cheese and started to eat. Finishing that, he checked his ever present necessities of war, hand grenades, ammo clips, water and bandages which he kept in his musette bag.

The sky above him was crystal clear for a change. He could see a flight of B-17 flying at 6000-8000 meters, heading possibly to Ploesti, Vienna, Wiener Neudorf, Debreczen, Munich, Blechhammer, Moosbierbaum or Regensburg.

The lead squadron, most likely the famous 817th under Maurice Raffel, flying out of Gioia, Italy, was trailing long, majestic contrails like a series of diamond necklaces.

Looking at those giant birds Edward smiled thinking that his German counterparts were ducking at the same sight. That was the payoff for air superiority. The Germans were probably not only ducking but hugging the ground. Infantrymen of all armies learned that lesson, especially Edward after Monte Cassino.

It felt good to be on the winning side for a change.

Several hours later he located with some difficulties his unit, which in the meantime moved to another nearby village. He reported to his C.O. Maj. Wieslaw Krzemien about his S.S. Col. Blau assignment.

"Well done Lieutenant. Too bad you couldn't capture him alive. We could have "pumped" for additional information."

"I doubt it very much, Sir. He was a very shrewd operator. I also wanted him alive but for altogether different reasons, Sir."

"Oh yes! That reminds me of a brief message we received for Capt. Michalski, regarding your wife, from our operatives in Cracow. Here it is: "Initial contact has been established with S.S. Hauptsturmfuhrer Helmuth Berger, Details to follow. Signed Kruk. "That is all we have on the subject, I'm sorry to say, Lieutenant."

"Thank you very much, Major. You gave me some hope, Sir."

"Glad to be of help. We are going to stay here for a while. You are billeted temporarily with a couple of the other officers in a bombed-out house until we find something more suitable. Just two more brief notices. Capt. Michalski should be back within 7-10 days and I have also assigned to you Corp. Eliasz Wachtel. He studied law in London and Paris, you probably could use a man like that in your department. He is also Jewish and he comes from Lvov area. You don't have any problem with working with Hebs?"

"No Sir, I don't."

"Very well than. Stop by tomorrow morning and see the duty officer. He'll have you present assignment. That is all Daszkiewicz, dismissed."

With his spirits uplifted Edward went to look for his "billet". What he found, any civilian seeing such a cellar, would have immediately declared it uninhabitable, but to Edward, the cellar seemed to be the safest place in the world, even though it smelled of cigarette smoke, sweat, brick dust and soot. The lack of running water was replaced by another luxury, hot food that the cooks provided.

Tomorrow was Sunday and he had an urge to go to church. The services were conducted by an Army Chaplain in a village church. The windows were blown out and the church itself was a mess but the services were very impressive. Most men were in combat dress and armed, from time to time their rifles leaning against the wooden pews would slip and hit the floor much to the annoyance of the congregation.

Edward ignored all that interference concentrating on his prayers:

"Our Father... which Art in heaven... Hallowed be Thy name... Thy Kingdom... Thy will be done..." His thoughts were with Czeslawa and Danuta as he left the church with a sense of comfort and well being.

Monday morning he went to the Company's HQ reporting to the Duty Officer.

"Good morning, Lieutenant. Here is the file given to me by Maj. Krzemien. It deals this time with criminal behavior rather than espionage or sabotage, so we think. Food destined for our troops disappeared and a number of fuel drums from the Motor Pool are unaccountable. This really worries us because of potential disaster. The case is a police work but at the moment we don't have anybody else to look into that Pandora's box. See what you can do to solve that case before Capt. Michalski's return. Any questions, Lieutenant?"

"No, Sir." "In that case good luck and I'm off. Here is your file."

Edward left Maj. Krzemien's office only to be stopped by a female soldier wearing no insignia.

"Begging lieutenant's pardon. Would you be Lieutenant Daszkiewicz?"

"Yes, madam."

"In that case please be advised that in the other waiting room, there is Corp. Wachtel waiting for you as per Major's orders."

"Thank you Miss, I'll go to get him."

Edward went to the waiting room where he spotted the slightly stooped figure of the only corporal with Semitic features. He walked up to him:

"Corp. Wachtel? I'm Lt. Daszkiewicz, I understand that you are looking for me."

Corp. Wachtel jumped to his feet and saluted: "Yes Sir, I was ordered to report to you, Sir."

"Welcome aboard, Corporal. What else do you know besides French and English?"

"I'm also fluent in German and am a fair stenographer."

"Excellent, you'll be a real help in our unit. By the way, the Major mentioned something about you being from Lvov."

"No Sir, I'm from Boryslaw, some 100 kilometers south of Lvov, Sir."

"I'm familiar with the town, had a very good friend living there. A fellow by the name of Henryk Kaplinski in Drohobycz where I come from, I had a professor in Gimnasium who taught us the Polish language and Literature, by the name of Wachtel. Any relative of yours?"

"It may interest you to know that Henryk Kaplinski is or was my cousin and Professor Wachtel was my aunt."

"What a coincidence. And now we are both in Italy fighting Krauts together. Do you wish to return home to Boryslaw?"

"There is nothing else that I think about. I'm only afraid what I will find there?"

"I understand you very well Eljasz. One of these days you and I will have a long talk. In the meantime there is a war to be won. Let's study our first case. Your legal training should come in handy. This case has to do with the theft of large amounts of food and the disappearance of 50 drums of fuel, a very serious crime in time of war. I'm not talking about small stuff. Everybody steals a little, either for vodka or a piece of ass. I've been a soldier long enough to know what goes on in kitchens or supply depots. The Russians would put the entire quartermaster unit against the wall and ask questions later. We are just a bit more civilized. We'll ask questions first and shoot those bastards later. What do you say to that, Corporal?"

"Lieutenant has a sense of humor, I'm glad to say."

"I'll tell you what, Corporal, you study those papers for a while and let me know what your ideas are as to how to solve this case. I've to attend to another function and will be back in a couple of hours. Should anybody question your presence, just tell them that you are with the Second Department under my command."

"Yes Sir, I'll do my best, Sir."

"I'm sure of that, Wachtel."

Should the truth be known, Edward didn't have a slight idea as to how to go about solving the case. He was hoping that Wachtel using his "Jewish head" will come up with answers.

Coming back some time later, Edward was not disappointed with his hunch.

"Lieutenant, I thing we've found a partial solution to the problem, at least the most important one, the disappearance of the 50 drums, 55 gallon each of fuel. It was a typographical error. Someone misread the poorly typed "30" drums and read "80" drums. The number "3" wasn't sharp enough. I've checked previous bills of lading thoroughly. It was 30 drums received and not 80. An honest enough mistake. The food is another case entirely. If that would be only one or two items it would have been a petty theft but so many items missing indicates that someone sold them to the black marketers, somewhere in Rome most likely. Let's start with the Supply Sergeant and put enough pressure on him and see where it may bring us."

"Wachtel, you're a genius. Your aunt would be proud of you."

"Thank you Sir."

"Let's go Corporal. My jeep is outside, I'll drive. It's just a couple of kilometers to the base."

They pulled in front of the heavily guarded supply depot. Edward introduced himself to the duty officer as a member of the 2nd Dept. and requested to see the Senior Sergeant Seweryn Klimczak. Amazing how fast Edward was getting things done, once he had mentions the 2nd Dept.

"You may use my office if you wish, Sir." The Duty officer suggested.

"Thank you, I shall do that. Please show me where it is and have Klimczak brought there."

It was a small room, used by the Duty Officers. To call it an office was a slight exaggeration.

There was a knock at the door and a man close to being middle aged, well fed with reddish complexion and a red nose that betrayed the affinity of alcohol, entered the room.

"Senior Sergeant Klimczak reporting as ordered." He shrewdly appraised Edward, paying no attention to the presence of Jewish corporal.

Edward didn't bother to acknowledge Klimczak's salute and report. Instead he turned to Wachtel and said:

"Corporal, let me have Klimczak's file." Seeing that Klimczak relaxed from standing at attention, he yelled at him at the top of his voice:

"Stay at attention, soldier, and don't make a move! Is that clear?"

There was no answer coming from Klimczak. "IS THAT CLEAR?"

"Yes Sir, very clear."

Edward reread the rile. Klimczak was a professional soldier since 1932, married to a German woman from Sosnowiec, near the German-Polish border, two children, his entire army life spent in the rear echelon, quartermaster's duties.

"Klimczak, I'm, Lt. Daszkiewicz with the 2nd Dept, here to investigate acts of sabotage and theft. Do you know anything about it? Now is the time to tell me, Klimczak."

"I don't know anything about it, Sir."

"Are you sure? Then what has happened to the 50 drums of fuel?"

"I don't know Sir. I swear by God, I don't know."

"Isn't that your signature on this receipt?"

"It is Sir, but I still don't know anything about those drums."

"Corporal, what is the punishment for stealing fuel in wartime?"

"Firing squad, Sir."

"Well Klimczak, that is what is going to be?"

"I swear by Christ that I don't know about those drums. Maybe someone stole it."

"Did you count those drums in the time of the delivery?"

"No Sir, I was busy with other chores."

"Then why did you sign those papers?"

"I asked the driver if the drums are all in, he said yes, and I signed those papers for him."

"Were you drunk at that time, Klimczak?"

"Maybe I had a drink or two but I wasn't drunk, Sir."

"Klimczak, I wasn't baptized yesterday. Just answer my questions, were you or weren't you drunk at the time?"

Klimczak dropped his head and kept silent.

"Listen Klimczak, it says here that you are married to a German woman. It smells of sabotage. I would hate to put a good Pole and a father of two girls against a wall. I'll make a deal. I'll drop the sabotage charges altogether just as long as you tell me what has happened to the food supplies. Do we have a deal, Klimczak?

Klimczak got to his knees and started to cry:

"I'm so sorry Lieutenant, I was drunk and sold them on the black market. With so much food coming I thought that nobody will miss it."

"What did you get for it?"

"I got 150 British Pounds and a pearl necklace which I thought I would give to my wife after the war."

"Corporal did you write all this down?"

"Yes Sir, here it is."

"Klimczak, read it and sign it. It is your confession."

"Klimczak signed the paper with a trembling hand without reading it."

"Klimczak where is the money and the necklace?"

"I'll bring it in, Sir."

"Corporal, you go with him and both of you come right back."

"Yes Sir." They both left the room.

Edward lit a cigarette, he was pleased with the progress of the investigation. It went better than he thought. By the time he finished smoking his cigarette, Wachtel and Klimczak returned to the room.

"Here it is." Said Klimczak handing over to Edward money and a small box containing the necklace. Edward counted the money. It was exactly 150 lbs. all in "fivers". The necklace was pretty but Edward wasn't sure as to the quality.

"Do you know something else Klimczak. The British 5 lbs. Notes look like the bogus bills printed by the Germans and the necklace is a fake too. And for this garbage you have betrayed your comrades in time of war? I pity you. You are looking at 3-6 months of hard labor and a reduction of rank to P.F.C., after all those years in the Army. You have 2 hours to transfer your duties to the next in line non-com. Corporal Wachtel will go along with you to see that everything is accounted for. Please no more tricks, because I'll add years to that sentence. Is they're anything you wish to say, Klimczak?"

"Could I be transferred to an active duty, Sir. Perhaps I can wash my shame with my own blood, Sir."

"I'll give it a thought, Klimczak. In the meantime see that everything is accounted for."

"Yes Sir. Thank you Sir."

"Klimczak, one more thing!"

Edward walked up to Klimczak and ripped off his army stripes.

"You are not fit to wear those stripes! I'll see to it, that you will be transferred to an Engineer combat battalion. The Army can't make you be a good soldier, but is sure as hell can make you wish that you were one. Now get out of my sight, you chicken-shit."

CHAPTER 41

To say that Maj. Krafchin was overworked would have been an understatement of the year. Gen. Gary had him working 7 days a week, 15 hours a day. Each report coming from the field had to be examined and proper steps taken, steps that would affect the lives of many pilots and airmen.

His hard work didn't escape the general's attention, who drove himself even harder. He once told Paul that he was working 8 days a week.

"Pardon me, Sir where did you get the eighth day?"

"It is because on Sunday I work twice as hard."

That was quite true. General and Paul made a very good team. Paul would never put his signature to a document without checking it thoroughly.

Paul had barely time to phone Cynthia at her home, but there wasn't any time to see her. In the course of the last few weeks he had just two visitors. One of them was his buddy, Capt. George Perry, who brought back his ring:

"Thanks Major for the use of the ring. We'll be grounded for a while for a little bit of R&R."

"You can have the ring any time you wish, George."

"I think that from now on we can manage on our own without the ring's magic powers."

"Very well then George, good luck."

The second visit was totally unexpected. It was Chaplain Jerome Rifkind, who brought him the ring in the first place, from his parents in Brooklyn.

"What brings you here, Padre?" politely inquired Paul.

"Had a long conversation with Gen. Cotshott regarding the

possibility of bombing certain targets in Europe, such as concentration camps and similar. He said that the decision as not up to him unfortunately. In the course of the conversation he did mention that you had lost your father. My deepest condolences Major. He was a very charming man."

"That he certainly was, Rabbi."

"Would you like me to recite prayers in his memory?"

"If you wish, Rabbi. I made my own peace with him. As long as I live, he'll always be alive in my memory."

"I respect that, Major. I would like to talk to you about something else. Can I tell you Paul?"

"Or course, Rabbi."

"Listen to me very carefully. The war should end in 6-12 months. Europe will be totally devastated. Reports that are reaching me are very hard to believe even though I know them to be true. The Jewish population in Hitler's Europe is being exterminated. The few survivors will look to America and American Jews for help. We'll need men like you, Paul to fly planes. Can we count on you, Paul?"

"Absolutely, but I'm in the Air Force, how can I be of help Rabbi?"

"Just remember when the time will come we'll be in touch, we'll be calling on you."

"Please do Rabbi, I will be continuing my father's passion, he was always concerned with the fate of his relatives in Poland."

"Are you up to reciting the prayers with me?"

"Yes, Rabbi."

Facing the east they both recited the prayers in Paul's father's memory:

> *"Lord, what is a man, that Thou has regard for him?*
> *Or the son of man, that Thou takest account of him?*
> *Man is like a breath,*
> *His days are as a fleeting shadow.*
> *In the morning he flourishes and grows up like grass,*

In the evening he is cut down and withers.
So teach us to number our days,
That we may get us a heart of wisdom,
Mark the man of integrity, and behold the upright
For there is a future for the man of peace.

Paul kept his eyes closed when he opened them the Rabbi disappeared without a word.

The intercom coughed up a "sweet" message:

"Paul where the fuck are you? I need you here on the double."

"Yes Sir, I'm on my way, Sir."

By this time Paul got used to Gen. Gary the "Hotshot" vocabulary. It didn't bother him at all.

"Paul, how was the visit with Padre? Did you know that Chaplain Rifkind was related to Alexander Good a Jewish Chaplain, who with 3 other Padres gave up their life jackets to four soldiers, who lost theirs, when the S.S. Dorchester was struck by a U-boat torpedo in the icy waters of Greenland?"

"No, I didn't know he was related, Sir."

"This is not why I've called you Major, I've got a job for you. You have to deliver some papers to the War Department in Washington, D.C. You are due for take off in three hours. I obtained a priority seat for you to Idlewild Airport in New York. From there you are to fly to Washington. Only, and I said only, after delivering those papers, get your ass to Brooklyn to see your mother. Got it straight, Major? Now get ready and be back for those papers. The attaché case will be fastened to your wrist. Under no circumstances can these papers fall in to the wrong hands. Is that clear, Major?"

"Very clear, Sir. I'll be guarding them with my life, Sir. Thank you Sir for the opportunity."

"Get the hell out of here and stop wasting my time. One more thing Major, you've got to be back within 8-9 days and don't you dare come back without your mother's "Mandlebread."

Paul was overwhelmed with the thought of seeing his mother.

The General kept his word.

He rushed to his dormitory to pack a few items of clothing and toilet articles needed for the trip, managing to put a fast call to Cynthia's parents to tell them that would be away for a couple of weeks on an assignment and was back at the office to pick up travel papers and a variety of vouchers. The attaché case was fastened to his left wrist. An Air Force driver was already waiting to take him to the airport.

To Paul's surprise the plane that was taking him back to the States was a B-17 converted to a makeshift passenger plane. The M.P.'s scrutinized his papers and saluted returning the papers to him. "Have a good flight, Sir."

He was welcomed by a pretty stewardess who brought him to the designated seat. The plane stated to fill up with high ranking Army brass, Red cross representatives, a couple of senators whose faces were slightly familiar from the press and a few minor movie stars flying with a U.S.O. group. The plane was full with the exception of two seats, one up front and the other one next to Paul. He was hoping for an empty seat that would give him a chance to stretch out a bit on the way to Greenland a refueling stop on the way to the States.

The plane was held up, awaiting the arrival of a V.I.P. The crew seemed to be very excited at the prospect of the new arrival, but Paul who was really tired and sleepy decided to get a bit of shuteye in the meantime.

He was awakened by the husky voice of Marlene Dietrich"

"Pardon me, Major, is this seat taken?"

Paul was sure that he was dreaming. "N…no, madam."

There she was, big as life itself, Marlene Dietrich the super star. She was even prettier and sexier than the silver screen would or could portray her."

"Do I need to introduce myself, Major?"

"No Madam, but I must. Paul Krafchin of A.A.F."

"Pleasure, Major."

Their further conversation was interrupted by a couple of reporters from" Stars & Stripes" and the N.Y. Times and their flash cameras.

"I do hope Major, that you don't mind the Hollywood hoopla?"

"Not at all, as long as they don't misspell my name or describe me as being married with six kids."

"Are you then married?"

"No, but engaged to a red head in Brooklyn."

"That is my luck. Everytime I do meet an interesting man he is either married or engaged."

"It can't be that bad. Half of the world's men are in love with you, Miss Dietrich." "Please call me Marlene."

"I'll do that, providing that you call me Paul instead of major." "You have a deal, Paul."

She was wearing a G.I. uniform, Air Force leather bomber jacket and fleece lined boots and like so many GIs she chain smoked Lucky Strikes. Each time she pulled out a cigarette, Paul would light one for her. She refused to smoke Paul's Camels, saying that 95% of doctors who tried Camels went back to their wives.

"Where are you from, Major I mean Paul?"

"Would you believe Brooklyn, N.Y.?"

"Wirklich?" A German word for "really" slipped out of her mouth. Paul, who took German in College and knew a bit of Yiddish from his parents, understood the word.

"I do understand some German. My parents come from Galicia what used to be Austro-Hungarian Monarchy. Can I tell you a story which might amuse you a bit on this long flight?"

"Go ahead, Paul."

"Do you know how the city of Cincinnati got its name?"

"I do not know."

"Well, some years ago two German immigrant women were in Ohio. One said to the other "Sie sind net" to which the other answered "Sie sind net" (you are nice) and that how the city got it's name."

Marlene Dietrich started to laugh so loud that everybody

started to look at her companion who caused such an outburst of laugh.

That laugh was also heard by Miss Dietrich's secretary because she showed up with a blanket, book and a few toilet items.

"This is my secretary," she said without bothering to give her name.

"How do you do." Something that "her majesty the secretary" ignored to acknowledge.

"Please fasten your seats, we are ready for take off." The Captain announced, causing the secretary to run to her seat.

"I really can't stand her. She is very devoted to me but when we travel she sits away from me. She doesn't like me to smoke cigarettes and this is our compromise, we sit separately. Paul why do you have that attaché case fastened to your wrist? What do you have in it that is so important?"

"Just letters from my fiancée, Miss Dietrich."

"Oh, we are back to being formal, Major?" She said flirtatiously. "In that case will you join me for a drink? Let's drink "Bruderschaft". Do you know what that is?"

"I certainly do, because after a drink I get to kiss you and call you "Du".

Marlene had only to raise her finger when two stewardesses showed up.

"May we have a couple of double Scotches, I believe that my secretary brought aboard a few bottles from my private stock?"

"Yes, madam, she did. I'll be right back. Do you like it with ice?"

Marlene looked at Paul questionably. "Yes, please."

A few minutes later they were both back, carrying the drinks and a bunch of salty peanuts.

"Prosit" "Bottom's up" They both raised their glasses giving a click. After a long sip of excellent Scotch, Marlene puckered her famous lips towards Paul. He gave her a gentle but sensual kiss.

"Paul, that was pretty good, we'll have to repeat it soon enough."

"The Air Force is at your service, Madam."

They finished their drinks just as the "secretary" showed up again.

"Miss Dietrich must get her rest. Please see to it that nobody disturbs her."

The "secretary" gave Marlene some pills and a black, cloth mask to cover her eyes.

Marlene swallowed those pills and put on the beauty mask and said to Paul in a sweet, practiced voice:

"Sleep well my prince, I'll see you in my dreams."

"Good night, Miss Dietrich." Try as he did, he had a problem calling her Marlene.

The combination of tiredness and fine whisky not too mention the intoxicating smell of his neighbor's perfume caused him to fall asleep at the same time as Marlene.

Sometime during the night she put her head on his should waking him temporarily. The only thought Paul had at the moment, was who would believe him in Brooklyn that Marlene Dietrich slept on his shoulder. He fell asleep disregarding her slight snore and the plane's strong vibration. They were not aware when someone took their picture while asleep.

CHAPTER 42

"Komm mit, Lisl. Follow me and make it "schnell."

Petrified she walked behind Sturmbahnfuhrer Berger. All her thoughts were with Danuta. She worried how Danuta will react when she'll find out that her mother was taken away. Will they ever see each other again? As soon as it will be humanly possible, she'll beg to be reunited with Danuta even it if would mean their joint demise. In the meantime she would have to rely on Jadzia's and Katarzyna's word.

They walked hardly a couple of hundred meters when Berger stopped. In front of a barrack was a Jewish inmate of undetermined age. If anything the man resembled a "musulman", whether sick or already hallucinating, the man ignored Berger's command of "Halt".

Berger took out his pistol and with its barrel lifted to the man's head. "Stehen bleiben" – Stand still you lousy Jew."

The frightened man finally understood the S.S.-man's order, but as hard as he tried to stand still, his body wouldn't or couldn't cooperate, it just kept shaking, tears were coming down his face and no sound came out of his mouth as he was trying to say "Don't". He knew somehow that these were his last minutes on this not so godly earth.

Berger moved three steps back, still holding the pistol aimed at the man's head. He stopped and slowly squeezed the trigger. The well practiced shot hit the man in his forehead. The man fell at first to his knees and then his upper torso fell backwards. The oozing blood covered the previously shed tears. The eyes were open and the fear and the surprise were still registered like on the lens of a camera.

Sturmbahnfuhrer Berger holstered his gun and if in an afterthought opened the fly of his pants and started to urinate, directing the stream of hot, yellow urine on the bleeding face of the dead man. The mixture of urine, blood and tears were being absorbed by the patient Polish soil.

Finishing his biological function he shook his penis to get rid of the last drops of urine and after buttoning his pants he said to completely horrified Czeslawa: "weiter gehen" "Let's go." His face was devoid of any kind of expression or emotion. Czeslawa's only thought after witnessing the whole scene: "Was this man also created the image of God?" – she wondered.

Her legs felt like they were made out of lead, she walked with much difficulty. Berger didn't pay any attention to her. He knew fully well that she would follow him. He still had another six bullets in his gun.

They walked to a building housing the Hauptwache, where his car was parked.

"Get in" he barked pointing to a Steier #2200 Kabriolet. He sat in the back of the car, too shocked to admire the luxurious, red leather seats. The guards recognizing Berger and his car opened the hell's gates.

The same sun and the same sky was also on the outside of the camp. How was that possible?

Berger drove in silence. Czeslawa kept quiet for different reasons. She was afraid that Berger would hear her teeth chatter. It didn't take Berger too long to reach the staff area and the living quarters of the commanders and lower ranks of S.S., which were built outside the camp and were well tended and meticulously clean. They served as a pleasant façade for the camp proper, which was surrounded by high electrified barbed wire fence and guarded from the watchtowers.

Berger's house was similar to other houses with its well kept manicured lawns. The only difference that Czeslawa could see were the colors of their curtains. The door of Berger's house was opened by a slightly obese brunette in her mid thirties.

"Mutti, I brought you a new Lisl. I think you may even like her."

"Gruess Gott Helmuth, the supper will be ready soon. Our Liliane didn't behave herself today, you'll have to punish her."

"Mutti, what else did she do?"

"She messed up her room, Helmuth."

"Don't worry Mutti, the new Lisl will take care of that. Just tell her what her duties are Liliane! Papa is here!"

From another room a small girl about six years old came out, dressed in a Bavarian dirndl, and ran up to her father. "Papa, papa, what did you bring me?"

He lifted her high and tossed her a few times into the air, much to the child's delight. "I brought you a new Lisl."

Czeslawa watched the cold killer playing with his offspring. Nothing ever prepared her for this.

"Lisl come, let me show you to your room." Frau Berger took her down to the basement of the house where a small room and bathroom awaited the new Lisl.

"Take off you're clothing and put them into this bag. In the closet are a few dresses I believe should fit you, but before you do that I want you to wash up. I don't want any dirt that you have brought with you from the camp in this house. You must be totally clean before I let you take care of Liliane or work in the kitchen. As soon as you wash up come up, you'll be fed and introduced to Liliane. She is a very sensitive child and you must be very good with her, if you know what is good for you," Verstanden?"

"Yawohl, Gnaedige Frau, I fully understand that."

Frau Berger went upstairs and Czeslawa looked into the closet, for clothing to change into. Whatever she found was heaven sent after wearing the same dirty inmate's outfit.

Warm water and a real piece of soap felt heavenly on her skin. If she could she would stay under the shower forever. The water seemed to cleanse not only the dirt and filth of the camp but also the terrible scenes she saw recently.

"Lisl, why is it taking you so long? Hurry up will you!"

"Sofort Madame, I'm coming right up."

Swiftly she dried herself and donned a dress that belonged most likely to her predecessor. She glanced into the mirror. A stranger looked back from the mirror. With the loss of hair and weight she looked like a creature from another world. In fact she was one.

She came up to the kitchen where Frau Berger prepared her a bowl of soup with visible pieces of meat.

"Today, you'll eat first and then wash all the dishes. Starting tomorrow you'll wash all the dishes first and only after you've done your work you'll eat. Is that clear Lisl?"

"Yes, Frau Berger."

"One more thing Lisl. We keep rabbits outside the house in the backyard. Your job is also to clean their cages and feed the animals. Later I'll show you where and how. Right now eat and do the dishes. Be back shortly. Those dishes should be done by that time. Any specks or left over dirt and you'll be doing all the dishes over again."

"It will be done correctly, Frau Berger."

Czeslawa quickly ate the soup, nothing ever tasted that good after camp's food. She started to do the dishes. In some of the pots she found burned slices of potatoes which she scraped from the pot and seeing no one around she ate it as well as porridge from a child's plate. She also found pieces of meat that looked like chicken but was much sweeter, probably rabbit's. She ate every morsel of food, not caring who had that plate before. She will eat anything to stay alive in order to save Danuta.

Very carefully each pot, pan and dish was washed, checking each item before she put it away. It was good that she checked because Frau Berger came to the kitchen to double check her work.

"Very good, Lisl. Come I want Liliane to get to know you." Czeslawa dried her hands and went with Frau Berger to the living room, where Herr Berger was playing with his daughter.

"Liliane, this is the new Fraulein Lisl."

"I hate her, I want the old one back."

"Now, now, Liliane be nice. The old Fraulein Lisl had to go to the hospital." Softly said Herr Berger.

Liliane walked up to Czeslawa and kicked her in the left ankle. Inadvertently Czeslawa grimaced from the painful kick.

"Liliane, this is not proper behavior, try to make friends with Fraulein Lisl."

"It's nothing Frau Berger, children often react that way in the company of strangers. May I ask Liliane to show me her room and her toys?"

"What a good idea" said Herr Berger "Liliane please take Fraulein Lisl to your room."

This time Herr Berger put a stress on the word "please."

Liliane hearing her father's voice took Czeslawa by the hand and led her into her room.

It has been seeming years since Czeslawa has seen anything as pretty as Liliane's bedroom. Everything in the room was done in light, friendly lemon-yellow colors. In the corner of the room, neatly displayed were Liliane's toys and stuffed animal. A small easel and a metal tin box with watercolors caught Czeslawa's attention.

"Liliane, would you like me to paint a real elephant for you?"

"You don't know even what an elephant looks like."

"But I do Liliane, I have seen one in the circus."

Not waiting for Lilian's approval she took out a brush from the box and within a few minutes Liliane had a picture of an elephant with a baby elephant holding her trunk. Liliane excited ran into the living room: "Mama, Papa, look what Fraulein Lisl painted for me."

They both came to see what caused all that excitement. The elephants looked so real that they could have walked almost out of the paper.

"Liliane would you like to have a tiger and a lion too? Maybe a giraffe?"

"Yes, please Fraulein Lisl." She was very polite this time. The

Bergers looked at each other quite pleased. The new Lisl had a good potential in their household.

Czeslawa kept painting until she used up all the available paper. Luckily she was rescued by Frau Berger:

"Liliane, it is time for you to go to sleep. Tomorrow Papa will buy you more paper and Fraulein Lisle is going to teach you how to paint, won't you Fraulein Lisl?"

"Of course, Madame, I'll be glad to."

"Herr Berger is going to read Liliane bed stories and he'll put her to sleep as always when he is home. You come with me because I want to show you where we keep the rabbits, how to clean their cages and how to feed them."

Czeslawa followed Frau Berger to the back yard of the house where in the wooden shack rabbits were kept in 12 chicken-wire cages. There Frau Berger explained to Czeslawa the best methods of handling rabbits, their feeding habits and frequency of cleaning those cages.

"Is that all clear to you, Lisl?"

"Yes Frau Berger, it is clear to me but it is also time consuming. If Madame will permit me I would like to explain my concern. You see I have taught art in Gimnasium for several years. Never have I met a child so obviously talented as your daughter. She has an inborn understanding of colors and light that most adults will never have in their lives. With proper training she'll become Germany's greatest artist. With your kind permission I would like to spend more time with her teaching the art of painting. As far as the rabbits are concerned, your husband can get someone to tend those rabbits. As a matter of fact, in my barrack, there is a girl by the name of Danuta, who used to take care of rabbits in her native village. I highly recommend that girl. She is honest and hardworking."

"Fraulein Lisl, I'm very happy to hear about Liliane, she is our only child and we certainly would like to see her talent developed. Herr Berger will take you to town to buy any art supplies you may need. I'll speak with Herr Berger to get the girl for the rabbits and now lets get back to the house."

By the time they both got back. Liliane was already asleep and Herr Berger retired to his bedroom.

"Lisl, one more thing before you go to sleep. Wash the floor in the kitchen, you'll be getting up everyday at 6. I'll show you what we eat for breakfast and how to serve coffee for Herr Berger, He often eats in bed. I must admit, for the first day you have done well. I hope you'll keep it up, for your sake."

"I will Frau Berger, I certainly will." Angenehme Ruhe "-Good Night."

With her morale uplifted with the possibility of rescuing Danuta from the clutches of the camp, she washed the kitchen floor before going to sleep. She fell asleep in minute she put her head on the pillow, oblivious to the noises coming from the squeaking mattress in the master's bedroom.

Czeslawa got up very early in the morning, even earlier than in the camp. After straightening out her room, she went to the kitchen where she located all necessary items needed for the breakfast and the local etiquette. By the time the half-sleepy Frau Berger came into the kitchen, everything was prepared.

"Gutten Morgen Gnaedige Frau" with a slight curtsy Czeslawa greeted Frau Berger.

"I see that you found everything. That's nice. I spoke with Herr Berger regarding our conversation. He promised me that he would bring the girl for rabbits and tomorrow he'll take you shopping for art supplies."

"Thank you very much, Frau Berger."

"Gutten Morgen, Mutti, did you sleep well my Schatz?"

"Thanks to you Helmuth, I slept very well indeed. Look, what Lisl did already this morning? She prepared a breakfast for us on her first day, so don't forget to bring that girl. What was her name, Lisl?"

"Danuta, Frau Berger. The "Blockalteste" will point her out for Herr Berger. May I now go to check on Liliane?"

"Let her sleep, Lisl. I'll get her up a bit later."

"Very well Madame."

Czeslawa seemed to have an over abundant energy. She performed her duties with relish, often smiling to Frau Berger. After Liliane got up she spent considerable time with her, hindered only by the lack of art supplies, which should be replenished in tomorrow's purchase. Today she awaited impatiently for Berger's return with "The rabbit caretaker."

Every few minutes she would glance out of the window looking for Berger's car. It seemed like an eternity by the time Berger pulled in front of the house. He stepped out of the car at the same time as a young slender girl, dressed in striped clothing also came out.

Czeslawa ran to open the door for them.

Right behind the big figure of Herr Berger was Janka Bialogora, Danuta's best friend in the camp.

CHAPTER 43

Someone was pulling his arm. "Heinrich, get up, please." With considerable difficulties Henryk opened his eyes, and if through a fog he recognized Maj. Scharf.

Slowly Henryk recalled yesterday's murder scene. It was his Astrid that was killed. Uncontrollably he started to cry. All his pain caused by the loss of his family, culminated paradoxically with the loss of Astrid.

"Now, now Heinrich, try to calm down. It is most unfortunate. People became beasts in this war, but you Heinrich must continue living and you must be strong. In a couple of hours we are going to bury Astrid in the nearby cemetery. It's all arranged. I'm so sorry Heinrich but that is how life is sometimes. I almost forgot to tell you, you have an important letter. Here it is."

"Letter? What letter? Who would want to write to me at this time?"

"Heinrich, this letter is from Gen. Vietinghoff, Astrid's father."

"Please read it to me, Major. I can't focus on anything right now."

"I see that Army Group North became Army Group Kurland, that means that Vietinghoff is no longer in Italy."

"Major if you don't mind, just give me the gist of the letter, please."

Major Scharf read the letter in silence and from the looks of it he re-read it once more.

"Simply put, the General welcomes you into his family and sends regrets, he can't be present at the wedding ceremony. He says further, that Astrid chose you for a husband and he trusts her choice. He mentions that according to Astrid's letter, the General has decorated you for bravery, although he couldn't recall the incident. His wedding gift for the young couple will have to wait till the end of hostilities and Germany's final victory. He hopes that your marriage will be blessed with many children and grandchildren. Best wishes e.t.c. Signed Gen. Vietinghoff. The General doesn't know yet what has happened to his daughter. I tried several times to reach his headquarters but I couldn't get through. I hope that Ivan didn't get a hold of him. Here is your letter, Heinrich, put it away. Look, the funeral will be held in an hour. Get up, I'll help you."

"Major, I'll take over" said Boeselager who just walked into the room. "Sir, you're wanted at the nurses station. There is some kind of medical emergency."

"I'll be right there."

Boeselager was very gentle and understanding with Henryk. He helped him to shave and to get dressed.

"Thank you Erwin, thank you very much, you are a real pal."

"I'm so sorry Heinrich. Astrid was a wonderful person and such a lady. She'll be missed by everyone who knew her. I'll go with you to the cemetery. The coffin is on the truck already. Some staff members also may join us."

Like in a drunken stupor, Henryk followed Erwin Boeselager to the truck carrying Astrid's coffin. It was only a few minutes by truck from the Sanatorium to the cemetery. The driver knew the road only too well, making that trip rather often.

A small group of people mostly staff members and the Dennhards awaited the arrival of the truck. Someone helped Henryk to get down from the truck.

The funeral service performed by a local priest rather than an Army chaplain was mercifully short. Henryk didn't hear a word of it. His thoughts were far, far away, in his native Drohobycz. Two gravediggers slowly lowered the coffin, a standard German army issue, on two worn ropes. Quickly the coffin was covered by shovels full of earth.

The priest came up to Henryk and said a few well meaning words and left before Henryk had a chance to thank him. He was shaking hands with people he didn't know. Someone attached a black ribbon to his tunic. The Dennhards approached him and offered a ride back to the Sanatorium and upon Boeselaer's urging Henryk accepted their offer.

"Look Heinrich, we have been very close to the Vietinghoff family. Astrid was like our own daughter. We don't know much about you, but as long as Astrid chose you for her husband, we'll consider you as a member of our family too. The day after tomorrow we'll be going to Schloss Elmau for a week or two. Come with us, you'll find peace there and solace, away from the Sanatorium and the painful memories. I'll speak with Maj. Scharf about it. He already mentioned a medical discharge for you. A change of scenery will do you a world o good. Trust us, we know what we're saying."

"Thank you Herr Dennhard, I'll let you know by tomorrow." Said Henryk getting out of the car in front of Sanatorium Dorfen.

Boeselager got somehow to the Sanatorium ahead of Henryk and waited for him in the vestibule.

"Heinrich, you must be hungry, you didn't have a morsel of food in your mouth."

"I'm not hungry, maybe just a cup of hot tea. I don't feel like seeing or speaking with anyone, I just want to be left alone."

"I understand your feelings. I'll keep everybody out of your room. I do know that Maj. Scharf wants to talk to you. Here he comes. In the meantime, I'll get you something hot to drink."

"Thanks again Erwin, I won't forget you."

Maj. Scharf apologized for not being able to attend the funeral: "Sorry, Heinrich I had an emergency and couldn't leave the operating room."

Henryk told Maj. Scharf about the Dennhards offer.

'I think that is a very good idea, you should take the advantage of the offer. Everything around here will only remind you of Astrid. In my opinion you are due for a medical discharge. This will take a bit of time. However, there is no problem with issuing an emergency furlough. I'll call the Dennhards myself about you, I'll also ask Boeselager to help you pack for a couple of weeks of furlough. For God's sake, both Astrid and I wanted you to live. We took tremendous risks to keep you alive, so don't disappoint us. You must live and you shall live Kaplinski, do you understand me? That is also a direct order, got it?"

"Yes Sir, an order is an order, Major." This time Henryk managed a weak smile. Uncharacteristically, Major gave Henryk a hug.

"Don't let me down, Henryk. My Jewish step father would be very angry with me."

"Don't worry Sir, I'll do my very best to stay alive. What a pity, I loved Astrid so very much."

By the time Erwin brought the herbal tea, Maj. Scharf was gone.

"What did the Major want?" asked Erwin Boeselager.

"The usual pep talk. He suggested that I get away for a few weeks from this stinking place."

"Do you know something, Heinrich, if someone would offer me a chance of getting out of this rate hole, I'd be the first to run. My advice to you, my friend is GO. This joint will be here when you do return. I guarantee it."

"Thank you again Erwin. Too bad that we didn't meet early."

"Enough of this bullshit. Here take this pill and go to sleep. I'll check on you in the morning."

Erwin left the room and on the outside door, he attached a note: "Not to be disturbed, doctor's orders."

The usual Sanatorium's morning noises woke Henryk up even before Erwin came into the room. Thanks to Erwin's pill, Henryk slept through the night not remembering any dreams. Stayed in bed trying to collect his thoughts and to plan his future steps. Try as hard he could he couldn't come up with anything. He would simply have to take a day at a time.

"Greeting Heinrich, I brought you your breakfast. I'm treating you like a big shot." Said Boeselager putting down the tray next to Henryk's bed.

"Maj. Scharf told me to tell you that you'll be picked up by Herr and Frau Dennhard at 11 o'clock sharp. I'm ordered to see that come hell or high water, you should be ready to leave. Is that understood, soldier?"

"Yes Sir, sergeant Sir. I can be packed in a few minutes. I just got to get to my regular dormitory to pick up my stuff."

"That is more like it. I'll go with you and help you pack. I want to make sure that you'll get the fuck out of here. One more thing, Heinrich, I have some money for you. Just spend it."

"I can't take your money, Erwin. Are you crazy?"

"Just take it and don't talk about it anymore. Come, let's go. It's getting late. I have also a small surprise for you. A gift from the staff – an elegant, crocodile leather valise. Those bastards probably stole it from rich Jews in Poland. We'll pack your stuff in it."

There was no sense or purpose of arguing with Erwin. They went to Henryk's dormitory and packed his belongings including the suit purchased by Astrid.

With Boeselager carrying his valise, Henryk went to say goodbye to Maj. Scharf and other members of his medical team.

"Good luck and try to relax, Heinrich."

"Thank you, Major and thank you sergeant Boeselager."

Exactly at 11 o'clock, Dennhard's limousine pulled in front of the gate. Their driver stored Henryk's valise in the large trunk in back of the car.

Entering the car, Henryk shook hands with both Dennhards, They were dressed in matching Bavarian outfits.

"Good morning Heinrich, we are so glad that you could join us. We'll be traveling about 80 kilometers southeast of here to Schloss Elmau. It's close to the former Austrian border. You'll love Schloss Elmau, everybody does since the philosopher Johannes Mueller back in 1916 set up his idyll, courtesy of a generous princes. His disciples followed and so did music and sport and this what we're doing right now."

The conversation in the car was light and surprisingly pleasant. The unpleasant subjects such as war or the tragic death of Astrid were avoided totally by the well mannered Dennhards.

They had reached their destination in comfort. The Elmau itself, seen from a near hill, looked like a great ship, sitting in its meadow, docked in a sea of wild flowers an expanse of Alpine scenery, frosted in white in winter, a tapestry of blue and green in summer.

They have checked in the Muellerhaus, a peaked-roof house, amid some short lived confusion. Eventually, their luggage was brought up to the second floor, where Dennhards were given a large suite. Henryk's room was across the hall from then, a small lovely room with a blue-tiled fireplace, paneled walls and a tiny marble bathroom. The view from his window was breathtaking. The Dennhards were right, the Schloss Elmau was a sight not to be missed.

Henryk was told that he had almost two hours of free time till dinner. A walk before dinner made much sense. The fresh, intoxicating, ozone laden air felt great in his lungs and replaced the Sanatorium Dorfen's disinfectant smells.

High ranking army officers and other notables, walking with their wives or mistresses would acknowledge Henryk's salutes often with a smile or "Gruess Gott". Most likely he was being taken for someone's adjutant in his corporal's uniform.

He went back to his room to change into a civilian suit. His low rank noncom's uniform wasn't the proper attire at Schloss Elmau.

He heard a knock at the door and Dennhards voice:

"Are you ready for dinner, Heinrich?"

"Quite so, madam, be right with you."

The Dennhards were elegantly dressed, he in his decorated dinner jacket and Gretchen in a long evening gown.

"We are glad that you have put a civilian suit. We would have a small problem explaining your uniform. We were ready to pass you as Gretchen's brother a soldier on medical leave front the front. We still may do it."

For many years the guests shared tables in the castle's dining room. This time the Dennhards and Henryk as their "relatives" were seated together with their long time friends, Count and Countess Dr. Lorenzo Mizerco.

The Count had typical Semitic features. No wonder that someone mentioned that Jews look like Italians or vice versa. The Countess as Henryk found out later was born in Friedrichsruhe to the family of Hohenlohe-Ohringen. She had met Dr. Mizerco in Heidelberg where he was the Italian Vice-Consul. They were married shortly after.

Gretchen told the Countess that Henryk was engaged to their friend's daughter, who unfortunately was killed. This brought up much sympathy and interest from the Countess directed at Henryk.

The dining room was artfully furnished and lit. The food was outstanding especially after eating Sanatorium's food for several months. The venison came most likely from the neighbor's hunt and Perigord truffles in puff pastry were made on the premises.

Beer is to Bavaria, what ice-cream might be to Americans. It came in different flavors in unlimited quantities. There might have been hunger in Germany but that was not evident in Schloss Elmau.

The service was very formal. Henryk even guarded clinking silver or glasses not to attract attention to himself. He also lowered his voice a bit, but six courses later, everybody at the table relaxed. The raised din in the dining room was more acceptable to Henryk's plebeian taste.

The Countess inquired if Henryk played bridge.

"I do regret Countess, but the army life is not very conductive for playing bridge. Perhaps now that I'm about to receive my disability discharge papers, I'll be able to devote more time to this game. That is of course if this darned war will come to an end. In the meantime, I would like to visit Italy, at least the parts that aren't occupied by the Allies. Do you think that a visa is required these days?"

"That should not present a problem Herr Heinrich, I'll ask my husband to issue you a "Laissez-passer", right Lorenzo? The Count, who was listening to the conversation held between the Countess and Henryk, shook his head.

"But of course, friends of my friends are my friends too. Just get me a couple of photographs and I'll take care of the rest. Luckily I have a few forms in my room. Hope that you'll enjoy Italy, even in these difficult days."

"Much obliged to you both. Tomorrow I'll go to the village where I'm bound to find a photographer. My dream of seeing Italy may yet become a reality."

Once he would get the papers and cross the border to Italy, he'll wait for the liberation by the Allies, one more disabled war veteran. A ray of hope came out of the trip to Schloss Elmau.

CHAPTER 44

Having concluded the Klimczak's case, Lt. Edward Daszkiewicz rejoined his unit. He noticed that the men in his company were cold, tired, worn-out, fed up and just a little scared. By this time they had seen far too many of their friends wounded, maimed or killed. The war seemed to be slowly grinding to a victorious halt. There was little point to sticking one's head out now and getting killed with the end of the war almost in sight.

Edward heard also one of the men muttering about him: "There goes a guy with more guts than sense." That description wasn't quiet accurate but for the time being will have to do.

A few days later, Captain Michalski returned from his furlough. He greeted Edward even more warmly than even before.

"Welcome back, Captain. You do look great."

"I must confess, Edward, I didn't feel like coming back."

"Why is that, Captain? Abandoning the only family you have ever known?"

"The fact is that I'm thinking of building a new one myself. Before I tell you about my own plans, I want to share with you some good news for a change. The S.S. man Berger in Birkenau was contacted and Czeslawa is out of the camp, living and working in his house. There is also a young girl there but evidently she is not your daughter Danuta. It is a little puzzling but that is all that we know at the moment."

"How did you find out about it?"

"The part of Berger being contacted by members of our underground, I found out from Maj. Krzemien. The rest I've learned from a dispatch while attending a staff meeting at Gen. Bronislaw Duch's 3rd Carpathian Division."

"Captain, what else can be done in their case?"

"Not much I'm afraid, but I did send a coded radio message to our cell in that area, to notify Berger that we shall release Col. Blau into Red Cross hands, once our people will confirm the freedom of Czeslawa and Danuta. Blau and Berger are old friends, I've a hunch that this may work."

"Captain, did you forget a small, insignificant detail, that Blau is already dead?"

"So what? Did I promise them Blau alive? No, Sir. Let's just be patient. We still have to find out what has happened to Danuta's whereabouts. As I said let's be patient. We have no other choice at the present time. I almost forgot to tell you that I've also met your favorite uncle Kazimierz-Jozef Daszkiewicz. He is a full colonel by now. I want you to know. He sends his love. Talking about love let me tell you how I've met mine and her name is Marcella Zurlini. Don't faint. We are going to get married."

"Mietek, are you totally nuts? You pick up a broad on a highway and a couple of weeks later, you want to marry her? It's crazy! Have you lost your marbles?"

"To the contrary, Edward. Do you know that certain feeling, when you have a bunch of keys and you do want to open a strange door and none of them fit? All of a sudden you do find the right key that fits the lock. What a relief that is. Listen to me carefully. She is the only woman made for me. I have never been happier with anybody else in my whole life. We understand each other perfectly, with or without words. I know it sounds crazy, I'll be the first to admit it but nevertheless it is true."

"Mietek, she is Italian and you are Polish. She has a child already, what are you going to do?"

"We are both Catholic and as far as the child is concerned I'll adopt her and treat her like I would have done with my own. We still hope to have plenty of Polish-Italian "bambinos."

"Captain, forgive me but I think you were in the sun too long. Your brains are scrambled."

"Maybe so, but I feel in my bones that once this war for "Deus at Patria" (for God and Country) will end, I'll find my happiness with Marcella in Italy or Poland, preferably right here in Italy."

"What do you know about Marcella, Captain?"

"All I need to know. She married a "black-shirt" fascist, when she was 3 months pregnant. Her husband an officer in the Italian Army was sent to Russia, where he managed to meet his "heroic" death at Stalingrad. After Emilio's death his upper class family spurned Marcella, claiming, that she entrapped Emilio into marriage. On the other hand, her own family being communists didn't want to have a "Fascisti" among them. As a result, Marcella and her daughter were caught between the devil and the deep blue sea. I did meet her parents, they are simple, hardworking people, similar to my own folks. I also met her favorite uncle, Professor Ugo Bazotta and his wife in Perugia. It was such a charming place with a dark, narrow streets, empty piazzas, unrestored palaces and overcrowded churches. It was once, I was told, a city resplendent with art. The Professor and his wife received us with open arms. I had at the time a couple of cartons of cigarettes, which I gave to Mrs. Bazotta and a few hours later those cigarettes were changed into a meal fit for a king. Starting with a soup of snails and fragrant porcini mushrooms followed by duck breast in sauce made with balsamic vinegar and fruit mustard. Dessert was a hot strawberry "crostata". All of that we washed down with several bottles of extraordinary Brunello di Montalcino. Just to think about it, makes my mouth water. Above anything else, Edward, that trip has given me the sense of tranquillity and renewal, that came from having been with Marcella and pondering about the continuation of our lives and enjoying the simple pleasures of well cooked meals and satisfactory physical proximity. I for one have discovered the healing power of Italy and an Italian woman, names Marcella. Does that answer all of your questions, Edward?"

"It certainly does. All I can do is to wish you both good luck."

The next day, Thursday October 26th, 1944 brought important news for Capt. Michalski and Lt. Daszkiewicz: U.S. and Britain recognized Italy, diplomatic relations were resumed by the

Allies. An American Ambassador Alexander C. Kirk was accredited to the Italian Government. Count Carlos Sforza a long friend of the United States became Italian Ambassador to the U.S.A.

"Captain Michalski, looks like the Krauts are retreating more and more."

"They are doing it, but much too slow for my taste. Don't forget Edward, we still have to penetrate and capture their Gothic Line holding up our northerly progress. I don't know if we would be sent in that direction or what might be more likely in our case. The Army may send our unit back to Rome. Personally nothing would please me more than to be with Marcella again. I also think that we have done more than our share fighting since September of 39. Don't you agree with me, Edward? Just the last campaign after Monte Cassino, the dry heat, dust, plus the constant vigilance against German snipers and those lousy booby-traps was more than I can take for a long while. Give me Marcella, Roma, a jug of wine and a loaf of Polish rye bread, preferably in that order."

"I second the motion. I'll be happy just having Czeslawa and Danuta. I don't need anything else, believe me. Mietek I want to thank you from the bottom of my heart, for being such a good friend, looking out for me and my family. I've lost one good friend, Henryk Kaplinski but I gained another in you. I have been blessed by the Virgin Mary."

"How do you know that you have lost Henryk?"

"Captain, he was taken to the German Army. Can you imagine a Jew in the Wehrmacht?" His chances were worst than a cube of ice in hell."

"Wait just one picking minute. Where would you hide a tree? In the forest, of course. He may still pull this one trick."

"I do hope so, Captain. I sincerely hope so, Mietek."

CHAPTER 45

A bad Atlantic storm shook Paul's plane like a dry leaf. He would have preferred to be in the cockpit of the plane instead of sitting like a sack of potatoes in the rear of the plane with the rest of the passengers.

"What is happening, Paul?" asked Marlene Dietrich still half asleep.

"Nothing special Marlene, go back to sleep. It's just air turbulence. Nothing to worry about, we'll be fine in no time at all."

Despite Paul's soothing words, the plane was encountering real rough weather. The wind was hauling like a pack of Siberian wolves and nobody on the plane had to be reminded to fasten their seat belts.

Paul envied Marlene's ability to shut everything off and continue with her beauty rest. Conquering the elements in the air, the plane reached the refueling stop in Greenland amid a snow blizzard. Luckily for everyone on the plane, the blizzard was short lived and a brilliant sun appeared on the horizon.

While the ground crew kept the plane defrosted, other service personnel kept removing the snow from the single runway and still another few attendants brought in steaming hot goulash and freshly baked rolls and plenty of hot coffee.

In addition to her ability to sleep in adverse conditions, Marlene also displayed a healthy appetite. Not only did she finish everything on her plate but asked and received seconds.

"That was pretty tasty food, Paul. Any idea when we'll take off?"

"Shouldn't take them too long. I can tell you Marlene that nobody can beat the Americans when it comes to putting planes into service. We are the best and the fastest. That's why we'll be airborne in no time."

"In that case I'm going back to sleep, Paul."

"You go right ahead."

Paul was right, in relatively short time the plane took off for Idlewild Airport in New York. Unlike the first leg of the trip, the second was smooth and trouble free. By noontime they had reached New York. In addition to the regular Custom and Immigration Officers there was a large group of reporters and photographers assembled outside the Customs area.

Marlene Dietrich freshly made up, held onto Paul's arm as popping flash bulbs almost blinded the pair.

"Sir, sir" a man with a press card attached to his hat addressed Paul: "I'm from the Daily Mirror, how well do you know Miss Dietrich?"

"We just met on the plane." His next question went to Marlene:

"Miss Dietrich, what do you think about the handsome Major, you're traveling companion? What is his name?"

"His name is Major Paul Krafchin and my answer is in the song: "Falling in love again."

Everybody but Paul loved that song. He was uncomfortable in the new role.

"Paul, how can I get in touch with you? Or perhaps you can get in touch with me. Here is my card, make use of it, please, pretty please."

"I'll do that as soon as my schedule will permit me." She kissed him so that the reporters could take more pictures.

They parted in two different directions. She by limousine to Manhattan and Paul was directed to a small commuter plane, which Paul disliked, claiming that they were made for small children. Still it was the plane for Washington, D.C. he was assigned a middle seat in the back row.

The flight to the nation's capital was a routine flight. There, an Air Force staff car drove him from the airport to the offices of the War Department building.

Although Paul had the name and rank of the person, whom he was ordered to deliver the papers in the attaché case, the problem was in locating him in that gigantic labyrinth of departments and offices.

The acronym of "SNAFU" must have originated in this edifice. Finally after being sent several times from one office to another, on different floors naturally, he actually stumbled on the right place.

A helpful sergeant pointed out to another sign of "FCFS" and asked him to take a seat. "Col. Frank McNeal will be right with you, Sir."

"Sergeant, what does "FCFS" stand for? I've been away too long. I don't recognize it?"

"It means "First come, first served."

The door from the other offices was opened by a gray hared colonel with the nameplate of Frank McNeal on his chest.

"Come in Major. I've been expecting you, Major Krafchin I believe?"

"Yes, Sir."

"Do come in and make yourself comfortable. Cup of coffee?"

"A cup of hot, black coffee is always welcome."

"How was your trip, Major?"

"Not bad, just a bit rougher than usual."

"While we're waiting for coffee let me have the attaché case. You'll be issued an official receipt for it. My staff and I will be studying those papers. It will take us a while. By the way how is the old Gary "the Hotshot?"

"He is in the pink, he sends you his best regards, Sir."

"Thanks. He and I are going back a few years. We met at Wendover AAFD in Utah. Gary is a very good man, who cares deeply about people under his command."

"That is how I'm here."

"How is it so?"

"My dad died recently and by giving me this assignment, I'll be able to see my mother and pay my respects to my father at the cemetery."

"My condolences, Major. Where does your mother live?"

"In Brooklyn, New York, Sir."

"Did you speak with your mother yet?"

"No, Sir. Had to take care of the delivery of the attaché case first."

"Look, we'll be busy going through those paper. Take your coffee with you to the other office, use the phone, just dial the extension #9 and give your mother's telephone number to the operator. Your call might be monitored."

"I haven't got any secrets, Colonel."

"Should we finish early with those papers, you still may catch a late plane back to New York. If not, we'll put you up for the night and get you the earliest flight out of here."

"I would appreciate that very much, Sir."

Paul went to the other office where he found the phone marked: "Authorized use only" He removed the receiver and asked for extension #9. The operator asked on whose authority this call was being made and the number he wished to be connected with.

"Please hang up. We'll call you as soon as the line becomes free."

Paul hardly finished his luke warm coffee when the phone rang: "We've your party on the line."

It was his mother. "Hello, Ma, how are you?"

"Paulie, is that you son?" Her voice was full of concern.

"Yes, ma. Are you alright?"

"Where are you calling me from?"

"Ma, I'm in the States in Washington, D.C. I may complete my assignment today, but it might be too late for a flight to New York. In that case, I'll catch an early flight tomorrow morning. Should be in the city by noontime. From the airport I'll grab a taxi straight home."

"Should I wait for you at the airport."

"It is not necessary Ma. I don't know when the plane will

land, the best thing for you is to wait for me at home. I'll call you from the airport. I've got to hang up now. I love you Ma."

"I love you too my son. I'll let Goldie know that you are coming. How long do you think, you'll be staying with us?"

"Couple of days at least. See you soon."

He hung up the receiver just as the sergeant came to the room:

"The Colonel needs you, Sir."

"I'm coming right away, sergeant."

"I just called you to let you know that everything is satisfactory. Here is your receipt for the delivery. We checked with the airlines. There is nothing available even with top priority. However you're booked for 8.17 A.M. Pan-American flight #645 to New York I'll have my sergeant drive you to a nearby officer's billet for the night. He will also pick you up at 5.30 A.M. This is the best I can do for you, Major."

"I'm much obliged to you, Sir."

"Major, just a few questions. Your 486th Bomber Group having four squadrons claims 187 missions, 3.862 sorties, total bomb tonnage 9.691 tons, missing in action 19 aircraft and other operational losses 12 various aircraft- how do you feel about those figures? Off the record, major?"

"On or off the record, Colonel, records were kept meticulously. There is always room for improvement, especially as far as sorties are concerned and bomb tonnage dropped. The unpredictable English weather has a lot to do with those numbers. Sometimes I believe that the English fog is the best friend that Luftwaffe has on the Continent. I'm sure that pretty soon we'll own the skies."

"You boys are doing a good job, I'll grant you that, but not as good as Col. Albert J. Shower's 467th Bomb Group. Those cowboys have unsurpassed records for bombing accuracy in the 8th A.F."

"If that is the case, we'll try to catch up and surpass, Colonel."

"That is the spirit, Major. I think that you're ready to hit the sack. Pleasure meeting you."

"Same here, Sir."

"Just one more thing, Major. Leave us your New York telephone number, we'll call you to let you know your return flight to England. What do you have 3 or 4 days furlough?"

"Colonel, please make it 4, got to see my girl too."

"No problem, Major. The war can wait another day. You've got it."

"Thank you ever so much, Colonel."

The sergeant took Paul's bag and drove him to the visitor's billets at Magnolia and "K". The assigned room was small but adequate to his needs.

"Sir, I'll get you some chow."

"Never mind, Sergeant. I'm so tired that all I can think about is going to sleep. As you know I have to be up nice and early."

"I'll have you awakened by 5 A.M. Will that give you enough time to get ready, Sir?"

"More than enough, I'll see you in the morning. Good night, Sergeant."

"Goodnight, Sir."

As soon as the sergeant left, Paul got undressed and went to bed. He fell asleep the same second.

Only repeated banging on the door woke Paul up. He glances at his wristwatch, it was exactly 5 A.M.

"Good morning, major. I brought you coffee and a cinnamon bun. That was all I could get at this hour."

"That is more than enough, sergeant. I'll be ready in a jiffy."

Indeed, Paul was ready in no time. The sergeant drove Paul to the airport where he boarded the #645 to New York's Idlewild airport.

A slight rain greeted Paul to the Big Apple. Getting a taxi on a rainy day in New York was a problem solved by displaying $20 bill. A checker cab took him to his home in Bensonhurst section of Brooklyn.

The door from his apartment was opened as soon as he knocked on it, using his teenage code.

"Paulie, how good to see you son." Paul held on to his mother for several minutes, they both cried from happiness.

"Ma, I missed you so much."

"I missed you too, don't stand by the door come in. Let me look at you. You must be starved. Let me make you something to eat."

"Ma, you didn't change a bit, maybe a couple more gray hairs."

"I had a very tough time with your father, may he rest in peace, and now that he is gone my life is finished."

"Don't talk "narishkeit" don't talk foolishness, Ma. What about me? What about future grandchildren?"

"First you have to get married. You are so busy with your Air Force, when will you have the time to get married?"

"Soon Ma."

"Make yourself at home. I'm going to prepare lunch for the two of us. Come to the kitchen so that we can talk, while I'm getting lunch ready."

"Go ahead, ma, I'll join you in a few minutes, I just want to wash up."

By the time he came out of the bathroom, lunch was ready on the small table in the kitchen.

"Ma, what do you hear from Goldie? How is she?"

"She is fine, she should be here by 4 o'clock. She wants to see you and tell you something very important. I promised her that I wouldn't tell you. But you're my son and my allegiance goes to you first, regardless of how much I'm fond of the girl. She met a boy who is very much interested in her and from what I can deduce, she is also interested in him"

"This sounds very serious. Who is the boy?"

"He is a Jewish refugee from Vienna. The Army selection board classified him as 4-F. He opened a dental laboratory and is very successful. I think they are talking about marriage. She is afraid that you may not come back from overseas with the shortage of men, as it is she didn't want to remain an old maid. I as a woman can understand her feelings."

"This is indeed big news, but if that's what she wants I will not stand in her way. It also happened, that I've met a lovely Jewish girl in London. Nothing serious as of now, but it may develop into more than a wartime romance."

"I was worried about you, Paulie. How were you going to accept the latest developments, but I see, that the war changed you too. You became tougher and more sophisticated."

"Ma, it isn't the end of the world. If she wants to build her life with someone else, I don't want to force her into anything that we may both eventually regret."

"It's a new world now. It is not like it used to be in the olden days, when a word given was a word kept, no matter what."

"Ma, leave it to us. We'll iron this out between us. To change the subject, I would like to visit pop's grave. Where can we get a car for the day?"

"You do remember Mr. Goldstein? He will be delighted to drive us to Long Island. All I need is to phone him."

"How about tomorrow at 9.30? We'll miss the rush hour traffic."

"I'm pretty sure that this will be OK with him. Paulie why don't you rest up a bit before Goldie comes. I'll wash the few dishes in the meantime."

"Don't you want me to help you with the dishes?"

"No, silly boy, who do you think does that for me everyday?"

He went to his room. Nothing was changed during his absence. He took of his shoes and jacket, loosened his tie and laid down on the bed thinking about Goldie. The news that his mother told him were a mixed bag of welcome and unwelcome news. No man, including Paul, liked to be dumped by his sweetheart, especially in time of the war, but Paul was no longer the same man, since he went overseas. London, blitz or no blitz, was full of pretty and willing females. Perhaps it wasn't meant for Goldie and him to be married to each other and with that thought he fell asleep.

Someone's moist lips were touching Paul's, waking him to the sight of smiling Goldie, whose red hair covered her face. Paul kissed her back, the way he always did, long and sensual.

"Welcome back, flyboy," said Goldie. "How are you? Judging from all those newspapers you're doing better than average. I've spent 6 cents on "The Daily Mirror" and "Brooklyn Eagle" to find out that our Paul and Marlene Dietrich are a subject of gossip columnists. Can you imagine, a nice quiet Jewish boy from Brooklyn is the new man in the romantic life of a world famous movie star?"

"Wait a minute, Goldie. I can explain it. She was on the same plane, coming over from England and we happened to sit next to each other and that is all folks. Believe it or not."

"A likely story. Tell it to all your neighbors, waiting for you in the living room."

"What? Let me put on my shoes and my jacket. Lets say "hello" to them and go for a walk. I need to talk to you understand?"

"So do I, so do I, Paul."

They walked hand in hand into the living room, where several Krachins' neighbors were busy reading papers about Paul and Marlene Dietrich.

"Here comes our hero, the lover boy!" Everyone wanted to shake Paul's hand. The ladies received a polite kiss on the cheek. Paul knew those people all his life.

"Tell us Paul, how it all happened?"

"There is nothing to tell. We flew on the same plane and the newspapermen blew it out of proportion. I guess they want to sell papers, what else? Mom, would never allow me to marry a German woman, right mom?"

"Right son. The young people want to go for a walk. They didn't see each other in a long while. We will see them when they come back."

"Paul, can I get an autograph before you get to be real famous." Said Mr. Goldstein.

"For you anytime, Mr. Goldstein. By the way are you available tomorrow morning?"

"I'm sorry Paul, I already told your mother, that my company needs my taxi in Manhattan tomorrow, but I'll let you have my own car. I'll park it in front of your house. It's a black Dodge 41. Here is a set of keys. The papers will be in the glove compartment."

"Many thanks Mr. Goldstein. You're a real friend." "Goldie let's go, otherwise these nice people will keep us here."

They walked along Bay Parkway towards the shore. The conversation was light, pleasant, reminiscing about the old days. They crossed the Belt Parkway reaching the area known locally as lover's lane with many benches facing the ocean.

"Sit down Paul, I've something to tell you."

"Can't I hear it standing up?" "No, Paul, you had better sit down." Paul never heard her using such a serious tone of voice.

"Alright then, I'll sit down."

"Paul, I'm pregnant!"

"Now I see why you wanted me to sit down."

"That is not all, I'm also married."

"WHAT! When did that all happen?"

"Well, I became pregnant about 2 months ago. Funny how virginity is like a balloon. One prick and all is gone."

"Never mind the jokes. When did you get married, Goldie?"

"We took our blood tests about 2 weeks ago and we got married in a civil ceremony two days ago."

"Congratulations Goldie, who is the lucky boy?"

"His name is Kurt Hallerman, he is a Jewish refugee. My parents and your mother don't know anything about it. Next week, Kurt and I are taking our vacations. We'll call our respective parents and tell them that we have eloped and got married by a justice of the peace and 7 months later we shall have our baby."

"You have everything figured out, what about us, Goldie."

"I'm very sorry Paul if I've hurt your feelings. I do love you if that is any consolation to you but that's how things are at the present time. I just don't know how to break this news to your mother. I'm really very fond of her. She is such a lady."

There was a long silence, which Goldie interrupted once more.

"Paul, I'm returning your gift, the gold watch, which you gave me before leaving for overseas."

"Goldie, please keep that watch. Let it be a friendship gift."

"I don't want it. Do with it whatever you wish."

"I'll throw it into the ocean."

"Go right ahead, it's all the same to me."

"I've a better idea. See that old Jewish lady sitting over there on the bench, reading a paper I'll give it to her then."

"It's OK with me."

They walked over to the woman reading the "Daily Forwards":

"Pardon us, madam, did you just loose this beautiful watch?"

She looked at the watch for a while and said: "Yes, this is my watch, I wondered what has happened to it? Thank you for returning it to me. You are such a nice couple and honest too. God bless you."

They walked back in silence till they came to the elevated station on the way back to Krafchin's residence.

"Paul let me say good-bye to you now. Please apologize to your mother for not coming back to the house. Tell her that I've developed a sudden migraine headache. I can't face her now. I'll call her in a few days and explain everything. Good-bye my darling, good-bye my knight on a white horse."

"Good-bye Goldie and good luck to you. God only knows you'll need it."

He watched her climb the stairs of the elevated station and soon she was lost among the rush hour passengers. Paul walked back home, somehow crushed by her words of being pregnant and married.

He entered his apartment just as his mother was drying the cups and the dishes. All of the neighbors were gone, thank God.

"Where is Goldie?"

"She sends her love but she had to rush home."

"Paul, is everything over between you two?"

"I'm afraid so, Ma."

"Would you like to eat something?"

"No, Ma. I just want to be by myself. What time tomorrow are we going to the cemetery?"

"We can leave the house by 8.45. I'll wake you up around 7.00."

"That's fine Ma, I'll be ready."

Paul went to the closet where his father used to keep the Canadian Club rye whisky. It was still there. He poured himself an 8 oz. glass and emptied in one lung gulp. A bit unsteady he went to his room, stripped down to his underwear and went to bed putting a pillow over his head to prevent his mother from hearing a grown man cry.

Next morning by the time Paul got up, his mother had breakfast all prepared.

"Ma, I'll just have a cup of black coffee for now. I'll eat when we get back from the cemetery."

Paul reminded her of her late husband. One could never push food on him either.

Mr. Goldstein's car was exactly where he said it would be. Paul took the Belt Parkway to the Southern State Parkway.

"Look for the Wellwood exit and the Pinelawn Cemetery sign, Paul."

"O.K. Ma."

The traffic at that time was very light. Once inside the cemetery, Paul's mother directed him to the Buczacz Society burial plot. He parked on a very narrow road and both of them walked towards Isaac Krafchin's monument. It was a simple slab of granite stone on which a large star of David was engraved along with the words of "loving husband and father."

As soon as she touched the stone she broke into tears. Paul picked up a small stone, as the Jewish custom and put it on top of the monument. Here his immigrant father was buried, a man who could never fathom the intricacies of baseball or American football but still made sure that Paul's homework was done everyday. Yes, thanks to him now, Major Paul Krafchin lived his and his father's American dream.

His mother gave Paul an old prayer book that belonged to his father. The open page was the Kaddish, which he started to recite, slowly at first and then more fluently. At the end of the prayer his mother said barely audibly: "Amen."

They stood quietly in front of the monument for several more minutes.

"Come Ma, let's go home. You may catch a cold yet, God forbid."

It was Paul who always felt cold when visiting a cemetery. Was it really cooler or his perception of it?

The fact was, Paul utterly disliked cemeteries, yet there was no escape from them.

"O.K. Paulie, let's go home. I'm sure that your father knows that you were here today."

"Look to your right, that's where Uncle Morris is buried right next to aunt Feiga. They died when you were hardly 3 years old. And this one, belongs to Cousin Milton, he died at 50, what a shame. He was such a nice man. Here are many of our relatives and friends buried in this peaceful place and not like our relatives in Europe. Only God knows where their bones are."

"You are right Ma, come, let's go, and get into the car. We'll have to thank Mr. Goldstein for the use of the car."

"He'll stop by this evening to pick it up. What would you like to do now, Paulie?"

"Ma, I would like to take you for lunch at Nathan's in Coney Island, I haven't eaten a good frank in years."

"Then let's go son. Just the two of us. People will see an old lady with a handsome major in the air Force. You are a major now or are you still a captain?"

"No, madam, I mean yes Madam, I'm a major now."

Paul drove to Coney Island where he found a parking space near the Amusement Park. At Nathan's Paul ordered 4 franks with sauerkraut and 2 knishes. His mother had just on frankfurter. The prices couldn't have been beat at 5 cents a 14" frank. The two root beers were on the house.

"Ma, don't you like sauerkraut on your frank?"

"No, Paulie, I get gas from it."

Feeling much better they walked on the wooden boardwalk until his mother said:

"I'm tired, Paulie, I want to go home. I'm not as young as I used to be."

They came home, just as the phone rang. The call was for Paul:

"Major Krafchin? This is Col. McNeal, how are you enjoying your stay?"

"Very much, Sir."

"Well, I'm sorry to disturb your furlough but we have sort of an emergency. Gen. Gary broke his leg in a car accident of all things and he needs you back as soon as possible. You are booked on tomorrow's pan-Am flight #684 at 10.48 A.M. Hope that we didn't screw your plans too much, Major."

"No, Sir, I'm ready to get back, Sir."

"I'll make it up to you personally, that is a promise."

"Who was that on the phone, Paulie?"

"The Air Force, I have a flight to London at half past ten, tomorrow morning, Ma."

"Must you leave so soon, son?"

"I must Ma, there is a war over there, they need me."

"I know that son, if you must, go with God. I'm so grateful to Him that we had the chance to see you. Too bad that your dad didn't see you."

"But he did Ma, you, yourself told me so."

"All I can say is" For gezunteheit und kum zurick gezunterheit. "Go in health and come back in health."

"I will Ma, I swear to you, I will."

CHAPTER 46

"Mutti, I'm home, I brought you a girl for Lisl. She is to tend the rabbits."

"Thank you Helmuth, I'm glad that you didn't forget."

"What is your name?"

"My name is Janka, Frau Berger."

"That is a bit too difficult to pronounce, we'll call you from now on "Die Kleine". You're here to take care of rabbits and help Fraulein Lisl with house chores. Is that clear to you Kleine?"

"Ganz genau, Frau Berger."

"Very good. Lisl will take you down to the basement. There in the corner is a folded cot for you. Lisl will show you around. After all she is responsible for you."

"Lisl, now that you have a girl you wanted, I expect you to spend more time with Liliane. Tomorrow, Herr Berger will take you and Liliane to town to buy anything you may need in art supplies."

"Very well Madame, can I take "Die Kleine" to the basement now?"

"Of course, go right ahead."

Once in the basement, Czeslawa embraced Janka:

"Jesus Maria, what has happened to Danuta? Why didn't she come?"

"It's not my fault, Pani Czeslawa. Berger came to our barrack, just as I've returned from work. He asked Katarzyna about Danuta's whereabouts. Unfortunately, Danuta's "Arbeits-Gruppe" was detained, because someone smuggled in carrots. Berger didn't want to wait. He said to Katarzyna that "one dumb Pollack is as good as another dumb Pollack" and he pointed me out, just as I was crossing the room. Katarzyna didn't dare to contradict him. I'm really sorry Pani Czeslawa, I know that you would have preferred to have your own daughter instead of me. But now that I'm here, what are you going to do with me?"

"I don't know Janka, I don't know myself. All I know is that God is testing me in ways that I don't know if I can handle. It's not your fault, child, come let me hold you in my arms."

They both started to cry each for different reasons.

"Pani Czeslawa, I forgot to tell you that Katarzyna gave me a cake of soap for you. You are to look inside it. I don't know where she got it?"

The soap was a slightly used bar, the words of "Warszawa" and "Carmen" were still visible.

"We'll look at it later, in the meantime put it in the bathroom on one of the shelves. You had better change into something else. Frau Berger doesn't like camp's garb. There are some dresses in the closet. Something should fit you. Here is also your cot. If you're cold at night you can come to my bed. Hurry because I have to show you where the rabbits are."

"Oh, I love rabbits, I really do, Pani Czeslawa, they are so cute."

If Janka liked rabbits, the rabbits liked Janka even more. To Czeslawa's amazement, all the rabbits congregated around Janka. Perhaps they liked the proximity of a younger human being. Frau Berger, who watched the whole scene, arrived at the same conclusion. After taking care of the rabbits, Janka helped Czeslawa serve dinner. Even capricious Liliane took wholeheartedly to Janka who looked really very funny in an oversized dress, causing Frau Berger to comment:

"Helmuth, we'll have to get her something else to wear."

"No problem, I'll bring her something from the camp's storage room."

"Lisl, tomorrow morning Herr Berger is taking you and Liliane shopping. Helmuth about what time?"

"I should be back for them around 10.30, Mutti."

"That's good. 10.30 is about perfect. You girls can clean up the kitchen, Lisl knows the routine by now."

"Of course Frau Berger, good night to you."

"Good night Lisl and "Kleine".

Whatever food was left over they both shared. Czeslawa made sure that the lion's share of the meal went to Janka. When the meal dwindled down to the last two potatoes, Janka started to sing"

"Deutschland, Deutschland ueber alles
zwei Kartofeln und das ist alles."

"Janka, in God's name be careful, someone may hear you."

"So what? I'll sing them something else."

"Child, please promise me that you'll be careful."

"Alright, I'll do that Pani Czeslawa."

They washed the dishes and the utensils. The pots seemed to gleam and so did the kitchen floor.

"Now we can go down to the basement. We have to be very careful with Berger. We must figure out how to get Danuta out of the camp. I see that you are very tired, child go to sleep Janka."

"What about the soap that I've brought you?"

"I forgot all about it. You stay here and I'll go upstairs to bring a kitchen knife to cut the bar of soap in half to see what's in it."

Czeslawa went upstairs and brought a knife. Cutting the bar about half through it, she encountered something hard. At that point she broke the bar of soap finding a narrow roll of paper. She started to read what was written on it with very small letters.

"What is it, Pani Czeslawa?"

"I don't know yet, Janka. It looks like the beginning starts in Latin followed by Polish."

"What else do you see?"

"Something about Jews. Looks like a poem of some kind."

"In that case I'm going to sleep, you'll tell me tomorrow about it."

"Go to sleep my child."

Czeslawa started to read the poem. It started in Latin with

words: "Excusatio propter infirmitatem" author's apology for the weakness of his talent:

"MY KADDISH"

"But the horrid storm
like a vicious, blood-thirsty beast
without mercy and commiseration
tore up and devoured my dreams
and annihilated my world.
Today, I want to say my Kaddish.
I will stand before the alter with a
"talis" woven from ashes and smoke
on my shoulders.
I will say Kaddish
With a voice so loud, so mighty,
That the foundations of the Universe
Will shutter and quake.
My voice will be so powerful
And so dreadful
That the seven heavens
Will rend and split asunder...
I will then call upon the Creator
Of all living.
And ask Him to be the tenth
And let Him say Amen.
Today I want to say Kaddish
For the lost Ten Tribes
And for the devastated locations
Of my birth place.
Today I want to say Kaddish
For my world which was
Inhumanly and beastly devoured
And lies under
Heaps of ashes and mire.

Today, I want to sayKaddish
For the gardens of my youth
And for the forest of my dreams
Both of them were utterly destroyed.
The garden became a graveyard
And the forest burned to ashes.
WOE To Me!
I used to sit under the shades
Of the twiggy firs
And the fragrant breezes
Caressed and fondled me.

Deeply moved by the poem, Czeslawa looked in vain for the name of the author. Unfortunately the name was erased when she unfolded the paper, the last word, the poet's name stuck to the soap.

Czeslawa looked at Janka, who slept on the cot with a sleep that, only the very young and the very innocent could sleep. Having a few moments to herself she got to her knees and started to pray, like she never prayed in her life. Waking up from a restful night she woke Janka gently,

"Please get up. We have work to do."

It took Janka a few minutes to adjust herself to the new circumstances. She was a quick learner.

"I have to serve Berger his breakfast in bed. Straighten both of our beds and come up to the kitchen."

"Good morning Herr und Frau Berger. Here is your breakfast. Liliane is still asleep."

"Good morning Lisl, I'll be back by 10.30 make sure that you and Liliane are ready."

"We'll be ready on time, Herr Berger."

After serving everybody breakfast including Liliane, she and Janka ate eggs for the first time in a very long time. She also changed into a better dress left by her predecessor in the closet. A gray coat, a bit too tight along with a black beret completed her wardrobe.

In an afterthought, she used a red paper wrapper from a chicory package, to add a bit of red color to her pale lips. Liliane was dressed by her mother.

A few minutes ahead of time, Berger came to the house.

"Is everybody ready?" "Yes, Papa, we are ready."

Liliane was sitting up front and conversing with her father. Czeslawa sat quietly in the back of the car.

Berger knew the 15-km ride to the town of Oswiecim from his previous visits to his uncle, a retired mineworker who lived in town. He took the Kolejowa street till the bridge over Sola River, reaching the area known as Zasole. He drove through the former Berka Joselewicza street named after a Jewish-Polish colonel. Berger as a young boy once counted a dozen synagogues, just on this one street. There were always many elderly, bearded Jews milling about the place. They always looked so unkempt. He remembered well, when his uncle took him to the Jewish store of Pan Wilbinger to buy him a new suit.

"Those Goddamned Jews, they always have better goods and cheaper prices than their Christian competitors. What I always do with those Yids, I Jew down the price and pay only half in cash and the other half I give them my promissory note, which I would pay if I feel like it or if I have the money, ha, ha, ha."

That was his uncle. He knew how to treat those Jews. The other store in the Market Place was Itzchak Sadger's. Berger would sometimes buy his school supplies, while on vacation from his own school in Danzig. Where ever he turned were Jewish stores. Most likely more than 90%. Even now he had to go to the former Jewish store of Riff to buy the art supplies. Thank God that this store is run by a former Riff's clerk a Volksdeutsch.

Berger parked the car a few blocks from the store. The street was simply too narrow for vehicular traffic. Berger is his S.S. uniform walked with Liliane holding her hand. Behind them walked Czeslawa. But there was also someone else paying close attention to Berger. It was a tall elegantly dressed blond woman who kept walking right behind them. When Berger, Liliane and Czeslawa entered the store, so did the mysterious woman.

The present store owner himself came to wait upon Berger.

"Please help my maid to find items she might need for my daughter's painting lessons. I'll just browse around in the mean-time."

"Very well, Sir."

Berger picked up a book from a stand "Bauhaus-Zeit Schrift" by Paul Klee. He didn't like his work in general and the "Plastik einer Blumenvase" the vase of flowers in particular.

"Good morning Herr Sturmbahnfuhrer, How are you?"

"Pardon me Fraulein, do I know you?"

"Not really, I'm sort of the fiancée to one of your men."

"Ach, so, did we actually meet? I don't recall, please refresh my memory."

"Not really, but I do have an important message from your best friend Winnetou."

"What did you say? Do you mind repeating it."

Czeslawa, whose back was turned to Berger in order to choose items from the counter, heard the entire conversation.

"I said, the message is from Winnetou." Berger's face became pale.

"What is the message?"

"He wants you to locate and free Frau Czeslawa Daszkiewicz and her daughter Danuta from Birkenau. They were originally arrested in Zakopane."

"Is that all?"

"Your friend Fritz Blau is held by the Allies and as soon as we have those two women, he'll be released in care of the Swiss Red Cross. It was Blau's idea. It's a simple exchange of prisoners. It happens in wartime."

"Why just these two women. Who are they?"

"I have no inkling, believe me."

"What prevents me from arresting you right on this spot."

"Berger, no theatrics, please. If I fail to report, a radio message goes to London and from there to wherever Blau is. He'll be shot by firing squad on the same day. They are not especially happy with his war record or yours for that matter. It is a deal worked out with Blau. It is very confidential. Listen carefully, I'm not going to repeat it. I'll be back next week, the same day, the same time. Let these women walk slowly in front of this store. We'll take care of them. Not until they reach a safe place will the Allies release Blau. It has to be the two women and not substitutes, we have their photos. Do we understand each other, Berger?"

"I'll do my best, Fraulein."

"It better be you're very best, because Blau's life is in your own hands."

"By the way Fraulein, you do speak an excellent German."

"So do you, Herr Berger, for someone born in Danzig, Auf Wiedersehen."

If Berger was dumbfounded, so was Czeslawa who listened to the entire exchange between Berger and the mysterious blond. Like most of the Poles, Czeslawa was aware of the tenuous strands of underground communications, which operated under the most repressive regime. Those strands were woven into a chain of command and intelligence, which retained its strength throughout the war. However she didn't think that she would personally be involved. She was deadly afraid of Berger, whose action she already had seen in the camp. To tell him something, may mean her and Danuta's life. Better to adapt an attitude of wait and see.

"Lisl, did you find everything you need? If so let's go home. I've a headache."

"Papa, we have all we need now."

"Very well, Liebchen, let's pay for it and go."

They drove in silence. Berger was in an obviously foul mood. He dropped them in front of their house and said to Czeslawa:

"Lisl, tell Madam that I'll be back later this evening."

"Yawohl, Herr Berger."

Carrying the purchases Liliane walked in the house. "Mutti, look what we bought."

"Very good Liliane, right after lunch you'll have your first lesson."

"Yes Madame, I'll see to it."

After lunch, Liliane changed into her play clothing. She was ready for her lesson, which Czeslawa started with an explanation of basic colors, how and to mix them effectively, the usage of different brushes, strokes and such. Liliane was a bright and eager student, perhaps not as bright as Czeslawa made her out to be, but nonetheless bright enough.

Frau Berger was listening to Czeslawa's lecture, noticing what, Liliane said to her mother:

"Mutti, go away, just leave me and Fraulein Lisl alone."

She left them without a word, satisfied that Lisl was doing a good job. She went to check Janka's work.

Janka was feeding her rabbits and singing a few bars of Franz Lehar's "Das Land des Laechelns":

"Dein ist mein ganzes Herz! Wo du nicht bist, kann ich nicht sein, so wie die Blume welkt, wenn sie nicht kusst der Sonnenschein! Dein ist mein schoenstes Lied, weil es allein aus der Liebe erbluht. Sag mir noch ein mal, mein einzig Lieb, o sag noch ein mal mir:

Ich hab dich lieb!"

"Bravo, Kleine that was very nice, I'm sure that the rabbits enjoyed the song."

Frau Berger was happy. Everything was working out so very well and tonight was their 10th wedding anniversary. She wondered if her Helmuth remembered it.

Berger came home or rather he stormed into the house. He was furious. Even his wife kept out of his way. As a S.S. wife she knew when to keep quiet. Czeslawa and Janka sensing Berger's mood made themselves almost invisible.

At dinnertime, Berger drank schnapps heavily, lost in his own thoughts. Seeing her husband in such a state, she broke the house rules:

"Helmuth dear, can I be of any help to you?"

"No Mutti, I'm trying to locate two stinking Pollacks. I went from one "Schreib-Stube" to another and there is no one by that name. I told all the clerks to find them, otherwise there will be hell to pay."

"Don't worry, Liebchen, they will find them. They are probably covering them up. When do you need those two?"

"In a week's time."

"By that time they will find them, if not, send another two."

"I wish it would be that easy. Mutti, I totally forgot our wedding anniversary. I'll bring you something in a day or two. Please forgive me."

The next couple of days were similar. Czeslawa kept spending more and more time with Liliane. Janka kept busy with the rabbits and chores of the house. Herr Berger was coming home in progressively fouler moods.

"Helmuth did you locate those two women?"

"Not yet, I'm checking everyday with all our lists and offices. No one seems to know Czeslawa and Danuta Daszkiewicz, dam it."

"But I do Herr Berger, If I tell you, will you set me free?" asked Janka.

"Of course my child, who are they?"

Czeslawa very quietly warned Janka in Polish to hold her tongue, but Janka didn't pay her heed.

"It's your Lisl. Her daughter Danuta is still in the camp, in my barrack, Herr Berger."

"Lisl, is that possible that you are the Daszkiewicz, that I'm looking for, day and night? Are we treating you so badly, Lisl? Tell me why you've kept quiet." He was white with anger.

"Forgive me Herr Berger. I was afraid to say anything. I want my daughter to live. She is such a young girl. She didn't do anything and neither did I. Someone accused us of being Jewish but we're Christian Poles. Anybody can see that, Herr Berger."

"Lisl, I don't understand it. You are almost like a member of our family. Liliane adores you. Why the secrets? I'll bring your daughter tomorrow. Will you then trust me?"

"Yes Herr Berger."

"Why do they want you, out of all people? Are you Rothschilds? Any ideas? Where or who is your husband?"

"I don't know that either, I swear by the Virgin Mary. My husband left and disappeared. I didn't hear from him in years. I wonder if he is still alive?"

"He must be alive because the Allies requested you. Lisl you are to be exchanged for an important German officer. Maybe your husband arranged this exchange. Anything is possible these days."

"I wouldn't know, Herr Berger."

"Enough already, Lisl or should I call you Czeslawa now?"

"As you wish Herr Berger."

"I'm thinking what will I tell Liliane?"

"Herr Berger, I do like Liliane. If you give me your word of honor that we won't be harmed, I'll come to see her once a week to teach her painting."

"Will you really do that? In that case you may have my word as a German officer."

"Very well Herr Berger. Will you bring me my daughter tomorrow?"

"But of course, by noon time the latest."

"Thank God it's all settled. Let's have a little wine. It's a dual celebration. Our wedding anniversary and your freedom. "Frau Berger finally joined in calming everyone.

"Best wishes Herr und Frau Berger." Did the murderer have a human soul or was that tactics to fool all of them? Thought Czeslawa, sipping a glass of red wine.

"Kleine, where does Danuta work? In which "Arbeits Gruppe?"

Janka informed Berger as to the exact Danuta's schedule. "I'll bring her home, don't worry."

But worry she did. She couldn't sleep a wink through the night.

The morning was excruciatingly long but by noontime, Berger arrived with a skinny girl in tow. It was Danuta indeed.

Czeslawa held Danuta in her arms for what seemed like forever. Tears of sheer happiness covered their faces. It was a miracle.

"How did Berger find you?"

"He came to our "Baustelle" and asked the "capo" for Danuta Daszkiewicz. She didn't know me by that name, so he put his gun to her head and asked her to produce Danuta in a minute, otherwise she would have been killed. Seeing that I came up and introduced myself. He just smiled and said, "So you are the one." I didn't know what he meant. Only in his car he told me that he was bringing me to you and here I am."

"Danuta, we are to be exchanged for a German officer, I think that your father arranged that."

"How is that possible, mama?"

"I don't know, my child, but let's thank God anyway."

The next day, Frau Berger received a telephone call from her mother informing her that her father was dying and wanted to see her once more. The following day Berger had a dual task to perform: to drop off Czeslawa and Danuta Daszkiewicz in front of the art supply store and later to drive his wife and Liliane to the railroad station for the trip to Chemnitz, where her father lived.

Czeslawa carried a small satchel with clothing that Frau Berger gave them as a departing gift. They both wore berets, to hide their shorn heads from curious eyes.

"Lisl, I mean Czeslawa, you stay in this area. Your people should pick you up shortly. Please remind them that I lived up to my end of the deal an I fully expect them to do the same." He left without so much as "Auf Wiedersehen."

They stood awkwardly when a beautiful blond whom Czeslawa has seen a week ago in the store came up to them and said in perfect Polish:

"Are you Czeslawa and Danuta Daszkiewicz?"

"Yes, Madame, so we are."

"I have regards for you from Lieutenant Edward. Please follow me and don't look back under no circumstances. You are on your first step to freedom."

Thirty days later Herr Berger received a letter from the Swiss Red Cross asking for instructions for the disposition of ashes of a certain Colonel Fritz Blau. At this point Sturmbahnfuhrer Berger, whose wife and daughter were killed in one of the most devastating air raids on Chemnitz, came home and promptly raped Janka, who stayed on with him. His next move was to shoot her exactly between the eyes and his last bullet was directed against his own open mouth.

CHAPTER 47

The very next day, after breakfast, Henryk took a walk from Schloss Elmau to the nearby town, locating a photo studio "Titian" without any difficulties.

Having his photographs taken in an area known for tourists, wasn't anything unusual. However, taking a picture in a civilian suit and then as other in a uniform, raised the owner's eyebrows.

"I'm being discharged from the Wehrmacht and I don't know which picture will be more suitable." That explanation was plausible enough.

"Ach, so! You'll have your pictures the day after tomorrow."

"Could you have those pictures made any sooner?"

"No, mein Herr. This is as fast as I can make it."

"Very well then, I'll stop by in two days, Auf wiedersehen."

Back in Schloss Elmau, Henryk kept basically to himself. The Dennhards knowing the gruesome details of tragedy, that befell Henryk, tried in earnest not to crowd him and the Count and Countess Mizerco followed their lead.

The same afternoon, an elderly postman on a bicycle hand delivered Henryk, an envelope containing the official Wehrmacht discharge papers, based upon his wound and mental condition. Enclosed were also various forms to be filled out.

At dinner time, Henryk announced: "As of today I'm no longer a soldier. I'm now a civilian."

"What do you intend to do now?" asked Gretchen Dennhard.

"I don't rightly know myself." It was as honest as answer as he could come up with. Countess Mizerco took over: "First of all, we have to change his luck." With these words, she removed from her neck, a coral pendant, carved into the ancient good-luck piece called the "corno" or horn, favored by the devoutly superstitious Italians.

"This will bring you luck, "Garantie a tout jamais" – lifetime guarantee."

It was probably a coincidence that good-luck piece started to work at the same time, and in the most unexpected way.

A tall, dark hared man with distinct Medditerean features approached their table addressing Count Mizerco in Italian. Count Mizerco in turn introduced the newcomer as his associate Dr. Giovanni del Forno.

"We are also old friends, going back to the time when we both were cadets at the Nunziatella, one of the oldest military schools in Italy. Those were the good old day, Giovanni."

Dr. del Forno was asked to join them for dinner. An invitation that was readily accepted.

"May I have a word with you before the dinner, Lorenzo? Will the ladies excuse us for a minute?"

"But of course." Replied the ladies.

Whatever the subject of their conversation was, it took a good half-hour to complete.

"Sorry, it took us longer than we thought it would."

"Lorenzo, is everything alright?" Countess Mizerco asked concerned.

"Yes, darling." But his facial expression spoke volumes to the contrary.

It was Maj. Dennhard who threw the proverbial stone into the still waters.

"Lorenzo, forgive me if I'm speaking out of turn. Are you in some kind of trouble, because of Italy's political move? Our countries are going separate ways. Does that mean that we as friends of long standing should do the same? I don't think so. If Italy wants to abandon the sinking ship, it's her business. I know that Germany alone will pay the price for it's ultimate defeat. Personally, I gave them my own down payment, my right arm. So in the name of our friendship, I'm asking you, do you need my help?"

"Lorenzo, if you permit me, I would like to answer Major's question. Can I be totally open with you Major?" He looked in the direction of Henryk.

Henryk wanted to leave the table to give them their privacy, but Maj. Dennhard held him down.

"I do vouch for this young man."

"Very well then. There is news and there is news. It is also a question of their interpretation. For instance, if a man bites a dog in Milano, it's news. If a man bites a dog in Naples, it's breakfast."

This metaphor caused a brief and uneasy laugh.

"Let me explain. We Italians have been involved in some very costly affairs, such as Ethiopia, Africa, Stalingrad, just to mention a few. Perhaps we are no longer the Roman Legions of the past, but artisans, painters, sculptors, musicians and lovers. And as such, we better learn and learn fast how to keep the lion of Albion and Uncle Sam with its huge and modern armies satisfied. To summarize it all, Lorenzo has been asked by his cousin, Count Sforza, to help with organizing a new and democratic government of Rome, which I may say, he reluctantly did agreed to. We need your help Major, in crossing the Brenner Pass, so that we may get back to Italy and now you have it all."

"I think it can be done. Do you have a car?"

"Yes, I have a long, black Mercedez-Benz limousine."

"Perfect. Do you have small Italian and German flags?"

"I have only an Italian flag, but what do you need it for?"

"You'll need them both, to attach to the fenders to look like an official car. We also need a chauffeur. Heinrich, you did say that you want to see Italy. Now there is your chance. Can you drive?"

"Of course, I'll be glad to drive."

"What kind of papers have you got?"

"My discharge papers and Count Mizerco is getting me a "Laissez-paser". All I need to do is to pick up my photos tomorrow and I'll be all set."

"I'll get you a chauffeur's cap. My next question is whether the Countess wants to come along? She can travel either as the wife that she is or as a secretary."

"We don't know that yet. We'll talk this over and let you know by tomorrow morning."

"I do have my papers and they are very impressive I may add. Nobody will dare to stop a German major, whose one empty sleeve will rest in his heavily decorated uniform's pocket. This is what I call using an arm that doesn't exist. You two, I presume have valid Italian passports?"

"Major, Yes. We do indeed."

"Well then, it's all settled. Tomorrow or the latest, the day after tomorrow, we shall start on our journey. One for all and all for one. Does that sound familiar?"

"Which one are you? Atos, Portos or Aramis?"

"Neither. I'm D'Artagnan."

"So be it. Tomorrow after breakfast, we'll go over our plans. Any changes or any new ideas will be jointly decided upon. Agreed?"

"Unanimously agreed, tomorrow is another day."

The next day brought the news that Countess Mizerco decided to remain in Germany and for several additional reasons, mainly logistics, the trip was delayed for another day, thus giving Henryk also a chance to pick up his photos needed for his new identification papers, which listed Henryk's occupation as driver and Polish-Russian-German interpreter.

The occupants of the car were well supplied with food and precious extra fuel for the trip to Brenner Pass and beyond.

The closer they got to the Brenner Pass, the more often they were stopped on the road. On both sides of the winding road, Henryk noticed camouflaged armored personnel carriers, several Mark III tanks with their 37mm guns, as well as Mark IV with their short and ugly 75mm guns, strategically placed near heavy zigzag barricades.

The two banners, flying in the wind and the impressive figure of Maj. Dennhard, sitting next to the driver, warranted but a superficial glance of the documents and were waved on.

At the Brenner Pass they were stopped by a tough looking border unit for a thorough check of papers and car contents. A sergeant brandishing a submachine gun came up to Henryk yelling: "Papieren!" Henryk coached by Maj. Dennhard remained unmoved.

"Papieren! Donnerwetter!"

"Mind your language, sergeant! Any questions you have address them in proper form. Is that understood, sergeant?"

The sergeant, an old timer, wasn't about to take crap from anybody, but it was the Major who continued:

"I think sergeant that you are drunk, get me your superior officer at once!"

"I'm doing my duty, Major. Let me see your papers."

"Not until you bring me you're commanding officer."

"I'm ordering you out of the car, Major or I'll shoot!"

"Oh, you will? Let me than come out."

Major Dennhard came out of the car and only then did the sergeant notice his missing arm.

"Yes sergeant, you were saying something about shooting?"

By this time, several other soldiers, their arms at ready, and a very young lieutenant came up to check upon the commotion.

"Lieutenant, are you in charge of this undisciplined bunch? Is this what our Army came too? My job is to make sure that these two diplomats reach Rome as soon as possible. They are on Fuhrer's special mission and what do we have here? Delays, delays and more delays. I'm afraid that I'll have to report your whole unit for insubordination and interfering with the Fuhrer's orders. What is your name, lieutenant?"

"It is not necessary, Major. Please show me your papers and you are on your way. I do apologize for my men."

The Major showed him his papers. Seeing those papers the lieutenant screamed at the sergeant:

"Get a 3 motorcycle escort for these people for the entire length of the Pass. On the double."

This time, the sergeant did as he was told. Three motorcycle riders with their sirens blazing were leading the limousine and it's flying banners through the dark, unlit Pass.

At the other end of the Pass the motorcycle riders turned back, each saluting the Major, who in turn saluted them back.

Unchallenged they drove some 50km till the next major road intersection, where the Major stopped a truck going back to the Brenner Pass.

"Gentlemen, I'm getting off right here. I'm returning home where I do belong. You on the other hand, should continue going south till you reach the allied positions. Replace the German flag with a white one, and introduce yourselves to the British or Americans as members of the new Italian Government. I wish you all God's speed. So long Lorenzo, so long Giovani and Heinrich to you I'll say "Mazel Tov." Hope to see you all after the war. With these words he boarded the truck waiting for him and waved to them using his only arm.

CHAPTER 48

As curses go, the Slavs have a clear advantage over their Anglo-Saxons counter parts. Their vocabulary in this respect is so much richer and juicer and yet when it came to vent his frustration, Captain Michalski used relatively mild words as "Psia krew" meaning "dog's blood."

He repeated this curse several times but his orders remained the same. Instead of going to Rome, where he hoped to see Marcella Zurlini, he was ordered by Maj. Krzemien to travel north to the most advanced units of the Polish Corps, facing the German positions.

This time his new assignment was a complicated investigation of the brutal murder of a British major Tony Alexander by an 18 year old Polish infantryman. The choice of the investigative team was up to Capt. Michalski, he therefore selected Lt. Daszkiewicz and Corporal Wachtel.

Told about the new assignment, Lt. Edward Daszkiewicz asked what made this case so complicated.

"To begin with, our 18 year old murderer Albin Pietrus is actually a 16 year old boy, who lied about his age, in order to join the Army."

"There is nothing unusual about it, many boys have done it."

"Wait, there is more. According to his file, Albin had a reputation of being a quiet, polite boy, who wanted to become a priest. Tell me Edward, is a future priest likely to be the material out of which murderers of British officers are made of?"

"Not really, Captain."

"Edward, listen to this. Maj. Tony Alexander is or rather was the nephew of no other, but General Sir Harold Alexander, commander-in-chief of the Allied Forces in Italy. Do you see the implications? The British are now holding Pietrus in their custody. He already confessed and now he refuses to speak to anyone. The problem and a big one too, is the fact that his uncle Gen. Alexander is the most competent, ever-patient and considerate British general. Half of his forces are Americans, French and us Poles. Who do you think he has most problems with? Yes, you guessed it. Our brothers. From drunkenness to insubordination to petty thievery and now the murder of his nephew. We have to get our asses to the area where Albin is being held "pronto" and that is near the city of Florence. Any questions?"

"Just one. When do we go?"

"Right now my friend, there is no time to waste. Just get a hold of Wachtel."

"Yes, Sir."

All the roads going north were full of military traffic. The Germans believed that the surest way of holding the Allies was to deny them their supply routes, but there were too many Allied Armies and not enough of German planes to stop them.

Capt. Michalski was behind the wheel and Lt. Edward Daszkiewicz was sitting beside him, allowing Corp. Eljasz Wachtel who was sitting in the back of the jeep, to observe the Allied units and the ever increasing optimism of those troops.

Capt. Michalski's single jeep, unlike long convoys, was often flagged down, mainly at crossroads of major roads by M.P.'s of different army units. Among others they were stopped by the unit of the 4th Indian Division. Seeing the Polish eagle on the white and red flag attached to the left bender of the jeep, the dark skinned Indian officer said:

"Your boys from the 3rd Carpathian Division replaced our unit just north of Ortona. Thank you or as you way in our language "Shookriya."

In addition to the Hindus, many inhabitants of Italian towns such as Loreto, Recanati, Osimo, Castelfidardo were kindly disposed toward their Polish liberators, even though some of the villages were flattened because enough bombs had found their targets.

Here and there, they have seen small groups of refugees, returning home from places that offered them relative security during the bombing or artillery exchanges of their own area.

Finally, Capt. Michalski's team reached the unit of the British 8th Army, which held Albin Pietrus in custody.

The tough looking and acting British M.P.'s refused Capt. Michalski's request to interview the prisoner Albin Pietrus.

"Sorry, old chap. It can't be done this evening. We'll need our own Polish-English interpreter as well as someone from Judge Advocate's Office to be present at the interview. Imagine that by tomorrow noontime, we could possibly set up the meeting. By the way, I'm Capt. Chartwell, Lester to my friends. Who are your teammates?"

"May I present Lt. Edward Daszkiewicz and Corporal Wachtel our legal council."

"Pleasure, gentlemen. May we offer you the hospitality of our unit? We can all have dinner at our Officer's Mess. For the night we'll put you up at the Officer's tent and the corporal will join the non-coms. Hopefully it is satisfactory to you."

"Your invitation is certainly appreciated, Captain."

There was very little they could have done. Another day or so couldn't possibly make a difference, one way or the other, thought Michalski, or could it?

Capt. Lester Chartwell, a Londoner as they found out later, turned to be a very congenial host. He saw to it that the Polish investigative team ate and slept in relative comfort.

Just before retiring for the night, Lester asked if he could speak with Capt. Michalski, privately as man to man.

"Of course, Captain. Let the two of us go for a little walk."

"Well Capt. Michalski, let me be very frank with you. We have a major headache on our hands. You see, your boy killed the nephew of Gen. Alexander. The problem with Tony Alexander, as you may find out yourself soon enough, was his fondness for young and pretty boys. Tony was briefly married, I think less than a month, but his homosexuality was well known in certain circles. What we do know is, that Tony offered your boy Albin a lift to the nearby village. The boy spoke hardly any English and here was a British major, being so nice to him. The kid as we can imagine was very much impressed and probably afraid of refusing the ride. We have pieced the rest of the story as best as we could. We found Tony's body with 16, I repeat 16 bayonet wounds, both Tony and the boy who appeared to be in shock had their pants pulled down. A half empty bottle of whisky in addition to much blood was also found. Recognizing the victim I swore my men to secrecy. And now you and I have a problem. Once the army newspapers will get a hold of this mess, the Polish-English relationship will go sour. I also would very much like to save the good General Alexander much undeserved grief. As I told you before, we have Albin's full confession in English. I doubt if the boy realizes what he has signed."

"Did Albin get medical attention at all?"

"Yes, of course. It was one of our Army doctors that gave him a sedative. The doctor was of the opinion that in a day or two, Albin should come out of his semi-shock. Do you have any ideas how to handle this case, Captain?"

"I can always take Albin off your hands and you, if you wish, you can claim that he was shot while trying to escape. There is however another problem. The kid is only 16 years old, too young to be in the Army altogether. You are right, it is a big mess. When do you think I can speak with him?"

"Not until tomorrow."

"We better find a solution to that problem because I would hate to see the headlines."

"I do know what you mean. See you in the morning, perhaps we'll find a solution by that time, Captain."

The problem was indeed solved but not the way both of them expected.

During breakfast on the following day, one of the guards ran up to Capt. Chartwell and said something into his ear, causing Lester's mouth to drop in surprise.

"Capt. Michalski come with me quickly!"

"What has happened?"

"Just come, will you!"

They both ran to the small well guarded building that housed the prisoner. The room that served as a cell was wide open. On the bed, sprawled in fetal position, was the body of a handsome youth in a pool of blood. His veins were cut with a piece of glass lying next to the body.

"How did that happen?" inquired Capt. Michalski.

One of the guards replied: "He committed suicide at night. We checked on him and he appeared to be sleeping peacefully."

"Where did he get the piece of glass?" Capt. Chartwell wanted to know.

"Probably on the outside, when we took him for a walk. There is plenty of debris all around."

"Did you check his pockets when you returned from the walk?"

"No Sir. We didn't, Sir."

"Well Capt. Michalski? What are your intentions now?"

"We have two dead bodies, nobody can bring them back alive any more. The unwelcome publicity is not going to help the war effort. In any case, I suggest that you announce that Major Tony Alexander died in hand to hand combat with the enemy. We'll notify the family of Albin Pietrus that he stepped on a mine, while clearing a minefield, and award him with a medal posthumously. This is going to be our official reaction. Of course, I will have to make a confidential report to my superiors. That report will be very confidential in every respect. We wouldn't want to impair the British Polish relations. I'll also arrange for the Polish burial squad to pick up his body, to give him a proper burial as well as a monument. As far as I'm concerned this case is closed."

"Thank you captain in the name of the British 8th Army for your cooperation. We have a few personal effects that belonged to the deceased. Would you like to have them?"

"Yes, we'll forward them to the family of Albin Pietrus. Corporal Wachtel please go with Capt. Chartwell and bring back those items. Don't forget to sign for it."

"Thank you again Captain. Wish we had met under more pleasant circumstances."

"Same here, Captain."

"Corporal, we'll wait for you by the jeep."

And wait they did, almost a full hour, growing impatient minute to minute.

"What the hell has happened with Wachtel? Did he meet some British Yids?"

"I see him coming, Captain, with two soldiers and a limping man in civilian cloths."

"Wachtel, what in the world took you so...." The rest of the words stuck in his throat.

He also didn't hear the two British guards asking him: "Do you know this man, Lieutenant?"

"Jesus, Maria Henryk? Is that you?"

"Yes Edward, it's me alright." At that point they were crying in each other's arms.

CHAPTER 49

The sun was beginning to shine brightly on early Thursday morning, as Maj. Paul Krafchin, after a tearful good-bye to his mother left Brooklyn for the airport, in Mr. Goldstein's taxi.

With his father gone and his relationship with Goldie turned sour, he felt a strange emptiness and sadness. The idea of going back to combat area was almost a relief.

"Paulie or should I call you major? Are you worried about your mother? Don't. She has lots of good friends and neighbors. She'll be OK. We'll look after her, I promise you."

"That would be very much appreciated, Mr. Goldstein. Oh, I just forgot to get something in Brooklyn for my C.O. Is there a bakery nearby where I can buy "Mandelbread"?"

"You are in luck Paulie. I have a cousin in Hewlett, who owns the best bakery on Long Island. It's not far from here on Peninsula Boulevard. The bakery is called "Butter Mill". They have the best stuff ever, I guarantee. How are you fixed for time?"

"We are in good shape Mr. Goldstein. I still have an extra half hour to take care of it."

"It wouldn't take us even 15 minutes. How many loafs do you want to take along?"

"I think three would be enough, Mr. Goldstein."

The "Butter Mill" bakery was crowded. A number of Jewish women were buying Challas for the coming Sabbath. The owner of the bakery noticing his cousin Goldstein with an Air Force major came right over to them:

"Gentlemen, what can I do for you?"

Mr. Goldstein told him what Paul needed: "Just three "Mandelbreads.""

"I'll be right back. Just wait a minute."

He came back real soon wearing a clean apron this time and carrying beautifully wrapped Mandelbreads. "I put in a couple of delicious cheese Danishes for your trip, good luck Sir."

Paul reached for his wallet in order to pay for his purchase, but the bakery owner wouldn't even listen:

"Just enjoy it and come "gesund" back to us, Major."

"Thank you very much. You don't have to do it." The man just smiled and went back to his waiting customers.

"That was very nice of my cousin. It was the first time I have seen him giving away anything to anybody. I guess war changes people."

"Yes Mr. Goldstein. The war plays tricks on people sometimes. Let's go to the airport. We haven't a minute to spare any longer."

"Hold on to your seat, Major. I'll show you what a New York City cabbie can do."

"I believe you Mr. Goldstein, just let's get there in one piece."

"I'll get you there safely and on time, I assure you."

There was no question about Mr. Goldstein's driving ability. He was an excellent driver.

"If my pilots could dodge bullets as well as you dodge cars, we wouldn't have a single casualty."

Mr. Goldstein dropped Paul off at the Idlewild Airport's main entrance.

"Paulie, don't bother taking your wallet out. Your mother already prepaid this trip, I swear."

"This is not one of your tricks, Mr. Goldstein?"

"No Paulie, this is on the level, "emes" the truth."

Once Mr. Goldstein used the Hebrew word for the truth, Paul didn't argue further with him.

"Well Mr. Goldstein, I just want to thank you for everything, you're such a good friend."

"Your most welcome Paulie. Have a good flight and come back soon."

Having a top priority clearance and ticket didn't help much, because everybody else on the plane had similar credentials. Still Paul was able to obtain a bunk head seat with plenty of room for his long legs. After some delay, the plane finally took off.

"Pardon me, Major, are you the same person who flew recently with Miss Marlene Dietrich on the same plane from England to the States?'

"I'm afraid so, but how did you know that?"

"First of all it was in all the papers and second of all I was with the plane's crew at the time."

"What can I do for you, Miss."

"Miss Dietrich left a book on the plane and a pair of leather gloves and I'm charged with sending both items back to her. Are you Sir in touch with her?"

"I do have her address if that could help. On the other hand, I'll be glad to send it to her."

"That's great Sir. I'll be right back with those articles."

A few minutes later she came back with a book, a pair of gloves and a cup of coffee for Paul.

"Thank you Sir. I'm much obliged. If there is anything you wish, please let me know."

Paul looked at the book. It was a German book titles "Vom Winde Verweht" by Margaret Mitchell, a German translation of "Gone With the Wind".

Paul had a smile on his face, wondering how would one say in German: "Frankly my dear, I don't give a damn." Unfortunately he couldn't say these words in either language to Goldie anymore.

The rest of the flight he spent sleeping, covered by an extra blanket brought by "his" stewardess and eating or reading, well supplied by the same source. Everybody went smoothly including the stopover. The landing on British soil was a bit too hard but without any mishaps.

The Air Force driver brought him back to the building, where his office was located.

He was warmly greeted by members of his office staff.

"Welcome back, Major. How is everybody back home?"

He answered their questions as politely as he could. He had a question of his own:

"Where would I find the General? In which hospital?"

"Hospitals and me? Are you crazy? You must have flipped for Marlene Dietrich worst than I thought. Come right here my boy!"

"Yes Sir, General Sir." It was Gen. Gary "the hotshot" himself. His left leg was in a cast all the way to his hip. Under his right arm he held a crutch.

"Major Krafchin reporting for duty, Sir."

"At ease major. Come right in Paul, good to see you."

"Good to see you too. You are looking better than I was told."

"Don't you ever believe the brass or the doctors. I'm fine I just can't move around. Now tell me how was your trip and how was your mother?"

Paul started with handing over the receipt for the delivered documents and briefly told him about his visit at home and the trip to the cemetery. Everything else that was private he kept private.

"By the way General, my mother baked you some "Mandelbread" and cheese danishes, a Brooklyn recipe."

"Thank you Paul and thank your mother in my name when you write to her. Sorry to have cut into your well deserved furlough. Because of that frigging car accident I was badly hurt. The fucking medics wanted to send me home. Me and Air Force General sent home because of an automobile accident, ludicrous. Who ever heard of it. I would be a laughing stock back home. So I told all the doctors to go and fuck themselves and then came back. And now that I'm here I need you badly. I can't get around as much as I would like. I need a bright, reliable, hardworking, knowledgeable, presentable and honest officer to represent me. Now because of your own publicity with Miss Dietrich you can even be more helpful. Let me explain because I see your puzzling look. We are in England and a man in my position must be also an astute politician. You see, the Brits see us Yanks as cowards. As in the First World War we entered late, after others had born the brunt of the battle. While you and I know only too well, what the "Mighty Eight" is doing and how many casualties we sustained and yet, they still call us cowards. Maybe they are plain jealous. Our G.I.'s are better paid and better dressed than they are. Also women from teenagers to grandmothers seem to be eager to trade their questionable virtues for luxuries from our PX stores. I don't have to tell you how popular our Hollywood films and dance music are. I can well understand their frustration. And now with those fucking V-1 "flying bombs" over southeastern England, the nerves of war-weary civilians and servicemen are quite frayed. On top of that, more and more G.I.'s are coming over, thus aggravating even more, the acute housing storage in the big cities."

The general had a sip of cold water and continued:

"Since we fight the same foe, we'll have to find a way to cooperate with the Brits and you my boy, better learn how to do it, because I can't. I also know that you've come here straight from the airport, so get the fuck out and get some sleep. That's an order. On your desk there is private mail for you and messages from some dizzy dame. I think the one we met in the bar. I want your ass in this office by 8.15 tomorrow morning "pronto". I have also some bad news for you. Your crate "Goldie Locks" was shot over Germany. Report has it that some crewmembers were seen parachuting over German territory, in the vicinity of Munich. This is as much as we know at the present time. I'm sorry Paul. I know how fond you were of the crew and plane."

"I'm sorry too General, very sorry indeed."

Paul looked at his ring on his pinkie finger. Perhaps if he would have left the ring with George Perry, maybe nothing would have had happened. However if he would have given George the ring, something bad could have happened to him. Perish the thought. Now he'll never know.

"Don't forget Paul tomorrow at 8.15."

"Yes Sir, I'll be here on time, Sir."

Paul went to his desk to check the mail Most of the mail was from his friends in the service. There was also a postcard from

Atlantic City, New Jersey a "wish you were here" type, signed by "ever loving Goldie." He looked at the date of the postcard. It was almost 5 months old. Next to the postcard was several identical, local messages from Cynthia "Paul, I miss you."

CHAPTER 50

Being guided by the mysterious blond, Czeslawa, walked along, holding onto Danuta for dear life. No, she wasn't dreaming, the blond talked to her in a voice full of confidence:

"Just keep on walking straight and don't look back." She urged.

They walked for several city blocks, twice encountering women who would say: "Good-good morning."

The blond would then squeeze Czeslawa's arm slightly and whisper: "These are our people. So far nobody is following us."

Czeslawa was afraid to turn her head, but from the store window sat at a particular angle. She could see for a brief moment the reflection of the street behind her. She really couldn't see much, because a large horse, who pulled a wagon loaded with hay, blocked her vision. At that point the blond said:

"Quickly, let's go into this door on your right hand side: "Czeslawa did as she was told, pulling Danuta's hand. It was dark, narrow passage or a corridor of some sort that had a door at the other end, leading to another street. While still in the corridor an old man who stood in a corner, gave the blond a small package, which contained as they soon found out, two ladies shawls.

"Please put them on. The coast is clear. Seems that Berger kept his word. On the other side of the street, closer to the corner on your left, you'll see a "droshky" pulled by two brown horses. I want you Czeslawa to board that wagon. Danuta and I will follow you in 3 minutes. Once we leave the town I'll give you further instructions. Is that clear?"

Czeslawa would have preferred not to be separated from Danuta even for a minute, but she had to rely upon the blond woman to lead them through this situation as well. She realized that all these masquerading steps were needed as precautionary measures. It was always better to be safe than sorry.

Czeslawa covered most of her head with the shawl and quickly crossed the street to the waiting carriage, to be followed by Danuta and the blond woman. As soon as everybody took a seat, the driver pulled the reins and the horses moved on.

"Well, we're on our way. You may call me Alina or Mrs. Dziedzic, whatever you wish. We're going to a farm run by a deaf and dumb couple. They will see to it, that you'll be properly fed. The house stands alone, there are no other houses in the near vicinity. I would like the two of you to spend time on the outside to get a bit of color to your pale, concentration camp faces. We expect that you will spend at least 2-3 weeks there. We need that time to prepare a new set of "Kennkarte" for you, at the same time your hair will grow a bit. Any questions?"

"Yes Mrs. Dziedzic. When can we get back to Zakopane?'

"Truthfully, I don't know. It is not up to me, we'll have to check with our people. Remember, we've put lots of effort into your escape. Surely we don't want to jeopardize it. By the way, that man Burczyk or Burczak, he is no longer a threat to you. You'll be glad to know."

"Thank God. He was the cause of our arrest. Can you imagine what that one Pole has done to other Poles? Mrs. Dziedzic please understand, we must return to our home in Zakopane. The Bujnickis are my adoptive parents. They are elderly people who need our help. Also, there I expect my husband to return after this dreadful war. He will be looking for us, of that I'm sure. We'll be fine and keeping a very low profile, like mice in a church behind a broom. To the very curious neighbors, we'll tell them that we've been temporarily detained by the Germans and released. The Bujnickis are well liked and respected people. There is no one that we know, who would wish them ill."

"As I've said, I'll discuss the matter with the right people and we'll let you know. As long as you wish to go back to Zakopane, we may prepare your papers under your own married name of Daszkiewicz."

"I think that would be the best, Mrs. Dziedzic. We thank you very much for everything."

"We are just doing our duty, Czeslawa. Look here we are already!"

The carriage pulled behind the house right into an open stable gate, away from curious eyes.

"You can come down now. I'll introduce you to Jan and Maria."

"How do we communicate with them?"

"With difficulty. They can read lips a bit and you can write notes, but not too often. They don't like to waste precious paper."

A man and a woman of nondescript age, dressed in well worn, peasant clothes, stood at the door to the house. Their hands and faces betrayed many years of hard work.

Mrs. Dziedzic pointed to Czeslawa and Danuta. Jan and Maria bowed politely and shook hands with them. Maria then took Czeslawa's arm and pulled it gently as a sign to follow her. Danuta out of curiosity went along. Maria brought them to a small but spotless room whose furniture consisted of two narrow, metal beds and a chest of drawers. The only decoration hung on the wall. It was a large wooden crucifix.

Czeslawa understood the room as their bedroom. Next was the outhouse, situated between the house and the stable. Coming back to the house, Maria brought them to the kitchen, where Jan prepared a small heap of potato and cabbage pierogis and slices of dark, pumpernickel bread. Maria pointed to the chairs and everyone sat down to the meal. After saying grace, they ate the food prepared by the unusual host and hostess.

Only now did Czeslawa realize how hungry she was. Danuta being the youngest, was always hungry and indeed she ate the most, to no one's objection.

"Mrs. Dziedzic, how can I get in touch with you?"

"You can't. We'll be in touch with you within a few days. Whoever will come, will have regards for you from Alina. In the meantime try to stay busy and help around the farm. Sorry but I must leave right now. Chin up."

She shook hands with Czeslawa and gave Danuta a hug. The driver of the carriage waited for Alina Dziedzic and soon they drove off in a direction opposite from Oswiecim.

Czeslawa helped Maria to clean up the table, earning a smile and a silent "Thank You."

She then pointed to herself and to the bedroom. Maria shook her head understanding the request. The turn of events were quite satisfactory to Czeslawa, she was free and with Danuta and hopefully on their way home in Zakopane.

She started to get undressed, when Maria after knocking on the door came into the bedroom carrying a pail of warm water and a towel. Czeslawa thanked her and heard something resembling a "Good-Night".

Both mother and daughter washed up, giggling like a pair of children. Having done that, they took out of their meager belongings, nightshirts and were in the same bed, holding each other, just to make sure that they weren't dreaming. Danuta was clinging to her mother like a kitten and like a kitten she was asleep within seconds.

Czeslawa on the other hand was thinking about their next few days. She glanced at the Spartan, meticulously clean room and at, the previously not noticed, small bookcase, easily recognizing her favorite authors Eliza Orzeszkowa, Adam Nasielski and Dolega-Mostowicz.

She had read those books what seemed like 100 years ago. The memory of those books brought a smile on her face and with that smile she fell asleep.

By the time Czeslawa and Danuta got up the next morning, Jan and Maria were up and working for a couple of hours.

On the kitchen table, they found a note in childlike handwriting: "Kasha and milk on the stove are for you."

"Danuta come here, this is our breakfast."

"I'm coming mother, but where are we?'

"We're safe and sound and that is most important. Eat your kasha and let's go outside. We have to help Jan and Maria and be patient until our papers will be ready. Do you understand that child?'

"Yes mother, I'm no longer a child."

After breakfast they got dressed and went outside to look for Maria and Jan. Czeslawa was given a pitchfork and Danuta a shovel. Their task was to clean the stable. It was hard work that had to be performed regardless of weather because the animals didn't know the difference between Sunday or Monday. Still, this work was better than the work in the camp.

Days spent on the farm, working very hard in fresh air and eating moderately well, brought color to their cheeks and no longer did they look like concentration camp inmates. Days passed by and no one from Alina's people showed up. That was a reason to worry. Those fears she couldn't share with Danuta, even though, Danuta kept asking her mother: "When are we going to leave this place and go home?"

"Be patient darling, all in good time."

It was easier said then done because a day later a German patrol stopped by asking questions, to which Czeslawa kept repeating: "Nichts verstehen, nichts verstehen". The Squad leader, a sergeant, replied something about "Stupid Pollacks" and left the house, killing two chickens on the way out.

The next day a visitor was very much welcomed. It was Alina Dziedzic, who instead of her elegant city dress wore a typical, local peasant garb. This time she arrived on a small panel truck loaded with timber. That woman was always full of surprises.

"Let's go girls and get packed, we're leaving immediately."

"Where are we going, Mrs. Dziedzic?'

"You'll be pleased to know you are going back home to Zakopane. We were told that everything there is peaceful. However, to make sure, we're going to stop a block or two away from the house. One of you will go in to check the place and come back for the other, agreed?"

"And how! You made us very happy and we thank you."

"Wait with your thanks until we get there."

They quickly gathered their belongings and said good-bye to their patriotic and yet totally unusual couple. Boarding the truck, Czeslawa managed to sit with Alina and an elderly driver. Danuta being young and more agile climbed onto the back of the truck, disappearing among various pieces of lumber.

Czeslawa didn't own a watch but she estimated that the trip to Zakopane took almost 3 hours. Somehow the old truck kept on moving slowly along the curved road, being stopped several times. It seemed to Czeslawa that everybody knew the old truck owned by "Firma Schlenker und Sohne"

Toward the evening the truck reached the vicinity of Bujnickis house.

"Stay here Danuta, let your mother check out the house."

Czeslawa with heart beating hard walked to the house. Her shawl covered her head and most of her face, wondering what she would find.

She knocked on the door, scared to breathe. A weak voice of Mrs. Bujnicki answered the knock"

"Who is that?"

"It's Czeslawa, mama."

Mrs. Bujnicki opened the door just as Danuta came running up the stairs. Both Czeslawa and Danuta fell into the open arms of Mrs. Bujnicki.

"Jesus, Maria! It is Czeslawa and Danuta!" These words were spoken by the old man Mr. Bujnicki, who didn't utter a word, since the cruel beating he received from the Gestapo on the day of Czeslawa's arrest. Everybody wept but Danuta was prancing about. They were finally home, unaware that Alina Dziedzic, gun in hand followed them, but seeing the family reunion, left them undisturbed in peace.

CHAPTER 51

It was the second time, except for Astrid, that Henryk's identity as a Jew was revealed. The first time by Maj. Scharf and the second time by Maj. Dennhard. That Maj. Scharf found out from Astrid, Henryk could understand, that Astrid wanted to share the secret with him. Being a doctor and having a Jewish stepfather who paid for his schooling, Maj. Scharf was unlikely to denounce Henryk to the Gestapo. Maj. Dennhard was another case altogether.

What pervaded his consciousness, and not unlike Plato's allegory of the Cave, it was evident to Henryk, that the reality of the time was far more heinous than the life of one single Jew, who to boot, served in the Wehrmacht.

Henryk suspected that Maj. Dennhard, who had lost an arm on the crumbling altar of the "1000 year" Reich, wanted to get back at his former idol Hitler, by saving a Jew for a change.

The other two Italians in the car couldn't care less about Henryk's background. All they worried about was how to get safely to Rome.

The closer they got to the front line, the worse the roads became. They encountered larger and more frequent potholes and craters. Henryk was primarily worried about the S-mines, which he considered, and rightly so, the most frightening weapon of the war.

Another obstacle was the "dragon's teeth", truncated pyramids of reinforced concrete about a meter in height in the front row, to two meters high in the back. They were usually staggered and spaced in such a manner, that a tank couldn't drive through. Also the pillboxes were numerous and better constructed, as he well knew. They were half underground, with cannon, machine guns and ammunition storage rooms and living quarters for the defenders.

It was a good thing that they kept moving, otherwise they were sure to catch a downpour of German or Allied artillery and mortar fire. As it was, they were several times shot at. All kinds of ordnance were exploding in much to close for comfort vicinity. At the same time, they were attacked from the air, by a single plane of unknown nationality. No one in the car was curious enough to stick his head out. In that case, quick thinking Henryk drove into the woods giving them a protective cover.

When stopped by the Germans, Count Mizerco invariably would ask the officer in charge, to kindly phone or otherwise inform the unit ahead of an arrival of a diplomatic car. Surprisingly, the request was so brazen that most of the commanders cooperated in getting them through. Only once did an officer say: "Sie sind verucked" "you are crazy, I won't have anything to do with your death. Go if you wish, I won't stop you."

Further down the road, already in no man's land, so they thought, they were showered from the air by "Safe conduct" – "Passierschein" leaflets, written in German and English, asking German soldiers to desert, promising a fair treatment if they did so.

At the last German fixed position, facing the Allies, the officer in charge of the unit, who introduced himself as Capt. Kurt Gabel calmly told them:

"Meine Herren" you are not going anyplace. It's getting dark and I'm not going to jeopardize the lives of two diplomats. You'll stay here and keep us company over night. Besides, we want you to see what we have in store for the Allies. And with these words he gave an order to open fire.

The concentration of German firepower was overwhelming with its violence, intensity and surprise. Artillery fire, 88s, 75s from well camouflaged tanks, 120mm mortars with apparently limitless supplies of ammunition hit the Allied side, creating a similar response. Only the well fortified pillbox saved their diplomatic skins.

As suddenly as the artillery duel began so it ended, giving them a few hours of respite. It was quiet in the morning, Henryk

0468-LEE

went to check on the car, he was sure that nothing remained of it, after last night's artillery performances. To his complete surprise, he found the car although riddles with holes, including windows and nonexistent headlights, the car started at the first try.

Capt. Gabel came up to Count Mizerco saying:

"Good morning, I really don't know what to do with you, arrest you or have you shot. I can't get through to my Headquarters. What do you think I should do, "Meine Herren?"

"Well Captain, I think that you should let us continue with our mission. It wouldn't look good on your war record having killed two diplomats and an innocent driver. Would Bismark or Fredrik the Great approve of such behavior? I doubt it very much. After all you are the regular Army or aren't you Capt. Gabel?"

"Yes, I am. We are not "Schweinenhunde" like the S.S. Go before I change my mind. At least make sure to stick out a white flag or a bedsheet."

"Thank you Captain. We don't have a bedsheet but we'll stick out a white shirt and again thanks for your hospitality."

"Follow this road in the southerly direction. There shouldn't bee too many mines on it."

"That is most encouraging Captain. We do appreciate your sense of humor."

"You're welcome but if I ever live through this war I surely will look you up in Rome."

"You do that, Captain."

Henryk drove very slowly on a badly damaged road for the remaining 300-400 meters separating the warring parties. While Henryk drove, both Dr. del Forno and Count Mizerco waved their white flag and a shirt from both sides of the car.

A short warning overhead fusillade of 50mm shells was their welcome to the Allied side. Henryk kept on moving albeit even slower. Their white flag was noticed by the two half-tracks that drove up to the car, machine guns at ready.

A twenty-one year old British lieutenant Brian Campbell, platoon leader, shouted in perfect German:

"Halt! Who are you and what is your mission?"

Dr. del Forno answered in English: "Sir, we are Italian diplomats, part of the new Italian Government. We wish to speak with your commanding officer.'

"Very well, please follow me."

Lt. Campbell's half-track turned around and Henryk followed him realizing that the second half-rack was right behind his Mercedes-Benz. With a half-track ahead of him, Henryk didn't have to worry about mines.

They drove for another couple of hundred meters, just beyond a small hill, where a large pillbox served as a forward staff quarters of the British 8th Army. A Union Jack flying in the wind told them clearly that they were with the British. The two half-tracks stopped and so did Henryk but for altogether different reasons he ran out of gas.

Lt. Campbell jumped out of his half-track, his side arm dangling from a web belt, loaded with extra ammo clips.

"Gentlemen, please follow me. May I see your papers." His clipped English had a trace of American.

Dr. del Forno and Count Mizerco turned over their diplomatic passports. Looking at the passports he gave his sergeant an order:

"Sergeant, frisk these gentlemen but gently. You'll forgive me gentlemen but this is Standard Operating Procedure, nothing personal, I assure you."

"Lieutenant, we have no weapons on us, neither has our driver. We are a part of count Sforzo's new Italian Government. Kindly notify your Headquarters as to our presence. Safe conduct papers and an escort to Rome would be highly appreciated. I'm afraid we have to ask for transportation as well since our car is beyond redemption."

"I'll contact our Headquarters on your behalf, but I have no authority on my own to issue such papers or provide you with transportation and an escort. In the meantime may I extend to you the hospitality of the British 8th Army. I'll arrange for breakfast for you. I'm sure that you prefer coffee to tea.'

"You have guest it right. Could you do the same for our driver? He remained with the car."

"I'll attend to it." He gave orders to that affect without leaving them for a single solitary minute.

Even Count Mizerco had to admit that Lt. Campbell was quite a charmer. A son of a British Army officer and a rich Southern California woman, Brian received the best available education on both sides of the ocean, spending several years in Europe. As a result he spoke French, Italian and German like a native. He had blown the lid off his Army I.Q. test. In this war, the sole requirement of the Duke of Wellington from his lieutenants is that they be brave, wasn't enough any longer. They had to be intelligent too. Brian was even more than that, considering his championships in tennis, chess and he was also a chemistry wizard. In him, America and Britain were throwing their finest young man at the Germans.

Having contacted his Headquarters, Brian awaited their further instructions while having breakfast with his unexpected guests. The conversation was held in English and Italian much to their delight.

Henryk stayed with the car, closely supervised by two armed soldiers, when another soldier brought him breakfast and plenty of hot tea.

"Sorry, old chap, we don't have bloody coffee, you'll have to drink tea."

Not knowing any English, Henryk had to resort to German, which o ne of the soldiers slightly understood. Henryk pointing to himself saying: "Poland, Polska, Polen, Polski."

"Oh, I see, he is Polish. We have many Poles with us. Maybe we can get someone to translate his words. Look there goes a Polish Corporal, let's call him over."

"Hey Corporal, come here for a minute."

It was Corporal Eljasz Wachtel, whom Capt. Chartwell and Capt. Michalski ordered to retrieve Albin Pietrus' personal effects.

"Corporal, this man claims to be Polish, can you verify it for us?

"I'll be glad to."

Corporal Wachtel looked intensely at Henryk, recognizing him at once.

"For God's sake, this is my own flesh and blood, my cousin Henryk Kaplinski."

"Eljasz? Is that really you? What are you doing here?"

"I could ask you the same question."

"It is a long story, I myself have trouble believing it. Come into my arms, let me hold you."

"Henryk, there is another fellow from our area, who knows you well."

"What is his name?"

"Edward Daszkiewicz, he is my lieutenant."

"Did you say Edward Daszkiewicz? I thought he was dead. He is my best friend, he saved my life. I must see him."

"Then come with me, I'll bring you to him."

"Corporal, where are you taking this man?"

"We are going to see my C.O. He'll also verify this man's identity."

"In that case, we'll come along."

"By all means."

They walked together towards the two officers waiting by the jeep for Eljasz Wachtel.

"Pardon us, Sirs. Does any one of you know this man?" The British soldier pointed to Henryk.

"Jesus, Maria! Henryk?"

Seeing them both in an embrace and crying, one of the Brits remarked:

"I guess this man has found his compatriots. We'll leave them alone and just report to Captain Campbell."

"Just get their names.'

"It's Captain Michalski of the Polish General Staff and Lt. Daszkiewicz. Let me spell it for you: D-A-S-Z-K-I-E-W-I-C-Z."

"That's a mouthful, Sir."

"You bet, soldier."

CHAPTER 52

Maj. Krafchin showed up in his office well ahead of the 8.15 A.M. schedule set by the general, he wasn't surprised to hear that the general was already there and hard at work. In a way, Paul was sorry for the general's immediate staff. He drove everybody hard and himself even harder. His approach heard even from afar, somehow sounded like the rumble of a tank battalion on the move through the cobblestone streets of a city.

Paul after a brief "Hello" and "Good morning" went to his own desk, attacking furiously the stack of papers awaiting his resolution. He divided all those papers into "very urgent", "urgent", and "can wait" piles. Working systematically and only taking time out for an occasional cup of coffee. Maj. Krafchin managed to reduce the stack to the remaining "can wait" file.

It was at that point that Paul was informed that the general called for an emergency staff meeting. It was nothing unusual. The general was tough and assertive, forever flexing his muscles. Still he had a way of illuminating matters of substance by examples rather than sweeping generalizations, to the point of near epigrammatic sharpness. At the same time, he would remain skeptical rather than cynical, pragmatic rather than dogmatic.

Paul took his usual seat in the Operations Room. The staff was already assembled and waiting for the general. The wait was very short.

"Gentlemen, please sit down and smoke if you wish. We reached a moment in our war with Nazi Germany, that calls for moving some of our air bases in England to airports of Europe. The need for such a move should be obvious to everyone in this room. While the idea is simple enough, the implementation of it is much more complex. It involves supplies, personnel, equipment and security to start with. We're waiting for our intelligence agencies to advise us which of those bases would be most suitable for our requirements. In the meantime I have prepared a questionnaire for each department, to deduce what their needs are in order to function properly.

There are two ways to get through it: To believe that everything is perfect as it is or to doubt everything. Both ways will save you from thinking. I, however, expect my officers to think and have the confidence in their judgements. That confidence should come not from always being right but from not fearing to be wrong once in a while. Before you smart asses will tell me, that the job of transporting air bases belongs to A.T.C. Air Transport Command, I just want to remind you, how chaotic their last performance was. I just don't want to repeat the same old story, when we had soup, we didn't have spoons and vice versa. With your input we'll minimize our losses and maximize our results. Our new bases will function from day one. Any questions?"

After a minute of silence, a few questions were raised. The General answered those fully.

"Any more questions? It can't be. I'll keep you here until someone will come up with an intelligent question."

After a long pause one of the younger officers spoke:

"So, where are you from general?" Everybody started to laugh including the general.

"An insolent pup! D-i-s-m-i-s-s-e-d!"

Paul got up with the rest of the staff, when the general called him over:

"Maj. Krafchin, I need to see you for a minute."

"At your service, General."

"Major, I have a job for you. Tomorrow being Saturday, I'm expected to make an appearance in Marble Arch, to address a British Ladies Auxiliary Group, tea and crumpets to follow. I don't feel like going there. Besides I'm much too busy as it is. Therefore I need you to fill in for me. Give them my humble apologies for not showing up myself. Feed them some B.S. on British-American friendship and cooperation. Answer their questions and above all keep on giving them your Pepsodent smile. Do that for me, son and you can have the rest of the day and Sunday off."

"Yes Sir! I'll be glad to, Sir."

"Come with me to my office, I'll give you their invitation. I think it starts at 10.30 A.M. The Brits will have a Rover and a driver from Transport for you. Good luck, son."

"Thank you Sir."

Although extremely tired, Paul decided to finish the remaining "can wait" file in order to clear his desk for the weekend. He accomplished that in another couple of hours, dozing off several times in the process.

When he reached his bed, all he could do was to take off his tunic, tie and shoes. The next second he was deeply asleep.

He could have slept much longer but the orderly assigned to the group of officers on that floor, woke him up:

"Sir, there is a British driver to pick you up, as per general's orders."

"Tell him to wait. I'll be down in 15-20 minutes."

"Yes Sir. I'll bring you a cup of coffee as well."

Once up, Paul was all action. It wasn't the first time that he had to get ready in a hurry. To mind came a song by Eddie cantor: "You're in the Army, Mr. Jones..."

"Are you Maj. Krafchin, Sir?"

A young Wren, dressed warmly was his designated driver. The thick stocking she wore, couldn't hide the beautiful shape of her legs.

"Yes, I'm Maj. Krafchin."

"Begging Major's pardon. I came to pick up a general. I guess we'll have to settle for a major."

"Don't you prefer a young major to an old general?"

"Not really. The young majors become old generals. I'll stick with young lieutenants, they have a long way to become just majors."

"I see your point."

She drove expertly through Chelsea, Kensington, Earl's Court and finally reaching Marble Arch and the schoolhouse, where the meeting of the British Ladies Auxiliary group was to take place.

The Chairlady introduced herself as Mrs. Trevor Armbrister, a tall thin and quite charming person, who listened patiently as Paul apologized for the General's absence.

"I guess he couldn't make it. Some of my ladies will be disappointed, I'm sure of that. Come with me to meet your audience. Where are you from, Maj. Krafchin?"

"I'm from Brooklyn, N.Y., Madam."

"How interesting."

Most of the audience consisted of middle aged, gray haired in most of the cases, ladies. Mrs. Armbrister extended General Cottshot's apologies and introduced instead, Maj. Krafchin of Brooklyn, N.Y.

Paul without preamble spoke briefly about the British-American cooperation, about the friendship between those two great countries, emphasizing the common language, even our variety, and the common front against Germany. He ended his impromptu speech with: "To FINAL VICTORY!" He received polite if slightly reserved applause.

It was Mrs. Armbrister who challenged her audience to ask questions about life in the States.

The first question came from a woman who identified herself as Mrs. Higgins.

"Are you the same major who is romantically involved with Marlene Dietrich?"

All the conversation in the large hall, decorated with British and American flags, stopped.

"Yes and No. I'm the same major but I'm not involved romantically or otherwise with Miss Dietrich. I'm afraid that the newspapers blew our chance meeting out of proportion. I just happened to fly on the same plane, scout's honor."

The more he denied the more questions were coming from the

floor. Some as innocent as what kind of perfume was she wearing to more personal: "are you in love with her?"

He responded: "Sorry, I don't know that much about perfume, I'm sorry to say." And "No, I'm not in love with her, although I must admit, she is a very attractive lady."

Realizing that he was in a quagmire, he motioned to Mrs. Armbrister to rescue him.

"Ladies, Maj. Krafchin has another speaking engagement this afternoon, therefore I suggest that we adjourn for tea. We wouldn't allow Major Krafchin to leave without it."

She then asked Paul to pose with her and another few ladies, for photographs for the local "The Sentinel" paper.

It became clear to Paul why the general didn't want to undertake this assignment, privilege of rank. All in all it hadn't been too bad. He rather enjoyed this unique experience.

"Thank You, Major, it has been a pleasure to have you address our ladies. Please give the General our fondest regards. Miss Flanigan will take you back to your unit."

"Thank you for having me and rescuing me. I enjoyed meeting you, Mrs. Armbrister."

"Same here, Major."

The Wren, Miss Flanigan came up to Paul:

"Where to Sir? Do you want to go back?"

"Not really. I still have some time to kill. Tell me Miss Flanigan, are we far from this address?" Paul gave her Cynthia Epstein's address.

"Not too far. It's in Knightsbridge, on the way back to your billet. Would you like to stop there? It's no bother."

"My friends live there, I'll just check to see if they are home. If not we'll continue on our way back to the base."

"Very well, Sir."

It started to rain. The cold, heavy raindrops were hitting the car's roof with hail's ferocity. They drove in silence, listening to the rain. Feeling chilled, Paul covered his legs with a car rug, left in the back of the car.

Miss Flanigan started to slow down the car.

"Why are we stopping?"

"I'm trying to locate the correct house number. We're already here, Sir."

"Very well then, Please wait for me. I'm going up to see if anybody is home."

"Very good, Sir."

Paul got out of the Rover and entered Cynthia's parents building. Although it took but seconds to do that, it was enough for him to get soaked by the rain.

Paul ran upstairs to Epsteins flat. He rang the doorbell twice, there was no answer. He tried it again, but this time he heard Cynthia's voice: "Just a moment, I'm coming."

Cynthia opened the door, dressed in a blue terry bathrobe, her head was wrapped in a Turkish towel, looking like she just got out of the bath and smelling of fresh Yardley soap.

"My God, its Paul. It has been ages. How are you? Do come in, Paul."

"I'm okay, just happened to be in your neighborhood. Thought I would say "hello" to your parents."

"You missed them. There is no one in the house but me. And here I thought that you came just to see me. Pardon my appearance, but I always look like that after taking a bath."

"Forgive me Cynthia for barging in on you without calling. It was very rude of me. Can I make it up to you by taking you out to dinner?"

"Nothing would please me more, Paul. Where is my kiss?"

"I have a driver waiting for me downstairs."

"Send him home, we don't need him. I've my father's car and enough Petrol to get you back after dinner."

"I'm off till Sunday afternoon."

"That's fantastic, Paul. You can stay here with us."

"I don't have anything with me, not even a tooth brush."

"Don't worry, we'll get you one. You can always use father's shaving kit and his pajamas."

"Very well then. I'll go down and release the driver. By the way, it's a she and not a he."

"My, my, aren't we getting up in this world?"

Paul wearing Mr. Epstein's mackintosh went down to Miss Flanigan, waiting in the Rover.

"Miss, I'll be staying here for a while. You're free to go back to Transport. Thanks for the lift."

"You are most welcome, Sir. Good night." Paul heard her starting the car as he walked back to the stairs.

"Fix us a couple of drinks and take off your wet clothing. I'll put father's black turtleneck sweater on the chair. Try it on. I'll be ready in a few minutes. It is not every day that a handsome major of the American Air Force comes to see me in my bathrobe."

"I'm so sorry, Cynthia."

"Your punishment is to take me out to dinner. The place I have in mind is just a few blocks away. We could actually walk over there, but if it is still raining we can take the car."

"Very well, Cynthia, can I bring you the drink?"

"Yes, but not too much."

"Bottoms Up!"

"Do you know something, Cynthia, one can get used to drink without ice, it tastes even better."

Half way through his drink, Cynthia came out dressed in a new lieutenant's uniform.

"Yes Paul, I've been transferred to the Supreme Headquarters Allied Expeditionary Force better known as SHAEF, your shield and sword. The promotion went with the job and now I work at Grosvenor Square, still as a historian. I do love my work."

"Congratulations Lieutenant, let's celebrate your promotion!"

"Sounds like a good idea. I think it stopped raining. We may as well take a walk. It will do us good to walk after the rain. The air is pure delight."

"What about your drink, Cynthia?"

"I don't drink much, I don't smoke, I'm what you Yanks call "a good girl."

"We'll have to amend the situation a bit."

"Wish you would, my life is getting boring."

They walked arm in arm for several blocks. Paul felt her warmth through his sweater and her wool-gabardine uniform. The streets were blackened and only Cynthia's torch lit their way to "The Golden Ox" pub.

"That's the place where servicemen and their sweethearts come to enjoy themselves and forget about the nasty war. The civilians are glad, too, because for money they can get more meat than their 4 oz. Weekly ration. Don't worry Paul, nobody starves in England. Fresh milk might be another matter. Why worry about milk when we have whisky."

They walked into a noisy, smoked filled room. Paul gave the head waiter 10 shillings:

"Give us a nice table, mate."

"It will cost you another 10 bob."

"You got it."

"What can I get you, Gov.?"

"Whatever is hot and strong and don't worry about the money."

"You Yanks never worry about the money, we Brits have to."

"Not tonight. We're here to celebrate this lady's promotion."

"Leave it up to me, Gov."

"You're on, mate."

Paul invested his money wisely because the waiter was a miracle man. He brought them hot and delicious beef Wellington and some fine, old scotch.

Food, whisky and the intoxicating smell of young bodies, combined with tobacco smoke, made a potent mixture, to which some reacted by singing and other by reciting poetry, that even the piercing wail of sirens couldn't put down.

One young lieutenant, barely out of his teens, got on the top of the table and started with:

"There was a young man from Kent,
with a penis so long, that it bent.
To save his wife trouble,

He put it in double
And instead of coming, he went."

The poem met with universal approval, several drinks were offered to that young and not too sober officer.

Not to be outdone, Paul got up and in his best imitation of the Kings English, he recited the only similar in style poem, he knew:

"There was a young priest from Siberia,
Whose life grew drearier and drearier.
To save him some fun,
He seduced a nun
And now she is a mother superior."

Bravos and free drinks were Paul's rewards. Some groups started to sing "Rule Britannia" other shouted "England Forever", getting an interesting response in the form of: "Scotland a wea bit longer."

Cynthia knew some people and they invited her and Paul to join them. The party intensified its tempo. Everybody spoke at the same time, without bothering to listen. Whisky and beer was flowing uninterrupted. A few drinks later Cynthia said to Paul: "I've had it, let's go home."

"Exactly my sentiments, let's say good-bye to your friends and I'll take care of the bill."

The friends wouldn't let them go without "one for the road" drink. That drink soon was changed to two drinks, the second was for "Bless 'em all."

It was rather late when they made their way home. Paul surely had too many drinks, while not completely drunk he became suddenly very tired and sleepy. The idea of taking Cynthia to bed crossed his mind several times, during the evening, but he didn't think that he could adequately perform.

To take his mind off he started to tell Cynthia about his trip to the States, the visit with his mother and in the moment of total frankness he told her about his break up with Goldie:

She did hang on to his every word. Half drunk he clearly remembered her words:

"Paul, I'm in the same boat. My fiancée was killed. I received official notification from the War Office."

"I'm sorry to hear it, Cynthia, very sorry indeed."

"It's the war, the stupid war. People do get killed as you know."

Paul was holding onto her as she was using the blackout torch. The narrow light emitting from it came across a big pile of rubble that before the bombings was somebody's home.

Slowly they had reached Cynthia's house. Walking up the stairs was another matter. Each leg weighed a ton. Whistling "Happy days are here again" he made it to the top.

It was Cynthia who put him into her bed. It was also her task to undress him, because he couldn't move. The only remark that he heard was: "Oh, God! What a waste of good material." Or something similar.

With each sleeping hour, Paul's body seemed to dissipate all the tensions and he slept soundly and peacefully.

It was late in the morning of the following day, when Cynthia's parents returned home and found Paul sleeping in Cynthia's room and Cynthia herself was sleeping in her brother's bedroom.

The only person who was embarrassed by this sleeping arrangement was Paul himself.

He could hear his father's words of disapproval: "Es past nyt" "It isn't nice."

"Good morning Paul and Good morning Cynthia. The way you've slept, the entire house could have been stolen from underneath you and you wouldn't have heard anything. Glad you are here Paul, we missed you."

"Paul went back to the States on an assignment but he still managed to see his mother." Volunteered Cynthia.

"How interesting, do tell us all about it."

Paul briefly described his trip and the time spent at home.

"Cynthia, how about a cup of tea for Paul? We are going to have lunch pretty soon."

"I'm sorry Mrs. Epstein, I've got to get back to my unit."

"Paul are we back to official Mrs. Epstein? What is this about going back? Cynthia tells me that you're off till this evening. Besides we're having a surprise guest, someone that you know very well."

"Who might that be?"

"If I tell you now, it wouldn't be a surprise anymore, would it? All I can say is that the person in question, is someone that you know and respect."

"Curiosity killed the cat, I'll say."

Someone rang the bell.

"It may be our mystery guest."

Mrs. Epstein opened the door and a man in civilian suit came in. Paul didn't have any difficulties in recognizing the man. It was his Air Force Chaplain, Rabbi Jerome Rifkind.

"Hello, everybody, Hello Major or shall I call you Paul? How are you my boy?"

"Very well Sir, how about you?"

"Never better. When the Epsteins told me that they met you, I was delighted. Well, today I came for a delicious lunch and stimulating conversation with these two historians on my favorite subject – Palestine."

"Rabbi, I suggest then that we start with lunch. Please follow me to the dining room."

"Forgive us Rabbi, this time the lunch might be a bit modest, however this time we have real milk for coffee or tea."

"Well, I brought you some chocolates and a few cans of "Carnation" concentrated milk."

"We appreciate it."

As soon as lunch was finished a heated conversation took place between the Epsteins and the Rabbi. Paul listened as the names of Chaim Weizman, Balfour Declaration, White Paper, national home for the Jews were mentioned over and over. It was all very interesting but Paul kept glancing discreetly at his wristwatch. Pretty soon he would have to make his move and get back to his base.

This time Cynthia must have read his mind.

"Sorry to break up this charming, debating society but our fly boy has to leave, much to our regret."

So, soon, Paul?'

"I'm afraid so. I'll be back and thanks for your hospitality."

"Paul, let me quickly iron your jacket, that got wet in the rain. It'll take but a minute."

Cynthia was neither a demure or obsequious English country girl. There was definitely steel in her mild mannered voice. Paul recognized the same fine quality as in his mother's younger days. There was no point in arguing.

"Paul, I'll be leaving too. My jeep is parked right outside this house. May I offer you a lift? I still want to talk with you."

"I appreciate that and am looking forward to it, Rabbi."

Cynthia handed Paul his freshly ironed jacket. She has done it with a smile, similar to his own mother's, when she did something for her husband. It was the look of love.

"I'm making too many comparisons with my mother. Am I falling in love? Thought Paul and his inner voice said to him: "You are poor boy, you are."

Paul said good-bye to the Epstein and turned to Cynthia. Before he had a chance to say anything, she said:

"I'll go down with you to the car."

The ever understanding Rabbi added:

"I'm going ahead to warm up the car." Giving them a chance to say their good-bye in private.

Cynthia stood up on her toes to reach Paul's lips. She kissed him passionately. It seemed to Paul, that her whole body was represented in that kiss. He responded in kind.

"Cynthia, something tells me that we're going to see much of each other."

"Yes, I know Paul. Take good care of yourself. I need you Paul."

One more brief kiss and Paul got into Rabbi Rifkind's jeep.

"She is a lovely girl, anything serious?"

"Truthfully Rabbi, I don't know yet. It might be. We both

just came out from a bitter experience and we both need time."

"Forgive me Paul, I didn't mean to intrude. Sometimes I think, that being a Rabbi, entitles me to know everybody's business and their affairs of heart."

"It's OK Rabbi. I understand that fully. What did you want to talk to me about?"

A drenching downpour of rain interrupted the Rabbi's answer. He had to concentrate on driving.

"To begin with, our conversation is strictly between the two of us, do you understand?"

"Of course, Rabbi, go ahead."

"Do you recall our previous conversation, Paul?"

"I do, Sir."

"The way I see it, this war will end unlike any other war. Consequently, there will be just two major powers left. The U.S.A. and the U.S.S.R. and the Jews will be caught in between those two. Great Britain and France will be of no consequence. Alarming reports are reaching us about the mass slaughter of European Jewry. I'm terribly afraid that only a small percentage will survive and where will they go? The U.S. Government sent back the "St. Louis" boat full of refugees, back to Germany. Canada with it's policy that even "one is too many", Australia, New Zealand? No one is interested in mass migration of the sick and poor refugees to their shores. Palestine might be the only option. The British with their pro Arab policy were always against the influx of Jews to their Mandate. We Jews will have to find a way to smuggle those poor people in, whether the British like it or not. We'll be needing planes and people who could fly them. Do I need to say more?"

"No, Sir, I read you loud and clear. I'll certainly give it a thought when the time will come. We still have to win this war first, don't you agree, Rabbi?"

"I do Paul, just keep in mind our conversation. It looks like we reached your base."

"Many thanks for the lift, Rabbi and let's keep in touch."

The sentry at the gate checked Paul's I.D.

"Maj. Krafchin, the general ordered to bring you in his office as soon as you return. Will you please follow me, Sir."

"What the hell now?"

"I wouldn't know Sir." The Sentry brought Paul to the General's office. Paul knocked at the door and heard the General's raspy voice:

"Come in."

"Maj. Krafchin reporting as ordered, Sir."

"At ease Paul, how did it go? Did you charm those ladies?'

"I think I did a good job. You probably can read about it in tomorrow's "Sentinel". You have the best regards from Mrs. Armbrister."

"Thank you Paul. Do you remember our meeting? I have on my desk already all the answers to my questionnaires. I know that Rome wasn't built in a day but if it were, I would have commissioned all those contractors. You look beat my son, go and hit the sack. We've lots of work for you to process all those questionnaires."

"Yes Sir, Good night Sir. See you in the morning, General."

He swiftly walked to the building where his room was located. On his bed he found an elegant, light pink envelope with a return address marked M.D. 993 Park Ave., New York, N.Y. U.S.A. He opened the letter that had an Air Force censure stamped on it. It was from Marlene Dietrich:

"Darling we belong together." In the rest of the letter she described her new 1.600 sq. ft. prewar co-op, about the paintings bought at the Sotheby's auction. One of a log cabin with smoke curling up its chimney and another by Carl Hirshburg of a couple picnicking in Connecticut. She also wanted Paul to know that she bought several brass bird-shaped doorknobs and described the parquet floors and the color of monogrammed towels, ending the letter with a quotation from her favorite song:

> "Falling in love again, never wanted to,
> What am I to do, I can't help it.
> I was made this way, I can't help it.

Ich bin fom Kopf bis Fuss aus der Liebe angestelt.'
Love M.D.

Paul read and reread this letter, not knowing what to make of it. At least I know that much, I have her new address where I can send her book "Gone With the Wind" and her gloves, which she had left on the plane. Good-bye Marlene, my heart is taken by Cynthia, I can't help it, I was made that way and I can't help it.

CHAPTER 53

Both Henryk and Edward looked at each other, disbelieving their own eyes. Each one thought that he was dreaming.

"Henryk, please pinch me. I just want to know if you're real?"

"He is real enough, trust me Henryk. The question is where do we go from here? We must return to our unit, the war hasn't ended yet. What do we do with you Henryk?"

"Captain, why can't we take him with us?"

"I doubt it Edward very much, if it can be done. He is a civilian, a Polish subject which is true, however, what I can see from here, the man was wounded or recuperating from him wounds. What we should do is to check with those Italian diplomats, he came with, to see what they have in mind for him. Come lets everybody hop into the jeep and drive up to see those "goombas".

Count Mizerco and Dr. del Forno were engaged in a heated conversation with Capt. Campbell, as Michalski's jeep with a Polish white-red flag, pulled in front of them.

Henryk introduced Capt. Michalski and Lt. Daszkiewicz to Count Mizerco and Dr. del Forno, who in turn introduced Capt. Campbell of the British Army.

It was Capt. Campbell who started to speak first:

"I've heard about your unbelievable meeting. I gather you have been good friends for a long time."

"Yes captain, since our childhood."

"A remarkable story."

It was now Capt. Michalski's turn:

"We would like to know what these diplomats have in store for Henryk Kaplinski? Unfortunately, we can't take a civilian with us. Do you have any suggestions?"

"We, ourselves, don't have any notion what to do with Henryk. First of all, we must report to Count Sforza. I'm very much afraid that we shall be very busy for the next few months. Henryk doesn't speak Italian, nor does he know Rome, therefore he can't be of use to us as a driver. As far as his Polish, Russian or German is concerned, we're still too far off from utilizing his skills in that department.

The only thing at the moment, that can be done, is for me to give Henryk a letter of introduction to a friend of mine, Gulio Romano, who owns the Hotel Sant' Anselmo at 2 Piazza Anselmo in Rome. In the past, we have used this hotel to lodge special guests, who for various reasons had to be less "visible" so to say. As soon as we get ourselves situated, we shall send for Henryk. We are fully aware, that Henryk drove us through mine fields at the risk of his own life. We Italians do not forget things like that, but not until we'll be functioning properly, can we do anything worthwhile for him. Henryk I also will give you the address of my own sister, to be used dire need only. It's Sophia del Forno at 49 Via Ludovisi. I'm afraid we can't do anything else for him. We must be on our way Capt. Campbell provided us with transportation and a driver. Henryk can come with us to Rome and we could drop him off at the hotel Sant' Anselmo."

"Well, Henryk that sounds like a temporary solution to your problem. I do know that Rome is crowded with refugees of all kinds, so to have a place of your own is great. Beside we do come to Rome very often especially Capt. Michalski. Don't worry, I'll be in touch with you, I won't loose you this time. We'll help you with food, cigarettes and clothing. You can take everything we have with us."

Capt. Campbell who listened intently to the conversation said:

"Let me also be part of this. I can get other items such as canned goods, tea, and sugar for him and what you have. Just wait for me, please. I'll be back in a few minutes."

"Thank you all, I'm overwhelmed."

Capt. Campbell came back with a large army duffel bag full of supplies, which he put into the staff car provided for the diplomats.

"We must be off. It's getting late, gentlemen."

Saying good-bye to Edward was very difficult. Both had tears in their eyes, they knew that come hell or high water they will be in touch again.

Henryk sat next to the driver, who introduced himself as Sergeant Malcolm. The diplomats sat in the back, engrossed in deep conversation.

Sgt. Malcolm spoke English only and a few words in Italian, thus Henryk watched the Italian countryside, the destruction of cities and villages in silence on the way to Rome. Without the knowledge of the Italian language he felt lonely and totally abandoned.

They were stopped several times by various army units, Sgt. Malcolm did all the talking. Only once were Count Mizerco and Dr. del Forno asked for their papers. Henryk, whom Sgt. Malcolm identified as the embassy's butler was totally ignored.

A few hours later they reached the Eternal City-Rome. Count Mizerco, for whatever his reasons, decided to drop Henryk off first. He introduced Gulio Romano to Henryk in German and then spoke to Mr. Romano in rapid Italian. They seemed to agree on something, that much was obvious to Henryk even without the knowledge of Italian.

"Well Heinrich or Henryk, we have to leave you here. Mr. Romano will take good care of you. He speaks German, so you'll be able to communicate with him. I don't know when I'll get in touch with you. Just be patient. Good luck and thanks."

Gulio Romano was a medium built man, about 45-50 years old. His jet black hair, sprinkled with some gray, was combed straight back. With a pleasant smile, he greeted Henryk in German:

"Welcome to Rome Herr Kaplinski, hope that you'll enjoy your stay with us. Please come with me. We have a small room and a bath on the third floor, I'm sure that you'll like it."

The room was indeed small, but nevertheless looked comfortable. It had a little balcony overlooking a courtyard that belonged to the adjacent church by the same name as the hotel. Henryk also admired the carved panels on the door of his room.

"Do you like your room Herr Kaplinski?"

"Very much Herr Romano. How much will I have to pay for it?'

"Don't worry about the money. You are a guest of the new Italian Government. We have problems with lack of food, which is in a short supply."

"Herr Romano, I have some canned goods, cigarettes and tea, perhaps we can trade them for something else that you need?'

"Santa Lucia! You speak like a real Genovese. What do you have to trade?"

Henryk took out of the duffel bag, which contained a few cans of Spam, package of tea and two cartons of cigarettes, British Players and American Camels.

"Herr Kaplinski, you're a rich man. I'll send my man Luigi to the market and you'll be surprised what he'll bring back. Why don't you put away your things, wash up from the trip and relax a while. I'll call you later, we'll have a bite together."

Henryk unpacked his few articles brought from Schloss Elmau and the items given to him by Capt. Campbell, Michalski and Edward. The additional canned goods, cigarettes, coffee and condensed cans of milk he put into the bottom drawer. Like in Poland or Germany these items were good as gold.

The bed looked inviting, he thought, why not take a nap. He probably could have slept longer but the noise coming from the courtyard woke him up. If not the noise, then the knock on the door would have done the same thing. It was Gulio Romano.

"Herr Kaplinski, please come down to room 204, just one flight below, I want you to meet my wife Fiorella. We'll have dinner together."

"Thank you very much, I'll be right there. Just give me a couple of minutes."

"Very well, see you downstairs."

The door to Romanos apartment was opened even before Henryk had a chance to ring the doorbell.

"Please do come in. Let me call my wife. Fiorella, Herr Kaplinski is here!"

A petite looking brunette with smooth dark hair and an olive complexion came out of the kitchen. She gave Henryk a smile, removed her apron and shook hands with Henryk speaking "solo Italiano". Gulio took over as an interpreter. "Please come to the dining room."

Large, massive, antique furniture crowded the room. Dark oil paintings in heavy frames hanging on the walls complemented the room further.

Although Henryk was in Italy a very short time, he knew that Italians unlike other people took their food seriously. The table was set for three people. Henryk would always remember his first meal in Rome, starting with bombolotti and sauce of spinach and parmesian cheese, a risotto with radicchio and prosciuto, followed by the main course, a sea bass served with perfectly cooked vegetables, washed down with a bottle of good Italian white wine.

The food was the best Henryk had eaten in a very long while. The conversation at the table turned eventually to the raging war and the role of the Hotel Sant' Anselmo.

"We belong to a certain group of Italian patriots who were never happy with Duce and his "Commando Supremo" Marshal Badoglio, or their claims that Italy was a major power and Benito a great warrior. Those claims backfired badly. Starting with the Abyssinian war, involvement in the Spanish Civil war, the very costly alliance with Germany, blunders in Africa, the Balkan campaign and finally his disastrous dispatch of an entire army corps to Russia is what caused his fall. Throughout that time, my hotel gave refuge to many people of different nationalities or political and religious beliefs. This was done by a clandestine support of such noble people like Count Mizerco and others. Sometimes the help would come from totally unexpected and surprising sources like the offices of Ulrich von Hassell who was German Ambassador to Italy or Philip, Prince of Hesse, no less than an Obergruppenfuhrer S.A., married to Princess Mafalda of Italy, and employed by Hitler as a reliable Party man on missions to Italy. I never understood what was beyond some of those moves. A lot of good has been done and you are today a beneficiary of that movement. You can stay with us as long as you wish or deem necessary. I almost forgot to give you your money from the sale of those cigarettes. Luigi has done well."

"I do appreciate everything you're doing for me, but I'll be happier if I could pay my share. Please take out whatever you need out of this money."

"Not this time. Should the time come that we would need your help we shall ask for it. Is there anything that you wish to tell us about yourself? You don't have to, only if you wish."

"There isn't much to tell. I'm a Jew from Poland, who somehow found himself working in the O.T. and later transferred to Wehrmacht. Although wounded was able to come to Italy where I have miraculously met my best friend, currently serving with the Polish Army. Had I been in better shape I would have volunteered to serve along, but I'm afraid that my fighting days are over, at least for a while."

"That is most interesting, so that you shouldn't feel too isolated, let me tell you that Fiorella and I are of Jewish descent. Our grandparents were Jewish, our parents converted to Christianity before we were born. We were raised as Catholics. Either way we're Italians for generations and generations. There is however another couple in the hotel. He is from Poland and she, I suspect, is German, although her Italian is absolutely fluent. You would expect that of an architect, a graduate of the University of Bologna. Where are you from in Poland?"

"I'm from the town of Drohobycz near Lvov, some call it Lemberg."

"Let me give them a call to see if they are home."

Gulio spoke with someone in rapid Italian on the phone.

Henryk heard his name and the name of his town mentioned several times."

"She is translating our conversation for her husband." Gulio enlightened Henryk.

"Multo bene, grazia mile. Si, si, subito."

"We invited them over for coffee. They should be here shortly. In the meantime, may I suggest, if you have some free time tomorrow, visit nearby Santa Sabina. It is a gem, a perfect example of fifth century basilica, full of light and space. Across the courtyard from Santa Sabina is a walled garden with a lookout, offering a panorama of the city and its cupolas. The best time to see the cupola of St. Peter's from there is when the sun ends its pink descent over the Mediterranean."

The door chimes announced visitors at the door and Fiorella Romano opened the door for them. A couple walked in. This time Gulio didn't have to introduce those people to Henryk because he knew them too well. It was Fraulein Luise von Spandorf and his fellow countryman "Panczyk" Edek Nadler, Henryk's Cracow benefactors.

CHAPTER 54

This time returning to their unit, Lt. Edward Daszkiewicz was driving and Capt. Michalski was sitting next to him. Corp. Wachtel was comfortable in the back seat.

"So, that was Henryk about whom you've told me so much."

"Yes Captain, he is the brother whom I never had. His folks gave me more warmth then my own parents. Besides we were in the Red Army together, captured by the Germans and together we have survived the O.T. It was much more difficult for him then for me."

"Corp. Wachtel, you're an actual cousin or aren't you, because you seem to be left out."

"Not really Captain, I'm about 4 or 5 years older than Henryk and I've spent most of my life outside the cities of Drohobycz-Boryslaw. We lived in nearby Sambor. The relationship between our families was a bit strained even before Henryk's father's death. Let me explain the reason for it. My mother married Henryk's father's brother. She never got along with her sister-in-law. This was going back some years, when both of them attended a wedding party wearing identical dresses made by the same dressmaker. I know it sounds funny especially in wartime, but that was then. I think it was my own mother who left the party and since that times the women hardly spoke to each other. Personally, I always liked Henryk, but didn't see much of him, since I lived and went to schools in other towns."

Further conversation was interrupted by a tremendous roar, coming from hundreds of American B-17 bombers flying overhead, at the top speed of 287 miles per hours, in a large formation wing tip to wing tip, spread as far as eye could see.

"These flyboys are the envy of the men in the foxholes. Bastards, they always have clean beds and sheet, good hot food and choice of women."

"We aren't doing so bad, Captain. At least when we're being shot at, we can hide, duck, run away or move about. But those guys are stuck in their planes. An enemy .50 caliber machine gun can make Swiss cheese out of the fuselage and wings. I'll take the artillery anytime."

"Alright already. Corporal, did you know that the crews of those bomber consist of officers and sergeants only?"

"How so, Captain."

"When the Air Force learned that the Germans treated sergeants better than privates in P.O.W. Camps, they made every enlisted man who flew over Germany a sergeant."

"That's the reason why I'm still a corporal, Sir."

"Not for long, Wachtel. You'll be getting sergeant's stripes pretty soon."

"Well thank you, Captain. Here we are back at the unit."

The sentry noticing Capt. Michalski's jeep, just waved them through.

"You fellows can go to your tents, I have to report to Maj. Krzemien."

"Very well, Sir."

Capt. Michalski looking for the Major was told, that he was at a briefing and to join him there. Maj. Krzemien was the briefing officer, holding a long pointer in his hand.

"Do come in, Captain and take a seat." He then lifted a piece of cloth that covered a large scale map of Northern Italy. Multicolored flags indicated various units of the Allied Forces and the small black swastikas-the German positions.

"Gentlemen, this is our jump off position for tomorrow's 5.30 A.M. attack. We'll open with everything we've got, operating under conditions of total air superiority. We have also trained our troops, over and over again, on grounds similar to the one we'll be facing tomorrow. I have complete confidence in our men. The other prerequisite of success in such an operation is a quick and efficient staff, to ensure rapid concentration of our forces and their mobility. To the west of us, the British have coordinated their units to our own efforts. Please come up closer to the map and examine your individual positions. I have prepared battle orders for each platoon. Any questions? Ask now, tomorrow might be too late."

While all the present officers came up to the map, Maj. Krzemien called for Capt. Michalski:

"How did the Albin Pietrus affair go?"

"Very satisfactory under the circumstances. The British buried a gallant officer and we a soldier. All bases are covered."

"Excellent, submit a detailed report in duplicate, my eyes only. One more thing, I received a coded message for you, which no one seems to be able to decipher. It goes like this:

'CDZBOJNIKI". Any ideas?"

"Not really, let me check with Lt. Daszkiewicz. He may have a clue."

"Take care of that matter, I'm very busy as you can see. Check with my adjutant, he has further orders and files for you. We have another nasty case. An officer and a non-com stole a truck and deserted our Division. Most likely they are still in Rome. Find them and have them court-martialed. Take you team and get to it by tomorrow. Don't forget to check with headquarters in Rome. They may have additional plans for you, possibly a permanent transfer to Rome and now I've got to get back to my briefing. Dismissed Captain."

"Good luck tomorrow, Sir."

"It will be alright, I feel it in my bones.

Capt. Michalski left the briefing hut looking for Edward. He found him a large, former German bunker serving as a dining hall, eating a bowl of soup.

"Hello again, Captain, would you like to join me for a bowl of soup?"

"Do you know something Edward, I didn't realize till now, how hungry I am, soup sounds just fine."

"Hey soldier! Bring me a bowl of soup, I'm starving."

It wasn't the regular time for a meal, but captains are known to bend rules once in a while.

"Edward, I've received a coded message from Maj. Krzemien. It might be for you, but I can't make head or tails of it. It goes like CDZBOJNIKI. What do you make of it?"

Edward was concentrating on the word just heard and then all of a sudden he started to laugh.

"It is so simple. The first two letters are Czeslawa's and Danuta's initials, letter "Z" stands for the Polish word "with", the word "BOJNIKI" is actually Bujnickis. The total meaning is that they are safe with Bujnickis. God almighty, that is the best news I've had in years. My prayers have been answered."

"I'm very happy for you. Come let me give you a hug. Now you have a goal in your life. In all that excitement I forgot to tell you that we're going back to Rome tomorrow. I have to retrieve our orders from Maj. Krzemien's adjutant. Please inform Wachtel, he is also coming with us. If we wouldn't be so tired, we could have left for Rome today. Because tomorrow morning, all hell will let loose. Our unit is going to attack, but we have to get our asses to Rome. There goes our glory."

"Don't complain, Captain, you'll get to see Marcella Zurlini."

"And you Henryk Kaplinski."

"Fair enough, let's get going. What time do you want to start?"

"If all goes well, we should leave by 8 A.M."

"Yes Sir, 8 A.M. it is."

Exactly at 5.30 .M. on the next morning, every piece of artillery, every mortar and machine gun opened fire. The barrage was unbelievably intense and the continuous engulfing explosions were overwhelming. This "concert" lasted a full hour and a half.

"There shouldn't be a Kraut left alive, after those fireworks, Captain."

"Don't bet on it, Edward. You don't know Krauts as well as I do. I still remember Westerplatte on September 1st, 39, when the German cruiser "Schleswig Holstein" opened fire on us at close range. I would hate to live through something like that once more."

"I feel with you but this time, we are the attackers."

"There is a lull in the fighting, may as well get cracking. Where the hell is Wachtel, it rhymes."

"He is loading up our jeep with supplies and fuel. He should be right back, Captain."

"Very well, Edward, I want you to drive. Last night I just glanced at the orders, I need to read them more closely. Also I have a surprise for our Corp. Wachtel."

"Here he comes, you can give him that surprise once we get on the road."

"Sergeant, are all our supplies in the jeep?"

"Yes Sir, but begging Captain's pardon, with those two stripes I'm still a corporal."

"No longer Wachtel, you're promoted to a sergeant and you're also entitled to wear a white/red ribbon around your stripes. Every non-commissioned officer will have to salute you. How about that Wachtel?"

"Thank you Captain."

"Don't thank me, it was Lt. Daszkiewicz who was after me to get you promoted. Sometimes I think he is one of your boys."

"Who knows, I might be one of them."

"Enough of horsing around. Watch how you drive Edward, let's not land in a ditch. I got to read those frigging orders."

It was quiet in the jeep, while Captain Michalski was getting himself acquainted with the contents of the file.

"What a mess. We have to locate and arrest a couple of deserters. Only God may know where those bastards are now."

"Do you have any photographs of those two?"

"No, just a lousy description. One is tall and thin and the other short and fat. Both have light hair and blue eyes. This will have to do for now. Just keep on driving. I'll try to take a nap. Last night I didn't sleep too well. The new Polish Headquarters are now located at 53 Via del Monte della Farina just behind San Andrea della Valle on Corso Vittorio Emanuelle II. Wake me when we get to Rome. I'll take over the driving."

0468-LEE

"Yes Sir."

Driving back to Rome, became a routine. Edward easily recognized towns and villages on the way to the Eternal City. They stopped once on the road to pour gasoline into the tank and take care of their biological needs, while the Captain slept. Wachtel prepared sandwiches made of Spam and crackers, which they ate as Edward drove.

Not until Edward saw the periphery of Rome did he relinquish the steering wheel back to the Captain.

"I know the City better, Marcella showed me around. I'll find the Headquarters because I must report to Lt. Col. Krzysztof Konopnicki, and old friend of mine since Westerplatte days, to see what assignments he has for us."

A large XVIII century building housed the Polish Headquarters where the heavily armed sentry checked their papers and called in their arrival.

"Col. Konopnicki will see you straight away. Are these men with you, Sir?"

"They are indeed."

"They will have to wait for you, Sir."

"Edward, this shouldn't take too long. Why don't you and Wachtel take a seat in the waiting room."

"Don't worry about us, you just go ahead, Sir."

The "shouldn't take too long" took over two hours.

"What in the world has happened to our captain? Asked Edward worried. The answer to that question was given by a pretty female corporal:

"You must be Lt. Daszkiewicz and sergeant Wachtel. Col. Konopnicki want to see you both in his office, please follow me."

The office was decorated with the ever present Polish flag and two large portraits of Gen. Sikorski and Gen. Anders.

"Lt. Daszkiewicz and Sgt. Wachtel reporting as ordered."

"At ease lieutenant and sergeant." Both Lt. Col. Konopnicki and Capt. Michalski were smoking cigars and being totally relaxed. The time element wasn't an issue at this meeting.

"Your Captain told me much about you two and that raised my curiosity. Besides I like to know the people I work with. Our Second Department is much feared and for good reason. We are a group, small in numbers and every man is very important to the Department. Capt. Michalski highly recommended both of you for future, permanent candidates of our Section. I have some doubts about Sgt. Wachtel. We don't have too many Jews in our Department. On the other hand, we don't have too many Poles with Wachtel's qualifications. I understand that you are also fluent in French and English, since I do speak those languages let's have a chat."

Lt. Col. Konopnicki started to speak French with Wachtel and a few minutes later he gave a big smile and turned to Capt. Michalski:

"This fellow speaks French like a born Parisian. Let's try English now. Please repeat "Betty likes butter better."

"Colonel, why don't we start with a Polish tongue twister: "drabina z powylamowanymi szczeblami."

"Let's stick with English."

The conversation was held in English, a language that Capt. Michalski understood but not too well.

"My Goodness, he can also pass for a Limey. Where did you study, Wachtel?"

"Not in Poland, as a Jew I wasn't admitted to Polish Universities." There was a note of bitterness in his voice.

"I do consider myself a Pole. My religion is or should be my own business. I'm not asking for this assignment. Should it be given to me, I shall discharge my duties as best as I possibly can. So help me God."

"Bravo Wachtel, I'm sure that we'll get along well. You're on 6 months probation."

"It seems Sir, that I'm always on probation."

"Well now Wachtel, mind your tongue. You're talking to a Colonel!" interjected Captain Michalski.

"Begging Colonel's pardon."

"Let's move along. Your team's assignment is to find those two deserters. One way or another you have a week to complete this assignment. We have other much more important things to worry about. Starting tomorrow, for your assignment, you'll wear civilian clothing. We have a warehouse full of captured men's suites and accessories. If you're missing anything, buy it even on the black market. Money is and isn't an issue, but I need a receipt for every zloty, pound, lira or dollar spent. Is that clear gentlemen?"

"Yes Sir, crystal clear."

"Your Captain has additional instructions regarding your assignment and housing. I'll ring for the Quartermaster, he'll issue anything you may need, including your choice of weapons. Good luck and good hunting. Capt. Michalski just one more minute. Lt. Daszkiewicz and Sgt. Wachtel you may leave now."

As they both left the colonel's office, they could hear his words:

"Give a Jew a finger and he grabs the whole hand. You better watch him, Michalski and keep me informed about your current project."

"Yes Sir, we'll do our utmost."

"I'm sure you will."

A short and portly sergeant-quartermaster joined Capt. Michalski's team:

"Please follow me to the warehouse. You may take anything that you need but I'm obliged to write everything down."

"So you should sergeant."

The warehouse was located in the adjacent building. In one of the large rooms, they found an assortment of men's suits jackets, pants, shoe and ties hanging on rack and laying on shelves. Going through that melange of clothing, they slowly picked the needed wardrobe in the right sizes. Most of the labels were in German, Italian and French origin. Capt. Michalski and Wachtel were the first to complete their garb. Edward after many years of wearing uniforms felt very strange in mufti, without the uniform, he was naked.

"Sirs, I'll have those things delivered to your rooms within an hour or two. I'll put them in valises in case you have to move from place to place."

"Good thinking, sergeant. Our rooms are 116, 117 and 218 at 55 Via del Monte della Farina. It's across the street."

"Well, we had enough excitement for one day. Let's hit the sack. See you all at breakfast and we'll discuss our next step."

"Fair enough, Sir."

Wachtel brought up the supplies and gears from the jeep to the respective rooms. By the time he finished with the task on hand, the sergeant-quartermaster delivered valises filled with the chosen items of clothing.

"Well tomorrow we'll be civilians for a change, hopefully a pleasant and a permanent change."

"Don't count on it, Sergeant."

Next morning three civilians showed up in the dining room, raising some brows. Being addressed as lieutenants and captains, the curious were quickly appeased. The new team like a chameleon adjusted to the new situation.

"Well fellows, any ideas where and how to start this investigation?"

"Do I call you Captain or Mr. Michalski?"

"You call me captain until I'll tell you otherwise. What did you have in mind?'

"Why don't we pay a visit to Henryk's landlord Mr. Romano. He surely knows Rome and its people. He may give us some leads or points. We may stop to see the British Military Police or their Authorities."

"May as well, let's see Henryk and Romano. We can always touch basis with the British later in the day. I would like to succeed without the British's help. They don't have to know about our problem with deserters."

After the breakfast, consisting of omelets made from powdered eggs and hot tea, they drove to Henryk's resident at Hotel Sant' Anselmo. The hotel's concierge told them that Henryk was in his room. A creaking lift took them to the third floor.

Henryk warned by the concierge opened the door for them and asked them in. There was another couple with him. They were introduced as Mr. Nadler of Boryslaw and his wife Luise.

"What brought you here so early in the morning and why are you all dressed in civilians?'

"We're looking for two deserters who stole an Army 2.5 ton G.M. truck."

"Were they a tall guy and a short one, looking almost like those two comedians Pat and Patachon, light hair and blue eyes?"

"How in the world would you know about them, Mr. Adler?"

"They offered me a truck for sale, which I needed for my growing business. I knew from the start that the truck was "hot". What I didn't know how "hot". Look here, this is Rome where people are trying to stay alive by hook or crook, if one can make a dollar, so much the better. After I gave them the agreed amount of money, they took their guns out and robbed me, plain and simple. They took everything including my gold Omega wristwatch, a present from my wife Luise. Can you imagine me being robbed like an amateur? Me "Panczyk" from Boryslaw? Wait till I get hold of them. They will see what a Boryslawer "Malach" can do."

"If you'll help we'll catch them. Whatever you do with them is OK with us, as long as they are alive for the court martial. Who knows, we may get a medal for rescuing them from the hands of black marketers."

"A deal is a deal, you are on."

CHAPTER 55

On X-mas Eve of 1944 the Germans launched their biggest aerial effort of the entire campaign in Northwest Europe, followed by a New Year's day air raid of 600 planes hitting British airfields at Eidhoven and Brussels, destroying 180 or more parked planes.

This was very discouraging because the U.S. Air Force had been after Luftwaffe's fuel supplies and airplane factories and now there were more enemy planes than before.

The intelligence reports reaching Maj. Krafchin's desk, spoke of German insufficient training time to become competent pilots and later what good were the new ME-262 twin-engine and ME-163 single engine fighters, when there was no fuel for them?

Paul also shares his C.O.'s view that was contrary to the opinion held by most of the staff officers, that Germany had lost the war. It was merely a question of tying up the loose ends.

Unknown to Paul, Gen. Carl Spaatz commanding the "Mighty Eight" Air Force, had given jet production priority among his German targets, second only to oil.

The German General Staff might have been stripped of its strategic and tactical prerogatives but it still maintained a skill in logistics that bordered on the miraculous.

By the beginning of 1945 most of the Air Force was stationed in France, but Paul remained in England "shifting papers from place to place" as he used to describe his activities. It wasn't quite true. Some of his ideas were helpful in keeping the B-17 and B-24 flying over targets in Germany even in bad weather, a technique first adopted by Germans for night bombing of London and improved by Americans. The planes would follow the radio beam of the lead an especially built B-24, to its target. That procedure accounted for fairly accurate bombings.

The German spearheads on the ground were under constant attack from the air and they were receiving no supplies. The Luftwaffe was now outnumbered and outfought. The German Panzers unable to maneuver because of the lack of fuel were abandoned by their crews, trudging morosely through the snow toward Germany.

That in itself was proof to Paul, that ideas and plans were only good intentions, unless followed by hard work and persistence.

His "London period" was a combination of very hard work and hard play. His every free moment was spent with Cynthia. He was drawn to her like a moth to fire and she in turn, would say, that she was attracted to him like an iron to magnet. They both fully realized that with the passage of time, their mutual attraction was inescapably interwoven.

Often, he would pick her up at the SHAEF's Headquarters, either for lunch or dinner. They reached a point in their relationship, Cynthia described as precipice. Sooner or later they would have to take a jump.

"When in the world are you going to make a dishonest woman out of me, Paul?"

"I would much more prefer to make an honest one by marrying you."

"Are you asking me to marry you, right in the middle of war?"

"Do you know a better time than the present?"

"It is a crazy idea, Paul but I like it. Let me think about it for a while. You caught me unaware. I do know that I love you. Like I've never loved anybody before, I feel good and secure in your arms. It is possible to spend an entire life with someone and still not know that person. With you it's different. I feel like I have known you for centuries. Does that make any sense to you?"

"As a matter of fact it does. Those are exactly my thoughts. In our case it's a combination of mutual chemistry and the Yiddish "bashert" – predestined. I don't have another explanation for it, whether intelligent or not, logical or illogical. All I know is that I want to marry you and share my life with you and what's more, I'm going about it starting with asking your parents consent and arranging for a religious ceremony before I take you to bed. I'll also have to get the Air Force's permission, which may take a while. So how do you like "them apples"?"

"I do like "them apples", especially your old fashioned Jewish approach to marriage. It is really funny in a way, because we Jews try to be like anybody else but at the same time we want to be different. Who knows, maybe we are different. Paul you always had my consent from the first time we met. If you want to speak with my parents, they will be delighted to see you this coming Sunday. Coincidentally there will be also our mutual friend, Chaplain Rifkind and other Chaplains of the Allied Armies. It should be very interesting. Can you make it?"

"Just try to stop me, you naughty child."

"Are you really going to ask my father for my hand?"

"Since he is a historian, I'm going to ask him for the origins of the Peloponnesian War; you silly goose. Of course I'm going to ask him for your hand, for both of them as well."

"Paul, I simply love you." With these words she left the table.

Paul sat for a while, watching the noon time crowd of people pass by. He felt good about his decision to marry Cynthia. He'll have to notify his mother, whose main concern always was, that he should marry a Jewish girl. He felt like saying to her: "Mom, with a name like Epstein, could she be Irish?" He started to laugh, sure that the people around him would say: "Another shell shocked Yank."

Back at his desk, Paul had the confidence in his opinions, the ease of expression, the range of knowledge about specific Air Force issues, and above all, the accuracy of his predictions, that was the envy of Gen. Gary the "Hotshot's" team. As his own rule, Paul discharged his duties fully, promptly and with enthusiasm, rather than using the "pass the buck" method. That attitude was appreciated by his C.O. Gen. Gary, who would often stop by Paul's desk and indirectly, ask about Paul's advice on variety of subjects.

"Don't get up Paul, I was just passing by. Have a little present for you."

"General today is not my birthday, what did I do to deserve it?"

"You didn't do anything, so is the present, almost nothing."

The General gave Paul a silver Zippo cigarette lighter, with the Air Force emblem engrave on both sides.

"It's beautiful General, I thank you very much."

"So, how is the Brooklyn kid doing?"

"Just fine, Sir. Have only one small problem, I want to get married Sir."

"Don't tell me, it's that Jewish broad we met in the pub?"

"The very same, Sir."

"Don't you know, son, there is a war out there? With so many women around, why in the world would you want to tie yourself down?"

"General, I just love her."

"Boy, you are serious, aren't you?"

"I'm losing more men to the British ladies than to the Luftwaffe. Paul, all kidding aside, this is a very complicated procedure. Is she pregnant?"

"No Sir. I didn't even sleep with her."

"Now I know for sure that you my boy are crazy all together. Are you sure that you're Jewish? Someone told me that Jews are smart. Maybe they are, but not this Brooklyn kid. Paul think about it for a month, if you still want to get hitched after that, I'll help you. Fair enough?'

"Yes Sir!"

"Wipe that silly smile off your face, Major."

"Yes Sir."

A few urgent matters at the Headquarters kept Paul busy that Sunday. By the time he arrived at the Epsteins residence, their living room was full of officers wearing different uniforms of the Allied Forces.

Mrs. Epstein noticing Paul at the door quickly ran up to him, kissing him on both cheeks.

"Welcome Paul. Cynthia has told us the good news. Our answer is an emphatic YES. Come, let me introduce you to our guests"

She started however with her husband:

"You do know your future father-in-law. Right next to him is Maj. I. Levy, Chief Rabbi of the British Army. Next is Chaplain of the Royal Air Force, Maj. Brodie. By the way Maj. Brodie has seen lots of action in Tobruk."

"How do you so, Sir."

"Come, come Paul, there are more people I want you to meet. This is Capt. Dr. Eszkoli a former Philology Professor at Sorbonne, I believe he is originally from Lodz in Poland."

"That is quite right, Mrs. Epstein. Pleasure Major Krafchin."

"You're not finished Paul, come and meet Capt. Hickman, Jewish Chaplain of the South African Army, sitting next to him is the Chief Rabbi of Egypt, J.E. Haim Nachum Effendi, advisor to the kings."

"It is an honor, gentlemen."

"Just two more, Paul and after that I'll let you see Cynthia. Here they are: your old friend Rabbi Jerome Rifkind and Major Steinberg of the Polish Army. I think he is from Lvov, am I right?"

"You're right Mrs. Epstein."

"Is that near Buczacz?"

"Yes Major Krafchin. I had relatives in Buczacz by the name similar to yours, spelled K-r-a-w-c-z-y-n. My cousin was Izak, who migrated to the States many years ago."

"Major Steinberg, you are looking at his son. I have seen my father's birth certificate and that is how he used to spell his name, the Polish way."

It was Mrs. Epstein who took over the conversation: "Gentlemen, a miracle has happened. Rabbi Steinberg just met his cousin's son, Maj. Paul Krafchin. What a coincidence!"

"Mazel Tov, Mazel Tov." Everybody came over to shake their hands.

Maj. Steinberg spoke a clear, if halting English, here and there getting stuck on the pronunciation of some words, soliciting help from Rabbi Rifkind in Yiddish. He wanted to know about Paul's family and was sorry to hear about the death of Paul's father Isaac.

"What brought you here Major, to the Epsteins home? You're not a member of the clergy, as I can see from you uniform."

"I came here to marry their daughter, Cynthia."

"With so many rabbis assembled in this room that shouldn't be a problem."

"Paul what do I hear, you want to marry Cynthia but when?" asked Rabbi Rifkind.

"How about right now?"

"You're not serious Paul, you're both in the Service. You must obtain permission to marry a foreign national, British or otherwise. There is a lot of red tape involved."

"I'm aware of that, but can't we get the religious ceremony done in the meantime, right here and right now?"

"I imagine it can be done. Let's ask first of all Cynthia if she is ready and the Epsteins. The whole thing is highly irregular to say the least."

Cynthia's answer was: "Paul you are crazy, what you Yanks call "loco", my hair isn't done and the dress is much to be desired. But what the heck, let's do it."

The Epsteins reaction was basically the same: "The kids want to get married, so be it. Rabbi Rifkind, since you are the U.S. Air Force Chaplain, will you please officiate."

"I'll be honored. We need a "Chuppah" or a small table cloth, to serve as a canopy, a cup of wine to make a blessing, a glass to be broken, a "talit" for Paul, which I'm sure we'll find in this house, a shawl for Cynthia and of course a plain gold ring."

Paul felt like kicking himself. He didn't have a ring, gold or otherwise, I'm a jackass.

"Paul, why don't you use my ring in the meantime, it should fit Cynthia's finger nicely."

Mrs. Epstein came once more to the rescue.

As Jewish marriages go, it was the most unusual wartime wedding yet. The canopy was held up by four swagger sticks of Chaplains of the Allied Armies. The ceremony was performed both in English and Hebrew, Rabbi Rifkind's words sounded clear as a bell:

"Do you Paul, take Cynthia as your lawful wedded wife?

Are you Cynthia taking Paul of your own free will?

. . . . as long as you should live?

What therefore God hath joined together, let no man put asunder.

The tradition requires of you Cynthia that you walk around Paul seven times held by your parents and that you should drink from the same cup. Amid happiness we do remember also the destruction of our Temple by crashing a glass object. Paul....."

Paul stepped on the towel wrapped glass. The ceremony was over. "Mazel Tov! Mazel Tov! Good Luck, Good Luck!"

Mr. Epstein brought out a vintage bottle of French Champagne. "I kept it with the intention of opening it on the day of final victory. Today is a special occasion."

Mrs. Epstein brought out of the kitchen several trays of small sandwiches and canapés.

"Sorry friends, I wasn't prepared for Paul's version of Blitzkrieg. We'll do it much better after the war. Everyone present is invited."

While everybody was munching on the food, Rabbi Steinberg was busy writing something. After he finished he went to each Chaplain in the room and asked for his signature.

"Cynthia, this is your "ktubah" a marriage contract, signed by seven rabbis of the Allied Forces. The Jewish law requires that the "ktubah" is kept by the wife. Again, our heartiest congratulations to Major and Mrs. Paul Krafchin."

Rabbi Rifkind addressed the present people:

"We are very happy for the young couple and our host and hostess, but as you know we came here to discuss ways and means of helping our Jewish brethren in Europe and elsewhere. If I may paraphrase Oscar Wilde's words "How narrow, and mean, and inadequate to its burden is this century of our." We are receiving at alarming rate, catastrophic news about the fate of European Jewry. The worst possible news have been confirmed by Capt. Rabbi Steinberg of the Polish Army-West. Poland as you very well know, had the largest concentration of Jews, close to 3.500.000 souls, unfortunately that is no longer true.

Judging by the progress made by the Allied Expeditionary Forces from the west and the speed of the Red Army coming from the east most of the military experts, estimated that the war should end within 3-6 months. The Allied world will celebrate its richly deserved victory and we Jews will have to face the greatest tragedy that has befallen our people, since the days of Babylon.

The question I'm putting in front of you is what are we going to do about it? And what are we going to do with the remnants of our people? Where are we going to put them? Can you tell me where and how?"

A very long silence took over the Epstein's house.

CHAPTER 56

For Henryk, Italy in general and Rome in particular became a place of many surprises. The unexpected meetings with Edward Daszkiewicz, his own cousin Eljasz Wachtel and his Cracow's guarding angel – "Panczyk" Adler, would change the course of his life. Of that he was sure, and so when Capt. Michalski and Edward came to his room at the Hotel Sant' Anselmo, his first question was: "Where is Eljasz Wachtel?"

"He is just fine. Col. Konopnicki transferred Eljasz to his own staff as a permanent interpreter."

"Why are you all in civilian cloth? Did the war end and nobody bothered to tell me?"

"We are on a special assignment to apprehend a couple of deserters and thieves by the name of Piotr Trzeciak, and officer no less, and a sergeant Bazyli Kaczor. Those characters also robbed your "Panczyk". We believe that those two are still in Rome. We got to catch them. "Panczyk" volunteered to help, he wants to settle his own score with them but where is he? He was supposed to be here at this hour."

Someone knocked at the door. "That is most likely your "Panczyk"."

"Good morning, gentlemen, are we ready to go hunting?"

"Yes, we are just about ready. Henryk, do you want to come along? You'll have a chance to see Rome?"

"I've nothing better to do, may as well come along."

"Remember, Henryk, those two "desperados" are armed and considered dangerous. Don't get involved. I would also like to ask our friend "Panczyk" to stay on the sidelines and let us do our job. Trzeciak and Kaczor are deserters and they must be apprehended by Polish Authorities. We have the legal right in this matter. Is that clear? We are going to start our search by visiting known hang-outs of black marketers and other shady characters. Our "modus operandi" will be as follows: I'll walk ahead with "Panczyk" and you two will back us up. I'm sure that Edward and I should be able to deal with them. Our jeep is downstairs, we'll drive as close as possible and walk the rest of the way. Driving to close may be counterproductive. Are we ready? Let's go to it."

Capt. Michalski drove the jeep towards the muddy, swollen waters of Tiber River. It rained the other day and when it rains in Rome, it pours. From there he drove near Circus Maximus and steep climb up its southern embankment, already halfway up the Aventine, close enough to Santa Sabina, Sant' Alessio and Sant' Anselmo, the three churches that crown the hill.

"Henryk, could you please stay with the jeep and "Panczyk" and I will walk ahead with Edward, following us some 20 paces behind. We want to check a few blocks."

"No problem Captain, I'll be waiting for you right here."

Henryk was watching this odd couple of Michalski and "Panczyk", totally different backgrounds and religions, but as their temperaments and outlook on life was concerned, they might have been identical twins. They understood each other by exchanging glances.

An hour later and disappointed they came back with empty hands.

"Let's move to Piazza Navona."

Here again, Henryk was left guarding the jeep while the investigative "trio" went to check out another potential hideout. The jeep became a curiosity center for a bunch of street kids. They asked for gum and cigarettes. He had on him a package of gum and a pack of cigarettes given to him by Edward, just this morning. Once he distributed them among the kids they lost interest and left him alone to admire the beauty of Piazza Navona a block away.

This time Michalski's team was luckier, someone did recognize the pictures of Trzeciak and Kaczor.

"I'm their brother-in-law, we were separated by the Germans and now I'm trying to find them, do you know where they could be?"

"They hang out usually around Piazza Di Spagna, mostly in the evening, when the girls come out. Sorry I don't know where they live, but you could locate them there or near the Spanish Steps."

"Thank you, you have been most helpful, Signore."

"We have several hours of waiting ahead of us, I'm hungry and am pretty sure that you all are too. Not far away from here, on Vicolo Montevecchio is a cozy pizzeria with wooden beams and tables, where pies are made with the typically thin Roman crust in a wood burning oven. Henryk, you'll love it it's so delicious."

"I never ate pizza in my life."

"You'll love it, I promise."

Wartime or no wartime, it was amazing to see how fast one could get results if one was willing to pay for it.

"Capt. Michalski was absolutely right, the pizza had a taste of heaven, but whatever the reason, the pizza only sharpened the appetite of the four young and healthy men. Michalski gave the waiter a British pound and asked for the classic Roman meal of pasta all'amatriciana. Told to wait, they waited impatiently till the dish of pasta, ham, tomatoes, tripe and lamb was prepared. The meal was well worth the wait.

"This is the kind of meal, that should be only served people sentenced to death."

"Do you have anybody particular in mind, Mietek?" asked "Panczyk" already on first name basis with Capt. Michalski.

"Not really, just generally speaking, it could be anybody. In the meantime, let's plan an ambush. You Henryk, please continue guarding the jeep, left unattended, the street urchins will steal every part, including the tires. Here are the jeep's papers, should anyone question you. We'll proceed in similar pattern. "Panczyk" and I will be circling the area around the Spanish Steps and the nearby fountain. Edward will walk toward us coming from the opposite direction. Whoever will spot those bastards first, will alert the rest of us, by combing his hair and slowly approaching them. Since they don't know our faces with the exception of "Panczyk" with whom they already had dealings, this plan may work out. We have with us handcuffs and pistols in case they should offer resistance. The most important is that they should show up, otherwise we would have to come back here again and again. Edward check your pistol. Are we all ready? Then let's go to it."

They left, walking apart towards the direction of Spanish Steps. It was an early dusk, the day was fighting a loosing battle with the night. Henryk felt a chill in the air. Noticing a folded, green woolen blanket that Capt. Michalski was using for back support, while driving, Henryk unfolded the blanket, wrapping himself in it, since he knew that he would have to spend considerable time guarding the jeep. He felt much warmer now. Having given away his own cigarettes at the previous stop, he took out of the glove compartment cigarettes belonging to Edward. He lit one, attracting the attention of a lady of the evening. Addressed in English and not being able to answer, he used German. It seems to Henryk, that the "lady" spoke a better and more fluent German than English. He could only admire the speed of acquiring a new language by members of the world's oldest profession.

"That's right. I speak a better German than English, had more time to learn it. While you "asnos" are killing each other, we have to feed our families and our children, "capisco?"

His answer was interrupted by three pistol shots coming from the general area of the Spanish Steps. Henryk threw the blanket back into the jeep and ran towards the Piazza Di Spagna.

A big commotion was caused by Edward holding a pistol against the chest of Sub-lieutenant Trzeciak. At Edward's feet were, shot through the chest, not stirring the body of Sgt. Kaczor and profusely bleeding body of Capt. Michalski with a quite visible knife, protruding from his left side.

Kneeling by the Captain was "Panczyk" trying desperately to

stop the flow of blood, using a handkerchief.

"Panczyk" what in the world has happened?"

"A few minutes after we left you, I encountered Trzeciak. We recognized each other at once. I pointed him out to Michalski, who tried to pull out his gun when Kaczor stuck a knife into him. Edward came to our rescue, he had his gun already in his hand. He shot a warning but Kaczor didn't stop. The second shot killed him. It was then when Trzeciak pulled his pistol but Edward was faster. His next shot wounded Trzeciak slightly in the leg. Seeing his own blood he raised his hands. Edward took away his gun and is holding him right now. Come get me something else to stop the blood."

A British Military Police staff car with an Italian "Carrabinieri" and siren blazing pulled in front of Edward, who identified himself as a Polish Army undercover officer on a mission of apprehending army deserters.

"Let's rush this wounded bloke to the hospital. You lieutenant and this man" pointing to "Panczyk" come with us.

"This man is not involved in this case. He is just a good Samaritan helping a wounded man, we don't need him. Let me just thank him for his help."

"Very well then, let him go."

Edward turned to "Panczyk" and said quietly in Polish "You and Henryk please bring the jeep back to the Headquarters. Wachtel will know what to do. I'll be in touch."

Two British M.P.'s were applying first aid to Capt. Michalski while the third called for back up.

"Mietek, for Christ sake, hold on, help is on the way. Please hold on." Michalski barely was able to shake his head. His face was becoming rapidly paler."

"Hospital, hospital, let's go to the hospital" begged Edward.

Michalski was gently put into the staff car. One of the Brits had to go with the newly summoned jeep into which they put handcuffed Trzeciak and the blanket wrapped dead body of Sgt. Kaczor. The British M.P. sergeant informed Edward, that the British will hold the prisoner in their custody, till claimed by the Polish Authorities.

Edward's main concern now, was to get Michalski to the hospital, as soon as possible. Guided by the "Carrabinieri" they drove to a small hospital on Via Nazionale near Piazza Venezia. Curiously, it was run by nuns and supervised by British Military personnel.

Capt. Michalski was taken on a stretcher straight to an operating room and Edward was asked to wait outside. He put a frantic call to Lt. Col. Konopnicki, briefly describing what had transpired in the last few hours.

"Stay with him and don't move any place. I'll be right over."

Edward was beyond himself with anger but he had to await the colonel's orders and probably an inquiry.

Lt. Col. Konopnicki arrived with a couple of armed M.P.'s and a doctor, wearing a whit coat over his captain's uniform. The doctor joined the British and Italian colleagues in the operating room while the M.P.'s went to claim the prisoner and the dead body of Kaczor. They were both now in Polish custody.

Both Konopnicki and Edward were pacing the floor of the waiting room nervously, chain smoking cigarettes. Edward repeated several times the botched up ambush.

"I understand, we can't win every skirmish, it happens. I'll need a detailed report in triplicate. Should anything happen to Michalski, I'll hang that son of a bitch myself."

Having said that they both became silent.

Finally after waiting, what seemed like ages, two doctor's came out, one Polish and one British.

"We lost him, Colonel. We tried everything. So sorry, Colonel."

CHAPTER 57

Even after spending several quiet and trouble free weeks at Bujnickis home in Zakopane, Czeslawa seldom ventured outside the house. Her own excuse was that she had to take care of Malgorzata and Cyprian Bujnicki, her adoptive parents. That was true enough, but fact was also that she acquired a real fear of German uniforms and of the "Granatowa" Polish Police, who worked for the Germans.

Czeslawa began relying more and more on Danuta, who like all teenagers knew no, fear. To augment their income, Czeslawa again started to paint and paint better than she has done in the past. Each finished painting Danuta would bring to the "Haus der Zakopaner Kunst" on Hauptstrasse. Herr Horst Fischer, proprietor of the store gladly accepted the improved Czeslawa's work because his inventory of Czeslawa's painting was depleted during her involuntary absence.

"Tell your mother to come to see me, I would like to speak with her."

"I'll tell her. She is busy taking care of my grandparents, Herr Fischer."

"Tell her to come as soon as possible. I've something very important to discuss with her."

"Thank you Herr Fischer, I'll tell her."

Danuta rushed home to tell her mother about Herr Fischer's strange request.

"I'll stop by tomorrow to see him. I wonder what he has on his mind?" Czeslawa worried because the only derived income was coming from Fischer's store.

The very next day, Czeslawa forced herself to get dressed and leave the house for the "Haus der Zakopaner Kunst." She was scared to walk the streets of Zakopane and what Herr Fischer may say to her. She certainly wasn't ready for surprises at this time.

Herr Fischer politely asked her to follow him to the back of his store, where he kept a small desk, offering her a chair which he never did before.

"Please sit down Pani Daszkiewicz." This was Czeslawa's second surprise, because Herr Fischer addressed her in perfect Polish. Not able to curb her curiosity, she asked him:

"Herr Fischer, how come you speak Polish so well?"

"Mrs. Daszkiewicz, I am a German, born and raised in the Polish City of Poznan. I lived among Poles and went to Polish schools. Does that answer your question?"

"It certainly does."

"Well, let me continue then. How was I to you in all our previous commercial transactions, Mrs. Daszkiewicz?"

"You were always correct and above approach. You have always kept your word."

"Well. I'm glad to hear it because I have a business proposition for you. I need someone to run the store while I'll be away. Someone who knows art and the German language."

"Where are you going Herr Fischer?" she kept calling him "Herr".

"Das Reich" wants me, despite my 60 years and severe diabetes. I gave "Der Fuhrer" my only son already. My wife Else, as you already know is wheelchair bound and since our son's disappearance, in deep depression. I was given two weeks to straighten my affairs prior to my induction. I'll just have enough time to show you around the store. You'll be my 50% partner. Do we have a deal, Mrs. Daszkiewicz?"

"Herr Fischer, I'm grateful to you that you've thought about me, but your offer caught me totally off guard. I need to think about it and speak with my family. I'll let you know within 24 hours."

"This is all I can give you, just 24 hours. Think about it, Mrs.

Daszkiewicz, it is a good store. The Jew, who had it before me, became rich in that store and left for America. If I don't come back it will be yours anyway? So what do you say?"

"You'll have my answer in 24 hours, Herr Fischer."

Deep in her thoughts with the unexpected turn of events she came home, but the day of surprises didn't end with Fischer's offer. At home, when she opened the door, she found in addition to Bujnickis, her smiling daughter sitting on the lap of Alina Dziedzic and next to her was a strange man, whom Alina introduced as Wincenty Dobrowolski.

"I'm glad to see you Mrs. Dziedzic, what brought you here?'

"Only good reasons. I came to check upon you and Danuta, to see how you both manage. After all I had something to do with bringing you here and also I wanted to bring you regards from your husband Edward. He is a lieutenant and doing very well according to his C.O. Capt. Michalski."

"We are all grateful to you. Can I speak freely?" She asked looking at Dobrowolski.

"Yes of course, Mr. Dobrowolski is with "Zegota" a Polish organization that helps the Jewish people."

"I'm not Jewish, I was only accused of being Jewish."

"We know that. Mr. Dobrowolski thought that in view of your recent experience, you might be willing to help."

"I feel very sorry for them. I don't know any Jews." She put her arms protectively over Danuta. "Maybe later but not now. I've got an offer from Herr Fischer to take over his store and don't know what to do?"

"Is that the "Haus der Zakopaner Kunst" on Haupstrrasse?"

"The very same."

"Unquestionably you should take it. It is very important to our organization to have someone who can have a good look at what is going on in the heart of Zakopane. Don't worry Czeslawa, we'll help you. You can trust us. The end of the war can't be far off. The Russians are striking with blitzkrieg speed that pales Germany's lightning marches through our land in 39 and France in 1940. It is payback time, Czeslawa. I'll be in touch. Mrs. Bujnicki, thanks for the tea and bread."

The next morning, Czeslawa went to see Herr Fischer, telling him that she accepts his offer.

"Very well, when can you start?"

"How about right now."

Herr Horst Fischer started to show her everything about the store, the stock, the art of displaying the merchandise properly, how to put the more expensive merchandise on eye level, bookkeeping and the polite way of waiting on a customer.

Danuta started also to work at the store, first by being a "schick Junge" an errand boy, progressing within a few weeks to a "stock boy". With Herr Fischer gone to defend his fatherland she was a big help.

On January 18th, 1945 Russian and Polish troops captured devastated Warsaw. Shoulder to shoulder, three crack Soviet Armies were driving westward across Poland along a twisting 450 miles front. They headed straight for Germany and were 260-288 miles from Berlin.

Nothing could stop the Soviet steamroller. In quick succession Lodz, Czestochowa and Cracow were liberated. German troops were retreating hastily towards the borders of the Reich. Berlin reports indicated that the Nazis might be pulling out of Poland entirely, writing off their 1939 conquest of the country.

More than 2,000,000 Soviet soldiers were committed to the huge offensive and Moscow dispatches said that, savagery unparalleled in four winters of war, raged on the Eastern Front as the Russians tore gaps in the German lines and split and re-split enemy groups falling back toward the Oder River-the Rhine of the East.

Zakopane a small, not of strategic value, town, not on the way of major army units, was liberated without much fanfare. The first victory-flushed Russian troops to enter Zakopane was a squad of six horsemen with their red-star adorned caps "unshankas" flapping in the air and their P.P.Sh. automatics on ready. Two of those riders, descendants of Ghengis Khan rode horses like an extension of the horses themselves must have whispered to them in Russian "davay na Berlin" let's go to Berlin. Riding through the main street the former Hauptstrasse they did notice a large red-white Polish flag flying over a new sign of "Dom Zakopianskiej Sztuki" that covered the old "Haus der Zakopaner Kunst". The more "gramotny" educated Russian sergeant remarked: "tam zhyvoot Paliaki" Poles live there. And thus the German nightmare ended for citizens of Zakopane.

CHAPTER 58

Ordered by his C.O. into being the "administrative type", Major Paul Krafchin was a "true believer" in air power, since becoming a pilot, at a relatively young age and spending his formative years acquiring top-notch flying skills in an Air Force squadron.

Even though sitting now behind a desk, he clearly understood problem that pilots, ground crews and other combat-support troops encountered. He was also fully aware that on average 5.000 American soldiers and airmen per day, entered the Continent.

Those young, patriotic Americans so eager to fight the Heinies, had to be taken care of and nobody did it better than the "Mighty Eights".

Many times, Paul was struck by the scale, scope and the very intensity of the war. Some of his unsolicited recommendations presented to his C.O. Gen. Gary Cottshot were remarkable for its broad and comprehensive approach to air power. The C.O., much to his credit, forwarded Paul's ideas to the General Staff. Unknown to Paul, serious considerations were given to Paul's doctrine of strategic bombing combined with the concept of conducting joint operations with the ground forces. His further suggestions of enlarging paratroop forces, capable of seizing and holding vital objectives behind the enemy lines and creation of a large air transport units, equipped with a mobile logistics system for keeping his own units well supplied, was well received and acted upon.

There was no doubt in Paul's mind that the American Air Force would emerge as the most combat-effective air force in the world. He also believed that the Luftwaffe failed to produce enough aircraft and above all, the right kind of aircraft. The ME-163,

ME-262 and the Arado 234 jet bomber just coming into production couldn't change the tide of the war anymore. It was too late.

Engrossed in his work he heard the loudest scream ever of "ATTENTION!!" by a member of his staff, Airman First Class Vinnie Caputo. This couldn't be Gen. Gary who very often would come to Paul's office leaving a standard order of "As you were" rather than has the staff jump up each time he passed by. Obviously someone else came in.

Paul got up from his chair and turned around to see a red haired, freckled-faced "Tooey" four-star USAAF General Carl Andrew Spaatz, surrounded by his ADC's and Gen. Gary Cottshot.

Paul stood at attention.

"You can close your mouth now, Major. I didn't bring any candies with me."

"Sorry Sir." Paul didn't realize that his mouth was open. It wasn't everyday that he spoke with a four-star general.

"So you are Major Krafchin. I've read some of your recommendations. Not bad, not bad at all. They do make a lot of sense to my people. How would you like to be transferred to my staff with a rank of lieutenant colonel? I'm sure that Gen. Cottshot wouldn't object."

"I don't know what to say, General."

"Yes, will suffice. I'll take care of the paperwork, Krafchin."

"Thank you, Sir." This Gen. Spaatz probably didn't hear because he left the room with his entourage, leaving Paul totally dumfounded. Where could that offer or rather order lead to?

As fate would have it, the transfer papers came in, but as Paul found out later, the papers weren't for him but for Gen. Spaatz who was sent to Guam on March 11, 1945. Paul was contented to stay at his post.

He never told Cynthia how close he came to be shipped half way around the world. Surprisingly enough, the promotion to lieutenant colonel that Gen. Spaatz spoke of came through on a very fateful day of Friday, 13th, 1945. The day that the President of United States, Franklin Delano Roosevelt suddenly died at Warm

Springs, GA at the age of 63, on the eve of his greatest military and diplomatic successes-the impending fall of Berlin.

If there was rejoicing in the Reich's Chancellery it was short lived, because a few days later, 845 German Planes were destroyed by allied fighters in a cataclysmic blow against Nazi Air Force. The Luftwaffe had been knocked out for good. The victory was in the air.

The news was all good. The U.S. First Army infantrymen and Soviet troops met on a broken bridge over the river at Tergau. The Russians were flying a red flag over the Reichstag.

The next day brought the news that the entire free world waited for so long: Hamburg radio announced the death of Adolf Hitler. The very best news came on May 8th: the war finally ended. Surrender was unconditional.

In London, what seemed like millions of people reacted in two sharply contrasting ways to the news of surrender of the German Armies. A large and noisy majority greeted it with the turbulent enthusiasm, especially the servicemen and servicewomen. The minority responded with quiet thanksgiving prayers at local houses of worship.

Paul tried unsuccessfully to reach Cynthia, was caught up in a wild, jubilant celebration of kissing, crying and laughing through tears and crowds. It was hopeless, he just couldn't get through the thick crowds. Coming back to his office, he found an impromptu party going full blast.

"Where the fuck have you been, Paul? Come have a drink with me."

"With greatest of pleasure, General."

"Paul, I just figures out that the fucken war lasted five long years, eight months and fucken six days. Can you imagine the balls of that fucken Heinie General Jodl, asking for mercy towards the German people and armed forces? I didn't think those bastards knew the meaning of the word "mercy"?"

"I guess not."

"The war is not entirely over for us Paul. We still have to fight those yellow-bellied Japs. Do you want to come with me to the Pacific?"

"If it is all the same to you General, I would prefer to stay right here."

"And what? Marry that Jewish broad?"

"The very same, Sir."

"Do you know something, Paul? I'll let you stay here. It is going to be my wedding present to both of you."

"Much obliged, Sir."

"Just name you're first born after me."

"Consider it done, General."

CHAPTER 59

Lt. Col. Konopnicki presided over convened court inquiry into the death of Capt. Michalski, putting the full blame on Lt. Daszkiewicz and his Jewish cohorts. What infuriated Konopnicki even more, was the fact that Lt. Daszkiewicz chose as his defending attorney, Sgt. Eljasz Wachtel.

The other two Military prosecutors assigned to this case, were Lts. Andrzej Pawlikowski and Zdzislaw Krasicki. Both were manipulated and influenced by high ranking and much older Lt. Col. Konopnicki.

After the charges against Lt. Daszkiewicz were read, Sgt. Wachtel took to the floor:

"If it pleases the court. . . ." Calmly and eloquently he started to build a defense against those charges. Starting with Maj. Wieslaw Krzemien who was assigned to the project of capturing army deserters a three men team, which was further, reduced to two men, Capt. Michalski and Lt. Daszkiewicz.

"Maj. Krzemien couldn't be reached for his comments on this case, due to being presently treated in an Army Hospital for ruptured appendix. It was also Capt. Michalski's idea to use a local informant Mr. Adler— "Panczyk" to help with the identification of perpetrators. The fact that Mr. Adler is Jewish has nothing to do with this case. As a civilian we have no jurisdiction over him, to order his presence in this court.

The knifing of Capt. Michalski couldn't have been prevented from Lt. Daszkiewicz's position. It was unfortunate like many other incidents in time of war. Still the Lt. Daszkiewicz managed to shoot Sgt. Kaczor and single handedly capture Lt. Trzeciak who is in our custody.

May I also bring out the distinguished military record that includes many decorations earned at Monte Cassino, not to mention his early days as an underground fighter and a patriot, who left his wife and child in order to join the Polish Forces, partially financing the transportation of Polish citizens from Roumania. In conclusion, Lt. Daszkiewicz- "acriter et fideliter" courageously and faithfully discharged all his duties, therefore, we respectfully request that all charges against him be dropped and an apology given to his fine officer. Thank you gentlemen."

It became very quiet in the makeshift court. Only a polite cough of the court's stenographer interrupted the silence.

"Thank you Sgt. Wachtel for the summarization. Please take your client, Lt. Daszkiewicz to the other room and wait for the results of our deliberation."

"Yes Sir." They both saluted and left the room.

"Eljasz, you have done an excellent job and I thank you."

"They really should dismiss the charges. They have no case."

"You're mistaken my dear friend. Konopnicki is after my hide, I can feel it. He is blaming me for his friend's death, besides we'll see soon who is right. Cigarette....?"

They smoked their cigarettes, deeply inhaling the Virginia's tobacco's taste. An hour later, Lt. Pawlikowski came into the room:

"We're ready for you, do come in."

"ATTENTION!" The court stenographer shouted as they both stood up.

Lt. Col. Konopnicki started to speak, quoting different articles and paragraphs of the criminal, military codex, behavior etc, etc.........therefore this court sentences you to a reduction in rank from lieutenant to master sergeant and an instantaneous transfer from the 2nd department to active front duties with an engineering battalion. Does the master sergeant wish to address this court?"

"Yes Sir. I'm not guilty of those charges. I've always conducted myself as a good Pole and even a better soldier."

"Master sergeant Daszkiewicz you're a good Pole, but good

soldiers do not cause death to their superior officers."

"Sir, we intend to appeal this verdict to a higher court!" interrupted Sgt. Wachtel.

"Your kind always does." Sarcastically added Konopnicki.

"By my kind, Sir, you do mean good lawyers of course?"

"Watch your language Wachtel! Don't forget, you're in a Polish Military court and not in a "cheder".

"How can I forget it, Sir. That's why I always keep my words soft and sweet one never knows when he'll have to eat them."

"DISMISSED!!! You have 24 hours to join you new unit. This court has been very lenient with you, Daszkiewicz."

Lt. Pawlikowski came over with transfer papers and sealed orders for Edward:

"For whatever it is worth, I was against the verdict, but was overruled. Wachtel, file an appeal, you never can tell in these cases. I'm really sorry Daszkiewicz, good luck."

"Thank you Sir for your kind words."

"What are you going to do now, lieutenant?" asked Wachtel.

"You may as well call me sergeant, I've got to get used to my new title."

"To me, you'll always be lieutenant."

"Thank you Eljasz, now I know for sure that you're from Drohobycz.'

"Was there ever any doubt?"

"No, never. Come, we still have our jeep, so let's go and visit Henryk and "Panczyk" I feel like having a drink or two. So let's use up those 24 hours and have some fun."

They drove to Hotel Sant' Anselmo just as Henryk, "Panczyk" and Luise were having tea. Eljasz told them in great detail what has transpired in the court.

"This is an outrage!" Fumed "Panczyk" –Adler. "How could they have done it? Is there anyone we can talk to about this case?"

"I appreciate your willingness to help, but do you think that a Polish colonel is going to listen to a civilian Jew in matters of military justice? Not in your lifetime, my friend.

I still think that I should have reacted a bit sooner, maybe I could have saved Michalski's life. I'll finish this war as a master sergeant. It isn't so bad. What are your plans fellows?"

"Thanks to Eljasz's recommendations, "Panczyk's" initiative and Gulio Romano's connections, we started to supply the Polish and British garrisons with fresh milk, bread and whatever else they can use. The pay us with cigarettes, coffee and their currency. I think we can build it up to a nice business, after all this war will end some day Edward you can join us whenever you're free."

"That is the best offer I had in a very long time. Thanks, but I must get back to my family, after that we'll see."

"We understand very well, as long as you have a few hours, stay with us for dinner. You have to taste my cooking." Said Luise.

"Very well, I accept but after the dinner, we'll have to get back. I got to get ready for my newest assignment. As long as I'll live, I'll be in touch with all of you through Henryk."

"You can write to me in care of this hotel. Gulio will forward your mail in case I move any place else. Then all is settled, agreed."

"Panczyk" had every reason to be proud of his wife's Luise culinary talents. She whipped out a delicious meal, which she elegantly served, considering the modest hotel's circumstances. Despite her aristocratic background, she could perform any menial task, faster and better than anybody else.

Once finished with coffee and cigarettes, Edward got to his feet:

"Well, the time has come to say good-bye. Thanks for everything, I do value your friendship above anything else." He kissed Luise, shook hands with "Panczyk" and embraced Henryk. No additional words were necessary, they understood each other without the benefit of a spoken word.

"Eljasz, let's go! I'm still the master sergeant."

"Yes Sir, You are Sir." Mockingly Wachtel repeated.

Driving back to their quarters they had plenty of time to say good-bye to each other:

"I'll file an appeal on your behalf and will stay in touch."

"You're wasting your time, but go ahead."

In his room, Edward had to remove the single solitary star from his uniform and attach the many stripes, indicating the rank of master sergeant.

Informed by the Transportation Officer of an army convoy leaving next morning for the location of his new unit, he obtained permission to join the echelon, based upon his present orders.

With his duffel bag, still clearly marked as Lt. Daszkiewicz, safely on the back of the truck, he rode in the comfort of the truck's cabin, listening to driver's songs and stories of his love conquests. Thus the few hours spent in reaching his destination were pleasant enough, thanks mainly to Jacek's youthful exuberance.

As per Lt. Pawlikowski's instructions, Edward handed over his sealed orders to the company commander Capt. Slomka.

"Very interesting, these papers tell me that you were with the 2nd Department as lieutenant and was demoted for causing an officer's death?"

"It was an unfortunate incident."

"Maybe it's one of your 2nd department's tricks, tell me, are you after someone in my outfit?"

"No Sir, I'm not. If I would have been on a special assignment I couldn't discuss the case with you anyway."

"I guess your right. I see from these papers that you have been at Monte Cassino and that you're the recipient of several decorations. That's very nice. By the way, are you related per chance to Maj. Jan-Kazimierz Daszkiewicz?"

"Yes Sir. He is my uncle?"

"What a coincidence. He was my C.O. A very good man indeed. Listen Daszkiewicz, I don't care whatever your reasons are for being here. I'm very glad to have a man of your caliber at my side, so welcome aboard. Get yourself all squared away and I'll outline your present duties. Any questions?'

"No Sir."

"Very well lieutenant, I mean sergeant, dismissed."

Edward joined the battalion in time to witness events, that

were heralded by the greatest use of air power in the history of Mediterranean theatre, the long awaited, all-out offensive in Italy, which began on April 16th, 1945.

Exhorted by their commanders to strike the blows that would mean final victory, the Fifth American Army, along with the British 8th and Polish units, hammered forward through the last Apennine barriers before Bologna. The Italian partisans helped to liberate the largest port-Genoa, moving toward Milano.

Edward's unit which burst out of the Apennines, swept the Po valley clean of the bulk of the Wehrmacht and cut off the remaining German troops in northwest Italy, by capturing Bergamo at the foot of the Alps.

It was at this place that Edward almost lost his own life, not due to the rare enemy fire but from shots coming from behind. He quickly ducked, pretending to be dead.

Slowly a crouching figure emerged and Edward noticed, through his half closed eyes, the ugly face of Seweryn Klimczak, the ex-supply sergeant, whom Edward caught stealing the Army's food.

Edward firmly believed that a first shot should be the last, because that meant that either you got your enemy or the enemy got you, and Edward was not in the habit of loosing.

"Klimczak, you son of a bitch. I'll get you for this!"

A rare now, German sniper's bullet, hit Klimczak in the chest relieving Edward of killing Klimczak himself.

After this nasty encounter, good news came in, confirming the death of Benito Mussolini at the end of April 1945, followed by a couple of days later by the death of Adolf Hitler, celebrated by Edward's entire battalion. The end was near.

On the 3rd of May 1945 the German Forces in Italy surrendered entirely. The surrender papers were signed on the German side, by Col. Gen. Heinrich von Vietinghoff-Scheel, Astrid's father and almost a father-in-law to his friend, Henryk.

The war ended for Edward and so many others on May 8th, 1945 but his problems as a Polish soldier, were far from over. The

0468-LEE

Big Three wrestled again over Poland and his future depended on the results coming from San Francisco. Much did he know that his country was going to be violated once more.

CHAPTER 60

"Colonel, there is a British lady officer by the name of Epstein, to see you Sir."

"Bring her up now."

"General, you'll see my ladylove once more, if you have a minute."

"I'm looking forward to it. I'm afraid that I didn't leave a good impression the last time we had met in that pub."

"You'll have a chance now to remedy the situation."

"Good afternoon, gentlemen>"

"Honey, do you remember Gen. Cottshot?"

"How can I forget him. How do you do, general?"

"Thank you. I'm just fine. Seeing you again, I no longer wonder why this big Palooka is head over heels in love with you."

"The general is too kind."

"Well, I have to run but you Col. Krafchin have an emergency 24 hours leave as of this moment. So take off before I change my mind. Good-bye Lt. Epstein and good luck."

"Yes Sir, General Sir."

"Paul, your general is very nice."

"For a slave driver he is OK. Let me just get a few things and I'll make like a banana and split."

"Come again Paul, I didn't quite get the meaning?"

"Forget it, it's Yankee humor. Come, lets you and I celebrate the end of the war in our own intimate way."

"I've a little surprise for you. Do you remember Alice Spencer a friend of Vivian Homes? The same one that let you have her apartment for a fling with Vivian?"

"That's not fair Cynthia. This happened long before I met you."

"It's OK Paul. I know it from Vivian herself. She told me that you are quite a lover. I have the keys to her apartment, but this time you are going to spend the night with me. Remember that according to the Jewish law we are married and I can't wait any longer to feel like the real Mrs. Krafchin."

"All right you naughty girl, let's go already. I'm not made of stone either. We are wasting precious time."

The apartment in Brighton was the same as Paul remembered it. This time however, he was with his wife Cynthia. It was the highest time to consummate the marriage. He was most gentle and considerate with Cynthia, he caressed her silk skin and sucked her hardened nipples till Cynthia shouted almost in pain: "Paul take me already."

Vivian was right when she described Cynthia as being a virgin, as incredible as it sounded in London during the Blitz there was still a virgin left.

They kept making love till the wee hours of the morning. With his love next to him and the knowledge that the war finally ended, Paul was one happy man.

Whoever said that nothing goes faster than a 24 hour leave, was right again and in as much as he hated the idea of leaving Cynthia, he had to get back to his office.

The atmosphere at the office changed altogether. Instead of constant pressure and emergencies caused by requirements of waging a war, everything became downright relaxed.

A few weeks later while bringing papers for the general's signature, Paul lost his equilibrium. Something was definitely wrong with him. He wasn't himself.

"Paul what is wrong with you?"

"I don't know Sir, I can't stand up."

"You haven't been drinking my boy?'

"I haven't touched booze in days."

The general let Paul sit and immediately called in medics.

Paul was rushed to the Military Hospital, where he was thoroughly examined by Air Force doctors. The diagnosis based upon a series of performed tests had shown an inner ear problem and a sudden case of vertigo.

"Colonel let me give it to you straight: "I'm afraid that your flying days are over. The inner ear condition will be cured by medication. The vertigo is another matter. It may become a regular reappearing phenomena or it may come once in a while or disappear altogether. We don't have enough hard facts in either case. We'll be submitting our report to the general, as per his instructions. Just between us, Colonel, if I were you, I would apply for an early discharge from the Air Force."

"Thanks Doc. I'll take this under consideration."

"Still, we want you to stay with us for a couple of days, just as a precaution."

"Whatever you say, Doc."

Capt. Dr. Gottlieb was right. The medication helped his inner ear inflammation and the vertigo subsided to the point that he left the hospital after a couple of days and reported back to active duty. He was told to see the general at once.

"How are you feeling Paul?"

"Much better General, thank you for asking."

"Paul, I was never a guy who beats around the bush. I've read your medical evaluation. The vertigo may come back in a most unwelcome situation. The war in Europe already ended. This is a good time for you to bail out. As it is, it will take you a couple of months to get all the papers filed. On lieutenant colonel's pay and partial disability, you'll be sitting pretty. Did you tell Cynthia all about it?"

"I didn't General, I wanted to know what has happened with me first."

"Whatever it is, this should not keep you from marrying Cynthia. I'll sign all the necessary papers. In the meantime take a few days off. You have worked hard enough."

"Thank you Sir."

"You're welcome. And Paul do it before they ship my ass to Guam."

While visiting the Epsteins, Paul had a chance to tell Cynthia about the new developments. Not wanting to scare his young bride, he told her only about the mild case of vertigo.

"It's really nothing, but the Air Force is stuck with so many pilots at the end of the war and it is looking to discharge many of them for whatever reason possible. Believe me, I won't be missed. I intend to leave the Air Force and continue with my education."

"Same here Paul. I'm leaving the Service because they aren't too keen on keeping pregnant women in their cadres."

"WHAT??"

"You heard me right, you're about to become a father. Hope you're not angry with me?"

"To the contrary. I'm very happy about it. If it's a boy let's call him Gary-Isaac, after the general and my father."

"Let's hope for a boy in this case."

"Did you tell your parents about it?"

"Not yet. You're the first one. Had to make sure that I was pregnant and not just late. What about you? Did you inform you mother about u s?"

"She beat me to it. She married a widowed neighbor, a friend of the family of long standing, a certain Mr. Goldstein a proud owner of a fleet of medallion cabbies in New York City. I'll try to call her or cable."

"Hello young lovers wherever you are" said Rabbi Rifkind who just walked in.

"How are you both?"

"I'm fine Rabbi but Paul over here has a problem. His flying days are over. For selfish reasons I'm glad about it. He'll be getting his discharge papers in the not too distant future."

"That is too bad Paul. I had other plans for you. However there is another option left. I'm sure that you are fully aware about the catastrophe that befell our people. The Holocaust survivors with no place to go are gathered in several Displaced Persons camps, being cared for by U.N.R.R.A. (United Nations Relief and Rehabilitation Administration). The biggest of those camps are in Landsberg, Feldafing and Foehrenwald, all located in Bavaria. We would like to have a young, energetic man with U.S. Military background to run the Foehrenwald D.P. Camp, some 30 km. from Munich. The present director, a Canadian woman by the name of Mrs. Henshaw has a too tough time running it. Besides she had only two more months till her contract with U.N.R.R.A. expires.

She is not Jewish and doesn't understand Jews and Jewish problems. I'll speak with my brother, Judge Rifkind who is a close friend of Fiorello LaGuardia, the present chief of U.N.R.R.A. I'll try to get you a 2 year contract and after that you'll be free to do what ever you wish. You'll be helping your own people in the most difficult time in the history. While being with U.N.R.R.A. you'll have all the PX privileges, salary paid in U.S. dollars, a private village and a couple of German servants."

"Rabbi, I don't know the first thing about running a D.P. Camp. I'm not a social worker, I'm a pilot or should say an ex-pilot."

"What is there to know? You'll get help from other U.N.R.R.A. officers, both naturalized American citizens and native born, speaking every possible European Language. Other Jewish organizations such as HIAS, O.R.T. Mizrachi and some Palestinian groups will also be of help."

"Sounds very interesting, but I would like to speak with your brother, before I undertake an important assignment such as this. I need more details before I make up my mind. Remember Rabbi, I need a couple of months to get my discharge papers. Why do you need an Army man to run the camp?"

"A prestige of U.S. colonel is needed with the Army that supervises the entire area. Trust me Paul, you are the right person for that position. My brother can be reached this afternoon at a cocktail party in honor of Marlene Dietrich, who is awarded the Medal of Freedom. It should make for an interesting evening."

"I don't know about that, Rabbi."

"Come Paul, that sounds like a lot of fun. I would like very much to meet the famous movie star, unless you have something to hide. Some say that you were romantically involved with her."

"Of course not. Let's go then."

The large hall was crowded with various dignitaries, high ranking Allied officers and the ever present reporters and photographers as Marlene Dietrich was awarded the Medal of Freedom, America's highest civilian honor.

Marlene Dietrich recorded lachrymose pop songs like "I'll get by", "I couldn't sleep a wink last night" and of course the very popular "Lili Marlene" with German lyrics. To be radioed to German soldiers in the field in order to make them feel homesick and morose.

In addition she did frequent, U.S.O. shows dangerously close to the front. There was a rumor that she has done some jobs for William J. Donovan of the Oh So Social, O.S.S.

Paul went over to her and offered his congratulations and at the same time he introduced Cynthia as his wife.

"You're a very lucky girl, I've tried to seduce him but unfortunately I failed. Good luck to the both of you." And she disappeared in a crowd of admirers.

While Paul and Cynthia spoke with Marlene Dietrich, Rabbi Rifkind located his brother, telling him about Paul. Whatever he told him met with Judge Rifkind's approval.

"So you're Col. Paul Krafchin and that must be the lovely Cynthia Krafchin nee Epstein. I'll go along with my kid brother's recommendations. Mrs. Henshaw will be leaving Foehrenwald D.P. Camp U.N.R.R.A. team #106 near Wolfratshausen and the job will be yours. I can't think of another more noble or rewarding job than to help thousands of survivors to start a new life."

"Paul please do it, for mine and your sake."

"Gentlemen, I'm yours."

CHAPTER 61

Life for Henryk at the Hotel Sant' Anselmo was getting better from day to day. Although delegated by "Panczyk", Luise and Gulio to the role of warehouse keeper, he performed his duties with relish, leaving the most difficult tasks of obtaining and selling needed merchandise to the "Three Blackmarketers".

Surprisingly, Luise was the most capable and enterprising person. Her knowledge of languages and her natural charm was the main asset in building up the business. With war ended, there was a pent up demand by the public for customer products including cigarettes, coffee, nylons, cosmetics, etc.

In a relatively short time they had a nice business going, buying and selling, which produced a healthy profit. In the course of those dealing, Luise came across a truck-full of Jaffa oranges for sale. The driver a Palestinian Jew, originally from Drohobycz, Poland recognized Henryk. They were schoolmates some years ago.

"I'm Chaim Klinghofer and you must be Henryk Kaplinski. What in the world are you doing here while your sister Maryla is in Wroclaw?"

"What are you saying? Is Maryla alive? Where and when did you see her?"

"Look Henryk" he lowered his voice. "I work for "Bricha" we smuggle Jews from Poland and Germany to Palestine. Recently I guided a group through two borders. Maryla and her family were supposed to join us but in the last minute, her child got sick. I'll be going again to Wroclaw in a few days, that's why I'm selling oranges to raise some money."

"Can I come with you? When are you leaving?"

"I'll take you. Be here in front of this building in three days at

6 A.M. should there be any changes in the plan I'll let you know."

"Chaim, is there anything that you need?"

"I really could use some cigarettes to "shmeer" border guards."

"Are "Camels" OK? Take the whole case."

"You mean it?"

"Yes, I do. Take it and be here."

"You bet."

That same evening Henryk informed his partners his reason for leaving Rome.

"I must get my sister from Poland out. Whatever my share is, please pay me out, if not all then part of it, and also deduct money for 12 cartons of cigarettes."

"We are sorry to loose you, come back to us anytime you wish. Your share is approximately 1.786 U.S. dollars and 164 British pounds. The cigarettes are our going away present. The best of luck and hope you'll be reunited with your family."

"Thank you very much. I still have a couple of days left, before I leave, I would like to show you where everything is located."

"Gulio asked us for a job for his 22 year old nephew. We'll take him in."

"Then all is settled."

The next day brought another surprise to Henryk: Edward Daszkiewicz showed up wearing a captain's uniform.

"Edward? What in the world is happening?"

"Crazy as it may seem, I was summoned to the Headquarters in Rome to see Judge Advocate, a certain Col. Kaszub. He overturned my verdict, on the basis of three separate appeals, filed by Eljasz on my behalf. Those appeals were supported by sworn affidavits from Maj. Krzemien and Col. Jan-Kazimierz Daszkiewicz, my uncle. My rank not only was restored but I was promoted to Captain. Needless to say my pay was adjusted accordingly. There were strings attached to it. I've to leave the Army and keep my mouth shut about my unjust treatment. I accepted both conditions and technically speaking, I'm as of now a civilian. I was also offered, sort of a bribe, to go to Munich and run a company of demobilized Polish soldiers to guard U.S. Army installations and warehouses. Good pay and an apartment goes with the offer. I, however, would very much like to go back to my wife and daughter in Zakopane. We are getting bad news from the homeland. The Polish Security Forces "U.B." run by Russkies are arresting the so called London Poles, especially officers. Maybe I can avoid that by smuggling myself through the still porous borders. That is also pretty dangerous."

"Edward, I was told yesterday, that my sister is alive and living in Wroclaw. I must see her. I know someone from a Jewish Organization who smuggles people across borders. If you wish you can come with me."

"Can you trust that man?"

"Yes, I can. He is a fellow Jew, a former classmate of mine. His job is to smuggle Jews out of Europe to Palestine."

"Henryk, but I am not a Jew."

"So what? If I could become a Christian for a while, you can be a Jew for a while. Funny you don't look Jewish."

"That's very funny."

"Do you have a place to stay, Edward?"

"Not really."

"Stay with me then. Chaim is supposed to be here within two days. We can be ready by that time."

"It's fine with me. By the way, did you see Eljasz? I would like to thank him for his efforts on my behalf."

"No, I didn't."

"He was also demobilized. He just left me a message that he was going to see a friend of his from Law school by the name of Menachem. Any idea who that might be?"

"I haven't a foggiest. Let's pack and take just the most needed and the most comfortable articles of clothing with us. I'm also going to hide some money in the lining of my coat. You may want to do the same."

It was still dark outside when the two of them showed up in

front of the building. A few minutes after 6, an old Fiat stopped with a screeching halt by the curb and Chaim came out:

"Henryk, I have a big problem on my hands. Our truck broke down and I have an additional six people, 4 men and 2 women, to bring to Munich. Who is the man with you?" Chaim asked in Yiddish.

"Edward Daszkiewicz a good friend of mine from Drohobycz-Boryslaw."

"He doesn't look like a Jew."

"He isn't, I do know him very well. He saved my life several times over. I do vouch for him."

"What seems to be the problem, Henryk?"

"Their truck broke down, unfortunately they need time to locate another truck. We're stuck."

"Who are the other people going to Munich?"

"They are Jews, former Yugoslav and Greek partisans."

"Give me 2-3 hours and I'll get you a truck. Can your friend Chaim drive me to the Polish Motor Pool? I'm entitled to transportation privileges, besides they know me from my 2nd Department days. Do you want to give me a lift?'

"Can we trust him?" asked Chaim in Yiddish again.

"100%".

"I'll drive you there and wait till you get the truck. After that we'll have to pick up the other six people, get Henryk and away we go. Agreed?"

"Excellent. Henryk please take my valise back to the hotel. I'll pick it up at the same time I'll be coming for you. Just be patient. We'll be there, don't worry."

Hours later, a truck full of people pulled in front of the Hotel Sant' Anselmo. Henryk put both his and Edward's valises on the truck, and said good-bye to his friends. There was enough room in the cabin of the truck for the Army driver, Edward and Henryk.

The driver a polite young corporal, whom Edward introduced as Corp. Piasecki, asked:

"Are we all in now?"

"Yes, we are Corporal. Let's go to Munich."

"Yes Sir, as the captain wishes."

For a while they drove in silence and then a light conversation on the subject of post war plans developed. The first one to tell about his plans was Corp. Piasecki:

"I have an uncle in Chicago. That's were I would like to go. And you captain?"

"I don't know yet. First I've got to see my family and then we'll see."

A few hours later, the driver showed signs of fatigue. Seeing that, Henryk volunteered to take over the wheel.

"In that case, you had better wear a military tunic, in case we're stopped."

"No problem."

They were stopped several hours later at the Italo-Austrian border. The papers were in order and the trip-ticket issued for 10 people.

"Are they all Polish?" asked the border guard.

"Yes, or course."

"How come some of you have dark hair and dark skin?"

"They are Polish Gypsies."

"Proceed!!"

Once they reached the Bavarian City of Munich, Chaim directed the truck to The Deutsches Museum, near the Saar River.

"Captain, I'm going to take my people including Henryk inside the institution where the Jewish Refugee Processing Center is located. As of now, we don't need your truck anymore, because by tomorrow morning you, Henryk and I will board a train to Weiden near the Czechoslovakia's border. From there I'll take over. Can you meet us here tomorrow morning-latest 7Am?"

"It's perfect Chaim. I have to see the place of my possible future employment. It is in Schwabing, Not very far from here. Also have the use of an apartment, so I'll be just fine. See you tomorrow at seven. Good luck to you all."

There were hundreds of refugees lined up in front of a few

tables. Unwashed men, women and children, all carrying a variety of luggage, from valises tied with rope to homemade rucksacks, were milling about, waiting to be processed to different D.P. camps.

Chaim approached a man sitting behind a desk in the farthest end of the big hall. After a brief conversation in Hebrew, Chaim's group was allowed to get in front of everybody else, much to the displeasure of the other people waiting in line already.

"You all will be going to be recently opened D.P. Camp Foehrenwald near Wolfratshausen. A U.N.R.R.A. truck will take you there with 10-12 other people. It is not far from here, about 30 kilometers a 45 minute ride." The clerk announced.

Chaim quietly said to Henryk: "While in Foehrenwald I want you to register yourself and your family. You will be issued "Zulage", your food rations, clothing and assigned housing. It is very important to be registered before the end of 1945. From Foehrenwald we intend to bring as many people as we can to Palestine, starting with young, healthy individuals. War veterans like you will be our priority."

"Do you expect a war?"

"One can never tell. Maybe the Arabs will disappear in the desert."

"In the mean time what do we do next?"

"Once we have taken care of all the formalities, we'll catch the next U.N.R.R.A. truck returning to Munich's Deutsches Museum. Tomorrow morning we're taking a train to Weiden, but today we have to go to Foehrenwald. I believe the truck is ready to take off. Are we clear on this?"

An U.N.R.R.A. 2.5 ton G.M.C. truck loaded with 20 people including Henryk and Chaim and their belongings left from Deutsches Museum to the Displaced Persons Camp Foehrenwald.

Henryk easily recognized the sights on the way: The Sanatorium Dorfen, the town of Wolfratshausen. He wondered if Dennhards and other people who were kind to him were still there. They probably would be shocked to know that Heinrich Kaplinski is a Jewish D.P.

He decided to keep quiet about that period of his life. The most important to him now, was to be reunited with his sister and her new family.

Three kilometers from Wolfratshausen was the location of D.P Camp Foehrenwald, U.N.R.R.A. team #106, whose main gate was guarded now by Jewish Police in civilian clothing, wearing armbands "D.P. Police."

They were let in without any fuss. The truck drove straight to the center of the camp and stopped in front of the "Verwaltung" administration building, where everybody got off.

The welcoming committee was personified by two men by the name of Zlotykamien and Chaver Davidoff, both of whom Chaim knew rather well.

"Shalom, shalom, ma nishma?" The conversation was held in rapid Hebrew, which Henryk had trouble following.

The partisans were registered and directed to the so called "Partisaner Kibbutz" where most of the tough looking men, wore Russian style leather boots.

Henryk managed to get himself and Maryla's family registered, even though he didn't have their married name. Chaim who was with him also didn't know, so everybody was entered as Kaplinski.

All the streets in Foehrenwald were named after American states. Henryk's address was now Florida Strasse #30. It was a small, three single room, house with one bathroom for all.

Henryk was lucky to have as a neighbor, a member of the "Verwaltung" Chaver Rubinstein.

When Henryk told him that he will bring his family in two weeks, Rubinstein told him:

"Don't worry, I'll watch your apartment."

The rest of the houses were an exact replica of Florida Strasse #30. Walking through the camp, Henryk noticed a large dining hall that served meals to the camp's inhabitants as well as a small hospital. Other signs were made by O.R.T. vocational schools. Garbage was collected by trucks, manned by Germans still in the Wehrmacht uniforms.

Chaim also found out through the grapevine that the present U.N.R.R.A. Director Mrs. Henshaw will be replaced by an American Jewish general.

"What would an American general be doing in a place like this?"

"So maybe he is not a general, maybe just a lieutenant as long as he has Jewish heart. I think Henryk that we have to go back to Munich. We accomplished whatever we needed, so let's go. The truck is waiting."

The receiving clerk at the Deutsches Museum, with whom Chaim spoke previously, suggested that they repack the contents of their valises into rucksacks leaving heavy objects and part of their valuables with him for safekeeping. Chaim approved the move.

After spending an uncomfortable night on a skinny mattress, put on the floor of a crowded "General Reception" hall they went outside the building where Edward was already waiting for them in a taxi.

"Zum Hauptbahnhoff bitte" and a few minutes ride, brought them to the main railroad station, busting at seams with crowds of people. In front of each ticket window there were long, slow moving lines of German refugees, traveling to their bombed or if lucky, undamaged houses.

"We can't stay here. Let's find the train going to Weiden, for a few packs of cigarettes any conductor will get us tickets and good seats. Follow me."

For a single cigarette they obtained all the needed information. The conductor standing in front of the 1st class wagon, bearing a sign: "Eintritt verboten" must have also been a magician, because the three packs of American cigarettes disappeared immediately in his pockets.

"Bitte sehr, meine Herren" he found them an almost empty compartment, where the other two occupants were a nondescript German couple, looking upon the newly arrived "Auslanders" with an upper class scorn.

"Henryk, how was that D.P. Camp?" asked Edward.

"Not bad really. It's going to be a bit crowded in the beginning with Maryla and her family but we'll be together and that is most important. Maybe later, I'll find something else for us. I have seen worse as you very well know. How about you?"

"I'll be a glorified superintendent in charge of 48 soldiers, guarding the American installations and warehouses. Some of those cutthroats will probably steal themselves. Why worry ahead? The pay is good, the apartment is nice, not too far from the place. Hopefully Czeslawa and Danuta will overcome their hatred of Germany until we'll get our visas to Canada. I stopped yesterday at the Canadian Consulate, they were very friendly to me, a Polish captain who fought alongside Canadian and British Forces."

"How do you know if Czeslawa and Danuta are willing to leave Poland?"

"I don't. I don't think that after the German occupation they are looking to a Russian one? If they won't come with me, I'll stay with them and wait for the U.B. to arrest me."

The train was moving slowly, making many stops on the way to Weiden, which they reached, in the late afternoon.

A small panel truck awaited Chaim and his friends. They drove for several kilometers on a narrow road, surrounded on both sides by a thick forest. The truck stopped in front of a temporary bridge.

"This is where we get off " Chaim spoke very quietly. "We shall wait here until it will get darker and walk the rest of the way. Do not talk and do not under any circumstances smoke. Should any guard approach us, you hit the ground and let me deal with him. Is that understood?"

"Chaim, Chaim, we are veterans, we do know what to do."

"I thought that you have forgotten the basic rules, so let's go."

They walked in a single file in complete silence with Chaim leading. Henryk was glad for the use of the rucksack suggested by the "Bricha" member. A valise in these circumstances would have been suicidal.

"Kto ide?" a sharp "who goes" in Chechoslovak sounded. Both Edward and Henryk hit the ground.

"Yam se priyatel, Chaim" – "I'm Chaim, friend." Chaim slowly moved toward the sound of the guard's voice.

Henryk and Edward didn't see the guard but heard laughs and loud enough "Nasledano"-"Good-bye".

Chaim backtracked: "The coast is clear. I'm just one carton of cigarettes poorer. We don't have far to go now.

They walked through a clearance in the woods till they reached a paved road.

"Now we have to wait for another truck or wagon."

It was a long wait, but eventually they hitched a ride to a small town on Czechoslovak side of the border. It was daytime already.

"From here we can get to the Polish border without any problems. At the Polish border I have to locate a certain sergeant, who will let us cross the border, for a fee of another carton of cigarettes per man. Should any problems arise at the crossing, remember, you are Jews returning home from German concentration camp, always stick to that story."

For another pack of buts they were brought close to the Polish border. A large white and red flag was visible from afar. They were in luck. The sergeant that Chaim was looking for was on duty. There was only a small problem: his price was doubled to two cartons per head.

"We're slowly running out of cigarettes, but we have no choice, we have to pay. I don't want these fellows to get used to foreign "Valutas", because their appetite grows from day to day."

Chaim went first and Henryk with Edward followed a bit later. The sergeant went to the bathroom leaving the border passage unguarded.

Once on the Polish soil they went to the open market and bought several bottles of homemade vodka "bimber", needed to bribe the Russian truck drivers.

"Here we're going to separate. Henryk and I will be going to Wroclaw and you Edward will be going to Zakopane, you know the area much better than I, so you'll be all right. Remember

Edward, we plan to leave Poland by the same route "the green border" only in reverse, in 10 days from now. We shall be leaving in the afternoon. Henryk's family lives near the Jewish Committee on Grzybowska 18. You shouldn't have any problem finding the place, hope to see you there with your family." Chaim shook hands with Edward, who developed a sense of respect and admiration for this young and enterprising Palestinian Jew, who was somewhat different from the Jews he had known.

Edward and Henryk embraced each other. Each was also worried about the future.

"Everything will turn up well, just come with Czeslawa and Danuta."

They went their separate ways, on different corners of the square market place. Edward was the first to get a ride towards Cracow. A few minutes later a Russian truck stopped:

"A kuda vam rebiata nada?' "Where to guys?"

"Na Wroclaw, tovarish."

"A vodka u vas yest?" "Do you have vodka?"

"Da, tselyi liter" "Yes, a full liter."

Henryk could never understand the Russian capacity of consuming large quantities of alcohol. To Chaim with his "kibbutz" upbringing it was a sheer enigma.

The driver dropped them off some 10 blocks from Grzybowska street. Walking through a mostly destroyed city, silent witness to incredible savage fights, they wondered how many years it will take to make it livable again.

"Henryk, don't think about Poland, think about Palestine a garden of Eden by comparison. Our people are not wanted here anyway."

Few more blocks and they were on Grzybowska: "Here we are, Henryk. It's upstairs."

Henryk ran upstairs two steps at a time, with his heart beating like a gong. Finally he'll see his sister Maryla. He knocked on the door and a young, slightly plump woman opened the door.

It was Maryla! Maybe a bit older and more mature but Maryla just the same.

"Maryla! My God, Maryla!" she recognized the voice before she recognized the person.

"Henius! You are alive thank God." They hugged and kissed, kissed and hugged, crying all the time, unaware that a man holding a small child came from the other room.

"I'm sorry Henryk, I forgot to introduce you to my husband Benek Morgenstern, from Sambor and our sweet daughter Lilka. Chaim it must have been you who found my brother I thank you very much for it. You must be hungry and tired from your journey so let me prepare some food."

"Don't worry Maryla, we're not starving. Let me hold the baby for a while. She is a beauty." "We do have some kielbasa with us if you need it. Let me give you some "weiche" American dollars, I'm sure that you could buy whatever you need with that money. Tonight I want to hear everything what has happened to you since you left home in June of 1941."

"I'll tell you everything you want to hear but first let me put the baby to sleep and fix you at least a sandwich. While you and Chaim eat I'll tell you my adventures."

"Go ahead, we can wait."

Benek took the baby to another room and soon a lullaby "I looloo" was heard. Maryla in the meantime handed Henryk and Chaim, each a sandwich.

"Well, I can write a book about my life in Russia, but it is going to be easier if I tell you, making it as short as possible:

I left Drohobycz with a group from my office on the 26th of June '41, the 4th day of war. We traveled by an overcrowded train going east. We didn't know the direction. East was all we knew. Just before reaching Kiev, our train was bombed twice and many people were killed. We changed the train for one going towards Kuybyshov. While I slept, my group left me alone stranded, hungry and full of lice. My meager belongings also disappeared. Somehow I kept going, living on "kipiatok" boiled water and the kindness of strange people that shared their last piece of bread with me. I've changed many trains and slept on floors of many railroad stations, waiting for trains, eventually I reached the City of Sverdlovsk in the Ural Mountains.

From there the authorities directed refugees to different factories and "kolhozes" collective farms. I was sent to "Kolhoz" named after Kirov in the village of Atchit, Rayon of Krasnoufimsk. The "Kolhoz" manager Tovarish Petrov, seeing that all I had on me was the dress I wore and a sweater full of lice, gave me some clothing that probably belong to his wife. I was given a single room in a house that belonged to an elderly widow on Pushkin street. She took a liking to me and gave me winter clothing, because winter came early in Ural. Wouldn't be for her kindness I surely would have frozen at temperatures I never heard of in Poland. The average winter temperature was minus 55 degrees Celsius."

Maryla stopped for a while to get a drink of water. Her mouth was dry. She continued:

"The times were hard for everybody in the village during the winter, especially for me who never lived on a farm. I was sent to "Liesozagotovka" to cut down big trees. It was a hard job even for men, but since men were send to the Red Army, women had to do that job. In order to earn your bread I had to meet certain "Norms".

My luck changed when I met Benek Morgenstern a fellow Jew. He was arrested by the N.K.V.D. with his entire family as an "Anti-social" element and sent to Siberia. They were later released as Polish citizens and made their way to Krasnoufimsk, where his parents died. His older brother was re-arrested and nobody heard from him to this day. Benek as a good dentist, got a position taking care of the "nomenklatura" and their families.

With his "Blat" connections, he soon got me out of "Kolhoz" to a nice house in Krasnoufimsk. Eating well for the first time in a long while, I gained some weight back. Looking more presentable, Benek proposed marriage. Since I loved him already, I said "yes". After our town of Drohobycz was liberated, we obtained the necessary papers, given mainly to former Polish citizen. We returned home. Not a single relative of ours escaped the Nazis and their Ukrainian collaborators. I went to our house to see what was left of it. The present tenant, a Ukrainian peasant, came out with an ax threatening to kill us all. If it weren't for Benek, he probably would have. The very few remaining Jews, who came out from hiding and some Christian Poles, started to move to Silesia in Western Poland and the newly liberated areas. We joined an echelon to Wroclaw and here we are. It is here where we met Chaim.

Henryk, we don't want to be here anymore. We don't want our child to grow up in this blood soaked land. I want to go to Israel and so does Benek. Enough of wandering, we want to have a place that we could call our own. A place where nobody is going to call me "dirty zhidovka". Henryk, do you want to come with us?"

"Yes, Maryla. I want to come along with you. We have been separated too long. Chaim here wants to leave Wroclaw in 10 days. That should give us ample time to get organized and to be ready for the trip. I have money to get the most needed items. We can't carry too much through two borders. We need to get to Munich, from there the "bricha" will take over. I'm also waiting for a good friend of mine, Edward Daszkiewicz and his wife and daughter to come to Wroclaw to join us. He is not Jewish. We were conscripted together in 1940 to the Red Army. He comes from our area. He is the fellow that helped me to survive the war. I owe him my life. I assure you, you'll love them. They are wonderful people."

"They are "goyim", I don't know. So far I had only bad experiences with "goyim".

"They are different, you'll see."

"Don't they say the same thing about us? Now Henryk tell me please about you."

"Forgive me Maryla but I'm so tired, all I can think about is sleep. We'll have plenty of time to listen to my story. Just put me anyplace."

Maryla made a bed for him by placing a blanket down on the floor.

"That's great, thank you sister."

The next few days they spent on getting ready for the trip. Henryk's money came very handy. Stopping by at the Jewish Committee, looking for newcomers and reading hundreds of notes attached to the wall. Some of them read as follows:

"Mania Weinflesz of Lodz is looking for her parents Izio and Sara Weinflesz."

"Moniek Bernstein from Warsaw seeking his sister Ewa."

"Anybody from Buchenwald Block #55 contact Abrasza Simonow at Grzybowa #7"

'Did anybody see Edzia Littman at Stutthof? Contact brother Siunek Littman, reward."

If he could, Henryk would have sent each of those "zetls", directly to the Jewish God. After all, it was He, who started the whole mess. They did meet a few friends from their hometown, some of them back from concentration camps and some from the Soviet Union. The latter groups were telling horrible stories of being attacked by the Polish N.S.Z. partisans. Many Jews were killed and robbed on the way to their homes in Poland, even though the hostilities ended, but not between the attackers and the victims. Hearing that, Henryk felt justified in his decision to leave Poland. By the 9th day being in Wroclaw, the modern version of "bondage in Egypt", they were packed and ready to leave. Henryk insisted on waiting one more day for Edward.

"He'll never come," said Chaim.

"I promised him I'd wait till the 10th day in the afternoon. If he doesn't come by that time we shall leave."

Later that day the Daszkiewicz family showed up. "I hope we're on time."

"Yes you are, come let me introduce you to my family."

One big smile and the women embraced, each attracted to the other. Seeing that, Henryk and Edward shook hands again.

"How was Zakopane?"

"Coming home and seeing my wife and my daughter was the happiest day of my life. I got on my knees and thanked the good Lord for his mercy. There was nothing more to keep me Czeslawa and Danuta in Zakopane. Cyprian Bujnicki died about a month after Czeslawa returned from Auschwitz. His wife, the gentlest soul in the world, followed her husband 17 days later. To top that loss, Bujnicki's relatives unexpectantly showed up. It was a very nasty situation, so here we're united in love and hope for a new life abroad."

The trip back to Munich was an almost identical reversal of the trip that Henryk, Edward and Chaim took. There was however one "small" difference.

They left Poland as a group of Greek citizens returning to Salonika. The Polish Authorities were only too glad to get rid of those "Greeks" through the "green" border but a few kilometers further they were stopped by another squad of Border Police and robbed of all of their valuables and money. Henryk's money kept in the lining of his coat was also removed.

Although instructed not to speak Polish, Czeslawa couldn't keep her tongue when one of the soldiers ripped off the gold chain and cross from her neck:

"Why are you steeling from Poles?'

"You're not Poles, you are all Zhids, you have stolen enough from us. Be glad that I didn't shoot you. Be on your way and never come back!"

Nobody was more frustrated and helpless than Edward Daszkiewicz, scion of a noble family and hero of Monte Cassino.

"If that is what we have to pay to get away from Poland, then it is worth it." Said Maryla.

Three days later they reached Munich. Edward took his family to the assigned apartment in Schwabing, assuming his duty as the commander of a Guard Company.

Henryk and his family settled in D.P. Camp Foehrenwald. To supplement his "Zulage" Henryk became an O.R.T. instructor in the camp's school, teaching young boys the art of carpentry. In his spare time he became the co-editor of the camp's newspaper "Bamidbar" and assistant coach to soccer team "Kadimah". It was in this capacity that he helped the Foehrenwald's team to win games with DP Camp Landsberg 3:1 and 1:0 with D.P. Camp Feldafing (also called Fickenfeld). While Henryk was busy with his activities, Dr. Benek Morgenstern opened a busy Dental Clinic, taking care of the Displaced Persons and their long neglected teeth.

The new camp director, Mr. Paul Krafchin, and American member of U.N.R.R.A. with the help of two new Welfare Officers, Helena Matouskova and Giselle Lachs, managed a well disciplined and safe settlement of 5.000 Jews of all ages and nationalities, on their way to different countries. The bulk of the camp's population consisted of Polish Jews. None of them wanted to go back to the country of their birth.

Only once did the camp encounter a major problem. It was the day, when American Military Police and the local German Police surrounded the camp, looking for black marketers, creating a panic among the camp's inhabitants: "They are going to kill us all."

The camp director changed quickly from his U.N.R.R.A. uniform into his blue Air Force uniform with a chest full of decoration, drove the jeep to the sergeant in charge of the "operation" "big-sweep".

Lt. Col. Krafchin told the sergeant in "polite" G.I. Language" "Get the fuck out and leave MY camp alone. I'm running this outfit, got it?"

"Yes Sir, 10-4 message understood Roger."

Nobody ever bothered the camp for the next two years, during the duration of Director Krafchin's contract with the U.N.R.R.A.

About the same time Edward Daszkiewicz and his family left for the maple leaf land of Canada from Bremenhaffen aboard the S.S. Marlin-Fletcher while Henryk Kaplinski and his newly acquired wife Sally and the Morgensterns with their two kids (the second was born in Foehrenwald) left for Palestine aboard the ship named "EXODUS".

E*P*I*L*O*G*U*E

50 PLUS YEARS LATER

In more than a half of a century many things did take place. Time takes a number on people, sooner or later and so.....

Henryk Kaplinski joined Haganah Forces in Israel in 1947. In one of many skirmishes and battles with Arabs, he was badly wounded in the same leg as in Italy previously, and this time, his leg was amputated, just above the knee. Drawing two, disabled war veteran pensions, one from Israel and the second from Germany, as a member of the Wehrmacht, he lived comfortably with his wife from Foehrenwald, Sally, in a small house on Rechov Hakibbutzim in Kiryat Chaim near Haifa.

Using the state of the art artificial leg supplied to him by Beit Halochem (House of Heroes) he is still walking ramrod straight, unlike many other silver haired senior citizens close to 80. Henryk and Sally were childless.

Maryla his sister gained considerable weight with each child. Her husband Benek as a dentist became a big success. From an apartment in Shikun Dan in Tel-Aviv, they moved to an exclusive area in Savyon or as some Israeli's call it Snob-yon. They were less lucky with their children. The oldest daughter went to Berkley in California, joined a cult and died of drug overdose. The oldest son, born in the D.P. Camp Foehrenwald was killed in 1967 fighting the Egyptians near the Suez Canal. The remaining three are doing well.

Edward Daszkiewicz upon entering Canada, obtained a job with General Motors Corp. – subsidiary in Downsview, Ontario, where he worked till his retirement at age of 62. Thanks to an employee stock option plan, he amassed enough capital to buy a charming villa on Rodeo Drive in Thornhill. Czeslawa opened a small art gallery, displaying mainly her and Danuta's work. The store prospered throughout the years. Danuta met and fell in love with an orthodox Jewish boy, a son of Holocaust survivors, while still in high school. She was shocked when her mother told her about her Jewish origins and wartime adoption. After trying for years to locate her biological parents, she finally married the boy who became a most successful corporate attorney in Toronto.

While officially Jewish, Czeslawa would cross herself anytime she was close to a church. They had four children all of them girls. Czeslawa adores those girls till the day of her death of cancer, and that was on the 49th year of her marriage to Edward. After Czeslawa's death, Edward a non-Jew started to study the Kabalah, always preferring the company of Polish Jews.

He and Henryk would see each other alternatively for Passover or Christmas in Israel and Canada.

Eljasz Wachtel came to Israel to join his friend Menachem Begin. He became one of Eichmann's prosecutors and eventually a Justice of the Israeli Supreme Court.

Adler – "Panczyk" (his real name) became a very rich man and moved to San Paolo in Brazil, where he died of old age. Luise went back to Germany, disappearing without a trace.

Lt. Col. Paul Krafchin returned to the States with his British wife Cynthia and Gary-Isaac, their three year old boy. His mother and her husband Mr. Goldstein baby sat for the young couple, while both of them attended their respective universities. Earning a Ph.D. Paul became a Dean of Social Studies at N.Y.U. his Alma Mater, He was always in touch with his former boss, Gen. Gary Cottshot.

Gen. Gary "the hotshot" spent several more years with the Air Force in Japan during the "Police Action" in Korea. Returning home he taught for a while at Military Colleges. His life ended, when a pick up truck, driven by a drunken red neck collided head on with Gary's Chevy. According to his testament and last will, he refused to be buried in Arlington National Cemetery. His resting place was in his beloved South Carolina's Myrtle Beach.

Should you visit the cemetery early in the morning when the air is still and sweet and as the waking sun casts an orange glow over the rustling sea waters, you'll see a large granite monument with engraved words: KISS MY GRITS next to General Gary Cottshot's R.I.P.

BIBLIOGRAPHY

Hitler and Stalin Bullock
Citizen Soldiers S. Ambrose
The Devil's Virtuosos Downing
Europe-History Davies
World War II Foot
Barbarossa A. Clark
Biographical Dictionary of W.W.II Boatner
Red Storm of the Reich Duffy
The Luftwaffe Corum
The Holocaust L. Yahil
Page One N.Y. Times

C. k. gimnazyum *Franciszka Józefa* w *Drohobyczu*

L. *3*

Świadectwo roczne.

50 HELLER

Daszkiewicz Kazimierz Józef

urodzony dnia *17 kwietnia 1902* w *Drohobyczu* w *Galicyi* religii *rzymsko-katol.* uczeń klasy *pierwszej B.* otrzymuje niniejszem za rok szkolny 19*16/17* świadectwo następujące:

Zachowanie się: *odpowiednie*

Postęp w przedmiotach nauki:		Wynik ogólny
Przedmiot	Postęp	
w nauce religii:	*dostateczny*	
w języku polskim (jako wykładowym):	*dostateczny*	
w języku łacińskim:	*niedostateczny*	
w języku greckim:	*%.*	
w języku ruskim:	*%.*	
w języku niemieckim:	*niedostateczny*	
w historyi:	*niedostateczny*	
w geografii:	*niedostateczny*	Do klasy następnej *nie* uzdolniony.
w matematyce:	*niedostateczny*	
w historyi naturalnej (*Zool. i botan.*)	*dostateczny*	
w fizyce i chemii:	*%.*	
w propedeutyce filozofii:	*%.*	
w rysunkach odręcznych:	*%.*	
w kaligrafii:	*dostateczny*	
w gimnastyce:	*dostateczny*	
Przedmioty nadobowiązkowe: w rysunkach odręcznych:		
w śpiewie:		
w stenografii:		

Liczba opuszczonych godzin szkolnych: *2.* ; z nich nie usprawiedliwiono: *2.*

Od opłaty szkolnej *nie* był uwolniony.

W Drohobyczu, dn. 30 czerwca 19*17.*

S. Jedliński dyrektor.

Jan Steinaing gospodarz klasy.

(969)

L. skł. 53 b. Gimnazyum.

NOTES

1 Russians
2 Peoples Army
3 Damned English
4 agreed
5 A Ukrainian derogatory term for Poles
6 I bend before you
7 shame
8 freebies
9 Racial shame
10 Good night and pleasant dreams
11 Be strong
12 High schools
13 God punish England